THE RIVEN TRILOGY

RIVEN | THE CYCLE | SPIRIT'S END

A.R. KNIGHT

RIVEN

THE RIVEN TRILOGY - BOOK ONE

1

———————

SHE'D BEEN dead for a month, but damn if I didn't love her.

Selena looked back at me from across the room, an ashen square occupied by swirling sheets of paper, a lone chair, and a closed door that Selena stood near. The walls were cracking, bits of mortar falling to the ground before getting swept up in Riven's ever-present breeze. Selena gripped the doorknob, but she wasn't going to open it. Not till I was ready.

My right hand slipped to the hilt on my waist, tied to my belt. My fingers fit into the creases on the leather grip. I lifted it free of the holster without a sound. As I held it up, the lash unrolled and played out along the floor like a snake waiting for its chance to strike. At the end of its long tail, the lash split into a pair of metal points. Points that glowed a faint blue.

"I've seen that enough times to not be impressed," Selena said. Her voice came with a thousand memories, scratches and scars underlining every word.

"It's part of my style," I said. I walked forward to the door and took Selena's hand off the knob. No reason to risk her for this. My gloved hand took her place, and I twisted.

The door opened inward, revealing an even greater disaster on the other side. Rubble from a caved-in roof spread across the floor, stone blocks split in half or smaller pieces scattered around. Dust swirled and danced in Riven's cold light. The same gray cast colored everything in this world. Sitting on the rubble, head between his hands, was a man. Or at least what used to be one.

His hair was thinning, some spare spidery wisps falling to touch his dirty white collar. A bow-tie hung askew beneath his neck, the lone spot of black until the man's torn trousers. He'd lost his shoes somewhere on the way to here. I noticed the watch on one hand, gold and shining. Rare to see something like that come through. Must have been a present, a treasured gift.

"Be careful," Selena whispered. "This one's got an edge."

"It won't get close," I replied, and raised the lash.

As my lash went into the air, its length whipping up and stretching over my right shoulder, the man looked up at me. No matter how many times I've seen their eyes, they never fail to send a shiver running through my nerves. Pale blue fire burned where their pupils should be. The sign of a spirit that's been consumed, that's lost what little remained of who they were.

"Now you've come again," the man said, standing. "Come to take what's mine, as you have so many times before."

"This will be the last, I promise," I said, and then I swung the lash. It went forward, snapping in the air. The lash wrapped around the man's neck, the metal points digging into the spirit. The points made the man's gray skin stretch and warp as they dug in, and then I twisted my wrist.

The lash turned the same color as the man's eyes. Blue fire tracing from my hand down the length of the lash and through those points into the man. The spirit howled, an otherworldly noise carrying all the pain the spirit had suffered to bring him here. To Riven and to let him stay.

As the blue flames covered the man, he fell to his knees and grew silent. Seconds later, I saw his eyes extinguish and twisted my wrist back. The lash returned to its normal black and, with a flick of my arm, I withdrew the coil and watched.

The man stood and walked towards me. I stepped aside, back into the room with the chair, and Selena moved with me. The man kept walking, right by us, through the room, and down the stairs at the other end. He would keep walking on a long journey until he reached the Riven's center. The thing that both made Riven necessary and terrible. The Cycle.

"I thought you said this was a bad one," I said to Selena. "He didn't even put up a fight."

"You heard him. He was angry," Selena said. "You always say to let you know when there's an angry one here."

"You weren't wrong. I heard him talk," I replied. "He didn't know where he was anymore. Thought I was someone else."

"I hate that. I hate it when they talk about before."

"All of them do that. Even you."

"But you saw his eyes. Mine aren't like that."

That's true. Any spirit with those burning blue eyes was lost. Needed to be sent back. I looked at Selena's face, the smooth curves in the long scar down one side. Her eyes were gray, like the rest of this place. But her body, the blouse and pants that she wore, those still held color. And there was warmth in her lips. Warmth that I felt as I leaned in and brushed them with mine. Selena took the gesture, then looked away.

"There are more of them," Selena said. "I keep seeing them, Carver. Keep seeing them running through the streets, losing their minds faster than before. I think they're feeding on it."

"Then we'll just have to work harder," I said. "I told you what's happening out there. A lot of lives are being lost. Riven is going to be crowded for a while."

"I feel it too."

"What do you mean?"

"The rage. The anger at all the loss," Selena said, pointing to her heart, and then her head. "It's like a sickness, festering inside. Whispering to me and telling me to lose myself in it and follow the feeling to the end."

I looked at her, studied those gray eyes for any hint of the fire. If you caught a spirit early enough, there were give-aways. Twitches and tells like clawing hands and snapping motions. The surest sign was a flicker behind the pupils, a spark that always led to the angry flame. Selena had none. I realized she was staring at my hand, my hand that still gripped the lash.

"You're bound," I said. "That should keep you safe. You can draw on my will, my life, whenever you feel that anger."

Selena nodded. The same nod that she had probably given to her husband when she was alive, quiet and confi-dent, but I could tell there was plenty left unsaid. She didn't explain, just turned and walked from the room. As I followed, a far-off bell clanged, ringing through the vast gray maze of Riven's city. That sound meant it was time to go home. Time to wake up.

2

———

THE FIRST FLOOR of the building consisted of a single room occupied by a lone table split down the middle, its two halves leaning down into each other. Square windows, with no glass, were bordered by empty bookshelves. Long ago cleared out by other guides. Before my time.

"How long had you been here before I found you?" I asked Selena.

She paused at the exit, a single doorway with the door no longer attached. Hinges hung off the sides at odd angles. The old door had been ripped off long ago. We didn't like leaving hidden places in Riven.

"Thirty days," Selena said. "Thirty days before Wiley lost his mind."

Wiley. Her last husband. The one that gave her that scar. After she gave him one far worse.

"The man? The guy upstairs?" I said. "He'd likely been here a week or more. Long enough to lose himself. You and your husband had each other for help. He had no one."

"You promise that won't happen to me?"

"As long as I'm alive, you'll be fine."

Selena stayed quiet. She did that a lot. Whether that was because I couldn't hold a decent conversation or because she had too many memories to dive into, I couldn't be sure. Riven was a place for silence, though. There weren't chirping birds. No noise from machines moving, crowds talking. Only the blowing of the wind.

I followed Selena into the avenue. Like the building we'd been in, the avenue was a mixture of ruins, empty storefronts, and unlit lampposts. A ghost town filled with literal ghosts.

We could see plenty of spirits, a dozen wandering the street as we looked up and down. Most were in various stages of being called. Pulled to the Cycle where they would vanish and find their way back to reality as a new life. Some, held through a stronger bond to something left behind, wandered with more purpose. Looked at the buildings with actual curiosity or longing. Those were the dangerous ones, the ones that would inevitably turn to anger if they resisted for too long.

Selena and I walked through them, passed by spirits wearing everything from rags to the wealthiest and most ostentatious of suits. There was no telling what a spirit would be wearing when they died.

Overhead an endless stream of thin clouds muted the light. Riven had no sun that I could see, only a constant gray cast. Ash filtered through the air. It was always there, had always been there, though none of the guides I'd ever asked knew where it came from. Not even Bryce.

My eyes moved to Selena. Even here she held her head high. That confidence, that willingness to confront whatever stood in front of her, I had noticed first. On the street not far from where I had crossed over. She had been fighting Wiley, right there on the road. Tearing at each other.

"I wanted to go," Selena said as we walked along. "Wanted

to be cycled. But then I kept seeing them, their mindless faces as they went on. I just couldn't do it."

"So you explored."

She turned like this every once in a while. Reflective. Curious.

"And I wrote," Selena said. "Don't forget that. You're going to memorize those and take them out of Riven, remember?"

"I promised, didn't I?"

"I've heard a lot of those."

"I keep mine."

We reached the main square for this part of Riven. On one side, opposite where we came in, stood a large clock tower. The hours themselves were meaningless here. But the count, the number of those hours you spent in Riven, that meant everything.

"Do you want me to walk you back?" I asked.

"I'll be fine," Selena said. A flash of disappointment. "You'll be back tonight?"

"Should be," I said. "All depends on what we hear today."

"Another one?"

"With the war, we have to keep in close contact. It's getting rough out there," as I finished the sentence my eyes took a jog around the courtyard. The large fountain in the center drew the most attention, spraying Riven's water high into the air. I walked over to it, held out my hand, and felt the splatters on my palm. Lifted it to my mouth and tried to take a sip. The liquid went in my throat, over my lips, but it tasted like nothing.

"Carver. Are you forgetting something?"

Selena held me captive with a small smile. It twisted the scar cutting across her face into a sickle, and I loved it. It seemed so fitting for this place, for Riven. Beautiful imperfection.

"I can't risk it here," I said. Her face fell, settled into a line.

"Sorry, Selena. If they found out, they'd blind me from Riven. Tonight though, I'll meet you at the apartment."

That didn't quite knock the sadness out of her eyes, but Selena pulled her mask back on. Flashed one last smile, then left me alone in the courtyard. I went over the clock tower, pulled the handle on the large double doors leading inside.

The spacious chamber was full of stacked bookshelves, racks with various weapons, each one labeled for the guide who owned it. Table and chairs sat in the center. And behind that, leaning against the far wall, was a line of beds.

I slid the lash into its holder on my rack. Pulled the long knife out of its holster on my left and slotted it beside the lash. The next rack over held a giant double-edged spear Bryce called it a voulge. Waving symbols were etched into the thing's pole. Bryce carved one every time he took out a ghoul. Something I hadn't done. Hadn't even seen. Bryce always said I was lucky for that.

I went over the beds, chose the one on the far right, and laid down. Almost as soon as I'd settled in, my eyes shut and sleep took me. I crossed over.

3

THE MORNING PAPER shot over my head as I woke up. The end of the tube came in over my window looking out over the streets west of downtown Chicago. The tube launched mail, paper, anything small enough to fit up from the ground and into my apartment, where it landed in a small basket.

The wall behind that basket, a jutting edge made just for this purpose, was padded with a thick cushion I'd nailed on when the first cracks from repeated impacts started to show. The start of the tube, at street level, had a small gate that only opened if you pressed the correct sequence of numbers on the keypad next to it. Prevented any kind of nasty bombs or pranks that people would otherwise send through the mail.

Outside the window, Chicago's hazy morning was beginning. The sun bled yellow through a smoky filter. Buildings played staccato in the distance, and in between their rises shifted the occasional hulking mass of a mech, given away by their belching smokestacks. The sky overhead was peppered with thick blotches of varying length. Zeppelins carrying passengers, products, or in the case of the large one persistently hovering over Lake Michigan, prisoners.

The cloudless March sky made it look like it would be a nice day.

I stood up and took the three steps from my bed to my kitchen, a squat affair with the table on one side, my icebox on the other, and the single oven in the middle. I pressed the button on the top of the icebox and it appeared to split in the middle, the cover rising to reveal two sides. On the left were the truly frozen items. An empty half, save for a bottle of Nikolai's Finest vodka. I reached for it then paused. Not this morning. There was a meeting that I'd have to be presentable for.

The other side was loaded with small packets of food. One, labeled Breakfast Number Three, was on the top and I grabbed it. Breakfast Number Three was the best, eggs *and* bacon. Only two of those per week.

I slid it into the oven and turned it on by rotating a small dial on the front. Sparks sprayed out the back of the machine as it spooled up, adding their singes to the black smears on the wall behind. Then I had the chance to actually take a look at that paper.

The usual headlines about the war dominated. Wins, losses, speeches by generals and politicians about how this was either the greatest time, or the end of time. I hunted for the numbers. They were buried, hidden in small boxes at the bottoms of the articles. A thousand here, another five thousand there. Each and every one of those would be going to Riven. Most would be angry. Everyone worried about the cost of war for the living, nobody seemed to care what it meant for the ones who watched the dead.

The oven dinged, a noise more seen than heard as the thing stopped its shower of sparks and the front door popped open. A pair of tongs hung on the wall next to the oven. Using its hook, a spindly metal grabber, I fished my breakfast out. I picked out my utensil from the container on the table, a tall cylinder with my name, Carver, embossed into it. A welcome gift from the other guides when I came here.

The utensil was a thick tool with a slider built into the stem. I slid it back a notch, hiding the spoon and revealing the fork. Stabbed it into the mix of bacon and eggs and stuck the salty goodness in my mouth. They'd done a real nice job with the taste on this one. A glance at the label on the package, Breakfast Number Three and, beneath, *flavored with cheddar.* That'd be why. Every once in a while the processors got a deal on something tasty and stuck it in. I took an extra minute to savor every bite of this one, as I probably wouldn't get another for a month or more.

Then a brief visit to the shared showers on my floor, always a crowded squeeze given the hot water for our building only lasted for an hour in the morning. 5:00 to 6:00. That's what you had if you needed a hot shower. Most days I didn't care, but today there were standards. Today I'd be going outside.

I put on an undershirt and the only sweater I owned. A faded green with the letters *C.R.* sewn into the back. My initials. Another gift, this one from a girl I'd known a long time ago. She would've laughed if she knew I still wore this thing.

Thick work pants, loaded with pockets, and then the coup de grace, my coat. A marker of status, this thing. Thick and long, originally black but now a dusty gray, with twin lapels stretching off the collar and down part of the front. A hood that tucked behind my neck and could be pulled out as needed. Only guides wore these, and they opened doors. Shut a few too.

As I left my place, I grabbed one more thing. My mask. The metal was cool on my face, but it settled under my chin and around my ears perfectly. Every year or so I had to take it in, get it adjusted. It had to fit tight. I rode the elevator down and as it opened I press the button on the side of the mask. A switch woven into the curling black metal with bits of topaz sprinkled in. I'd wanted it to look like embers in the night, and the guides had delivered.

I pulled over the hood, and stepped onto the sidewalk. The mask started filtering out dust and dirt from the air. The lenses dulling the sunlight's bright edges from my eyes.

The streets were crowded, the masses generally going in my direction. Making their way to the trains going either into or out of the city. The streets themselves busy with ranging carts. Treaded steel beasts hauling cargo or passengers arrayed on lines of benches. Wheels crunched into gravel, sprinkling the sidewalk with pebbles.

The train station was a block away. Its looping entrance arch watched over by a three-story tall mech. The machine stood on four legs that bled into a squat sphere of a body. Lights coated the bottom, directed wherever the driver chose. Twin smokestacks on top sat still, they'd only belch when the mech was moving. On the sides of its body were a pair of thick guns, their bullet belts streaming down and wrapping around the machine so that it seemed to be literally cloaked in golden death. These days, most people looked up at the mech and smiled. Waved.

I did too.

4

I NODDED to the conductor as I stepped on the train. Behind me, the next passenger pulled out her chit and the conductor punched it. Another perk of being a guide? Free rides. The train car was crowded this morning, but a pair shuffled away from a bench and let me sit down.

I took them up on the offer and settled in against the window. It was as cool on the train as it was outside, a temp I was comfortable with. In the summer, wearing this coat wasn't always a pleasant experience, but without it I didn't get the perks. So even if I was liable to become a pool of sweat, I wore the damn thing.

Across from me, a man and his son stared open-mouthed at my face. Their masks were of the ordinary variety, a plastic covering that did its job but nothing more. That lack of personality was echoed by the man's uniform, the plain white shirt and trousers. An average briefcase, one that probably didn't even expand when opened. Didn't even have a shock lock.

The kid, though, made up for the boring outfit with a healthy helping of personality. His eyes seem to get wider and wider the more he stared at me. I smiled back at him, but he couldn't see it from beneath the mask.

"Got a question?" I asked the kid.

"No, he's fine," the dad said.

"Let him talk," I replied and nodded at the boy. The dad gulped, but kept quiet. "Come on kid. Not every day you see a guide."

"What's it like?" the kid blurted. "Over there?"

They always asked the same question. The same one that can be found answered in any magazine in any given month. None of these people ever read anything.

"Riven. Not 'over there'," I said. "You want to know what it's like? It's like walking into a nightmare. The scariest thing you've ever seen and it only gets scarier every step you take. Eventually, if you live long enough, you realize you can't be scared anymore. That the things you were scared of, well, now they're scared of you."

I thought the kid's eyes were to pop right out of his head. But he got himself pulled together enough for follow-up.

"What were you scared of?" the kid asked.

"You ever see a body?" I said and the kid shook his head. The dad next to him kept getting paler and paler. That's the thing that happens when the stuff you only hear about in stories turns out to be real after all and closer than you think. "Well you've got these chopped up, mangled people wandering the streets and they're getting angry every second that they're there. They're frustrated that they have to live in this terrible place where there's no sunlight, no real food or drink, nothing to do but think about what you've lost, and eventually they forget who they were. Then they find someone to take it out on. Someone to tear apart because that's the only thing they can think of to do. Those people are what I was scared of."

The kid was into it, nodding like he wanted me to go on.

The dad looked like he was going to be sick. He grabbed his son's hand and stood up as the train started to move. Pulled the kid off the bench.

"We've got to move up for next stop," the dad stammered, leading the kid away.

I barely had a moment to myself before another body slid into the bench across from me. A woman, going by the cream dress, one already showing stains at the edges from the air. Her mask, though, that caught my attention. Not the cheap stuff, but a silver plate with weaving white ceramic around the eyes. The usual filters over the nose and mouth bordered with gold. Flashy.

"So you're a guide," the woman said. I spread my hands, palms up. Didn't the coat make it obvious? "That likes to scare children."

"Riven should scare children," I said.

"But it doesn't scare you."

"Not anymore. You go anywhere enough times, even the strangest of places start to feel ordinary."

"Have you been far over there?"

Far? A word like far didn't really apply to Riven. Where you were over here, affected where you came out over there. I'd never seen a map of the place, but all of the guides crossed over in different parts of the city. Maybe just outside. That's where the spirits were, and that's where we stayed. No reason to explore a world of horrors.

"I've seen enough," I said. Outside the window the train was drawing closer to the city center. The wide apartment structures like the one I lived in were gradually being replaced by taller offices, wide warehouses for factories, and the occasional metallic buildings that housed laboratories. The places that experimented and invented the things that would go to the factories and then to our homes. Most of the laboratories were thick and windowless, owing to their tendency to explode. Or catch on fire.

"Then you know what's happening?" the woman tilted her head as she asked the question. I got the impression that she didn't think I had a clue. Her voice, coming through that mask, had the same sort of tone I got from Chicago's finest when they asked if I could find a murder victim in Riven. That I was a problem that had to be endured.

"The same thing that's always happening. More spirits to wrangle."

Now her eyes lit up. Apparently I'd found the right word.

"More spirits. So you've noticed?" she asked.

"We've all noticed. When you've got a war this big going on, Riven's going to get a little crowded."

"And when it gets too crowded?"

"Don't think that's going to happen," I said. "We've got enough guides, and Riven is a bigger place than people think."

The train whistled to a stop, one before mine. The woman glanced outside the window, then turned back to me, digging into a pocket in her dress. She pulled out a card and a pen, scribbled something on it, and then handed it to me.

"I think your world is about to get a lot more dangerous than you expect," the woman said standing up. "I can help you."

I turn the card over in my hand. On one side was a floral design, a simple slogan reading "find your peace" and a number to call. On the back, in her handwriting, was a street address. Not far from where we were now. I looked back up, but the woman was already gone.

I took a deep breath as the train stopped at Union Station. You want a real taste of Chicago, you came here. Preferably in the morning, when Union Station was a pit of chaos. Everyone going somewhere, and everyone else trying to sell them something for the trip. I followed the crowd out of the train car and onto the platform where my ears were blasted with shouts for a thousand things I didn't need.

It was a weekday, so most of the goods for sale were targeted at workers going to their places. Newspapers, food packages for lunch, shoeshines or lint rolls. One guy, wearing a halter over his neck that connected to long portable shelves, sold tubes of whitener. Guaranteed to remove pollution stains from your clothes. Whenever the sellers caught me in their eyes, though, they fell quiet. Guides weren't anyone's target market.

Another benefit to being a guide? Even though I was in a crowd, everyone kept their space. It was like moving in my own private bubble. Plenty of room to breathe, to look around, to walk without tripping over someone else's shoes.

So long as you don't mind the stares, it was a good deal. At least, it was until the reporter showed up.

"Carver!" Opperman said, appearing as if by magic on my left side. He held a scribe tablet in front of him, a nifty little gadget that recorded everything we said as punches on a thick paper. By running those punches through a player later, the paper would re-create the sounds we made and, thus, the words we spoke. "Care to comment on the war this morning?"

"War is bad," I said, not stopping.

The main plaza of Union Station was miraculous place to see. I still remember my first time, when my train arrived from the east coast. The station's ceiling covered in tubes sending packages and letters to the various platforms where they would be loaded in mail cars and shot across the country. Each of those tubes colored so that, plastered up against each other, they formed a painting. A great circle with three colors; green, black, and blue that represented Chicago's main industries. Food, mechs, and research. The Spire of Humanity graced the center. The tall tower at the heart of the city. The seat of government for the middle third of the country.

A giant display of train times, standing on a copper tube, sat beneath the painting. Each departure and arrival tracked and entered by a team of people working switchboards around the base of the column. All in plain view because, so I'd heard, the operators wanted people to know how much work it was keeping their trips on time.

"That's it? That's all you've got?" Opperman continued.

"What did you want me to say?" I replied. "Save yourself some time and tell me what you're fishing for."

Opperman nodded, his head bobbing violently. Sometimes I wondered if the man subsisted only on coffee. His movements were so jerky and his voice went so fast that it sounded like one of those children's toys wound up too tight.

"Have you seen it?" Opperman said. "The spirit that's causing all the problems?"

Now I turned my head, looked at him through my mask.

"Causing all the problems? What spirit?"

"My sources tell me—"

"What sources?"

Opperman shrank back a step. "You know I can't tell you."

My hand moved to my waist but there was nothing there. I wasn't in Riven, I didn't have my lash. Even for a guide, traveling around the city armed was a good way to get in trouble. Chicago was weapons-free, like most of the country. If you weren't in the military or enforcing the law, you'd find yourself in a cell before they even bothered asking questions.

"Then I can't trust your information," I said.

"Come on, Carver. You how this works. You give me the story, and I drum up support for the guides. Make sure you have the funds you need."

"I haven't seen it," I said. "Don't know what you're talking about. If you want, I can tell you about the spirit I wrapped up this morning."

"Anything interesting? An angry widow claiming she was wrongly murdered? Maybe a kid?"

"How about a man driven to despair by this rotten city?"

Opperman rolled his eyes, but kept pace with me as we neared the exit.

"Carver, I can't get that above the fold. Maybe page three. How about an opinion piece?"

"What kind of opinion do you want?"

"Do you think the guides are able to handle an uprising? A mass of angry spirits led and directed by one even worse?"

An uprising? That was a new term. Angry spirits weren't exactly disposed to cooperation. They tended to, you know, tear each other apart. Opperman leaned forward, staring at my mask. Holding the tablet up. The guy thought this was an important question. So I bit back my sarcasm. There were benefits to having the biggest paper in town on your side.

"Look, Chicago has three guides alone, and there are hundreds across the world. More than enough to deal with a bunch of angry spirits," I said. "Remember, we're still sane. They're not. Even if they have numbers, we've got the brains. The equipment. Riven will be fine."

"If it's not?"

"You'll know, because all of your dead friends will come back to find you. And you won't be happy to see them."

Opperman switched off the tablet, slipped it in his pocket as we went through the door and out into the street. He held out his hand and I shook it.

"Now that's the quote I was looking for," Opperman said. "I'll try to get the story in for the afternoon. Evening edition at the latest."

"Can't wait."

Opperman turned to walk down the street, opposite of where I was going. I let him get four steps away.

"Opperman. Your sources have any more useful info, you be sure to get it to me," I said. "If there's really something dangerous out there, there's more to worry about than selling papers."

The reporter held up his hand and kept walking. The man stuck to his principles, had to give him that. As I turned towards Ezra's, I couldn't stop thinking about what he'd said. One spirit ruling a bunch of others? I'd never seen that before. Never heard of it. Even when Riven was crowded, Bryce said, there still wasn't any organization. Just one big angry mob of ghosts waiting to be sent on their way.

This time wouldn't be any different.

6

EZRA'S LOOKED over the river, stuck between a pair of bridges at the base of a bank. From the outside, all you saw were the thick gold letters hanging above the door. Nothing more than the name flanked on either end with the guide insignia. A circle in the middle and four lines spaced around the outside. They didn't quite form a square, leaving the corners blank, but the impression was clear. Those lines kept the circle from expanding, kept Riven from breaking out.

Ezra's door, unlike Union Station's, was a purifier. Most stores were these days. I opened the first metal and glass entrance and stepped into a small room. Big enough to hold two or three people. The door shut behind me and I pulled a small lever on the wall to my right. The movement opened a seal, leveraging air pressure to force the dirty haze back out into the city. The lever crawled back up and by the time it clicked back into position the air inside the room was clean. A snap announced the inner door unlocking, and I pushed my way into the best bar in Chicago.

The first thing anyone notices about the inside of Ezra's, and the first thing my eyes went to even after all this time, was the automatic orchestra hanging above the bar. It was massive, covering the length of the back wall. Instruments carved out of wood, brass, and canvas made a collage that appeared to go deep into the wall behind. As though you were actually looking into an orchestra pit.

Beneath the carvings, an intricate set of speakers piped music in from the player behind the bar. Like Opperman's tablet, the thing ran on reams of punched-in paper. I'd watch them load it a time or two, the bartender slotting in a scroll that weighed twenty pounds and letting it play.

If you weren't sitting right at the counter, a crimson stained bar, Ezra's had more than its share of tables and cushioned chairs. Fake candles hung from the ceiling on wires, their flickering light pointing down as though they might drip wax right on your face. It created the illusion that it was always late at night, always classy, always mysterious.

"You going to stare that thing all day, or are you going to sit down and have a drink?" Bryce, my mentor and Chicago's oldest guide, said to me from our table.

Ezra's wasn't all that crowded in the morning. A few nights shifters drinking off their hours. A dozen more putting off the start of the day with some coffee and eggs. Bryce already had a pair mugs in front of him, each of them ceramic, the same color as the bar. I sat down, leaving my coat on. Bryce hadn't taken his off either. He had, however, set his mask on the table. An emerald and white affair that looked like frost-kissed vines. I did the same. No need for the things in here.

"You want to tell me where you were this morning?" Bryce said. The man spoke in tender tones, rusty at the edges from decades in the city. Despite the question, I could see in his eyes and his raised eyebrow that it wasn't an interrogation.

"Tracking an angry one. Took care of it," I said. The steam

coming off the coffee said it was just about the right temp. I lifted it up, took a sniff, that hot bitter caramel curling through my nose and a second later down my throat. Pleasure burn.

"So you hit your quota?"

"One over, actually. You?"

Bryce grinned. It was a stupid question. The man carved up spirits like a runner carved up miles. Every single one another routine, something to be dealt with. The more he wrangled in a session, a single night in Riven, the better his score.

Watching Bryce at work was fascinating. Sometimes he would line up angry spirits, lead them all to the same avenue, with them growling and yelling at each other, and then use that voulge of his to carve through them all in a single dash. If what I did was work, what Bryce did was art.

"Glad you're getting better," Bryce said, and here his smile faltered. "Word is things aren't always going to be so easy."

"Speaking of, I ran into Opperman this morning," I said. "He hinted at some sort of controlling spirit. One that was keeping all these war casualties in line. Giving orders. You ever hear something like that?"

Bryce took a long drink of his coffee. Then shook his head.

"Ghouls come close. They're terrifying enough, but they don't make friends. They don't lead. Did Opperman tell you anything else?"

"I tried, but he wouldn't give up his source."

"Maybe we'll find out on the call."

The whole reason we were at Ezra's that morning was the call. A chance to get our orders from up above. Normally only happened once a month, a couple hour-long breakfast chat about which region had the highest numbers, or if anyone had a new guide to introduce. A fallen one to remember. Lately, though, the war had bumped these up to every other week.

"You ever have frequent calls like this before?" I asked.

"Happens every so often. If there's a big event and we need to step up the guiding, or there's some new practices going into effect. Like when we first split the regions."

Riven wasn't all that large. For a long time, the guides had all been based in London. Now, they were spread out all over the world. Recruitment happened in every area. Regions had designated times to patrol Riven. Guides worked around the clock to keep the spirit count low.

"It was crowded back then, right?"

"Every hunt, every night was a chance for disaster. And glory," Bryce said. "All of us would go to Riven at once and we'd spend the night slaughtering spirits, catching ghouls that had pulled together during the day. It was harder, and we lost a lot of good guides."

"Still," I said, glancing down in my coffee. "Wouldn't mind seeing one of those someday."

"With what's going on now? You just might."

Bryce pushed himself back from the table and I followed suit. We grabbed our mugs and headed towards a small door left of the bar. Our logo was pasted on the outside. Bryce reached into his pocket and pulled out a card with the cut out of the circle and lines. Slid it into a slot in the door and it unlocked.

In the room sat a table and chairs. A gadget took up most of the middle of the table. A squat box with the speaker on top. There was only a single switch. When Bryce tapped it, the speaker rumbled with static as it connected to the line.

Time to get our orders.

7

A VOICE on the line was already talking, the rolling baritone of the guide leader, Piotr. I'd never seen the man, only heard his voice, but I imagined the body behind that much bass would have to be huge. Thick. With a thousand cigars consumed in the making of it.

"With the continued disruption in our European region due to the war," Piotr was saying. "Other regions will need to increase their quotas. This is on top of the increases made to account for the war dead."

Piotr sighed, audible through the line. In the background, hints of whispers made their way through. Bryce looked like he was listening intently, so I matched his expression. It was important information, sure, but hardly a surprise.

"I was told by our Athens sect that a ghoul was sighted just hours ago," Piotr said. "They did not manage to track it down, but it is evidence that we are not working hard enough. Riven is a dangerous place, and it only becomes more so as we let our efforts falter."

Piotr kept going, but I fixated on the ghoul. It hadn't been caught. There was one in Riven right now. Ready for me to find and take. I glanced at Bryce, but he didn't meet my look. Would probably consider it immature excitement anyway.

"Lastly," Piotr said. "Take care of yourselves. This is not the time for bravery, but for cooperation. Hunt together. I have had to replace five guides in the last month, and that is far too many."

That was news. Five guides. Now both Bryce and I looked at the empty chair on the far side of the table. Alec never came to these calls, preferring instead to spend the time hunting spirits or hunting love in Chicago's dark corners. Bryce let Alec go, though, because the guide was absolutely vicious in Riven.

I'd seen him carve up five spirits in a row, a group of enraged lab workers decimated in an explosion that morning, still in their coats. They had come at Alec as a group, and the guide had held up his hand, warning me back.

Then he'd begun what Alec called his *dance*. Gauntlets made of serrated silver lined Alec's arms up to the elbows, and with the same snap of the wrist that activated my lash, Alec set them glowing blue. The first spirit, howling, came within reach and Alec sidestepped the charge. Let the spirit blow by and, with a right backhand, smashed the spirit in the back of its head. At the same time, Alec's left hand jabbed out into the second one. As the gauntlets struck, their edges ripped holes in the ethereal skin of the spirits, igniting their bodies with blue flame.

Using the second spirit as a shield, holding onto it with his left hand, Alec forced the next two spirits to step around. The last one, though, felt braver than its fellows and jumped over Alec's burning spirit shield. I was going to yell, but Alec saw the move and stuck his right hand into the sky. The leaping spirit impaled itself on the fist, while Alec let the burning body go from his left hand. That left a symmetrical moment, Alec with a spirit held in the air above, and a pair surrounding him on either side.

As the two spirits lunged at him, Alec pulled his fist out of the spirit in the air and skipped back, landing three feet away on his toes. The two spirits collided in the space where Alec had been. Alec used their moment of confusion. Jumping forward, Alec brought his gauntlets together in a sweeping arc in front of his chest, collecting the spirit's heads along the way. They met in the middle, bursting into blue fire and collapsing.

A moment later all five spirits rose again, calm and dead-eyed, and began their last walk to the Cycle. Alec turned to me, tipped his wide brimmed hat, and—

"You weren't paying attention," Bryce said, breaking me out of the memory. I noticed the speaker was silent, switched off.

"I drifted," I glanced again at the empty chair. "Wondering about Alec."

"I'd say he can take care of himself," Bryce said, frowning at the space. "Except for Piotr's warning. None of us should be out there alone until the ghoul is dealt with."

I nodded. "When, then, do you want to hunt?"

Bryce looked at the clock hanging in the room, a black and gold piece on the wall. The carved yellow hands turned slowly against black numbers. Still early.

"Two," Bryce said, his face sliding into a frown. "I have to head to the Spire today. There are, unfortunately, some new members of our esteemed government that doubt the dangers of our work and would seek to reduce its funding."

"What are you going to do?"

"Scare them. I've found the best way to teach new bureaucrats is to make them realize all they could lose," Bryce said with a shake of his head. "Yourself? Any events today?"

"Going to go for a long walk," I said. "It's been a while since I've gone around down here."

Telling Bryce about the woman on the train wouldn't get me anything other than an inquisition. Either an admonishment that I was listening to non-guides talk about Riven, or a stern warning not to look into it without him along. Nothing against Bryce, but I didn't need him for everything.

"I'm envious," Bryce replied. "One of these days, I'll pass off the role of liaison to you, and then I'll be the one enjoying strolls."

"Yeah, like that'll happen," I said.

"One day," Bryce said as we stood up. "One day, Carver."

Back out on the street, after Bryce had made his way off towards the city center and that tall black spike reaching towards the sky, I took out the card and read the address. Less than a mile away. Time to take that walk.

8

THE ADDRESS WASN'T EVEN a building. It was a building-to-be. Blocks and bars stuck out of the ground at the construction site. Workers were gathering, looking at the plans on a giant rolling board. Nearly eight feet high, the metal board resembled a series of overlapping drapes. Levers on the side raised and lowered sections, each one with a different level or diagram presented. I watched the shifting plans for a minute, then double-checked the card. This was definitely the place, only the place didn't seem to exist.

"Can I help you, sir?" a worker, this one's uniform bearing the blue slash across gray cloth that indicated a foreman.

I held up the address so he could see.

"Oh, that's over here. Beneath the site," the foreman said, his face breaking into a confidant's smile. "Didn't expect someone like you to want to see them, but I'll show you where to go."

"See them?"

The foreman glanced at the workers, then back at me with a slight shake of his head, nodded for me to go along with him. We moved around the board and kept walking along the edge of the site into what would be an alleyway once the building was finished. The foreman leaned in as we went.

"Being truthful, sir, these people are making our work here a pain. They're a mess for morale. Nobody here likes thinking about the other side," the foreman said. "You wouldn't be, uh, planning to get rid of them, would you?"

I stopped walking. The foreman took another step before he realized and looked back at me.

"Be straight. Who lives here?" I asked.

The foreman's eyes brightened. A chance to make his case, no doubt.

"The worst, sir. The worst," the foreman said, moving closer to me and sinking his voice to a whisper. "You know the type. The ones who pretend to do your work."

Ah. That explained the woman's attitude. Sneaks, we called them. Everyone called them. People who had the gift to go to Riven, but who either couldn't be, or didn't want to be, a guide. Constantly getting themselves killed by spirits they didn't know how to deal with. Sneaks sold their gift to desperate people, ones looking to send a last message or, maybe, to hear one. Searching for proof that a missing friend might be dead.

"Our work has nothing in common with a sneak's," I said. "We keep people alive, a sneak profits on one's love for the dead."

"That's what I mean. The worst people," the foreman said. "You'll find the stairs a little further ahead. They have the basement. I, uh, I must be getting back, you know."

I nodded and the man dashed away to his board. Sneaks. I squared my shoulders, went ahead to the drilled-out stairs heading down to a heavy door. There was a knocker, and a handle. I pounded twice. Waited. Pounded again. Still nothing. So I tried the handle. The latch clicked and the door swung open, revealing a short, dim hallway leading to a wide room. I walked in.

On either side of the hallway sat a pair of shut doors that I ignored. The middle room appeared to be lit by candles, long ones stuck into the walls and a candelabra on large stone table in the center. In downtown there wasn't a reason to go without electricity, so why were they using candles? Then, above, I heard the pounding start. The construction, of course. Perhaps they had no power here. As I went into the room, however, any curiosity about the candles disappeared.

All along the walls, nailed between the candles, were thick canvas maps. Dark lines stood out, with plenty of lighter versions beneath that'd been partially erased. Developed as they'd gone along, then. The map's method didn't interest me so much as their contents, however.

For the maps were of Riven and of its different regions. I'd never seen any maps like these before. The guides didn't bother. The majority of the spirits were in Riven's main crumbling city, so there wasn't a need to venture outside of it. Here, though, Riven expanded into a world I'd never imagined.

The city alone covered three of the maps, streets broken out in their wandering lines. The maps were covered with different colored markings. Red, blue, and yellow dots scattered throughout. Their placement seemed to be at random, as I couldn't distinguish any pattern to them. Where our clock tower stood, there was a black star. I looked and found other guide entrances to Riven, marked with black stars as well. All of them. This group of sneaks wasn't a bunch of fools, they had plotted out where we were most likely to be.

I moved to the next set of maps. I'd never been outside the city walls, but close. A journey with Bryce to show me that Riven did not truly end at the city's edge. On one side, a vast plain with waving white stalks of grain. Never harvested, always blowing for eternity in that dead wind. The map here had fewer dots, no stars.

The next one covered the region on the city's west side, a dense forest. One I'd never seen but, by Bryce's account, a place to avoid. Angrier spirits stayed there, monsters we didn't have to face to keep Riven in line. The Cycle stood beyond that forest, and the map dwindled in detail the deeper into the woods it went, eventually dropping into blank canvas.

The third map on that side of the wall appeared to go beyond the plain, and it also disappeared into nothing. An outline of some buildings, but none of the city's detail. No interior sketches. I'd never heard of a second city, but if it followed the same trend as the forest, then perhaps it was too dangerous to be worth exploring.

The last wall of the large room was split by another hallway and had one blank map hanging in the available space. *The Mountain* written on it in deep black marker, but nothing drawn below.

"A pity the guides are trusted with a world they do not even know," said a woman's voice behind me.

Something hit the back of my head and thrust me into a world of darkness.

9

I'D HAD HANGOVERS BEFORE, but waking up to this headache was in another realm entirely. As if thought boulders were being thrown inside my brain, shattering against my skull. I didn't even want to open my eyes. If I'd been at home, I'd slip into Riven. A different world, a different body. Easier to work it off over there.

"We're not killing a guide down here," the woman's voice. A familiar one. "Too many would have seen him."

Now I forced my eyes open, let the real pain bleed in. I was in a chair at the table in the center of the room. On the other side of it, the woman I'd seen on the train that morning was talking to a shabby man. Mangy coat, dirt-stained pants. A scarf tied tight serving as a mask. Then I noticed the bar held in his right hand. Looked like it might've been pilfered from the construction site up top.

"He saw the maps, Anna. He knows what we're doing," Scarf said, the cloth muffling his voice.

I tested my hands. Found out my wrists were tied to the chair I was sitting on. Thick dark cable wrapping around the wood. More castoff from the construction site. I wondered if the foreman knew how much he was losing to these people.

"Did you think of how he found this place?" Anna said. "I gave him the address."

"Why in Riven's name did you do that?"

"We need help, Laurence," Anna said. "You know as well as I do that more of our targets are angry now. It's too dangerous."

"Good to know," I announced. "Thanks for the information. Mind letting me out?"

The two of them started, then Laurence raised the bar. I stared at him through my mask, trying to communicate the many, many ways I would make him suffer if he hit me with that again. Then Anna pressed her hand to the man's chest and pushed him away. She, still wearing her white mask, stood over me.

"How's your head?" Anna asked.

"Got a show going in there," I said. "But I've tuned it out for the moment."

I shifted my wrists. Tried to remind her that they remained shackled. Anna didn't make a move.

"How much did you hear?"

"Doesn't matter," I said. "You didn't say anything interesting."

"You had to find a cocky one," Laurence said, sitting in another chair. Letting the bar clang against the floor. "Only thing worse than a guide is one with a mouth."

"It's a fact," I said. "Riven's dangerous? You think we don't know that? We've got people in Riven all day, every day, wrangling spirits to keep the numbers down. Getting hurt. Dying."

Anna sat back on the table, folded her arms across her chest and looked down at the floor. I jiggled my wrists again. There were limits to my vast patience.

"At least you're armed," Anna said. "We're left to run and hide. Which is why we need your help."

"Already helping. Or I would be, if I wasn't tied to a chair. If you'll please let me out, I actually have things to do today."

"You know who we are?" Anna met my stare with serious eyes.

"Yeah, you couldn't hack it as a guide and now you're here selling snake oil to people who'd give anything for one more message to their kid. Their husband. That girl they loved down the street," the acid pity dripping from my voice was intentional.

"There we go. That's what I was waiting to hear today," Laurence muttered.

"We bring people closure," Anna said.

"You exploit their pain."

I couldn't see her face under that mask, the long silence had me picturing a series of angry responses crushed into control. "What about your pain, Carver? Anything worth exploiting there?"

Carver. My name. She shouldn't have known that. I preferred my anonymity. Used it as a cloak, a shield from less than pleasant beginnings, the dangers of the present, and a muddy future. As long as I had that cloak, I could be anyone I wanted. I had no past.

"Repressed all that years ago," I said. "Time to let me leave."

I wanted to push her about my name. Figure out where she'd found that information. Only I was late. Bryce would be waiting.

"I have an offer," Anna said. "One that I think can benefit us both. I'll send you descriptions of spirits we're looking for. You can let me know where they are, or if they're already crazy. In return, I'll help you find your mother."

"I thought sneaks only worked in Riven?" I asked the

question to cover my surprise. Anna not only knew my name, but also knew that I'd never met, never seen or heard anything about my mother? Not that orphans were exactly rare. Even in Chicago, plenty of kids lost parents to disease, war, or a machine gone wrong. Still...

"I go where my clients need me . So you'll accept?" Anna replied.

"If it'll get me out of here."

Laurence unlocked the cuffs and I sprung free from the chair. Rubbed my wrists and didn't wait for another word before I walked across the room, up the stairs, out of the building. Flipped on my mask's respirator as I stepped into the dirty air and rumbling noise of Chicago's downtown.

Anna could send me her list. Now that I was free, I had no obligation to answer. No way would a guide help a couple of sneaks. As for my mother, I'd never known her, and I'd made it this far. Even if Anna's offer was real, even if she had information, I didn't need it.

I SWUNG my legs out of the bed and looked over at Bryce as he raised the cup from the small table. Riven threw its muted gray light into the clock tower's windows, the usual flakes of ash fluttering around the room. It always took a moment for my body to catch up with the new sensations. The hard switch from the smells and sounds of the city to Riven's blank expanse. The first couple of times it was jarring. Now I'd learned to give myself a moment to sink in to the new reality.

"I'd say you're late, but you already know." Bryce said.

"Sorry, the walk ran long."

Bryce didn't ask for a follow-up. Just nodded and drained whatever was left in the cup. Drinking here was more of a joke than anything. Whatever liquid existed bubbled up through pipes that no one had ever built. Came out of faucets no one had ever installed. Tasted a pure and perfect nothing. Like drinking air. Most guides didn't bother, but I think Bryce found it calming. A bit of normal in a strange world.

"Grab your gear," Bryce said. "With that high quota, we've got a lot of work ahead."

"Can't wait."

Armed with my lash and the usual assortment of guide gear, I followed Bryce outside. My partner had his giant voulge strapped to his back, the blades at either end gleaming against the murk. Bryce raised a finger and I took a small tube from my belt. Held it up and pressed in a button on the bottom. A bright blue light shot up into the sky, split and sparkled azure color above the dead city. Right over the fountain, which I figured was a nice touch.

Over the next couple of minutes other sparks shot up and appeared in the sky. Red, gold, green. Each identifying another set of guides at work. One area, to the south, showed no flash.

"See, this is what happens when you take too long," Bryce said.

"You know you've been wanting to go back."

It had been a while since we had last gone into the Warrens. Of the places to go hunting in Riven, the Warrens were, well, less fun. Or more, depending how you looked at it. Bryce chose to shake his head and walk towards the south. I followed.

The streets around our clock tower were mostly deserted. A few blank-eyed spirits wandered down the avenues. So many guides came through here that anyone even close to changing would be wrangled within moments.

On the right side of the street, beneath a bending lamp post, was a melancholy man. You could always pick out the interesting ones by how they stood. A spirit that had simply gone out on their own time, wasted away from a disease or old age or passed off in their sleep, those always looked lost. Ready. As though finding their way in this next life. This guy, though, he wore a set of army fatigues. The vest and pants with the whole pack attached. What drew my eyes to him was his face, the open mouth, a silent scream stamped onto his expression. A giveaway of a person who hadn't meant to die. Who couldn't believe where he was.

"How long you think for that one?" I asked.

"I give him a day. Maybe two."

"You want to wrangle him now? Save some time?"

Bryce hesitated. Then shook his head. Potentials were always a risk. You could usually get the drop on a spirit that wasn't angry yet. They wouldn't be expecting the guide to strike, but if you messed up, or if the spirit proved better than you expected, there was always a chance it could go wrong. One of the first things I learned about Riven is that you don't go picking fights you don't need.

"There's always a chance he'll be cycled," Bryce said. "Always a chance."

"If he bites me later, I'm blaming you."

It took nearly twenty minutes of walking to reach the Warrens. You could always tell you'd arrived by the way the crumbling buildings rose higher and higher, coupled by more and more stairs leading down from the sidewalks, below the ground. If Riven had ever been a real city, this is where the masses would've lived. Bryce paused between a pair of tall towers. The guides called them the Ghoul's Gateway.

"Any chance we'll see one today?" I said as Bryce looked the two towers up and down.

"It's been almost fifty years since the fight that named these things," Bryce said. "Don't get your hopes up."

"Someday."

I knew the remark, the comments about facing a ghoul always got under Bryce's skin. Sure, we'd all known guides that hadn't made it. Maybe it was disrespectful to hope for danger. At the same time, though, I wanted to see a legend live.

There were a couple of ways guides started a hunt. You

could wander around and hope you stumbled upon something interesting, but that usually meant relying on luck. Or lots of time. Neither of which we wanted to waste in a place like the Warrens. So instead we had a couple of tricks.

"Let's listen," Bryce said. Not a bad call. The Warrens were tightly packed, with plenty of spirits wandering through these rooms. Using the resonator made sense. I took the small box off of my belt and placed on the ground. The box itself was covered with mesh, wires that would vibrate if they were hit by a certain frequency of sound. Sound that Bryce and I couldn't hear. The sound of a spirit losing its mind, a scream too high frequency for our ears. I flipped the small switch on the top of the box and we waited to see what the Warrens had for us today.

It only took a minute for the resonator to vibrate. With the heat of the vibration, the wires closest to the sound glowed a faint orange. That pointed us in our direction. Straight up the street, deeper.

"That was fast," I said. Getting a strong signal out here meant one of a couple things. Either we were really lucky and we had a spirit real close by. Or, worse, we had some strong waves coming in. Which meant either one very, very angry spirit, or a whole bunch of them. "We get a whole group, maybe we can fill our quota in a single fight."

"I'll take ten single spirits over a group any day," Bryce said. "It might take longer, but you're probably going to be alive at the end of it."

Holding the resonator in my hand, we walked down the street. Followed the tinting of the wires as the glow shifted from straight ahead to going right. The sound led us down an avenue, towards a tower that was holding together well. Few cracks in the outside walls, no collapsed floors. The base was built as an ornate restaurant, silver letters above proclaiming it *The Castle*. Above the restaurant stretched at least eight floors of a hotel. A hotel that had never been occupied, just as the restaurant had never served a single meal. At least, not so long as the Riven we knew had been around.

Bryce pressed on the door, a thick revolving one with four slabs that slid against the tile floor. Slid well too. Riven was a study in paradoxes. Some things wore down, others kept working as though the elements never touched them. I had asked Bryce about it before but he had shaken his head. Said that Riven had its own rules, and whomever wrote them wasn't around anymore to explain.

"Be ready," Bryce said as he stepped into the lobby. It took me a moment to see why. The floors and walls were chipped, gashed. Chunks were missing, and not the usual crumbling of decay Riven had elsewhere. These had all the hallmarks of collateral damage. Irregular slashes and tears in the sides, an entire corner carved out of the dark wood desk that in some other time and place would have served as the greeting spot for customers.

I uncurled the lash and let it dangle behind me on the floor as we moved through the lobby following the marks of the fighting. Equipped the resonator back to my belt, flipping off the switch. We were too close now to bother taking up a hand with a tool that had no use with a spirit grabbing for your throat.

The damage led us back through the restaurant, a line of overturned chairs and broken tables suggesting the fight hadn't been going in a good way. The goal was always to get your spirit wrangled as fast as possible, as cleanly as possible. Drawn out fights always had the possibility of driving other spirits to investigate, bringing in more enemies than you could handle. The carnage here suggested something more desperate.

Bryce froze as we neared the back of the restaurant. Held up his hand. Folded down his fingers so that only two pressed together and pointed straight up. The symbol for silence. A moment later I heard the reason why. The gnashing and scrambling, the tearing of a spirit in its frenzy.

I wasn't a fan of this place. Too many things my lash could get stuck on. Too tight. But a guide didn't have the luxury of choosing where he worked.

Bryce pushed his way through the swinging doors into the kitchen. There, lying on the central island where food would've been prepped, was a body. On top of it, chewing away with its hands covered in blood, was the ragged form of the spirit that had lost its mind. Another soldier, though this one's outfit suggested he'd suffered his death at the hands of the enemy's guns. Holes peppered the spirit's uniform, bullet-sized pock marks rippled up and down his arms. Some spirits came to Riven as they wanted to be in their mind's eye, their ideal form. Others, too swept up in their own tragedy, came the same way as they left life.

The voulge's edges flashed blue as Bryce, with his right hand, whipped the weapon off of his back and brought it, as he ran forward, slashing at the spirit. The move was fast, but the spirit was faster. He rolled off the body and behind the island as the Bryce sliced the air where the spirit had been.

"Pincer," Bryce said, moving around the island to the left. I went right. The spirit stood, looked at each of us in turn. Blood ran down his ruined face. A hole where half of its mouth had been. No wonder the spirit was angry, his death had been the thing of horrors.

As I moved directly across from the spirit, I swung the lash over and across the island. The lash was ten feet long, more than enough distance to strike the spirit. Only as my arm flipped the weapon forward, I felt a body tackle me from below. A new spirit drove me into a counter and I rolled away from its grasping hands. Another soldier, though this one less torn up than our first friend. Hiding among the dishes and pans beneath the island.

The spirit lunged at me again and I threw up my arms to block his grasp, dropping the lash and gripping the spirit's scrabbling wrists with my hands. His mouth hurled soundless curses at me and I stared into those bright blue eyes, burning with pale fire. Then I brought my knee up into his stomach and slammed the spirit into the counter on my left.

"There are three!" Bryce shouted from across the kitchen.

The rattle of metal on tile announced another spirit bursting from beneath the island, thankfully not on my side. I let go with my right hand and jacked the spirit in the face, trying to keep his biting teeth from getting a grip on my fingers. The punch knocked the spirit back a few steps, gave me just enough space to draw my backup weapon, the standard-issue long knife that every guide had. Twisted the hilt and the blade glowed blue, ready to wrangle.

On the other side of the island, Bryce danced between the other two spirits. The quarters were too tight for his voulge to be any good as one large weapon, so Bryce had pulled the neat trick of splitting it into two separate blades. He stood with his back against the cabinets, one blade facing each of the spirits on either side of him. Trying to delay till I could come for help.

My target gave a ripping howl, or tried to; his throat wasn't in the best shape, the wound that had probably killed him slashed through his vocal cords so that the scream came off as a crackling wind. Then he charged. I stepped forward with the knife, hoping the spirit would just impale himself and make this easy. But the soldier had just enough experience to dive below the blade and hit my legs, knocking me down.

I felt the spirit's hands digging into my ankles as I tried to roll away. But he wasn't letting go. Was trying to get behind me as I struggled with my face against the floor. Not good.

Then the spirit was on my back, climbing towards my neck. I felt the hands on my throat, the cold clammy grasp of bloodless fingers.

"Should have stayed down," I said. I stabbed my knife over my head, into the air where I hoped the spirit would be, and felt it bite into the thing's skin. The spirit's fingers loosened and he rolled off of my back. I sprang up and glanced at him, but the blade had done its work. The pale fire was gone from the spirit's eyes and the only thing left was a blank gaze. In another minute he would start his long walk to the Cycle.

"If you're all done over there, I could use some help!" Bryce yelled.

Oh yeah. Guess that would be the nice thing to do.

11

BRYCE DOVE across the island as the two spirits flanking him charged. As the guide rolled off the other side, he somersaulted, landing on his feet with his back to the spirits. Without waiting, Bryce whirled around, slashing the blades behind him. If the spirits followed him across the island, they'd have been caught in the attack as they came across. Except they didn't.

"Not as mindless as their friend," I said as I picked up my lash.

"I'll take the left," Bryce replied. The man never was one for mid-fight banter.

That left me with Swiss cheese man. Bullet riddled and bloody, the spirit came around the island towards me. I cocked the lash in my right hand, wrist ready to whip the weapon forward. The spirit's pale blue eyes locked on the lash's tip. If I just came at him, the spirit would be ready to dodge. He'd proven himself more capable than your average enraged ghost. In my left hand, I held the long knife. That was going to be my real weapon.

I took a step forward with my left leg as the spirit moved in, swung with my right hand and cracked the lash. The tendril swung through the air straight towards the spirit's head. As I started the move, the spirit, with his right hand, swept a pan off of the island and shifted it in front of the lash, blocking the strike.

What the spirit didn't block was my follow-up. As the spirit focused on the lash, I stepped in with the blade, cutting beneath the pan. I felt the knife bite in, but only to the spirit's clothes. That bulky uniform had my strike missing wide left. The spirit pressed forward, allowing my blade to get tangled up in his uniform and pressed the pan into my face.

Another dirty fight. I turned with the spirit as he pushed and used my grip on the long knife to shove the spirit forward. I stuck my right foot out and it collided with the spirit's ankles. Tripped the bloody bastard. My long knife cut its way free in the motion, so that when the spirit hit the floor, sprawling out, I was ready to close the deal.

"Duck!" Bryce yelled and I didn't second-guess, just dropped to the floor. Over my head I felt the rush of wind as the second spirit flew by. A reckless dive, one that would've taken my head off without Bryce warning me. The second spirit bounced off the wall and turned, standing up, arms spread with a pair of serrated knives in his hands. And then one half of Bryce's voulge sliced through the thing's face and embedded itself in the wall behind.

The spirit at my feet started to scramble away, but I pinned him with the knife. Right in the calf. The blue fire shot down the blade and into the spirit, draining away his rage and leaving him lying there, senseless. For the first time in what felt like forever, I took a deep breath. A pointless breath, as there wasn't really air in Riven, but it felt good anyway.

"Sorry," was the first thing Bryce said after he retrieved his weapon from the wall, the split-headed spirit falling to the ground. "I've never seen one turn away from a fight and go after someone else."

"Me either."

We studied the body lying on the island, the source of this whole thing. The outfit was easy to recognize. A guide, though not one from Chicago. A newer one, going by the slim toolset on his belt.

"You know him?" I asked. Bryce nodded.

"Part of the latest class. He shouldn't have been out here alone," Bryce said. "The name was Felix. Out of Europe."

"You going to tell Piotr?"

Bryce nodded. "It's my job."

Then, without warning, Bryce slammed his fist on the island. I backed up a pace.

"He shouldn't have been here. His mentor, where was he?" Bryce said, though I could see wasn't really talking to me. "We don't have enough guides for this. We can't lose people because they decide to play lone wolf. Especially not now."

"Bryce," I said. "Think about it. We came in here, saw one spirit, and thought it would be easy, but there were two more hiding. Felix probably had the same set up. Saw one, got ambushed."

"Spirits don't ambush," Bryce said.

"These just did."

Bryce chewed the scene for a moment, glancing around the island. Then he snapped his voulge together and slung it over his back.

"I have to go report this," Bryce said.

"Three is short of our quota," I said.

"The quota won't matter if we're getting killed. Guides

need to know that some of the spirits aren't the usual mindless drones. If they're setting traps, then Riven's a lot more dangerous than it used to be."

Which was just what I'd asked for, right? More danger?

I needed to learn to shut up.

I DROPPED Bryce back at our headquarters; the old clock tower in the fountain-centered courtyard.

"Try to find Alec, if he's in here," Bryce said as he went through the door.

"Yeah, I'll keep an eye open, but I think Alec only gets found when he wants to be," I replied.

Bryce nodded. "Be careful. If you're chasing your quota, don't go following any spirits down alleyways. If these were a trend…"

"Don't worry. I can handle myself."

"Felix probably thought the same," Bryce held up a hand, then vanished through the door. I was not jealous of the conversation he was about to have. Any dead guide resulted in a massive review. An investigation into what led to the fatality, and what could be done to prevent the next one. That's why we now carried sparkers and tried to work in pairs as much as possible. All of our tools had come about through failure. Survival today due to the deaths of those that came before.

Leaving the courtyard, I struck out to the west. Unlike the

Warrens, the buildings here weren't as tall, weren't as run down. As though whomever built them had an eye for beauty rather than simple efficiency. Along the avenues I walked, two-story shops and bungalows with swooping fronts and faded marquees dominated the sides. Had this been a real neighborhood, I imagined it would be filled with families on a night out. People looking for restaurants, a play, or a chance to see the newest fashions on display. Here, in Riven, it was like walking through a half-realized dream.

I paused in front of a larger building. This one went three high stories, the tallest one on the block, each floor separated from the one beneath with small balconies bordered with weaving iron made to look like vines crawling up the side. My favorite place in the neighborhood. The place Selena and I chose for her.

"You around?" I said as I walked into the third-floor apartment. Furniture in Riven was, by its nature, a dull gray affair, but Selena and I had found enough interesting pieces to give her apartment a sense of character. A long thin table sat in the living room, surrounded by a few different types of skeletal chairs. One metal, one wood, and another seemingly made of wicker. It was a mystery how anything like wood, made from something that been alive, could exist in Riven, but it did.

The walls of the place were decorated with hanging, unframed, drawings. Selena's. Most were of Riven's cityscapes, the scenes she saw as she wandered. A couple were portraits of people I didn't know. One, of a girl and boy, I assumed were her children. I hadn't asked, and she hadn't offered an explanation.

"I'm outside," Selena called from the balcony.

I went by the kitchen, a galley-style affair that was point-less in the food- and drink-less land we were in, and out through the opening onto the balcony. No door, no barrier for the nonexistent bugs here. Selena had her hands on the railing, looking out over the city. Riven's endless haze gave the vista a fog effect, the rows of structures collapsing into the mist in the distance as though the world vanished into nothing.

"It's a nice day," I said.

"They are always nice," Selena said. "One of the things I miss the most, and I didn't realize it until the other day, is a bit of rain."

I followed her eyes up to Riven's cloud-smeared sun. Or moon. It was hard to tell exactly what hung behind the cover. All we knew was that it was always in the same spot, never moving, giving Riven the constant pale cast.

"Look at it this way, it's never cold here."

"It never changes," Selena said. "That's a strange thought, isn't it? That what I want more than anything else, is change?"

"You might be in luck," I said. "We found something different today."

Selena turned away from the sky and looked at me. That scar, those big beautiful eyes. Still no hint of the pale blue fire. I swallowed away the nervous flutters that always bustled up the first time I saw her face. Even now, there was so much packed in that simple look that I had to prepare myself before I could continue.

"Bryce and I, we found a dead guide. The spirits that tore him apart, they were working together."

"I thought all of the angry ones were mindless?"

"That's what I thought too. I wanted to ask if you'd seen anything strange?"

Selena shook her head. "But it's not like I'm looking for them. Unless I'm with you, I try to stay away from the angry ones."

"Probably a good idea. You'll keep an eye out?"

"It's not like I have much else to do," Selena said. "I wander around the city and, eventually, I come back here and wait for you."

I didn't know what to say to that. It wasn't like I could gift her something new. I didn't even know what she wanted. If, beneath all the grief at her past life, she wanted to find something here that could take that away, or if she just wanted to stay for a while and live with her memories. Eventually she would go to the Cycle, as would all of us.

"Nicholas wants to talk," Selena said after a minute's silence. "He's got something he wants to show you."

"I suppose it's been a while," I said. "You want to go for a walk?"

"Aren't you afraid we'll be spotted?" Selena's voice slid into a mocking tone. "That you'll be seen with me?"

"Anybody says anything, I'll just pretend I'm wrangling you," I replied, slapping a smile on my own face. The joke didn't get the reaction I was looking for. Selena looked away and nodded. Someday, maybe, I'd understand how her mind worked.

Back on the street we continued west. Towards the edge of the neighborhood. The spots for Selena and Nicholas made sense because they were quiet. Like Selena was saying, angry spirits had a tendency to find each other. To go where other spirits already were. We saw few wandering around here, this part of Riven. Was never sure why, just that it was empty. Maybe Riven's creators wanted to keep the area pristine, and so kept most of the foul things away. The other bonus was that guides rarely went here so Selena and I had to spend less time ducking into alleys to hide.

"Do you ever think about your family?" Selena said as we crested a hill, the street bending through what would've been a beautiful park in the real world. Leafless trees stood in plots of dead grass. Shells of bushes lined the sidewalks. On the other side, the nice neighborhood fell away into a long series of broken factories and warehouses. If I wanted to fill my quota, I'd be able to do it there, no problem.

"What family?" I said. "Bryce?"

"No," Selena said. "I mean, the ones you love. I think about mine all the time. Every day."

"I think about you, if that's what you mean," I said. "I don't really have anyone else."

"So you say."

"You think I'm lying?" I said, guiding us to a bench to sit down for a minute. Once we reached Nicholas, it'd be hard to have a moment to think. "I've never known anything other than the guides."

"You've never tried figure out where you came from?"

"What's bringing this up?" I asked.

Selena wrapped her arms around herself, took a slow look around the park. "We used to come to places like this, when I was alive. I loved to run and play. My mother, father, we would go here and have picnics on the days when he didn't work."

"That's not really an answer."

"Isn't it? Most people, they have childhoods full of memories. Of their parents, or friends, or family. I'm trying to find yours."

"Why?" I said. "They aren't very interesting."

"Because a woman has a right to know a little about the man who's trying to win her heart."

"I can tell you that I didn't go to a park like this," I said. "I can tell you that I went to a series of schools. That I moved around a lot as certain houses, guides, had the space to take me. I was never around anywhere long enough to make real friends."

"That's sad."

"That's life," I replied. "Only, now that we're talking about it, you're not the first person today to bring up my family."

Selena gave me a questioning look and I told her about Anna, the sneaks, and the offer about my mother.

"You're not going to help her?" Selena asked when I was done.

"Why? She'll just get herself killed running around Riven. Better if her work fails and she does something else."

"That's her problem," Selena said. "What matters is that Anna might help you find out who she was. Your mother."

"I'll think about it," I replied.

"I'll help you," Selena said, her hand reaching out and grabbing my wrist. "It'll give me something to do. Something to fill the time here."

I wanted to say no. To tell her that risking herself in this whole mess wasn't worth it. But looking at that face, feeling the pressure from her hand, I didn't want to take that away from her. So I nodded, then stood.

"Come on, let's go see Nicholas," I said. "Whatever new toy he has is bound to be thrilling."

So long as it didn't kill me.

13

Nicholas Salzer. A man so brilliant he blew himself up in a west side lab district not long after I came to Chicago. I found him in Riven two days later looking around, trying to take notes using a rock and a wooden board he'd found on the street. Like Selena, I'd helped him find a home.

In return, Nicholas built my lash.

The building we chose for the lab was a squat, wide structure that might've been used for machining, or maybe as a school. Inside was a large empty space. Nicholas seemed to take the vacancy as a challenge, and filled the building with random junk he found wandering through Riven.

Selena and I came up to the front door, one that had been wood when we first found the place, now replaced with a slick steel slab. Worked metal was a rare find in Riven, but the factory district near here had a fair share for the taking.

There wasn't a handle on the door. Only a button on the right that, if pressed, would set a series of lights aglow in the lab. Nicholas insisted the lights were a better way of alerting him, as there was usually so much noise that a bell would go unheard.

I pressed the button and winced. A habit. More than once, Selena and I tried Nicholas's inventions and found them to be a tad more dangerous than the inventor had explained. Nicholas blew himself apart here in Riven with unsettling regularity. Pulled himself back together through the simple magic of not being alive in the first place.

The door popped open. Literally popped. Shot off its hinges and fell over to the side, bits of smoke rising from where the door been attached.

"That wasn't quite the result I was looking for," came the breezy voice of the inventor. Nicholas, wearing a set of makeshift goggles, nearly disappeared into his large, very stained and burned lab coat. His waving hand stuck out from the wide sleeve like an island in an ocean. "Answering the door was getting to be too much of a hassle. I thought, perhaps, a more automatic means might save me some steps."

"How many times are you getting visited?" I asked. So far as I knew, Selena and I were the only ones aware that Nicholas existed.

"Oh, just you. And Selena, of course," Nicholas replied.

"So you're building this to save yourself time for one visit every few days?" I asked.

"It's really more of the principle," Nicholas said. "It's something that is less efficient than it could be, therefore, I must do what I can to fix the problem."

"Also, we're in Riven," Selena said. "It's not like we don't have time."

"Right. Time. I've been thinking about that," Nicholas said. "Do you know the extent of your binding ability?"

Nicholas addressed the question to me, but I didn't know the answer. A guide could, as could a sneak if they really tried, bind a spirit to Riven. Prevent the Cycle from calling them. Leave the spirit in limbo, essentially.

There was always a chance a spirit could grow angry, and

so guide rules forbade binding a spirit unless you had a good reason. Nicholas and the things he made qualified as a reason. Selena, well, that was complicated.

"Let me know if you start feeling any weird urges. Or if you start getting angry," I said. "Don't want you deciding the best use of your inventions is to go killing me or anyone else."

"No urges beyond the usual," Nicholas said, his eyebrows popped. "I'm glad you're here. I've got something fun for you to try."

"What are the odds it'll kill me?" I replied.

"If you pointed at yourself, high. Point it anywhere else, low," Nicholas said, ushering us inside.

The lab was arranged into a large U shape. Long tables, made from smaller desks and other furniture cobbled together, were arranged along the outside walls. In the middle, compiled tools and stacks of books sat on the hard floor. Books, in this case, being sheafs of paper that Nicholas had filled up with notes and bound together. Paper that Nicholas had made on his own by processing the wood that could be found around Riven.

On the back wall sat a boiler, hooked up to a mechanism that leveraged steam to generate electricity. How Nicholas powered his lab in a world that had no other options.

Nicholas led us to the central part of the U, a workbench that had on it a crossbow. It wasn't the basic kind that I recalled from medieval tales. No, this one was longer, bulkier. A lever along the main shaft cycled between three separate series of bolts. I reached for it but Nicholas blocked my arm.

"Now, here you are talking about how you hope I won't kill you and then you go grabbing for it?" Nicholas said, a laugh tweaking the edges of his voice. "You might think that this is just a simple crossbow-"

"Believe me, I don't think that at all," I interrupted.

"I suppose it is a tad obvious. I couldn't find an efficient way to hide the extra bolts. Trust me, I tried."

"I'm guessing there's a reason for the different types?" I asked. Looking closer, the bolts were shaded. Feathered with different colors. The first set was black, the middle blue, and the last orange.

"No, I just did this all for fun," Nicholas said. The scientist's sarcasm was like getting hit with a wet sack of flour. "Of course they're different. The first ones are your run-of-the-mill bolts, they'll shoot through a spirit and pin it to the wall. Or, you know, do a number on any living thing you run across."

"I'm not planning on killing a guide anytime soon."

"Not saying you would. Only saying you can," Nicholas said. "Moving on. The blue ones you can probably guess. They give you a shot at wrangling a spirit from afar. The orange ones, well, it's best if you see those in action."

Without waiting for my reply, Nicholas picked up the crossbow from the table. From the way he hefted it, I could tell the thing wasn't going to be light. He shifted the lever on the shaft to the third setting, the orange bolt. Then he pulled the crank on the right side. As the crank turned, an orange bolt slipped out of its slot and shot up to the front of the crossbow where it latched into place. As Nicholas continued turning the crank, the string tightened, pulling the bolt back into a firing position.

"Now, it's probably better if we try this outside the lab," Nicholas said, looking around. "I'd rather not rebuild this whole place."

Outside, on the street, Nicholas moved us to the center and aimed the crossbow towards the factories. He pointed it at a large container a couple hundred yards away, one probably made for holding industrial liquids in another time and place. Then, without any warning, he raised the crossbow and pulled the trigger.

The orange bolt streaked off down the street and struck the container, bursting into a fiery lightning that crawled around and arced off to the surrounding building and even to the ashy flakes in the air. The burning rays jumped from object to object, expanding in a bright nova for a dozen yards or more in every direction before slowly petering out and leaving only charred wreckage behind.

"Riven has unique physical properties," Nicholas said into the silence. "I'm still learning how it works, but the possibilities are very interesting."

"How hard is it to make more of those?" I said.

"Selena and I have been making expeditions. Finding the materials," Nicholas said, glancing at the woman with a thankful smile. "So long as we continue, and Riven doesn't get too dangerous, keeping you supplied shouldn't be an issue."

"Have you noticed more angry spirits way out here?" I asked.

Nicholas nodded. "I don't go exploring as often anymore. There are voices on the wind. Spirits, loud ones, talking with each other. Making plans. The kinds of things they should not be doing."

"Note them for me," I said. "I'll make sure they get taken care of."

Nicholas handed me the crossbow and backed away a couple steps. I held it up, shifted the lever to the regular bolt and turned the crank. Ready to fire. Then I lowered it.

"This thing have a holster?" I asked.

"What do you think I am?" Nicholas replied. "An amateur?"

14

———

THE GUIDES CALLED it the Tar Pit. The part of Riven's city made up of broken down factories. Containers, like the one Nicholas shot with the crossbow, littered the landscape and were full of unidentified sludges, liquids, or worse. After saying a brief goodbye to Nicholas and snagging a quick kiss from Selena, I went on into the Tar Pit to fill my quota.

Bryce and I needed to get ten, and we had wrangled three back in the Warrens. That left more than enough fun for me. The crossbow hung across my back, a new weight I wasn't especially fond of, and I'd have to be careful about rolling anywhere with that thing, but if someone hands you an amazing weapon, it's worth putting up with a few inconveniences.

Fifty yards into the Tar Pit and I was surrounded on all sides by the cracked, massive buildings. Tall and wide, the factories took up blocks at a time. Smokestacks, silent and ominous, lanced into the sky. Fences bordered dusty lots, their chain links as often splintered and unwound as they were together. All in all, it gave the impression of a war zone whose war had ended decades earlier.

It wasn't a good place to be alone.

I kept my eyes scanning the windows, what few of them there were. My ears hunted for the sounds of spirits venting their rage. The resonator might have worked, but the thought of giving up a hand to hold the thing made me hesitate. Normally, the Tar Pit wasn't a hard spot to find prey. Something about the desolate nature of the factories seemed to attract spirits who wanted space to rage.

I was so focused on the factories around me that I almost didn't notice the spirit standing in the middle of the road. But when something has its eyes deadlocked on to you, you eventually feel the itch. Especially when it's not friendly.

The spirit was a large one, a man standing tall and straight. A wide-brimmed, stovepipe hat sat on his head. Strands of scraggly hair leaked beneath the hat to below the man's chin, collecting into the collar of his ragged suit. The gray jacket cloaked over a white undershirt and brown suspenders. In one hand, the spirit held a three foot-long hammer with a fixed spike driven into one end. On the other wrist was a gauntlet that vanished up the suit's sleeve.

It was rare to see a spirit even notice the environment around it. Seeing one actually picking up weapons... that was a whole other level of dangerous. I stopped my walk ten yards away and stared at the man. The spirits eyes held no pale fire, no sign that it had given into the chaos.

"Strange place to stand," I said.

"Any place here is strange, wouldn't you say?" the spirit replied.

"Maybe. All the same, I'm wondering what you're doing here."

"That's easy. I'm waiting for you."

I moved my right hand to the lash and took it off the belt. "Heard that a lot today. Why?"

"What's your name?" the spirit asked.

"Why?" I replied. The man shook his head.

"Because it's what people do when they meet."

I paused. Spirits normally didn't ask questions. At least not beyond the usual set wondering where they were, how they got to Riven, how they could leave it. They definitely didn't want to know who I was. Then, today had already been one for the surreal. Might as well keep riding that train.

"Carver. Carver Reed," I said.

"You can call me Graham," the spirit replied, though I hadn't asked for his name. "Tell me, Carver, do you want to see the most amazing thing?"

"In Riven?"

"In anywhere."

Graham was starting to really mess with my head. Spirits didn't offer this kind of stuff. Didn't play games. Whatever was going on here, I made up my mind to wrangle and send Graham to the Cycle. He wasn't playing by the normal rules, which meant he was dangerous.

"Show me," I said. Maybe Graham would give me some clues as to what made him who he was.

Graham half turned back down the street and gestured with the hammer. "It's a short walk this way. You're not too tired, are you?"

"Seeing strange spirits with hammers like yours has a way of waking me up," I replied.

We walked and I kept my distance, always staying a few paces behind Graham. My eyes crawling around to make sure the spirit wasn't setting me up for something worse.

"You ever think about what a terrible place this is?" Graham said.

"Not really."

"Of course not. You get to run away. Go back to where you can feel the sunlight on your skin. Taste real coffee. Feel the world spin beneath your feet."

"Pay real rent. Breathe terrible air."

"Those are nothing," Graham snapped, glancing over at me. "Any spirit that has to look around this place for more than an hour would take every disadvantage of your world for another chance at it."

"They had their chance. Some live a long life before they come here. What's your point?"

"You and your brothers and sisters drive spirits to be cycled. Force them out of this place and into nothing. Why not go the other way? Bring them back?"

In front of us, the street ended in a large building with a curving roof. It took up more space than Union Station. The doors facing us spanned half a block, standing one after another waiting for a crowd. Graham went right for them.

"Even if we could. Even if we could bring every dead spirit out and make them alive again, that would be chaos," I said. "So many spirits don't even retain their identities. What would you do with them?"

"I would give them another chance," Graham said. He grasped the handle on one of the doors and pulled it open.

Unlike the sliding door back in the Warrens, this one screeched in protest as old joints ground against each other. Inside, there was nothing more than darkness. Graham stepped into it and disappeared. I waited for a minute, and then a flickering light burst out of nothing. Graham, now holding a torch, showed up back in the doorway.

"We're almost there," Graham said.

"Can't wait."

I followed Graham into the building. Images of Felix, torn apart on that kitchen island flitted about my mind. This is exactly what Bryce was saying not to do. Go alone with a strange spirit into an area where you could be trapped.

We walked deeper down a wide hallway, until Graham's torch stopped fluttering off the walls and its light disappeared into a blackness too thick to overcome. Graham paused, turned to look at me.

"When was the first time you felt that?" Graham said. "The feeling that you're not just like the rest of them?"

"What are you talking about?"

"Carver Reed. Where'd you get that family name?"

"It given to me. I kept it."

My right hand gripped the lash tighter and my left moved towards the long knife.

"Ask them," Graham said. "Ask them where your name came from."

"Ask who?" I replied, but Graham didn't seem to be listening. He'd turned back to the wide open dark.

"And when you do," Graham said. "Tell them that the dead are ready."

Graham leaned back and threw the torch. It whirled through the air, spinning into the dark. As it rose, the torch's light bounced off of girders and bars holding up the ceiling, and that light reflected into the corners of the factory.

Standing there, standing everywhere, were spirits. Dozens. Hundreds. As one, the torch still flying in its arc, the spirits turned to look at me. Pale blue fire roaring in their eyes. Then the torch hit the ground, broke apart and died.

In the darkness I heard the screams of the spirits as their feet pounded against the ground. Graham's cackling laugh echoed off the walls as the damned descended upon me.

15

As my heart jumped into my throat and my eyes bugged out at the sight the pale fire streaming towards me, training took over. My left hand abandoned the long knife and grabbed the sparker. I spun to where I thought we'd come from and pressed the button, holding the tube out in front of me.

A blue spark launched out through the dark. It went down the corridor, and exploded against the line of closed doors. I ran after it. Behind me, Graham's laugh fell away and the only noise was the growling chase of the spirits.

I was five paces away from the doors when the first spirit grabbed my coat. I nearly fell, the sudden jerk stopping me and dragging me sideways as the spirit's own momentum kept it moving left. I turned with the motion, trying to keep upright, and faced back down the corridor. In the dying embers of the blue spark, all I could see was an endless line of pale fire eyes. Some stood on top of each other, crawling over the other spirits or crashing them to the ground. A stampede for my blood.

I backpedaled and, a moment later, smashed the spirit on my back through the doors and out into the Riven street.

The Tar Pit loomed around me again, the sight of Riven's cold light bringing me just a bit of hope. At least until the spirit dragged me down.

The spirit crushed itself beneath my body, the crossbow digging into it, but its arms were still tearing at my clothes. More were coming, leaking out through the door and charging at me. With my right arm, I flicked the lash at the oncoming wave. The lash wrapped itself around the leading spirit and I jerked its feet out from under it. The spirit collapsed and the ones immediately behind it tripped over its body. Bought me a second of time.

I rolled off of the spirit, tearing myself from its grasp, and scrambled away. Pulled up to a crouch just in time to catch the spirit's swing. The spirit looked like an old woman, wearing a ragged dress, but she swung with plenty of rage. The fist struck me in the chin and knocked me to the ground. Beneath me, the crossbow made an angry crunch as it struck the stone street.

As fights went, this one wasn't going very well.

The spirit closed again, her wild old eyes matching her manic grin as she went for my face. Only now I'd had time to grab my long knife. I stabbed it up as I rose, taking the spirit's punch on my forearm as I drove the blade in. The knife's blue flame swept up and into the spirit, driving the rage out of her eyes. The old woman slumped forward as I pulled the knife free.

Then I looked up, and wished I hadn't.

Surrounding me was a line of spirits easily three or four deep with more streaming out of the factory every moment. Dead was too nice of a word for what I was going to be.

"Carver! Getting a little brave over there?" a voice from up the street shouted.

I couldn't see the speaker, but I knew that accent. Alec. "A few more than I expected!" I shouted back.

Some of the spirits started to turn, but they weren't fast enough. Alec crashed into the outer line, and I saw spirits fly, their bodies wreathed in blue wrangling fire. Too many wrangled for just one guide, even Alec. Then I saw the other guides wading in, throwing knives, axes, spears. He'd brought friends.

The spirits weren't done. They were rage incarnate, and they came at me anyway. The three closest to me rushed forward, hands outstretched. Clawing for my face. I cracked the lash wide, sending that blue tip in an arc around the three of them, biting into the right shoulder of the far one. I ran after the swing, tightening the lash around the three as its fire cleansed the first spirit.

With the lash keeping them from moving, I finished the last two spirits with the knife. I looked around and saw a true battlefield. At least a dozen, and maybe more, guides were sweeping by me, led by Alec. They hacked, slashed, and burned their way through the disorganized spirits.

Or they did, until some whistle we couldn't hear, some call that only the spirits could answer, caused the horde to turn away and run. To scatter back through the Tar Pit and leave us panting and standing amid a crowd of wrangled spirits waiting to walk to the Cycle.

Not all the guides had made it through unscathed. Some were scratched, others held arms or favored legs that bled from more vicious strikes. Yet all of us appeared to be alive.

"Where is Bryce?" Alec said. "I only saw you go in there."

"Long story," I said, then blinked. "Are you following me?"

Alec shook his head. "Graham. That's the spirit's name, right?"

I nodded.

"I've been tracking him for weeks now. I've seen traces of this, this gathering, but never so many spirits in one place."

"You think he's the one behind it?" I replied.

Alec looked back at the factory. "I don't know if it's just him, but he has an agenda. He's not corrupted. Not enraged."

I relayed what Graham had told me, but left out the part about my name. The part about asking the guides who I was. I wanted to ask Bryce first and get his opinion.

Most of the guides, including Alec and I, went back to the clock tower or other bases. The time was drawing late, and I had a lot of questions. Questions that Riven couldn't answer.

1 6

My eyes opened to catch the last glimpse of the sun setting on west Chicago. Even the last few minutes of blaze orange and violet clouds were such a different palette than Riven that I laid there and soaked in the color. After hours in Riven, I tended to think I wouldn't see anything other than ashy gray again.

Then my eyes fell on the small stand of collected mail shot in by the overhead pipe. On top of the usual assortment of bills and advertisements sat an envelope with my name on it. Inside were three pieces of paper. The first one a note:

Carver,

Enclosed you'll find a list of people we're looking for. Names and brief descriptions. If you happen to find any while wandering Riven, if you wrangle them or notice they're on their way to being cycled, let me know and I'll be grateful. You can find me most evenings at the Broken Beaker in the lab district.

I know you're probably thinking that helping sneaks doesn't fall in with your normal mode of doing things. I'm hoping I can persuade you otherwise. As a sign of good faith, I've included a little bit more about your mother in this envelope. I hope we can work together.

Anna

The second page was the list of names and descriptions. Children, wives, husbands, the list was long. I shook my head as I looked at it. Spirits weren't exactly the talkative type, you had to catch them in the right mood. You had to get lucky. And Riven was a big place. It wasn't like I could just stroll down the street and call out some names and they'd come running. I folded it up and stuck it in my pocket anyway.

The last sheet was a surprise. It was a formal paper, thick white with the letterhead of the main Chicago medical center across the top - the Spire of Humanity set into a red aid cross. Immediately beneath, in thick letters, were the words *Notice of Death.*

Katherine Reed was found dead this morning in her room, having apparently passed in her sleep overnight. Prior to this incident, Katherine had expressed difficulties with her recent pregnancy and childbirth and had been admitted to the psychiatric ward after repeated assertions that she was being threatened.

Beneath the note were some signatures of doctors and the medical examiner. And beneath those, a scrawled line.

I couldn't find the rest of her records. The hospital said they were lost.
-Anna

Died in her sleep. An answer to a question I'd never bothered to ask. At least now I knew she wasn't out there somewhere. I hadn't been abandoned at birth.

I sat down on the bed and reread the certificate. Took in the doctors' names. People to find later, perhaps. Now, though, I had more urgent problems. The spirit named Graham had a death wish for me and an army at his back. I needed to talk to Bryce.

If anyone knew how to tackle Graham, he would.

We met at Ezra's, as usual. When I got there, Bryce was already a couple rounds in. His face and its dead frown said as much about his day as did the empty glasses in front of him.

"They don't care," Bryce said. "Piotr says too many guides are dying to bother with the particulars for each one. That nobody has the time anymore."

"I hate to say it, but I kind of agree with Piotr on this," I said, taking the first sip of an amber ale. I found the malty flavor played well with the lingering aftertaste of Chicago pollution. A frothy, stinging drink. "I nearly died this afternoon."

Bryce looked up, slanted his head in a questioning look.

"Went hunting the Tar Pit and found a spirit. He was holding a hammer, and he talked to me."

"Holding a hammer?" Bryce said.

"Yeah, one with a spike in it. Had something on his wrist too, but I never found out what that was. A goofy outfit with a top hat."

Bryce sat back in his seat after the description, rubbed his chin with his hand. I waited, but Bryce didn't say anything and eventually nodded for me to continue. Not exactly the reaction I was expecting.

"Graham led me to this big abandoned building. There were hundreds of spirits inside. All angry. If Alec and a bunch of other guides hadn't arrived, I'd have been dead," I said.

"Hundreds?" Bryce said. "It's been a while, but it wouldn't surprise me if the war created a breach."

"That's I was thinking. Now, I mean. Then, I was mostly just panicking," I replied. A breach appeared when large numbers of people died near each other, particularly in traumatic fashion. All of the spirits dumped into Riven at a single point and, due to both the number of spirits and the way in which they got there, the whole group became angry very quickly. When a breach was found, groups of guides would work together to close it.

"It probably won't be the first," Bryce said. "Large-scale wars, you're going to get things like this."

"What I didn't understand, what I don't understand, is why they listened to Graham."

"Because Graham isn't a normal spirit," Alec said, coming into the bar and sitting down next to us. "He was a guide, long ago. A good one. Better than you."

"Thanks," I said. That was Alec for you, delivering the unvarnished truth.

Bryce was nodding. "I suspected when Carver mentioned the hammer."

"So wait, he was a guide?" I asked. "Why hasn't he been wrangled then? I thought that was standard policy."

"A spirit must be caught to be wrangled. Graham, you see, he's very good at getting away. At being found only when he wants to be," Alec said.

"So you're saying the spirit of a dead guide is hunting me?"

"Hunting you? I don't know why he would," Alec said. "But with the three of us, I bet we can catch him and ask him, politely, what he's up to."

"First things first," Bryce said. "If you really found a breach in there, we've got to close it before it gets any worse."

"Two hours?" I said. "So long as I'm down here, I want to take care of something."

Bryce and Alec nodded. I finished my drink, and left. With Alec there, I didn't want to bring up what Graham had told me. About letting the spirits back through. About asking for my name. Nothing against Alec, but he didn't need to know everything.

Back outside, my mask on, I jumped a short train heading towards the lab district. If Anna had found out more about my mother, I wanted to know.

18

THE LAB DISTRICT was the opposite of everywhere else in the Chicago. The opposite of Riven too. Brightly lit with more technology than the rest of the city combined, stepping off the train into the lab district's sparking avenues buried my questions beneath frenzy of light and noise.

On either side of the broad avenue in front of me, buildings glowed with gas tubes of every color. The center of the street was closed off to normal traffic because a new zeppelin was getting ready to launch. A warbling man with a looping horn boosting his voice declared that this zeppelin was powered through batteries. A thousand fans working on top of the ship to provided the charge. A horde of workers, scientists, and students clustered around the zeppelin as it started to rise in the air.

Two blocks to the left, the colors were more muted, a concession, one of the few, made to sleep around here. Cheap hotels specializing in hourly rates and single bedrooms targeted the frantic pace. The lab was the home, and when you needed to sleep, the hotels gave you a place to pass out, shower, and then get back to it. Between the larger facilities, bars and diners showed off cheap beers and fast food. Others offered exhibition galleries to go with their beverages, a chance to taste the excitement with your cocktail.

Past the zeppelin, which slowly crawled up the sky, I found the Broken Beaker. Standing outside, white mask on and watching the experiment, was Anna.

"You weren't kidding," I said.

"It's my favorite place in the city," Anna replied, not bothering to look away from the zeppelin. "The energy here is addicting."

"You don't get enough excitement in Riven?"

Anna laughed. Then shook her head. "When I'm there, I'm not looking for dangerous spirits. Most of the time, I'm finding a loved one and reading them a note from their daughter. Not so thrilling."

"Speaking of, I'm not sure I'll be able to help you," I took out the list of names Anna had sent me. "We don't exactly write down the details of every spirit we see."

Anna nodded back towards the Broken Beaker. "Talk about it inside?"

She led the way. Which was good, because I would have fallen over. Or turned around and left, without her. The Broken Beaker wasn't my kind of place. Not like Ezra's, with its classic dignity. No, Anna's favorite bar was a blend of humanity's brightest lights and loudest sounds mashed together in an overwhelming blast to the senses. Beyond the array of tables dominated by scientists and students shouting inches from each other's faces sat a large stage on which, at the moment, a contraption resembling a train car ground out a ferocious noise.

"It's demo night!" Anna shouted into my ear. "Tonight's theme is noisemakers!"

"Great!" I replied, wondering how many minutes we'd be in here. Having functional ears was, you know, a perk.

Anna grabbed my hand and led me through the crowded floor towards a side wall. More specifically, to a spot that sported a picture of a sunflower. She pressed it, and a door swung inward. The room on the other side was cramped and featureless, except for a second door with another flower, this one a fragile-looking lily.

"Sound damping," Anna explained, somehow sensing my confusion even though my mask was still up. Her words proved themselves a second later as we went into the Broken Beaker's back half, a quiet array of couches and low tables overseen by walls of chalk bearing scribbled equations. The only sound was the bartender rattling cocktails.

"Marginally better," I admitted as we snagged a spot.

"A lot of people don't realize this is even here," Anna said. "Great place to meet clients."

"Which is what we were talking about?"

"All business, aren't you?" Anna replied, slipping off her mask.

"I nearly died twice today," I copied the move. The air felt good on my face, even with the scent of booze underlining every breath. "Makes you rethink small talk."

"I'd ask how, but I can imagine."

"Bet you couldn't. Not this," I said, enjoying her questioning look. There was something fun about holding information from a sneak. "I'll tell you later."

Anna shrugged. Waved for the bartender's attention and then held up two fingers. "I hope you like gin."

"There are worse things to drink," I said. "I wanted to ask you about—"

"Your mother."

"Lucky guess."

"The paper says she died," Anna said. "Only I don't think that's true. At least, not the way they said it happened."

Her comment knocked me back for a moment. Not what I'd been expecting.

"What do you mean?"

"Died in her sleep? Your mother wasn't very old. She wasn't in the hospital for injuries," Anna said. "I get a lot of requests to talk to the dead, Carver. Guess how many just turn up that way without a scratch, and without any investigation?"

"You're really running with this."

"It's not all hunches," Anna said. "But I can't tell you anymore. Not without a favor."

"I already said I couldn't help with the list," as I spoke, the bartender dropped a pair of wide-bottom beakers on our table, each one bubbling with a set of gin and soda. Limes wedged into the neck.

"That was just to get Laurence off my back," Anna said. "I was hoping he wouldn't be there when you came by. What I'm looking for, Carver, is to be one of you."

I took a long drink. Felt the pine needle gin run down my throat. Glanced around the bar to make sure nobody I knew was around.

"There's not a chance," I said. "They'd never give you approval."

"Why not? I can get to Riven. I'm savvy."

"Because you're a sneak."

Anna's eyes narrowed and she leaned forward across the table. "That's something you're going to have to come to terms with. That's the deal. You want to find your mother, you get me in."

Anna picked up her beaker and slammed it, finishing the cocktail in a single pull and then stood up. Walked away.

"He's buying," Anna said to the bartender as she pressed the flower and left.

Getting a sneak to be a guide was impossible. We were chosen young, evaluated when, as kids, we had our first crossing. You came tumbling down to your parents, your teacher, and talk about how you spent the night wandering around another world. Then the law kicked in and you were sent to the nearest guide headquarters and evaluated.

I drank my way through those memories in the Broken Beaker after Anna left. The constant shifts between Riven and the real world, teaching you to control the crossing. To link your own bed to a place on the other side. If Anna hadn't been accepted as a guide, there'd been something wrong. There were no second chances.

And if Anna wouldn't help me find my mother, I knew someone who could.

19

I'D NEVER BEEN in an army. Never stood rank and file with comrades and looked across some vast plain at an opposing force. But standing on the street in Riven with a score of guides around me, staring at the factory that I'd run out of only hours before, I felt a surge of energy, pride, confidence. There were a hundred angry spirits or more, and we were going to go in and wreck them.

"Positions!" Bryce called. He was the senior guide there, the leader for the mission. At his call, ten guides on the edges split out and moved around the factory. The rest of us went forward. Into the teeth.

The first spirits rushed towards us a minute later as we neared the doors. They burst out, scrambling, yelling and grasping at the air with their hands. These weren't the smart, tactical ones we'd encountered in the Warrens. Just your usual rage-filled ghosts looking for some sort of vengeance. We cut them down.

My lash sliced forward with crack after crack, lancing through and wrangling one spirit after another. Still, I was only one, and other guides chose arms more suited to mass attacks.

One, her arms pumping, launched what seemed like an infinite supply of small knives into the waves of spirits. Wrapping her body was a copper construct that, with her motion, cycled knives from a pack on her back down along her arms and right into her hands.

Another swept aside two or three spirits at a time, swinging the largest ax I'd ever seen. Its double-sided head fell into a haft with blades along each side, catching spirits running inside its reach with blue fire. They didn't stand a chance.

When we broke through the doors, Bryce, myself, and three other guides pulled their tubes from our belts and launched sparks down the corridor. The blue, green, and red fires hit spirits while showing the way forward. The sparks provided the signal.

The guides back at the doors saw the flashes and sent their own sparks up to the guides on the roof, the ones who'd moved around at the start of the fight. Those guides punched holes in that roof. They used hammers and spikes to create holes and rake back metal slats. Riven's gray light streamed in as we pushed forward, giving us our first real look at the breach. The first one I'd ever seen.

It looked like a puddle, a huge one in the middle of the factory floor. A watery mass that, instead of reflecting the world above it, showed a different landscape beneath. The battlefield in the real world where all the soldiers were dying. They crawled up through the breach, as though swimming out of a pool. Splashing their way up and into Riven.

I ducked the wild swing of another spirit and paid back his aggression with a stab of my knife. Looked up and saw that we were close. Only a few feet away from the edge of the breach.

"Carver, you want the honors?" Bryce shouted above the chaos.

"My pleasure!" I replied.

Bryce, his voulge in one hand, reached under his belt and pulled off an ancient device. I recognized it from training. A stone slate with a sapphire in the middle. A sapphire that glowed with the same pale fire burning along our weapons and in the eyes of the spirits we sought to quell.

"It's ready," Bryce called, and then he threw the object to me.

As more spirits crawled up from the breach, their hands grasping the edges of the factory floor and pulling themselves out of the muck, I ran towards them. Above me, guides provided cover, launching arrows, firing single shot rifles with burning bullets, or dropping down to crush spirits up close.

I stepped on the breach and my shoes felt like they were being sucked into the mud. Bits of the real world splattered on the my ankles as I ran forward. A breach had to be closed from the center. If even a little bit escaped the reach of the device, the breach could reopen. I felt the hands of spirits brush my feet as they crawled up, but the newest spirits would take a moment to comprehend their surroundings. That moment was all I needed.

Once I got to the center, I pressed down on the sapphire in the device. Every part of it, the gem, the stone, turned teal as energy flooded out. The light gushed like a river and poured off into the breach. Flooding its surface and sealing it off. The hands of new spirits retracted, fell back through the muck as the light ran over the breach. They would still be coming to Riven, but now they would be separated, would wander, and perhaps would be cycled without the need of a guide to get them there.

Then I stood in the center of a factory floor, surrounded

by a score of exhausted guides, and many more glazed-over spirits starting their long walks to the Cycle.

"Well done," Bryce said, slapping my back and reaching for the device. "This was a small one. If the war gets worse, we'll see breaches double or triple the size.

"That goes for the rest of you too," Bryce announced to the other guides. "We found this one by accident, but there might be others already. Keep your eyes open. Don't hunt alone. If we catch the breaches early, they'll stay small, and we'll stay alive. Good work."

"He's right, you know," Alec said to me as we moved out of the factory. "You shouldn't go alone. I won't be watching every time."

"I'd find it a little creepy if you were," I replied, and Alec laughed.

WHEN BRYCE and Alec went back to the clock tower, I went in a different direction. Dating someone in Riven wasn't much different than doing it in the real world. Still had to stop by from time to time. Find places to go. Experiences to share. The dinner options were a little lacking, but we figured it out.

Selena was in the middle of another one of her drawings when I showed up. This one showed the Tar Pit, and she was halfway through one of the tall smokestacks, a stark line reaching towards the top of the paper. Paper that Nicholas undoubtedly gave her.

"You're still alive," Selena said as I went through the door. "When you didn't say anything, when you didn't come back after going to the Tar Pit, I figured that was the end."

"That's grim," I said, pulling out one of the wicker chairs and plopping into it.

"You'll have to forgive me. My mind doesn't run to happy places all that often," Selena set her pencil down and leaned back in her chair. "How was it? Did you meet your quota?"

I gave her the details. Graham, the scrambling, the near-death experience and then coming back with the others to close the breach. Through it all Selena just stared at me, nodding every once in a while.

"I don't know how I'm supposed to feel about that," Selena said when I finished. "On the one hand, I don't want you to die. On the other hand, that would bring you here, forever."

"Until we both went crazy. Or to the Cycle."

"It's going to happen eventually, right?" Selena said.

"Not so long as you're bound," I said. "What's with all the fatalism lately?"

"I'm a person," Selena said. "Or, at least, I was. I need more than just sitting here."

"I'm not enough?"

Selena laughed. "You're not here all the time. Even if you were, I don't think it would matter. I need more. More than wandering around with Nicholas looking for random things so he can build his inventions. More than these drawings."

"I might have something," I said. I had thought about taking the task to Nicholas, seeing if he had any ideas, but Selena might be even better. "There's a spirit. His name is Graham. I need help finding him."

"You want me to do it?" Selena look skeptical.

"He said something to me. Said that he thought that we should be working to bring spirits back. Back to the real world."

"Wouldn't that be disaster?"

"If we did it for all of them, sure."

Selena's face changed as she understood what I meant. Her hand went to her hair, twisting a pair of strands between her fingers. What she did whenever she was really, actually, interested in something.

"You think I could get back?" Selena said.

"I don't know. But we could try," I said.

"They'd never let you stay a guide if they found out," Selena said.

"I'm already risking that with you."

"You know," Selena said. "Sometimes you really come through for me. Other times, I can't tell if you care. But this, if you're willing to try, would mean everything."

I lived for that look that came over her eyes then. That hopeful, wanting glance that said I was the only thing she was thinking about at that moment. That my future and hers were one and the same and that we could get anything we wanted. Be anything we wanted. Together.

Selena stood up from the table, took my hand, and we left the half finished drawing of the smokestack and all thoughts of Graham behind.

THE POUNDING on the apartment door ruined the moment. I rolled off the bed, the hard palate barely a foot off the floor, and shrugged my way back into my clothes. Selena was faster, throwing a dress over her head and going to answer the knock.

"Is he here?" I heard Nicholas's voice around the corner.

"I'll be out in a minute," I said. Getting the belt back on and situated took a second. Then slinging the crossbow over my back took another. Finally, after slipping on the gloves that kept my hands from getting bit off by angry spirits and I was ready to go.

Nicholas, however, clearly wasn't. The man's lab coat was torn. Spirits didn't bleed much, but they could get roughed up plenty and Nicholas had scratches all over his face. His goggles hung askew, one of the lenses missing.

"They told me to find you," Nicholas started as soon as I came into sight. "Told me that you would be here, that they would stop if you came."

"Stop doing what?" I asked.

"They're tearing apart the lab! They're ruining my experiments."

"Who is 'they'?" I said as Selena bounced her eyes between the two of us.

"Graham. Or at least that's who they say they're working for. Spirits. Not like ones I've ever seen," Nicholas said. "They talk but they're not angry. There's no fire in their eyes. But they're destructive, determined. Actually, they'd be a rather intriguing study if they weren't wrecking everything."

"Well, I can fill tomorrow's quota today," I said. "You two stay here."

"I don't think so," Selena said. "You said that Graham nearly killed you earlier. I can't sit by and just let that happen. If you go, we go too."

I didn't argue. She wasn't wrong. The three of us left Selena's apartment and went down the street, over the hill, to Nicholas's lab. Standing in front of it were a pair of spirits. They didn't look like soldiers, and they were dressed in the same sort of formal wear that Graham sported. Dirty suits and tall hats. Nicholas was right, no fire in their eyes.

The one on the left held a large cane and rested on it. The one the right had grabbed hold of something from Nicholas's experiments. A spiked bar that had blue fire channeling between the needles.

"Heard you were looking for me?" I called as we came closer.

"Got a message for you. From Graham," the one with the cane said.

"I'm all ears."

"He says it's time to come home," Cane said. I expected a laugh, maybe some sort of manic grin, but the spirit's face stayed serious.

"What, that's it?" I said. "No explanation?"

Now Cane got all squinty-eyed. Clenched those knuckles

around his fancy stick. I gave the lash a twitch, made sure they saw it hanging ready.

"Are you sure you can handle both of them?" Nicholas whispered behind me. "They look rather intimidating."

"Selena, keep him out of it," I said, then put some distance between us by launching myself at the Graham's two spirits.

To their credit, the spirits weren't surprised. Cane went forward at my move, trying to close the distance so the lash wouldn't be so effective. Spike, as I nicknamed the other one, hung back, waiting for an opening. Which was fine with me.

I swept the lash low, banking on Cane getting inside the pointed tip. He did, but the rest of the lash hooked and wrapped around Cane's ankle. I pulled the lash tight and Cane crashed to the ground in front of me. My left hand went for the knife. Easy pickings.

"Watch out!" Selena's yell jerked my head up in time to see Spike copying his friend's assault.

My lash was still tight around Cane's ankle, and Spike's club was coming in fast, so I dropped the lash and rolled left. Coming out of the move, I reached behind my head and pulled out the crossbow. Held it up as Spike adjusted his advance.

"Careful," I said. "This thing hurts."

"I'm already dead," Spike replied. The spirit had a point.

I turned the crank anyway, slotting a normal bolt and, as Spike went for a swing, I fired the crossbow in his face. The bolt struck Spike in the nose, the shock of the hit robbing Spike's swing of its momentum, but not all of it. The club hit my left arm and I felt piercing pain as one of the spikes drove in.

A spirit in Riven doesn't have real blood. Doesn't feel or operate the way a body does. A guide, or a sneak, or anyone crossing over, though, they bring part of their physical selves along for the ride. Get your knee shattered here, it would be broken back home. Get your ear chewed off, good luck hearing anything after you crossed back. So when my arm went hot with my own blood, I screamed.

Then I hit back. Literally struck Spike with the crossbow and pushed him to the ground. Dropped the weapon and reached across my waist with my right hand and pulled the knife free. Spike's broken face, split by the bolt, stared up at me in mangled rage, but I hesitated. No pale fire. None. Even in a situation when the spirit should be losing control, Spike didn't look lost.

Cane tackled me. Rammed me off of his partner and threw me onto the hard stone of the street. The knife bounced from my hand along the ground. The pain would have been excruciating. Would have thrown me into shock. Should have.

"There will be moments," Bryce's voice flew through my panicking head. *"Where you will be at the very edge. Where you will be one breath away from the end. But you will still have that one breath. Use it."*

Cane moved over Spike, barreling down toward me like a nightmare version of a carnival barker, cane and suit blowing wide, top hat long gone and revealing a head of wispy hair.

On my belt, my hand found the spark tube. I pulled it out and pressed the button as Cane raised his namesake weapon to bash in my skull. I filled his eyes with burning blue fire.

Spirits might not bleed, but damn do they still hurt. Cane reeled back, roaring out something I couldn't understand, and I pushed myself back to my feet. Kept after Cane, kicking him in the stomach and pushing him back into Spike. Cane fell over his friend, landing on the ground hard.

I went over and picked up the knife. Tried to flex my left arm and couldn't. Not good.

"Ready to give up?" I said, my voice pained. Weak.

Spike, he of the split face, didn't reply. Not sure he was capable of it. Cane just growled and scooted himself back off his partner, who tried to get up as I stabbed him. The knife's blue fire ran down the hilt and over Spike. As the spirit's eyes went blank, I felt a surge of relief. One down.

Then Cane was on me again. I swept up the knife to block his swing, but Cane's strength was incredible, his namesake bashing away my hand. The knife flew to the other side of the street, bouncing away. I backpedaled and Cane followed.

"You could have come with us," Cane said. "Could have made this easy."

"That's not really my style," I replied.

Cane responded with a bigger swing, going for a two-handed head-knocker. I ducked forward, getting inside the attack and leading a right shoulder charge into Cane's midsection. His elbow connected with my temple, sending the world spinning as we fell over.

My eyes blurred in and out of focus as I rolled off of Cane onto my back. It was like my nerves were scrambled. Directions were getting lost en route to the muscles they were for. I closed my eyes for a second to try and correct myself, and when I opened them, Cane stood over me.

One, two, three quick strikes with the cane to my chest. Jabbing straight down. Not going for the kill, not yet.

"There's a price to be paid," Cane said. "Always a price, where I came from. When I paid it, I wound up here. Now, it's your turn."

I tried to come up with a retort. Tried, and wound up coughing blood as Cane delivered another shot to my gut. Then he stopped, scowled at me.

"Except he doesn't want you dead," Cane muttered, his eyes twisting up and looking above. Like the man was getting a communication from the beyond. Or having a stroke, if spirits could have such things.

Selena smashed Cane from behind. I didn't even see her, just the end of Spike's club driving into Cane's back. The blue fire wrapping the spikes, the fire that had done nothing to me, burned its way through Cane. He dropped his weapon and collapsed.

"Next time," I coughed. "A little sooner?"

22

As a guide, there was a certain indignity about being carried by a pair of spirits. However, given that I was a messed up hunk of battered flesh at the moment, I shelved my pride and let Selena and Nicholas drag me along the streets back to her apartment.

In between the spasms of pain from, well, from everywhere, I tried to figure out why Cane hadn't bashed my head in. He'd had the chance. Could've turned me to pulp right there on the street. Something, no, someone said no.

There weren't many ways to control spirits. If you were a guide, you could bind one or two, like I'd done with Nicholas and Selena. I couldn't make decisions for them, but they knew that if I let them go, the Cycle would compel them quick. Or they'd lose their minds and become a target for my lash.

Bryce had spoken a few times about Ghouls being able to control spirits in their vicinity. Their sheer menace collected spirits and warped them in the same way a cloud of perfume twisted the minds of men late at night.

These two were following Graham's orders. Another *spir-*

it's orders. I'd heard Graham call off the horde outside the factory near the breach. There must be something he was doing that could tie these spirits to him. One more reason I wanted to find Graham and get some questions answered.

"Are you still with us?" Selena asked as we neared the clock tower. "I'm worried if they find us with him..."

"He is still breathing," Nicholas said. "Which, despite being unnecessary here, shows evidence—"

"I'm alive," I said. "Bryce and Alec just went back. They shouldn't be here."

"You can talk!" Nicholas announced. "Excellent! I'd feared the blow to your head had scrambled your mind."

"Oh, it did," I replied. I managed to get my legs under me long enough for Selena to open the clock tower's door. Then it was a short series of steps to the main chamber. I counted each one of those steps in searing stabs from my abdomen.

"Straight to the bed, please," I said when we made it into the main hall. "I need to cross back."

Not that my real body would feel all that much better, but the thing about Riven is that there wasn't any alcohol. Or doctors and hospitals. But mostly alcohol.

"Carver, a question before you go," Nicholas said as Selena laid me on the mattress.

"Go for it," I replied.

"About my lab? I took the liberty of checking inside while you and Selena were dealing with those goons and it seems they were thorough. My work has been set back considerably."

"Can you rebuild it?"

"I would question the effort," Nicholas said, looking at the floor and wringing his hands. "If this Graham knows where it is, then I should think he might attack again."

"Then move it to the apartment," I said.

"What?" Selena and Nicholas said together.

"It's got room. Selena, you said you were lonely. Why not?"

"The steps would make moving equipment difficult," Nicholas said, but his wandering eyes gave away his thoughts. "But it would be more secure. Having Selena nearby would make it easier to experiment…"

"I'm not your plaything," Selena said. Nicholas bowed his head in an apology, then went to go check the door, make sure the courtyard was still clear.

"Talk it over," I said. "I'm sure you'll work something out."

"So long as he remembers that it's my place first," Selena said, then she turned back to me. "I'm going to go look for Graham. Like we talked about."

"Now? After seeing what he did?" I said the words, but didn't put much punch into them. If Selena was able to find Graham, learn more about what he wanted, then it would be worth the risk.

"That's why I have to try," Selena said. "He's just going to keep hurting us."

I could feel the blurred edges of my vision closing in. Crossing back and forth from Riven was like falling asleep, only instead of sinking into any dream, I had to drift my mind towards where I wanted to go. In this case, back to my little apartment, to my bed tied to the clock tower. In a normal situation, without my blood dripping from the hole in my arm, it would be simple. A habit, like walking or blinking.

Now, with the constant ache, I couldn't maintain the picture. I was falling unconscious, not shifting over. And if I collapsed here, I might not ever wake up.

"What's wrong?" I heard Selena talk, her voice sounding far away.

C'mon, Carver. I forced my eyes back open, beat away the blurred edges.

"I need to be numbed," I said. "I can't concentrate."

"Numbed?" Selena said.

"Get Nicholas here," I said. "He'll have an idea."

Selena yelled for the scientist while I clung to consciousness. My stomach lurched. Something burned in my chest. Wouldn't be surprised if Cane had done deadly damage, despite trying to keep me alive.

"You have any morphine?" I asked Nicholas as he came in the room.

"Have you forgotten where you are?" Nicholas replied. "Riven lacks the necessary ingredients for any chemical drugs."

"The pain's keeping me from crossing," I said. "It's getting worse."

Nicholas glanced at Selena and shook his head slightly. Scientist out of ideas. That wasn't good. Selena turned to me, and I must have looked terrible because her eyes quivered and her mouth fell slack.

"Don't tell me," I said. "I don't want to know."

"Be quiet," Selena said. "Focus. Cross over, Carver."

I was about to slide into sarcasm and say that was the whole problem, when Selena leaned over and kissed my forehead. The slight pressure, the warmth from her lips blunted the pain. Not a lot. The stinging, raging ache from my stomach and arm were still there, but quieter. Countered by Selena's affection.

Her lips moved, crossing my forehead and making their soft way down the side of my face. I closed my eyes. Sank into that sea of near unconscious, and, with Selena's soft voice whispering in my ear, I latched onto my home and didn't let go.

"Cross over, Carver."

23

IT WAS NOT A GOOD MORNING. I awoke from the crossing like I'd run a marathon while taking a gut punch every mile. At least, that's what it felt like. My muscles, particularly in the left arm, were sore. My stomach was nauseous, and I stumbled out of bed to the bathroom upon waking up. Things weren't pretty.

But I was alive.

After far too many minutes putting myself together, I fell out of my apartment to the train station and got on the next line downtown. My body wanted to lie there and suffer, but giving Graham time to plan another attack was what we in the guide business would call a bad plan.

Ezra's was more crowded earlier in the morning, the clock barely pushing 7:30. Third-shifters saying goodbye to the night. Bryce would still be here, though. He'd told me before that his wife did some sort of government work downtown, had to be in the office early, and they regarded the morning train ride together as a sacrosanct ritual of their relationship. Bryce probably enjoyed the hours of coffee and reading in Ezra's that followed just as much.

With my usual mask-and-coat getup, I approached the bar. The air was hazy, a build-up the papers attributed to the factories ramping up war production. Exactly what we needed. More pollution, more dead soldiers clogging Riven. Great times.

"Carver!" Speaking of great times, here came one. Opperman waved from near the door. "Haven't seen ya, and guess what? There's another quote needs giving!"

"Can't you find another guide?" I replied, trying to walk past him, but Opperman shifted himself in front of me.

"Bryce doesn't even look at me anymore," Opperman pouted. "I don't even know the name of your third guy."

"Some journalist you are."

"I focus my efforts on what matters to the people," Opperman said. "And what matters right now are the rumors that guides are dying left and right!"

"They are?"

"Don't you know?" Opperman gave me a quizzical look, his recording tablet punching holes. "Riven's more dangerous than ever, or so they say. Catastrophe as more guides are mauled by angry spirits!"

"Who are your sources again?"

Opperman wagged his finger. "C'mon, Carver, give me a response. Tell me, what're you going to do about it? How are you going to keep the people safe?"

I paused for a moment. Bryce would ream me out if I gave any sort of promise to Opperman. On the other hand, someone had to talk to the media. Keep the public informed and, hopefully, paying for us to keep Riven clear.

"Tell you what, Opperman," I said. "How about we trade. I'll give you an opinion, if you do a little digging for me?"

"Digging?"

"There's a, um, nasty spirit I'm dealing with in Riven," I said. "Need to find out more about her. Can you look and see if there are records of a woman named Selena? She was killed by her husband?"

"Here? Or anywhere? Because, you know, I can't—"

Selena hadn't ever told me where she died, but we'd talked about Chicago before. While spirits could pop up all over Riven, most of the time they were concentrated to certain areas. That's what made wars so dangerous. Whole districts of Riven could get overwhelmed as so many people died in a single spot on Earth. It seemed like, with the current war ramping up, the Tar Pit was going to be a mess.

"Somewhere in the Midwest," I said. "You're the journalist, do the digging."

"My part of the deal?"

"Look, being a guide has always been a difficult job. A lot of risk. Not a lot of reward," I said. "With the war going on, things are going to get dangerous. But we've kept the world spinning for centuries, and we won't stop now."

Opperman nodded when I'd finished. "That's what I needed. Now, smile!"

The reporter waved behind him and a woman I hadn't noticed ran up to my face. On her shoulders, she wore what looked like a jumble of metal parts. On her head was a massive lens. She pressed a pair of buttons, one in each hand, and the lens blasted me with light.

"Your picture," Opperman said as the woman backed away. "Should get on the front page!"

"I'm wearing a mask," I replied.

"Even better!" Opperman exclaimed. "Guides are mysterious, scary, and that's what you are."

"Thanks," I said, brushing past him. "Selena, remember."

"Sure thing, Carver," Opperman said to my back as I slipped into Ezra's.

Bryce was at our usual table, immersed in the morning edition. Ezra's had its music playing bright ragtime, pianos bouncing along at a frenetic rate. Bryce looked up when I sat down across from him, narrowed his eyes when I took a pour from his coffee.

"Feeling spicy this morning, Carver?" Bryce said.

"Got the crap kicked out of me last night, Bryce," I replied. "Just happy to be alive."

That bled into an edited recounting of the encounter with Cane and Spike. I left out Nicholas and the lab, Selena saving me, and turned it into a two on one slugfest that had my physical heroics carrying the day, albeit not so well that I'd dodged any harm.

"You and Alec have the same problem," Bryce said when I was done. "Both going out alone. Against orders."

"There aren't enough of us," I said. "What orders am I supposed to obey? The quota, or sticking together?"

Bryce set down the paper and rubbed his eyes. The same look he did any time I confronted him with an impossible question.

"You have your sparks with you?" Bryce said.

"Always," I replied. "I forget to shoot them."

"Please don't. They'll save your life."

"Know what else might save my life?" I said. "Telling me what you know about Graham."

Now Bryce sat back, confused. "Did you see him again?"

"These guys, they said they were working for Graham. That's right, spirits working for each other," I glanced around Ezra's, no Alec in sight. "I didn't mention this earlier, but Graham talked to me. The first time."

"Saying what?"

"Essentially that he wanted a way out of Riven. Back here. For him and all other spirits."

"That sounds like Graham," Bryce said. "Not that I knew him well, but he wasn't one to settle. Always pushed the limits for a guide. Like you, dove into one messy situation after another."

"How'd he die? Spirits?"

Bryce shook his head. "Illness, if I remember right. It's been a long time, and I was going through training."

"Then how is his spirit still around, if he died that long ago?" I asked.

"When a guide dies, out here, they can last for a long time in Riven because they know what it is. How it works," Bryce said, his eyes sliding into a thoughtful stare. "Even so, the Cycle should eventually get them. I'm not sure how he's lasted so long."

We talked for a while longer, me taking the opportunity to get my own coffee and sip the steamy brew. Then Bryce took a long pause, staring over at the bar. I followed his glance, realized he wasn't looking at anything in particular, and took in my mentor's face.

Bryce was looking, and this felt strange to think, old. Or rather, used. Slight wrinkles threaded his face, and Bryce's eyes were rimmed with tangled red. Strands of gray intermingled with his auburn hair.

"You can probably tell," Bryce said when he caught me looking. "I'm getting tired. Decades in Riven will catch up to you."

"Didn't want to say anything."

Bryce reached inside his coat pocket and brought out a book. Leather-bound. Only, on the inside wasn't pages, but pictures. Bryce handed the book to me.

"Take a look," Bryce said. I obliged, flipping through. Black and white smiles flashed back at me. Bryce, his wife, their two children. As I turned the pages, I noticed that all of the pictures with Bryce were around Chicago. In their house, or a park. Pictures elsewhere just had his wife and the kids.

"You never leave?" I said.

"Do you?" Bryce replied.

I hadn't thought about it, but the answer was no. No I didn't. Chicago was my area, and even though I could cross into Riven from anywhere, I might not appear in the same place. Wouldn't be able to respond to a crisis. And guides didn't take vacations.

"You're going to retire?" I said.

"Soon," Bryce said. "When the war calms down, I think. I want you to take my place."

"Not Alec?"

Bryce smiled. "You think he would want it? Having to police the other Chicago guides? Make pitches to the city for support?"

We both laughed at that one. No way would Alec and his ego work in that environment. He'd probably have us run out of town in a month. Then Bryce turned serious again.

"You ever think of having a family?" Bryce said.

"Never really had one, except for you and the other guides," I replied. The remark brought my mother's strange death floating back through my head, and I frowned.

"Probably for the best," Bryce said. "This life isn't a kind one."

I nodded. Took the last drink of the coffee. Family. I'd had one once. For a moment. Maybe it was time to find out what happened to it.

24

The Chicago Medical Center. Or the CMC, as the newspapers called it, took up five blocks south of downtown. From the top floors, I'd been told, you could make out the lake on a clearer day.

This was not one of those. The haze was thick, making the strings of lights directing patients and visitors to the entrance less of a decoration and more of a necessity.

As I walked towards the main doors with a dozen others, tinny speakers played recorded messages when we stepped on certain plates. Directions for patients, guidelines for visitors, and so on. By the time I was standing in the purifying room, the haze sucking away, I felt I knew every little detail about how CMC worked.

I wanted to see the doctor that had presided over my mother's treatment. Whose name was on the certificate Anna had sent me. Thankfully, he was easy to find. Because he was also my doctor, and the physician for all of Chicago's guides.

"Carver Reed," Barrington Farth said to me from behind an enormous pair of spectacles. The glasses, which always took a second to get used to, weren't just lenses. They had a series of gadgets attached to them that allowed Barrington to zoom in for a closer look, register air quality, and, so he'd told me once, even pick up the frequency of a heart beat from inches away.

"That's my name," I said.

"You're early for your annual check-up," Barrington said, glancing at a folder with my name on it.

"Not here for that. Thanks for taking the time to meet on short notice," I said.

"My contract with the guides requires it," Barrington replied. "What do you need, then?"

"I wanted to ask you about this," I said, taking out the certificate and setting it on Barrington's absurdly crowded desk. Papers and knickknacks, tools that had no purpose I could discern, littered the dark wood surface. Barrington leaned over, so close that I thought his wrinkled skin might droop down and touch the sheet.

"Your mother," Barrington said. "I'd ask how you acquired this, except it's here, so such a line of inquiry would waste our time. You want to know how she died?"

"Sure, let's start with that."

"It was a long time ago," Barrington said slowly, dredging up the memory while reciting it. "But a patient like Katherine stays with you. If only for how much she fought to bring you into the world, and how fast she went after."

"Fast?"

"Yes. Even in the lead-up to your birth, she had been claiming people were coming for her. Other guides, even. It was the start of a problem that would kill her."

"Other guides? You mean my mother was one?"

Barrington gave me an odd look. "Of course. You didn't know that?"

"Not many people talk about my parents, doctor."

"No, perhaps not," Barrington said. "At the time, my

priority was to ensure she made it through the pregnancy. Her obvious psychosis could be dealt with later."

"Except it wasn't."

"No. She had you, and then within days, she was gone. We'd transferred her to a safe ward. She was monitored. Few visitors. In the end, however, Katherine slipped away."

"You have no idea why?"

Here Barrington paused. I could practically see him measuring and discarding words. Picking the proper phrase.

"I wouldn't say that," Barrington said. "I did an autopsy, after all."

I waited. The doctor put his elbows on the desk, leaned forward, pushed his massive spectacles towards my face.

"It's hard to tell what goes on with a guide's body when they cross over. On the outside, it resembles sleep. Or a coma," Barrington said. "On the inside, that's an open question. So when your mother expired, I took the chance to see."

Then he paused. As though remembering that talking about dissecting a man's mother right in front of him might not be the most polite thing in the world.

"It's fine," I said. It definitely was not fine, but I wasn't here to be emotional. This was about finding what happened to my mother. "Tell me what you found."

"In short, it was multiple organ failure," Barrington said. "I assume something happened to her over there. She was crossing quite frequently, you know. I think it helped her stay sane."

"What do you mean, 'assume something happened to her over there'?"

"The damage must have come from a Riven event. It wasn't natural," Barrington shrugged. "If she'd been a normal patient, a normal person, I'd have said she'd been poisoned."

I woke up back in the clock tower. My body was still sore, but the hole in my arm didn't exist. My stomach wasn't a pillar of pain. Crossing worked miracles. I stood up and stretched, enjoying the muscle ache because of its familiarity. I could deal with this.

Barrington left me with questions, but there wasn't time to tackle them now. Alec, by way of Bryce that morning, had asked for help with a hunt. We had our ten spirit quota to fill for the day, and with Bryce pulled into another hours-long diplomacy session in the real-world, it was up to Alec and I to keep Chicago in the black.

"This fountain is a mystery," Alec said to me as I left the clock tower. He stood beside the basin, staring at the not-water as it flowed. "Riven has no power. A questionable relationship with physics. Yet, here this fountain pours."

"Chasing answers here is a mistake," I said. "Riven is Riven."

"Tsk tsk," Alec said. "That sort of attitude will leave us stuck where we are now, forever. Better to ask 'what is Riven'?"

"Someday, when I have time, I'll put that question to the test," I replied. "You said you had something?"

"The ghoul that was found? It is still around," Alec said. "One of the guides told me while we were closing the breach. It's far, so nobody has bothered going after it yet. Until now."

Normally, I'd be ecstatic. A ghoul! The very thing I kept harassing Bryce about. A chance to push my abilities to the max against the most frightening creature Riven had to offer. Except, after Cane's beating last night, I wasn't feeling thrilled about going into combat against a giant beast.

"I thought you would be more excited?" Alec said to my uncertain face. "Bryce told me that you always wanted to fight one."

"I had a rough night."

"Then what better way to recover than by risking life and limb?" Alec said.

"I could think of some," I said, but the curious itch was growing. I might be in rough shape, but who knew when I'd get another chance? Not only were ghouls rare, but you had to be in Riven at the right time or other guides would take it down first. "Fine, let's go."

"Not very enthusiastic, but it is a yes, nonetheless," Alec said. He walked away from the fountain, heading east. Away from the Tar Pit, which was west of the clock tower, and the Warrens, south. Normally, the east was a quieter district. A series of wide squares and misshapen structures. Like someone playing with brick and mortar got carried away.

"Why the gauntlets, Alec?" I asked as we walked along.

"Why?" Alec replied. "A family tradition, my friend."

"Family tradition?"

"I'm a fourth generation guide," Alec said. "These gauntlets are over a hundred years old."

"Is there going to be a fifth generation?" I needled my friend, and Alec laughed.

"Perhaps, but I don't think now is the best time for talk of family," Alec said. "The world is in a dark place, and Riven even more so. Better I help cleanse the streets than take time away for children."

"If you say so."

"What about you, Carver?" Alec said. "Have you found a love of your own? Do you hope for your own family one day, like our dear leader, Bryce?"

"I don't know," I said, Selena dashing through my mind. "I've got other priorities, I guess."

"Other priorities, the man says. Then that is what I will say too. Other priorities," Alec kept up the grin. "Then, until we find that love who steals our hearts and makes us long for quiet nights with our families by the fire, let us wield our lives like a sword for the guides."

"Anyone ever tell you that you're crazy?" I said.

"All the time, Carver. And I never deny it," Alec said.

After making our way through the area surrounding the clock tower, we saw more spirits. These weren't the wandering dead that went through most of Riven. People who'd been killed of old age or accidents. No, most of these bore the hallmarks of disease, and the same one.

You could always tell a disease death in Riven because the spirits, like the war dead, looked the same as when they fell apart. No ideal form, no relaxed way to go. The suffering transformed their spirit as it had warped their last days in life.

The spirits we were seeing? Their hair, when they had it, was matted to their faces from sweat. Their arms and legs were thin, wasted away. Their eyes twitched open and closed, a sure sign that they'd spent most of their waning days asleep. The ones not moving towards the Cycle were sitting, staring into nothing.

"This is bad," I said. "Where is this happening? I haven't heard of a plague."

"The war is across one ocean," Alec said. "This is across the other."

The streets broadened, blended in with broad courtyards surrounding strange buildings. One to my left appeared to be a half-finished castle. A turret spiraling upward, with chunks missing from the walls. Spirits sat on the stones like visitors to ruins, watching us as we went by.

To the right were the Watcher's Tears. A series of stone bases that curved upwards to pointed tops a dozen stories high. Some of those points had been blunted, broken off with their blocks shattered on the ground beside them. Where the name had come from, I didn't know.

"Have you ever been out of the city?" Alec asked as we went.

"In Riven, you mean?"

"Yes, here," Alec said. "To the walls?"

"Never been that far."

"You know, Piotr says that there is nothing worth exploring beyond this place," Alec said. "But I think he is lying. Or he chooses not to see."

"Have you been?"

Alec nodded. "To the eastern edge. Where the streets drain away to wide fields of the whitest grass you have ever seen. There are few spirits. But Riven goes on."

"Why?"

"See, now you are asking the right questions. Why, indeed. What is the point of this place? If it is just a house for the dead, why bother with all the rest?"

In front of us, slowly growing to tower over dead tree-lined boulevards and scattered structures, was The Palace. Double the size of the factory in the Tar Pit where we'd closed the breach, The Palace was a giant building covered in ornate carvings. Symbols that I couldn't understand, that I'd never heard an explanation for. Domes dotted the roof, entirely black. The darkest things I'd seen in Riven's eternal gray.

"It's supposed to be here," Alec said, looking around. "Unless someone was rude enough to take it from us."

I looked around, noted the lack of spirits. Where there'd been dozens wandering earlier, The Palace was empty. The grounds were clear. That just made things creepier.

"Ghouls aren't supposed to be hard to find," I said.

"Perhaps we need to make it easy to find us," Alec replied. Before I could say anything, Alec pulled his spark tube from his belt, pointed it towards the sky, and triggered it. Blue sparks flew up and burst.

A moment later, the ground shook. A noxious roar, a mixing of anger, liquid lungs, and spit, echoed across the stones.

"You see? We just needed to say hello," Alec said.

2 6

One of the side benefits of crossing to Riven was that, when it wasn't getting beat up, my body in Chicago slept. I'd cross back and feel rejuvenated. It also meant that I never really dreamed. Or if I did, if my brain back in Chicago whirled through nightmares while I slaughtered spirits in Riven, I didn't experience them. So while I'd say the ghoul looked like a nightmare come to life, the truth was, I didn't really know.

The ghoul was a slathering mass of arms and legs. A ball with appendages formed of other appendages, the result of sucking up countless spirits on its raging path through Riven. Eyes and mouths interspersed the spaces between the limbs, some of which held stones, wooden boards, and other rubble as weapons. Countless shards of ruined clothes, furniture, and other body parts roiled in the mass.

Perhaps the worst part was the pulsing, the shuddering rhythm that shook through the ghoul's body every two or three seconds. The limbs bounced when that happened, with occasional loose bits falling off the ghoul's body to the ground, only to be grabbed by one of its passing arms and shoved back in.

"That is, truly, the most disgusting thing I've ever seen," I said. "And I've seen some awful stuff."

"I must agree," Alec replied. "I shall take no small amount of pleasure in ending its miserable existence."

Alec straightened his arms as the ghoul continued its orbit around The Palace towards us. The gauntlets Alec used changed when he snapped his wrists, sliding out metal plating to coat his forearms. Inch-long spikes shot out along the length of the weapons, each one glowing with wrangling fire. He reached into his coat and pulled out his mask, the Riven version of the thorny vine one he wore back in Chicago.

I slipped my black and gold mask on, then reached over my back and pulled out the crossbow. Slid the lever to the blue wrangling bolt. I brought it up, turning the crank, and noticed Alec staring at the weapon.

"That's a nice piece of work," Alec said. "After this, you will tell me who made it for you."

"A friend," I replied. The bolt snapped into place. Ready to go. If the shot worked, the bolt should wrangle the ghoul just like any other spirit. "Let's see if we can take the easy way out."

I pulled the trigger, sending the shot sprinting towards the ghoul as it came closer. The bolt struck the ghoul's gross flesh and sank in, bursting into blue flame. The ghoul howled, an unearthly scream that ricocheted around my ears like the sound of rusty metals scraping against each other.

Then the ghoul flailed, arms patting at its body, grasping for the bolt. One of the arms snagged it from the growing pit of pale fire and held the bolt away. Nicholas's invention kept burning, sending searing blue lines down the ghoul's arm. The creature dropped the bolt on the ground, still furiously batting at the burning area on its body.

The blue fire died. Smothered out by the ghoul's arms, or by its sheer size, I didn't know. The lower left quarter of the ghoul's body was a black ruin, another first. Normally the wrangling fire didn't actually burn. At least, not physically.

"Interesting," Alec said. The ghoul shifted the burned area away from us, and, with its dozen mouths gnashing, charged. "Now the real fun begins."

"Your concept of fun needs work," I said, but couldn't deny that part of me was happy Nicholas's bolt hadn't ruined the ghoul. It would have been too easy.

The ghoul's charge was more of a shamble, catching itself on its mass of limbs and rolling forward. Arms cycling towards the top threw stones and rocks at us in an endless stream of projectiles. I sidestepped one, then two, while my arms worked the crossbow. I jumped the lever to the orange bolt, the fiery one, then noticed Alec was running towards the ghoul. If I used that, I'd burn him up. Back to the wrangling bolt.

I felt the rock smash into my hands, a flash of white pain. The crossbow flew out of my grip, skipping across the stone. My right hand went numb. My left ached. Not a great start.

Even though I couldn't feel my fingers, I knew where my lash was. I drew it, then circled to the right of the ghoul. Alec, about ten yards in front of me, rolled beneath a pair of large thrown stones and then used his momentum to jump in the air. He struck the ghoul with a wild yell, his gauntlets catching hold. Then he began to tear the ghoul apart.

One arm held on while Alec used his other to grab the ghoul's many limbs and break them off, piece by piece. The spikes on his gauntlets drove into the ghoul, weakened the arm or leg Alec was grabbing, and then Alec ripped it off and flung it to the ground.

A particularly long, thin arm went for Alec's head and I

snapped the lash. It snaked out, wrapped around the arm, and its blue-tinged tip bit into the wrist. I yanked, and the lash's pale fire burned the limb away. Its charred remnants broke from the ghoul and landed on the ground.

The creature howled again, this time its screech inflected with pain, but not panic. Not fear. Not yet.

The ghoul rolled, bringing Alec towards the ground. Where the guide would be smothered beneath the creature.

"Jump!" I shouted, as if Alec couldn't tell what was happening. He was trying to scramble up the front of the ghoul, but couldn't move fast enough. At the last moment, just before vanishing beneath the ghoul's bulk, Alec grabbed a passing leg and swung himself out of the way, rolling across the stone courtyard.

I snapped the lash again, decimating the leg Alec had just used to save himself, but the ghoul didn't even notice. It started to reverse direction, rolling towards where I stood.

"We need a new plan!" I said. "There's too much of it to take apart!"

"Couldn't agree more," Alec said, picking himself up. "I like that crossbow of yours. Try it again?"

"I'll need cover," I said, ducking another thrown stone.

"Consider it given," Alec replied.

I broke into a run, getting out of the ghoul's way. Alec sidestepped the mass, then jumped on the ghoul again, pulling up the creatures side and leaving charred scars.

In three long strides, I made it back to the crossbow. Somehow, the weapon still worked. Whatever Nicholas had used to make it, the man knew his stuff. I slid the lever back to the wrangling blue bolts. Then I heard a scream.

The ghoul had Alec lifted in the air, a trio of long arms holding the guide's gauntlets wide, while more arms and legs kicked and punched Alec's body. One vicious swipe raked long, broken fingernails across Alec's face, leaving a trail of bloody marks.

There wasn't time to take chances.

I shoved the lever to the orange bolts, turned the crank as Alec struggled. Another rock hit me on the shoulder, but I ignored the pain. It wasn't dislocated, I could still hold the crossbow, and that's what mattered. I raised the weapon, aimed it beneath the ghoul, and fired.

The bolt struck the ground at the ghoul's feet, expanding in an orange bloom. Rays reached out and latched onto the ghoul's legs and dangling arms, climbing them to the creature's body. As I'd seen the bolt do to the container in the Tar Pit, the blazing rays disintegrated every part of the ghoul they touched.

When the ghoul roared again, mixed in with the noise was a new tone - fear. As its bottom legs were eaten away, the ghoul collapsed. Its arms still held Alec as the ghoul dropped into the expanding flames. I'd hoped the bolt's blast wouldn't extend far enough to get Alec, but with the ghoul literally falling apart, bringing Alec closer... I broke into a run, dropping the crossbow.

"Carver!" Alec yelled as the fire came closer. "I can't get out!"

"On it!" I replied. Because the rays focused the fire on whatever they could grab rather than burning freely, the ghoul had become a pillar of burning orange light. I ran close, close enough to try something stupid.

With the flames burning up, brushing the bottom of Alec's coat as the last of the ghoul disappeared into the writhing heat, I cracked the lash. It flew, wrapping itself around Alec, and jabbing its pointed end into the fabric of the guide's coat.

"Roll!" I said, and then twisted and pulled, yanking Alec

free of the ghoul's melting arms. I braced myself as Alec fell, using my legs to push us both away from the fire. The lash held, hopefully giving Alec enough momentum to clear the flames. When I felt the lash start to drag, I turned back to see if I'd torched Alec alive.

MY LASH STILL WOUND around Alec's body. Filaments of smoke curled up from beneath the guide, but the man's breathing chest gave away that he lived.

"So, that was your plan?" Alec said, still lying on the ground. "Burn the ghoul and I in one go? Make it look like an accident?"

"Absolutely," I said, gripping Alec's hand and pulling him to his feet. "Nobody would ever suspect a thing."

"Au contraire, they would, because who could ever believe you would be able to kill a ghoul, much less moi?"

"Anyone ever tell you you're insufferable?" I said, winding up the lash and sticking it back in its holster.

"My mother, every day since I was born," Alec said. "But enough talk. We killed a ghoul, Carver! That is worth celebrating! I say we head back, go to Ezra's, and regale the masses with our tale of victory."

"This really went to your head, didn't it?"

"I prefer to work alone for many reasons, Carver, but I would be lying if I didn't say one of them was keeping the glory for myself."

Alec continued singing his own praises, with the occasional mention of me, during the walk back to the clock tower. Eventually I tuned him out. Replayed the fight in my mind. We'd been lucky. Without that crossbow, the ghoul would have torn us apart. I'd have to thank Nicholas.

"So I will see you at Ezra's?" Alec said as we slipped into the beds in the clock tower.

"You might have to take this one on your own," I said. "I've got plans tonight."

"Plans, eh?" Alec said. "What could be better than celebrating our victory?"

Before I could reply, Alec held up his hand. "Don't tell me. It will only make me pity you all the more."

"Always a pleasure, Alec," I said. The guide grinned at me, then collapsed on his pillow. I followed, and crossed a minute later.

A cloudy afternoon gave me a moment's surprise. I thought I was still in Riven, the gray making the two worlds come a little too close together. I turned over, saw my minuscule apartment and knew I was home.

As had been the trend, I took stock of the mail stack and found a package sitting on top the usual pile of bills and ads. On the flimsy box was a note, pinned several times to make sure it wouldn't fall off on the vent ride up.

You didn't tell me it was local! Finding Selena was easy - plenty of headlines. I've included some here for you.
You owe me at least three juicy quotes for this!
- Opperman

Inside the package were a set of articles. All of them from Opperman's paper and written over a series of days. I took the longest one, the last one, out first.

. . .

Revenge of the Ruined

Selena Kairis isn't known to many of you, but rest assured, by the time this article is over, you will feel nothing if not sympathy for this doomed woman. She was killed by her last husband, who wielded a cleaver in making an end of his wife. Selena did not go quietly, however, as she delivered her own fatal stab to her husband's back. A discerning reader might wonder which attack came first. With Selena, there is no question.

Kairis was Selena's maiden name, and it remains hers despite three marriages. And, before this last one, two other likely murders. Both of them in Chicago, and both of them declared accidents. The first husband, a Matthias Ferber, found squashed on the ground beneath their tenth story apartment. Alcohol was blamed, broken bottles throughout the place. Selena, sobbing in the living room, given the innocence due a properly weeping widow.

The second, Bruce Evers, of an apparent heart attack at the old age of thirty-three. Selena again at the scene, again describing a mess of a marriage full of drink and drugs. Of failed business and failed love. Whether Bruce committed a secret suicide or Selena assisted, it didn't matter. Our Selena was set free.

The third looked like it would stick. Wiley Rose, a stable butcher that, by all accounts, found himself in love with Selena's sad story. Two children later and it seemed Selena's bad luck had disappeared. Until both mother and father turned up dead in bloody fashion.

Wiley, it turned out, was not nearly so stable as he appeared. Friends had driven the man into debt, and the growing pollution in Chicago was forcing expensive adjustments to keep his meat pure. Selena responded to the stress in the same way this reporter, and the Chicago police, now believe she acted in every other situation. Remove it by means of untimely demise. Except Wiley wasn't a drinker. Wasn't a drug user. Their house had no second story to fall from. So Selena turned to more direct means.

I put down the article. The implications were clear. Selena had murdered her husbands, had escaped punishment, until the last one proved harder to kill.

When I'd met Selena, it was in a side street not that far from the clock tower. I'd been hunting an angry spirit in the area, the resonator taking me right to it. The spirit had been a hulking man, the pale fire of rage in his eyes. Selena had been backing away as the man went towards her.

"How could you ruin everything?" the man had said as Selena retreated down the street. I unfurled the lash, walking towards them. "Things weren't perfect, but they were going to get better!"

The man broke into a run at Selena, who turned and saw me.

That moment is one I hope I'll remember forever. Her eyes lighting on me and her mouth dropping open in a yell for help, her face crying with what I thought was fear. Now, I think, it was the last goodbye to a life she'd chosen to end.

I closed the distance and, as the man reached out to grab Selena, my lash struck. Wrapped around his chest and pierced into his stomach. My blue fire washed his away, and a moment later the man stood stock still and stupid.

"What did you do?" Selena asked me.

"Gave him what he wanted," I said. "Peace."

The man turned and walked away, towards the Cycle. Selena held my arm. A murderer clinging to one more victim.

Part of me wanted to go right back into Riven, find Selena, and talk to her. Confront her with the article and get her story straight. Learn if the only thing she wanted was another person to get close to and, when things took a turn, end.

But it was getting towards the evening and I had another mystery that still needed solving. Barrington had said my mother was a guide. Had died a strange death. If there was anyone that might have more information, it was Anna. And now was prime time for the Broken Beaker.

The Lab District at sunset wasn't quite the madhouse it would turn into later. For one, too many people were still pushing papers and bubbling brews in their buildings for the streets to be too crowded. For another, the alcohol hadn't been flowing long enough.

Anna met me in the back room. Or, I should say, I found her there. At the bar, taking a long slug of something dark with an empty glass beside her.

"Rough day?" I said, pulling off my mask and sitting.

"You think being a sneak is easy, don't you?" Anna said, leaning her head on her elbow and turning to me.

"Never said that," I replied.

"Sorry," Anna said. "I'm just looking for a target."

"Me too. You can go first, if it'll make you feel better."

"It's nothing. A nice client that's going to get a bad end," Anna said. "She was paying to see what happened to her father, and I could see that she wanted to believe that he hadn't died in the war."

"You found him?"

"Running around the Tar Pit. Which, by the way, is turning into a disaster area."

"Avoid it," I said. "We closed a breach there yesterday."

"Not everybody has the luxury of playing by your rules," Anna said. "I saw the pale fire in his eyes, but there wasn't anything I could do about it. I'm going to meet with the girl tomorrow, tell her that her father's in there."

"You're going to tell her that he's a mindless, enraged ghost?"

"I'm going to tell her that he's at peace, making his way to the Cycle," Anna said, taking another pull.

"I could make that happen," I said. Thought that was the right thing to do; offer to wrangle the spirit. All it got me was a glare.

"You can. I can't," Anna said. "That's what's messed up about this situation."

I was about to speak, but Anna kept going, bowling me over with a string of words, slurs sliding in here and there as the drinks she took caught up with her. "They never tested me. My parents kept it hidden. Ignored it when I told them about my nighttime walks on the other side."

"That's illegal."

"Thanks, I know that," Anna said. "I think they believed I'd grow out of it if I wasn't trained. That I'd have a shot at a normal life lived in this world. Except it doesn't stop. If you don't know what you're doing, you'll still cross over. It's dangerous."

"The guides have clinics for people who flunk out or retire. They'll train you how to avoid Riven," I ordered my own beer. Something about the direction of the conversation told me it'd be better with a drink.

"I didn't want to avoid it," Anna said. "Like all of you guides say: getting to see the truth is a gift. Why give that up? Only, I couldn't find much else to do, until I found the sneaks."

"But now?"

"Riven's getting more dangerous," Anna said. "You see that. You know it. Bet you're all laughing there with your gear thinking about all the sneaks getting taken out by spirits. Chewed to pieces in that gray mess."

"That sounds like us. Laughing as others die," I said.

"Then why don't you help us?" Anna said. "Do more than just warn us away."

"That's why I'm here," I said and Anna bit off her next remark in surprise. Gave me a wary look. "I can't make you a guide. Not yet, anyway. But I can help you."

"How?"

"Guide gear is only for, well, guides," I said. "Only I happen to know someone who can get you something to fight with. Something that'll let you take care of those spirits and give your clients some peace."

"Who?"

"He's in Riven," I let a smile cross my face. Anna looked so suspicious it was funny, like I'd put in all this effort just to trick a sneak into a bad situation. "There's a catch, though. What do you know about my mother?"

Anna laughed. "Sorry, Carver. I'm not telling you that. Not until you come through. I said you had to make me a guide, but if your magic man turns out to be a real thing, if I get my tools, then I'll tell you."

There's few things as frustrating as getting locked away from what you want. My mother died, and I wanted to know why. Anna was the next link in that chain, but here she was, playing a hard game. That Nicholas could build her a weapon, I had no doubt. The problem was one of time.

Riven was getting worse, and Graham was coming. I didn't want another Cane crushing my head in while I still had so many questions.

"Deal," I said. "Tonight, we go to Riven together."

"Think about it. A guide helping a sneak."

"Don't remind me," I said, taking a long drink.

"I'm going to. This whole time. You, a guide, need a sneak."

"Stop it."

"No."

29

THE FIRST CHALLENGE was finding out where Anna crossed over. She'd mentioned that it was somewhere south of the clock tower, near the Warrens. Made sense, as most people dying in the usual ways showed up there at some point or another. Sneaks wouldn't have to venture too far to find their targets.

As I went south from the clock tower, I saw plenty of sparks shooting up from various parts of the city. Guides were getting out in force lately with the war picking up and Riven getting more dangerous. Had to keep ghouls to a minimum, had to keep breaches closed. Normally I'd have been happy to see so much activity.

Now it would just make my job harder. I couldn't be seen with Anna, or I'd have to have a real good story for why I was leading a sneak around Riven.

I'd told Anna to wait for me when she crossed. Running around wasn't going to do anything more than getting her killed. She hadn't taken that line very well, throwing me a raised eyebrow and replying that she'd been running around

Riven as long as I had, thank you very much. I switched tactics and said I'd never find her if she moved around, and that worked a little better.

"I'll give you half an hour," Anna had said at the train station before we split.

It had to be getting close to that time. I was at the entrance to the Warrens, the Ghoul's Gateway. Without Bryce, the crumbling arch was ominous. Less a lead-in to excitement and more a warning of terrors beyond. My hand drifted to the lash.

"You're awfully slow for a guide," Anna said, stepping out from behind the arch.

"You're a terrible listener," I replied, unwrapping my fingers from the lash's grip. "Told you to wait where you crossed."

"Figured you'd have a better chance of finding me here," Anna said, looking up at the gateway. "So where's this friend of yours?"

"Hold up," I said. "There's a lot of guides around, so some ground rules. First, I lead."

"You're the one who knows where you're going."

"I'm going to leave you here if you don't stop interrupting me," I said and Anna leaned against the arch with a shrug.

"Thought you could take it," Anna said. "What with all your brave talk."

"Look," I pushed past it. "I need to have a reason you're with me if we get found. That's going to be that you're a spirit I bound. Because you have information on another angry spirit."

"I do, huh?"

"Yeah. Make something up if they press you."

"That's all? Just make something up?"

"I thought that's all sneaks did."

Now it was her turn to get defensive. Made me feel good.

The walk back to Selena's apartment, now also Nicholas' lab, was made mostly by ducking into alleys, using the periodic spark showers as signposts to be avoided. I listened for any noise. Fighting, footsteps, conversation. Anna, for her part, focused once we started moving and kept quiet.

After an hour, twice as long as it would've taken on a normal night, we made it to the apartment. Nicholas greeted us at the door, taking Anna in with a close look from his goggled eyes.

"Assuming this is your friend?" Anna said. "Cause if you were to ask me who was making weapons in Riven, a person decked out in goggles and a lab coat would be my first guess."

"I'm Nicholas Salzer, at your service," the scientist said, extending a dirty, gloved hand. Anna glanced at the offered palm, hesitated, then shook it with gusto.

"Anna Blanc. Pleasure," Anna said. "Carver's been telling me about your prowess."

"Years of hard work pays off," Nicholas said. "Was doing quite well for myself back in the real world. Unfortunately, explosions can be a tad unpredictable."

"Nicholas, stop scaring her," I said, more afraid that Anna was going to ask Nicholas for the full story. We'd be here for hours, time I didn't have. "She needs a weapon. You have any lying around?"

As I finished talking, I went by the scientist and into the apartment. From the doorway I'd caught a hint of changes, and once I went through, wow. Gone was the long table Selena and I used to sit at. Even the chairs had been pushed to the edges of the room. A new, smaller, boiler was out on the balcony, pipes streaking into the apartment and wrapping through a long series of machines that I couldn't identify.

Some were obvious - a forge for heating metal, a stove that appeared to have several boiling liquids on it, and then three other contraptions that dominated the rest of the space that I couldn't identify.

"I don't have one ready-made, no," Nicholas said. "Despite your predilections, Carver, I'm not a store. I do not have limitless stock on demand for you."

"Selena really lost the battle for this place, didn't she?" I said, continuing my inspection.

"Selena?" Anna said from behind me.

"My co-habitator," Nicholas said. "She was generous enough to support the mission at the expense of her own living space, yes."

"Where is she?" I said.

"Outside, watching the storm of sparks your fellows are setting loose," Nicholas said. "Now, when you say weapon, what are you looking for?"

"Something for her," I said. "Easy to learn."

"Strong and deadly," Anna countered. Nicholas took a slow look at her.

"You're not a guide," Nicholas stated. "If you are not a guide, then do you have any formal training in the arts martial?"

"I'm savvy," Anna said. "I know how to throw a good punch. Enough bar fights have taught me that."

Nicholas rubbed his chin, his wispy beard. He kept staring at Anna with an intensity that, with anyone else, would have been creepy. I knew, though, that behind those eyes numbers were dancing a tango that would end with some devilishly cool device.

"I have it!" Nicholas announced. "Only, I cannot make it here. Or rather, I can, but I'm missing the necessary pieces."

"Of course you are," I said, and Nicholas shot me a glare.

"It was you who told me to abandon my lab," Nicholas said. "Were we still there, all this would take is a night of work. Now, however, I'll need you two to go back to my former residence and collect a few items."

"We'll do it," Anna said. I sighed.

30

I FOUND her on the balcony, staring at the sparks popping up into the sky. Selena looked radiant in the gray light wearing a new dress that I'd never seen before.

"Nicholas made it for me," Selena said, without looking at me. I watched a series of amber sparks ripple across her eyes. "A gift for letting him move in here. I didn't even know you could make dresses in Riven."

"Nicholas is a talented guy."

We said nothing for a moment. Behind me, back in the apartment, I could hear Nicholas telling Anna more about his planned weapon. She was peppering him with questions and, if there was one thing Nicholas liked, it was answering inquiries.

"I found him," Selena said. "Graham."

"Where?"

"We spoke," Selena said, and now she turned to me. "He wants me to bring you to him."

"That sounds like a trap."

"It is," Selena said. "I don't want you to go. You told me he might have a way of bringing me back, and I think he does, but it's not a good one."

"Even if it's the worst thing Riven has ever seen, I don't have a choice," I said. "Graham's a danger to everyone, including you and Nicholas. I can't just let him run around out there."

"I thought you'd say that," Selena slipped into a sad smile. "Always running towards adventure."

"You're not so different," I said. I wanted to talk about what I'd found, what Opperman had told me, but there didn't seem to be a good way to bring it up. What would Selena think if she knew I'd had her investigated?

"It's easier when you're already dead," Selena said. "Who's the new girl?"

"She knows something about my mother. In exchange, I'm having Nicholas set her up."

"Nothing else?" Selena raised an eyebrow a millimeter.

"And get on your bad side?" I laughed. "I've got enough people trying to kill me. No thanks."

I leaned in, slid my arm around her waist and brought her close. Tried to find a line, something smooth to say, and settled for a kiss. Selena didn't back away from it.

"We've got to go get something for Nicholas," I said. "But when I get back, we're picking this up where we left it."

"So you do like the dress."

"I love it," I said. Gave Selena a nod and turned to go back into the apartment.

"Carver, don't get yourself killed out there," Selena said.

"Not the plan," I replied, then walked back inside. I really needed to work on my goodbyes. 'Not the plan'? What kind of a phrase was that?

"Let's get going," I said to Anna as she and Nicholas huddled over a desk where the scientist was sketching something. "I've got things to do tonight."

The Tar Pit was getting a little too familiar. One of those places where I didn't want to spend a lot of time, but now here I was again. Nicholas's lab sat in front of us, the main doors still broken from Cane and Spike's visit last night.

"You set him up nice," Anna said. "I'm assuming that you've bound both of them?"

I glanced at her. It wasn't common knowledge that a guide could keep a spirit around if they wanted. "I might have."

"Heard that's not easy to do," Anna said, leaving the sentence hanging there.

I could've told her that the process was arduous. That you first had to befriend the spirit, or at least get it to accept what you were going to do. Then you had to find an area that the spirit could call home. A place that would be safe. For Selena, that'd been her apartment. For Nicholas, his lab. After that, well, it took a handshake. A kiss. Some form of physical contact.

I'd bound two spirits, and binding more than one was very much frowned on by the guides. Binding was disruptive - it kept spirits from the Cycle and established permanence in a world that didn't want any. Not to mention there was the potential for exactly what Selena and I were doing. Guide - Spirit romances were so forbidden as to be blinding offenses. Guides would take you and strip your connection to Riven. Then charge you with the literal crime so you rotted in prison too, just to kick you in the teeth.

"It's not fun," I said. "But for the right spirit; it's useful."

I didn't let Anna get going with her next sentence, but walked fast inside the lab. Nicholas had us questing for a pair of parts to get Anna's weapon put together. First was a chain he'd been building as an eventual substitute for my lash. That was easy - the chain hung on a crude hook slammed into the back of the far wall.

The lab apart from the chain was a study in random destruction. Materials and machines were scattered around. Tables overturned and shattered. Yet, even with a cursory glance, it didn't look like things had been so ruined as to be irreparable. If we could guarantee Graham wouldn't be a problem anymore, then Nicholas would be able to come back here without much fuss.

"I'm not seeing the ball," Anna said, digging around. That would be the second item we needed. Nicholas described it as a beige sphere. I had asked what it did and he said that he'd show us when we brought it back.

"I have it," said a new voice, soft and strong. Leaning on the lab's door, the beige sphere held in her hand, was a spirit wrapped in a tight series of ashen bands. Her shoulders and arms were bare, but the bands covered the rest of her, leaving her eyes and her straight hair the only other parts visible. Rising over her back, I could see a pair of handles. Or hilts.

"Guessing you're not going to give it to us?" I asked, drawing the lash.

"Do you work for Graham?" the spirit asked.

"Who's Graham?" Anna said at the same time as I was saying "No."

"Then you can't lead me to him?" the spirit said, ignoring Anna and looking at me.

"Don't know where he is," I said. Anna flipped glances between the two of us.

"Then you're no use to me," the spirit said. She turned to leave.

"Give us the sphere," Anna said, her tone way too aggressive for someone that had no weapon. The spirit paused, turned to look at Anna.

"Do you know where you are, girl?" the spirit said. "Because threats here must be backed up by something more than words."

"They are," I moved forward, snaking the lash behind me. With a flick, I could have the lash streaking through the air towards the spirit's face.

"I suppose I could use the practice," the spirit murmured. Then, with a snap of her arm, she threw the sphere at me. I caught it with my left hand, but the motion meant I didn't crack my lash.

The spirit used that moment to draw the weapons on her back, a pair of wooden batons with metal hooks on the top end. Batons with the telltale line near the grip that indicated they could be twisted to ignite wrangling fire. A guide's weapon.

I danced back as the spirit came at me with a spinning flurry of blows. The edges of those batons blurred by inches from my face. But those inches were the difference between dead and alive.

I snapped the lash back, then cracked it forward as the spirit whirled into a half-crouch, glaring up at me with her batons ready. Then she did exactly what I'd hoped.

The lash blitzed forward and the spirit stuck one of her batons in the way. The baton blocked the strike, but the lash wrapped around the spirit's weapon. With a snap of my wrist, I whipped the baton out of her hand and sent it flying across the room.

The spirit made the most of that vulnerable instant, charging into me. She used the baton in her left hand to strike at my right elbow, pinning my lash back. I felt her empty right hand reaching for my long knife. Couldn't let her get that and poke me to pieces.

I grabbed the spirit's wrist as she made another grab for the knife and twisted it. I should have been strong enough to break it, but the spirit moved with my force, jumping and twisting so that her legs wrapped around my face. My eyes bulged as her knees pushed into my temples, her hand still pulling for that knife.

Not what I'd expected, but if there was anything I'd learned as a guide, it was that most fights were dirty. The dead had no dignity. So I turned around, stumbling, and then ran at the wall behind me. I felt the spirit try to release my head, try to scramble away, but I held her legs with my hands, trapping her.

Just before we struck the wall, the spirit arched her back, threw her arms out in front of her towards the wall, and, as we hit it, pushed. The sudden opposite force coupled with my legs hitting the wall to knock me, still holding the spirit, on my back.

The spirit rolled off of me as I coughed up air. She hadn't escaped unscathed. I stood up and followed her as the spirit limped back to her baton, her left wrist hanging at a strange angle. Probably broken from the impact.

"For a guide," the spirit said, looking back at me. "You're a clever fighter."

She picked up her baton, then, and came at me again. My left hand went for the knife, but it wasn't there. As I looked up at the spirit, I realized why. Her wrist was at a weird angle because of her grip on the knife. Hiding it along the length of her arm.

The spirit with my knife ran at me, pointed right for my throat.

"Carver!" Anna yelled from across the lab. In my peripheral, I saw her throw something at me. The other baton. I caught it as the spirit hesitated. Staring at me.

"What, you're done now?" I said.

"A trade," the spirit said suddenly. "The knife and the sphere for the baton."

I glanced at Anna. Even if the spirit had some sort of

fancy trick planned, I felt better without her having the knife.

"Deal," I said. The spirit threw the knife at my feet. I looked at it. Thought about picking it up and just going after the spirit with both weapons. Only, the spirit had no pale fire in her eyes. She had an agenda. She seemed to want to hurt Graham.

I gave the spirit her baton back. She took it and, without another word, bolted from the lab.

"Was that strange?" I said, watching the door the spirit had fled through. "Because that seemed strange."

"She was killing you," Anna said. "Not very impressive for a guide."

"Please, that was all part of my plan. Get her overconfident, then surprise," I said.

"Right," Anna said. "That's what was going to happen."

I ignored the remark. Went outside and saw the sphere on the street, left there as promised. Picked it up and ran my fingers over its smooth surface. It seemed to be stone, something Nicholas could have found anywhere in Riven.

"Come on," I said to Anna as she followed me out of the lab, chain in hand. "Let's go. Next time a spirit jumps me, it'd be nice if you had a way to help."

ON THE WALK back to the lab, I kept turning over the banded spirit in my mind. While Riven had plenty of spirits in states between losing their minds and on dead-eyed journeys to the Cycle, before Graham, I hadn't encountered any that were calculating. Aggressive but not out of control. Now, counting Cane and Spike, there'd been four in the last couple of days.

Anna and I passed by a trio of spirits, standing on the thin sidewalk and staring at each other, confused. Newcomers. Sharing that lost and dazed stare amongst themselves.

"Hold this," I said, handing the sphere to Anna. "I want to try something."

I went up to the trio and waved my hand in front of their faces. They looked like travelers, sporting jackets and trousers meant for a trek. Victims, perhaps, of an accident or disease in some edgy frontier. As my hand passed in front of their eyes, they tracked it.

"What're you names?" I asked them. They turned at the sound of my voice, but said nothing. Angry spirits, like the one Selena found days ago, clung to their personality. To a warped version of themselves. Others, especially if they had some expectation of death, understood where they were and managed to bring part of themselves to bear on it. Gained a voice, even determination. Until the Cycle washed it away.

These three, though, they were what I expected. Whomever they had been at the moment their lives left them was gone.

"What are you doing?" Anna asked me.

"Confirming that Riven still makes sense," I said. "At least in its own way."

We left the spirits and kept going back to the apartment. The trio hadn't helped me figure out why the banded spirit bothered to attack, but at least Riven wasn't turning to a murderer's row of hostile spirits around every corner. I only knew one way, though, that a spirit could gain that level of reasoning, come up with goals beyond tearing the throat out of the next thing it saw. That was through binding, which a guide could do, which anchored a spirit to Riven through a piece of the guide himself.

Graham suggested another. That perhaps a strong-willed spirit could survive on its own. Even bring other spirits under its power. If that was true, and Cane and Spike suggested it was, then Graham might be able to form his own army. Bring bands of armed, deliberate spirits to sweep ambush and annihilate unsuspecting guides. He was more dangerous than ever.

I opened the door to the apartment and froze. Nicholas stood in the middle of the living room, holding one of the blue-tinged crossbow bolts and wearing a dark cloth vest with indigo lines running through it.

"You've returned!" Nicholas said as he saw me. "Now, the test can begin!"

Before Anna or I could say anything, Nicholas stabbed himself with the crossbow bolt, blazing blue fire up and around the scientist. I felt a sudden rush as Nicholas severed our connection. Ran forward to try and pull the bolt out of the scientist's chest, but Selena stopped me. Caught my arm as I went into the apartment.

"He thinks he has a way to stop it," Selena said as we watched Nicholas collapse to the floor. "To block the Cycle. It would mean you wouldn't have to bind us anymore."

"This is his idea of how to test that?" I said, incredulous.

"If it doesn't work, you'll rebind him," Selena replied.

"You chose some weird spirits," Anna said.

The fire burned down around Nicholas, eventually vanishing and leaving the spirit lying on the floor. We all watched him. Waited. I'd never seen a broken binding before, had no idea what would happen next.

"Nicholas, you still there?" I said to the scientist's prone form.

He didn't reply.

"Should we poke him or something?" Anna said.

"Wait," Selena said. "Give him time."

Nicholas eventually stirred. Stood up on his feet, his back to us.

"So if this worked?" I said to Selena.

"He said he should be himself," Selena said.

When Nicholas turned around, though, I didn't see any trace of my friend. His eyes were as dead as any of the spirits I'd wrangled before. As devoid of comprehension as the trio on the street.

"Nicholas?" Anna said to the scientist. He didn't say anything. Stared past us, towards the door. Took a step forward.

"Right," I said, moving in front of Nicholas. "This one's gone on long enough."

I reached out, put my hand on the spirit's shoulder, and found our connection. Brought the two of us back together, and re-bound the scientist to me. When it was done,

Nicholas blinked and, behind those eyes, I saw the shimmering intelligence that had been missing a moment before.

"I take it the experiment failed?" Nicholas said.

"It did not go well," I said. "You went blank, and were about to march on out of here."

"I'm sorry, Nicholas," Selena said.

"That's all right," Nicholas said to her. "Experiments are meant to fail. Are meant to be tried again. Eventually, if one follows their hypothesis to the end, the idea is confirmed to be possible, or..."

"Or we have no other choice," Selena said.

"Right," Nicholas seemed to deflate. "If we cannot devise a means to suppress the Cycle, then we are tied to Carver here. When he eventually passes, then we will lose our anchor."

Selena nodded, then slipped away, out towards the balcony. We watched her go.

"Nicholas," I said. "Do you think you're close?"

The scientist sighed, shook his head. "Without a better idea of how the Cycle works, I'm afraid I am only guessing. The vest was meant to suppress the frequencies your resonator picks up. I had hoped, perhaps, the compulsion came through along those lines."

"Keep trying," I said. "You might get lucky."

Anna held up the sphere, and Nicholas brightened. "There's no better cure for a failed experiment than conducting another one!" Nicholas said. "Now, bring that bauble over here and lets get started."

32

After Nicholas declared we'd found the right pieces, and that it would take him a day of focused effort to put the thing together, Anna left to cross back over. I went out to the balcony, where Selena was still standing, watching the occasional spark.

"So you're still tied to me," I said. "I hope you're not *too* disappointed."

"So clever," Selena said, rolling her eyes. "So funny."

"I can't help it," I said. "Part of who I am."

"It's good that you know who you are," Selena said. "It's easier to lead the life you're looking for, that way."

The hard swing to the serious. I had already made up my mind to leave Opperman's material alone for now, but if Selena wanted to dig into that side of life, I was ready.

"Do you know who *you* are?" I asked her.

"Me?" Selena said. "Sometimes I think I'm just a woman who wound up on the unlucky side of life. Other times, I think that everything that brought me here is my own doing. That it's who I am."

"What brought you here?" if Selena wanted to confess her

past, and thus make revealing Opperman's work unnecessary, I'd take that chance.

"Choices," Selena said. "While you're living it, life moves too fast for reflection. Here, though, in Riven, you're presented with as much time as you need. All the evidence of lives lived wrong."

"The other spirits."

"I look at them and wonder how they died," Selena said. "Is that strange?"

"That's basically my job. So, I hope not."

"Right, but its different for me. I want to know, did they deserve it?" Selena said.

"Because you did?"

Crap. That was the wrong thing to say. I knew it as the words came out of my mouth, and it was confirmed when Selena frowned at me.

"What did you say?" Selena's voice didn't hold the anger I expected.

"That you think you deserve to be here?" A chance to change my words, to dodge the swinging ax, but no. I went for it. Because I knew I wanted to have this conversation. To find out whether the Selena I knew was a fraud, whether she was using me as some new affection before stabbing me in the back, or finding a way out of Riven with Graham.

"I do," Selena said, not even bothering to fight. "Then, so do most people. I've done terrible things, Carver. Even so, they're not so awful as others. I didn't die terribly, this scar notwithstanding. I didn't suffer through a disease. I didn't watch my children die. I wasn't mutilated or drowned. It was instant. One moment there, the next, here. If you hadn't found me, I'd be gone entirely by now."

"We all go eventually."

"Only that's not really true, is it?" Selena said. "Graham's idea. The binding you've done. Spirits can live forever, and maybe come back."

I studied her expression as she said those words. Looked for any sign of malice, or her eyes slipping away from mine as she lied. There was nothing. Only honest conversation.

"You're going to take me to him," I said.

"Yes," Selena replied. "Together."

"What if he *can* crack Riven? Open a way back?"

"I'll be the first through the door," Selena said.

"Even if it would hurt everyone on the other side? Even your children?"

Selena's face went sad for a second, and she turned back to Riven's torn skyline. "For another life, I would do anything."

The words chilled me. There were a lot of terrible things Graham might offer her for that chance.

"Are you ready?" Selena said. "He'll be there tonight, but we can wait. If you're tired."

I was. I was exhausted and burnt after this conversation. After the fight with the spirit in Nicholas's lab. But I was sick of Graham. Sick of what he was doing to my life.

"Let's go," I said. "Take me to Graham."

3 3

The building wasn't natural. Wasn't in its original Riven state. I could tell from the imperfect shards placed on the square roof. From the bars put into the windows and the broken mortar around them. Could tell from the large deep wood door with new hinges covering the entrance.

The windows hadn't the slightest glow. No sound came out of the place, which was a half-block in size. At least three stories. A big place for a single spirit to bother with.

"He's here," Selena said at my questioning look.

"How's he want us to come in?" I said. "Knock? Break through the door?"

At my words, Selena walked forward, took the handle that sat on the right side of the door, and pulled it. With silent grace, the door large enough for Selena and I to walk in side by side swung out towards me.

Inside, the entrance held a single bench and clear stone walls. A passage went back briefly before opening into a wider room.

"Boring, but I guess its functional," I said.

"Focus, Carver," Selena said, this time a flash of worry

darting across her face. With all that talk of getting out of Riven alive, it was nice to see she still cared.

"Making stupid statements is how I focus," I said, peering down the passage. "I'm finding the lack of a greeting suspicious."

"Follow me," Selena said. And so I did. Down the passage, where the lack of windows made the world dim. The room beyond, however, lacked a ceiling. Riven's light poured in. I guess in a world without rain or anything other than gray nothing, missing a roof wasn't a problem.

One thing caught my eye.

"There he is," I said to Graham, standing at the end of the empty courtyard. The ash that fluttered through Riven's air had been collecting here, had built up until it formed a loose carpet.

"Indeed, here I am," Graham replied. "Thank you, Selena, but you may leave us now."

I wanted to tell her to stay, but stopped myself. What would she do? Would Selena blindly obey Graham and make it obvious I was screwed, stab me in the back? Or get herself hurt trying to help me?

"Be careful," Selena told me. "His weapons aren't only physical."

Graham gave the comment a nod, and then Selena walked back the way we'd come. Shut the door to the outside and disappeared. Leaving me alone with captain top hat and his hammer.

"Why'd you wreck Nicholas's lab?" I said.

"Because he was making things that don't belong in Riven," Graham said. "That crossbow you wear on your back. That was never meant for here. Riven is where you get up close with the lost, and by doing so earn your own self."

"That's a bunch of crap," I said. "You've told me, told Selena that you have a way out of Riven. What is it?"

"So direct, Carver," Graham said.

"You remember that you used to be a guide?" I said. "That your job was to keep Riven safe? To keep spirits locked in?"

"Look where it took me," Graham said.

"Tell me how," I repeated. Either Graham would tell me how, and then I could share it with the rest of the guides, and potentially Selena, or he wouldn't. In which case I would wrangle him and send Graham to the Cycle.

"Some things are better shown, I'm afraid. If you'll come over here, lie down, then we'll get started?"

"That's not happening," I said. "If you're not talking..." I reached for the lash.

Graham smiled, a creepy affair as his eyes opened wide, dragging his wrinkled, scraggly face up around them. "With pleasure."

Graham broke into a loping run, setting the spiked hammer over his shoulder and holding the hilt. His left hand, still sporting the gauntlet, pumped with every footstep. I flipped the crossbow off my back. Raised it, and fired.

On the walk over, I'd slotted in a normal bolt and cranked the weapon. Figured having a ready-to-fire shot wouldn't be a bad plan. Graham tried to dart out of the way, but wasn't fast enough. My shot caught him in the shoulder, spun him around and to the ground.

I drew the lash and snapped it as Graham tried to push himself to his feet. I hit his leg, but Graham twisted his ankle away from the pointed end. Still, the lash tore away parts of the spirit's clothes and the skin beneath.

I sent the lash forward again. This time at his chest, an easier target. Except Graham's left hand snaked out and caught the lash. Held it tight. I did nothing for a second. Stunned. A whipping lash was fast, so fast that I couldn't believe anyone could catch it. Graham would have had to anticipate the move, already getting into position before I'd snapped the lash.

Then the spirit pulled hard. Yanked me forward. By instinct, I dug in my heels, and realized what a bad call that was when Graham used the resistance to pull himself up to his feet. He lunged, swinging the hammer. I dropped the lash and darted back, the spirit's swing catching only air.

I pulled out the long knife. Sidestepped to Graham's right, towards the side with the hammer. His weapon took space to get a good swing, and if I could close, get inside his reach, there'd be openings. I kicked my right foot, throwing up a cloud of the ash that'd gathered on the courtyard floor. It flew towards Graham's face, and as soon as my foot hit the ground, I pushed off towards his right side.

The spirit didn't move fast enough, the ash forcing him to block his face with a hand. I cut in, grabbing his hammer arm with my left and stabbing with my right. I felt the knife bite in and expected the pale fire to burst out, crawl over Graham and end the fight.

Only it didn't. The knife burned blue, but Graham jerked free before any pale fire touched his clothes. Swiped the hammer as he back-stepped. I couldn't get out of the way, the hammer catching my left shoulder as I tried to keep a grip on the knife.

Graham couldn't get much power behind the hit that close to me, but there wasn't a light way to get slammed with a large hammer. The spike brushed my shoulder, the rest of the head crunching me down to the ground.

I used the momentum to roll, ignoring the ache from my left side. A second later, the hammer struck the ground where I'd fallen, denting the courtyard's floor.

"There are two ways, Carver!" Graham continued. "Two ways to bridge the gap between Riven and your world. One, you already know."

Graham let me stand up. The spirit wasn't pushing his attacks. Why? "Clog Riven with spirits?"

I felt something against my foot and noticed I'd rolled near my lash. Without taking my eyes off of Graham, who seemed content plucking the crossbow bolt from his left shoulder, I crouched and regained my lash.

"Yes, and what a terrible choice that would be," Graham said. "Chaos. No control over who went across. At one time, though, I thought that would be the only way."

The crossbow was behind me, only a few feet away. If Graham stayed on his monologue, I'd have a chance to get it. Get another shot off. This one straight into the spirit's busy mouth.

"Until I found you, Carver," Graham said. "Until I found out who you were."

I paused. "What do I have to do with anything?"

"With you, Carver, I can control the breach. Control the bridge between Riven and our home," Graham said.

"Giving you control has to be the last thing I want," I said, yanking up the crossbow.

I didn't see Graham launch the hammer. Didn't see it whirl through the air. I only felt it when the spiked end embedded itself in my chest and pushed me into the wall.

I felt my ribs break. Couldn't focus. My vision pulsed, shook at the edges. But I could see Graham walking towards me, that same manic grin on his face.

I grabbed the spark tube from my belt as I slid onto my knees. Standing was too hard. I pressed the button on the tube's end. Didn't even watch the sparks fly high into the sky and burst.

"Unfortunately, Carver, you don't have to be awake for this. Only alive. At first," Graham said, coming close. "Or perhaps it is fortunate. I hear it's much easier to die in one's sleep."

3 4

GRAHAM REACHED OUT, grabbed the hammer, and pulled the spike out of my chest. I slumped forward. For some reason, my body didn't want to stand up. Didn't want to do anything. There was pain, sure, but on top of it sat an overwhelming sense of defeat. Of being broken.

"Why'd you bring me to the factory?" I said. I wasn't really talking, more wheezing out the question. "If you wanted me alone, you had me then."

"The other guides were there," Graham sounded annoyed. "That one that's been trying to track me, he was following you. None of the spirits would have killed you, if they'd won. You would have been saved."

Graham crouched in front of me, gripped my face with his hand and lifted it up. "The eyes are perfect. The hair, just like hers."

"What?" I coughed.

"I wanted to be sure," Graham said. "Now, we can begin."

Graham grabbed my shoulder and pulled me forward, dragging me along the ground. In front of my eyes, Graham's hammer swung low, bouncing off the surface with every step the man took. Tiny sparks flew with each contact. Mesmerizing.

And then Graham dropped me, right in the center of the courtyard. Turned me so my eyes faced Riven's gray sky. Graham seemed to fall inside himself, as though thinking hard on something. Then his eyes snapped wide and he smiled at me.

"A little while longer and then everything will be ready," Graham said. "I truly hope you've enjoyed your life, Carver, and that at the end you can feel well-lived."

Truth was, I wasn't paying attention to what Graham was nattering on about. That's because, flashing in the open air above our heads was a series of blue sparks. A face appeared, looking over the edge. Graham, staring at me over his hammer, didn't notice Alec.

Didn't move until the guide slammed down on Graham from above, knocking the spirit down into the ash. Alec didn't give Graham a moment to recover. Jabbing the spirit with his gauntlets, spikes digging in, Alec launched Graham across the courtyard. The spirit rolled to a stop near the edge.

"You are still alive, Carver?" Alec said to me. "I know we are late, but you choose the farthest places for your fights."

"Sorry," I said. The weakness in my voice killed Alec's friendly grin. His eyes narrowed, and he looked over at Graham.

"We will get you home," Alec said, all joking gone. "Hold on, my friend."

I turned my head to follow Alec as he sprinted towards Graham. Alec led with a right jab, his left swooping for a deep upper-cut. Graham, recovering faster than Alec expected, twisted to his left, dodging the jab and putting Alec out of position. Graham kicked out with his leg, catching Alec in the stomach.

The guide took the blow and wrapped his arms around Graham's leg, pushed up. Tried to break the spirit's knee. Then I saw what the thing on Graham's wrist was for.

Graham clenched his left hand into a fist and the gadget pumped. A short wire shot down the gauntlet, appearing to glow blue as it went, then flew off Graham's wrist right into Alec's neck. The wire snapped, choked Alec, and then crackled with pale fire. Alec dropped Graham's leg and fell to the ground, rolling, trying to free himself.

Graham went back towards the hammer. Made it three steps before, with a whistling noise, a spear landed in the spirit's chest. No, not a spear, half of Bryce's voulge. Graham looked down at it, surprised.

"Graham!" Bryce called from the courtyard's entrance. "It's time for your mistake to end."

Spirits couldn't die a second death in Riven, but they could be hurt. Weakened and wrangled, sent to the Cycle. Graham reached for the voulge and pulled on it, breaking it free from his chest and letting it fall to the ground. I noticed, though, that he straightened slowly, his smile gone and his eyes lacking their manic sparkle.

What Graham didn't notice was that I was crawling, tugging my way through pain and agony towards Alec. I heard Bryce run through the courtyard behind me.

"You look familiar," Graham said, his voice lead now. Dead with effort.

"What I look like doesn't matter," Bryce said. "What does is that you don't belong anymore. The Cycle calls, spirit."

In front of me, Alec writhed on the ground, his neck turning black where the fire burned. His hands, protected by the gauntlets, were trying to pull the wire off and failing. I grabbed the knife on Alec's waist, and pulled it out of its holster.

"Be still, Alec," I whispered. Alec obeyed, somehow

calming his pain enough to stop struggling. I slipped the knife against the wire, a dark line coated with burning blue, and cut through it. As soon as the wire split, the fire vanished.

Metal clashed behind me and I turned to see Bryce engaging Graham in a deadly dance. Bryce had nabbed the half on the ground and, his voulge still in two parts, Bryce was a dervish, sidestepping, parrying, and getting under Graham's longer hammer blows. I could see Graham was slower too, the injuries catching up to him.

The spirit wasn't talking anymore either. No cocky asides or strange questions.

"No rest yet," Alec muttered, massaging his charred neck. The guide rose, then turned to the fight.

Graham noticed, and as his eyes caught Alec, Bryce struck with the side of the voulge, knocking Graham in the head. When Graham straightened, Alec stood next to Bryce, ready.

"This is the end, spirit," Bryce said, twisting the handles of his voulge. The weapon's edges glowed with blue fire. At the same time, Alec twisted his wrists, his gauntlets wreathing themselves with the same flames.

Graham, leaning on his hammer, looked at the two guides. Then his mouth opened in what seemed like a silent scream.

I heard noises above, on the building's second floor. The simultaneous pounding of feet. A spirit landed in the court-yard, then another. And a third. Jumping from the balconies lining the open space. Two landed between Bryce, Alec and Graham.

These weren't normal spirits either. Like Cane and Spike, these had weapons. While they didn't have the pale fire in their eyes, they had murder.

"Run!" I croaked at my friends. It wasn't worth having them die for me. Especially as I was feeling worse. My body's will to push through the injuries was fading, pain again overtaking my ability to do anything other than curl up.

Graham was the first to look at me, and I saw something in that sinister expression I did not expect. Concern.

"Carver cannot die here," Graham said, speaking to Bryce and Alec. "An exchange. Your lives for his."

"A deal we should take," Alec said to Bryce. "As much as I hate admitting it, we are not favored in this match."

"Agreed," Bryce said.

The spirits parted, allowing the two guides to get to me. To life me up and carry me from the courtyard.

"Live, Carver!" Graham said as they carried me out. "Come back to me, and do what you were meant to."

The words followed me into unconsciousness, chasing me into the dark of Riven's oblivion as Bryce and Alec carried me through its gray streets.

35

I HADN'T DREAMED in decades, but when I saw the tree above me, its bare limbs stretching towards a ghost sky, I thought I'd found my way into one.

"Carver?" Selena's voice stirred into my ear. "How are you here?"

I turned to look at her. Selena stood at the base of the tree, eyes wide.

"Selena?" was all I could think to say.

"Graham's plan didn't work, then?" Selena said to me, coming closer. "Or did it?"

Selena reached out a hand towards my chest. Her fingers touched the edge of my coat, the edge of my shirt, the edge of me, and passed through.

Selena raised her eyes to mine, drawing her hand out. "You're not here. Not all the way."

"I'm not dead," I said. "At least, I don't think so."

"Not yet," Selena said softly, her face looking down. "You're close. Almost a spirit."

"Where did you go?"

When Selena looked back at me, her eyes shone with

tears. "I'm leaving, Carver. Going to where Graham can't make me hurt you."

"Make you?"

"You've seen it," Selena looked behind her. I could see, in the far distance, the outlines of the Tar Pit smokestacks. "He can influence spirits, but that's not all of it. I could have resisted. Could have pushed him back."

"You wanted to cross," I said the words knowing they were true and yet not blaming her for it. Not hating her for wanting to go back to life.

"I did," Selena said. "I still do. That makes me dangerous. I tried to help, when Graham was focused on you. I found your friends. Led them towards the fight."

Selena passed her hand through my own. I didn't feel anything other than a cool otherness, a sense that my body and mind were in two different places.

"They saved me," I said. "You saved me."

"I don't know," Selena replied. "If you're here, then it might be too late. If you die, then I won't be bound. I've done enough hurt, Carver. I'm done with it."

"Where will you go?"

"To the Cycle," Selena said. "It's always there, you know. Like a song my daughter used to sing in the summers. Easy to ignore, but if you listen, you can find it."

Selena leaned in, her lips searching for mine. And when they met, I felt nothing. Selena's face passed into mine, and then drew back. She laughed.

"Appropriate, don't you think?" Selena said. "For a last kiss between ghosts?"

"Don't leave," I started. "It's not your fault—"

"Stop," Selena said. "Focus. Stay alive," She took a step back. "When you wake up, try to remember me."

Selena left me there. I tried to follow, but my legs weren't listening. The dream state left me stuck beneath the tree, able only to look after her as Selena went through the barren park and over a hill.

I felt a tug, like a heavy wind pulling at my back. The edges of everything blurred. The dead grass flowed together. I tried to focus on Selena as she went further and further away. As she vanished.

Then a mar. A dark spot in the fading scene. Another person.

Following Selena through the park, moving slow. The spirit from before, in Nicholas's lab. Dark and banded, her hair flickering in the wind. I tried to yell, to say something, but my mouth didn't work. My body wasn't there. The world was pulling away.

At the last, the dark spirit turned and stared at me. I could see her eyes, the roiling heat burning in her gaze. As she turned back towards Selena, I woke up.

"COME BACK, CARVER," Bryce said as he slapped my face in the clock tower. "Pull it together."

My eyes flickered open and brought with them a thousand aches. It was getting really old waking up this way. Deserving to die.

"Good," Bryce said, then he looked behind me to someone else. "Alec, bring the salt."

As I groaned, lying there pathetic in the bed, Alec came over with a small bowl. In it, clumped, was the dried up essence of Riven's non-water.

"Inhale," Bryce said as Alec put the bowl beneath my nose.

When I breathed the crystals in, my chest expanded with an icy chill. The freezing sensation went throughout my body, stretching to the ends of my fingers and my face. Every instant of pain obliterated in the face of that cold.

"Now, cross," Bryce said. "Don't wait."

At first I thought the cold itself would prevent me from focusing on anything, but I embraced the chill. Used it. Sank into the numbing ice. In that frozen bath, I found my apartment and fell towards it.

I woke up for the third time in an hour, only this time I was in my own bed. In Chicago. In the real world. To be sure, I stood up, raised my arms to test if my body listened. I looked outside the window and counted the zeppelins coasting by in the sky, which was an emphatic blue. Early morning.

My chest still hurt. While washing myself off in the cramped bath I shared with others on my floor, I traced the bruising around my lungs. A particularly dark circle where the hammer's spike had pierced. Every breath carried with it a sting.

But I was alive.

I showed up at Ezra's close to lunch time. A couple of hours later than usual, but I figured Bryce would be understanding. What I didn't expect, though, was to see Piotr sitting at our table. Having coffee and chatting with Bryce. Alec there as well, looking exhausted and wearing a shirt with a high collar that hid his neck.

Piotr was a giant of a man. Tall, thick, and coated with long white hair to go with a full, snowy beard, the leader of the guides complemented his physical stature with a deep navy cloak. Gold-lined tracings of the guide logo, that circle and incomplete square, appeared at random on the outfit. Looking at the man gave me a sense of power, of stature, and his warm smile as he saw me made the inspiring whole come together.

"Here's the missing man," Piotr announced when I came in. "Carver, Bryce tells me that you had a close call last night."

"Wasn't my best hunt, sir," I said.

"Any hunt you live through is a good one in my book," Piotr replied.

I was about to sit down when Piotr stood and looked towards Bryce, who gestured towards our private room in the back. It was so much easier to get service out here that we didn't use it except for calls. Or meetings that we wanted kept secret.

The four of us crowded into the small chamber and I grabbed my own mug of the dark stuff. The taste of something hot and real was a wonderful sensation. Especially when, for much of last night, I'd thought I was never going to experience it again.

"Thanks," I said before Piotr could get started. "Both of you. For everything."

"If you keep ignoring my rule about going alone," Bryce said. "I'm going to let Graham have you."

"What I'm curious about is how we found you," Alec said. "Eventually we saw your sparks, but before that there was this beautiful voice. It kept saying you were in trouble."

"Strange," I lied. "I don't know what that would've been."

"Riven has its peculiarities," Piotr interjected. Alec looked like he wanted to press the point, but Piotr ignored the guide. "I'm here to talk to you about one of them.

"There's a tower on the southwest side of the city, at the very edge of the Warrens. A number of guides have gone near the area and disappeared. What I'd like to know is what's going on. Is it a ghoul, a breach? Or something worse?"

"You want us to take a look?" Bryce said.

"With the recent casualties, there aren't many full city complements left. Much less ones with your level of experience," Piotr said. "Consider it a favor to me. If the tower is indeed a problem, don't engage. Report back and we'll organize a large effort."

We spent the next hour talking over the tower's precise location, the identities of the missing guides, and when we'd go on the trek. Piotr pushed for doing it that night and Bryce agreed. My mentor's words about guides never getting vacations buzzed in the back of my mind. Here I was, barely scraping through, and they wanted to throw me into the fire again.

Still, this was the path I'd chosen. If I didn't want to walk it, I could get blinded from Riven and set loose. Which wasn't going to happen.

After Ezra delivered sandwiches and we'd devoured them, Piotr stood up.

"I think I've said all that needs saying," Piotr said. "I'll be back in the morning to see how it went."

Then the leader of the guides turned to me. Stuck out his hand. I shook it, hesitating a second.

"Carver Reed," Piotr said. "It's been a long time."

Piotr walked out of the room. Bryce and Alec followed soon after. I sipped the rest of the coffee, confused.

I'd never met Piotr before in my life.

"YOU'RE LATE," Anna said to me as I walked into the apartment. Back in Riven, my injuries were gone. Physically, anyway. Mentally, hah, let's not talk about it.

"It was a busy morning," I replied. Walked past her into the noisy mess of the living room. When Nicholas went full on into a project, his sense of cleanliness vanished. Most of the machines were churning away, and Nicholas himself was bent over a workbench.

"Nicholas?" I said, raising my voice over the noise. "Is Selena here?"

I hadn't seen her in the bedroom or through the window on the balcony. I remembered the vision from the night before, but had no idea if that was real.

"I have seen no sign of her since she left with you," Nicholas replied without looking up. "Have you lost her?"

"She left," I said. I felt heavier. Selena was gone. Once she made it to the Cycle, everything that she was would be erased. Everything we had shared in this gray city of the dead would only live in my memories.

Nicholas stood up from the workbench, turned around

holding a two-foot long metal rod in his hands. At one end was that beige sphere, locked into the rod.

"She left?" Nicholas echoed. "Not what I would have expected from her. She seemed so hopeful after yesterday."

"It was an impossible dream," I said. I could feel Anna's eyes on my back, and Nicholas waited for more, but I didn't say anything. Didn't want to get into Graham and all the rest. That wasn't what we were here for.

"Anyway," Nicholas said after a too-long silence. "I'm finished early. This is your weapon, Anna. It is a mace, with a special flourish."

He presented it to her, and Anna raised the weapon gingerly. I could see the muscles tighten in her right arm. Heavier than she expected.

"Now," Nicholas continued. "When you carry the weapon, you keep it like this. When you have a fight in tight quarters, you keep it like this. But when you have room? Then, you change it!"

Nicholas reached above Anna's grip and twisted. The sphere fell off the top of the mace and dangled for a moment, until, with a click like a gear winding, a ring of inch-long spikes popped out. Pale fire made its way down the chain, starting from the rod, and eventually covered the sphere.

"Is that not a perfect weapon?" Nicholas said. Anna, staring into the fire with her mouth slightly open, nodded.

The best place to learn a new technique was the Warrens. Populated with spirits, but with plenty of other guides around if you got into trouble, the Warrens were as safe as danger got in Riven.

Anna and I made our way through the Ghoul's Gateway, Anna cradling the mace in her hands.

"He gave you the holster for a reason," I said, looking at Anna's back. "It's going to be more comfortable than carrying that thing."

"I want to get used to holding it," Anna said, and I didn't bother arguing. Everyone has their quirks.

"Hold up," I said some minutes later as we approached the middle of the Warrens. From my belt, I pulled off my resonator, set it on the ground, and let it do its thing.

"What's that?" Anna asked, and I told her. "So, wait. You're saying you have this tool that lets you find angry spirits and you never told me? That could be so useful!"

"It's for guides only."

"I thought these were too," Anna waved the mace around. "Besides, you seem to be bending all kinds of rules."

"I do what I have to."

Anna rolled her eyes. "What's with you today? You're sad. Moping around. Does it have something to do with the other spirit? Selena?"

On the ground, the resonator glowed orange. North, but not quite back where we came. We'd be walking alleys to get to the target. And doing it quietly. I'd already popped sparks to indicate we were in the area and keep other hunts away, but a guide could always be chancing by.

"I have a lot of questions that need answering," I said. "So after this, when you learn how to use that thing, you're telling me about my mother."

"That was the deal," Anna said, her tone different. Distant. Good. I didn't want a sneak thinking she was my best friend all of a sudden.

Anna kept quiet as we made our way north, following the resonator. The tool became brighter as we drew closer, bringing us into a ruin of what would have been a seven-story apartment building. A basic structure, with stairs running up the center.

"Ready?" I asked as we went in.

"Been waiting my whole life for this," Anna said. "A chance to wrangle a spirit? I'm ready."

I couldn't stop a small smile. That's what I'd said too, on my first time. Bryce had been there, watching my every move. Now, I'd do the same with Anna.

Except if we were caught together, I'd lose access to Riven forever.

3 8

THE SPIRIT WAS in the next room, and we could hear it growling to itself.

We were on the fourth floor of the apartment building, and it was ugly. Cracks lined the floors and walls. Doors were nonexistent. What furniture there was looked like it had been torn apart with absolute fury. One chair had legs in multiple apartments. Fuzz from cushions meshed with the ash floating in the air.

"You'll go in first," I said to Anna, who stood in the hall next to me. "Say hello. When it turns, you'll confirm that it's the target, then you swing."

"No special dance? No ritual?" Anna said, laughter in her eyes. I shook my head and waved her forward.

Anna rounded the corner into the room and I followed. The spirit was hunched over the ruins of a bed. It was really just a splintered wooden frame and a single pillowcase, but the spirit, a middle-aged man, caressed the frame with a slowness at odds with the noises coming from his mouth.

"Hello?" Anna said. Taking me literally then.

The spirit paused. Straightened. Then turned his head to

look at Anna. Glowing bright in his eyes were the telltale signs of crazy. Pale blue fire.

"You're not my wife," the spirit said.

"Correct," Anna replied, raising the mace.

"Then you don't belong here," the spirit replied. He bent down, snapped off a part of the bed frame. Anna smashed him in the face.

The spirit crumpled to the ground, groaning. Anna glanced back at me, grinning.

"He's not gone yet," I said, leaning against the door frame. Anna jerked back as the spirit made a grab for her leg. "You have to use the flail."

"Oh. Right," Anna twisted her weapon, the sphere popping off, spiking out, and growing the blue fire.

The spirit was back on his feet, one hand holding the bed frame and the other his head. It moaned, lurching towards Anna. She met the advance with a two-handed swing of her flail, the chain pulling the sphere hard and fast behind the rod. The spirit put up its bed frame piece to block.

Anna's flail simply shattered the spirit's poor defense, blowing apart the wood and continuing on to crumple into the spirit's chest. The blue fire spread out and enveloped the spirit.

"Your first wrangling," I said a moment later as the spirit walked by us on its dazed path to the Cycle. "Well done."

"Thanks," Anna said. She glanced down at her weapon, back in mace mode. "Have to remember the fire."

That's when we noticed the noise from the next room. A crying sound. A young one. I pulled out the resonator and confirmed. The signal guiding us to this building had been strong. Looks like the sound was coming from more than one spirit.

"You ready for round two?" I asked.

"Ready," Anna replied.

"Then lead on."

Anna went past the splintered bed frame, deeper into the apartment. An empty living room with a balcony, and then a second bedroom. Sitting in the middle of it, a girl. She looked up as we entered, her eyes a perfect burning blue.

"What happened to you?" Anna said to the child.

The girl tilted her head. She was wearing a flowery dress, one that I'd seen in Chicago kids going to parks. It lacked a certain charm when the kids wore their masks along with them, but here, on this spirit, the dress was perfect.

"You're not my mommy," the girl said to Anna. Then she looked at me. "You're not my daddy."

"That's right," Anna said, squatting to get eye-level with the girl.

"Anna," I said. "That's not a real girl anymore."

"I'm not a real girl?" the spirit said, standing up. She barely came up to my waist.

"You are," Anna said. "You were."

I caught the slight change, the tense of the girl's calves, but Anna didn't. Wasn't ready when the girl lunged at her. I pulled Anna back and the girl's grabbing hands fell short. Anna scrambled away, back to her feet, as the girl hesitated. Unsure which of us to target.

"Don't think of her as a girl," I said. "You have to see them all as spirits; things that need to be cycled."

Anna nodded, but she held the mace loosely. When the girl lunged again, Anna tried to counter, to bat the girl away with the weapon, but Anna didn't put enough effort into the swing. The mace went high, the girl ducking under it and attacking Anna's leg. Grabbing and crawling up Anna's coat. Biting and clawing her.

"Stop it!" Anna yelled, but that wasn't going to mean anything to a spirit. The girl reached Anna's face, her mouth opening and going for Anna's cheek, when my lash wrapped around the girl's body, pulled her off Anna, and cloaked the spirit in blue fire.

We both watched the girl as the fire died away, as her eyes blanked and she stood up and walked from the apartment. The only sound was Anna's hard breathing.

"They're not people," I said. "They're spirits."

"I know. I know that," Anna replied. "It's just hard sometimes."

"You can't let it be. One mistake with nobody around to help you and that's the end of it."

"I get it."

"I'd agree, but the only way we'll know for sure is when you make it through the next few nights alive," I said. Harsh, maybe, but Bryce had said much the same to me. Riven didn't do charity. Didn't give people an opportunity to learn.

"I think I'm done for tonight," Anna said, staring at her mace. I didn't argue.

When we reached the bottom floor of the apartment building, I paused.

"Now, about my side of the deal?" I said. "Tell me about my mother."

"I'VE BEEN THINKING about how to tell you," Anna said. "I think it'll make the most sense if I go back to the beginning."

"I'll walk slow," I replied as we moved through the Warrens.

"Remember when I met you on the train? Came up to you with the card?"

"It's not easy to forget. Most people don't approach a guide."

"Right. That wasn't an accident. I knew you were going to be on that train," Anna said. "I knew because I'd been following you."

"Someone hired you?"

"Why else does a sneak do anything, right?" Anna said. "All about the money and that's it, according to you."

"Prove me wrong," I said.

Anna laughed. "Prepare to be embarrassed. I wasn't hired to follow you. I was hired to find your mother."

"Find her? But she's dead?"

"In Riven."

"She would have died decades ago," I said. "There's no way her spirit would still be here."

"That's what I thought when the client told me. When I found the death certificate," Anna said. "The client told me he was confident she was here somewhere, and I believed him."

"Why?"

"Because the client was the lead guide for Chicago."

"Liar," I said without thinking. "Bryce would never hire a sneak."

Anna took the opportunity to dish me another glare. Her annoyed face went well with the broken side-street we were going down. A smattering of lampposts leered over the cracked road, storefronts full of shattered glass stared out at us. Spirits wandered by on their winding paths to the Cycle.

"Apparently you're not listening," Anna said. "Because he did. Told me to look for a Katherine Reed. To search Riven, and, if I found her, to tell him immediately."

I decided to drop the Bryce issue for the moment. I could bring it up with him later. "Did you? Find her?"

"Close," Anna said. "It took a long time. A lot of asking random spirits, following rumors and riddles. Eventually, I found where she lives. Which is how I found out about you."

"What do you mean?"

"She's keeping a diary," Anna said. "Writing down bits and pieces. I think it's so she doesn't lose herself entirely."

I thought about Selena, her talk about falling out of sync with herself. Losing what she was to Riven's unchanging eternity. "Do you have the diary?"

Anna shook her head. "I read it for a while and then ran out of there. The later entries weren't pretty. She's getting angry, Carver, and I didn't want her to find me there."

We'd reached the busted-up building that served as Anna's crossing point. The place looked like it'd been a cheap hotel. Floors full of crumbling identical rooms. A faded sign out front missing half the name, so that the place looked like it was called *The Grand Reg*.

"So you found the diary," I said. "Why didn't you go to Bryce with that?"

"I wanted to find you first," Anna said. She looked away from me. "Because I thought I could use the information. Use you."

"You did," I said. "Congratulations."

"I'm not proud of it, but I'm not sorry either," Anna turned back to me, defiant.

"You can make it up to me," I said. "I'm busy tonight, but tomorrow you'll take me to my mother."

"You sound like you're giving me an order," Anna said. "I don't like it."

"Says the person who just admitted to using me?" I replied.

"We made a fair exchange," Anna replied. "But I'll do it. Have to admit, I'm curious to see where this goes."

"You're not the only one."

Anna crossed over a minute later, leaving me alone again on Riven's streets. The walk back to the clock tower gave me plenty of time to think. My mother, still alive in Riven. As a spirit, anyway. Maybe not yet angry. She could tell me what happened to her.

Tell me who I was and where I came from.

I PRESSED a small switch outside the front door to Bryce's house. A three-story thin building in the middle of a quiet neighborhood on Chicago's north side, Bryce and his family lived in comforts worthy of a guide who'd been patrolling Riven streets for decades.

The switch, when I pulled it, bounced back up. On the inside of the door small light would've come on. I heard the chime as it sounded. The usual way to say hello.

Running thumps came a second later, the patter of small feet and then a click as the center part of the door twisted to reveal a lens; a way for them to see who was on the outside. I waved at it. The children, a boy and a girl, stepped back from the door giving nervous glances at each other. My mask was a little scary, my large black coat didn't help.

The door jerked open and Bryce stood on the other side.

"Carver. A little early for dinner," Bryce said. "Not that we were expecting you?"

"Sorry, but I didn't want to wait," I said.

"What for? What's this about?" Bryce asked, turning back to the kids for a second and waving them away.

"You have somewhere we can talk in private?" I said. As much as I wanted to ask Bryce about the sneaks in front of his family, I figured there was a chance things could get emotional. It wasn't entirely out of the question that anger could come into play when you get to talking about how your mentor, your best friend in the city, decided to have your family investigated without telling you.

"In the back," Bryce said. "Come in."

I stepped in through the door and Bryce shut it behind me. As soon as the door clicked closed, I heard the purifiers kick in. Sucking the haze out and leaving the inside air refreshed. I pulled off the mask and hung up my coat.

The inside of Bryce's house was like the perfect family home. Warm lights glowed along their wall strips while the smell of cooking food, food infinitely better than anything I made in my apartment, floated through the vents. The kids had ran away from the door and were back in the living room, off to my left, fiddling and fighting with the radio. On the walls were paintings and pictures, every professional one matched in size by a drawing from one of Bryce's two kids. Even the earliest ones, the smatterings of paint or sketches with a marker that bore no resemblance to anything.

Seeing all of it told me why Bryce didn't have people to his house. Why I'd never been inside before. This place was a sanctum, a castle apart from the deadly terrors of his daily life.

"This is something else," I said.

Bryce laughed. "It's something you only understand when you have them," he said, nodding towards the kids.

"It looks like a lot of work."

"Think of all the free art?" Bryce said. "And it's refreshing to hear their laughs after a long night in Riven."

Bryce led me back behind the stairs, past the kitchen to a

room that had a series of windows and a booth around a table big enough for eight. I looked for a door to close but there wasn't any. Then Bryce flipped the switch on the wall. All the noise from the kids, from the house, and outside vanished.

"Dampener," I said. "How much did that cost you?"

"It was a gift," Bryce said. "From Piotr. When I had the kids. Did you know that they're twins?"

"Didn't catch that."

"Piotr said I would need a place to get away. He was right," Bryce said. "You wanted to talk? This is where to do it. No one can hear what you say."

"I met a sneak," I said and waited for Bryce's reaction. The guide sat back in the booth, but otherwise didn't let anything flicker across his face. "She told me about my mother. That you were looking for her."

Now Bryce rubbed his chin. "I figured this was going to happen sooner or later. Especially when the sneak disappeared."

"She didn't. She went looking for me instead."

"It was a risk that it would get back to you. One I don't regret taking," Bryce said.

"Going to have to give me more than that," I replied.

"How much did she tell you about your mother?"

I relayed what Anna had mentioned. What I'd found. About her death after giving birth and the evidence that she still lived in Riven. The only time Bryce showed any expression was at the end, when I mentioned the diary.

"She was my mentor. Katherine taught me everything," Bryce said. "Like I taught you. When she died, I didn't understand. It was so sudden and the doctors had no explanation. Then I found her. In Riven. Katherine wouldn't talk about what happened, but she helped me anyway. For years we continued working together over there. She would lead me to breaches, or find angry spirits for me to take care of. Until a few years ago. Until you arrived."

"What do I have anything to do with it?" I said.

"You're asking the wrong person," Bryce said. "At first I thought maybe she'd finally gone over to the Cycle. Guides can resist the call for a long time, like Graham. If they have enough reason they can stay. I thought that reason was you."

"But she left. That doesn't make sense," I said.

Bryce stood up and went behind me to a cabinet in the wall. Opened it and took out a bottle of something dark and spicy. Poured a couple of glasses.

"Katherine did a lot of things without talking to people," Bryce said. "Kept a lot of her own secrets. Still, it wasn't like her to just disappear. At the same time, I had you to train. Chicago to run. A family. I didn't have the time to look."

I took a long sip of the drink. Felt the whiskey light up my tongue and traced its sweet fire down my throat and into my stomach. If my mother was in there, if she had stayed around this long, then there was a chance I could still find her.

"After the tower, after the mission, I'm going to have the sneak take me back to where she found the diary," I said. "You should come with."

Bryce nodded. "Your mother was a wonderful teacher. If she's still there, I would love the chance to see her again."

We spent the rest of the drink talking. Bryce sharing memories of my mother with me. Hunts they went on, and more random details, like what she preferred to drink. Where she liked to eat in Chicago. For the first time my mother began to seem like a real person.

"Why didn't you tell me all this before?" I said as we went back to the front door. Dinner was ready, and I had no right to keep Bryce and his family from their food.

"Because I was ordered not to," Bryce actually seemed

angry. "Piotr himself told me not to bring it up. Not till you were ready, and that he would decide when that was."

"You're breaking the rules?" I said. "Didn't know you had it in you."

"We already talked about it, remember?" Bryce said. "I'm retiring. I don't care about the rules anymore." He glanced at a clock ticking away along the wall. "Better get going. We're meeting Alec in a couple of hours."

My mother. The guide that a trained Bryce. I couldn't, no, I could believe it. But what stuck with me more on the train ride to my apartment was the idea that she might still be there. Waiting for me.

"One more hunt, mother," I muttered. "Then I'm coming for you."

Riven felt different with a group of guides. A trio like ours made the dark shadows tame. Like we could beat anything and anyone. I wanted some angry spirits to come out. Another ghoul maybe. It would be so easy.

Alec led us through the Warrens, towards where Piotr's tower stood. We passed guides on the way, groups out filling their quota. Most greeted us with a wave, or a short conversation, but their faces brought my mood down.

"Things aren't going well are they?" I said to Bryce. "Everyone looks stressed. Tired."

"The war is getting worse. You've been outside of the loop," Bryce said. There was a bit of accusation in that voice. Hinting that perhaps chasing after Graham might not be the best use of my time. "We're closing breaches almost every day now. And we're finding them later because there's too many."

"Is anyone trying to talk to the countries? Tell them the risk?"

"That's why Piotr's here in Chicago. He's spending all day

at the Spire trying to pitch our case. That whatever they're fighting over isn't worth it if Riven falls apart."

"If it does, then their wars won't matter," Alec chimed in. "We'll all be dead anyway."

Bryce did not look amused.

Beyond the Warrens, the large apartments dwindled into smaller bits of buildings. Stores, warehouses, and broad tracts of land covered in containers. Train tracks went through and off to anywhere, nowhere. After thirty more minutes of marching we could see Riven's wall in the distance and, rising above it, the tower.

At first I thought it was just another apartment building, a lonely one rising up from a bunch of single-story homes. As we got closer, though, I realized the tower wasn't like the rest of Riven. Not an ancient construction of unknown origin. This thing had been built by our hands. Or by spirits.

From the outside, the tower looked like a hodgepodge of materials. Stone stacked on top of stone, but in different shades. With different design. The tower was a product of stolen stuff. A collage of crap pilfered from other buildings and shoved together.

"If that isn't the ugliest building in Riven," I started.

"It is," Alec said. "My question is why? Who would build something like this and for what purpose?"

"I think that's what Piotr wants us to find out," Bryce said.

At its base, the tower was as wide as a block. Massive. The top was easily a dozen stories high. Thankfully, the door was easy to find. A hole in the mashed up stone. Like the rest of the tower, the door had been made with crude nails and boards stripped from other homes.

"Who wants the honors?" I asked.

"I don't suppose we should knock?" Alec said.

"Piotr said guides were dying here," Bryce said. "We don't need to let them know we're coming."

Bryce went by me to the door and, voulge drawn in his right hand, pulled it open. The door wasn't locked, and the hinges didn't make any noise. The inside, unlike the gray of Riven, was lit with soft yellow fire.

We walked into the first room. The fire came from a series of small torches that lined the pool in the middle. A pool filled with more of Riven's strange water. Behind it, climbing up the wall, was a stair. Along the sides of the room were more doors leading to who knows where.

"I'm going to admit it. This is not what I expected," I said.

"Stay quiet," Bryce said. "Keep your eyes open."

"Welcome, welcome, welcome," a hearty voice exclaimed. Coming down the stairs was an enormous spirit, fat and wearing what looked like a robe made of bedsheets. "I'm so happy you came. The master has been waiting for more friends."

I glanced at Bryce, Alec did the same. Our leader stared at the fat spirit, his mouth slightly open.

"Who is your master?" Bryce said, recovering.

"Oh, you'll meet him," the spirit said. "Of course, we must be polite. The master so doesn't like the ash in the air. I'm afraid it's all over your clothes."

The spirit gestured at us. He wasn't wrong. Any long walk in Riven was going to leave you coated in ashy stuff.

"If you'll kindly step into this pool and wash yourselves, then we can begin," the spirit said.

"Wash ourselves?" I said. "Does your master know where we are? Cleanliness isn't exactly a thing here."

"Carver," Bryce said.

"It's quite all right," the spirit interjected. "Remember, it is you who chose to come in to my master's tower. Therefore, it is you who should abide by his wishes."

"Where is your master?" Alec said. "Can we talk to him?"

The spirit pointed to the pool. I looked at the water. The

clear liquid reflected the flames from the torches, creating blurry shades of yellow and orange along the walls of the room. Guides occasionally drank the non-water and it didn't seem to have any effect. But I'd just had the salt of it the other night and it had chilled me to the core.

"I don't like this," I said.

"Agreed," Bryce said. He turned to the spirit. "We'd like to see your master. We're not going to wash ourselves in the pool."

The spirit's bright smile shifted to a deep frown and he shook his head. "I'm sorry, there really is no other way."

"I bet we can climb up the outside," Alec said.

Bryce nodded and the three of us turned back towards the exit. Only to see, standing in front of it, three other spirits. Also dressed in robes. Armed. Not with the usual rocks and sticks that spirits might find, but with swords. Long knives in their off hands. Guide weapons.

Around us the doors on the floor opened and more spirits came out. All of them had guide weapons - spears, axes, and more exotic ones. At least a dozen, maybe more.

"So many," Bryce said. "So many guides here."

"The master has many friends," the large spirit said. "He always wants more. Please, wash yourselves."

We were outnumbered and the spirits looked like they knew how to use those weapons. There was a chance we could fight our way out of here, but the odds didn't look good.

"The pool," I said. "That's my vote."

"You see this?" Alec said. "These weapons, they came from the guides that died here. We either fight our way out, or we share their fate."

"We don't have a choice," Bryce said. "We'd be slaughtered. We take the chance on the pool."

"If we die in there," Alec said. "I'm going to find both of your spirits and beat them to death again."

The three of us went into the pool. I felt the water seeping along my boots, up my legs and up to my waist. It was cold, so cold. In seconds I lost all feeling in the lower half of my body.

"Please wash off your arms and head," the spirit said. "Then we'll be ready to go see the master."

I glanced at Bryce and Alec, who shrugged. I reached my hands in the water, felt my fingers go numb as I cupped some of the stuff. Lifted it up to my head and poured it on.

4 2

"IT'S TRULY fascinating how we can go back and forth. About how you have to be conscious, and yet unconscious. We put ourselves in two places at once. We are not truly alive here in Riven, but dying here, we die there."

I opened my eyes and saw the gray Riven sky above me. Only, there was glass. A skylight. An actual skylight in Riven. I'd never heard of someone being able to make that here, not even Nicholas.

I realized my hands were tied. My legs corded onto a board. I could turn my head; saw Bryce to my right and Alec to my left.

"Only the truly fascinating part happens when you kill a man while he's crossed into Riven. Then you have a true marvel. For he's not a spirit, no, not quite. But no longer a living thing," I couldn't see the speaker, but could tell he was in front of me. I tried to sit up, but could only lift my head forward, and not far enough.

"At first it seems like this purgatory would be worse than actually dying. You want to go to the Cycle. Then you find that perhaps all is not as bad as it seems. You find purpose, even in this place."

"Bryce?" I called. "Alec?"

"I'm awake," Bryce said. "Who are you?"

"Who am I?" the speaker said. "That doesn't really matter anymore does it? My spirits call me master. Before? I had a name then, when names mattered."

"Who is this guy?" I said. "I think he's lost it."

"Oh I have," the speaker said. "There's no denying it. Which is why I'm trying to get it back. Trying to find my way out."

"Graham?" I didn't think that's who it was, but I couldn't help but try.

"Don't talk of him," the speaker's voice burned. "That man has no idea what he's doing. He's reckless, arrogant. I prefer a more methodical approach."

"Barth?" Bryce said. "Is that you?"

"Barth?" the speaker said. "I suppose that may have been, once. I suppose that it may be again. No, no, will be again. That's right. Concentrate."

"I thought you died years ago," Bryce said. Our heads were still strapped down, I watched Bryce stare at the ceiling and talk to the man. The speaker scurried into view. A hunched-over lanky figure wearing the same robes as the spirits. Pale and ghostly. He leaned over Bryce.

"Time is measured in moments here," Barth said. "Death is not the release some prefer to believe. For some it is a trap. A trap that they have to find their own way out of."

"What are you talking about?" Bryce said. "Let us go."

"Oh I will," Barth said, running a finger along Bryce's chest. "The way out is just a matter of finding one. Just one is all you need."

Barth scuttled out of sight, back to the other side of the room. I heard him messing around with various objects, clattering things against the ground. Bryce continued to ask for release, but Barth didn't bother to answer.

"Now here they are. I can't choose, you see. Too hard to know who should go. These can help," Barth said.

A moment later I heard a trio of knocks, small objects bouncing off the floor. When the noise stopped, Barth giggled.

"Why look at that. It's number two. What an excellent choice," Barth said. I felt my board lurch, slide along some lever until I was upright, my feet a foot above the floor. Beneath me, looking up at my face with a broken grin, was Barth.

On the ground I saw what had made the choice. What had made the noise. A trio of skulls. Two of them resting with their eyes looking up at me, the third on its side.

"You see? Your friends? They chose you," Barth said.

43

WHEN YOU'RE TIED DOWN, you feel like all you want to do is escape. I wanted to break my arms and legs free and run. Having a trio of skulls at my feet didn't exactly calm me down. Neither did the crazed glint in Barth's eyes.

"Bryce, I think I might be in trouble here," I said.

"Stay calm," Bryce said. "Look for a way out."

A way out. With my arms and legs tied? There wasn't an easy option. In front of me Barth returned to his desk and dug through a pile of random tools. Some knives, a hammer, and a couple of saws among other, smaller, knickknacks. I got the distinct feeling that any and perhaps all of them would be used on me.

I touched my fingers to the board. Wood, but frail. Thin. If I pressed against it, maybe I'd have a chance. I tried to clench my fists and hit them against the board. They bounced off. I couldn't get enough force. Barth, meanwhile, hummed a tune. One I recognized. A song from twenty years ago but that still played on radios today. Barth hummed the simple jingle while he straightened his murderous tools.

"Lean forward," Alec said from my right. "I can see the lever holding you. It's not very strong. You can throw it off."

Okay. Another thing to try. I lunged my head forward, tried to pull my body with it. The board groaned but didn't shift.

"Again," Alec said.

Barth seemed oblivious. Laying out the tools to the side. So far, two knives and that little hammer. Was not looking forward to whatever he was going to do with those. I went forward again. This time I heard a crack, the board starting to give way at the back.

Barth heard it to.

The strange man turned to me, his eyes blazing. "So you like to play with things that are not yours. Break my toys. That is not very nice. New friends should be respectful."

"I'm definitely not your friend," I said.

"Not yet, maybe," Barth said, grabbing a long thin knife and coming towards me. "Soon you will be."

As Barth reached towards me with the knife I went forward again. This time the board snapped free and I fell ahead. Smashed myself into Barth as he came close and knocked us both to the ground. My forehead hit his, and the world jerked for a moment. The ropes holding my arms and legs kept me from catching myself, so as a I rolled off Barth, my face smashed into the floor. Not my best move, but at least I was free from the lever.

Barth was muttering some incomprehensible nonsense as he pushed himself away from me. I reached for the knife, my hands still tied but, without the lever holding me in place, I was able to slither myself across the floor. Shove with my toes and my hands towards the blade that Barth dropped. The madman seemed too distracted to notice.

My left hand closed around the hilt of the blade when I heard a scraping noise. I couldn't look up, couldn't see what

Barth was doing, but that sound probably meant pain was fast approaching. With my left hand, I spun the blade around, twisting the hilt through my fingers to bring the edge to rest against the cords. Now it was a matter of getting a strong enough grip to actually cut them.

"Carver, roll right!" Bryce said. I didn't think; kicked off the floor with my toes and tried to shift the board. I felt the wood hit something soft, and Barth squealed in pain. I heard him fall to the ground, another clatter as he dropped whatever tool he'd picked up from the table.

I adjusted my left hand again, trying to get a solid grip. I finally had it between two pairs of fingers, and worked the knife up and down. The cords were thick and I didn't have much pressure. Or time.

"Help me out," I said. "What's he doing?"

"Friends shouldn't talk out of turn," Barth replied. Not who I was hoping to hear from.

"I can't see enough," Bryce said.

"He's got the hammer," Alec called. Then I felt the impact. Barth had jumped on my back. On the board. Pressed me into the ground. He hit the board behind my head with a hammer, pressing my face into the stone. Grinding my jaw into the rock.

The weight also pressed down on the blade in my hand. Pushed it against the cords and let it cut faster. A couple of seconds later and I felt the sting as the knife cut through the cords and into my own wrist. I focused, leaned hard on my right side as Barth continued to pound with the hammer. The lean gave my freed left hand just enough space to plant my palm against the ground. I pushed.

Barth was a small man and when I shoved the board over he flew off and rolled across the ground. I grabbed the blade again and, with my free wrist, cut my legs and right hand loose. Stood up from the board in time to see Barth swinging the hammer at my face. I got my right hand up, caught Barth's wrist before he could bring the hammer down, and then ripped the hammer away from him.

"Didn't your mother ever teach you to play nice?" I said, brandishing both weapons.

Barth shrank away, dancing back behind his desk. "New friends are nasty. Not very nice at all. If they don't want to see the way out, then they will stay here, in the dark."

The man give a bloodcurdling shriek, and I heard pounding on the stairs. The tower shook as Barth's spirits responded to their master's call. This place was about to get really, really crowded.

44

I THREW the hammer into Barth's face, smashing his nose and knocking out his scream. He collapsed behind the desk. I went to Alec, who was a few steps closer than Bryce. Slashed his left hand free.

"Behind you," Bryce called. I let go of the knife and spun around. The fat spirit that had greeted us stood at the top of the stairs wielding a familiar lash. The friendly face he'd worn was gone, replaced by malevolent insanity. With his eyes wide and mouth gibbering nonsense, the spirit attacked. Snapped the lash at my face.

If there was one thing I knew, it was how to get around my own weapon. I dove beneath the crack as the spirit attacked. Tucked into a role and somersaulted into the spirit's ankles. Like knocking down a building. The spirit tumbled back and fell at the head of the stairs. I heard outraged cries as other spirits tried to shove past the new blockade.

I saw Alec, having freed himself, stand over Bryce and cut him loose. I grabbed the arm holding my lash, tried to tear it free. But the spirit was strong, shoved me away and stood up as we wrestled. Used his bulk to push me into the desk. The stone edge pressed into my back as the spirit bent me over.

"A little help here?" I called.

"There are too many," I heard Bryce's voice, strained. Spirits were running up into the room now. In a moment we would face the same overwhelming odds as the bottom of the tower, be killed in the same fashion as we would have then.

With my left hand grappling for the lash, my eyes staring into the blue-black void of the spirit's pupils, I scrabbled around the desk with my right. As my back exploded with pain, my spine rubbing into the stone, my right hand landed on something it could grab. I shoved it into the spirit's face.

A saw blade is quite a bit less effective when used as knife, but even glancing off the spirit's mouth, the attack bought me some surprise. The spirit leaned back slightly, gave me just enough room to slip out from under him. I wanted space. A chance to figure out some plan of attack.

Bad idea.

The spirit snapped my lash again and this time I couldn't move fast enough. The lash wrapped around my legs and threw me to the floor. I felt the point scrape around my knee but ignored it. Had to ignore it. The spirit was coming right at me with his left fist raised, which would hurt a lot more than the lash. As I raised my right hand in a pathetic defense, I noticed something.

I still held the saw.

The spirit punch down towards me and I twisted the saw blade up to meet his fist. The spirit punched into the tines and howled. Jerked his hand back and took the saw with it. With my left hand, I grabbed the lash's cord, still wrapped around my leg, and pulled it free. The spirit didn't notice, was more focused on the saw sticking out of its hand. Understandably.

I stood up as the spirit yanked the saw free. As he looked

towards me, I struck out with the lash and took him down. Wrapped my weapon around his neck and purified him with wrangling fire. The spirit collapsed and I took a breath.

On the right, Bryce and Alec were faring better. They'd managed to trap most of the spirits on the stairs. Kept the fighting to where the two of them, armed with the knife I'd handed Alec and a strange curving sword that Bryce must've picked up from another spirit, could limit the number of enemies at once.

"Get to Barth," Bryce yelled. "We can't hold them forever."

I nodded out of reflex; Bryce definitely wasn't watching me. Turned behind the desk to see where Barth had fallen. Only to find he wasn't there. A new door, however, was. A section of the wall behind the desk was open, a dark path that required crouching to get through. There were no torches along the walls, no light whatsoever except, in the distance, a gray glow. Coming from that glow was Barth's babbling voice.

I stepped along the tunnel, moving slow in case of any sort of strange trap or ambush. Normally in Riven I wouldn't have suspected anything. Spirits weren't the type to lie in wait. Only this one, Barth, seemed to play those kinds of games. At the end of the hall I stood up into what looked like a bedroom. A flat mattress on a stone floor. Scattered papers, some bound together. Ashy wood sticks piled in an urn. Going by what I could see on the paper, Barth was using the ash to write with.

"I am so close. So close to finding the way. You cannot abandon me now. I need more chances," Barth was pleading out loud to the air. But to what? To who? I stayed still as Barth shook his head, as though receiving some sort of an answer.

"I know you said this was the last group. But there are always more. I'm so close," Barth continued to whine.

"Graham is a monster. He will turn on you. Not I, your loyal friend."

"Who are you talking to?" I said. Bryce and Alec were fighting for their lives out there. I couldn't sit here listening to Barth babble to nobody.

Barth turned slowly, like a person waking from a long nap. Glared at me. "You were supposed to be my key. Now I have nothing. He has abandoned me."

"Good for him," I said. "Call the spirits off or I end you. Now."

I held out my lash, making it very clear exactly what would happen if Barth didn't follow my instructions.

To my surprise, Barth opened his mouth and spoke in that frequency only spirits could hear. A moment later, the man gave me a sideways nod. "What you want, it is done. My friends have retired back to their quarters."

"Speaking of friends," I said. "Let's go back. You're going to tell us everything."

45

BACK IN BARTH'S experimental chamber I found Bryce and Alec leaning against the desk. Both had nasty gashes, cuts, and bruises from fighting with the spirits, but at least those enemies had disappeared. The spirit I'd wrangled had already walked off on his journey to the Cycle.

"That was your doing, yes?" Alec said, looking at me. "How did you make them go away?"

"I made Barth a compelling offer; your lives for his," I said.

"Barth," Bryce said, turning to look at the man. "What happened to you? I heard you were killed. Years ago."

Barth shifted his eyes between us, giggling to himself. He wrung his hands.

"Can he still talk, or has he lost all of himself?" Alec said.

"I didn't touch him," I said. "He can talk."

"I've been here for so long," Barth blurted. "Yet no one knows how to tell the time. So long and always working. Always trying."

"What were you trying to do?" Bryce said.

"He told me to find a way back. That we would need one.

That he would need one. So I searched. Searched for so long," Barth continued. "This place? There are doors that can be opened. Can be walked through if you know where they are."

"He's not talking about the tower, is he?" Alec said.

"Sounds like Graham," I said. "Talking about getting out of Riven."

Barth's eyes lit up at the word. He became even more excite, swaying now as he spoke. "Yes, Riven. That's where we are. That's where we don't belong. I was trying to find a way to open the door."

"And the spirits?" Bryce asked.

"Guides," Barth replied. "One of them might be the key. Open the passage back. You sleep and you come over here, you are a door. I was trying to open it."

"How many guides did you kill?" Bryce said, his voice changing to a darker mood.

"So many. So many over the years that cannot be counted," Barth said, and then his face dropped. He stared at the ground. "Now it is over. He is letting me go."

"Who is letting you go?" I said. "Is that who you were talking to, back there?"

Barth shook his head. "My master does not let me see his face. Or know his name. I must do as he commands, until he releases me from his service."

"It sounds like he's released you already?" Alec said.

Barth cackled. We shrank away from the man. There were something crazy going in his eyes. "Released. Yes. After one more task."

The tower started to shake. A growing boom echoed up from below. I grabbed onto the dust to study myself while Alec and Bryce leaned against the wall. Chunks of stone fell from the ceiling, shaken loose. Cracks appeared in the skylight.

"I have failed, my master said. Failures must be buried with their friends," Barth said.

"I say we leave," I said.

"Seconded," Alec said. The three of us made quick steps to the stairs. Bryce and Alec started down and I took one look back at Barth, waving for him to come with, but he ignored us. Simply stared up at the skylight as it shattered, tears running down his grinning face.

I flew down the stairs after Bryce and Alec. My feet barely touch the steps as they swayed back and forth with the tower. There didn't seem to be other floors, just a long spiral down to where we saw the glowing pool and the torches. Falling rock splashed by as we tried to make our way along the sides. When we passed by a stone-carved window I looked out, glanced down to try and see what was happening.

Wrapped around the base of the tower were the spirits, hacking and bashing and tearing apart the base. Using guide weapons to shatter stone and destroy the foundation. A normal person, with normal energy, might have found the process impossible. But the tower was rickety from the start, and the spirits were tireless. They swung with every ounce of might they had every single time.

The tower began its final collapse. I felt it from the window, the walls weaving in and the steps starting to pull away. I grabbed the outside, reached to the window frame and pulled myself through. Pressed my legs on the frame of the falling rock as stone and glass shredded my back. Jumped into the gray haze.

I DIDN'T SEE the roof that I landed on, but I felt it. My shoulder slammed into the hard stone and I felt a pop, but aside from that searing pain, I rolled to a stop alive. Used my right hand, the shoulder that still worked, to push myself upright. I was on a small house with a pointed roof. The slant probably saved my life. I looked at the tower, or where it had been, and figured I'd fallen ten to twenty feet.

Now the tower was a pile of rubble and broken boards. Around it stood the circle of spirits, at least fifteen. The destroyers of their own home. They stared around, lost with their former master buried in that pile. Somewhere in there, too, were Alec and Bryce.

I crawled to the edge of the roof, hung down and dropped the remaining eight feet. Managed to keep my balance and made it to the ground. I went over to the rubble and looked at it. Tons of rock and broken wood. Twisted beams and crumbled mortar. No way I was going to clear it all by myself.

There was another option, if I could pull together the energy.

The spirits all around the tower were familiar. They wore guide coats and clothes, and most still held weapons made for guides, ones that could, with a twist or a tap, produce that pale blue fire. From what Barth had said, it wasn't hard to make the connection. All of these spirits that he'd bound, every last one of them, had been an experiment gone wrong. An attempt to find the door back to the real world. Every time it failed, Barth bound the guide into service.

The one closest to me was an older woman, bearing a pair of lethal-looking pick-axes. At least I assumed that's what they were, short handles with pointed heads on them. She stared at me as I walked up.

"You were a guide once," I said, making things up as I went along. "Now I'm giving you a chance to help your friends. To do one last thing for who you were."

The woman tilted her head, stared at me, her eyes blank. I'd never tried to bind a spirit that had already been bound, but nobody had told me couldn't be done. I reached out with my right hand and grabbed hers, which still held the pick.

"Help us save them," I said. I focused on the touch. The feel of the woman's hand on mine. The spirit's skin was cool, but I fought past that. It was like tracing a point of pain, a pinprick or a bug bite somewhere on your body. Only here I was looking for a way into hers. A spot where my life could bleed into the shadow of her own.

When I found it, I took a breath and gripped her hand tight. It felt like a rush of blood to my face. Who and what I was, a living person crossed into Riven, flowed through that pinpoint into the spirit and tied her to me. A moment later her eyes lost their blank look and her face fell into a smile.

"My name is Teresa," the spirit said. "I was a guide once."

"I know, and now I need you to save two more," I said. Pointed to the rubble. "I need you to dig them out. Find Bryce and Alec under there."

Teresa nodded, let go of my hand and started to dig. Hauled one block after the next off of the pile. I went to the next spirit, and the next and the next. Bound them one after another. Each one took a bit of myself with it and by the tenth spirit I was struggling to the next one. Limping and pale. Gulping Riven's non-air with heavy breaths.

The rubble was clearing. The spirits were tireless, shifting off the tower and it's garbage. Diving underneath and hunting for any sign of Bryce or Alec. After I bound the eleventh, I collapsed onto the ground and watched. My left shoulder ached, and the rest of my body didn't want to move. It wasn't tired so much as dead. There simply wasn't enough of me to do anything other than keep me awake.

Barth must've been a incredible at this, to bind so many spirits. Years of practice. Or maybe the cost of keeping a spirit went down over time. Or maybe that's what drove him insane. Losing so much of himself for so long.

One of the spirits give a shout, and then, with another's help, pulled Alec's body from the rubble. He was wet. Soaking. He must've dove into the pool as a way to save himself.

"Alec," I said as the spirits carried the guide over to me. He didn't respond. I didn't really expect him to. "Lay him down. Press the water from his lungs."

The two spirits did as I asked and began compressing his chest. There was a chance that his bones were broken, but I didn't think that would matter if the man was already drowning. Two presses in and Alec started to cough. Spat up water everywhere, but he was alive.

Another shout came up and soon Bryce was lying next to Alec, his body more battered, also soaked from the pool. The water that had captured us at the start, had served to save our lives. Both of the guides were broken, lying there unconscious but alive. I had to get them back. Had to get me back.

Thankfully, I had plenty of help.

47

I BRACED MYSELF, but it didn't matter. I still let out a yelp when Bryce shoved my left shoulder back into its socket. We stood beneath the clock tower, surrounded by the spirits I'd bound. They all had the glazed look of the lost in their eyes. I'd released them, one by one when I took hold of their hands and, like soaking up the warmth from a fire, drew my own life back.

"After all the hits you have taken," Alec said, leaning against the wall next to the door inside. "This isn't too bad, no?"

"Pain is pain," I said. "It hurts."

"I don't like your decision," Bryce said to me. "You should be crossing, with us. Recover and then come back tomorrow night."

I shook my head. "I have to go. I don't know whether it will last until tomorrow."

I knew what I said sounded dumb, and Bryce's arched eyebrow didn't do anything to calm that feeling. Except, I couldn't tell him about Selena. Couldn't say that I needed to go after her, find her, and either bring her back or protect her from the dark spirit I'd seen in the vision. Retiring or no, I didn't think Bryce would be a big fan of our guide-spirit romance.

"Let him go," Alec said. "Sometimes a man must be by himself. Find his own way."

"Trust me, self-discovery has nothing to do with it," I replied.

"Then be careful. You have your sparker?" Bryce asked.

I nodded. Somewhat incredibly, the spirits had been armed with our weapons. Had worn our guide belts. I'd only noticed when we got back to the clock tower, but it made sense. Might as well arm your spirits with the best weapons available. Having bound them, they didn't reject my request to return our stuff.

"I'm going to find Piotr and tell him about what we saw," Bryce said. "Tell him about Barth. He might have an idea of who Barth was talking to."

"I'll meet you at Ezra's when I'm done here," I said.

"Don't go getting yourself into much trouble," Alec said. "We won't be running around to save you."

"Stay away from Graham," Bryce said. "When we're ready, we'll take him together."

The two guides went back to clock tower and crossed over. I started the long walk south. I tried to remember from my vision where Selena had been going, and I thought I recognized the park. On the far edge of the Warrens, back towards Barth's tower but then curling further south than west.

I was tired. Despite Bryce's first aid efforts, pain poured in from everywhere. By this point, though, that was starting to be the usual state of affairs. Every step, every twitch another opportunity for my body to remind me that it was not happy.

The walk gave me a bit of time to reflect. Barth and

Graham both seemed to have the same master. Someone that had power over them. Either through binding or other leverage. The way Barth had been talking, it seemed like this had been going on for a long time. Years.

They all wanted a way out of Riven. Which meant that this master, whomever he was, was probably already here. The only other option, the only people that could bind spirits to their control, were guides. To bind a spirit for years and exert that level of control? To command Barth to trap and murder his friends? To force Graham, that deadly force, to do his bidding? Whomever this master was, I wasn't looking forward to meeting him. If I lived long enough to do it.

After an hour I reached the park. At the very edge of the Warrens. On the south side, the big apartment buildings disappeared into the parks which bled into what we called the Shambles. By far the worst part of the city, at least in terms of what was left. Crumbling half built homes, buildings collapsed against each other, streets that weren't paved but were only chunks of rock that wound around remnants. If there was a war zone in Riven, this place was it.

It was also the fastest way to the wall. Once you got the wall, you could leave. Once you made it outside, though I'd never been, it was supposed to be a straight shot to the Cycle. So as I walked into the Shambles I saw plenty of spirits, some bearing the blank-eyed look of lost ones heading to the Cycle on their own. Others the mute march of a wrangled soul. Ones that had met the wrong end of a guide's weapon and were now on a straight path to destiny.

Here, though was the end of my clues. Behind me stood the tree that I'd seen when I was half dead. Where I stood now, smashing down some white threads of grass, was where Selena had walked. Where the dark thing following her had passed.

48

FOR THE FIRST time I wished I had a sneak with me. If Anna had been there, I'm sure she would've had some idea for how to find Selena. Part of me wanted to turn back right then. Cross over, give tonight up as a first attempt and then come back later with Anna. But the bigger part of me realized that Riven was getting worse. If someone like Barth was out here hunting and killing guides, and Graham was doing the same, how much time did I really have before one of them caught up with me?

So instead I tried something new.

The first street that I walked down was crowded. Plenty of spirits bustling out of the city, but a few stood around watching the procession. Those were the ones I was looking for, the ones with a little bit of themselves left. The ones that could hold a conversation.

I went up to a woman who, sitting on a listing bench, looked like she was counting the spirits walking by. Her mouth moved silently as her eyes tracked each and every one.

"You still here?" I asked, coming up beside her.

"Depends on what you mean by here," the woman said, turning to look at me. "I'm not so sure where here is."

"You ever hear of Riven?" I said. Because spirits came from people dying anywhere, there was no guarantee that they knew that Riven existed. Many had no idea what had happened, only that they were somewhere else and didn't feel normal. I'd found the spirits who understood were easier to deal with. Less prone to panic.

"I have no idea what that is," the woman said. "If you're asking if I know that I'm no longer alive? I think that's rather obvious."

"That's something, anyway," I said. "Can I ask you a question?"

I tried to be polite with spirits. Especially when I'm just getting started. It's hard to know what could trip a spirit off, send them into a rage. With the streets crowded, the last thing I wanted was a fight that would attract attention, or even bring other spirits to the brink of anger.

"You've already made me lose count. Well over nine thousand in the last four days," the woman said. "So I suppose you can ask, yes."

I didn't flinch at the number. Who knew how many people all across the world went through Riven? How many were sent on by guides, how many more naturally went to the Cycle. Nine thousand just on this street? Who knew if that was a lot, or a little?

"Have you seen a woman with a moonlight dress? Her hair is auburn, down below her shoulders. She has a scar on her face," I said.

The woman shook her head. "I'm only counting. I don't recall anyone like that."

Before I could say anything else she turned back to the

street and started again. At one. She'd probably continue like that, counting onward and upward until the Cycle finally took hold of her. Still, as Riven existence went, that was one of the better spirits I'd seen.

The next one was a young man in soldier's fatigues. Surprising that he looked so normal. Standing there in the middle of the street playing games with the spirits as they walked by. On one he pulled down a pair of trousers. On another, he tussled their hair. None of the spirits cared. They moved on without reaction.

"Having fun?" I said to him.

"Fun?" the man said. "There's nothing else to do. I'm waiting for something to happen. Waiting for one of them to have a reaction, to come at me. Anything to feel even a little bit alive."

"They tend to respond to aggression," I said. "But you can't really hurt each other. You'll just wind up losing what's left of your mind."

"The thing is," the man said. "I thought I lost it when the artillery fired. Then I woke up here and all my mates were gone. Wandered around this place for three days and then found this line of people. Figure I'll just keep going with them, but it gets boring walking all the time, you know?"

"Have you seen one?" I said, giving a description of Selena. The man shook his head.

"Only got here a few hours ago," the spirit said. "Can't help you there."

"I've seen her," came a crusty voice from behind us. A head poking out of a window on a building that looked like it at once held a store but was now a crumbling pile broken boards and brick. "She passed here yesterday. Looked awful scared for a spirit."

"Do you know where she went?" I asked. I would have felt

better if the spirit came out of the building, rather than hiding behind a window, but I wasn't in a position to choose.

"I followed her," the voice said. "I know where she went. I can show you if you give me that knife of yours."

Striking deals with spirits. Another one of those things guides weren't supposed to do. Except there's one thing the spirit didn't know, and that's the fact that I could end it at any point. Wrangle and clean up what remained of his sanity and send him on a quick trip to the Cycle.

"I'll give you the knife if you take me to her," I replied.

The crusty voice made its way out of the building. I did a double take. The spirit wasn't an elder, but a gentleman in his thirties. Maybe even younger. Only he leaned over and walked with a broken bit of board that served as a cane. I would've said it didn't make any sense except spirits came to Riven in their own best image. Came with what was left of their minds and what they happened to recall. If the spirit was so used to hunching over, so used to having a cane and talking with a voice ground to gravel by age, then that was what he became.

We left the pranking young man behind and the spirit with the cane led me deeper into the Shambles. Off of the main path and through winding alleys bordered by buildings in various states of collapse.

"You're a guide aren't you?" the spirit said.

"Good guess," I replied.

"Wasn't a guess," the spirit said. "The only ones who come after spirits in Riven are you guides."

I felt something at the end of that sentence. Like a lingering question, a phrase left hanging in the air as though the spirit wanted me to ask for more. So I did.

"Why do you say that?"

"Because I don't think you're after the spirit. I think you're after the guide following her," the man said.

"The guide following her?"

"A real nasty piece of work," the spirit said. "Not one that I'd like to meet when I go to the other side."

The other side. Not many people called it that. Guides didn't have the patience for it. If you're angry, you're angry. There weren't sides to cross. There weren't emotions and feelings to protect. In Riven, it happened to every spirit at some point and that's all there was to it.

We came to a split in the alley, three branches heading off in different directions. In front of us was a larger home, two stories and still mostly put together. In fact, as I looked at it more closely, the building looked clean. Maintained and repaired.

"The spirit you want is in there," the man said. "Now about our deal. The knife."

"Why?" I asked. "What do you want with it?"

The man shook a little. Closed his eyes for a moment. "Some days are better than others, but I feel it coming on. The call is growing. When I lose it, when I lose who I am, I want to be able to end it."

"You won't be able to," I said. I'd heard that before too. Spirits that knew where they were, knew what was coming. Wanted a way to wrangle themselves, erase who they were as they fell into an angry mess. "You've got two choices. Give in and go to the Cycle now, or hold out, lose yourself, and then a guide will find you and set you on your way."

"I said give me the knife," the spirit argued. "That was our deal."

I reached under my belt and grabbed a knife with my left hand. Held it in front of me. The spirit turned and reached for it, his eyes bright. I twisted the hilt, sent the blue fire down the blade, and stabbed it into the man before he could react. I could see his eyes go wide as the fire rushed up and down his body.

"You wanted to be free," I said. "Now you are."

I sheathed the knife as the spirit, walking straight and leaving the cane on the ground, started his journey to the Cycle. I started mine into the house.

49

For the first time in Riven, I encountered a locked door. When I twisted the handle and tried to pull the door open at the back of the house in the Shambles, it didn't move. Beneath the handle was a keyhole. It was new, shiny, and unlike anything else that I'd seen in Riven. At least anything outside of a guide base. Whomever lived here had resources, knowledge, and, perhaps most importantly, the will to make a home in this world.

So I set out to destroy it.

First I tested the door by force, pushing against it and getting nowhere. I didn't want to do a shoulder charge given the sorry shape of my left arm, still aching from my jump out of Barth's tower. I could lead with my right, but if I hurt that arm, I'd be useless.

I gave the door a kick and got nowhere. Except, I heard a noise coming from inside the house. Muffled. I leaned close to the door, stuck my ear against the wood and listened.

"Is there someone out there?" the voice barely came through, like a blunted whisper. I recognized the pitch. Selena.

I took a look around. The alleys dividing the house from the other buildings were wide enough to make scaling up a different structure and jumping onto the house a risky move. I went around to the front and found what had been a second door but it had been bricked over.

There were three windows, all on the second story. Others on the first floor were sealed in like the front door. Whomever lived here wanted this place as a fortress, not a home.

I took out my lash and tied the end of it around the back door's handle. Walked back as far as I could, until the lash was tight. I pulled it across my chest, gripped the lash hilt with both hands and tugged. I couldn't keep my grasp. I felt the door start to give, but as it moved the lash slipped out of my burning hands.

I needed a better grip.

The answer was right in front of me. In the street. The cane left by the other spirit. A lever I could use to increase the pressure. I took my lash handle and some of the slack in the line and tied the end of the lash around the cane. Then, holding the cane in my hands, I pushed. Put all my weight into it. Behind me the door groaned and I heard the crackle of wood giving way, splintering under more pressure than it could handle. With a crackling roar, the door fell free to the ground.

I ate a mouthful of dirt as the sudden loss of resistance shot me into the alley and sprawled me along the stones. But what were a few more scratches at this point?

"Selena?" I called as I went in the house. "Are you up there?"

The inside or at least the part where I entered, was immaculate. The walls, while still bare stone, were clean. Any cracks had been patched over, broken blocks replaced. The floor was smooth stone. Like a modern house back in

Chicago before any wood was laid down. Ahead of me, on the ground floor, was a dark room. Without any windows the only light that came in was from the door that I'd just torn open. The room looked empty.

"Carver?" Selena replied. "I'm up here."

To my left was a set of stairs leading up. Stone steps with boards placed over the top to make for easier footfalls. Also, I noticed when I stepped on the first one and it creaked, a good way to detect an intruder. I made my way up and walked into the strangest room I had ever seen.

The entire second story was a single large chamber. It may not have always been so, but now the whole place was patterned over with boards along the ground. Windows let in gray light, illuminating a series of rudimentary wooden. Tables covered with tools, weapons, and books. And, tied to one of them, Selena. In the same dress she'd worn in my vision. Only instead of one scar on her face, Selena looked like she'd taken the brunt of a hundred blows.

"What happened?" I said coming over and cutting her free. "Who's doing this to you?"

"Carver," Selena hugged herself and glanced around. "Carver, it's your mother."

5 0

I SHOULD HAVE BEEN MORE surprised. My mother? The dark spirit following Selena? The comment sank in and washed off me. Perhaps I'd seen something of myself in the spirit's eyes when she had turned back, hazy and distant in my half-dead vision.

"Where is she?" I asked.

"She comes and goes," Selena replied. "I don't know where she is now. All she talks about is Graham, and you."

"Me?"

"That's why she took me," Selena said, glancing down. "She wanted to know everything about you. What you're like. Your hobbies. All of it."

"She beat you up for that?"

"No. She hurt me because Graham told her to," Selena went over to one of the tables covered in books. "I think he has some power over her. Controls her like the other spirits, except not everything. Sometimes, she even says she's sorry."

I followed her, looked down at the books. They weren't the kinds that I saw back in Chicago. More like binders with papers shoved between the covers. Cheap organization.

Selena opened one and we looked at the first page. Unlike Barth, my mother had access to pencils. Actual writing tools. Stolen from a guide base, most likely.

"I see her writing in these all the time," Selena said. "I think it's her diary. I hear her repeat things to herself, like she's trying to remember."

"Don't you want to leave?" I said. "Get away?"

"Remember when we talked about family? When I told you about mine? This is your chance to find yours."

Selena pointed to the first sheet of paper, the first entry. Dated just a few days after I was born.

June 21st, 1890

At least, that is what I think the day is. Hard to tell in Riven. If that is correct, then I was murdered three days ago. Killed because I chose to love the wrong person. Bryce, though, is still here. Still helping me set up this place. He's agreed, if I start to fall apart, to bind me.

June 22nd, 1890

We've made the plans. Bryce agreed to keep an eye on my son, Carver, who is still alive. I'm not sure why. But at least I will know his life, if only secondhand. It gives me some hope in this ruined world.

I looked up from the table. Bryce had a hand in everything. Even though I'd bounced around from guide to guide as a child, even moving around the country, it had always been Bryce showing up to take me from one place to the next. He hadn't been doing it out of charity. He'd been doing it for my mother.

"Who killed her?" Selena wondered aloud, continuing to flip through the pages. "I can't find where she says."

"She might not know," I said. "The hospital said she died in her sleep."

"Here, look at this one," Selena pointed to another entry farther along.

October 10th, 1896

We met again today. He says he's still holding on, but I'm not so sure. I don't know how he can survive so long without being bound. Bryce cautions me against the meetings but he can't understand. I suppose Bryce could use the binding, could compel me not to. I don't know that he has the courage.

"Who is the 'he' she mentions?" Selena asked.

"I don't know," I said. "She might name him in an earlier entry."

Bryce had bound my mother. Kept her alive in Riven all this time. He'd told me that she disappeared when I started coming in. Had Bryce released her then?

December 25th, 1900

Carver continues to grow. Bryce tells me that my son has crossed over. That he's already approved for training. At once I am filled with joy at the idea of seeing my son and filled with fear that the guides understand what he is. Even Bryce doesn't know. The risks are so great.

"If we had the time to read all of these," Selena said. "instead of flipping through..."

"Go to the end," I said. "The last ones."

Selena nodded and we moved down the table to the last set of pages. These hadn't yet found their home between covers. Unlike the first entries, the writing here was fractured. Ideas didn't seem fully formed and the handwriting skipped around. Jagged edges to rounded letters, words written over others.

April 6th, 1917

The spirits say our country has entered the war. Bryce tells me that Carver is doing well. I fear Graham is stronger. I need to find him.

The next few entries rambled. Lacked cohesion.

"Bryce must have released her at some point," I said, and Selena nodded. "But why?"

"I think your mother is the only person that can answer that," Selena said.

June 3rd, 1917

I saw Carver today. If Graham comes for him now, my son will not survive. Perhaps, though, I can find an opening. Graham is distracted. Extended. All it would take is a single strike to end all of this.

Two days ago. My mother had been watching me. From where?

We both heard it. The creak of the stairs. I put myself in front of Selena and drew my lash and knife. If it was my mother, there was no telling what she would do, and I would be ready.

The spirit walked up the stairs without hurry, taking each step and, at the top, turning to look at me. Just like the spirit had in my half-dead vision. Her wild hair bled down into the bands covering the rest of her body. The same spirit I'd seen at Nicholas's lab, the same one who'd stopped the fight as soon as Anna called my name.

"Carver," the spirit said, staring me straight in the eyes. "You shouldn't have come."

51

"Sorry, I didn't see a sign," I said to the spirit. "You should really warn people to keep out."

The spirit cocked her head at me.

"Also," I said, nodding back at Selena. "I wasn't leaving her."

"Didn't she leave you?" the spirit said. "That's what she told me."

That cemented it. The banded spirit in front of me, batons showing on her back, was the spirit that had interrogated Selena, was my mother.

"She had her reasons," I said. "I'm here for mine."

The spirit moved closer. Shifted so that nothing stood between the two of us. Selena stepped back, towards a corner of the room. Getting out of the way.

"I wondered for twenty-seven years if this day would ever come," my mother said. "Some of those days I wanted nothing more than to see you. To tell you of this world and the one you live in. To share the same love my own mother shared with me. Other days, I wanted to destroy you and the threat you present to everything."

"People keep saying that," I said. "Nobody tells me why."

"Because of who you are, Carver," my mother said. "The product of love between a spirit and a living person."

Now I was confused. "I was born in a hospital, not in Riven?"

My mother reached over her shoulders and drew out her batons. The motion was slow, deliberate. I saw her eyes close briefly as she readied herself.

"Your father died before he should have," my mother said. "I think you know that love does not end with death."

Her eyes slipped past me to Selena. Yes, I knew what she meant.

"So what does that mean?" I said.

My mother didn't give me a clue, didn't give me a hint, just rushed me. Both batons swinging up over her left shoulder in a twin strike towards my face. I sidestepped, flicking the lash around the leg of one of the tables and pulling. Sliding the table into my mother's side and sending her rolling across the floor. Katherine Reed caught herself on the wall.

"It means you're a key, Carver," my mother said. "That, with you, they can create a breach that goes both ways. From Riven to the real world and back."

Which is what Graham kept talking about. My eyes flicked to Selena, who didn't look surprised. Graham had told her. That's why she'd led me to him in the first place. A chance at getting back home. Barth was probably looking for the same thing, only without the precision. Kill enough guides and he might get lucky.

My mother pressed off of the wall in a running start. Jumped onto the nearest table, scattering her own diaries, and sprung towards me. I tried the lash again, hooking another table and twisting it on its side like a wall. But

Katherine was too fast. She skipped over the top of it and tackled me.

I hit the floor and tried to roll. Tried to get my coat between the batons and me. Protect my face. She struck my left side first, the small hooks on the end of the batons tearing through the fabric. I dropped the knife and grabbed her right hand mid-swing. She raised the left, this time aiming right at my eyes.

"You're going to kill your son?" I said, and my mother hesitated. Then I threw her off of me. Rolled the opposite way and scrambled to my feet.

"I don't want to," my mother said, straightening. "Graham doesn't want that."

"Who cares what Graham wants?" I replied.

"I must," my mother said. She broke into another run, but this time whipped a baton towards my face. I brought up my left hand and blocked it, the impact numbing my left arm, but it freed up my right hand to strike with the lash.

I caught her legs, wrapping around her knees and bringing my mother crashing to the floor. She hit hard, her arms not ready to catch herself, and groaned.

"Sorry," I said, and meant it. The point on the end of the lash was in my mother's ankle. If I twisted the grip, I could send the wrangling fire into and over her. Cleanse her clean. But that might mean losing answers. "What does Graham have on you?"

"I am bound to him," my mother said.

"I thought Bryce bound you?"

"For a time," my mother said. She struggled against the lash, but I placed my foot on her back, pressed her down. It didn't feel good, but I figured it was a better option than letting the fight get back on. "Until Graham broke it."

"He broke it?"

My mother, trapped against the floor, still managed to nod at the batons. If she used them on herself, the fire could cleanse, could break a bond. "It… frayed me. I shouldn't have tried to take Graham alone."

"That was after we found you in Nicholas's lab?"

"I was following Graham and saw you," my mother said. "I hadn't seen you since you were in my arms. I thought you were another of Graham's soldiers. Nothing has made me so happy as seeing you that day."

"You tried to kill me."

My mother laughed. I kept my foot on her back. "I'm far from perfect, Carver."

"So you found Graham?"

"Eventually," my mother sighed. "We were equals before, Carver. A pair that hunted Riven's spirits in tandem, bringing down ghouls and worse without a problem. Only Graham has changed. Another mind lends him strength. When we met, I tried and failed to break him free. He bound me."

"I'm going to release you. Now."

Before my mother could object, I twisted the the hilt of the lash and sent the fire streaking down the cord. The pale flames crawled over her, burning brighter, without heat, before dying out. I stepped off of the spirit and watched as she rose to her feet, stared at me without emotion or intelligence.

"She's gone?" Selena said.

"No," I said. "It's more like she doesn't know how to use herself."

For the first time in my life, I reached out and took my mother's hands in mine. She looked at our grip as I felt for the pinprick, the point at which I could join my life to hers. And when I found it, I sent a part of me into her.

"Mother?" I said. "Katherine?"

She looked up at me and, instead of a blank nothing, her face had the hard edge of driving desire.

"Carver," my mother, bound to me, said. "We have to free your father."

52

GRAHAM. As she said the words it all fell into place. My father was the one that had died early, fallen ill and passed before his time. A guide that had crossed over as he faded from life in the real world and so remained a spirit in Riven.

"I have so many questions," I said. "Only, we're running out of time."

"Out of time?" my mother replied.

"I've already been in Riven too long," I said. "I have to cross back."

We made quick work of the jaunt back to the apartment. Dodged guides when we saw them, but Riven's growing danger served to keep us hidden. Nobody searched for spirits anymore, not when breaches were right in front of you.

I left my mother in Selena and Nicholas's apartment, where they promised to stay until the next night. Exhausted and sore, I went back to the clock tower and crossed over.

It was late morning in Chicago. I'd been in Riven for a long time, nearly twelve hours. My body back home felt refreshed, but sluggish. I ignored the stack of mail, went to the train, and downtown to Ezra's.

I CAUGHT Alec on the sidewalk outside of Ezra's, on his way to somewhere else. He didn't look thrilled, but brightened and when he saw me.

"Ah, the brave one. Good to see you're still alive," Alec said.

"Tried my best, but I'm still here," I replied. "Bryce in there?"

"Bryce is in shock, I think," Alec said. "Piotr thanked us for Barth, then said the guides didn't have the men or the time to investigate another crazy spirit. I waited for Bryce to explode, but our man is like a stone."

"Bryce is one-of-a-kind," I said. "You have a minute?"

Alec shrugged and, when I asked, followed me back into Ezra's without complaint. Standing in the air purifier was a normal delay in any day. Now it made me anxious. Everything had me on edge. I wanted to sit down, have some coffee, and get some opinions.

Bryce was standing up as we walked in and, after seeing our faces, the man sighed and sat back in his chair. Waved his hand at the bar for another pot of the black stuff.

"Thanks," I said, sitting down. "I need some of that."

"You look like it," Bryce said. "Alec fill you in?"

"There's no way I can get any help?" I said.

Bryce nodded. "The breach count is too high and the number of guides we've got too low. Piotr ordered us not to go after Graham."

I was shaking my head as soon as Bryce finished. "Not an option."

"Are you hearing this, Bryce?" Alec said. "Perhaps Carver spends too much time around me. My bad habits are starting to rub off."

I ignored him, looked right at Bryce. "I found my mother. I found Katherine."

Bryce took the information in and sat with it for a moment. I took a sip of the fresh coffee and Alec took turns looking at each of us; wondering who was going to talk next.

"How is she?" Bryce finally asked.

"You can ask her yourself," I said. "Tonight. You two are going to help me, and Katherine. We're going to go after Graham."

"We didn't do so well with that last time," Bryce said.

"It wasn't fair. An ambush," Alec interjected. "Another try, with all of us together? Graham has no chance."

"Agreed," I said. "This time we'll have my mother helping us too."

"If Piotr finds out that we're disobeying orders," Bryce said. "He could blind us."

"You're talking like an old man," Alec said. "You, the one who is retiring? What concern could you have?"

Bryce laughed. "How you've made it this long without getting blinded is a mystery to me."

"Piotr would never dare," Alec said. "I'm far too charming."

"That's definitely the reason," I said. I launched into the

details. Explained about Katherine's house in the Shambles. About how Graham had bound her. How they thought I was a key to cross back from Riven into the real world.

"He's not wrong," Bryce said to Alec. "They keep it quiet; that the right guide can serve as a gate."

"How do they do that?" Alec said. "How do they turn a living, breathing, guide into a hole between Riven and reality?"

"It's not easy," Bryce said. "From what I understand, from what Katherine told me, is that it takes killing the guide in Riven and in the real world at the same time. The spirits meet in the middle and create the hole."

"I've got a solution," Alec said. "Carver, I'm sorry, but if we kill you now then we are all saved, correct?"

I glared at him. "Ha."

"So it's tonight then," Bryce said. "We go after him. One more time. Bring an end to it."

THE FRAME WAS UP and the crews climbed all over the metal-work at the construction site where, what seemed like an infinity ago, I'd followed the directions on Anna's card. This time the foreman took a look at me and turned away, didn't bother to wave. I hadn't cleaned out his sneak problem. Too bad.

The door was open when I walked down the hallway to the room full of Riven maps, I didn't bother being quiet. Laurence gave me a scowl as he came out of one of the back rooms to greet me.

"Didn't think we'd see you again," Laurence said. "Since you decided to do nothing for us."

"Is that what she told you?" I replied.

"No help with the spirits, she said."

"Trust me, Anna is getting her own benefits from this relationship," I said. "Speaking of, she around?"

Laurence glanced behind them. "She's back there. Wrapping up a consultation."

I took a seat at the table and let my eyes run across the maps. Laurence sat across from me.

"So how far have you gone?" I asked, gesturing at the maps. "Beyond the wall?"

Laurence laughed. "You guys really stick to your spots, don't you? Of course I've been beyond the wall. We can't just take the first spirit that walks into our path. We gotta work for it. Sometimes we get clients looking for someone that died a week ago. They're not sitting in the center of town waiting to be found."

"What's out there?" I asked.

"Beyond the wall?"

"I'm curious."

"Depends on your perspective," Laurence said. I could see the change in his stance; he leaned forward over the table and his eyes lost a bit of bite. His mouth moved away from the frown and into a thoughtful line. "I think it's beautiful. Rolling forest. Not alive, of course, but the white trees with the dark leaves, the mountain in the distance, you should see it.

"That's just south and west of the city. Towards the Cycle. We haven't gone much in the other ways, but I've come close. One direction it looks like plain white grain as far as you can see. In another, it's rocks and hills. Like whomever put Riven together was trying to see how many different places they could cram into one little world."

Behind Laurence the door opened and a haunted-looking man came out and scurried by us. Didn't even bother to look my way, or notice my mask. Behind him, Anna walked up to the table and took a seat next to Lawrence.

"He was telling me about the adventures you have outside the walls," I said.

"Laurence likes to play a dangerous game. It's not fun out there," Anna said. "You think the spirits are mean inside Riven, try going beyond the walls. Things there will tear you apart in seconds. We go in groups, and we're always ready to run."

"Clients have to pay big if we go outside," Laurence interjected.

"How about him?" I said nodding after the man who just left. "Is his case a big one?"

"Another lost loved one," Anna said. "Only a day old. We'll find her, probably still in the Warrens."

"What I really like about the two of you is how you so obviously care for your clients," I said.

"Now you're one to talk," Laurence said. "All you do is burn people's memories into oblivion. You don't give a crap if they were someone's father, son or anything. Wrangle him and let him go. You ever think maybe their families would want to know?"

"Laurence," Anna said. "Now's not the time."

"Fine," I said. " You want to disagree on how we do things? Tell me how you can keep Riven from being overrun while still telling every family that their uncle went crazy and tried to take a chunk out of us."

Laurence opened his mouth but, at a look from Anna, shut it and leaned back in his chair.

"Why are you here, Carver?" Anna said to me.

"We're going after Graham tonight," I said. Told her all about my mother. The plan with Bryce and Alec. "I don't want you in the fight."

"So why did you come at all?" Anna said.

"Because I want you to cross over with us. Then follow us and keep your eyes open. If something looks strange, or there's a trap, I'll give you my sparker. You launch it and warn us if things look weird."

"I can do that," Anna said after a minute's silence. "But I need you to help me first."

"Help you with what?" I said. "If you need cash, I can get

Bryce to pay what he owes you for the investigation. You did find my mother, after all."

"No, back in Riven," Anna said, glancing at Laurence. "Do you have time now?"

"Anna," Laurence said. "I don't think—"

"What is it?" I asked.

"We'll have to cross over," Anna said.

"You're being evasive," I replied.

"Because I don't think you'll like it," Anna said. "If you want my help tonight, though, you have to help me now."

Laurence looked annoyed that I was being asked. Which made me want to say yes. Besides, I had hours yet before tonight, before our raid. "Fine," I said. "Let's go."

Anna led us to the back rooms, a pair of small chambers that only held beds. She went into one, shut the door. Gestured for me to use the other. As I went in, Laurence grabbed my arm.

"If you hurt her..." Laurence said.

"I won't," I said. "I need her for tonight. She'll be safe."

"She'd better be," Laurence met my eyes. "You're not the only one that needs her."

I CROSSED OVER INTO A STURDY, windowless room. Stacks of random stuff littered the area. From makeshift weapons to sketches of Riven's territories, to lists of active investigations hanging on the walls. Anna was already there, setting her mace into its sheath. I was unarmed; all of my gear besides my coat was back over at the clock tower.

"Cozy," I said.

"It doesn't attract attention," Anna said. She seemed distracted, not looking my way or bothering with her usual snappy replies. Without anything further, she opened the door out and led us away.

The room sat in the basement of a ruined apartment building, its upper levels leaning to the side and crumbling away that any guide would avoid the building for fear of its collapse. I pointed that out to Anna and she shrugged. Kept on moving through the Warrens. Every so often the two of us ducked into a storefront or slipped down an alley to avoid a passing pair of guides. I didn't recognize any of them - other regions of the world were active at this point of the day.

"Stop," I said as we hunkered down behind a collapsed wall and waited for another group of guides to pass. "I've gone along with you this far, but I'm unarmed and have no idea what you're leading me into."

"I need you to teach me," Anna said. "To bind a spirit."

"Why?"

"You've heard about the disease on the other side? The one that's spreading?"

"A little?"

"A couple of people I care about caught it," Anna said. "They didn't survive."

On the street in front of us, the pair of guides went by, looking at their resonator and oblivious to us.

"Anna," I started, but she was already moving. I followed, frowning. I wasn't in a great position to argue against binding spirits, but I'd barely made it away from Barth's tower with my life. Every unnecessary binding took a part of you away, strength and vitality that might be better kept at home.

We reached a dilapidated ruin, a store that was nothing more than a collapsed roof and a single, empty doorway.

"They're in here," Anna said, ducking in. I followed her in where the roof filtered some of the gray light, casting shadows throughout the rubble.

At the back of the building, after stepping over and around chunks of broken wood and rock, Anna leaned down and opened a trapdoor, grasping and hauling on a metal ring. The door banged open, scattering ash flakes into the air. Someone had hung thick glass along the stairs leading down. Riven's gray light reflected its way into the depths, letting us see where to set our feet.

"You did this?" I said.

"It took a long time," Anna replied. "Glass is hard to find."

At the bottom, the light illuminated a short hall that

ended in a dark iron slab. Lifted and pressed, with crude hinges, into a faltering doorway.

"Laurence helped," Anna said as we went up to the door. "We had to dodge so many guides setting this up. I think that's part of why he's so hostile towards you."

"Everybody has their reasons," I said. "What's behind the door?"

Anna didn't say anything. Just reached out, grabbed the edge of the slab, and pulled it open. The slab creaked as it swung, revealing a room in shambles, and a pair of spirits inside. That's when I noticed Anna had drawn the mace.

The spirits turned towards us, a man and a woman. I caught the resemblance in the slight light. Their faces, height, everything matched the sneak standing next to me. I also saw the pale fire in their eyes.

"They're your parents," I said.

"I need you to help me bind them," Anna replied, not taking her eyes off of the spirits. Both of them were edging towards the doorway. "Make them whole again. Like you did with Nicholas."

"How long, Anna?" I said, stepping back from the door. From those burning eyes. "How long have they been down here?"

"Almost a year," Anna whispered. "I found them right away, after they passed."

The two spirits started to growl, to hiss. Crouched and readied themselves to run at the door. I grabbed Anna and pulled her back, slammed the slab shut.

"Your parents aren't in there anymore," I said. "It's been too long. They didn't even recognize you."

"I... I thought you could bring them back?" Anna said. "I thought binding would...?"

"A bound spirit is shielded from the Cycle," I said. "From its call. Like my coat keeps me safe from their bites. Binding doesn't do anything to the spirit beneath. The things in there aren't your mother and father anymore."

Anna stared at me. Not a single tear dropped down her face. "I had hoped," Anna said. "Except, I think part of me always knew. When they stopped talking to me, when their eyes shifted, that they were gone."

"That's why we can't bind everyone we love," I said. "We have to find them fast, before the anger takes hold or the Cycle claims them." I put my hand on her shoulder. "You can give them peace, Anna. Send them on their way."

This time, when I opened the metal slab, the two spirits were waiting by the door. They lunged, right into Anna swinging her burning flail. Anna's aim was true, and moments later the two spirits, black-eyed and blissful, walked up the stairs and outside of the basement.

"I'm sorry," I said.

Anna didn't reply. She walked up after her parents. I followed, and we looked at the two spirits as they wandered down the road together into the hazy distance.

"I wanted to become a guide to save them," Anna said after a long moment.

"You did," I said.

Anna nodded. We stayed there in that ruined building, watching the ash drift and swirl along the empty apartments, until Anna gave a heavy sigh. "You did you part," she said. "I'll be there tonight."

"Thanks," I replied. "There's one more thing we need to do first."

WHEN NICHOLAS OPENED the door and I saw my mother standing behind him, I was stunned. What a change a single day of freedom could do for you. She'd lost the banded outfit and, with Selena and Nicholas helping, now wore more traditional guide garb. With the cloak I'd brought her from the extras in the clock tower, she looked less like a terror of the night and more like a real person. The grit and grime from decades running around Riven wasn't entirely gone, but she looked fresh.

"It feels strange," she said when I gave her the compliments. "For so long I've been on my own. Whatever I could cobble together out of the things I could find."

"Well, if you really try..." Nicholas started before I held up a hand.

"Not everyone has your talents, Nicholas," I said. "So you think you're ready?"

My mother nodded. "Graham is only going to get worse. He's going to find more breaches and compel more spirits to follow him."

"I've been meaning to ask," I said. "How is he doing that? Is he actually binding all of them?"

Katherine shook her head. "He talks to them. Graham's been a spirit for a long time, Carver. He calls to them in the voice that you cannot hear and gives them a cause, a home for the lost."

"You're saying Graham's forming relationships with these spirits?"

"I'm saying that when you die, you cross into Riven devastated and alone. Graham speaks to you. Tells you what you are, where you are, and then offers you a way home," Katherine glanced towards Selena. "It's a persuasive speech. The promise of a new life works on the hardest of hearts."

"When I first met Graham, he led me to a factory. Ambushed me with an army of spirits, only all of them burned with anger. I didn't think a spirit would listen to anything past that point?"

"It would be more difficult," Katherine said. "However, wouldn't surprise me if Graham found a way to connect with them. A rock rolling down a hill is difficult to budge, but if the effort is large enough, you can change its course."

"If I might change the subject?" Nicholas interrupted. "I would like to show you my latest tool? I believe it will be quite useful."

"One of these days, Nicholas, I'm going to teach you how to talk like a real human," I said.

"I believe that is an opinion, Carver," Nicholas said. "My motor speech is not unqualified for—"

"I get it," I said. "Please, talk?"

"Look," Nicholas said, then he rushed over to a table that had a coat lying on it. A large, thick black number. He held it up and in the gray light I could see a series of lines running all across it. Down the back, along the arms, as though the entire thing were an art piece instead of clothing. "It is beautiful, isn't it?"

"Nice design," I said. "Only, I already have a coat."

"You'll like this better," Katherine said. "Trust me."

Nicholas gave my mother an appreciative nod. He slipped the coat on. Shrugged. When Nicholas moved his shoulders, all of the lines on the coat lit up briefly. Went bright blue for a second before flashing back to the normal color.

"If a spirit touches one of these, they'll burn," Nicholas said. "Selena and I, with the help of your mother, tested it earlier today. Perfect for wrangling when you're desperate."

I ditched out of my coat and tried on the new one. A perfect fit. If what Nicholas was saying was true, and my mother seemed to agree, and this was a great addition.

"Nicholas," I said. "Have I ever told you how wonderful you are?"

"Not enough," Nicholas said.

"Remind me to tell you next time," I replied.

I looked around the living room with the new coat on, but didn't see Selena anywhere. Katherine caught my roaming gaze and nodded outside. The balcony. Of course. Selena's favorite spot in the place. I figured a do or die mission against Graham required at least a cursory goodbye. Just in case.

I FOUND Selena outside on the balcony looking over the skyline. There weren't as many sparks right now - the hour was a little odd. Too early for the night crew while the day would be wrapping up their hunts. At least for my part of the world.

"You really like it out here, don't you?" I said.

"Like?" Selena replied with laughter on the edge of her voice. "It's more that this is the only part of the apartment that's open. Nicholas has taken it all over. And now with your mom there, it's crowded."

"You need to breathe."

"I was never one for crowds," Selena said. "I prefer my own freedom."

"That's a little dramatic, isn't it? All you have here is freedom. You could go anywhere," I said.

"I don't know that I really could," Selena turned away from me. "If I venture much beyond this place, I might be found by another guide. Might be attacked by an angry spirit. Or I might find someone like Graham, who can mess with my head."

"We're going after him tonight. You won't have to worry about him anymore," I said.

"You know what?" Selena replied. "I still like it. Worrying. Having something to be afraid of. You always talk about how you love the hunts and going out there and having adventures. I like it too."

"I was thinking about that," I said. "After this, once Graham is out of the way? Let's go. I'll get Nicholas to make you some gear and we can hunt together."

"Go with you?"

"Bryce and my mother? They went on hunts for decades together. She was a spirit whole time. I can teach you, and we can be a team. Explore all of Riven together," I said.

I watched her face. I didn't know how she was going to take the idea. On the one hand, it had to be more interesting than her current existence wandering the streets around the apartment. Playing test subject for Nicholas's experiments. On the other, she'd never been trained. She wasn't a guide, or a soldier. Violence might be in her nature, but not the same way as it was for me.

"Yes," Selena said, and for the first time in a long time, her smile looked genuinely happy. "I might not like all of it, but anything would be better than this. Besides, I would get to see you in action more often. See whether all the bragging you throw around is really earned."

"Believe me, it is," I replied.

"That means you have to come back alive tonight," Selena said. "You can't let Graham win. Because now you owe me."

"I owe you?"

"You do. I'm the one that led you to your mother, after all."

"I believe I rescued you?" I said.

"Only because I let you," Selena said.

I pulled her close then. Laughing. There were few

moments in my life where I've been able to do that. Just enjoy seconds of free fun. No angry spirits attempting to kill me. No sarcastic undertones about how everything was grim and dark and doomed. No, for that moment on the balcony, Selena and I were two people enjoying one another and delighting in our words.

I heard a new voice come in through the apartment. Bryce, and my mother's happy exclamation at his arrival.

"I guess it's time to get ready," I whispered.

"I guess so," Selena said. "A kiss for luck?"

"Make it two," I said.

5 8

Back inside the apartment things were like a family reunion. Bryce and Katherine hugged each other and launched into questions and stories about what had happened over the last few years. Alec pulled Nicholas aside and asked him about the various things in the room. What this machine did, whether Nicholas could make Alec something fun. Selena and I, we stood and watched. When Anna came in a minute later, the whole thing was thrown into entertaining chaos yet again.

"The sneak!" Bryce said. "She arrives."

"She's carrying a weapon," Alec noted.

"A weapon?" Nicholas said. "That's a most rudimentary term. What Miss Anna carries is a thing of art. A wrecking ball that is nonetheless the embodiment of finesse."

"Nicholas is right - I'd avoid the wrong end of that one," I said, stepping into the fray. "Introductions all around. Then we should go. I'm guessing Graham's not going to let us walk right in like last time."

"I hope not," Alec said. "All of us together? How unsatisfying if our foe is not at his best?"

239

As names were exchanged and roles described, I noticed Bryce flicking his eyes to Selena and I. Selena, who stayed towards the back, gave her name and nothing else when it was her turn. I'd probably have to answer questions about that later and, if this were a month ago, the thought would've had me worried. Now it seemed so trivial. Who cared? With everything at stake, there was no reason to worry about some love in my life.

It took another hour, but we finally left the apartment. The five of us, myself, my mother Katherine, Bryce, Alec, and, trailing behind, Anna. She hadn't pushed against the role of reinforcement. I think seeing the kind of experience we had on the front lines communicated the type of fight we were walking into. That, perhaps, she wasn't ready for this yet.

The walk to the Tar Pit seemed faster this time. Maybe it was because we all kept talking, laughing on our way to what promised to be a difficult fight. Like I said before, Riven takes on a different cast when you're traveling with a group. The deadly doesn't seem so deadly anymore. The gray ash was more like snow. The ever-present muted light seemed dramatic, creating the perfect atmosphere for us to visit a final end upon our adversary.

We were four blocks into the Tar Pit, blocks away from the building we'd fought Graham at earlier, when our target strode out in front of us. Graham still wore that same top hat, carried that hammer with the spike, sported the long overcoat. That maniacal grin.

"Katherine!" Graham called. "I see you swapped sides. That's a shame."

"Amazing what free will can do for you," Katherine said. "You should try it sometime."

"If you think free will is amazing, have a look at this,"

Graham replied, then brought a pair of fingers to his mouth and whistled. At least, that's what I thought. I couldn't hear anything. Katherine, though, winced.

"This isn't going to be good," Katherine said. "Get ready."

A moment later the ground began to shake, a rumble of hard thumps pounding their way towards us. Alec threw me a look and I knew exactly what he was thinking. Ghouls.

They burst onto the street, two of them. Different than the one Alec and I had fought. The one on the right barreled towards us in a rolling mass. Instead of an endless supply of arms and legs, it seemed as though this ghoul was only made out of the former. No eyes, no mounds, just a thousand arms hooked into a central ball.

The one on the left, that was even worse. It moved slowly, a pair of giant two-story legs curled up into a ball with a maw full of teeth. As though a million smiles had been shoved together, all their mismatched incisors jammed into one another to form a jagged infinite.

"We'll take the one on the right," Bryce called.

"We?" I said.

"Katherine and I," Bryce said. "Like old times."

That left Alec and myself. I waved to Anna to fall back fall back. Stay out of harms way. Then I faced the monstrous thing.

Each of the ghoul's toes were as large as I was. Their gnarled nails protruding like dirty sheets of glass towards us. Alec threw a wink my way.

"At least this one doesn't have arms," Alec said. He ran towards it.

"Wait," I said. Drew my crossbow and flipped one of the orange explosive bolts into the slot. Turned the crank as the ghoul came closer. Aimed. Fired straight into its mouth.

My aim was true, but then, from the ghoul's mouth, a

giant tongue snaked out and batted the bolt away. The missile struck a factory roof and exploded, well away from the ghoul.

"Guess we'll need to try something else then," I said lowering the crossbow.

"Besides, such a technique is no fun," Alec said.

Alec met the ghoul's feet head-on, rolling underneath an attempted kick and then, springing at the back of the leg, Alec grabbed hold of the ghoul's calf and climbed up. His serrated gauntlets left burning blue gashes everywhere they touched. The ghoul howled its displeasure but didn't seem to have a way to get to Alec, or at least, that's what I thought until I saw that tongue come out again.

The slimy thing snaked out, around and back behind its own leg, gripping Alec and pulling him off. Alec struck the tongue with his gauntlets, but the spirit ignored their burning pain and flung, with a sharp crack, the guide to the ground. Alec bounced off the street and lied there, groaning. Not our best start to a fight.

The ghoul came closer, reached up a foot to step on Alec, and as it came down I rushed underneath and jabbed upwards with my long knife. The ghoul's foot stomped onto the point and it howled, a crazed scream that bore no resemblance to anything I'd ever heard before. High-pitched and ripping with static agony. Like an emergency radio broadcast losing its signal.

The ghoul tried to raise its foot back off of my knife and lost its balance. Fell backward and collapsed its bulk onto the street. I followed the fall, climbed over the foot and began running up the leg, uncurling my lash as I went.

I saw the tongue come out, looping its way into the air. Pointing at me and darting down. I snapped the lash and it wrapped around the tongue as it came towards me. Pulled to the side, jerking the tongue to the right as it went by, missing me by inches. Then I twisted my hand and sent the pale fire running along the lash through the point and into the tongue.

The ghoul spasmed at the pain, ripping the lash from my grasp and flailing around trying to get the burning cord off. That gave me time, time to run up the rest of the leg to the edge of that mouth. I pulled the crossbow off my back, used a lever to crank a blue bolt in place, when the ghoul started to snap towards me. To stand up.

If I fell from the lip of the mouth to the street, I was going to get hurt, badly. Or worse, I could fall into those teeth and get carved up into a thousand pieces.

"Stay focused," Alec called and, as the ghoul tried to get its feet under it, my friend carved his way into the ghoul's right ankle. Pounded on it with his gauntlets and burned through the support lifting the ghoul upright. I kept myself balanced, my feet on the edge where the ghoul's leg ran into the bottom of its mouth. Precarious, but as long as the ghoul was lying on the ground, I could stand.

The lever clicked when the bolt was tight and I aimed it into that gnashing maw, around the flailing tongue, and fired. This time the ghoul couldn't deflect it, couldn't dodge it, and the wrangling fire burst out inside the beast. An inferno of pale blue reckoning.

Unlike the first ghoul, the one Alec and I had fought around the Palace, this one didn't disintegrate into nothing. Rather, the wrangling fire split apart the spirits that had come together to form the ghoul in the first place. The blue fire spread up and down the length of the ghoul's body and out of it crawled a dozen soldiers, their spirits looking around in utter confusion. They'd stand that way for a moment until the Cycle took hold and began urging them along their final journey.

I picked up my lash from where, when the tongue ceased

to exist, it'd fallen. Then I looked to see whether Bryce and my mother were still alive.

59

THE EASIEST WAY TO describe how my mother and my mentor fought was to say that it was like watching a tornado of razor blades. The ghoul looked hapless and lost as it flailed its many arms around, trying to catch Bryce and Katherine. My mother, with her hooked batons, used every swing to give herself leverage for her next one, looping around the ghoul at lightning speed and leaving slashes of blue fire everywhere she touched.

Bryce, his voulge split into two halves, stabbed and rolled along the outside of the ghoul, darting in and out of the grabbing arms and leaving burning holes wherever he struck. By the time our ghoul finished disintegrating into a mess of spirits, its opposite was less a creature and more a ball of blue gashes. In a few moments after that, the pale fire lines that the two guides had left were burning up and over the ghoul.

Another ten soldiers emerged from the ghoul's vanishing corpse, blank-eyed and ready for the Cycle.

"I think we killed ours through luck," I said. "They took care of theirs with skill."

"You mean you didn't intend for me to get thrown into the street?" Alec said. "Because I was hurt and you didn't seem to care."

"I was waiting for my moment."

"Next time, perhaps you wait a little bit less, yes?" Alec replied.

"I don't know, it worked out pretty well."

Alec shook his head and walked over to greet Bryce and Katherine. Showered them with compliments on their victory. I looked for Graham, but the man had disappeared.

"He vanished right away," Anna said, coming up. "I guess he didn't think his creatures would win."

"He's buying time," I said. "Or maybe he thought he would get lucky."

"With what happened to Alec, he wasn't far off."

"You have to take close calls as victories," I said. "Especially in Riven."

"Especially tonight."

After we collected ourselves, the five of us continued heading deeper. Towards Graham's building. Katherine and Bryce chattered back and forth most of the way, commenting on how nice it felt to be back together doing what they did best. It almost made me jealous, seeing the two of them talking so fast with one another. A relationship with my mother that I would never have. That close friendship and the bond of countless shared experiences. At least, I didn't have it then. Maybe now there was a chance.

Graham's building stood in front of us, glowing from the inside. It was hard to tell from what, but in the gray light of Riven it looked as though some sort of green lightning flashed from inside the building steps. We all stared at it, out there in the street, in silence for a moment.

"Anybody have any guesses?" I asked.

"Not a guess," Katherine said. "There's a breach in there. A big one."

"That's what he was waiting for," Bryce said. "He must've noticed so many soldiers crossing through at this point. Claim the building and waited for the breach. If we don't take him tonight, he's going to push farther."

"There's no if," I said. "Graham is going to the Cycle. We're ending it."

"Anyone ever tell you that you have a flair for this sort of thing?" Alec said. "The dramatic, I mean?"

"It gets old, doesn't it?" Anna said.

"I'm trying to pump us up," I said. "Trying to be a team player here."

"We all appreciate it, Carver," my mother said.

"Thanks," I replied. It was time to get this fight underway.

The strategy was simple. Bryce and I go in the front door while Alec and Kathryn scale the wall, get up that second story and take care of any ambushing spirits so Graham couldn't get the drop on us like he did before. Anna keeps an eye on the outside, let's us know if there's problems coming in. Fires the sparker if she needs to. Ideally Bryce and I would keep Graham engaged long enough for Katherine and Alec to complete the sweep, the four of us trap Graham in the courtyard and finish it.

Bryce and I made it all the way to the front door before things fell apart.

I REACHED for the twin handles on the door to get into the building but, as my hand came close, the doors blew open. The force of the wood knocked me back down the steps. When I looked back to see what slammed the doors open, I saw a mad spirit biting at my face. Then Bryce's voulge cut through the spirit and flung it away, burning it up with pale blue fire.

I scrambled up to my feet and was set on by another pair. I worked the knife and the lash; sending the first one to the ground with pale blue fire wrapping around its legs while I kept the second dancing away from the knife's point. There were more spirits behind it, a wave of them bustling out through the door. Bryce whirled into them, going through a dance and sweeping the voulge up and down. Raking through spirits as they tried to grab hold of him.

There was no place for caution here. Slowing down would mean being overwhelmed.

"Should we help?" Alec yelled from the outside of the building. He was almost at the second level, my mother already climbing over through the open windows.

"Stick to the plan," Bryce said, the man was braver than me. I wouldn't have minded Alec's gauntlets right about then.

I charged the second spirit and caught it by surprise, lunging forward with my knife and spearing it. The spirit fell away, blue fire crawling all over it. I continued up the stairs, back to the door. I'd fought with Bryce enough times to know how to work with them, how to use the lash to catch any spirits that he missed with the spear and soon we were making our way through. Spirits fell one after another, caught by the pointed burning end of my lash or Bryce's voulge. Except there were always more, and they clogged the hallway. Bryce and I would get tired eventually. Make one mistake and get torn apart.

"When I yell; dive back," I said. Bryce grunted an acknowledgment, dodging a spirit's raking hand. I noticed all the spirits here were wearing soldiers uniforms, but different ones, with various countries' styles on them. Riven didn't discriminate, and neither did Graham. The soldiers who'd died bitter enemies of each other were working together to kill us.

I slipped the lash back in its holster and drew the crossbow, flipped the second of my three orange bolts into the firing slot and turn the crank. I watched as I turned the lever. Bryce ducked under a pair of grasping arms, only he wasn't quite fast enough, their hands grabbing and tearing at his coat. Another two spirits dove at his legs, knocking Bryce on his back. Bryce swept the voulge down across his body, cutting off the spirit's wrists and freeing himself from their hands, but the endless wave was going to crash over him.

"Get back now," I called and pulled the trigger. Aimed the bolt just above the first row of spirits. As it flew, the bolt sank just enough to strike one in the back. I didn't see the impact, but saw the orange blue explode upward and outward, its rays decimating their way through the ranks.

Every time Nicholas's energy leapt to another spirit, it feasted on the creature and then jumped to the next one.

As Bryce scrambled back, the front wave of spirits surged forward. Reaching for him and trying to escape the doom at their backs. One by one they went up in the orange fire. The last one, its hand an inch from Bryce's feet, evaporated into nothing.

"What was that?" Bryce said.

"Secret weapon," I said, looking at the empty hole in front of us. "Let's go."

"They're gone," Bryce said, looking at the empty hall. Standing up and matching my stride. "I don't know what's going to happen if those spirits don't make it to the Cycle."

"Promise I won't use it too much," I said. I figured there were always more spirits. It wouldn't matter a whole lot if a few dozen never made it home. I hoped.

We scrambled down the hallway and looked into the courtyard. Or, what had been the courtyard. The ash-covered grounds where I'd been torn apart last time were covered in the glowing green mess of a breach. On the other side of the hole we could see the bright flashes of an ongoing battle. A trench full of bodies as bullets flew back and forth and exploded in front of our eyes. A portal to a world just as deadly as the one we were in. A window into our home.

"You think I'm a monster," Graham said, stepping out from behind a pillar. "You think it would be so terrible for all of these poor souls losing their lives in a meaningless fight to come back and have another chance. And I'm the evil one?"

"That's not the way it works," Bryce said. "It's a one-way road. There are no guarantees. No second chances."

"Then you won't mind following in their footsteps," Graham said. The spirit that had been my father charged Bryce and me, his hammer raised. Behind him, from the breach, more spirits crawled out. Whatever time the crossbow had brought us, it was running out.

251

Bryce snapped his voulge together and met Graham's strike head-on, clashing his weapon against Graham's hammer swing. With his left, Graham raised his fist and sent a burning wire right into Bryce's face. The wire wrapped itself around Bryce's head and lit up, causing Bryce to backpedal and drop his voulge.

Graham followed, raising the hammer for another swing, when I hit him with my lash. The whip curled around Graham's hammer arm and I pulled it back towards me, spinning the spirit around and bringing his malevolent gaze to meet my own.

"Haven't we already had this fight?" Graham said. "Don't we know how it ends?"

"This time it's going to be different," I replied and pulled back on the lash again, drawing Graham towards me while keeping his hammer arm extended. No way for him to swing the hammer with any momentum. I had the knife ready in my left hand. Until a spirit tackled me from behind and drove me to the floor.

I felt Graham jerk the lash out of my grip as the spirit on

my back clawed me through my cloak. I thought about activating the coat Nicholas had given me and burning away the spirit. I held back. Graham didn't know about the coat, and I wanted to keep my surprises hidden.

"Incoming," Alec yelled, landing next to me and pulling the spirit off. His gauntlets wrangled the spirit and their flame culled its anger. "No ambush on the second floor. All of the fun is down here."

"Thanks," I said pushing myself to my feet. I looked up as Katherine joined us on the ground, mixing it up with Graham already. Trying to keep him off of Bryce, who was busy peeling off the burning wire. My mother was faster than Graham and kept him moving, occasionally landing strikes with the batons while Graham used the hammer more to create distance than actually try to hit her.

If I could get behind him, with my knife...

"I'm going to need some help," Alec said, looking behind me. I turned that way and saw another five spirits climb out of the breach, their pale fire eyes turning towards us.

"Keep them busy," I said. "We get Graham, this fight is over."

Not entirely true, but I figured if Graham was gone then dealing with more spirits wouldn't be a problem. So I ran at Graham's back as Katherine circled him away from us. Ready to thrust a stab in between Graham shoulders. As I closed, I noticed my mother's eyes slip away from Graham to meet mine, and that was all the clue that Graham needed. He turned a swipe of his hammer into a full spin, bringing it to meet me. I had to throw the knife up to block and the hammer battered it away, sending it bouncing along the ground and leaving me weaponless.

Katherine tackled Graham from behind, striking him with her batons. The baton's blue fire burned, but Graham shrugged her off, threw her side into the wall at the edge of the courtyard.

"He's too strong," Bryce said. "We have to work together."

My mentor stood, slowly. A burning line crossed his face, running along Bryce's nose and cheek, then around and behind his head. Bryce held his voulge was up, set his feet. I drew the crossbow and Graham looked at both of us, laughed.

"Even with all of you here, you can't hope to win," Graham said. "You'll be overwhelmed in minutes. Torn to shreds."

"Careful," I said. "Your crazy is showing."

I fired a blue bolt right at him. Graham moved fast, ducking it, but the move gave Bryce an opening. His voulge slashed across Graham's shoulder, and Bryce quickly turned the swing, sending the voulge back, point first and stabbing into Graham's back. Pinning Graham down into the ground.

"I can't hold them!" Alec yelled.

The call came at the worst time. Bryce and I looked and saw ten spirits, with more crawling up behind them. Alec was a dervish, slicing up the spirits as fast as he could, but I saw more than a few scratches on the guide. As I looked, four spirits converged on Alec, two grabbing his arms while the second pair raked at Alec's chest and face.

"Help him," Bryce said. But we'd taken too long. Graham caught the hesitation and, still on the ground, swept Bryce's legs out from under him. With the voulge still sticking out of his back, Graham stood. Turned to me.

"Carver," I heard my mother's voice, glanced as she threw my knife back to me. She jumped into the fray next to Alec, batons flying and scattering the spirits holding my friend. Buying us a bit of time. When I turned back, Graham raised his hammer.

"Come on," Graham said. "Show me that you deserve to be a guide."

I hefted the knife, tiny next to Graham's hammer. But before my father could come after me, he screamed. Pain, surprise. Bryce had knifed Graham in the leg. Bryce was about to twist the hilt when Graham, reaching behind his back, pulled out Bryce's voulge and, in one smooth movement, stabbed Bryce with his own weapon.

I yelled, but I wasn't sure what. My vision went hazy, a film of red cast over everything. Anger in terror and frustration boiling over at seeing my mentor and teacher for these last twenty years struck so terribly. The voulge stood up like a sinister grave, marking Bryce as he shuddered on the ground, speared.

Knowing nothing else, seeing nothing other than Graham standing over Bryce, I charged. Took two quick steps and leapt at the spirit. Graham twisted at me as I hit him and knocked him over Bryce. Drove him into the wall and stabbed with the knife. But even then, even with surprise and reckless anger working for me, I couldn't catch hold. My knife tore through Graham's coat but he slithered out of its reach. Pulled me aside and pushed me away.

"If you had given yourself to me," Graham said. "Then your friend would still be alive."

"Never," I said, though Graham's words struck home. I could have. I could have given him the path he wanted. The path back and none of this would've happened. I saw, in the corner of my eyes, Alec and my mother overwhelmed by the growing number of spirits. Driving them back towards us, raking and tearing at their arms and legs. In front of me, limping, weak, but still deadly, Graham. One hole back to the real world, one life, and this could have all been erased.

"Don't give up," I heard Bryce's voice; slight, scratched. "Close the breach."

I saw on his belt the same device we'd used earlier, the tablet with the sapphire. It glowed. Ready.

I returned Graham's glare with one of my own. "I'm not done yet."

I threw the knife at Graham and he raised the hammer for the block. I used that time to run towards Bryce, reach down and scoop the device, off of his belt. Ran towards the center of the breach.

"Give me an opening," I shouted. The two guides, one current, one former, pressed their backs to one another and then, using broad strokes, cleared out a path. A small hole through which I could see the rippling green glow of the breach and the war happening on the other side.

I ran through that hole, squeezed between a thousand grasping fingers and dove into the center of the breach. Pressed down on the sapphire and felt its glow explode out around me. Azure tendrils reached out into the green and began to tear up and shatter the image of the real world, to bring Riven back together.

The spirits stopped fighting as the sapphire's tendrils reached out and caught them too, wrangled them as the device closed the breach. Except one.

Alec didn't see Graham coming, didn't see the hammer as it smashed down into his back, the spike crushing through his coat. With his left hand Graham blasted my mother with another wrist wire, circling around her leg and knocking her to the ground. As I stood up from where the breach had been, Graham looked over at me.

"If you want her, follow," Graham picked up my mother with his left hand and dragged her away. I ran to Alec's crumpled form, sprawled out on the ground. A dozen pacified spirits stared at us.

He wasn't in good shape. Alec's chest barely rose and fell, his eyes were closed. I looked over Bryce and saw the same.

The man's hands weren't moving. The voulge still stuck there, pinning my mentor to the rock. I wanted to help them, to drag them back to the clock tower, but if I let Graham get away than this was all for nothing.

"Forgive me," I said as I stood up and walked away.

I went out to the street. Graham was a block away, moving quickly with my mother in tow. A pair of shadows sifting through Riven's haze.

"Anna?" I called.

"I'm here," Anna said, stepping out from behind a building.

"Shoot the sparker," I said. "Bryce and Alec need help."

The blue sparks launched into the sky. I had her use all of it. Create a show. Any guide seeing that would know there was something wrong. Any guides in the Tar Pit, or the central part of Riven's city would see that and come running. If Bryce and Alec were going to make it out of this alive, it would be up to them.

6 2

My HEART BURNED at leaving Bryce and Alec behind. Nobody wanted to abandon their friends. But if I didn't follow, Graham would have my mother. He'd just set up another breach. Find another army like the one we'd already dealt with. Anna looked at me like I was crazy, but she stayed by my side.

"You sure they'll be found?" Anna said.

"There'll be dozens of guides in Riven right now," I said. "Some would've seen the sparks, they'll come. They'll come."

"What happened in there?"

I told her as we kept moving. Replayed the desperate fight, the back-and-forth against the overwhelming number spirits coming from the breach. We had expected a breach, but not for one so large, with spirits so angry.

As I talked, we kept moving after Graham. Anna matched my speed, and we caught up to the spirit. As we closed, Graham looked back at us, my mother in his left hand and the hammer in his right. I could see my mother wasn't moving. He'd either knocked her out, or threatened her with something so terrible that kept her from fighting.

"If you come any closer," Graham said. "It will be the end of her. Follow me, at that distance."

I thought about using the crossbow. Taking a shot at Graham's back. But the statement made me curious. Follow where? Graham was taking us westward, towards the edge of Riven's city. Towards the wall.

"She said you were my father," I called to Graham as we moved. "That you two were a team. Why would you do this to her?"

"You don't always have control," Graham said, and for the first time I picked up a note of sadness in his voice.

"We met a spirit, his name was Barth," I said. Anna, next to me, took the cues and kept silent. Must've been a sneak's instinct; to listen when there was important information at play.

"Barth was a fool," Graham said. "He had no method. All he had was hope."

"What do you have?" I said.

"I have you," Graham said. "I have my son. The key."

We left the Tar Pit and moved into the last bit before the wall. A section of wide open pavilions. A place that would've served as a market back, if, Riven had ever been a real city. In front of us, the wall appeared through the haze. Five stories high and made of stacked stone.

I'd only seen the wall on a couple of occasions, both long journeys with Bryce. Few of the wall's stones had any cracks, and the stairs on the inside that led to the ramparts were all there. As though Riven's city devoted what energy it had left to keeping the wall intact.

"Who is controlling you?" I said. "Barth mentioned you, mentioned a master."

"I can't tell you that," Graham said. "The Master forbids it."

"You never mentioned anything about a master," Anna said to me. "I thought this was all about Graham?"

"Tonight it is," I said. "Tomorrow, maybe not."

Graham led us to the stairs up the wall, to a tower next to the gate leading outside. With my mother still in his arms, Graham began the limping walk up to the top. We followed, waiting until Graham gave us the nod to come up behind him. Halfway up, Graham told us to stop.

"Here you'll have to make a decision," Graham said. "Carver. You've come this far. You've seen your friends fall. Your mother captured. How much more are you willing to lose? I asked you once about a gateway home. Now I ask you again. Give up yourself, and save the ones you love."

I paused. Took a deep, unsatisfying breath of Riven's non-air. If I charged Graham now, he'd either kill my mother or use his better vantage point to strike me down. So I did the only thing I could.

"Take me," I said. "I'm done."

"What?" Anna said, her eyes going wide as I went up the steps and left her behind. "Carver, what are you doing?"

"Don't worry," I said. "It's just the end of the world."

I stepped out onto the top of the tower. Behind me, Riven spread out like a charred ruin. Its gray and ashen structures falling apart forever. Still, it was a home of sorts. I'd wondered its alleys, climbed its buildings, and explored its secrets for so long that it didn't seem like an alien place. In fact, I realized, Riven was more of a home to me than Chicago. Than the real world.

On the other side, over the wall, a dense forest began a hundred yards from the gate. Interlocking trees of white and thick clusters of black leaves. Not truly alive, not entirely dead. The forest continued on to a horizon where, barely, I could pick out the outline of a mountain. Somewhere back there, according to rumor, was the Cycle. If I looked over the wall to the left I could pick out spirits working their way around from the Shambles and entering the forest on the long walk to nothing.

"The Master wanted this place," Graham said. "Likes the view, I suppose."

"I don't care, let's get this over with," I said. Graham set my mother down, and I saw her eyes open. She looked at me, her face curling into a question. I lied down on the cold stone next to her, and reached out with my right hand, found hers, and gripped it tight. Graham stood over us and raised the hammer.

I saw it. The same look Graham had in his eyes earlier, the same expression Barth had. He was receiving instructions.

"I have been getting here," Graham said to nobody. "We are ready to begin."

We laid there, my mother and I, for what felt like forever. It was moments, but when you have maniacal spirit standing over you with a giant spiked hammer, the seconds feel long.

"He's not there?" Graham said, glaring down at me. With his left hand, he gripped the collar of my coat, and pulled me up. "Where are you? Back home?"

"Nowhere you'll ever find me," I replied, then did as Nicholas said. Shrugged my shoulders and let the lines on the coat ignite. Graham jerked back as the fire ran up his arms. I was ready for the fall, caught myself and made my move. Took the knife from my belt with my left hand and stabbed forward, twisting the hilt. Graham didn't expect it. The knife slid between his ribs and the pale fire spread out over his body. There was nowhere to slip away. No way to dodge.

As the fire crawled over him, Graham's eyes met mine. He smiled.

I STOOD OVER MY FATHER, or the spirit that had been him. As the pale fire died away, Graham stood up and stared at me with blank eyes. No expression on his face. Ready to go to the Cycle.

"Bind him," my mother said. "We need what he knows."

I reached out and took Graham's hand. He looked at me, then down at our grip. Expressionless. His hammer sat on the ground next to us. Just a moment ago, he'd been perhaps the deadliest thing in Riven. Now, he was nothing. I could just let him go all the way to oblivion. Instead, I searched for the pinprick. Found it, and nearly passed out.

I was exhausted. I already had three bound spirits. My mother, Selena, and Nicholas. Another would take too much out of me. I might be able to walk, keep that sarcastic mouth of mine, but in a fight? I would be useless.

Thankfully, I wasn't the only one in the tower.

"Anna," I said. "You want to be a guide?"

"I don't like the way you're saying that," Anna replied, coming up the steps.

"I need you to bind him. Take Graham, and make him yours."

Anna hesitated. "Are you sure that's the right thing to do?"

"It's the only way," I said. "If we ever want to figure out who is behind this, we'll need Graham. I'll walk you through it."

"Please," my mother said. I glanced at her and saw something I didn't expect to see in her eyes. She was giving out a pleading look. I realized she didn't want Graham to go. Didn't want to lose the man that she had loved, the man she'd worked with for decades. Didn't want to see him vanish into nothing just when she'd found her own way back to a new life.

Anna saw that. Or at least, I thought she did. Because when Anna looked at me next, her face was determined. Anna walked up and took Graham's hand, pushing mine out of the way.

"Tell me what to do," Anna said.

"Concentrate on your touch," I said. "Where you feel his hand. You'll notice something small, like the tiniest poke you've ever felt."

"I feel it," Anna said, her eyes closed. "What do I do?"

"Focus on it," I said. "You'll feel it open, like a drain wanting to suction you away. Let it."

The only clue was her sharp intake of breath. Anna shivered and her hand clenched even tighter on Graham's. Then it was over. When binding a spirit, you knew when you'd filled that well. When the drain stopped asking for more. Anna stepped back from Graham, let go of his hand. My father's spirit looked at her, still in that ridiculous hat, and nodded.

"Thank you," Graham said.

6 4

THE DOORS OPENED on the eighth floor of the Chicago Medical Center. I took a breath; the sweet sterile real air coming in through my bruised lungs. Stepped in with Anna behind me and walked past a series of patient rooms towards a large one in the corner. One that had a doctor I recognized standing outside studying sheets of paper.

"Carver Reed," Dr. Barrington Farth said as I walked up. "Who's this, a new addition to our group?"

"Anna," Anna said. "And, maybe."

"Not up to me," I said. "Anna, this is Dr. Farth. He oversees any problems the Chicago guides have."

"Two of those problems are in there right now," Farth said. "Close calls. I'd prefer you keep to the usuals; broken bones and bruised egos."

"They're alive?" I said.

Dr. Farth looked at me over his glasses, his eyes at once skeptical and admonishing. "I believe they'll stay that way. Though I'd be more confident if they kept out of Riven for awhile."

I nodded and Dr. Farth stepped aside, waving us in. The

room had two beds facing a large window looking out over Chicago's cityscape. Each of those beds held a guide. Bryce in one, Alec in another. Of the two, Alec was the only one awake, and the heaviness of his eyelids said consciousness was hard to maintain at the moment.

"Tell me, you took care of him, correct?" Alec said.

"She did," I said, nodding to Anna. "He's bound to her now."

"That would be a feisty binding," Alec said. "Be careful not to lose him. Would hate to have to clean up after your mess."

"I'm not the one in the hospital bed," Anna replied.

"I shouldn't be here long," Alec said. "Just broken ribs. And a punctured lung. Crossing isn't as effective when you're nearly dead."

"Giant hammers will do that to you," I said.

Bryce stirred in the other bed. It was hard to look at him. His skin was pale, and the jagged red outline of a burn traced its way around his eyes. From what I could see, large bandages wrapped around his chest. Evidence of more than a few injections to kill the pain. He pulled himself awake anyway.

"I know what you're thinking, and I can still see that ugly face of yours," Bryce said. "Graham didn't quite blind me. Didn't quite kill me."

"You heard what I said?" I replied. "Graham's done with. It's over."

"It's not though, is it?" Bryce said. "For you, anyway."

"What you mean?" I replied.

"Barth and his master? You're not going to let that go are you?"

"Eventually," I said. I meant it, but I wasn't in great shape. Alec and Bryce weren't either. Anna was fresh to the experience. Charging back in after some unseen enemy that had managed to control two of the more powerful guides out there wasn't what I wanted to do that afternoon.

"You should know," Bryce said. "I'm not coming back. I said I was retiring, and this is it. You'll have to tell Piotr for me."

"You're not coming back?" I said.

"I should be dead," Bryce replied. "It was a miracle those guides from New York found us. Brought us back and kept us awake long enough to cross. Dr. Farth says some of these wounds won't heal. I can't risk leaving my family behind."

We kept talking for a while longer, but I didn't remember much after that sentence. My mentor was gone. Wasn't going to be back with us. If we were going to go and find this Master, Anna, Alec, and I would do it without Bryce.

"Carver," Bryce said as we made to leave the room. His eyes had closed, Alec was already asleep. A real sleep. "Finish it. Find the one who did this to us. Make them pay."

"I will," I said.

Anna and I split on the way to Ezra's. She had to touch base with Laurence and get back to some of her clients. I had to have an unpleasant chat with the leader of the guides.

Piotr looked confused, sitting alone with the coffee at our table. When I came in, the man gave me a halfhearted grin. Stood up and reached out to shake my hand. As I told him what had happened, that grin replaced itself with a frown. At the end, he shook his head.

"A guide retiring in a time of war," Piotr said. "If it were any other, I would call him a coward. But Bryce has put in more years than most of us."

"He deserves it," I said.

"Of course," Piotr replied. "Though I'm disappointed that the three of you disobeyed my orders. Went after that rogue spirit despite the risks."

"But we won," I said. "Graham is gone."

"To the Cycle?" Piotr asked.

I wasn't sure how to answer the question. Anna wasn't a guide, and therefore was forbidden from binding spirits. I could say that I bound Graham, but then Piotr but want to know why. That wasn't a road I was ready to walk. So I just nodded. I'd tell Piotr everything, when it made sense. The leader of the guides sighed at my gesture.

"Then at least one more soul is put to rest," Piotr said. "Now, with Bryce leaving and Alec incapacitated, Chicago is in need of a leader. A guide to represent the city. You."

"I'm not ready," I said without thinking about it.

"It doesn't matter," Piotr replied. "There's no one else. I have to leave, today. I'm heading overseas to try and do what I can to put an end to this war. I leave you in charge of the city, Carver Reed. May you protect her well."

With one last sip of his coffee, the leader of the guides left me in charge.

I THOUGHT my apartment would be a wreck. When I got up to my floor, I noticed my door was knocked ajar, hanging out on one hinge. Whomever had gone in there had done so in a hurry. Inside, though, the only messy thing was the bed. Sheets thrown away to other sides of the room. Evidence they had been moved to check if I was underneath.

I figured the plan had been to kill me in both worlds at the same time, except they couldn't find me in this one. The danger with Riven and crossing from places you didn't know is that you couldn't be sure where you'd come in. You might be miles from where you wanted to be, or appear in a dangerous place without any of your equipment. Without any backup.

So before we started our run last night, I moved what I needed from the clock tower to the Warrens, to the small room that Anna and Laurence crossed into every time from the construction site. Nobody had been here when Graham was ready with his hammer, and if the lock wasn't going to open, why destroy the key?

I put my door back as best as I could, laid down on the

bed, and crossed into Riven. I didn't expect them to come back for me, whomever it had been, because unless they had me strung up and ready to die in Riven, it wouldn't do any good to kill me back home.

The apartment was crowded now. Nicholas working at a feverish pace to load out Selena, Katherine, and now Graham. The four spirits were huddled together the living room, discussing what they wanted for weapons and tools, and when I entered, they fell silent and looked at me. I held up a hand in a friendly wave.

"Any ideas?" I said.

"I'm working with him," Katherine said. "Unfortunately, it seems whomever bound him did a good job covering his tracks."

"It's like there is a hole in my mind," Graham said. "A blank spot."

"Try and find a way through," I said. "Because I don't think he's going to stop. Whether that's coming for me, or tormenting others."

Selena came up and took my arm. "Let me show you something Nicholas made for me."

We went to the balcony. Selena wasn't wearing the same dress she had been before. Now she wore a thick coat, one that reached down to her ankles with sleeves that covered her wrists. A guide cloak, with her hair pulled back tight. She turned away for a moment and reached into the coat's pocket, and pulled out a pair of blades. One, long and thin. Like my knife. The other, thick and wide. A cleaver brought to larger proportions. Meant for more than cutting meat. Along the cleaver's front edge, spines struck out like angry teeth.

"Nicholas made it from some of his old machines," Selena said. "He thought it would be fitting."

"You were killed with something like that," I said.

"That's why it feels right," Selena replied. "Now I need practice. A teacher."

Selena looked at me, and then out from the balcony. The occasional spark lit up the gray sky as Riven continued its constant dance. Spirits coming and going, guides finding and finishing the ones that wanted to stay. For the last few days I hadn't been filling a quota, I'd been hunting a single spirit. It would be nice to get back to the usual, until we found the Master.

"Are you ready for your first lesson?" I said.

"I've been waiting for a long time."

"Just because I love you," I said. "Doesn't mean it's going to be easy."

"Nothing with you ever is," Selena said.

CARVER'S ADVENTURES *continue in The Cycle.*

THE CYCLE

THE RIVEN TRILOGY - BOOK TWO

Selena hacked the dead man with her cleaver. The spirit was young, cloaked in hospital rags, and vicious. Blue flames poured from the edges Selena's weapon and curled around the spirit's snarling body. His eyes glazed over into blank nothing. Then I snapped my lash.

My lash whipped forward and snagged the outstretched arm of another spirit reaching for Selena's neck. Gnarled hands betraying the spirit's own mind, her perception of herself as she crossed to Riven an old woman. Also wearing a hospital gown. As were all the spirits in the courtyard, near the large palace where Alec and I had fought a ghoul not too many nights ago.

"Behind," I said, and Selena whirled, going low with her cleaver while I held the spirit back. Selena made contact and the spirit howled her rage before the pale fire burned it away.

"You can't forget that," I said. "Your back is always vulnerable."

"Not when you're around," Selena said, giving me a quick smile. Not much time for talking. More spirits climbed out of the breach, a glowing pit on the flagstones in front of us that, like a pond reflecting the sky, showed a hospital ward on the other side.

A containment unit housing so many dying from the disease. They called it the flu, and it was wrecking the world. It would wreck this one too if we didn't close the breaches fast enough. To my right, a pair of spirits worked together to annihilate their brethren.

Graham, looking like an out-sized carnival barker and sporting a spiked hammer, swept raging spirits aside with long swings. That gave space for Katherine to work, her hooked batons carving up and propelling her from one spirit to the next, wrapping each one in blue flame as she moved.

"It's almost ready," Anna said from my left. She held a tablet with a blue sapphire in the middle. A device centuries older than I was, a product of unknown creation that had been passed from guide to guide and now found itself in the hands of a former sneak.

"On it," I said, grabbing my large crossbow from its holster on my back. With Selena providing cover, I clicked the lever on the left side of the stock to load up bolts tinged with blue, and then turned the right crank. Slotted one, aimed, and shot a spirit just as it turned toward us, its eyes awash with the same blue glow as our calming fire. The bolt hit the spirit in the chest and fire burst out, matching its eyes. But when the fire finished crawling over its body, the spirit's eyes were plain, blank. Ready for the Cycle.

Fired again, and a third time. Each bolt wrangled a spirit with blue fire. Each one bought us a bit of time. Brought us one step closer.

"It's ready," Anna said. "I'm going for it."

I pushed the lever on the crossbow, switching to the normal, hard-hitting metal bolts. I tracked Anna as she ran towards the center of the glowing breach and fired at any spirits that came close. Each bolt slammed into and shoved away a pair of outstretched hands, wild and crazy eyes, and gnashing teeth.

"Back up!" I yelled to Graham and Katherine. Selena caught the words too, ran behind me, and kept going. They had to get out of range.

Anna reached the center of the breach and pressed in on the sapphire. It sank into the tablet, slick blue lines shooting out in all directions, tendrils reaching for the edges of the glowing portal. They lanced through any spirits, enveloping them in that same blue glow. The raging ones in hospital rags turned to simple bodies, standing there without a thought left in their heads. Other tendrils grabbed the edges and pulled them closed, shrinking the portal against the flagstones until, seconds later, there was nothing more than the hard gray rock of the courtyard beneath our feet. Another breach closed.

"It gets easier every time," Selena said as she walked back to my side.

"These spirits were sick," I replied. "Patients that weren't strong. Some breaches are harder than others."

"Oh come on," Selena said. "Can you at least say I did a good job?"

"You're getting better," I said. "Still have to watch your back. If I wasn't there, you'd have been caught."

"Who cares?" Selena said. "I'm already dead."

I shook my head. Didn't have a good come back for that one. Just because Selena was a spirit and couldn't actually die again, didn't mean she couldn't get hurt. Didn't mean she couldn't wind up broken and weak and waiting to recover. "Even if that's true, I bet Nicholas wouldn't like repairing all your stuff."

"He lives for it," Selena said.

That cockiness. That was a new one. An unexpected bonus of bringing Selena into the more dangerous parts of this life. She'd wanted to add adventure to her endless days in Riven and had taken to it like a rat to a sewer. I couldn't suppress a laugh.

"Is that enough for your quota?" Graham said. "Or has Piotr increased the number again?"

"Still at one breach," I said. Which was a ludicrous amount. We'd never had an expectation to close a breach on every night in Riven before. Normally, it was a set number of spirits. Three, four, maybe even five that we had to find and reduce to walking mannequins heading for the Cycle. That far-off place where Riven cleansed the dead.

"It's not getting any better," Katherine said, panning a slow look around the courtyard. "Every time we're wandering around, there are more. And more guides to go with them."

"Piotr's been recruiting," I said. "There's no telling when the war is going to end. We're taking everybody we can get."

"Except for some people," Anna said. She handed me the tablet and I slotted it back in my belt.

"I'm working on it," I said. "Sneaks don't do themselves any favors."

"Not everybody can afford to be noble and righteous all the time," Anna said. "Some of us need to get paid to survive."

"The guides were always too stuffy," Graham said. "All pomp. All bravado."

"Quit it," Katherine said. "You loved them just as much as I did. Besides, without being a guide, you wouldn't have met me."

"And then I wouldn't exist," I said. "Come on, let's get back to the apartment. It's almost time to cross back."

6 7

In the few months since we'd freed Graham, there had been one objective for the apartment: to expand. The usual routine was to clear a breach and hit my quota, and then come back to this place and clean the next floor down. Put in new doors.

Scavenge materials and work with Nicholas to prep the new living space.

The nutty scientist now had the ground-floor lab that he wanted. As we came back, Nicholas was audible from a block away, buzzing around with his machines. How the man managed to craft working ovens, generators, and other miracles from Riven's desolate ruins stunned me. But then, that's why I bound him in the first place.

The second and third floors belonged to Graham and Katherine, with Selena taking the top for herself. The tall and thin building now resembled an actual residence. We made furniture, stripped what cloth we could find in other places to put together bedsheets and even some semblance of carpet. The whole thing an exercise to make the spirits feel more like the humans they once were.

"Do you like it?" Nicholas asked as we walked in. He gestured to a far wall on which he'd carved a map of the city. Hooks, little spikes, were driven in nearly every inch. On some of those hooks hung glowing blue dots. "Each one is a breach. The stones work like your resonators. The breaches pulse a certain signature. A wavelength that I can catch with these little gadgets."

The scientist held up what looked like a pair of beads fused together with a wire running around them. Next to the map Nicholas kept a bent metal barrel full of the things, with a thick lid on top. Nicholas led us over to it, continuing his explanation. "I leave one out, and when it picks up a signal, because every single breach is slightly different, the wire vibrates and the beads glow blue. Then I measure the frequency to determine the distance, and that tells me roughly where it is." One of the dots on the map faded. "And that tells me when a breach has been sealed. Genius, right?"

"You never cease to amaze," I said.

"So does this tell us where we should be going?" Anna said. "Or where other guides are more likely to be?"

Nicholas stared at her for a moment. Then hummed, tapping his lips. "I suppose I haven't thought of that. Perhaps that's the next thing. Find a way to track where the guides are going."

"Now if you could do that," I said. "Then you and the others would be safe."

"The guides would be safe, you mean," Graham said. The spirit wasn't wrong. That spiked hammer of his could probably take care of most of the guides we had. With Katherine beside him, I would pity any poor guide that tried to wrangle them.

"All the same," Katherine said. "It's best if we avoid each other."

"I love it, Nicholas," Anna said and the scientist beamed at her. "Keep going. And, speaking of guides, it's time for me to check out."

"Anna," I said. "Come by Ezra's in the morning. I've got something for you."

Anna nodded. Her exit prompted the rest of us to make our own. I went with Selena to the fourth floor, the top. I thought it funny how we'd filled the apartment with furniture. Things absolutely meaningless to a spirit in Riven. Selena didn't need to sleep. She didn't need to eat. She never, barring injury, became tired. No day to shade and night to light in the perpetually gray monotone of this world.

When you walked into her place, it looked, it felt, like a home in a world that needed none.

"You're bringing her to Ezra's?" Selena said as soon as we'd shut the door behind us.

"She doesn't know yet," I said. "But Piotr approved the application. She's going to be inducted as a guide."

"She already is, more or less, right?"

"If guides caught her in Riven with a weapon that could wrangle," I said. "They'd probably try to blind her."

"Sometimes I wonder if that would be so bad," Selena said. "Never having to come back to this place again?"

I followed Selena through the living room, back to normal after Nicholas moved down below. Selena covered the walls with her black and white drawings, mostly cityscapes that Selena could see out from the balcony. Where we went now.

Off in the distance, over the gray tops of buildings, the occasional shower of colored sparks flew through the air. Guides communicating their positions to one another. Riven looked the same as it always did. Full of buildings with no real architectural pattern. Some bearing the pointed, targeted stone of centuries ago while others had the sheer walls and multistory design of more modern cities. Though no one could recall ever seeing a building come up in Riven, the variety of design made it hard for me to accept that it had all been created at once. One certainty, though; Riven was falling apart.

Walking the streets was a tour through disaster. Some buildings crumbling in their entirety, others only in pieces. A floor collapsed here, a wall knocked over there. The decay continued to spread through Riven. Partly due to the fighting; the endless waves of angry spirits trashing things in their fury until a guide put them to rest. Partly due to the mysterious, gradual decline of this place. A dying world.

I glanced up at the gray sky, a permanent mist blunting the white light above. Ash flakes filtered down around us; a constant presence floating along on a breeze that came from nowhere. Like snow that never melted, that wasn't cold.

"It's a gift," I said. "Everyone else has to sleep. Has to dream. I get to spend these hours here with you."

"You're such a sap sometimes, Carver," Selena said, but I caught her smile. "It's much better now than it used to be. Thanks for taking me along."

"You're getting good with that thing," I nodded to the cleaver locked into a holster on her belt. The jackets we wore, long trench coats that provided protection, weren't always the easiest to fight in. They were heavy. The long sleeves and flapping cloth could get in the way. But Selena learned fast and she came with on all of our raids.

I wasn't sure if my girlfriend being a murderous expert with a cleaver was comforting or not, but it fit that she'd learned to use the weapon that killed her.

"I want to go with you," Selena said. "When you go after him."

"We don't even know where he is. Who he is," I said. "I've only heard him called 'the Master'."

"We found your mother," Selena said. "We can find him too."

"So long as he doesn't find us first," I said.

"If he does, we'll be ready," Selena replied with all the confidence of one who couldn't die.

6 8

I JERKED AWAKE IN CHICAGO. Even after years. I would fall asleep in my bed in Riven's clock tower, the base from which our Chicago guides operated, and wake up in a world full of color. With whirring machines and, outside the window, swarms of drifting zeppelins. The war burned abroad, and Chicago's industries changed to suit the country's needs.

I glanced over at the growing pile of mail underneath my vacuum tube. A funnel that sucked letters up from the street and shot them into my apartment. The latest paper sat on top. Above the fold ran a piece by my most and least favorite reporter, a guy by the name of Opperman.

"Death by disease, or war?" the headline ran. I skimmed the article, wincing at the endless hyperbole Opperman employed. Every battle a glorious victory or horrendous defeat. Every death multiplied to the thousandth in its cost to humanity. Every outbreak of sniffles the next doom to sweep the land.

I used to laugh at pieces like these. The ridiculous notion that that I lived in the world described by these pages. Not anymore. The articles weren't all embellishment. They weren't proved false by the facts at play. Opperman had finally found a world that suited him. One that brought more disaster every day.

I slipped on my mask, a black and gold number that hid my face, that combined with my coat to announce to the world what I was. A guide. A special kind of creature, worthy of both respect and fear. Living proof of a place nobody wanted to know.

Which give me plenty of room on the crowded streets, and even earned me a mechanical nod of deference from a passing pilot in his mech. The giant two-legged things, twenty feet tall, were everywhere these days. Their twin smokestacks looming above the metal barrels of their guns, belching hot black into the air. Stomping around and making sure their dire threat brought peace to the streets.

As times go, there had been better.

Crowds filled the train downtown, as ever. Life churned on, and so the throngs of businessmen, scientists, and everyone that supported them continued making their treks to their respective parts of the city. Suits to soot-stained coats to mechanics in greasy overalls - all the classes came together in common movement.

I always had my own seat. My own space. At first I'd been troubled by the fear that came over everyone's eyes when they saw me, that nervous look that shaded their glances. A reminder of a nightmare they never wanted to believe. Now I enjoyed stretching my legs.

Ezra's defined *classic*. A fixture that made itself known to anyone passing by. The gold letters on the outside, and that deep crimson veneer that said a trip into this bar had the potential to change your life. At least for a drink or two.

For me, at 8:30 in the morning, coffee would be that drink. I slipped inside the door and stood for a minute in the purification area. Dirty air, that musty grime of Chicago's, filtered out as purified sweet stuff came in. I pulled off the mask, its respirator no longer necessary, and went inside my favorite place in the city.

"You are here. I was beginning to have my doubts," Alec said to me as I walked in. He sat at our usual table, a circle big enough to sit six, though the two of us were often its only occupants, now that my mentor, friend, and former leader Bryce had slipped away to a quiet life with his family. Alec already had a pot of coffee sitting there, this time with three mugs instead of two.

"I don't think Anna is used to getting up early," I said. "I'm usually the first to cross back by a long shot."

"One of many changes she will need to be making," Alec said. "Anna cannot be both sneak *and* guide."

"Once we start paying her," I said. "She'll be able to afford to leave that life behind."

We spent the wait swapping stories. I told Alec about closing the breach last night; our team of five wiping through spirits and sending them to the Cycle. Alec did what he usually preferred, running around alone, picking off angry spirits when they didn't see him coming. Of course, our current quota made that harder. It would be suicide to try and close a breach by yourself.

"I join up," Alec said. "It hurts, but I need to make friends anyway. Find a different group every night, help them close a breach, and then I go do what I want."

"Look at you," I said. "A team player. Never thought I'd see the day."

"These days are full of surprises," Alec said, nodding back to the door.

Anna stood there, in her usual working woman's attire, looking lost. Of any place in Chicago to go, a sneak would find Ezra's the least accommodating. It'd been a guide meeting place for centuries. And sneaks, people that were able to cross into Riven and did so without approval or training from the guides, were definitely not welcome.

"Anna," I said. "We're over here."

She flashed a grateful smile, and took a seat. I slid across a mug full of coffee to her and she stared at it, then looked up. "I'm more of a tea person."

"Oh, the first error already," Alec said. "Carver, I think we made a mistake."

"We can't all be perfect," I said. "She'll just have to work harder to make up for it."

"Sorry," Anna said. "I thought I heard you needed more guides? I don't think now is the time to get picky."

"Truth," I said. "Which brings us to why you're here."

I nodded to the bartender, and the gentleman brought out, from behind the bar, a crate and carried it to the table. From his waist, bartender took out a small device, an opener, and slotted into the lock in the center top of the crate. The bartender turned his wrist and moved the opener in a circle, winding the gears on the crate and eventually popping the thing open, its flaps falling to the side and revealing the contents.

A new mask, white and silver and looking like curled smoke. A card with her name. Beneath both of those, an official coat. Long and thick, and emblazoned with the circle and bars that declared its wearer a guide.

"Does this mean what I think it means?" Anna said.

"Over my strenuous objections," Alec said, disarming the comment with a wink.

"We'd like to make you an official guide," I said. "If you accept."

"Is there any doubt?" Anna replied. "Why wouldn't I?"

"You have to give it up," I said. "You can't do both. A sneak can't be a guide."

Anna passed her eyes between Alec and I, thinking. Then

she nodded. "Riven is getting too dangerous for sneaks anyway. If I can help make it safer, then it would be the right thing to do."

"She's a noble one," Alec said. "This is the worst idea."

"Be quiet, Alec," I said. "Welcome to the guides, Anna. We're happy to have you."

"If we're going to have to take her on," Alec said. "Then the only way I accept is if we celebrate." He looked at Anna's full coffee cup. "Please tell me you're okay with beer?"

"Now that I enjoy," Anna said, and Alec gave an exaggerated sigh of relief.

69

I'LL BE the first to tell you that I like a good drink. Or several. And that being a guide comes with the most wonderful way to avoid a hangover. Just cross to Riven and all my problems went away. Hunt spirits for a few hours, and when I crossed back I'd be feeling fine. So that evening, on the train back to my apartment, ginned up from all the, well, gin, I looked forward to crossing over, finding Selena, and maybe a breach or two to put to rest.

I had my own pair of seats on this route, a double facing me wide open even as other people stood in the center of the aisle. Nobody wanted to look at me in my mask. Nobody wanted to get on the wrong side of someone they might run into after they've died, someone who made souls cease to exist. So I wasn't expecting anybody to bother me. So when a man sat down across from me, and maybe the alcohol helped, it took me a minute to notice.

He didn't say anything, just stared at me and out the window at the passing cityscape. I gave him the once-over. He wore a cheap mask, not carved metal like my own, but one made of cloth and rough edges. No style. The could be said for the rest of his clothes. A workman's vest and a ratty jacket, trousers stained and worn. I couldn't quite make out his eyes beneath that mask, but the man's slouch suggested they would be tired.

"Funny how no one likes to sit across from a guide," the man said by way of a greeting.

Took me a second to compose a reply. I'd settled into the silent stupor that so often takes travelers on trains, rising back to consciousness only when their stop is called. "I don't mind."

"It's like being afraid of your destiny," the man said. His words, the leaden tones in his voice, shook me out of my boozy haze. People didn't usually say lines like that, much less to someone they didn't know. Even less to a guide.

"I suppose you could say that," I said. "But not everyone needs a guide to get where they're going."

"Especially not one like you," the man said.

I straightened up. "What was that, again?"

"Carver Reed," the man said. "I've been trying to find you. Riding these trains back and forth most days for the last week."

If I'd been sleepily sobering up before, I woke up now. I'd been hunted before, in Riven, by the kind of spirits you don't want to go up against. Here in Chicago, in the real world, people didn't know my name. Not unless they were a guide, or I knew them personally. I didn't advertise.

"Now," the man continued. "I see you're getting a little bit nervous. I'll contend that you ought not to be. And also contend that you ought to stay seated."

The man shifted his jacket enough so that I saw, hanging from a shoulder holster, the dull bronze of a pistol. When the man saw that I'd noticed, he closed the jacket again, but left his right hand on the weapon.

"Is this how you always make friends?" I said.

"Only the ones I want to keep," the man said. "I feel like it's only fair, as I know yours, that you know mine. Inman."

He extended his left hand across the gap between our seats. I wanted to spit on it. Or slap it away. But I wasn't armed. My weapons lived on the other side. So I gripped his hand with mine and we shook in a single pump.

"Well, Inman, you've come onto my train. You've made a subtle threat. You going to explain why?" I said.

"I will," Inman said. "But before I do, we're going to get off this train."

We were not at my stop. In fact, we were coming up on a switch point. A station where, if you wanted, you could jump to trains heading farther west, out of the city and into the country. The station itself was snarl of stairs and platforms, trains running in and out in a constant blare of whistles. Chaos or perfect efficiency depending on your perspective.

Inman gestured for me to get up as the train slowed to a stop, and I didn't argue. Survival took priority, so I followed orders. I didn't really want to get shot, or start a fight with the guy on the train. Also, I had questions. What did he want, and why go about it this way?

We crossed the switch point, walking along an overpass above various tracks that rattling as trains crossed beneath us. The smoke billowed around the glass enclosing the overpass, so it looked as if we were shrouded in momentary fog. We went passed the city routes, a couple heading north and the one heading south. Stopped at the thick rail going west.

"Gun or no," I said "I'm not going to leave the city."

"You will," Inman said. "But we're not going far. Only to the river."

"The river?"

Inman shook his head. "I forget how little you city folks know about your country. The Mississippi."

I knew the Mississippi. Of course I did. It didn't come to

mind right away because I never left Chicago. Never needed to, and being a guide meant staying put. Crossing at a new place brought risks. Never knew where in Riven you might wind up.

"Are we going fishing?" I said.

"If you want to call it that," Inman said. "We're aiming to catch something a little different. You're the bait."

"That doesn't exactly make me want to go with you."

"What if I told you that the man we're trying to catch is the one that bound your father. That tried to have you killed. That murdered your mother?" Inman replied.

The Master. They were after him too. And they had a plan, or at least it sounded like it. I must not have reacted fast enough, because Inman kept going.

"Now we know it's not your fault," Inman continued. "You were just born, but sometimes existing has a way of forcing people's hands. I've lost too many friends to that man, and I don't even know his name. With you, I think he's desperate. Sees you as his only chance. Which gives us an opportunity."

Two hours of slight conversation later, the train pulled into the station, doors sliding open in front of us. This time, when Inman waved me forward, I didn't hesitate. If they wanted to catch the Master, if they wanted to kill the man that had brought my family so much pain, I'd be their bait.

Nobody wore a mask. After years in Chicago's packed pollution, I noticed that first. The people pouring off the train around us, greeting friends and relatives, all had their faces out in the evening sunlight. When I breathed, the air had a different flavor. Not the sweet sterile taste of Ezra's and other purifiers, but instead heavy with nature. The sense and textures of wildflowers and pine needles, the burning smoke of fires not for forging industry but for cooking food.

Around the station, as far as I could see, stretched arcing tree-covered bluffs racing alongside the endless churn of the Mississippi River. The town we'd stopped in nestled amongst the limestone cliffs, curling back away from the river and up into the hills.

Inman pointed down the road, a gravelly affair crowded with animals. Horses. A couple of small jalopies, but otherwise the neighing creatures were the order of the day. You didn't see those on Chicago's streets. Nobody wanted to clean up after them, so once you hit the city limits, you stabled your horse and rode the trains like everybody else. Or you walked.

Inman led me to a trio of horses, all brown, and all, Inman explained, the gentlest of mares. Another man sat on the third horse, wearing a guide's coat and looking at me as though I were some kind of a traitor. The man's glare matched his angry beard, a gnarled mass of black and gray that seemed to be taking over his face. A stained charcoal hat sat on his head, the wide brim casting shade across his eyes so that their green appeared to glow in the setting sun.

"I see you found him," the man said. "You know how to ride?"

"Not a clue," I said. "Not much use for it in the city. Or in Riven."

"Then today, you learn," the man replied. "Climb into the saddle, hold on to that little knob in front of you, and I'll lead her."

"It's not too far," Inman said.

I watched Inman climb into his saddle, then tried to copy the move. Stuck my right foot in the stirrup and then swung my left leg over. It would've worked, I'm sure, if I'd had a looser coat. Something that didn't get snagged on the end of the saddle. I wound up flopping my way over and wriggling around with my chest pressed to the horse before finally getting myself arranged.

When I sat up, I saw Inman repressing a chuckle and the other guy shaking his head. The crowd joined in. Claps and whistles. Nothing like a little humiliation to keep your ego in check.

"This is Mead," Inman said as we started moving along. "You might've noticed he was a guide."

I bounced around on the horse, trying to adjust to the constant motion. I slid back and forth in the saddle and tried to keep hold of the knob in front of me, alternating between that and a death-grip on the horse's hair. For her part, the mare didn't seem to give a crap about whatever I did. She followed Mead and his guiding hand on the rope tied around her bridle without complaint.

"I might have," I said when it felt safe to talk, to take a bit of my attention away from staying in the saddle.

"You might've noticed that he doesn't much care for you," Inman said.

"I might've."

"Mostly because you buried his friend beneath a tower of rubble," Inman said. "Which is how we know about you at all."

"Barth?" I said. That spirit had been another one working for the Master. Barth had performed murderous experiments in hopes of finding a way out of Riven. He'd murdered guides in his tower, and with each failure, enslaved the subject to join his bound spirit army. All in the hopes of finding a way back to life he once had.

Then Barth picked the wrong fight with Alec, Bryce and I. Tried to bring his own tower down on top of us and wound up caught in it.

"That's the one," Inman said. "We'd been preparing our own move on the tower. We wanted to try to free him. Send him to the Cycle. Then you took care of it for us."

"Sounds like I did you a favor," I said.

We turned up out of the town onto a winding trail to the bluffs. The narrow pathway curled beneath leafy trees, adding the sound of songbirds to the crunch of hooves on dirt and rock.

"I think Barth deserved what he got," Inman said. "But some of us thought he could be saved. Some of us thought that if we'd been able to get him back, Barth would've told us where to find the Master. Now all we've got is you."

"How did you even find me?" I said. "I didn't see anyone there after the tower fell."

"Spirits talk plenty once you bind them," Mead grumbled up front.

"We found some of Barth's old spirits standing around the remnants of his tower," Inman replied. "So now you understand. You owe Mead, really. His right to be the one to help his friend."

His right. Sure. Barth had been doing his experiments for years by the time we took care of him. Mead hadn't been in a hurry. But I didn't bother saying that. Bryce had pressed a cautionary attitude into me, despite my attempts to ignore it. In Riven, caution meant being calm around spirits that hadn't already turned. Keeping a spirit from getting agitated meant saving your own life. I wanted to keep Mead from deciding I'd make a better bait with a few cathartic bruises.

Inman didn't talk for a while after that. Perhaps the glowing embers of the sun setting behind the bluffs, filtering its purple orange rays through the branches of the trees mesmerized him as it did me. The flickering wings of bats replaced the birds, their chirps and chimes swapped with buzzing bugs. I sat in silence. Experienced it.

Didn't have this in Chicago.

Eventually we came into a campground; a series of tents and ramshackle cabins set up around a large fire pit. Another ten to fifteen men and women worked around it, cooking food and cleaning, doing laundry in a washing well set up nearby. I felt like I'd fallen down a hole and come out several centuries ago.

"What's the point?" I said as Inman helped me off the horse. "Living way out here, you can't be on our calls. Can't be connected."

"We're not guides anymore," Inman said. "We don't have any need to pay attention to what you're all doing."

"Why?"

"Eventually you get sick of following orders. Especially when you're told to forget your friends."

Inman pointed me towards one of the cabins and I, ignoring my growling stomach, went. People turned to glance at me, but most didn't stop their work. Disciplined. In the cabin were pair of cots, if you could call them that. More like bedrolls with blankets on top. Inman gestured to the one on the right.

"Go ahead. Lay down and cross over," Inman said.

"No dinner?" I said.

"You'll get plenty to eat if we make it through this."

"You know, if I cross here, I won't have anything," I said. "No weapons, nothing to help."

"You're the bait," Inman said. "The bait's not supposed to help."

I thought about protesting, but Inman pulled out that pistol of his, held it at his waist. No choice but to cross. Which I didn't mind. In spite of everything, I wanted to meet the Master. Even if it killed me.

71

Normally Riven presented the same scene when I crossed over: a stonework room with a line of beds beside me, a rack of weapons in front, and a stone table and chairs for waiting until my friends joined.

Here, I crossed over onto a pile of grass. Not the summer kind; the wavy green and soft stuff of childhood dreams. These stalks were crinkly and white. Like walking on dried straw. Or a scrub brush. Trees rose up around me, blocking Riven's gray light, their spindly branches sprouting black leaves in all directions. I had my coat, my mask and nothing else. The things I carried on my person crossed over with me. No lash, no knife, no defenses.

Felt a hand grab my arm and pull me along. I turned and saw Mead's set face, the glower beneath the man's scraggly beard.

"It's this way," Mead said.

"Didn't you quit the guides because you didn't like their orders? And yet, here you are ordering me around?"

"This is more important than your sarcasm," Mead said, but at least he dropped my arm and let me walk behind him.

Unlike the trail through the bluffs leading to the campground, the forest in Riven had no scent. Nothing other than the usual bland blankness of Riven air. I breathed it in, even though I didn't have to. One of the first things they taught a new guide, told you when you cross over to hold your breath as long as you could. Then you found you could do it forever.

We reached a gap in the woods, one that Mead and the others had made. Trees had been cleared, their stumps ringless and solid gray. One by one the former guides showed up and formed a ring around me, pushing me towards the center. Inman came, gave me a nod.

"So is this a sacrifice, or what?" I asked him. "Because this doesn't seem like a trap to me."

"We don't know where he'll come from," Inman said. "But we know he'll try to get to you."

"How are you going to draw the Master to me?" I said. "You want me to dance? Sing a song?"

Inman laughed, shook his head. "Carver, in another life, I imagine we would've had a few good times together."

Minutes later, the ring tight and everyone standing ready, their hands on their weapons, Mead brought two fingers to his lips and whistled. I couldn't see them, but I assumed there were other people that lit the fires. Raw flame, not the pale blue wrangling kind, shot up the trees around us.

I saw them now, the ragged sheets and paper and wood gathered from elsewhere tied up around the trees. The fires caught quickly and burned upwards, climbing the gray trunks and lashing into the black leaves. The sudden burst of color threw me, played with my eyes and a mind that expected nothing other than the endless gray. Real ash joined the omnipresent flakes as the fires engulfed trees around the square.

"You think he'll see this?" I called Inman.

"We know he's around here," Inman said. "Tracked him this far. But he keeps slipping. Which is why we need you."

I watched from the edges of the ring, the backs of all the heads of these guides waiting for their chance to exact vengeance for some wrong or another. I wished that I could've stood with them.

Especially when the screaming started.

72

THE SHOUTS CAME from beyond the ring, in the flickering darkness outside the flame-lit clearing. I watched, but none of the guides shifted. Nobody displayed any signs of panic as the howling drew closer. The same wail I'd heard a thousand times. A wave of angry spirits pouring from a breach, ones pulled together to form a mob of horrors. Left unchecked, the source of the howls, that screeching rage, might form a ghoul.

One of the guides raised her hand, pointing with her hatchet. I looked that way and saw, at the edge of the courtyard, a figure. A tall, thick, cloaked person. In the firelight, the man's black robes shimmered, laced with gold filament. His face hidden by a ridged, obsidian mask, as though forged from volcanic rock. In both hands, down at his waist, he held a long, wide blade that went half his height and perhaps more.

As the ring around me turned their attention to him, the man raised the blade and jammed its point into the ground. As soon as the edge made contact with Riven's earth, if it could be called that, the screeching that surrounded us shifted, like a siren in the distance suddenly turning towards me.

The spirits descended out of the dark.

The guides drew their weapons with their own cheers and battle cries. Most were names, some I recognized, of guides that had fallen over the years. Friends lost to this nightmare world. I watched as they met the crash of spirits head-on.

Only these weren't the scraggly rabble Selena and I had fought earlier, the sickly and desperate. The confused and lost. No. These spirits were bound, these were trained and hardened and though they came at the guides without more than stones and scraps for weapons, they moved with purpose and they moved together.

The spirits weren't in soldier's uniforms or the rags of the hospital-bound. Instead, they were uniformly different. As though coming from a dozen times and places. Some wore armor of an Eastern past, while others raged in little more than loin clothes and thin robes.

I watched a guide swing at one with a pair of long knives, blitzing slashes and weaves only to see the spirit backpedal out of reach and, after a near miss thrust, a second spirit dove from the dark at the guide, rending and tearing at his face.

On the other side, Inman and Mead worked together. The latter using a pair of short spears to stab and withdraw, sending one spirit after another away with blue fire. Inman complemented the man with a pair of pistols, weapons I hadn't seen much of in Riven. You never knew how many spirits might be around the next corner, and running out of ammunition meant running out of your life. But Inman's guns popped one after another, sending shots into the spirits and opening them up for Mead's wrangling stab.

I kept rotating, tried to keep my eyes everywhere at once.

The ring still held, but its boundaries were getting loose. Spirits clawed closer and closer as guides fell or shifted out of the line. I tried to keep my eyes everywhere, minimize the chance that I could find myself attacked without defenses. I had to be ready to run.

A fist hit my shoulder and knocked me to the ground. I rolled with the impact and wound up on my back, pushing away from the towering figure standing above me. The Master himself, carving in through the ring.

"Carver Reed," the Master said, his voice a hollow baritone, like the low notes on an organ. "I'll be taking you now."

The Master's held his blade in his left hand and reached for me with his right. I leaned forward and grabbed his wrist, pulling him, trying to trip him up. The Master braced himself and, instead, yanked me to my feet. Then he pointed outside the ring, to somewhere in the distance.

"Walk," the Master said, ignoring the continuing fight. He had good reason to. More spirits kept pouring out of the dark and the guides were overwhelmed. One after another fell to the tricks and traps of the Master's devious army.

"I'm really not feeling it," I said.

"You know what I want," the Master replied. "To open the gate, you're the only one that needs to die. If you don't walk, I'll make sure everyone you love dies as well."

I take threats as seriously as the person who makes them. If I don't think they can pull through, if I think they're punching above their weight, then I'd laugh and move on. With the Master, I started walking.

"You're not taking him," Mead announced, diving at the Master with his spears stabbing. I watched the guide attack, his first strike heading straight for the Master's chest. The great sword sat too low, too far away to be brought up to block. So the Master twisted, allowed Mead to come ever so close to sticking the Master on the point of a spear. So close, but not close enough.

I heard a crack, the report of Inman's pistol, and the Master grunted. The large man brought his right hand up to his shoulder where I could see a tear in the coat.

"That's for Barth," Inman said. "This is for everyone else."

The guide raised his other pistol, aimed right at the Master's face, and fired. The bullet struck the mask. It hit that shimmering rock, and bounced off. Blew a chunk away, revealing a hint of skin in that shadowy light. A glint of teeth. And then the Master moved.

Mead turned from his strike and stabbed at the Master's back, a hair too slow. The Master ducked forward and charged at Inman. Mead's spear grazed the Master's coat, but missed the flesh. Inman worked his first pistol, slotting another bullet, raised it, and then the Master's sword swept up and carved the man in half like I would cut a slice of bread.

I wanted to yell, to do something, but my hands were empty and my throat had lost any voice it ever had. I could only think to run. I saw Mead's wild-eyed face as he leapt with spears flashing forward and the Master, in a smooth motion, swinging his great sword around to meet the attack, and then I turned away to the forest.

The gray dark beyond the burning trees had me stumbling over the brittle grass. My eyes recovering from the bright orange light. I tried to remember where I crossed over, where Mead first grabbed me.

If visible terrors filled Riven's dense city, its forest; dark, quiet and creeping, gave rise to more insidious fears. My mind conjured up grasping claws, raking arms, and the hideous faces of those old, enraged spirits. Every step brought me past another tree, under another branch where any hell might lurk.

Bryce had spent years drilling the fear from me. Forcing reaction from panic to poise, to treat the unusual with calculated tactics. Then, I'd had weapons. Friends. A chance for success. Here I ran alone from a merciless enemy with allies in the shadows.

And yet, my feet flew with purpose. I pushed away numb frenzy gripping my nerves and focused on the grass, on the rays of gray light slipping through that canopy. I found my path and pressed on.

I recalled the tree had been near, the depression in the grass that indicated guides had used the spot as a bed more than once. The screaming behind me grew softer, more sporadic as the remaining members of Inman's band shared his fate.

There. The flattened bed of grass, nestled in between the roots that large damned tree.

I dove onto the grass, turned over, and closed my eyes. Shut away the dead.

73

WHEN I CROSSED INTO RIVEN, the camp had been bustling with activity. When I crossed back in the dead of night, only the insects and the far-off cries of a loon gave me company. I didn't move. Not for a minute, anyway. A body lied in the bed to my right. I could see it through the scattered bits of moonlight bleeding through the cabins loosely thatched ceiling.

I recognized the face. The coat. The bronzed pistol on the ground next to the limp hand. No breath came from those lips, no rising and falling chest to denote the living human body. Inman had died in Riven, and so he died here as well. Whatever that had been, whatever their thought to ambush the Master had been based on, it hadn't accounted for the numbers. They hadn't known what they were going into, hadn't known what they were drawing out, only that they could.

I stood up and walked from the cabin and around the campsite. Bodies were scattered on bedrolls, in the other small cabins, around the dying embers of small fires. Not a single one still alive. All of these guides, these former guides, had given themselves to a doomed mission.

I wanted to despair right then. They didn't need to die. All of these guides could've helped with the breaches, could have helped keep Riven alive. Instead they been hacked to pieces going after one person. One soul. A waste.

But they had known where to find him. The Master. Now I had a clue; the forest. West of Riven's city, and large. Only, their clearing could've been anywhere beneath its dark leaves. So I searched the campground for anything that might give me a location. A place to travel to so I could find the Master again. Anything that might help me avenge my brothers and sisters.

I knew that if I hadn't been on that train, that if Inman hadn't found me, then tonight wouldn't have happened. All these people would still be here. Or if we'd found the Master sooner. If Graham, Katherine, Alec and I had downed that monster, then these people would still be alive.

Selena would be shaking her head at me right now. I could hear her voice, telling me that I couldn't take responsibility for other people's actions. That everyone is who they want to be. That Mead and Inman and the rest of the guides knew what they were doing, and accepted whatever fate their actions would bring them.

Dwelling on death wasn't a luxury of our lives.

I found the map in the last cabin, pinned to the wall above Mead's motionless body. His spears hadn't struck home, apparently. Or if they had, the Master had taken Mead down with him. With nobody else in the camp moving, I didn't think it likely.

In the silver wisps of light, Mead's beard and emerald eyes, which had propped themselves wide open in the hideous state of the dead, struck me with a strange fear. A wild man meeting his wild fate. Would I, too, one day look like that? Alone and frozen in perpetual struggle against an unseen end?

I shook my head. Stay in the present, Carver. You're not dead yet. I tore my eyes from Mead's visage to the wall above him. The drawing.

Like Anna's maps in her hideout beneath the construction site in Chicago, the large sheet of paper held a crude drawing of Riven's city coupled with a more intricate mapping of the forest. Lines indicated routes that had been walked, pathways from a circle I assumed to be the clearing and whether or not, marked with red Xs, they'd encountered hostile forces. Words next to each of the Xs denoted the number of spirits found, whether those spirits, if captured, mentioned the Master. Towards the upper left part of the map the forest cut off into a swooping line. Two words written explained the shape.

The Mountain.

Below those words, on the edge of the line, written in jagged handwriting: *He lives here.*

The map fell off the wall when I pulled on it, rolled it up and shoved it into my coat pocket. Went back to the cabin with Inman's body, and took the pistol. Robbing the dead might seem disrespectful, but good weapons were valuable. I had a feeling Inman would rather see it used than lying there moldering away on the bluff. Patted down his pockets and found a smattering of bullets. Inman had left his pistol loaded, too. If he'd had to shoot me, Inman had been ready.

I went over to the horses, the whole group of them in various states of sleep and nervous wakefulness as I approached. The thought of trying to ride one back to the train station in the dark almost made me laugh. Almost broke the mood. Instead I opened the gate to their pen and walked away. Who knew when, if, anyone would come here.

No reason to sentence the horses to a starving prisoner's fate.

Eerie shadows and illusions drifted along with me on my walk back to the town. I kept drifting into recollection, playing back the fight, and then the snap of a twig or an animal's surprised cry would jerk me back to the present. The short crossing to Riven and back didn't help - my muscles ached, my head eyes and throat dry and itching, my bones bleached and weary from the stress and the climb to the campsite.

So I held to the one positive. The one thing that made all of this misery worth it. I knew where to find him. The Master wouldn't be hiding much longer.

74

I MADE it to the station by dawn and bought a ticket for the first train back to Chicago. Grabbed a newspaper and a stiff coffee for the ride and stood on the platform with a ragged band of commuters. They and I shared that quiet bond of a common destination, communicated by avoiding each other's eyes and keeping any words to absolute necessities.

The train roared in from the west, a great, hulking mass of steel and burning coal. Black smoke pitched out through a series of thick stacks. Whistles announced the boarding time and spindly metal gates shunted aside to let us climb on. Again I found myself left alone, my own corner of a car isolated as passengers clustered elsewhere.

I unfolded the paper, my companion for the ride, and I fell into its conversation. Yesterday, Opperman had the prime headline and today his bold name plastered across the paper's top line again.

We'd joined the war in Europe. Whole bands of zeppelins crashing into each other above men and mechs blasting away in the trenches. Gas bombs flung back and forth, sending soldiers into delirious and deadly spirals. Ground wasn't being gained, but lives were being ground. Calls for sign-ups were increasing. The last peace talks had scattered to ashes amid the latest casualty reports. Desperate nations had scheduled the next attempt to start in a week, in New York, but Opperman gave a peaceful resolution low odds.

Humanity seemed resigned to burn itself to ashes.

Compounding the fighting were continued, frightening notices of contagion. Sickness spreading through America's major cities, sweeping from one borough to the next. The disease had come from overseas and, like the war, seemed intent on ruining everything it touched.

Masks were said to be effective, and avoiding the sick. I heard it there on the train. A cough, two rows ahead. A woman with a child.

And another; across the aisle from me. An older man staring out the window with a handkerchief pressed to his face. Even though we were miles yet from the city, the air still tasting clear, I pulled out my mask and slipped it on. Made sure the respirator worked.

Sometimes I had to remember that this world could kill me just as easily as Riven.

Still, even if the countries pulled themselves together, even if the scientists made a miracle cure to keep us all from falling victim to disease, none of it would matter if the breaches kept forming in Riven. None of it would matter if the dead clawed back into our world. None of it would matter if we couldn't find the Master and stop him.

I looked down at my coffee, the steam rising from the tall cup, I wanted a drink. And not this kind.

75

"The Mountain?" Graham said when I told him about the map. "That's not close."

We were back at the apartment, the whole group of us. I'd insisted. Only Alec, disappeared off on some rogue hunt, didn't show. So far the response had been skeptical. Even when I talked about Inman, Mead, and their sacrifice.

"We've tried to go there before," Katherine said. "When Graham and I were still alive."

Katherine paused for a second, I could see her struggling with the word. The idea. I'd never been a spirit, but I imagined part of it meant knowing all the time that you were no longer, well, you. Selena had talked about how she missed the tastes, the colors, and the sounds of the real world. She missed living.

"What I'm trying to say," Katherine continued. "Is that you can't make it there in one night. It takes days. You'll have to cross back before we get there."

"Then we'll try," I said. "I'll go as far as I can. At least to the border of the city. Once you get beyond that, there won't be other guides in your way."

"The forest doesn't need guides to be deadly," Graham said. "There are reasons why we don't go there. Why the guides don't follow spirits beyond the walls."

"You're not helping," Selena said. "And it doesn't matter, right? We can't be killed."

"There are worse things than death in Riven," Katherine said.

"We have to try, don't we?" I said. "Holing up here does nothing."

Graham and Katherine shared a glance, their faces shifting from concerned frowns to resolute lines in light of each other's eyes.

"Carver's right," Katherine said. "As much as I don't like it, we gain nothing by sitting here."

"We'll make the trek," Graham echoed. "Just know it won't be easy."

"You mentioned an army of spirits?" Nicholas said to me. "By my count, we have significantly less than an army here. Even if we make it to the Mountain, I fear we would face impossible odds."

"I think Inman's group took care of some," I said. "And they drew attention. They made a big burning flag and stood beneath it. If we can find a way to get close to the Master without him knowing, then we might have a chance."

"And if you get rid of him, then the spirits go too," Graham said.

"So that's the plan?" Anna said. "We march off into the woods, Carver and I stop at the border, and then we hope the three of you can take care of the Master by yourselves?"

"Four of us, I believe," Nicholas said. I looked at him, raised an eyebrow. "It's time I acquired some field experience. After all, my inventions are only capable of solving the problems that I know of. And quite frankly, I'm running out of problems to solve."

"Any objections?" I said.

"So long as I'm not the one taking care of him," Graham said. "We find the Master, he's mine."

"I'll watch Nicholas," Selena said. "I don't want any part of the Master and his sword. I've already been cut enough for one existence."

We gathered up our things and started the long walk towards the city wall. We went west, through the factory district known as the Tar Pit. Where not long ago we staged a series of fights against Graham, trying to stop him from doing what the Master wanted. To stop him from killing me and opening a way back to the real world.

On the way we avoided the scatter-shot sparks launched into the sky by guides on patrol. Avoided breaches and their angry spirits when we could. Graham and his hammer, Katherine and her batons, Selena and her Cleaver, Anna and her mace, and my lash. Nicholas, behind us, carried a large pack holding gadgets that I didn't understand. He called them his experiments, and told us to be patient whenever we asked what one did.

After several hours we reached the border, the long wall that circled the outside of Riven's city. Unlike the crumbling buildings, it stood strong and solid, several stories high. Kept intact through some force of will that none of us understood.

The gate was open, a wide archway beckoning us to the forest beyond. I could keep going, but if we stayed in Riven too long, our bodies back in the real world would deteriorate from hunger, or dehydration. Like sleeping for days. There had been more than one guide that had spent too long in Riven and found themselves unable to cross back, their body desiccated and dead back home.

"Straight west for another day or two, and then curl north," I said. "You should be able to see the Mountain and then find his tunnels. Find the Master and end it."

"We won't fail," Graham said.

"Always confident," Katherine sighed.

"Life's more fun that way," Graham replied.

"Says the man who wound up enslaved to the guy we're trying to kill," I said. "Try to make it back alive, all right?"

"Alive? Carver, we're well past that," Katherine said.

And then, behind us, Nicholas exploded. I saw it in my mother's eyes, the sudden burst of color over my shoulder. The lights arcing up into the sky and then breaking again and again. Nicholas threw the bursting device onto the street. The rest of us ran to the sides for cover as the device, a small cylinder, eventually stopped spitting the sparks into the air.

"I'm sorry, I'm sorry. It's all my fault," Nicholas exclaimed, running over to us. "It's my panic button. Useful if we were ever under grievous attack. It copies the same spark pattern of a group of guides under assault."

"I noticed," I said. "That means all of you had better run."

"Run?" Anna said.

"Nicholas called every guide within miles to the spot," I said. "If they're still here, we'll have to explain why we've got a bunch about spirits armed to the teeth marching out of the city."

"I'd be interested to hear that explanation," called a voice from down the block. I looked, heart sinking, and saw a squad of five guides staring at us. "Because breaking our laws means a blinding, or worse."

I STEPPED out in front of my friends and held my arms wide so the other guides could see I wasn't hiding anything. "We're taking them to the Cycle."

"Taking them?" the leader of the squad said. The five of them spread out to cover the avenue, their leader front and center, holding a pair of vicious serrated blades. He stared at me from behind his mask, vibrant red with blue flecks. "I didn't think we were in the escort business."

"These spirits are special," I said. "Too dangerous to let go."

"Is that why we saw the panic sparks?"

"An accident," I said. "Nothing more."

I heard movement behind me. Not good. If Graham or Katherine decided to get hotheaded, then guides would lose their lives. Lives we couldn't afford to waste.

"So you've bound a few spirits," the guide said. "Breaking one rule. Now you're allowing them to draw arms against other guides, a violation of another rule. And you've called us off our quota to come save you from nothing at all."

"You're taking this a bit too seriously, don't you think?"

Graham said from behind me. "We're going about our own business. Business that's nothing to do with you and yours."

"Graham, shut it," I said.

"Your spirit has a mouth on him," the guide said, then pointed at Graham. "How about we strike a deal. You wrangle that spirit right here, now. Then we let you go and don't report this."

"That's not going to happen," I said. "For your own good, turn around and don't look back."

"We heard rumors of guides falling away," the leader said, shaking his red mask back and forth. "Enslaving spirits and doing terrible things. I never thought those rumors were true, until now."

"Carver, I don't think he's going to let us go," Anna whispered.

I didn't want this. We should be fighting the Master, not other guides. But I had to choose, and the Master took precedence. I couldn't let this unlucky band of guides stand in our way.

"Don't kill them," I said. Loudly. I rushed the leader. Took three steps, pulled out my lash and snapped it forward as I came within range.

The guy brought his serrated swords in line, catching the lash in one and trying to hack at it with the other, but I pulled the lash back, yanked the sword out of his hand and flung it to the other side of the street.

On my left, I saw Anna and Selena shape up against another guide holding a thin rapier to go with an arm-coating thick cloth. Meant to take the brunt of a scrambling spirit's attack and facilitate a quick counter.

Graham and Katherine lined up against the other three. Standing between them and Nicholas.

"This isn't your fight," I said. The guide in front of me

shifted into a stance, leaning forward with both hands around his remaining sword.

"It is now," the guide spat, and then he charged. I cracked the lash again, this time slipping it between his legs and wrapping around an ankle, sending the guide sprawling. He tried to roll out of the fall, but I yanked the lash back, tightening the grip around the ankle and sending his roll out of control, leaving him sprawled at my feet. I looked down at him.

"End it," I said. "You won't win."

The guide growled at me and made a grab for my ankle, tried to sweep my leg out and send me crashing to the ground. Only I'd seen that move a time or three. Back stepped out of reach. He started to get up, and then I pressed the point of my long knife to the top of his head. He froze. the first good sense he'd shown.

I glanced left, keeping the point of my knife steady, and watched Selena and Anna go through their awkward tango with the rapier-wielding guide. Selena's cleaver didn't give her the reach to get close, but she moved to guide's side, drew her attention from Anna circling the other way with her mace.

"Why would you do this?" the guide I had pinned said. "With all the problems we're facing? Why now?"

Anna charged at the back of the rapier-wielding guide with her mace. It looked good until, as Anna swung her weapon at the guide's back, the guide rotated and shoved her shielded arm in the way. At the same time the guide stabbed towards Selena with the rapier, forcing her back. Or at least, that's what I expected to happen.

Selena, her left-hand empty, reached out and grabbed the rapier and yanked it by the blade out of the guide's hand. Selena's palm bore a brutal gash, but the guide, weaponless, held up her hands. If I were human, a cut like that would've hurt, would have ended my ability to use that hand until it healed. For Selena, the cut would vanish in an hour. An annoyance and nothing more.

"What we're doing," I said. "Is trying to stop Riven from becoming worse. You have to believe me."

On my other side, I saw Katherine and Graham dispatching their guides. Using the hammer, the blunt side rather than the spike, Graham kept two of the guides at bay while Katherine blitzed the third with a dizzying array of jabs and swipes. Too much for the man's large ax to handle. Three swift strikes to the man's stomach and Katherine swept her legs low, tripped him and knocked the guide over. The ax clattered to the ground.

"I have to believe you," the guide in front of me said, a low laugh bubbling up through his lips. "I don't have a choice, do I? If I resist, you'll kill me. You kill all of us."

"We're not going to kill you. We just want you to leave us alone."

Before Katherine could get to his side, the two guides facing Graham charged. One, a burly man with a large metal spear, came in point first. His partner, a lithe figure bristling with knives, feinted in. Graham swung his hammer to stop the spear wielder's charge and didn't catch the knife thrown by the other. The blade embedded itself into Graham's shoulder as his hammer collided with the spear, knocking both of them away.

I saw the blue spark, the pale fire ignite from the lithe guide's hand and trace along a wire I hadn't seen, speeding towards Graham's body. Only my father moved too fast. He dropped the hammer, reached across his chest and, in one smooth motion, drew out the dagger and threw it back at its owner. It struck in her stomach as the fire ran down the link to the hilt, the blade, and over her.

I left my hostage, stuck the knife back in my holster and

ran towards the guide. The burly man, who dropped his spear, met me there.

"I'm taking it out," the man said reaching for the knife. The blade still glowed with the fire, the blue burning along her body.

I knocked his hand away and instead twisted the small device around her wrist, the source of the wire that plugged into the knife. The fire went out and dwindled away along the length of her. "Withdraw the knife, you might hurt her even more. What she needs now is to cross back."

"We're not close to our home," the burly man said.

"Then run. Carry her and go," I said.

"Carver," Anna said from the other side of the street. "Are we letting them leave?"

She said my name. Up until that moment, there was a chance that we hadn't been identified. Guides didn't see each other very often, at least not outside of Riven. Names weren't well known, faces were often hidden by masks. Now, there would be no dodging this mess. Unless we killed all of them.

"Let them leave," I said, banishing that dark thought. "We're not here to kill guides."

The burly man didn't hesitate, grabbed his fallen friend, hefted her in his arms, and ran away down the street. Back towards the center of the city. The other guides grabbed up their weapons, and followed. The leader, the one that I'd had kneeling beneath my blade, turned back to me after he'd put some distance between us.

"Carver Reed," the guide said. "You are a traitor to our order. And I'll see to it that you pay for this."

"I can catch him," Katherine said.

"Let him go," I said. "It doesn't matter anymore. The Master is the only thing that does."

But my words didn't do anything to melt the block of ice forming in my stomach.

WE LEFT them at the gates leading out of the city. Left them with instructions to keep moving on, to go out into the forest and find the Master. To finish him and stop this mess. What I didn't say, what I didn't tell Anna, is that they might not have much time.

I rode the train downtown, got off at Union Station, and had my hand on the door into Ezra's when I felt a tap on my shoulder.

"Haven't seen you in a while, Carver," Opperman, the newspaper reporter who, in his gray suit and thin, newspaper-branded, mask said. "I'm guessing you've been busy?"

"Do you read your own stories?" I replied.

"No, I only write them," Opperman said. "What do you think? Is Riven going to explode? Are we all doomed?"

"Probably," I replied. "Know what a breach is, Opperman?"

"Isn't that where a lot of angry spirits come out at once?"

"It's like an infected wound. One that bleeds and spreads its disease out from the sore. If it's not treated," I said. "It spreads and eventually you die. A breach is like that. And Riven is getting full of them."

For once I left Opperman speechless. Trying to find a way to turn my words into a headline. So I left him and walked into Ezra's purifier. But before I shut the door, Opperman raced in behind me.

"Just once," Opperman said. "I think I'm going to need more from you than a line. This is a chance, Carver, a chance to really tell people what you do. Why they should care."

The purifier sucked out Chicago's dirty air and a moment later the inside to Ezra's stood in front of us.

"Nobody wants to know," I said as I stepped into the bar. "They can't do anything about it. You'd be adding another nightmare to their lives."

"We could stop killing each other," Opperman replied.

I would've laughed at the idea. The thought that guides simply saying a bunch of dead spirits clawing back into the real world could end a war. Piotr, and my former mentor Bryce, had been trying that already for years now. It hadn't worked. It never did. The enemy in front of your eyes made an easier target than the one in the shadows.

Alec sat at our table, and not alone. Two other guides stood up as I walked in, their coats a lighter cast than mine, and I recognized their names and faces. From Detroit, not a far train ride from here.

"Carver, please sit," Alec said. "You know why they're here."

"Because they wanted to give us a visit?" I replied.

Polk and Derringer, those were their names. Polk a wiry man with a penchant for stroking his wispy beard every chance he got. Derringer an athlete, strong and a fan of talking like it. The number of times I'd heard Derringer shout loud agreement with anything Piotr said, well, let's say it'd been a running game between Alec and I. Bets to see how often we'd hear his bellowing roars of approval.

"You're breaking rules," Derringer said. "They exist for a reason, Carver. Just because you were the head of Chicago, doesn't mean you get to disregard our principles."

"And even though you think you're right, doesn't mean you are," I said.

"Nina nearly died, Carver," Alec said. "As it is, she's in the hospital over there in New York. Serious internal injuries."

At least she'd lived. Whatever they were planning to do to me, if the guide Graham had injured hadn't survived, it would've been much worse. "They attacked me."

"With good reason," Polk said. "What were you doing with all those spirits anyway? Planning something sinister, no doubt."

"What does it matter?" I said. "I'm assuming Piotr told you to come here?"

"I said we wouldn't need them," Alec said. "But Piotr insisted. Said that you would resist."

"What do you think Alec," I said. "Should I? Should I resist?"

"We're going to blind you," Derringer said. "Keep you from doing this ever again. So yes, resist. It would make it more satisfying."

I kept my eyes on Alec. Watched his face. He knew all about Graham and the others. Knew about the Master, and what we were trying to do. I could tell he didn't want any part of this. When his eyes met mine, I shook my head slightly. No need for him to sacrifice himself here. If they blinded me, then Alec would be the only one who could take my place. Find Selena, Graham and Katherine. Continue to fight.

"You've got a deal," I said, and made a break for the door. Blinding meant cutting off my access to Riven. Burning away what allowed me to cross over. Polk and Derringer weren't going to take that from me.

I heard a loud crash from behind me, Derringer swearing.

"Oh, I'm so sorry," Opperman said. "Always so clumsy before I've had my first cup of coffee."

I shut the door to the purifier behind me. Stuck my mask on, and ran out onto the streets of Chicago. A fugitive from my own friends.

7 8

I RAN AT RANDOM. Trying to get away from Ezra's. I took a turn left here, right there. Gradually heading towards the lake, but otherwise without a destination. A problem with being a guide is that you don't make many friends. At least, not those outside your own field. As my field wanted me out, I had to look elsewhere.

Which left two places: the construction site, with Anna and the sneaks. I didn't want to cross into Riven from the construction site, because I didn't have any equipment there. I'd be in the Warrens without a weapon, at the mercy of any guides or spirits that happened to be waiting. I needed to get back into the clock tower and get my things out.

My second option would bring me there.

I figured Alec and the others would be watching the trains, so instead I looked for one of the small motoring taxis drifting through the streets. Small vehicles with benches on the outside and slat roofs over the top in case of rain. Downtown, the things ran on tracks laid in the streets. Tracks that funneled electricity up through their wheels. All part of the efforts to reduce pollution. Farther out, near my apartment, larger oil-burning buses were the norm.

As a taxi trundled past, with only one other person on the opposite side, I took three steps, reached out and grabbed a pole and hauled myself into a seat. Reached over the long console in the middle of the taxi and plugged in my stop by setting a green pin into the map of downtown Chicago. The map's edges were the limits of the taxi's coverage.

My pin would be the second one on the taxi's journey. I'd been lucky. The other passenger had placed his destination in the same direction. His black pin marked the first stop, and only blocks from my target. I sat back and thought.

It would take Alec, Polk, and Derringer time to cross over. Time to let everyone know that I had fled their attempted capture. Alec would doubtless be given my position as Chicago's lead guide. They might give Anna a pass as she'd been inducted less than a day. The other guides we fought wouldn't even have known who she was. I hoped Alec wouldn't go after her either.

I had to keep the other guides from blinding me. So long as I could cross to Riven, my binding on Katherine and Selena would stay. Keep their spirits sane.

I needed to evade capture long enough for my parents to take care of the Master. After that, well, I could take it one problem at a time. Go into hiding and find a better plan.

Maybe I'd turn out like Inman and the others; living outside the city and crossing over on my own vigilante efforts. Help the guides from the shadows. It would mean losing some comforts, sure, but I would still have Selena. There would still be us.

It took an hour, but the taxi eventually trembled to a stop on the street corner I'd been waiting for. I got off, looked up and down the block. Didn't see anything. The sidewalks their usual deserted. The small yards left to their own scraggly weeds. Whatever could grow in the grime. Nobody would be outside at this time of the morning. Everyone either at work or indoors; anywhere you weren't breathing in the terrible air.

I had tried it once, on a bet from Bryce. The goal being that I could take more than three breaths without coughing. I had lasted one. Drinking in the air around here felt like inhaling dry mud. Thick, grainy, and tasting of a million disgusting things. So I kept my mask on, and its respirator did its job.

I knocked on the door; a deep brown oak number in front of a two-story house. Brick and quaint. Squashed between a pair of similar buildings. The kind of home I wouldn't have minded owning one day, assuming I lived that long. I expected to hear the patter of feet, the yelps of children, but there weren't any.

Right. School.

When the door opened, the face I saw my mentor's tired face. Sad and bent.

"Get inside," Bryce said to me. As I stepped by him, he peeked out the door and looked up and down the block. "You weren't followed?"

"I don't think so," I said. "I moved fast, and I don't think Alec really wanted to catch me."

"I don't know," Bryce said. He shut the door and the house's purifiers kicked into action. "He came by this morning. Earlier. Told me what happened. He thinks you've gone too far."

"Too far?" I said. "He was there. He fought Graham."

"He won't risk his life for you. Here," Bryce said. "Take off your mask. Let's get you downstairs. Where you can't be seen."

I followed Bryce through his house and down a flight of stairs below the ground. Through a room packed with boxes and a large furnace with a pile of wood nearby. Summer heat left it unlit, the iron cool and dark. A bed for one sat in a back room, surrounded by clutter.

"What do you mean?" I said as I looked around.

"Alec 's been with the guides longer than you," Bryce said. "Depends on them for his lifestyle. I'm not saying it'll be easy for him, but if it comes between you and everything he knows and depends on; I'm sorry Carver."

"What about you?" I said.

"I'm retired," Bryce gave me a grin that died almost as fast as it came. "But I can't risk my family. You can stay here for now. Not forever."

"You should know," I said. "We know where the Master is. Graham and the others, they're going for him right now. This whole thing could be over soon."

"That's why I brought you down here," Bryce said. "I figured you'd want to cross."

I looked down at the bed. A wimpy frame, a small mattress. Not what I expected from the man who'd been Chicago's lead guide for over a decade. "This leads to the clock tower?"

"It doesn't look like much," Bryce said. "But it will get you there. Before you ask, the reason it's down here, in the basement? My wife came down every morning I crossed to check, in case something went wrong. To keep my children from finding their father's body."

MY EYES OPENED in the clock tower, the center chamber a mix of wood and stone with a line of beds on either side of me. The weapon rack in front holding my lash, my long knife. For the first time waking up in here felt wrong. Like at any moment I could be attacked by a fellow guide. By Alec. My sanctuary was one no longer.

These were odd hours for our region. Noon back in the real world, when most of our hunts happened at night. I took my gear off the rack and left the clock tower without interference. Made it past the fountain without any guide seeing me. Spent the next half an hour ducking through alleys and avoiding the occasional sparks launched into the air from groups of guides on patrol.

I wondered if sneaks felt this way; always watching over your shoulder and looking around corners to make sure you weren't about to be caught by a guide or torn apart by an angry spirit.

As strange as it had felt to wake up in the clock tower and feel like an intruder, going into the building Nicholas, Graham, Katherine, and Selena had occupied felt even stranger. Nobody home. Devoid of any of the spirits for the first time in months. Nicholas's machines were still there on the first floor, quiet and cool.

I wandered through my parents' place on the second floor; it was utilitarian. Arranged to provide maximum sight lines to entrances and exits, and they had placed a ladder alongside the balcony, one that could extend all the way down to the ground. Ever ready in the case of an emergency.

Checking to see if they were home, that's what I told myself. If they'd already come back from fighting the Master. Or maybe failed to find him and returned. Except, I knew they wouldn't be there.

I'd come to the apartment because it might be my new home. Without the clock tower, I needed a base. The apartment, with Selena, my parents, and Nicholas made the best candidate.

I made my way up to Selena's balcony, where we shared so many hours talking and watching the shiftless sky. Watching the sparks break over the city roofs. I wanted to try something I'd never done before. Something I'd only ever seen with my life hanging on the edge of ruin.

Barth, the mad guide that had tried to kill us in his tower, he'd talked to the Master from a distance. Had a whole conversation in a room without the Master even there. Graham, about to kill me on top of Riven's wall, had been ordered to stay his hand from afar. If the Master could do it, then why couldn't I?

I didn't know how to start. I didn't have instructions, no easy option like flicking on a light switch. Or humming a song. Instead, I tried to find the missing pieces of me. The parts that I had given to Selena, to Katherine, to Nicholas to keep them sane. The connection that bound me to them.

The hollow parts weren't hard to find. Like a tongue feeling for a missing tooth, or sore throat that had disappeared. An expectation reflexively looked but not found. And that missing tooth or that sore throat, each one, each missing piece had a spirit tied to it.

I found Nicholas first. The connection tying the two of us together feeling cool and distant. Like stumbling on a new bump on my skin in the dark and not being quite sure where it was. Only, when I pressed, focused on that feeling, shadowy sensations came through. As though touching something through a cloth. Nicholas's experiences at that moment; his temperature, his emotion, the sense of the world around him. Perhaps I could reach through the other way.

"Nicholas," I said. I spoke the word aloud, and, as much as I was able to, tried to press it through the connection. Thought the word at the link between us. Then I felt the shock. The flare of surprise come through our bond.

"Can you hear me?" I sent through. Another wave of surprise. Then a pause. Followed by frustration. "Try to talk back."

I waited. Felt the frustration growing in our link. And then it died away entirely, faded to a calm. What was he doing? I opened my mouth, about to speak again, when I felt a chill rush.

"Carver?" I couldn't hear her voice, at least not in the usual way. She came through more like a sensation. Like when you imagine someone talking to you in your head. "Where are you?"

Selena had figured it out. I latched on to her voice, or my rendition of it. "I'm back at the apartment. Can you hear me?" I said.

This time, instead of frustration, I felt the warm glow of happiness. Surprise mingling with a smile. "I can," Selena said. "In a way. Are you all right?"

"I'm better now," I said. "It's been a rough day. Are you making progress?"

"We're still in the forest, but moving fast. We can see the Mountain now, whenever the branches clear up enough for us. We should be there soon, Graham thinks."

"I'm sorry I can't be there," I said.

"I wish you were," Selena replied. "But it's nice to know I'm saving you for once."

"I could get used to that," I replied.

I listened to her describe the forest, talk about how the group was getting along. The four spirits venturing on. Graham getting more annoyed with Nicholas every time he stopped to try another experiment. Katherine playing mediator. Selena, well, she was enjoying the chance to explore. To get out from between the crumbling canyons of the city for a little while and see something new.

I don't know how long we were talking, sending our words over miles and miles, but it ended when the apartment door swung open. It ended with a voice I knew saying my name.

"You shouldn't have come back here," Alec said. "If I couldn't find you, then I wouldn't have to kill you."

8 0

I DIDN'T SAY anything to him at first. Instead, I focused on sending one last message to Selena. "I've got to go," I said. "If you don't hear from me again, I love you."

"Look at this, now you are talking to yourself," Alec said.

"I can still reach them," I said, turning to face my friend. "Just like Graham and the Master."

"So you are the same now?" Alec said. "You will start getting the same ideas? Binding more spirits? Find guides more loyal to you than our order?"

"You know I wouldn't do that," I said.

"I do?" Alec said. "We fought to save your life, Carver. To keep this world and ours apart. Now here we are, on opposite sides. Do I chance everything by playing nice? Walking away? I feel like the risk we are taking is letting you live at all."

"Think about what you're saying," I said. Scrambling here, trying to keep Alec talking. My back leaned against the railing of the balcony, a thirty-foot fall to the ground. Alec stood between me and the door. No easy way out.

"Prove me wrong," Alec said. "I am begging you, friend. Show me a better path."

"You have to trust me," I said. "We're almost there."

"If you are, then may the guides damn me for what I am about to do," Alec said.

He ran at me, those gauntleted fists of his swinging low. No time to bring out the lash. I grabbed the knife and stabbed forward as Alec closed. But the guide jumped, grabbed the frame of the balcony opening, and swung his feet at me as my knife stabbed air beneath. The kick knocked me into the railing, almost threw me off. I ducked as Alec swung for my head.

He missed with that one, but the right hook was just a feint for a left. Alec's metal fist connected with my kidney, an organ that didn't exist in Riven, but that hurt all the same. Alec grabbed me as I started to fall back over the railing, and threw me into the apartment. I bounced off Selena's table and landed hard against the wall.

Every time my back hit something, I felt the pressure along my spine as the crossbow shaft jammed against it. This time, that jarring ache gave me an idea. Alec walked in towards me, slow.

"I do not love this," Alec said. "This is not fun."

"Great, I was real worried," I muttered. My right hand grabbed the hilt of my lash. I stood up, stared Alec straight in the eye. Ignored the nausea coming up from my rollicking stomach, the bruising ache from my back.

"I promise you," Alec said. "After this, I will continue your hunt for the Master."

"Aren't you a regular saint," I said. I raised the lash, and Alec flipped the table towards me. Launched it with both arms. I shifted my shoulder to block it and the table pressed me to the wall. Alec came after. A series of quick jabs into my side.

I rolled away and Alec let me escape, let me get some distance. If I'd been a spirit, or someone he truly hated, those gauntlets would've kept pounding me until I was nothing more than mush.

"Who told you?" I said. "Who gave the order to blind me?"

"Polk and Derringer were at Ezra's when I arrived," Alec said. "They told me it came from Piotr. Hours earlier."

"Piotr didn't want to talk?" I said. I once again had my back to the balcony, Alec advancing towards me.

"He is a busy man," Alec said. "Enough of this, Carver. It's time to go."

Alec darted forward, the same run-up to a punch that I'd seen him do a hundred times. I flicked the lash towards his feet, to the left. Alec moved fast, jumped over the strike, only I wasn't aiming at him. The lash wrapped itself around the leg of the table and I pulled it tight as Alec came through the doorway to the balcony.

The lash's cord swept up through the doorway and caught Alec's ankle. Tripped him and sent him flying into the railing. I ran back through the other way. Slipped the lash back in my holster and reached over my shoulder to pull up the crossbow. Locked in an orange bolt as Alec picked himself up and turned towards me.

"You know what this can do," I said, leveling the crossbow at Alec.

"You would burn down this building," Alec said.

"I don't exactly have a lot to lose," I said.

"What is your offer?"

"Let me leave. You can say you didn't find me, we can forget this happened," I said. "Then, after I deal with the Master, I'll come back and you can blind me."

Alec stared at me for another moment. Weighed the options. Nodded. "Go. But I will keep looking for you. Next time I won't be alone."

I didn't give him a chance to change his mind. Ducked out of the apartment, ran down the stairs, hit the ground floor and dashed out into the streets. Like Chicago, I went at random but always with one general direction in mind. I had to make a stop, and then I would have to cross back. I had no doubt Alec would be waiting at the once place I could do that.

The clock tower.

8 1

I WATCHED the clock tower from the top room of a building across the courtyard. Looked right over the fountain at the guides standing in front of where I needed to go. Three of them, and Alec stood in the middle.

Crossing out of Riven meant tying yourself to a location. My body, my real body, sat in Bryce's basement. That bed linked to this location in Riven, the clock tower. Every time Bryce crossed from that bed, he would appear in the same place over here. It's how we managed to keep our equipment where we needed it. How we determined which regions guides around the world would patrol.

It wasn't all that hard to find a new place to cross over from the real world. You needed somewhere you could fall asleep. Some guides were so good, so able to relax on any floor, that they could cross in and out anywhere. That didn't work for me, but maybe I needed to rethink my comforts. I'd never been able to cross over without a cushion or a mat. Somewhere safe. Getting *out* of Riven, though, only had one option. Had to go out the same way you came in.

That meant the clock tower. Finding my bed and crossing back. I didn't think Alec and the other guides would just let me by without a fight.

But I hadn't come empty-handed. My lash, my knife, I'd left those back in the Warrens. Where Anna and Laurence crossed over from their hideout beneath the construction site. A place, so far as I knew, Alec and Bryce didn't know existed. The one thing I'd brought with me?

The crossbow.

The orange bolted loaded from the fight with Alec was still ready for action. I went over to the crumbled wall that faced another street, out of sight from the guides in front of the clock tower. Aimed the crossbow at a house half a block down. Fired.

My shot zipped across the street, struck the building, and burst into orange fire. The blazing rays climbed up and down the house, and left towards the buildings around it, spreading into an all-consuming nova. I backed up and glanced out back towards the clock tower, and saw what I'd hope for. Alec and the other guides running across the court-yard towards the blossoming burn.

As they passed by my spot, I dashed down the stairs and sprinted across the courtyard. Behind me I heard their shouts, Alec calling for them to search the nearby buildings and keep their distance from the fire. At the entrance to the clock tower, I took a second to look back. To make sure Nicholas's invention wasn't going to roast the entire city.

It looked like solid spiderweb, orange burning lines lancing from place to place, connecting with stone, wood, or wandering spirits and flaming into a new nova. At the edges, though, the intensity faded. The jumps were shorter. The lines smoked and died. I hadn't destroyed the city to make my escape. At least, not entirely.

"It was an ugly block anyway," I said to myself as I slipped inside the clock tower. I shoved the crossbow beneath the bed as I jumped in it. Not that I expected it to remain hidden, but I could use any minutes they spent not knowing I'd already crossed back.

I closed my eyes, and slipped back to Chicago.

8 2

Bryce's basement had no lights, felt like midnight, even though I knew it was only mid-afternoon. I curled out of the bed and felt my way along to the stairs.

I took the steps up slowly, testing each one for creaks. Bryce had given me a chance, and I didn't want him to die for it. Or suffer. The sooner I left his house, the sooner he could claim I'd never arrived. The sooner his family would be free from the risk I carried with me.

I heard thumps from the front door, exclamations of welcome from Bryce and his wife as their kids came home. I took the opportunity to slip from the basement and head back to the kitchen. Went by the nook where, not long ago, Bryce had told me about his quest to find my mother. Back when things had seemed so much simpler.

Out the back door, my fingers catching the metal frame as it closed to muffle the noise. An empty lawn, a plot for a garden that would never grow. An alley where, every so often, crews in large trash tanks would trundle by and collect the refuse. Only when I lost sight of Bryce's home did I give myself a chance to breathe. To take in the summer weather filtering through my mask and beneath my coat.

I'd taken one step towards my new life. Now came the second.

The construction moved fast. When I first came here months ago, there had been piles of steel bars and a plot of land. Now a frame loomed seven stories high. Powered winches and pulleys shoved material up and down, back and forth, while workers sporting various equipment welded, tied, or measured every new piece. A foreman stood at the base with a monoscope, flipping through the various lenses to zoom in on his team's activity and shout out instruction.

Nobody noticed, or bothered, to call out my presence as I walked behind them. As I slipped around the edge of the construction site and headed down a steep set of stairs. The door had a knocker but I ignored it. Twisted the handle and went straight in.

Down the main hallway, beyond a pair of rooms that were always closed off, and into the center chamber. Dominated by a big table with scattered bits of food and drink on it, the room drew my eyes to its walls. To the maps hanging there, outlining parts of Riven in detail ranging from perfect to light sketches and theories. Candles burned. Still no electricity down here.

I reached inside my front coat pocket and drew out the map taken from Mead's cabin. Unfolded it and tried to find where, if, it matched the ones on the wall.

"You ever think to knock?" Laurence, Anna's partner and a generally unappreciative fellow, said to me as he walked in the room. "We're not your apartment."

"Now you are," I said. Laurence looked confused, which was the point.

"They kicked you out?" Anna said, following her partner

to the room. "We were waiting here, like you said. But I didn't think they would actually do it."

"The rules are clear," I said. "Hurt another guide and you're going to get blinded."

"You didn't hurt her."

"Graham did," I said. "Close enough."

"He's my spirit," Anna replied, drawing a questioning look from Laurence.

"Don't say that," I said. "If they don't know, then they can't come after you. I've already taken the fall."

"That's the first smart thing I've ever heard you say," Laurence said.

"Someday, Laurence, we'll be friends," I said.

"Hey, you give me a weapon like hers, I'll call us good," Laurence said. "Till then, you're just a guy that shows up every now and then who gives me grief."

I went towards the wall, towards the map of the forest that hung from the back. Held up Mead's map to it. They were close, but the sneak's map had more detail. More symbols.

"Is this your map?" I asked Anna, she shook her head.

"It's mine," Laurence said. "I do the exploring, Anna handles the clients. What do you have there? You draw a map of your own?"

I relayed the story. The kidnapping on the train, the ambush attempt on the Master. Anna had heard most of it before, but it was worth taking the time just to see Laurence's eyes bug out.

"On my way back, I found this map. That's how we know where the Master is," I said. "You've got more on your version. Like this one spot, here."

I pointed to the large red circle, directly on the path between the city and the Mountain. Shaded in with the words *avoid at all cost* next to it. Laurence came close, put his finger on it, humming to himself.

"Yeah, I remember what that is," Laurence said. "It's a ghoul. A real old, nasty one. I studied it for a while, kept out of sight. Seems to stick to that area, which is why I drew the circle."

"It's right on the path," Anna said. "They might walk right into it."

"The path to the Cycle?" Laurence said. "Because that's the route you're looking at. It's why think the ghoul's there in the first place. Plenty of spirits walking by, and it snaps them up."

"Wait," I said. "You're saying the Cycle is in the Mountain?"

"I mean, I've never seen it," Laurence said. "But I've come close. Tracked enough spirits to see them go into those caves and never come back out."

"It could be on the other side," I offered, and Laurence shrugged.

"Maybe. I'll tell you right now, you go anywhere near that ghoul, you better be ready. It's not normal."

"We have to warn them," I said to Anna.

"How?" Anna replied.

"I've got a new trick to show you," I said. "Let's cross."

8 3

THE WARRENS. A miserable mess of sprawling apartments, crumbling buildings, and lost spirits. If you wanted to hide, the maze made for a good spot. We crossed over into the basement of one of those buildings. A six-story monolith bland in every way except for its height. We didn't wake up in beds, instead I stood up from a mat with ratty pillows on the ground.

"This place could really use an upgrade," I said, stretching out.

"Oh, I'm sorry it's not up to your standards. I'll get right on that," Anna replied.

"You should," I said. "The better your site is, the easier the crossings get. If you're under pressure, every bit of comfort helps."

"Why would we be under pressure?" Anna replied. "Oh yeah. Because now every guide in this place is hunting us."

"You should be used to that," I said. Sneaks weren't exactly targeted by guides, but they found Anna skulking around and talking to spirits, guides would take care of her. They would give her a choice. Give up her location in the real world and get blinded. Or die, right there and then, for interfering with Riven and the spirits of the dead.

"I thought my sneaking days were done when I became one of you guys," Anna said.

"I thought they were too."

Anna led me to the top of the building. I didn't know whether or not height would make things easier, but we could see farther. Had a better chance of noticing any guides before they got to us. If we had to, we could run and the guides wouldn't know where we crossed from. We had to keep our exit hidden. I didn't have a crossbow anymore, didn't have a good way to create a distraction so we could dash by and cross over to the other side.

Anna watched as I reached into myself and felt for those missing pieces. As I tried to open the channel between Selena and I. Last time, I'd felt the wave of emotions coming back through. The rush of feeling and sensation, like a breeze on a dead wind day. Only now I felt nothing. As though my mind ran into a hard wall. I tried Nicholas, my mother, and they were the same.

"I'm not getting them," I said. "Try Graham."

I walked her through it and Anna closed her eyes and concentration. In a minute later open them, shaking her head.

"Nothing," Anna said. "I can feel where he should be, that part of me that isn't there, but when I tried to connect with it... I couldn't feel anything."

"I don't know what that means," I said. "They might be dead. Cycled. Or maybe a guide found them and they've been wrangled apart from us."

"Wouldn't that give us back the parts of ourselves?" Anna said. "When the binding is severed, don't we get ourselves back?"

I nodded. The sneak had a point. Those parts of me were

still missing, which meant Selena and Katherine and Nicholas were out there still. Stuck in that forest somewhere.

The forest. A place we couldn't get to. Unless...

"I have an idea," I said. "We're going to have to take a little trip."

FOR THE SECOND time in years I rode on a train heading outside of Chicago. This time, nobody pointed a gun at me. Much nicer sitting with Anna and watching as the city trailed off into grain-filled fields.

"Have you ever been out here?" I asked her.

"Plenty of times," Anna said. "Sometimes clients write me. Or wrote me, I suppose. They didn't want to come in the city, so I would go out to them."

"Quite the service," I said.

"We charged them for it," Anna said.

"Did you ever feel bad?" I said. "Taking advantage of people's grief?"

"Do you ever feel bad? Sending people to oblivion that they can't escape?"

"I didn't ask for this," I said. "But no, it's my job, and it's a necessary one."

"That's how I felt too," Anna said. "If people want closure, and I can give it to them, then why shouldn't I?"

Another time I would've pushed her on that point. I would've made an argument about how it's harder for people to move on if they think about the one they lost wandering in that desolate wasteland. Hard to get over disaster if they think they could still, maybe, have one last conversation with that person. But I didn't. I stayed quiet and let Anna have her moment out the window.

Who was I to define right and wrong?

An hour later the train pulled into the station. The last one of the day, the sun setting over the bluffs. It felt familiar, like when I came there last. Only this time there weren't any horses. No gruff former guides waiting to escort me up into the wilderness. Just Anna and I walking along the road.

Some people spared us a glance or two, but, like in the city, people preferred to pretend we didn't exist. Carriages called out to other passengers to ask if they wanted rides and ignored us. Even some of the horses shied away as we walked past the posts.

Once we were away from the station and walking the path that led towards the bluff, I pulled off my mask. Anna followed suit.

"I wondered when you were going to do that," Anna said. "I feared I'd forgotten some rule."

"The air is better out here," I said. "But if you've been reading the papers, listening to the people, there's a lot of disease. We're not immune to that."

"You're paranoid," Anna said.

"Cautious," I replied.

We continued up the path, going up and around rocks and underneath the wide trees. I kept scanning the canopies for the bats, those funny creatures flitting in the twilight. So unlike birds with their spastic patterns.

"Carver," Anna said, her voice in a whisper. "I think there's someone up there."

I paused and followed her pointing finger. There were lights ahead. Not the flickering of a campfire, but electric.

Plenty of them. I nodded towards the side and Anna went with me into the brush. We moved slow, stepping over ferns and between the scraggly branches of newly grown trees, but if anything came up or down that path they would have a hard time seeing us.

At least eight uniformed policemen and their horses stood around the campground. Poking around and loading the rigid bodies into carts. I don't know why didn't think of it. Of course a massive die off out here in the woods would attract attention.

I reached in my coat and felt the hilt, the metal of Inman's pistol. Not that I had any kind of experience with these things, but I worked with the weapons I had.

"You're not going to fight them," Anna said.

"I don't want to," I said. "I think if we wait, they won't stay all night."

"You want to just sit here?"

"I don't see any other option."

We hunkered down beneath a large bush, bugs swirling around our heads, and watched as the officers continued digging around. Calling to each other whenever they found something interesting. I laid my head on my hands, and watched as the sun finished its descent and plunged the forest into night.

"Hey," Anna whispered. "I think they're gone."

I open my eyes. Stunned for a moment. I'd actually fallen asleep. Taken a nap. Probably for the first time in years.

The lights were still there, electric lamps set up and plugged into a large box of a battery. The lights illuminated a sign that said *Keep Out - Active Investigation*. Beyond that, beyond the ever present wildlife, there were no noises.

"Keep your eyes on the ground," Anna said as we moved closer. "They'll have triggers to keep animals away."

"You've done this before?" I said.

"Not everything we get paid for happens in Riven," Anna said. "I learned how to get around."

"Remind me to stop underestimating you," I said.

We made our way to the campground and over to the cabin where I crossed over not two nights ago. Where Inman's body had been. The police had replaced it chalk mark. A small note saying a body had been here.

"This is it," I said. "If we cross over here, we'll be in the forest."

I told her to take the bed that I'd gone in. I slipped into Inman's. I didn't know precisely where I'd cross over, but I figured we be able to find each other. Either that or we'd be arriving alone, without weapons, into a forest full of danger.

I AWOKE under the gray grim trees. Those black leaves shaded the pale light, casting dark shadows all along the dead ground. The breeze blew, rippling through the branches, adding a lifeless chime to the place.

There were some marks on the ground, flattened parts of broken stems leading towards the clearing. I followed them, hoping Anna would do the same. Before long I'd returned to the same spot where I'd seen Inman carved in two, where so many former guides had fallen. The scars were there. The black lines running up and down the trees, weapons scattered about along with the occasional bit of cloth. Pieces torn from guide coats and masks. Otherwise, there were no bodies. Riven didn't have those. Not for long, anyway.

I'd seen it happen before. A guide falls and, in the aftermath, their bodies slowly disappear. Their spirits awaken elsewhere in Riven. Or sometimes right on top of their corpse. As the energy faded, so did the body, and the spirit started its walk to the Cycle.

"You weren't lying," Anna said as she stepped into the clearing and looked around.

"You thought I was?"

"No," Anna said. "I guess not, but your sounded strange. A bunch of guides massacred by an army of spirits and a crazy villain wielding a giant sword?"

"For Riven? That's almost every day," I said.

"For you, maybe. At least now we have weapons," Anna said. The sneak had a point. We had crossed over empty-handed, all of our gear far away in the Warrens. There were plenty of weapons scattered around the clearing and I didn't their former owners wouldn't mind us taking them. We both fished around for something we knew how to use.

In the middle the clearing, I found Inman's two pistols, his long knife and a pile of spare bullets. Not my favorite weapons, but the guns were small enough to take along. I slipped them into my pockets. Took the knife and then found a longer sword on another body. No lash, but I could use the edged weapons.

"Check this out," Anna said. I looked her way and saw her holding what looked like a long chain with handles on either end. Along the length of the links were tiny spikes, serrated edges meant for cutting. "What do you think?"

"That doesn't look easy to use," I said. "And tonight is not the time to learn on the fly."

"I'm going to take it," Anna shrugged.

I helped Anna find another couple of knives to slot in her belt and then we looked around. There weren't a lot of markers for where to go. If I remembered Mead's map correctly, then the Mountain stood northwest of here. The path the others had taken would be straight north.

"I agree," Anna said. "How can you tell directions? There are no stars."

"Look," I said, pointing towards one part of the clearing. The grass there was decimated, trampled under more pounding feet than any other part. "If most of the spirits came from that way, and the Master lives in the Mountain, then that would be where we want to go. We just follow the tracks."

Anna didn't argue, and we set off through the woods. Anna played with the chain. Practiced whirling around, and nearly took my head off once or twice. Still, I'd rather she knew what to do with it when the time came.

It felt like hours, but without any moving sun or changes in light, it was impossible to tell time in Riven. Eventually, in front of us, a crowded line of spirits appeared. They walked, blank-eyed and without speaking, through the forest. Towards the Cycle. Ghosts shifting through the trees.

We came to the edge of the path and watched them. The long line of soldiers, sick patients, and normal men, women, and children in a long walk towards the last moments of their existence. Wandering Riven, you saw people of every color and background, every race and origin. Some crossed over covered in tattoos, or piercings, while others wore elaborate headdresses and spiritual robes.

I'd never seen them all at once. Never noticed how many hundreds and thousands of spirits must be walking this road every minute of every day. How few must be losing their minds in order for us to keep Riven safe.

"It's almost beautiful," Anna said, her eyes running down the line. "All of them, from all these different places and they're all at peace."

"For now," I said. "I never realized. If all of these spirits turned, there would be no way. No way we could hold them back."

"The world is a big place," Anna said.

We watched for a while longer until, shaking my head, I pulled Anna between a pair of dead-eyed soldiers and we made it to the other side of the path.

"Let's keep walking along. If I remember right, on

Laurence's map, that circle is somewhere up ahead," I said. "If anything took Graham and the others, it would be that."

"You think we can fight it?" Anna said. "Us? Alone?"

"Alec and I fought ghouls and won," I said. "Anyway, we don't have a choice."

"Oh, that makes me feel better," Anna sighed.

We marched along with the spirits, matching their steps and staring off into the woods, looking for any sign of our friends.

IT WASN'T hard to see where Laurence's red circle began. Off to the side of the path, to our right as we walked alongside the spirits, was what looked like a giant hollowed-out tree. A stump as tall as the other trunks in the area. Its open-air top a ridge line of broken bark reaching up towards the sky.

"What do you want to bet that's where Laurence found the ghoul?" I said.

"You're the expert on these things," Anna replied.

True. While I hadn't hunted many ghouls - the first one only came with Alec a few months back - you could spot the telltale signs: torn up sections of Riven, a lack of angry spirits, and a general sense that you were not where you should be.

"What's messing with me is that ghouls normally crop up when there are bunch of angry spirits in an area," I said. "All of these spirits are passive. Or they've been wrangled by a guide back in the city."

"Do ghouls age?" Anna said. "Does anything age in Riven? Maybe there used to be spirits here. Laurence said he thought the ghoul looked old."

The sneak had a good point. Riven didn't seem to change all that much, except the slow deterioration of its buildings. A crumbling as much to do with the fighting between angry spirits and guides as any sort of natural force.

"It's possible," I said. "Normally anything big enough to get noticed gets taken care of quick."

"I'm saying we don't know what this thing is," Anna said. "If we try to think that this is something we've seen before, it could be a bad idea."

"So be ready for anything."

"Right," Anna said.

We left the spirits behind and walked up to the stump. Searched our way around its base. The stump's bark a fading brown, unlike the gray forest. Patterns and textures lined the wood, unlike the featureless trunks of the other Riven trees. Whatever had once grown, whatever had produced this stump, had been something unique.

"There's an entrance," Anna said. She walked a few steps ahead of me, around a curve in the stump. I followed and looked. Saw something less an entrance than a torn hole. Jagged edges and splintered chunks of bark surrounded a space twenty feet wide. Light vanished into that hole, bending into the ground.

"This seems ominous," I said.

"We crept into a campground full of bodies, looted the weapons left over from murdered guides, walked along the trail with thousands of other spirits, and now you're saying this, this is the ominous part?" Anna said.

"I stand by it," I replied. "Never walked into a tree before."

"We're both getting a lot of firsts today," Anna said.

We took our first steps through the entrance into the stump. My hand drifted towards my belt where, normally, I'd have a sparker. Something to shoot light out in front of me.

Without one, we descended into the dark with only the faintest glimmer of reflected gray following us.

The air changed as we went down, thickening and growing pungent with the smell of rot. An usual smell in Riven, where souls didn't decay. Something lived down here. Or had lived.

The pathway stayed wide enough that Anna and I could stretch our arms around us and not hit an edge. That didn't give me a lot of confidence. I preferred any monsters to be smaller than me. Strange how rarely that happened.

The ground beneath our feet changed over from dirt to polished wood. Only, as I knelt down to feel the smooth ground, it felt like rock flattened by ocean waves through years and years of pressure. The kind of stones you would find on a beach, smooth and clean.

Just as the last bit of light winked out behind us, we saw a flicker in front. A whisper of a glow sneaking out around a bend. We followed it, taking each step slower than the last. Noises, the shifting growls and grumbles of a large creature making the most of its next meal echoed their way down to us.

"I didn't think ghouls had to eat," Anna said.

"I don't think this is just a ghoul," I said.

When we turned the corner, I wasn't thrilled to see I was right.

In front of us, bathed in the light from a hole in the stump's roof overhead, hung a gnarled mass of roots, plants, and bodies. Spirits ensnared in vines and branches, a roiling ball linking to the outsides of the stump through veins of wood and pulsing green stems. The sphere sat suspended in the center of the stump, like a marble caught in a spider's web.

As we watched, the thing moved and shifted. Morphed and sent bits of itself crawling up and down the stems, arms and legs reaching out and being drawn back. Occasionally a face appeared, small and rough in the mass, but always with its mouth open in a wide and silent scream.

"Of all the horrors in Riven," I said. "I've never seen one like this."

"Laurence wasn't lying," Anna said, her voice devoid of feeling, in total shock. "I don't even know what to call this. What it is."

"Wait, look closer," I said. I could see along the sphere, along the stems that held the ball up, there were cuts. Deep gashes and burns. Wounds suffered in a fight, and some of them still dripped bits of phosphorescent goo onto the ground. "It's hurt."

"Graham," Anna said. She straightened, looked at me. "I feel it. The part of me that I lost."

"What?" I said, but followed her words. Felt for my own connections, that piece of myself long since given to Selena. And found it. For the first time in years, my body and soul were whole. Which meant...

"They're gone," Anna said. "That's the only way the binding breaks, right?"

I nodded. Selena, I couldn't feel her anymore. She'd given that part back to me. Or had it taken from her. I gripped the sword I'd taken from the guide's body and drew it from my belt.

"There's only one way to get them back," I said.

I took the lead, running into the central chamber with the sword in my right hand and one of Inman's pistols, loaded and ready to fire, in my left. I almost fell. My legs moved faster than before. My muscles felt stronger, lighter. Even my eyes were sharper; I caught the changes in the flickering gray as the beast shifted its tendrils and limbs around, picked out the numerous wounds delivered by our friends.

I was whole.

Not that the ghoul cared.

I didn't see any eyes, but it noticed us. With snapping, crackling noises the ghoul withdrew its connections to the stump. Ripped off the branches and veins until its mass slammed into the stump's floor. Those whipping, swirling tendrils slithered into an array around the ghoul's body, pointing at us.

"That's not good," Anna said. "I liked it more when it was sitting still."

"I'm feeling its just getting started," I said. "You take your chain and see if you can keep it busy. I'll go for the kill."

Not that I had any idea of the best way to do that. Figured

a headlong rush at the center would do. Sink the sword in, twist the hilt, and let the blue fire do its work. I heard Anna shout as she sprinted away to my right, that bladed chain waving through the air. The ghoul turned, the sound of its body grinding against the ground as its waving brown and green mass shifted towards Anna. I took the opportunity to charge.

The ghoul's main body, framed by pulsing emerald tendrils, sat in front of me. The round surface looked like a ball, perfectly round except for where the tendrils emerged. Beneath the surface I could see the shifting faces, arms, and legs as they twisted and turned within.

After seeing the Master's dark cloak and his huge sword, a normal nightmare seemed refreshing.

I made it ten steps before the first tendril swatted at me, a thin vine swiping down from above and looking to flatten me into the floor. I saw it cracking down, twisted and slashed upward with the blade as the vine came streaking towards my head. My sword cut in to the attack, but did nothing to stop it. The vine crashed me to the ground and coated me in goop running from the cut I'd made. The stuff felt warm, sticky. Unpleasant. I felt the vine wrap itself around my chest and with my left hand I raised Inman's pistol. Aimed right at the ghoul's center mass, a target too big to miss. And pulled the trigger.

The gun went off with a roar. The shot popped into the monster's ball, scattering a chunk of ghostly flesh off of the thing. Otherwise, the ghoul didn't seem to notice. As the vine lifted me up, I noticed the ghoul didn't cry. No roar coming from the beast. No angry howl. Only the gravelly crackle and whistling wind as its body shifted and moved.

"Could use some help?" I yelled as the vine dragged me through the air. Smaller tendrils branched off of the vine, threading their way between my arms and legs. The plant squeezed, my limbs going numb. My right hand, weaponless, was pinned to my body. I couldn't exactly reload the pistol either. If something didn't change soon, the ghoul would squash me into pulp.

I saw the chain whipping by my face, wrapping around the vine. The chain's edges bit in and cut all the way through, severing the ghoul's tendril and sending me back down to the ground. The vine cushioned my blow, hitting first and bursting into in a sticky pile of ichor. I blinked away the slime, amazed to discover that I did, in fact, still live.

"Now it's your turn," Anna yelped from across the chamber. I looked and saw her beating away a pair of vines with her knives, stabbing them as they came close. Above her, a branch shifted into position; straight and hard.

"On my mark, roll left," I said, my hands scrambling to reload the pistol as I came up to a crouch. "Now!"

Anna dove to her left as I fired the pistol. The branch swung to follow, which took it right into the path of my shot. The bullet exploded into the wood and scattered chunks all over the place. The main body of the branch fell down and landed on the twisting vines turning to chase Anna, trapping them onto the floor.

"Nice shot!" Anna said.

"I'll take it," I said. I holstered the pistol and drew my knife, grabbing the sword off the ground as I ran back towards the ghoul. Two more vines arced towards me, but now I knew how fast they moved, and dodged. I sidestepped their grasp, then planted my foot on the end of one and swiped down with the sword, cutting it off. The vine flailed around, twitching and leaking the same blue glowing goo as the other parts. Every time I thought Riven had run out of ways to be disgusting and horrific, it proved me wrong.

The ceiling shook. The stump rumbled and it took me a second to see why. The ghoul's other branches had rotated up and bashed at the hole, letting in more light and sending chunks of wood taller than me raining down to the ground.

"What's it doing?" Anna said, running over past me towards her chain, a vine trailing after her.

"Running away," I said, no idea whether that was true. So I went after it.

I closed within a few feet of the ball and leapt towards it. As I jumped, wood chunks raining down around me, the ghoul lifted itself towards its new, wider opening. I swung the sword and felt it bite in to the ghoul's skin, or whatever it was. And found myself hanging by my own blade. The stump's ground fell away beneath me and, with a yell, I swung my left arm up with the knife. I stabbed the knife into the ghoul, giving me a second handhold.

The ghoul rose up above the stump, its vines and branches breaking out into the sky and smashing through the canopies of nearby trees. I clung to my blades, keeping my grip tight. I wouldn't be able hold forever, and if I fell from here, well, Anna would be cleaning up my splattered remains.

The ghoul moved off the stump, shifting over the forest floor, using its branches to stab into the ground and move itself along in lurches. I tried to twist the handle on the sword, to activate the fire, but I didn't have the leverage. Even trying to cut free might cause me to plummet to the surface. My arms burned. I needed to move.

With my left, I went for it. Withdrew the knife and stabbed higher up. Then, with my right, I pulled out the sword. The move sent me swinging back as the ghoul jerked over the dead grass. My left wrist ached, but I held on, and lunged back at the ghoul, sticking my sword in a little higher. For its part, the ghoul ignored my climb as it walked. I took a needless breath, then repeated the steps. Inching my blades foot by foot up the ghoul's body until I reached the top. Until I stood on the thing's head.

And saw where we were.

Beneath us, beneath the swirling twitching massive vines and branches, was the infinite line of spirits marching towards the Cycle. The ghoul began to feed. One after another, its vines and branches scooped spirits up from the path and shoved them into its spherical mass. Pressed them into its skin, even where I'd cut it. Wherever the spirits touched, the ghoul grew larger. The cuts healed. New vines started to sprout.

We were running out of time to beat this thing.

I raised the sword and slammed it down into the top of the ghoul. Went to turn the hilt, when I saw a face in the skin below. Selena's eyes, that vicious scar, they looked up at me blank and unseeing. The sparkle I'd become used to no longer there in her dead gaze.

I hesitated.

The ghoul hit me hard, sent me flying off its head with a thick vine. Small leaves actively grew around me, spreading their small tendrils between my arms and legs and wrapping them around my neck.

"You're not playing fair," I said, immediately regretting opening my mouth as more plants shot their way inside. The vine tasted like spinach, full of iron and bitterness. I ground the leaves in my teeth. If the ghoul wanted to tear me apart, well, I'd make it pay. Give it the full power of my gnashing gums.

The vines swung me through the air, suspended me where I could watch as the ghoul continued feeding. As it grew stronger, pressing the helpless spirits into itself one by one. I saw one of the spirits running, catching a vine and riding it towards the top of the ghoul. Just before the spirit smashed into its skin, I saw its arms move, a chain fly out and wrap itself around the vine.

That wasn't a spirit. Anna had caught up, and she cut herself free. Fell towards the ghoul and landed near my sword. As the vine grew leaves in front of my eyes, coloring the world a lighter shade of green, I saw Anna climb over to the sword and twist the hilt.

Blue fire ran down the blade and streaked out over the creature, running down its sides and up its vines and along its branches. I felt my vine shiver, the leaves withdrawing out of my mouth and wasting away. Shriveling to nothing as they held me twenty feet above the ground.

I fell.

8 8

I DIDN'T KNOW the spirits that I landed on, the ones I crushed down into the dirt, but I thanked each and every one of them as I stood up. Around me the unending march continued, only now around this part of the path swarms of spirits stood staring at the trees around them. The lives consumed by the ghoul over its long reign.

"Carver!" Anna said. "Where are you?"

"Over here," I said, not really sure where here was. I looked around, scanning the faces. Before too long, all of the spirits would head towards the Cycle. There were hundreds of them. I had to find Selena. Graham, Katherine, and Nicholas too.

Anna shoved her way through a crew of centuries-old sailors. Their ornate coats contrasting with their swarthy appearance. She looked rough; bruises across her face and more than a few cuts and splinters sticking out from shredded parts of her clothes. Going by the multitude of aches and pains bouncing their way through my body, I gathered we both looked terrible.

"I can't believe we're alive," Anna said as soon as she came up to me.

"Why?" I said. "We're guides. This is what we do."

"Stop it," Anna said. "This is not what guides do. Guides handle one or two angry spirits in a back alley in the city. They don't attack a giant creature that's covered in whirling death vines and then act all cocky about it when they luck their way into victory."

"I don't know what you're talking about," I said. "I left the sword there for you. I knew you'd get to it."

Anna stared at me, mouth open and her head shaking. "If my hand didn't have at least three splinters in it, I'd smack you right now."

"Have to save your energy anyway," I said. "We still have to find the rest, bind them again, and then cross so we can put ourselves back together."

"No. You wait one second," Anna said. She stared me in the eye, her face fierce. "We did something incredible. You're going to take one sentence. At least one sentence, and acknowledge that."

She was right. The ghoul we'd defeated, who knows how long that thing had been here? How many spirits it had feasted on? We knew it had bested Graham and Katherine, up to this point the deadliest duo of guides I'd ever seen. Anna and I, and let's be honest, mostly Anna had beat the creature through a combination of luck, skill, and determination. I felt bad about doubting her, about insulting her abilities, because she had proved herself one of the finest guides I'd ever seen.

"Any time now," Anna said, picking a splinter from her shoulder.

"Fine. You are amazing. That was incredible. I'm glad we're not dead. Can we go now?" I said.

"I guess that's all I'm going to get."

"You guess correctly."

We spent a long time sifting through the souls. Wandering through crowds of spirits and inspecting their faces. Hunting for familiar outfits. We eventually found them, all four together, beginning to walk at the edge of the crowd.

If you've ever seen someone you loved look at you like you don't exist, then you would understand what I felt seeing Selena. I walked up to her and she turned to look at me. Her eyes met mine and I saw none of her in them. No recognition, no thought.

When I had released Graham from his binding to the Master, he'd retained some of that personality. He'd still been, to some degree, himself. Ghouls were different. They devoured spirits, crushed them into nothing. I didn't know if I could ever get her back.

I had to try.

Anna watched as I took Selena's hand and felt for that pinprick. Felt for that connection to bring us together there in that gray forest. When I found it, I poured myself into her. My body wilted as my energy sapped through our touch, as what gave me life passed through into her. It found a home, and I felt the bond grow. A tether between our souls formed out of mine.

"Carver?" Selena's voice poured like chill water on my face. I hadn't realized I'd shut my eyes, but I opened them and saw her looking back at me. Not the dead-eyed spirit, but Selena herself.

"You're back," I said.

"It feels good," Selena replied, looking down at her hands gripping tightly. "I don't remember any of it. Nothing after the ghoul attacked us. Now here you are."

"I'm sorry I wasn't there," I said.

"It's not your fault," Selena said, and then she smiled. "I

think we almost had it. Graham and Katherine were keeping it distracted while I protected Nicholas. He prepared something that exploded. Or that meant to explode. But we didn't see all the vines."

"It had a lot of those," I said. "And they tasted awful."

Selena raised her eyebrow.

"Never mind," I said.

I bound Nicholas and Katherine again, waking them from their slumber. Anna did the same to Graham and after replaying the fights and the challenges to each other, all of us went back to the stump to retrieve their weapons.

It felt strange, giving up those parts of myself again. I'd grown so used to being without them; always being slower than I should be. Tiring faster. Being my full self had felt good. Right. Maybe someday I'd have that again.

"Carver," Anna said as everyone stood assembled. "We should probably go. Cross back. We've been over here for a long time."

"Can you keep going?" I asked my parents, Selena and Nicholas. They nodded.

"That thing caught us by surprise," Graham said. "I don't think the Master is a giant monster full of vines. We'll take care of him."

"If we can," I said. "We'll try to come back the same way tomorrow night. Meet you at the Mountain."

"I like that idea," Nicholas said. "It'll give me time to study the surroundings. Find a plan."

"Plans," Graham shook his head. "Run in with a hammer held high, now that's a plan."

Anna and I left them to carry on, made our way back past the line of spirits, to the clearing, into the beds of grass and crossed home.

89

I OPENED my eyes to the wide black barrel of a gun, and behind it the furrowed brow of a police officer. He wore the standard blue and copper uniform, the metal winding through the cloth around various badges and devices. He gave me a moment let me collect my breath. I glanced to the right, noticed Anna staring at the weapon.

"Now that you're both awake, I'm hoping you won't mind giving me some answers," the officer said. "It's been a while since I've had someone decide to fall asleep in a crime scene. Particularly when that someone doesn't want to wake up."

"We were in Riven," I said before Anna could get any ideas. "We're guides. We were trying to figure out what happened."

"Guides," the police officer said. "Guides way out here. Just happening to come by after all the others died."

I could've said anything. I could lie; protest that we were innocent and that we'd only stumbled on the cabin as a place to spend the night to complete our quota. Or I could tell the truth, say that I'd been here the night the guides were slaughtered, but all that would get me is an interrogation. Questions about why I hadn't gone directly to the police. So I went with option three.

"It's guide business," I said. "Riven is a mess, and we're trying to clean it up. The group here made mistakes, we came to fix them."

"Did you now?" the officer said. "Why don't you stand yourselves up, and come with us. Then you can tell me all about exactly what mistakes were made."

"Gladly," I said. Not that I had a clue what I was going to say. If they actually checked with the guides about my name, they'd find my fugitive status right there.

"Carver," Anna said. I held up my hand.

"Don't say anything," I said as we got up from the beds and followed the officer from the cabin. "The less you can implicate yourself, the better. If we're lucky, you'll still be a guide after we get out of this."

Several more officers milled around the campground outside. When they saw us come out, one of them took off a pack and reached inside. Pulled out a pair of what look like collars.

"What are those?" Anna whispered.

"Shock collars," the police officer said. "Normally we keep them for sneaks. Anyone who feels like Riven is a place to run off and hide. I wouldn't advise crossing while wearing one of these."

"It reacts to your breathing. If you start to even out, like you're falling asleep, it'll zap you." I said. I'd had a short, ugly experience with those while being trained. A demonstration to show what would happen if you went astray. I had no doubt that Polk or Derringer had one back at Ezra's and, if I'd waited a moment longer, they would've tried to clap it on me.

"You're really ruining this whole guide experience," Anna said.

"Bad timing on your part," I replied.

"Since you're both so talkative," the officer said. "How about you tell me about those mistakes?"

I went into a censored version of the story, spinning a tale about how all of the people here were former guides, how they had tried to break a hole through Riven back to the real world. About how that hole didn't work out. Attracted a lot of spirits. Too many. The guides' own ambitions had cost them their lives.

"Sounds like they were a real batch of evil men and women," the officer said when I'd finished. His deadpan hadn't changed at all. No idea whether he had bought the story. "But here's the funny thing. We and all the other departments around Chicago, for hundreds of miles, received a notice last night. About a guide who'd gone his own way and refused the justice your kind insists on delivering itself. Included in this notice was a description. One you happen to resemble. It also included a note about a mask. Black and gold. I think you'll agree that the one you're carrying there holds those colors."

The officer clapped the shock collars are on each of our necks. They felt tight, cold. Every time I swallowed or took a breath my throat scraped against the metal.

I saw Anna's eyes flicked towards me. Shook my head slightly. Four officers, two of us. We might've been able to win, but there are some things you don't come back from. Binding spirits, even injuring the guide in Riven, those were different. Here in the real world, these officers had family, friends. A blinding, getting cut off from Riven forever, still meant you were free. Not locked in a prison cell.

"It sounds like you've already made a decision," I said.

"Maybe I have," the officer said. "I think you'd better start walking. On the way there, back to the station, you're going to give me the real story. Because right now I have a cart with twenty bodies in it and no one to tell me how they got there."

"You're not going to understand," I said.

"Trust me," the officer said. "I long ago figured out that this world doesn't provide easy answers. Doesn't give clear explanations. But eventually someone will come around and ask for them all the same. I don't need to understand, I need to be able to say why."

So as we marched down to the station I retold the story. Told him about the man in the cloak with the big sword, and the army of spirits that slaughtered those that had made the camp. The officer took it all without interrupting, and finally nodded when I was done.

"Now that is a story I can believe," the officer said as we walked up to the train station. "Not because it sounds believable, but because the way you said it proved that *you* believed it."

Waiting at the top of the station's steps were Polk and Derringer, their eyes bearing a deadly glint. Derringer favored his right arm, and when he saw that I'd noticed, shot me a spicy glare. They would be the escorts. Lovely.

"We'll take these two from here, officer," Polk said.

"You should know," the officer said. "They've both been cooperative. For fugitives, the best company. Even helped me clean up my investigation."

"We'll take it into account," Polk said. We followed them onto the train and they pointed us to a pair of seats.

"Straight to the hospital this time," Derringer said. "Right into surgery. Your game is done, Carver." Then he turned to Anna. "Too bad he dragged you into this. I heard you had potential."

"Fun while it lasted," Anna replied.

The train blew its horn and started rumbling off, back towards the city. To the knives that would cut away Riven forever.

90

Polk and Derringer sat on a bench across from us, staring at me with narrow, suspicious eyes. Their mouth's twitched. Derringer coughed once into his wrist, then returned to his glare. As though they were waiting to ask me a question, but were waiting for me to do something first. Me, with a shock collar around my neck and cuffs on my hands.

Guess I'd better get started.

"Seems like a lot of effort for one wounded guide," I said. "They're pulling two of you from your quota just for this?"

Derringer glanced to Polk, giving me their order of operations. Polk could play the lead and Derringer would be the muscle. The ease with which they slid into their roles had me wondering how often they'd done this. Were they Piotr's go-to handlers whenever a guide stepped outside the lines?

"You know what's funny, Carver," Polk said. "We were in Detroit. We were filling our quota. Then Derringer and I, we went to our normal meet up spot. Like that bar you've got in Chicago. Ezra's?"

I nodded. Polk spoke with a bad affliction, a habit of

emphasizing the wrong syllables. Like an actor learning how to talk by watching silent films.

"Like that one. Only when we got there, Piotr was sitting at the table. Waiting for us. Now I don't know when last time was you saw him. But to me, to Derringer here, Piotr looked old," Polk widened his eyes, made a helpless shrug. "Looked tired. Like he'd been in a lot of fights. Had a lot of nights in Riven, and a lot of days back here battling for the survival of all of us. You know what Piotr says? You know what he tells us as Derringer and I sit down?"

"That you're doing a swell job?" I said.

"He tells us that there's this new kid, this guy he thought would make one heck of a guide, would make such a good guide that even though he's only been part of us for a few years that he deserves to run Chicago. Derringer and I, we're looking at each other like hey, we've both been doing our work for more than a decade, and we're not getting anything. But we're quiet. We take it. Because that's what loyal guides do," here I could see Polk start to shake. His forearms trembled, hands gripped the bench tightly. Derringer put a hand on Polk's shoulder. "So when Piotr tells us it's a guide that he thought was the next big thing? That the man whose helping us dig out of these dark times, tells us that this wonder kid has gone and hurt one of our own. Has broken our rules. We didn't take long to jump on the train."

"You didn't even ask him why, did you?" I said. "Why he thought I was doing this?"

"Oh, no," Polk said. "Should we have? Should we have interrogated him? Tried to question the man who single-handedly keeps our order alive? Or do you, you know, give him this one. Seeing as all the evidence is on his side."

"I'm being hunted," I said. "That's why I'm here."

"Who isn't being hunted?" Derringer said. "You? Me? All

of us got spirits after our hides. All of us are dealing with one terror after another every night."

"Your understand," Anna said. "The people coming after Carver aren't like the spirits. They're trying to find him. Just him."

"Why is that?" Derringer said. "What makes you so special?"

I paused. Part of me wanted to spill the beans. To say to them that I, by an accident of birth, could be the end of everything. But then, why would they believe me? Why would it matter? If they were going to take me in any way, then who cared?

"Let's say that I'm not just a guide," I said. "Because of my parents, I can be used by someone else."

"Ain't that mysterious?" Polk said. "Aren't you special?"

"Hear that Polk?" Derringer said. "This guy thinks that he's better than us."

"That's not it," I said. "You have to let me go. Keeping me puts Riven at risk."

"You talk about how you're getting hunted in Riven," Polk said. "Sounds like there's a simple solution for you. We take you back to the hospital. We get you blinded. Then guess what? No more Riven. No more getting hunted. You're safe. Piotr's happy."

"Everybody wins," Derringer said.

I didn't have an argument against that. They were right, to a degree. Blind me, I couldn't be used to create a hole out of Riven. Only, that would still leave the Master out there. Would leave whomever came next at the mercy of his schemes. I couldn't let that stand.

"What about the people hunting me?" I said. "Who's going to deal with them?"

"Why don't you give us all the details," Polk said. "We'll take care of it for you. Derringer and I. We'll hunt them down. Send that nasty spirit into the Cycle. Along with those spirits you bound over there."

"Polk, don't take any offense, but you two wouldn't stand a chance against my friends," I said. "If you do blind me, the best thing you could do would be to stay out of Riven for a while. Because they'll find out who cut me off, and they won't be happy."

Polk laughed. "Threats? You're something else, Carver."

"Not a threat," I said. "It's a certainty."

Polk sat forward on the bench, his elbows on his knees. "Know what? Alec? He says he knows all about where you've holed up your pals. Soon as we blind you, we're crossing over and taking care of them. I don't care how good you think your spirits are - they'll be outnumbered. Outclassed."

"You broke the rules, Carver," Derringer said. "It's what you deserve."

Outside the windows, the fields began to pepper with buildings. Streets broke between the yellow and green acres of early summer. Sunlight washed the world in gold.

I wanted to go back to Riven's gray.

Dr. Barrington Farth looked the same staring down at me, preparing to cut me off from Riven, as he had when he told me how my mother died; clinical, distant, methodical. Alec had strapped me down into the hospital bed, Anna similarly confined next to me. They called it surgery but the blinding really amounted to a small incision under the temple. Snipping part of the brain.

There were potential side effects.

"It used to be that we would hit you on the side of the head particularly hard," Barrington explained. "As you might imagine, this led to some unfortunate trauma. A higher likelihood of death. This way is rather pleasant."

"You're really selling it," I said.

"Carver, be quiet," Alec said. He stood in the corner, near the door, supervising. To make sure Anna and I didn't try something weird. We still wore the shock collars. Ready to zap us if we tried to escape by going to the other world.

"First you'll be feeling a slight prick as I numb you," Barrington continued. "Then the actual procedure will only take a moment. Simple slice, a few stitches, and you'll be free of your burden."

"You think this is fair," I said to Alec.

"It's not my position. Not my decision to make," Alec said. "I'll let them know."

He meant Selena. Graham and Katherine. Nicholas. That only applied if he could get to them fast enough. If Alec could cross to Riven in time to tell my parents what had happened before, freed of their binding, they journeyed to the Cycle and disappeared forever.

Barrington turned to a small table and loaded a syringe, sticking the needle into a small vial and filling it up with clear liquid. I should have felt panic. Dread. Instead, my mind fogged with the malaise of the inevitable. I'd tried, and I'd failed. I only hoped it would take long enough so that the others could finish their mission. Find the Master and eliminate him before the blinding set them free.

"Hey Alec," Polk called from the hall. "Bryce is here. Says he wants to talk to you."

"I thought you'd retired?" Derringer asked, his loud voice carrying into the room. I didn't hear Bryce's reply.

Alec caught my eyes and shook his head. "He shouldn't have come for you."

Alec stepped out of the room and I heard their voices back and forth. Polk and Derringer interjecting as Bryce protested the treatment. The injustice of my sentencing, that Anna had no right to be included in it. Polk countering that Piotr made the call and, as guides, they had to obey his orders. That's when I heard the punch. A thud in the hallway. Polk's muffled groans echoed into the room.

Barrington turned at the sound, holding the syringe in the air like a weapon, and then the doctor shrugged and backed into the corner of the room. Another pair of strong hits and a yelp from a nurse, and I heard another body hit the floor. Bryce walked in, rubbing his knuckles.

"These new guides never learn how to fight outside of Riven," he said to me as he reached over the bed and undid the straps. "They've got their fancy toys over there, but ask them to engage in an old-fashioned brawl and they fall apart."

"What are you doing?" I said.

"Alec told me what was going on," Bryce said. "I objected to it. There are more important things right now than punishing a guide for a little injury."

"They won't let you walk away from this."

"I didn't want to face my family every day knowing I'd let this happen to the son of the best guide I've ever known," Bryce said. "It's worth the risk."

Bryce pressed the latches on either side of the shock collar, held them down for a full ten seconds. The collar ground as its gears turned. It popped off, one side opening to let my neck slip out. I could have held the release down myself - shock collars normally paired with handcuffs, and the time for the collar's gears to unlock gave guards ample opportunity to intervene.

"I'm gathering there won't be a procedure today?" Barrington muttered from the corner.

"You gather correctly," I said, getting out of the bed and pulling on my coat.

"You'll need to leave the city," Bryce said as he unshackled Anna. "If you stay here, they'll find you. My guess is, after this, they forget about the blinding and go for more permanent solutions."

We walked from the room and headed down the hallway, passed the unconscious forms of Polk and Derringer. Alec watched us, arms folded, as we went by. I expected him to say something, maybe a threat or jeer. Some measure of acknowledgment. But whatever war Alec waged went on inside his head and he stayed silent.

Outside the hospital Anna and I turned towards the train station. The quickest way out of the city. Bryce didn't move with us. He looked north, back towards his house.

"You're not coming with?" Anna said.

"I'm not leaving my family," Bryce replied. "If they choose to blind me, I don't care. I'm done with Riven anyway."

I held out my hand and when Bryce took it I pulled him into a tight hug. "Thank you, for everything."

"Don't go wasting my gesture," Bryce said. "Leave."

We left my former mentor and ran through the streets. Towards the train station and, hopefully, a way out of town. While not as big as Union Station, the trains near the hospital had some options. One went south, toward St. Louis, and others wrapped east towards Detroit. I kept my mask off, breathing the harsh air and drawing stares, but if there'd been any sort of release about me then going without the black and gold mask would buy me some cover.

"You there," shouted one of the station's policeman, gesturing at me with his baton. "What's your name?"

I glanced around, pushing Anna away for me. Trying to get her some cover. I walked out of the line for the tickets, pretending not to hear. The policeman repeated his question and I kept moving. His whistle blew and I ran. Back up the steps and out onto the sidewalk. I coughed, my rapid breathing pulling too much harsh air for my lungs to cope with. I jammed on the mask, started the respirator.

The officer lunged at my back and I felt him grab my coat. I twisted with the move and shrugged him off, sending the officer tumbling to the ground. Three more were heading my direction, pounding up the station steps. So I took off.

The streets around the station showed signs of a new age

for Chicago. Wooden stores and offices were being torn apart to make room for forged metal. Ever present construction. Small zeppelins carrying materials bobbed overhead, guiding people and beams to their proper places. Shifting crowds of workers in the late morning moved their mass of bodies along the streets or in the automatic taxis. Every so often, as I darted between crowds, I caught sight of one of the city's mechs, the tall two or four-legged beasts that, with stacks belching smoke, rumbled their way on patrol.

I burst through the crowd and found myself in a large intersection, bustling groups crossing in shifts to blue and red signals on ten-foot posts. At random, I went left. Down a long sidewalk that stretched in front of a row of offices claiming various legal representation. The kind of office I could probably use right about then. In front of me, as the block ended, a black metal leg pounded into view. Followed by another.

The cockpit of the mech, a half oval with a glass windshield set over the top, a pair of large guns beneath, swiveled to point my way. Its barrels trained on me, and I paused. Raised my hands.

"Carver Reed," the mech announced, the pilot's voice catching a mechanical twist coming through the machine. "You're under arrest, and any action taken without our consent will result in your immediate execution."

9 2

ANNA GRABBED my shoulder and pulled me into the alleyway. Out of sight of the mech. Then she continued, yanking me further with a vice-like grip on my wrist

"I can run my own," I said, trying to break my hand out of her grasp.

"Then do it," Anna said, but she let me go. Anna kept moving, taking a right at the next break between the buildings and bursting out onto the street behind the mech. Running across the road, darting between a pair of taxis and into another alleyway.

I followed, wheezing through my respirator. To say I didn't go on too many runs was an understatement. Exercise came in fits and starts. Workout sessions to hone techniques with Bryce. Push-ups on the floor of my apartment. There weren't other options.

"Where are we going?" I said when Anna finally took a second to breathe.

"The airfield," Anna said.

"I thought you were getting train tickets."

"They were watching the trains," Anna said. "The officers

had pictures of us. There was no way would we get on one."

"Oh, but a zeppelin's going to be so much easier?"

"If we're lucky," Anna said and then she took off again.

We broke onto a large thoroughfare heading west. A wide street with multiple taxis, surging crowds, and plenty of police hunting for us, their blue and copper masks bobbing between more common outfits. Anna kept her head down and ducked between groups, trying to stay out of the open. I followed suit, except there were some things the shorter, smaller girl could do that I could not. Like be inconspicuous.

"I've got them!" a voice bellowed behind me.

"You're the worst," Anna said.

"You could've just left me there," I replied as we broke into another run. As mechs turned to track us and the officers chased, we kept swerving in and out of people. Trying to prevent any clear shots. It worked, at least for a while. We made it three blocks up before the constant whistles and cries of alarm cleared the streets.

When a mech spools up its gun, it sounds like a strobing whine. A clear signal you're about to be torn to a million tiny pieces. I caught up to Anna, grabbed her, and jumped into a storefront. Smashed through the glass windows as the sidewalk blew up in gunfire. Sparks flared behind us, bullets bouncing into the street and through the window that we'd crashed to pieces. One advantage of being covered with a coat and mask is that the glass didn't manage to cut us. Some new scratches in our clothes, but no blood.

"That's a neat trick," Anna said. "Adding vandalism to our charges?"

"We're still alive, aren't we?"

"Can't argue with that," Anna said and we took off towards the back of the store. It was full of dresses and shirts, blouses and pants. The people inside ran behind the sales counter or ducked in the racks of clothes. Anything to get them out of sight of the two crazed people fleeing through their store. Behind us officers came in through the door, yelling and blowing their whistles.

We blew through the rear, past rows and rows of clothes that didn't make it to the front of the store. Clerks stared at us as we went by and I repressed the urge to wave. Not the best time. We went out the back door, into another alley.

"This way," Anna said, turning right and running parallel to the wide street we'd nearly been killed on earlier.

Another block down the alleyway and I heard officers behind us, catching up. We did our running in Riven, these guys did it here, in the real world. Where their muscles give them one heck of an advantage.

"Need a new strategy," I gasped as our feet pounded pavement.

"Here," Anna said. She cut into the back of a restaurant. Right to the kitchen where serving staff and chefs were prepping for dinner meals. I followed, banging against pans and pushing people out of the way. I think I muttered apologies, but I can't be sure. Chaos navigated by instinct. Trying not to die.

We ran out through the front of the restaurant and onto a smaller street. Anna swung left, then dove in between a pair of buildings heading back the way we came. Anna slowed, crept to a crawl as we went down the alley. Hid behind a large bin for trash and watched as groups of officers ran by. Chasing after our trail.

"Won't they think were heading for the airfield?" I said. "Given that's where we were going?"

"We weren't," Anna said. "The main airfield's that way. The one we're going to? It's much smaller. South."

I'd heard of that one. A few flights a day to major cities. Only luxury class zeppelins, the ones that would take longer but gave you a scenic route. A chance to really enjoy your time above the clouds.

"We're escaping on the slow ships?" I said.

"Wasn't aware you were on a schedule," Anna said.

That stopped me for a moment. I supposed I didn't have anywhere to be. Waiting for Graham, Katherine to go and take care of the Master. Until they succeeded? I just had to survive.

"Point," I said.

"Okay, let's go," Anna said and we ducked back into the wider alley and shot down the road in the opposite direction we'd started. This time, when we hit the crowded street, there were far fewer officers. None of them scanning our faces. Why pay attention for fugitives when they'd been on the run in the opposite direction?

It took another hour of walking but we made it to the South airfield. There in the center, on a giant cleared patch of grass, sat a zeppelin as large as a football field. Its numerous fans spun in the wind, idly keeping the zeppelin in place. Long ropes tied the craft to the ground as people boarded. They walked up a long stair connected to a platform with wheels at the base. A series of uniformed officials took tickets and welcomed everyone on.

"So I'm guessing you have the money for this?" I asked Anna. "Because I didn't plan on buying cross-country air tickets today."

"We won't need it," Anna said. She made a beeline for the ticket counter, for one line in particular. One man who looked at her with beady eyes when she stepped up in front of him and smiled.

"Calling in the favor?" the man said.

"Time to get out of Chicago for a while," Anna said. "You have room for two of us?"

"With the war, there's plenty of space. People don't seem to like leisurely travel when the world is falling apart."

"Imagine that," I muttered.

The man stamped out a pair of tickets and handed them the Anna. Wished us a pleasant trip. I waited until we passed the pair of officials checking tickets, until we walked on the aircraft, to ask what that whole exchange was about.

"If a client can't pay," Anna said. "I ask what else they can do. Whether there's something that might come in handy later. He said that he could get me a free trip on one of the ships in exchange for doing him a favor in Riven."

"Not a bad deal," I replied.

The inside of the zeppelin matched Ezra's classical charm. Ornate woodwork and long, electrically-lit hallways glowed with warmth. Mustard carpet matched the deep brown doors and walls, and room numbers carved in polished bronze hung above every cabin. We traced our way past a series of dining rooms, small library, and a wide viewing gallery with windows on every side and even a large glass section in the floor.

"Ever been on one of these?" I asked Anna. She shook her head. "Me neither. Maybe, when we're not being hunted, we can try this again. Actually enjoy ourselves."

"You guides ever get to do that?" Anna said. "Enjoy yourselves? Because everything we've been doing since I joined has been risking our lives in one way or another."

"You have to find the moments," I said.

"Next time you see one, mind letting me know?" Anna said.

We reached our cabin and Anna put in the key, twisted it in the lock, and opened the door. A pair of beds nestled against the walls in an otherwise spacious room. Windows everywhere looked out onto the field. When we were in the air, those let us see in every direction. A bottle of wine nestled on a shelf in the wall, with glasses. Snacks littered an accompanying table, cheeses and sausages. A note welcomed the passengers to the luxury cabin. Anna's contact had more than come through.

"Anna?" I said. "This is one of those moments."

9 3

AMID THE CABIN'S OPULENCE, my eyes focused on the two most important things in the room. The beds. As soon as we were both in the cabin, I shut the door behind us and locked it. Our friends were getting towards the Master and, if we wanted to find them, if we wanted to help them, we had to move.

"Do you think the beds are linked?" Anna said.

"The ship looks new, so I'm hoping no," I said. If nobody had used the beds to cross to Riven before, then they would be untethered. Open. Anna and I would be able to focus on a particular spot in Riven and cross there. From then on these beds would be tied to that spot forever. Of course we could try to use the floor if the beds didn't work, but you still had to be able to fall asleep. Waking up from a long session in Riven on a hard surface usually meant a stiff body, a day spent regretting the night before.

"So what's the plan?" Anna said, lying down in her bed.

"I say we visualize the stump. The only place I can picture to that's going to be closer," I said. You couldn't just name a spot in Riven and go there from an untethered bed. You had to know it. Be able to guide your spirit there as it crossed over.

"The stump it is then."

I lay down on the bed, took off my mask, and stared at the ceiling for a minute. Officially a fugitive. On the run from both guides and ordinary police. On the off chance they searched the ship while we were in Riven, they would take us in without a fight. Lock us up and, assuming we were even able to cross back, we would find ourselves in cells. On the other hand, if Selena and the others needed help and we sat here too nervous to do anything, then everything was worthless. Then the whole sacrifice, the injured guide, would have no benefit.

We had to hope that there was nothing coming for us. That our luxury cabin would kiss the skies without police dragging us out of it. I heard Anna's breathing even out as I closed my eyes. The last time we crossed we'd nearly been killed. This time wouldn't be any different. We were going to find the Master and put an end to this.

94

We joined the line of spirits making their way away from the stump. That long crowded stream of souls of every shape and form marching towards the Mountain in the distance. Again, we were weaponless. A problem to solve when we caught up to the others.

I relished the calming walk through the forest after the rapid-fire sprints from the officers back in Chicago. So long as I didn't focus on the thousands of the dead, the quiet walk let me relax. The leaves shimmered in the breeze and neither of us spoke. Took the opportunity to collect ourselves.

I tried at one point to reach out to Selena and I felt her, sent some reassurance through our bond and received her warm respond. Not frantic, not scared. They weren't fighting anyone yet.

The Mountain rose gradually on the edge of our vision, hazy through the endless waves of gray and floating ash that made up Riven's air. Eventually, though, we hiked up to the entrance. A wide portal cut into the side, perfect and spaced twenty yards wide to allow the throng of spirits through. Graham, Katherine, Selena, and Nicholas were waiting.

"You didn't try going in?" I said.

"We did," Graham replied. "Explored a fair bit. Even found some of these."

Grand gesture behind them. A pile of various weapons and robes, cloaks and coats sat there. Most of it looked like guide gear, but old, cracked and torn through use. Some bore versions of the guides symbol in different sizes, some etched or stitched with simple fabrics. Rather than the thick leather that made up most of our new gear, a number of these were made from thin cloth. Almost rags.

"What does this mean?" Anna said as she sifted through the weapons, looking for something she could use. "None of this stuff looks standard."

"It means that the guides weren't always in Riven's city," Katherine said. "Or someone, sometime, brought this out here."

"The spirits that the Master brought to murder Inman, they didn't have weapons," I said. "They were smart, but just used their hands and mouths. If he had these available, why not use them?"

"I have a feeling they're meant for others," Graham said. "This one, for instance." Graham pointed at a particularly vicious-looking sickle whose point carved into a forked tongue. A serpent's ridged scales made up the rest of the curving blade. "That's the same sort of weapon that Rainier, one Chicago's first guides, wielded. Might even be the same."

"Why would it be here?" I said

"Things don't age in Riven," Nicholas said. "It's possible that someone found it. Collected the weapon and brought to the Mountain. Or even that Rainier died and left it here."

"There's one person that'll be able to answer those questions," Selena said.

"Selena makes a point," Graham said. "We're here. We're ready. Let's do the job."

I picked up the sickle, and a shorter sword. Longer than the knives, and broader, but the two felt good in my hands. Anna, for her part, found a simple mace with spikes jutting out of its head. Similar to what Nicholas had made for her.

Then, with me in the lead, we joined the line of spirits and headed down into the Mountain to find the Master.

And end him.

WE HIKED through the opening into the Mountain, the yawning gray rock closing around us and blocking out the sky. Deep down the tunnel, past the ends of Riven's gray light, blue flickered on the walls. The same pale cast that burned in the eyes of angry spirits and lit up our weapons when we attempted to send that anger into oblivion.

"Where do you think it's coming from?" Anna said, nodding down the tunnel. Spirits shuffled by us, continuing on their journey towards the Cycle.

"Take a look around you," I said. "It's coming from where they're going."

"This would be the proper location for the Cycle," Nicholas said. "If the Cycle is indeed in the base of the Mountain, then that makes the Mountain and all of its rock the only thing holding the Cycle at bay."

"If the Cycle is something that can actually be held," Katherine said. "I've never seen it."

"You might get your chance," I said and then kept walking. I'd never been in a cave before. At least, not the natural kind. Chicago had plenty of underground paths, but they were made of metal and stone. Weren't traveled by an endless mass of spirits.

As we went into the cave, the air itself became clearer, Riven's ashy haze didn't reach far into the depths. Outside light vanished, replaced by the blue glow. It reflected up and down the cave walls, their shiny surfaces serving as mirrors to the sapphire cast. Every so often a path branched off to the side, and every single time I glanced at Graham and Katherine and they shook their heads.

"That's where we found the gear," Graham said after the first one. "Every one we explored ended with a small circle and a cushion of leaves and grass. Weapons and coats lying next to them. The closer to the entrance, the older the gear."

"It sounds like people crossed over here," I said.

"My impression as well," Nicholas said. "There is evidence that the guides once used the Mountain as a base."

"But not anymore," I said. "No guide I know has ever been here. Most probably don't even realize it exists."

"Why would you need to?" Graham said. "All the fun is back in the city. These spirits are long past needing our help."

Eventually the cave opened into a large chamber with a central flat, rocky space. Around that circle, the spirits continued walking a sloping stair into the depths. The circle held one thing that made me pause. Towards the back, against a wall, sat a makeshift bed, scattered sheets and a ragged pillow. The great sword I'd seen the Master wield hung behind the bed, a pair of spikes pounded into the rock serving as a rest for the sword's hilt. Next to the bed, on the ground, his same hooded cloak.

"I think we found him," I said.

"Except he's not here," Selena replied. "Only, why would a spirit need a bed?"

"It means the Master is not just a spirit," I said.

We surrounded the bed. For being such a deadly figure,

the Master didn't live in luxury. The clock tower I'd used for years in Chicago stood in luxurious contrast to this spartan existence.

"So what do we do now?" Graham said. "Wait?"

I almost said yes. Almost said that we ought to stand with our weapons drawn so that when the Master crossed over we could strike before he had a chance to blink. But a scraping noise of a sword drawn from its sheath drew our attention. Had us turning as a group towards the downward stair and, on it, a spirit wearing nothing more than a ragged robe, holding a long blade I recognized from other guides on the opposite side of the world; a katana.

"Those weapons do not belong to you," the spirit said.

"You are?" I replied.

"Takeda," the spirit said. "Former leader of the guides. And destroyer of thieves."

Then Takeda, destroyer of thieves, ran. Dashed down deeper into the cave, pushing past spirits and disappearing.

"You remember your history?" Graham asked.

"Takeda lived two centuries ago," I said. "I don't understand how he can still be here."

"I say we go ask him," Graham said.

We split up; Graham, Katherine and I resolving to chase Takeda down the steps while the others watched the Master's bed. I figured they would be able to handle the Master as he crossed over, taking shape defenseless on that pile of cloth.

The three of us ran after Takeda, circling deeper into the bowels of the Mountain. The blue light brightened to the point where it almost hurt my eyes, forcing me to squint until they adapted. I pushed past spirit after spirit as the path tightened. Narrowing until only two bodies could move abreast. The ceiling shrank, brushing the top of my head and forcing me to duck. And then I found it. We found it. The source of our salvation and our ultimate end.

The Cycle spanned an immense space in front of us. Its radiant blue spun off as far as I could see and beyond. A lake of churning cerulean aura. In front of us, forward on a flat expanse that trailed into a single point, walked the spirits. They moved to the very edge and without breaking stride walked off and fell into the Cycle. Takeda watched them, katana still drawn. Next to him stood an even older spirit with nothing more than a long staff and a plain tunic. Together they turned to us as we walked in.

"Do you find it beautiful?" Takeda asked us. "You should, as you'll be sinking into it soon."

"I've seen better," I said. Which was a total lie. If you could stare into the sun, and the sun were as big as the sky, then you might understand what it was like to see the Cycle up close. I had to focus on the ground, focus on the spirits, because staring at that blue meant sinking into it and never coming back.

"Tell us," Katherine said. "How are you here? After so many years?"

"We will not honor the thieves with answers," Takeda said. He nodded at the other spirit, who turned his face towards us. Some terrible fate had torn the spirit's face away, the mouth a mangled mess. Nose broken off. His bones were charred black.

"Zolin," Graham said. "Leader of the guides back in 1500. A monk. His temple burned and destroyed by Spain as they made their way through Mexico. With him in it."

"So now there's two of them?" I said. "Both former leaders? Both far older than any spirit should be?"

"It's a troubling coincidence," Graham said. "One I think we can rectify."

Graham pulled his hammer off of his back, held his gauntleted wrist ready. Katherine drew her batons, and I raised the sickle. Really wished I had my lash. My knives.

Going up against some of the best guides that it ever lived, I'd rather do it with weapons I knew how to use.

"Are you ready?" Takeda said. He pointed the sword, that long katana, at us. Countless spirits walked by, oblivious to the world around them.

"Let's go," I said, and ran forward.

9 6

GRAHAM MADE A BEELINE FOR TAKEDA, while Katherine split off to engage Zolin, leaving me with a choice. Which parent did I love more?

Easy. Graham had tried to kill me so many times; my mother deserved my help. So I slipped by a soldier's spirit, pulled ahead of my mother, and swept the sickle forward to meet Zolin's swing. Zolin caught the strike on his staff and wrenched the sickle away from my hand. My weapon flew across the room and bounced off of the cave wall. Zolin's disarm swept his staff wide, leaving room for me to stab him with the sword. The blade stuck into Zolin's side and he replied by whipping the staff back and knocking me away.

I bowled into a trio of spirits and sat up to see my mother battering Zolin, my sword still sticking out of his body, with her batons. She drove the monk back with a flurry of blows, each baton running a rhythm of strikes up and down Zolin's body. I noticed that my mother took special care to strike my sword as well, driving it deeper. Desperate, Zolin dropped the staff, ignored my mother's batons as they clawed into his arms. He grabbed my mother and threw her to the ground.

"That's not fighting fair," I said as I tackled the monk. I gripped one of my mother's batons, sticking in Zolin's body like my sword, in my right hand and driving it into the wasted space of the monk's mouth. Zolin groaned, more a buzzing whine without a tongue to shape the sound, and flailed as I pushed him back towards the edge of the platform. I stuck my leg behind Zolin's, and sent him tripping back over the edge. As he fell, I reached with my left hand and snagged my mother's other baton. The short sword fell with Zolin into that blue oblivion.

"Carver! Look out!" Graham called. I whirled back and held the batons up in time to catch Takeda's blade. The katana came at my face, and bounced off the batons. The force threw me back, my feet brushing the edge of the cliff. Takeda readied for another swing when I saw my father's hammer slam into the spirit's back and knock Takeda to the ground. I shifted away from the edge, gained some distance. Graham bore a number of deep cuts along his arms and legs. Takeda hadn't gone down quite so easy.

Graham reached the spirit and, as Graham grabbed his hammer off the ground, Takeda turned with a sweep of the katana, swiping towards Graham's stomach. As the katana swept up, Graham fired a burning wire from his wrist. It wrapped around Takeda's hand and lit on fire. The spirit dropped the katana and howled in pain. Pain that my father, with a two-handed swing of the hammer, put to rest.

Both of us pushed the motionless Takeda off of the cliff, into the Cycle. Two guide legends erased, and neither one gave us any answers.

"Disappointing, isn't it?" said a voice behind us. A voice I knew. Cloaked and holding his sword at his waist, point touching the ground, stood the Master. His obsidian mask shone in the Cycle's blue light, still chipped from Inman's desperate shot. "They've been down here for so long that they've lost their edge. Nothing more than pitiful memories."

"How did you get here?" I asked, trying to shrug off the dark scenarios flashing through my mind. The Master being here meant he'd crossed over and none of the others had stopped him. Which meant Selena, Anna, and Nicholas were either dead, or captured.

"You've already found the spirits here. Leaders of the guides from centuries ago. How many more do you think there are?" the Master said. "More than your friends can handle, at least."

"If you hurt them..." Katherine said.

"You'll do what?" the Master replied. "I know you, spirit, and you don't have the skills to make me sweat."

"Maybe you haven't noticed that you're outnumbered," Graham said. "Three on one doesn't make for good odds."

"Do I look afraid?" the Master replied.

This was it. I could almost feel it, as though destiny were pulling us in to this one fight. One chance to get rid of the person behind the danger and death that had followed me for so long. Except I couldn't get Selena out of my head. I needed to know she was okay. Needed to make sure Selena, and Anna, and Nicholas weren't dead. Or about to be.

So I charged the Master, holding my sickle in one hand and Zolin's long staff in the other. Not an ideal combination, but this wasn't a time for perfection. The Master turned the sword, holding the blade straight behind him, and then stepped forward and swung it to meet my attack. As I closed, I planted the staff into the ground and pushed, jumped and swung my feet forward. I felt the sword swish beneath me, felt it take a part of my coat, as I kicked the Master in the chest.

I hit the ground, looked to see the Master picking himself

up. I rolled forward and dove at him, tackling the man and bringing him to the floor with me.

"Go!" I said. "Save the others, and then come back for me."

Would my parents listen to me, or would they try to exact their own vengeance? Either way, I couldn't pay attention. The Master knocked my hands away and, somehow, lifted me up and threw me to the side. I caught myself on the wall, glancing towards the stair to see Katherine and Graham vanishing up it.

"It doesn't matter," the Master said, following my look. "They're running into a trap."

"What, that army of spirits you had before?"

"Those aren't any spirits, they're all guides. Or they used to be," the Master said. He picked his sword up off the ground and turned to face me. My sickle looked awfully small in comparison. "Many of them so old that they didn't even have weapons. Or the ones they used have broken over the ages, leaving them with nothing more than what they can scrounge."

"Why are they still here?" I asked, part of me wanted to attack straightaway. Part of me wanted to throw everything against the Master. The other part of me knew I held a small sickle and, with that sword, the master could cleave me in half without thinking about it. I had to hope that Graham and Katherine, that the others would come back and together we could overwhelm the Master. So I tried to keep him talking.

"A pact," the Master said. "One that is becoming unnecessary."

"A pact?"

The Master took another pair of steps and scraped the sword along the ground in an upward swing towards my torso. I back-stepped out of the reach and danced along the edge of the platform, near the cliff with the Cycle spreading out behind me. The Master followed my moves, but with indifference.

He didn't want to kill me.

"As you now know, Carver, you can be the path out of Riven," the Master said. "A controlled valve to relieve the pressure in these dark times."

"You make it sound so simple," I slipped between the ever-flowing stream of spirits. If nothing else, the ghosts of people past would make good shields against any sword swings.

"It should be," the Master said. "If you cannot see what is happening, that Riven is collapsing, then you are more blind than I expected."

"So the only way to save Riven is to give you what you want?" I said. "That's convenient."

"Again I make the offer, and again you refuse," the Master said. "If you will not change your mind, then I will keep you here, trapped in Riven, until your sleeping body can be found."

"Try it," I said.

Instead of answering me, the Master turned towards the stream of spirits. I followed his eyes and, mixed with the common people and soldiers flooding down to the Cycle, moved a pair in medieval tunics. Strong and without will, they shuffled to the edge and jumped into the Cycle with the others.

"With every victory your friends earn," the Master said. "I grow stronger. With every broken binding, your hope dims. Now, Carver, I think it's time to shut that mouth of yours. The passage will open with your life, it does not require anything more."

The Master hefted the sword and swung, cleaving a line

through the spirits and scattering their bodies across the ground. He stepped into the gap, his glare coming through his mask into my eyes. I backpedaled until I felt my foot brush the one thing that could get me out of this alive.

As the Master ran forward I bent down, grabbed Takeda's katana, and thrust it like a spear. The Master slid to the side, brought his sword crashing down on the katana and battered it from my hand. Takeda's weapon flew away over the cliff and into the Cycle, joining its owner in the next life. But it had bought me a moment's momentum.

I lunged in with the sickle, tried to get inside the Master's reach. Leaving the great sword in his right hand, the Master met my strike with his left hand. Grabbed my wrist as the sickle closed in on his head and held it firm. I stared into that black rock mask, those eyes hidden under the dark of his hood, and tried to find some measure of humanity.

The Master tried to bring the great sword back, I gripped his right wrist with my left hand. We grappled, our strength measured in my desperation and his determination. I heard the Master gasp, not out of surprise, or fear, but of delight. His left hand twisted my wrist back, pushed the sickle away, and I used the push to back up from the Master and get out of the sword's range. Where the Master had found that sudden surge of strength, I didn't know.

"Another binding gone," the Master said. "Carver, save your friends. Stop this futility."

The Master let me get my distance, let me circle him and put my back to the spirits, to the path back up the Mountain. Again the Master took his time, toying with me. I saw his gaze sweep back to the stair; another odd spirit amid the horde. Another one in older dress, but this one I recognized.

"Pierce," I said. The Master nodded. "He died 20 years ago?"

"I bound him on that day," the Master replied, following my retreat around the room.

"How?" I said. "How could you manage to bind all of them?"

"So many questions," the Master said. "What does it matter?"

He hefted his sword again, and when he came towards me, I threw the sickle at his face and ran. I wouldn't win that fight. Not with a weapon I didn't know how to use, against an enemy stronger than me, and who seemed to have every advantage. I skipped up the stairs, pushing and knocking spirits down around me. Trying to create any obstacle I could to keep the Master from pursuing. Or least to buy me some time.

I made it back up to the landing, where the Master's bed sat, and saw a slaughter. Graham and Katherine were working alongside Anna and Selena, with Nicholas watching, as they carved into a long line of spirits. Former guide leaders, most of them weaponless, all of them charging in with reckless abandon to be fought and wrangled by my friends.

The Master sacrificing his army for himself.

"They're bound to him," I called. "With every death you're making him stronger."

"Then what do you propose we do?" Graham said,

smashing his hammer into the face of another elder spirit. "We have to fight, or they'll tear us apart."

"Then don't wrangle them," I said. "Keep the fire out."

Selena, her cleaver glowing, twisted her wrist as she bit in to the next spirit. The fire went out and, instead of falling to the ground blank-eyed and ready to be cycled, he spirit lurched away, grabbing at its injured throat. The spirit would recover, eventually, but it still took strength from the Master.

"Carver, behind you!" Anna called. I turned and saw the Master, sword high, hacking through spirits as he made his way up the stairs.

"Graham, Katherine. We have to take him together," I said. "Selena, Anna, you keep the other spirits back."

My parents heard the call and twisted away from their targets. Selena stepped in to cover as the three of us turned towards the Master. I reached for my belt, and realized I had no weapon. Graham glanced at me and laughed.

"Better leave this one to the two of us," Graham said. "You're only going to get in the way."

He wasn't wrong. I needed to find a weapon, and fast. I backpedaled away as Katherine and Graham engaged. They kept the Master pinned on the stairs; Graham's hammer forcing the Master to intercept with his great sword. Katherine tried to get behind, to batter the Master with her batons. As she moved, the Master back-stepped down the stairs and cut his great sort in a high arc to his left. The blade cut into Katherine's leg, knocking her down with a scream.

A spirit tackled me from behind. A crazy maniac with the beard longer than my torso. His hands clawed for my face and I batted them away. We rolled across the floor as I tried to get my elbow under the spirit's chin to force his snapping teeth back. We hit a rock wall, stopping our tumbled with me on my back. The spirit pressed his knee up into my stomach, twisting my intestines and sending my vision spinning. One of the spirit's hands reached back, elbow cocked and ready to deliver a fist into my eyes, when I saw a flash. Nicholas stabbed the spirit with one of the crossbow bolts he'd carried for me, back when we'd first left the apartment, when I still had the weapon.

The bolt burst into blue fire, wrangling the angry spirit. I pushed the idle body off of me, another soul restored to the Master.

"Thanks," I said to Nicholas, climbing to my feet. "Got any more of those?"

Nicholas shook his head. "I've already used several."

I turned back to the stairs and saw Graham mounting a frantic defense as the Master fought his way back up. He was swinging faster than he had before, the strikes more precise. Graham did everything he could to keep the hammer bouncing the sword away. The Master turned a cross swing into an overhead stab. Graham swung the hammer up from the ground, and deflected the blow, but the Master wheeled with the momentum, bringing the great sort back around faster than Graham could halt his own hammer swing.

The Master yelled, a bellow of pain. Katherine had clawed her batons into his legs. Lying there, grievously wounded, she delivered a strike that saved Graham's life, such as it was. Graham did not waste it. My father twisted his shoulders sent the hammer smashing into the Master's head. The blow struck the black crystal mask and shattered it, sent the Master staggering back down the steps.

I locked on his face. Clear in the blue light of the Cycle. The old eyes, the thick white beard, long gray hair of Piotr, living leader of the guides.

I WANTED to ask a thousand questions. A thousand things I wanted to say in that instant when I saw his face. When I saw that Piotr had been behind all of the attacks, the binding and suffering of my parents, and the threats to my friends. Before I could voice any of them, though, I heard Anna cry behind me.

"There's too many!" Anna sounded frantic and I turned. They were overwhelmed. Five spirits were driving Selena and Anna back, all of them bearing multiple wounds, strikes that should have wrangled the spirits. Instead, the cuts meant nothing to those already dead. Using the blue fire, though, would only make Piotr stronger.

I had to make a call. If we stayed and didn't finish Piotr in a minute, we'd be overwhelmed. If we left, assuming we made it out, who knew when we'd make it back here.

Behind me, Graham continued his desperate defense, Piotr's toothy smile growing with every swing. In front of me, Selena yelped as a spirit raked her forearm. We couldn't win.

"We have to run," I said. "Use the fire!"

Selena and Anna didn't hesitate, once more cloaking their weapons in blue flame and slashing their way through the spirits. I pushed Nicholas after them.

"Carver," I heard my father yell. "Get them out of here!"

"Working on it," I replied. Not that I was doing much. What I wouldn't have given for my lash. For those knives right now. Selena and Anna, they were doing work. Ducking underneath scratching nails and sidestepping shoulder charges to deliver stabs and jabs, crushing hits with Anna's spiked mace, and sending one spirit after another to blue burning doom.

I followed Selena, Anna, and Nicholas up the stairs towards the exit. Glanced back to my parents, still holding Piotr on the stairwell. Piotr looked like he was playing, testing the reach of the hammer. My mother was on the floor, holding her injured leg. Unable to move. Unable to run.

"Keep going," I said the Nicholas and the others. "Keep running until you're outside and then keep running still."

"What are you doing?" Selena asked, turning back.

"I can't leave them," I said.

"I can help you."

"Protect Nicholas," I said. "He'll need you."

Selena nodded, then reached inside her coat and pulled out her long knife. It seemed pitifully small next to the great sword, but I counted one weapon better than none. So when she tossed it my way, I caught it and nodded my thanks.

"Remember Carver," Selena said. "We need you too."

I took the comment and started back down the steps. I didn't have any intention of dying here. I didn't plan to let my parents die either.

Back in the circle, Graham and Piotr engaged in a deadly dance. As I stepped into the clearing, I saw my mother make another move. Darting with her remaining baton, dragging her left leg, she lunged at Piotr's back. The strike a second slower than she used to be. Piotr caught the motion and continued his swing, turning with the blade back to catch my mother's baton.

Piotr's sword sliced through the baton, and if my mother hadn't fallen to the ground, he would've taken her apart too. Piotr whirled with the swing, shifting his feet and bringing the blade back up and over his head. Swung down towards Graham as my father's hammer slammed towards Piotr's chest. They struck each other, Graham's hammer crushing into Piotr's cloak as Piotr's sword cleaved into Graham's shoulder.

Graham's blow staggered Piotr and he went to one knee, leaning on the great sword. But only for second. Then Piotr rose back to his feet and towered over Graham, crippled on the ground. Piotr raised the sword, and Graham shot a wire from his wrist. It wrapped around Piotr's right hand, burst into flame, and Piotr stumbled back, trying to pull the wire off and shifting the sword to his left hand.

I went towards Katherine, reaching for her, but when she saw me my mother pulled away. "Get out of here, Carver," she said. "For once, let us save you."

I started to reply, but my mother stole the words from my mouth. She grabbed the broken half of her baton, and charged Piotr, still struggling with the wire. Swiped the clawed weapon at his face, and struck home. Opened a long gash along Piotr's cheek, but it wasn't enough. Piotr twisted his left wrist, sending blue fire streaming down the length of his sword. Even with only one hand, strengthened by the return of so many of his spirits to the Cycle, Piotr put an end to Katherine with turning stab.

"Go," Graham said, pulling himself to his knees. "Don't let it be for nothing!"

I saw my father launch another burning wire into Piotr's

face and reach for the knife in his belt, and then I ran. I pushed through the spirits, shoved past the blank faces of the dead. I didn't stop to think about anything other than the next foot in front of me until I was out in the forest. Anna, Selena, and Nicholas were waiting, looking at me with hope that died as they met my eyes.

"It's over," I said. "Go back to the city."

We fled. I felt a part of me, the piece that I had given to Katherine, return as our binding broke. I heard Anna's gasp as Graham's borrowed piece came back to her. I'd lost the parents that I had barely known. Taken by an enemy that at last had a face. A name.

Piotr.

When we reached the stump, Selena and Nicholas kept going. A long run back to the city. Anna and I, though, we had to cross back. I didn't know when we'd be able to catch up with the two spirits. We needed to find a bed that hadn't been used, or that could cross us back into Riven' city.

That could come later. Now I wanted to breathe. Find a drink and remember my parents. Nurse my growing anger.

We crossed back into the zeppelin. The windows of our room showed a spotted sky as the airship buzzed over one of the Great Lakes. Maybe Michigan, or maybe we were farther. The sun setting, that Golden orb lighting the tops of the clouds in purple and orange fire.

"I'm so sorry," Anna said as she sat up.

"It's not your fault," I said, my voice flat.

"We could have done more," Anna said. "We let him come in. Cross over. There were so many spirits that we didn't notice."

"We didn't know," I said, standing up. "We couldn't have known that he'd bound all of them. That every single one we wrangled made him stronger."

Anna said nothing for a minute. I embraced that silence. We'd come so close. Had hit Piotr's base with numbers, at the right time. Only we didn't know what was inside, and Anna and I were missing our weapons. Whether that would have even made a difference. Graham had been one of the strongest fighters I'd ever seen, and my mother wasn't any slouch either.

Piotr had demolished both of them, barely getting hurt in the process. Going after him again would be suicide. So rather than think on it, I decided to solve a simpler problem.

"A drink?" I said.

"Yes please," Anna said. "There's this bottle right here."

I shook my head. "I need something harder."

The two of us made our way to one of the dining areas, to a long metal counter with a sign overhead labeling it the *Sky Bar*. At various ends of the letters small fans turned through some mysterious power. Beneath the sign a pair of bartenders mixed up concoctions from a plethora of vices. A rotating menu declared specialties from where we were flying over at that moment in time. I asked for vodka. Anna ordered her gin. Both on the rocks.

Why did I feel so torn up? So shredded by the loss of two people who, less than a year ago, I didn't know existed? That I thought had abandoned me? Even when I found them, Graham and Katherine weren't alive. They couldn't come over for dinner, go on trips, or enjoy coffee on a cold morning. Our only bonding experiences had been frenetic fights for Riven's survival.

Yet I couldn't seem to summon words. Every sentence that came to my mouth died as the fight with Piotr replayed itself over and over and over again.

How many mistakes I'd made. How many opportunities I'd had to reverse things. Why hadn't I grabbed Selena's knife earlier? Why did I let the katana fall, or kept the sickle? A dozen other choices all turned wrong as I relived the moments.

"How do you deal with it?" I asked Anna. "With your parents?"

"This," Anna said, raising her glass. "And the memories. The times we laughed. The hopes and dreams we shared with each other. I cling to those."

"Wish I had those to turn to," I said.

"You do," Anna said. "How many times did you explore with them over the last few months? How many times did you get to do what you *live for* with the ones you loved? I'd say that's lucky, regardless of how it ended."

"Ghoul hunting as treasured family bonding time," I gave a short laugh.

"There's worse things," Anna said, her eyes stuck to the windows looking out over the water below.

I nodded and took another sip the chilled liquor. The vodka felt good on my tongue, a warm nova in my stomach. I figured a trail of the drinks would eventually lead me back to the cabin, and to a hopefully dreamless sleep. When I woke up, I'd be...

"Where are we flying?" I said, realizing I had no idea of our destination.

"New York," Anna said. "Sorry if it's not where you want to go, but I figured we didn't have time to be picky."

"It's fine," I said. "We just have to figure out how to get back."

"What's your plan?" Anna replied. "We went in there with everything we had and lost. We're fugitives out here too. There are places we can hide, but not forever."

"I'm not going to hide. We have to take down Piotr," I said.

"Maybe you didn't hear me," Anna said. "We tried that. It

didn't work. Without Graham and Katherine, we'll be slaughtered."

"Only if we try the same thing."

"I'm listening."

"We hit him here. Outside of Riven. He won't have his sword, he won't have an army of spirits to help him," I said.

"You're saying we try to murder the leader of the guides?" Anna said. "I don't think that's going to work."

"Anna, it's either him or me," I said. "Or, worse, we keep dancing around each other until Riven breaks open and we all lose."

"Is stopping Piotr is going to save Riven?" Anna asked.

"I don't know," I said. "But it can't hurt."

"Carver Reed," a familiar voice said as a hand clapped on my shoulder. "Didn't expect to see you on this ship."

I turned into the questioning face of Opperman, the newspaper reporter who seemed always pop up at the strangest times. He wore more than his usual working coat. A level of finery and sophistication that I'd never seen Opperman adopt before, and he didn't look too comfortable in the outfit. A beggar sneaking into a play, or a nice restaurant.

"What are you doing here?" I said.

"Flying to New York, same as you," Opperman said. "Say, how did you fare back there? Those couple of thugs get their hands on you?"

"Not yet," I said. I glanced around, didn't see anyone watching us. "I'm trying to keep a low profile for that reason."

"Well then, you might want to try not looking like a guide," Opperman said. "Especially on a ship to New York for the peace summit."

"Peace summit?" Anna asked.

"Indeed. It starts tomorrow," Opperman said. "I'm covering for the newspaper. Everyone's going to be there."

"Everyone?" I said.

"Everyone that matters," Opperman said. "Even the leader of your own group, that Piotr fellow, is making speech. You sure you're not going?"

I shook my head. "Just needed to get out of the city for a while."

I saw the change come over Opperman's face, the eyes turn from genial conversation to that hard-edged look the reporter had whenever he was hunting for a quote. The man had a nose for a story and once Opperman found the scent, he wouldn't be deterred.

"Mind giving me a clue why?" Opperman said. "The guides having a fight? if Riven's in danger, then the world ought to know."

"It's nothing to do with the rest of the guides," I said.

"Is he right?" Opperman asked Anna. "Also, forgive my manners, I don't believe we've met, Miss?"

"Smith," Anna said. " I think Carver's got the right opinion on this. Nothing to talk about."

Opperman sat back in his chair and appraised us. "So you're saying that the two of you, and by the look of it you're both guides, are on this ship and *not* going to the summit that literally everyone else on board is heading for?"

"A coincidence, really," I said.

"An unfortunate one, then," Opperman swung his head to the right. "Aren't those the two fellows that were trying to grab you in Ezra's?"

I followed his eyes and saw Polk and Derringer, sitting at the table across the room. They hadn't noticed us yet, which might have something to do with the fact that both were bandaged, sipping wine, and looking thoroughly the worse for their fight with Bryce.

"We didn't see them get on," I said.

"We went right into Riven," Anna said. "I don't know how long the ship stayed docked after we boarded."

"We've been in the air for some hours now. I should say we're somewhere over Ohio," Opperman said. "You say you crossed over? And did what? Anything I could file as a story?"

"Opperman, shut it," I said. "We need to get back to our cabin without those two knowing we're here."

"You'll need a distraction," Opperman said. "I think I can provide one, for a story."

"If you can wait until after the summit is over I can give you one heck of a story," I said. "Above the fold, as you say."

"If you were anyone else I wouldn't take your word," Opperman said. "But a reporter needs to protect his sources, and you, Carver, are one of my best."

I downed the rest of my vodka, and Anna shot her gin. I nodded for Opperman to commence whatever plan he had cooking. The reporter stood up from his chair and wandered over to the two guides. Took a seat at the table. Started talking. I watched their eyes as the two guides slowly recognized Opperman as the man who'd knocked them down back in Chicago, when Polk and Derringer had first tried to arrest me. I could see them glazing over at Opperman's barrage of questions.

"Time to make a move," I said. "You go first. They don't know you as well."

Anna nodded, slipped out of the chair and made her way through the dining room. She crossed through the crowd and, as I walked, neither Polk nor Derringer looked up at her. One down, me to go. I shrugged out of my coat and held the heavy thing in my arms. Underneath I only had a plain white shirt, a tad less distinctive than the guide coat.

In front of me were tables and chairs, people mixing in

and out as they decided on afternoon meals, cocktails, or more. Polk and Derringer were on the left side, so I veered right. Went around one table. Scooted behind a large gentleman who seemed intent on eating an entire cow by himself. A waiter in front of me handed out champagne to everybody around a larger table. I slipped behind her and kept moving. Almost clear.

I heard a rattle behind me, a tinkle of glass as someone's flute whacked against the tabletop and shattered. Someone yelped and I turned, against my own judgment, to see what was going on. The large man with the steak was beating on his own chest, his face turning purple. A couple of waiters ran over, one was trying to dislodge whatever chunk of meat had found itself trapped within his throat. All eyes went to the struggle. Then I felt a pair on me.

I looked to my right and saw Polk and Derringer, their eyes dead set on mine.

I ran.

WE DASHED through the airship and back into our cabin. As the door shut, I looked back in the hallway and didn't see either of the two guides there. We'd either lost Polk and Derringer, or they'd taken too long to get up from the table. If we were lucky, Anna and I would be able to hide in our room.

"Until we land, anyway," Anna said to my remark. "There's not exactly other ways off the ship."

"When we're on the ground, I feel like we can find another way out," I said. "In the meantime, we'll just have to be careful. "

"You mean starve?" Anna said. "Stay in this room for the next day?"

"Did you think the fugitive life was a glamorous one?"

"For a second I dared to hope," Anna said, sitting down on the bed. "Did you hear what Opperman said?"

"Piotr's going to be in New York," I said. "We'll have a chance."

Anna opened her mouth to reply when a crackling noise came from the hallway. A gravelly, distorted voice spoke.

"This is your captain. We've been informed that there are a pair of potential criminals on board our aircraft," the voice said over an intercom. "In order to ensure the safety of our crew, and our passengers, I'm ordering everyone to return to their cabins until further notice. We will be conducting a cabin by cabin search until the suspects are found and apprehended. We apologize for the inconvenience, and hope you understand that the safety of our guests is paramount."

Not good. A cabin by cabin search? I looked around the cabin, confirmed there were not, in fact, a bevy of hiding places. Squeezing beneath the beds seemed like a poor choice.

"So do we wait?" Anna said. "We could stand by the door, ambush them when they open it?"

"We can't fight all of the guards on the ship," I said. "This isn't Riven. We don't have our weapons."

Which meant we'd have to try another way. Staying in the cabin was a nonstarter, but the mass thumping going on outside, feet pounding on the hallways above and below us as people scurried to their cabins… that meant opportunity.

"They won't search the crew area," I said. "If we can hide there, we might stand a chance."

"It's as good a plan as any," Anna said.

I opened our cabin door and looked into the hallway. People running back and forth, yammering at their spouses and friends. Ducking into cabins and slamming shut the doors. I threw my coat on and we left. Took a right turn and headed away from the dining area and the bar, towards the ship's engines.

A stairwell at the end of the hall led up and down, next to it stood a door marked, in bold white letters: NO ADMISSION - CREW ONLY. I turned the knob and found it locked. Anna pounded on the door before I could suggested trying another route. A moment later the knob turned and the door opened, an irritated serviceman already talking on the other side.

"Did you lose your key again?" the serviceman said before realizing we were not, in fact, part of his crew. I pushed him back through the doorway, clapping my hand over his mouth. Anna slipped in behind me and shut the door. I pressed the crewmen up against the wall, a narrow one lacking the finery of the passenger quarters. Further along I could see the hall split into a series of catwalks and compartments, space for churning engines, mechanical parts, crew bunks, and bathrooms.

"You're going to take us to the engines," I said to the serviceman.

"The engines?" Anna asked.

"We can't hide here for another day until the ship reaches New York," I said. "We need to bring her down, now."

The serviceman, eyes wide, tried to nod. I didn't move my hand. Not giving the guy a chance to scream.

"Now, we're a pair of guides that you're leading on a ship inspection," I said to the serviceman. "That's what you're going to tell anyone we run into. Don't try anything, or I'll snap your neck. Then I'll cross over to Riven, find your spirit there, and make sure you go straight to the Cycle."

The serviceman tried to nod again, more frantic than before. I let my hand fall away and he sucked in a large breath. My left hand balled into a fist, ready to sock him in the kidneys if he tried to shout. Guess the serviceman didn't want to risk his life for no reason, as he stepped away and waved us down the hall.

"Follow me," the serviceman said loudly. "If you want to see the engines and make sure they're safe, I'll take you right to them."

"We're turning into real criminals," Anna whispered to me. "First evading arrest, now taking a hostage?"

"You can always say I pressured you into it," I said. "Threatened you, blackmail, take your pick."

"What about you?"

"I don't know," I replied. "I'll figure something out."

The serviceman led us past the bunks in the bathrooms, through a series of black metal catwalks bordered by gaskets blowing steam, shifting and churning pistons, and a maze of pipes. Copper lights hung from the ceiling by threads of wire, their yellowed glow giving a rich bronze cast to the world. Apparently most of the crew members were helping with the search, because the back rooms were deserted. Only a skeleton set making sure things were running well.

Valves covered the engine room. Large and small wheels controlling the pressure and fuel leading to various fans keeping the zeppelin aloft. A woman stood there working them in a pressed royal blue uniform. She turned as the serviceman entered and regarded us with the baleful stare of someone interrupted out of deep concentration.

"Now is not the time," the woman said. "We're executing an altitude change to get through a rough patch."

"They wanted to talk to you, Wynn," the serviceman said.

"We need you to bring the ship down," I said, cutting right to it. "The criminals on board are dangerous. They could disable the vessel. We don't want fatalities."

Wynn stared at me, then moved her eyes to the serviceman, then to Anna. "Who are you?" Wynn asked.

"I'm a guide," I said. "We're trying to catch a pair of fugitives."

"Right," Wynn said. "The only person who can tell me to bring the ship down is the captain. You want to change this flight, you talk to him."

We didn't have time for that. Not to mention that the odds of us getting all way back out of this area and to the bridge without running into problems were zero. Time to cross another line.

"Wynn, let's make this real simple," I said. "The world is at risk. We're the only ones who can save it. In order to do that, this ship needs to be on the ground, now."

Wynn raised her eyebrow. "I already told you. The ship stays up unless the captain tells me otherwise."

Anna pushed past me, walked right up to Wynn and pressed her into the valves behind her. "Listen, Wynn. He's telling the truth. We're not above doing what we need to do get it. Either you take the ship down now, or we play a game where I see how many of these valves I have to twist to send the ship into a dive. Which do you think gives you a better chance to live?"

Wynn shifted her eyes between the two of us. "I'll do it."

Anna turned back to me. "See? You're not the only one who can talk tough."

I barely saw the move, the change in Wynn's expression as she shot an elbow into Anna's side. The mechanic reached up and slapped a button next to the valves, one labeled emergency assist. Overhead alarms began to go off.

And to think, for a second I'd thought we might actually pull this off.

THE SERVICEMAN DECIDED to be a hero and came at me as Anna and Wynn struggled by the valves. He punched like a man who had never fought before, wide and slow, afraid of hitting his target. I ducked the swing and swept my leg through his, tripping him to the ground. I glanced behind us, to the hallway where we'd come in from, and hoped to find a door. Nothing. Any reinforcements would have easy access.

I heard a yell, and turned back to find Wynn on the floor. Anna went to the valves and started twisting the wheels. Shutting them at random.

"I don't think—" I started.

"You're going to bring it down and kill us all," Wynn said from the ground, then pushed herself off of the floor and jumped into a low tackle.

I felt the serviceman grabbing at my ankles and stepped away, raised my foot and threatened to stamp on his face. The serviceman caught the gesture and held up his hands. Why risk yourself when reinforcements had to be on the way?

I felt the airship lurch as the whole world tilted on its axis and sent us falling to the right. My shoulder rammed into the side wall of the room, the metal pipes providing nothing in the way of cushioning. I heard shouts from up the hall. Crew members having a hard time keeping their own footing as the ship twisted and turned.

Anna kept herself up right, hands gripping a pair of valves while Wynn held onto Anna's coat. Trying to pull herself forward.

"Then tell me how the land," Anna yelled to the mechanic.

"You can't do it all from here," Wynn replied. "It takes a captain to steer."

Anna reached up and dialed another valve to the right, sealing it. "He'll get the idea."

"You're insane," Wynn said.

"We're desperate," I said.

I felt my stomach climb up my throat as the ship entered a steeper drop. Fans were shutting off as the listing craft accelerated towards the ground. Towards a very messy landing.

"Fine!" Wynn said. "Reopen the one on your right. After five seconds open the one on your left. They'll equalize."

Anna did that, twisted the valves open. Gradually I felt the ship start to pull up out of it suicide dive. My ability to stand came back and I pushed myself off the wall. Just in time for the serviceman to come at me again.

He opted for the less precise method of the shoulder charge, running right in at my chest. The serviceman pinned me back against the wall as I wrapped my arm around his neck, slung my left foot behind his ankles and once more slammed the man to the ground. This time I didn't let up. Gave him a vicious kick; the man going limp. I'd never knocked someone out here before. Only in Riven. More lines being crossed, and all because of Piotr.

Wynn pushed Anna to the side, using the ship's

momentum and Anna's larger coat to drag shove my friend away from the valves and throw her to the floor. I moved to help, then paused as two more servicemen ran into the room, these brandishing stun batons. Two on one, and I had no weapon. So I did the only thing I could.

I ran for the valves. Crossed the room as the servicemen started after me. I spun as many valves as I could to the right. Wynn tried to stop me, but Anna reversed their positions, clinging to Wynn's back and forcing her to her knees. An ugly fight.

The airship lurched again. I heard the serviceman yell as they were driven back in the wall. I copied Anna's technique; kept my hands in the valves. I felt as though I were hanging from a cliff, the valves my only handholds.

"You have to open some or you'll kill us all," Wynn pleaded.

"Not until there's no other choice," I said. "This ship's landing."

There weren't any windows in the engine room, no way of telling how close to the surface we were. Adrenaline and nausea shot through me, my stomach flipping end over end. I didn't fear dying, really - so far as deaths went, going out in an airship crash seemed to be one of the better ones. Only, I didn't want to kill all the others on the on the ship. The other passengers had no idea they'd boarded the wrong ship. Piotr's catastrophe shouldn't hurt them too.

"Tell me when," I said to Wynn.

"Now," Wynn said. "Do it now. At least two of them."

Wynn might've been lying. I couldn't tell. Like she'd played Anna. If the ship would right itself and we'd be captured. If Wynn had told the truth, though, and I did nothing, everyone would die. So I turned the valves. Opened them and felt the fans churn as the airship struggled to pull itself upright.

Other alarms added to the cacophony. I didn't know what any the noises meant, but I assumed I was doing something right. An assumption that proved true a moment later with the first loud crack from somewhere up front. Followed by another and another. A section of the hallway ripped away in a brief flash of a brown tree trunk, pine needles scattering everywhere. Branches tore through. One after another.

We were going down into a forest.

"Hold on!" I yelled to nobody and everybody. Because I couldn't think of anything else to say. Because everything in front of us vanished into a massive green, brown, crackling terror. I kept my grip on the valves, ducked my head into my chest and tried to survive.

103

SUNFLOWERS GREW EVERYWHERE. Yellow, brown, and tall. I saw them outside of the ship, I saw them within a few feet of me as I pried my fingers loose from the valves and took a fleeting step forward. We had crashed through a forest and, somehow, the captain had put us down in a wide field. The walkways in front of us had been torn away entirely. Wreckage scattered all around, but the engine room held. The thick pipes providing shelter.

Around me the servicemen groaned. Wynn looked unconscious, and I pulled her away to see Anna trapped against the wall. Her eyes closed and a gash marring her forehead. Probably where Wynn had fallen into her. I picked Anna up, hefted her in her coat. Stood on my aching knees and walked away from the ship.

I ducked under bars and beams, the occasional burst of steam spraying hot wet air over my face. Pieces of torn canvas whiled in the wind, slapping around like the wings of an enormous bird. Shouts for help and rescue rang out as people realized they weren't dead. I kept walking. Crunching over the plants and getting out from beneath the vessel.

The field was huge. Stretching for hundreds of yards. Every inch of it covered in tall sunflower stalks. I tried to shield Anna from their leaves, kept her face covered by her coat. Warm summer sunlight blazed at us, super-heating me, causing sweat to run out of every pore. I didn't know where we'd landed, but staying by that ship and getting captured would make the disaster worthless.

Eventually we reached the forest at the edge of the field and there, underneath the shade of the trees, I risked a look back. The airship looked like a beached whale, its great bulk sliding slowly to the ground as the zeppelin deflated. I could still hear cries, and saw at least one or two riders on horseback had come galloping up to the vessel. Help would be coming. Those who could be saved, would be saved. I hoped Opperman was among them.

"You thought I was reckless before, Selena," I muttered to myself. "Wait till you hear about this."

I went for another hour through the woods, walking over pine needles and taking in the smells of ferns and blooming flowers. Chirping birds and the scuffles of animals in the deep. Anna dragged on my arms, a consequence of time more than weight. Our coats - I'd taken off mine - had to be tucked with us. I made frequent breaks and pauses to catch my breath. Stops to make sure Anna still breathed.

"Carver?" Anna spoke up as I trudged along, the day sinking deeper into the afternoon. "Where are we?"

"I have no idea," I said. "But we're alive."

"My head hurts," Anna said.

"You've got a nasty cut," I replied. "I'm hoping we can find somewhere to set you down soon, because my arms are going to give out."

"Oh," Anna said. "I think I can walk."

"That would be lovely."

I helped her to stand, and Anna immediately fell against

me. Her legs had power, she could move, she just needed support. So we kept walking as afternoon dwindled into evening and the sun fell behind the horizon. I did not want to be stuck in the forest all night. We didn't have any camping gear, no food or water, and Anna needed treatment for her cut.

"Over there," Anna said, pointing. "Do you see it?"

A small town's twinkling lights flickered in the twilight, peeking between tree trunks and low, leafy branches. I'd been looking for salvation the entire time, but now that we'd potentially found it I paused. A farmhouse maybe, someplace where odds of us running into other survivors were slim. A town only a few hours walk away from a crash? We wouldn't be the only ones heading there.

"Carver," Anna said at my hesitation. "I don't think I can keep going."

"Then let's get you some help," I said, and we turned towards those burning lights. Being free wouldn't help us if Anna died, or if her gash became infected.

The town grew. As we came closer and left the forest, I realized the dense tree trunks blocked much of the town from view. Traffic; motorcars and horses and a rail line, washed their noise over us as we approached. We didn't have a good way to cover Anna's gash, something that would draw commentary if seen, so as we came close Anna found a bench on the side of the road. Kept her head low and her hair covering the wound.

I continued into the town, trying to find some form of first-aid. A place we could stay that wouldn't ask questions. And hoped our crimes hadn't beaten us here.

A BROAD AVENUE, caught between old and new, cut through the center of town. Between motorcars and horses sharing the street, kicking up dirt and mud as they went by to the scattered flickers of neon signs going up outside storefronts and saloons, I realized that Chicago's common luxuries hadn't spread everywhere. No automated taxis, a lack of paved roads, and, on the other side of things, clean air.

My mask hung inside my coat, in the breast pocket designed to carry it. First there'd been Inman's camp, and now this town. I resolved to get out more. Find more places where the world wasn't best experienced through a filter.

I scanned the windows and the marquees, trying to find something that indicated a doctor. Some sort of a hospital or clinic. I passed by places selling food, drink, and virtually everything else a person might need. A small clock adorned every light post, their hands adding a mechanical cadence to the buzz of the place. People shuffled about without the hurried, frantic nature Chicago. Their eyes fell on my coat and didn't slide away but lingered, instead, with the curious fascination of seeing a legend come to life.

I made it a block and a half in before I saw the glowing heart hanging in a front window. Inside, through the glass, I saw the usual white coats of nurses and doctors tending to a smattering of patients covering the range from early evening drunk to late afternoon farm accident. A perfect spot.

I smuggled Anna to the place, keeping her head down and pressed into my chest, as though she were suffering from some sort of grief or cold, even though she wore her coat and the night was warm. Whatever attention we attracted quickly drew away to the roaring sound of another engine, the laughter echoing from a nearby bar, or even just a glance up at the starlit sky.

Out with Inman, that night in the bluffs; my first time to really see the glittering canopy that hung above us every night, that Chicago's endless glow made invisible. The town split the difference, its lights washing out the smaller stars but letting the brighter ones poke through. Part of me wondered if Riven lived on one of those, a place hung up somewhere in the cosmos that we happened to travel to when we crossed over.

Inside the clinic, a nurse took one look at Anna and leapt into action. Set her down on a chair, swabbed the wound with a wet towel, and set about to stitching it closed. Anna took the whole thing without talking, staring forward with a glazed look in her eye. Exhausted. Like me.

"Where did she get this?" a doctor asked me, stepping up to watch as the nurse finished closing the wound.

"Running through the woods," I said. "Tripped and fell."

"Aren't you a little old for those kinds of games?" the doctor said.

"Apparently not," I said.

"It's none of my business," the doctor said. "But you two appear to be guides, correct?"

I said nothing for a moment. Weighed the answer. With

the coats we were wearing, however, it would be obvious. I nodded.

"We're leaving town as soon as she's ready to go," I said.

"Look at her," the doctor said. "Look at you, for that matter. You're in no state to go anywhere. Let me recommend you a hotel, nice and discreet."

"Why?" I said. "What do you want?"

"I want nothing," the doctor said. "I have a daughter. Her name is Ada, and she is one of you. Lives east of here, in Pittsburgh. Is it true what they say, what I've been hearing, that it's getting worse over there? On the other side?"

"It is," I said. "War, disease, they hurt as much over there as they do here."

"I know you probably think those of us here don't care," the doctor said. "That we don't understand what you're doing. It's not true. We just don't know how to help."

"This helps," I said, gesturing it Anna. "Giving us places to sleep. Food and water. Those help."

"Then we will do what we can," the doctor said. "When she's done, the two of you can leave. No payment necessary."

I looked at Anna's face, her sagging eyes as the nurse cleaned up the stitches. "You mentioned a hotel?"

"It's a block further in," the doctor said. "Called *Pine's Rest*. Tell them we sent you and they'll treat you well. Remember that she has to get those out in a few days."

Minutes later the two of us were walking down the street towards the hotel. Anna kept her eyes crawling over the scenery. I tried to keep her standing straight.

"What were you talking about with the doctor?" Anna asked.

"For once, someone was saying thank you," I said.

"I bet that's a rare thing for you," Anna replied.

"I liked it better when you were quiet," I said.

The *Pine's Rest* stood five stories of ordinary. Without the doctor's direction, I would have kept walking by. *Pine's Rest* had a small sign and dim windows, a lack of energy. Then again, we didn't want attention. I definitely didn't want excitement. For that, the *Pine's Rest* fit perfectly. We booked a room on promise of paying in the morning and went upstairs. A pair of twin beds in a small space that made me reminisce about the airships comforts.

I didn't have much money left on me and I didn't think Anna did either. If we were going to book passage all the way to New York, then the *Pine's Rest* would have to go without. Another crime to add to our growing list. A part of me despaired at how easily I came to that conclusion. Such small time acts no longer seemed to have relevance in a world growing darker and more desperate.

"I'm going to cross over," I said.

"I don't think I can," Anna said. "Not tonight."

"You could feel better on the other side?"

"Carver," Anna said "haven't you had enough adventure for one day?"

"In this world, yes."

When I lied on the bed, the thriving hum on the street outside the window pouring in, I felt the pull towards sleep. That threat of diving deep into that unconscious pool. Rather than follow that pull, though, I focused my mind on Riven and attempted to cross.

105

I LUCKED OUT. The bed never been used before by a guide. It had no anchor in Riven, and so when I focused on the apartment I shared with Selena and Nicholas, I woke up right where I wanted to be.

Selena stood outside on the balcony, leaning over the edge and staring out over the city. As though nothing had changed.

"You made it back," I said.

"We ran the entire way," Selena said. "I never realized how different we are over here. We never tired, Carver. I never had to stop and catch my breath. Never felt my legs give out. I ran right up to the door."

"Not everything about being a spirit is a disadvantage," I said.

"I kept expecting it to happen. It was scary when it didn't. When my legs kept moving," Selena said, then glanced at me with a worried glint to her eye. "Look at me. Here I am talking about not getting tired, when you must be exhausted."

I told her the story. Bringing down the zeppelin and the

running through the forest while carrying me in my arms. Selena took the whole thing while barely batting an eye. At the end she nodded her head gave me a sad smile.

"It seems like our lives are one mess after another," Selena said. "I'm glad you made it."

"I wouldn't mind a bit more calm," I replied.

I reached out and took her hand. I'd never quite become used to how a spirit's touch felt in Riven, that lukewarm, almost placid feel. The lack of real blood moving through their veins. But I held on, threading my fingers through hers.

"So what are we doing now?" Selena said. "Carver, I don't think we can do another attack on the Mountain."

"I agree," I said. "As much as I'd like to think we can beat him, Piotr's too strong. Anna and I are on our way to find him on the other side, where he won't have his weapons. His spirits. If we take him out over there, that will break his bindings. Piotr might even go right to the Cycle by himself."

"You really think that'll work?"

I shrugged. "It's all we've got."

We stood in silence for a minute, watching the sparks flare. Then Selena let go of my hand and pulled me in for a tighter hug.

"I'm sorry you never got to say goodbye to them," Selena said. "If it matters, Katherine and Graham were wonderful during the trip out. Were amazing to get to know while we stayed here in this apartment. They were always funny, always enjoying every moment together. Whether they were fighting spirits or not."

A side of my parents that I never saw. Yes, we had a chance over the last couple of months, after freeing Graham, to catch up with each other, but most of our nights had been spent chasing ghouls and closing breaches. Wrangling spirits to keep Riven whole. Not a lot of opportunity for family togetherness. Not a lot of opportunity to grow bonds between mother and father and son.

"Tell me more," I said. "Did you ever talk about their past? Who they were or what they wanted to be?"

Selena paused. Then spoke slowly. "Carver, you may not understand, but it feels strange to talk about life when you're no longer living. I don't talk about my children, or ask you to try to find them, because it feels like that part of me is no longer here. Katherine and Graham were the same. We only talked about what they'd done in Riven. Their adventures together."

"Never once?" I said. "My mom never talked about how she died? Or what brought her and Graham together?"

Selena shook her head. "I'm sorry. Maybe we weren't close enough."

We stayed out there for a while longer. Talking, touching, and reveling in a moment without horror and violence. Sometimes I needed a reminder that those moments could actually happen in Riven, or outside of it.

"I'm going to go back to her house," I said. "I bet her diaries are still there. I never finished reading them."

"I'll go with you," Selena said. "There's no reason to stay here. Also, Nicholas is hard at work at something new."

"Something new?"

"You'll have to ask him. You remember him talking about the Cycle, how he wanted to learn more about it? I guess seeing how it worked in the Mountain gave him an idea."

We went downstairs to the bottom level, on the ground floor, and found Nicholas bent over a table. A lot of the machines that have been in the room had disappeared. When I asked the scientist he gestured towards the mound of metal and tubing and other scraps gathered together on that table.

"Riven isn't booming with raw material," Nicholas said.

"So I'm converting it. I think the end result will be well worth it, however."

"What's that result going to be?" I asked.

"I'll know it when I find it," Nicholas said. "Right now it is only an idea. Something that might solve all of our problems if it turns out to be true. Or, if it's not the case, then I'll have merely wasted days and days of effort."

"Is that all?"

"Your tone implies that perhaps engaging in such random activities is, in fact, a waste of time," Nicholas replied. "I can assure you that it is not. Especially when time has no endpoint, provided you stay alive."

"Whether I live or die isn't looking too certain right now," I said.

"Don't take too long," Selena chimed in. "You know how we like your toys, Nicholas,"

"Toys?" Nicholas said. "Katherine and Graham never called them toys. I suppose it is too much to ask that I get some appreciation."

"We love you Nicholas," I said.

"If you really loved me, when you get back from wherever you're going, if you could bring another bit of metal. Any metal really, but I would prefer something thick. Iron or steel. If you would be so kind," the scientist said.

"We'll keep our eyes open," I said. Metal in Riven? Rare even if you weren't specifying a type. Where we were going? The Shambles? We'd be lucky if we found anything usable.

I wasn't going there for the scientist or his experiments. I was going there because, while Anna recovered, I wanted to find out what it really happened to my mother.

106

SPIRITS ALWAYS CROWDED THE SHAMBLES. The derelict build-ings and broad streets providing ample room for the horde of spirits to run through on the way to the Cycle. More now than before. Less defined. The soldiers that used to make up so many of the dead running through here had thinned out, replaced by old and young. The diseased.

The word continued to be that the plague was spreading. More and more people suffering from what they called the flu. Selena and I moved among them, using the spirits for cover as we made our way through the district. Dodging guides along the way.

My mother's house stood open, the back door ajar as we left it those months ago when I found Selena there, a captive of Katherine's when Graham and, by extension, Piotr had bound her. Upstairs sat a series of tables stacked with pages covered in my mother's handwriting. I wanted to dive into those journals. To explore my own past.

Selena went to the far side and broke into the pages. I didn't have a specific goal, except to try to find out more about what had led my parents together. What had led to my mother dying shortly after my birth. To get there I shuffled through page after page of notes, discussions on various hunts Katherine had gone on with Bryce. Wondering paragraphs asking what I'd been doing. Feedback from Bryce on where I'd been moved to and who I lived with.

I'm not sure what I expected to find in the pages, what I thought would be revealed to me about my mother. I found that the life of a spirit in Riven shared many of the same problems I had on the other side. Boredom, a desire for purpose, and dreams were all there. Thoughts of choices not made haunted my mother's days. Joyful anecdotes about finding fascinating buildings, or meeting a spirit that hadn't yet gone astray and delving into a conversation. If anyone could say they had lived after dying, my mother had done so.

"Carver," Selena said. "I think I found what you wanted."

I went over and reached for the the first page that Selena was holding, but she moved it back.

"It's not easy reading," Selena said. "I can just tell you what it says?"

"I have to know," I said. "My mother said Piotr killed her. I need to know how, why."

Selena handed me the page without another word. Slid beneath it the next few. A stack of entries. I started to read:

I feel as though I'm starting to lose more of these memories. The things that have led me to this place, and who I am. As though my grasp on reality is fading. So I'm writing them down.

This memory starts in the spring of 1889. On a raid to close a breach. Some skirmish on the other side of the world that brought a lot of hapless soldiers into Riven at once. As happens when countries forget that their wars don't just affect the living. Graham wielded that hammer of his, a ridiculous weapon. One that gave him such a small window of flexibility. I remember laughing at it, saving him from a group of spirits that made their way inside his reach.

Rather than being haughty, or dismissive, Graham chose to play game with me. Challenged me to ever-increasing feats of stupidity here in Riven. Like anyone, I enjoyed pushing myself to the limits, so I didn't refuse. Together we soon were going on nightly adventures. Drawing closer and closer to each other. Until, six months later, Graham told me he was dying.

Told me that, on the other side, he had a disease that was eating away at his heart. I had never seen him over there. In Riven only. He lived on the West Coast, and I in Chicago. What point was there in journeying across the country to find each other when we could do so every night?

He made me promise. Promise to bind him when he died. When he felt he was going, Graham crossed over and stood with me next to him. I held his hand and he told me when he felt the cord binding him to his body sever. I replaced it with my own.

The next few pages talked about how they continued in Riven. How their love grew despite having no connection on the outside world. My mother started spending more more time in Riven, often crossing back only to wake up, eat, take care bodily needs, and then dive back in. At least until that fall.

I could feel it. Though I didn't know how. I was pregnant. With child. I didn't believe it at first, but I found myself having to cross back more often. Sickness presented itself at regular intervals. I was often tired. Graham promised to keep filling my quota while I was otherwise occupied. Because he was not present in my world, that was all he could do.

I scoured the libraries during the days. Spoke to other guides I felt I could trust. Even told Bryce, the new guide that I was mentoring at the time. Throughout history there had been a number of these children, born of spirits and people mingling in ways that, perhaps, were not intended. Most went on to lead the same lives that I or Graham or Bryce might live. Some, however, became targets.

As the summer wore on and my due date grew closer I noticed more attention paid to my activities. Guides not assigned to Chicago moved to the area, claiming they were visiting for other reasons. Neighbors I'd never spoken to noticed me in the halls. Asked me when I was due.

It wasn't long before I began to see them at night, before I crossed over. In the shadows during the day. I could feel them outside my apartment door. Waiting. I knew why. They wanted to take my child and use him, use him to bring the worlds together.

I secured Dr. Farth's promise that no one besides the medical staff would be allowed to enter during my labor. That no one would have access to my child beyond those required to keep him alive. But Dr. Farth had allegiances beyond my own. He had just been given the assignment to care for us, the guides in Chicago. He would not give it up for me.

It was on the night after Carver had left my arms to go away with the nurses that the first of the attempts was made. I do not know what was used, only that it was slipped inside my food, and when I refused that, my drink. I hid in Riven, replacing my weak body with my strong Riven half. Until eventually I too felt that cord slip away. That last tie to the world and my son.

Bryce bound me eventually, but Graham had disappeared. The price of our brief romance was my life, and, I could only imagine, that of my son.

107

I PUT the last sheet down and stared out the windows into Riven's gray. I had it now. The history that led to me. The suspicion and fear that consumed my mother in her last days as she felt Piotr's thugs closing in. She'd known my condition, and accepted that Piotr would kill her for it.

The most terrible part, though, was that Katherine didn't feel like she could even try to stop it. At least not over there, in the real world where she lived alone. In Riven she had a chance; with her weapons and her friends. How strange that Riven, her salvation, had become more dangerous to me than the world she left behind?

"Carver," Selena said, moving over near the stairs. "I don't think we're alone."

I moved my hand to the lash. We had grabbed my equipment from Anna's place in the Warrens on our way over here. It felt good not to be relying on random weapons, but instead on the familiar gear that I'd worked with for so many years. Selena drew her cleaver and the two of us took up position, me looking over the stairs from behind and Selena ready to spring if the intruder made it to the top.

The stairs creaked as someone walked up. The moment any heads appeared, Selena would be able to take it off or I would be able to loop the lash around their neck.

But when I saw Alec's face, I hesitated.

"Don't kill me," Alec said. "I'm not here to fight."

"What if I don't believe you?" I said.

"This isn't about us. This isn't about you," Alec said. "They're going to cleanse Bryce."

Cleansing. Blinding was the usual punishment, a severing from Riven. A cleansing amounted to the capital degree. Taking your soul in Riven and sending it into the Cycle. Wiping you out in both this world and the other. Reserved only for the most severe offenders. I'd never heard of one ever being sentenced. More of a cautionary punishment than something actually delivered.

"Why?" I said.

"Because he helped you," Alec said.

"That's ridiculous," I said. "Why aren't they just blinding him?"

"Piotr wants to make a statement," Alec said. "He says that the guides cannot be divided at this time. That we must all be together. However, cleansing Bryce is not the way."

"That's not the only problem with Piotr," I said. I brought Alec up to speed with the details. Who the Master really was. What happened to my parents. At the end of it, Alec reached out and shook my hand, then pulled me into a hug.

"I am sorry for what I have done," Alec said. "Will you forgive me?"

"Just this once," I said. "Next time, maybe give me a little more credit? Besides, I feel like knowing you never caught me is punishment enough."

"It will haunt me for the rest of my days, no doubt," Alec said, then looked over at the stairs. "We have to hurry. They are already taking Bryce to the Cycle."

"One question," Selena said. "How did you find us here?"

"Easy," Alec said. "I knew Carver could never leave you. So I watched your apartment until he appeared. Love always makes for easy prey."

"You're so creepy," Selena said.

"And you, *mon frier*, a spirit with a cleaver, are not?" Alec replied. Selena glanced at the blade in her hand and shrugged.

"Glad we could agree," I said, nodding towards the stairs. "They're taking Bryce? Let's go save him."

As we walked down the stairs and outside the house, Alec pointed to an object leaning against the entry wall. My crossbow.

"I thought, maybe, you would like it back," Alec said. "I found it beneath the beds. Hidden like a child's toy."

"Alec, I think this is the first gift you've ever given me," I said, refusing to acknowledge his judgment of my chosen hiding place.

"I recall giving you your life more than a few times," Alec replied.

I couldn't argue with that one.

108

FOUR GUIDES, with Bryce in the middle. They were nearing the gate to leave the city through the Shambles, the stream of spirits making their way around and giving the guides plenty of room. Bryce, for his part, walked with his head up and his eyes gazing forward. Hands tied behind his back with a length of chain. Seeing my mentor a prisoner filled me with deep anger at ruined justice. This wasn't right, and Bryce walked in irons because of me.

"We're outnumbered by one," I said. "I'll take a shot with the crossbow, try to even it out. Selena, you get Bryce out of there. Alec and I will handle the other three."

"I can fight too," Selena said. "You don't have to protect me."

"He's not," Alec said. "Bryce is the most important target, and we don't want to kill the guides."

"If you can get Bryce away, then we can leave," I said and Selena nodded. Looked like she understood why I didn't want her carving up the guides.

We were in the bottom floor of a building a block behind the guides, a block of dry road and damned spirits marching out of the city. I went up to the second floor, climbing a stair that wobbled with every footfall. Riven's rot claiming the house piece by piece. Crept out onto an overhang, praying that it would hold my weight. It creaked and I heard something snap beneath me, but it stayed up. I lay down and set the crossbow in front of me, looked down the length of its shaft, and set my sights on the rear guide.

I loaded the normal bolt. Not enough, hopefully, to kill. Only incapacitate. As the front guide started underneath the open gate, I fired. Pulled the trigger and, without waiting to see whether the bolt hit, dropped off the overhang and hit the street running.

Alec and Selena were out in front of me. Dashing along the side of the streets to stay out of the spirit crowd and sprinting towards the quartet of guides. Or, I should say, a trio. My shot had found its mark. The rear guide stumbled away from the rest, clutching at his back. The other three were losing their chance to get ready, looking at their companion and not paying attention to their approaching adversaries. Which was exactly the point.

Alec, gauntlets ready to work, sprang out from behind a pair of spirits and tackled the guide on the left. He appeared to wield the standard set of guide gear, the one given to new trainees. A sword and a knife, simple and deadly.

The one on the right, my target, had the same combo. The leader in front looked like the only experienced one. She held a pair of short axes, double bladed, with more hanging from her belt. As Selena closed, the lead guide shoved Bryce to the ground and held her arm back to throw one of the axes.

"Duck!" I shouted. But I didn't need to. Bryce rolled and kicked the guide in the knee, knocking her off balance and forcing her to catch herself on the ground with a hand.

The guide on the right stepped up to meet Selena, his

sword stabbing out in front. A maneuver that would work well against mindless spirits with no thought for their own safety. A move anyone with a functioning mind could dodge without a second thought. Selena sidestepped the strike to the right, smacking the sword aside with her cleaver and engaging with the long knife. Going for a nonlethal stab into the guides leg.

The new guide had some skill, though. He saw the strike coming in and back-stepped out of reach. Out of reach for Selena, anyway. My lash came by Selena's right side, whistled over and wrapped itself around the guide's wrist. I yanked him to the right, away from Bryce and giving Selena a clear path to my mentor.

"You don't have to fight," I said as I used the lash to throw my target to the ground. "We want Bryce. Don't want to hurt you."

"Then you shouldn't have come," said a voice to my side. The guide I'd shot put his pain behind him and stepped towards me. He swapped out his long knife for second sword, and swung the long reach weapons at the same time. Overhead, a massive all-in attack that would be fatal if it hit.

If it hit.

I dove towards the blades, ducking into a roll to get beneath the slash. I felt the swords whistle over my coat as I came out of the somersault into a tackle, hitting the guide in the waist and bowling him over. The guide let out a pained yell as his back hit the ground and I realized he hadn't removed my crossbow bolt from his shoulder. A shoulder now planted into the hard street. I took the moment of shocked pain and used it to throw away his weapons, kicking them out of his hands to the side. They disappeared beneath the trample of spirit feet.

"Carver," Alec shouted. "A little help?"

I turned and saw Selena dragging Bryce away, helping

him get up to his feet while Alec danced with the two other guides. The lead one, her twin axes moving, kept Alec on the defensive. He had to constantly shift his gauntlets to get in the way of the strikes, sparks flying every time the edges struck Alec's metal. The other guide, the sword and knife wielder, circled behind and looked for an open strike.

The guide focused too intently on Alec to see me coming. To see my lash before it wrapped around his leg and dragged it out from under him. I sent the guide crashing down, his head striking the street and falling limp.

"You're clear," I called.

Alec caught the words, blocked one more strike from the lead guide's swinging ax, and went on the offensive. Two quick jabs that forced the guide to stick her axes in front of her face for defense. A move that exposed their hafts for Alec to grab. He did so, then kicked the guide in the chest. Used his grip on the axes for added force, and as she fell back, pulled the axes free.

I turned my right, the first guide back on his feet, sword and dagger ready. Only he didn't look quite so eager to engage.

"I repeat," I spoke. "You don't have to fight this one. Back off and we'll let you go. Then you can help your friends."

The guide glanced over to his leader, who was reaching to her belt to draw new axes. She stopped as Alec moved closer, raising her own axes and showing her what might happen if she continued to fight.

"We yield," the leader said. "We're done. You can have your prisoner."

"For once, a good decision," Alec said.

"Take him now," the leader said. "But we'll send up the sparks as soon as you leave. You'll be tracked. Found. You can't hold onto him forever, and we'll make sure you share his fate."

"We could kill them, too," Selena said from the side as she used the cleaver to hack off Bryce's chains. "Hard to use a sparker when you're dead."

"How about we take the sparkers with us?" I said. "A little less lethal, I think."

I barely finished the sentence before the the guide with the bolt in his back, sitting up from the ground, stuck his hand in the air and launched the sparks. The rapid cadence, achieved by holding down the trigger and letting more more of the gas ignite, signified an emergency. Alerted any guide nearby to come for help. We were out of time.

"Run!" I yelled.

And we did.

109

T HE FOUR OF us sprinted back through the Shambles, heading north towards the clock tower. We had to get Bryce back to where he had crossed into Riven in order for him to cross back out of it. So he could hide. I handed him my knife, giving him something to defend himself with. Kept my lash ready.

"Alec, take the lead," I said and my friend nodded. I dropped to the rear while Selena stayed near Bryce.

We ran through the streets, dodging around spirits and racing against popping sparks as guides seeing our flight launched them through the sky. Now I knew what it was like to be an angry spirit, hunted and chased throughout the gray ruins of Riven and its city. Not pleasant.

Towards the edge of the Shambles, where they bled into the park leading to the Warrens, we had our first test. A pair of older guides. Each wearing thick, damaged coats and carrying large halberds, spears with an ax edge on one side and points on top and behind. The guides looked almost identical. I knew them. A pair of twins from South America, known for working in tandem so tightly that they effectively fought as one.

"Selena, you keep Bryce moving ahead. We'll rejoin you later," Alec said. Selena listened, peeling off with Bryce to the left and into the park while Alec and I went straight for the pair.

"Alec," the first one said. "I cannot say we expected this. How many hunts have we been on together, and now you would fight against us?"

"Mateo, I did not plan this," Alec said. "It is Piotr's doing. His hands molding this conflict."

I came up beside Alec and we stood five feet away from the pair. Almost within reach of their halberds. At Alec's words, they tilted their heads, squinted their eyes.

"Piotr," Mateo said. "Piotr didn't free the prisoners. Piotr didn't hurt the other guides. Piotr didn't break Bryce free."

"Those are all symptoms," I said. "Piotr is the cause."

"Or perhaps you are," Mateo replied. "If you wish to discuss it, however, put down your weapons and come with us. We won't hurt you."

I was shaking my head before he finished. "I'm sorry Mateo, Anton. We can't."

They nodded in unison. Then set their halberds forward. I would not relish this fight.

Alec struck first, darting in as Mateo, on the left, attempted to step forward with his halberd. I cracked the lash to the right, striking towards Anton's face. The man shifted, sliding his head to the right and dodging the lash's strike. Moved towards me and brought the halberd in for a wide slash. I back-stepped, but not far enough. The point of the halberd gashed into my side and sliced along my coat. Left a searing cut in my abdomen. I winced and tried to push down the pain. No time for that here.

Anton kept coming forward, reversing his cut to swing back from the other side. If I'd had my knife, I could've tried to catch the spear. Instead, I did the only thing I could and flicked the lash again. This time, mid-swing, Anton wasn't able to dodge my strike. As his halberd's blade fell toward my side, my lash struck into his chest. The pointed ends piercing through his coat and causing Anton to stagger back, remove some of the momentum behind his cut, so that instead of being bisected, I had another long gash along my left side. Happy to make that trade.

I didn't relent, couldn't relent. As Anton stumbled back, I cracked the lash again and again. Each strike opening new holes on the guide's chest, arms, and legs. None of them truly serious, all of them debilitating. Taking away his momentum and his focus. And then Anton dropped the halberd. Let the weapon clattered to the ground at his feet. I didn't stop. Kept driving him back until I stood above his weapon, and only then did I let the lash go quiet and hang down by my side.

"I'm sorry," I said to Anton, who knelt on the ground and bled from a dozen cuts. "I'm sorry, but you didn't leave me any choice."

I turned left to see Alec take a blow from the halberd's shaft to his chin. Mateo had drawn my friend in close, and, rather take the long swing, jerked the butt of the halberd into Alec's face. Now, as Mateo pressed the advantage, I knelt, grabbed Anton's halberd off the ground, and threw it at his brother.

It wasn't a great toss - I was no expert at throwing spears - but it was close enough. The weapon slid between Mateo's legs, biting into his thighs and knees and sending the man sprawling. Alec took advantage. Ran up and disarmed Mateo, kicking the halberd away and pinning the guide to the ground.

"Surrender," Alec said.

Mateo glared up at him, whatever spirit of fellowship that

had existed between us extinguished in traitorous fashion. "You can have your victory, and we will have our revenge."

Mateo's words stuck with me as we ran through the park, catching up with Selena and Bryce on the other side. We entered the Warrens and the maze of large apartments. They would have their revenge. How many guides were saying that about us right now? Were planning to advance their own status, or avenge their friends, by taking us apart? I was starting to think there would be no way back from this. No recovery.

My days as a guide were done.

The clock tower swung into view, after another hour of dashing and hiding, ducking between stores and counters, weaving between masses of spirits on the move. Even using breaches to our advantage, drawing guides into the eruptions of angry spirits. I had no idea if some of our friends fell trying to find us. If, led into the breaches, they were overwhelmed and torn to pieces. There would be time for that later. Time to bring Piotr a reckoning for all the terrors that he had wrought.

We crossed the courtyard, around the fountain bursting Riven's water into the air, and led Bryce into the clock tower. Selena shut the doors behind us and barred them with Bryce's voulge, still in the weapon rack where he had left it.

"I can never thank you enough," Bryce said to Alec and I. "For all you've sacrificed for me, for my family. If you ever need anything..."

"Let's start with getting you back home," I said. "Go, cross over so we can get out of here."

Not that we knew what Bryce would find on the other side. Perhaps a jail cell. Maybe another guide or two waiting to exact some punishment. But we had to start somewhere. Give him some chance.

Bryce lay down in the bed and concentrated. I saw his

eyes close and waited for his body to fade. But he didn't. Bryce sat there, in full form. After several minutes passed and Bryce still hadn't left us, I moved over. Took a close look. He breathed evenly, he hadn't sustained wounds. There shouldn't be any difficulty. Then his eyes popped open.

"They're blocking my way back," Bryce said.

"What?" I said.

"My body," Bryce said. "They're keeping it asleep. With drugs. I felt it as I crossed back, I felt myself slipping away into a dream. If I let that happen, that I might never get back here. I might never wake up."

"Alec," I said, turning to my friend. "If he can't cross, then we have to save him on the other side. Break him free. You're the only one that can do it."

"I don't think they'll let me into the hospital, not after this," Alec said.

"Hey," Selena said from over the by the doors. "There are noises outside. I'm hearing guides talk. I think they're planning something."

I went over to the door while Alec and Bryce tried to talk strategy. Tried to look between the doors outside, but all I could see was shifting gray and a bit of the fountain. A burst of orange. A smell of smoke. I looked around us at the wood and stone chamber and realized the guides didn't have any interest in fighting us. They were going to burn us down.

1 1 0

"Is there another way out?" Selena said.

I shook my head. "Not that I know of."

I told Bryce and Alec about the burning, though the smoke coming in from under the door made it unnecessary. The gray and white smoke floated way up to the top, trapped beneath the roof. The sheer height of the building would give us some time, but it was going to get hot in here very soon.

"I can't cross back," Bryce said. "There's no way out."

"Selena and I can't either," I said. Then I glanced at Alec. "Alec, go. You're the only one that can leave. Go back."

"Leave the rest of you? I'm not a coward," Alec said.

"You're no good dead," I said. I looked back towards the door, the first flicker of orange popping through near the hinges. The smoke thickened - I couldn't see the roof above anymore. "Go back. Find Bryce. Get him free."

That was a compromise Alec could accept. He slid onto the bed, closed his eyes, and faded a minute later. That left the three of us in the middle of a building rapidly turning black as flames crawled their way inside.

"Any ideas, Carver?" Selena asked.

"I've got one, but you might not like it," I said.

"I don't think liking it matters anymore," Bryce said. "What's important is whether we make it out alive."

"That's not a guarantee," I said, pulling the crossbow from my back. Moved an orange bolt to the front and cranked it into firing position. "This thing is going to cause a lot of destruction. I'd stand back."

"You're going to bring down the building on top of us?" Selena said.

"Just be ready to move," I said. "Bryce, if you want your weapon, now's the time."

Bryce nodded, went over the door and grabbed his voulge out from the locks. And winced. "It's really hot."

He ran by me as I lifted the crossbow, aimed my shot at the front wall. The door facing the fountain. If things went right, the bolt would explode and burn through, collapsing the the structure and causing enough chaos for us to get away. If things went wrong, the clock tower would collapse and bury us in rubble. Or we'd run right out into certain death at the hands of the guides.

I pulled the trigger.

The bolt launched out and embedded itself in the door, or what was left of it as the fire made a meal out of the building. The bolt popped and expanded in a blooming orange nova, a spreading swirl of superheated light that devoured the rest of the door. Branches launched out like electricity, tendrils snapping out and grabbing on to other parts of the tower, climbing and expanding and consuming the entire front of the building in a wave of heat and light.

Around us the structure groaned. Wood and rock began to fall as supports vanished, either annihilated by the fire, the bolt, or crumbling beneath the pressure. I pulled Selena to the ground, crawled beneath the table that had for so often served little purpose inside a place we didn't spend much time. Bryce joined us, squeezing in as rocks and boards chipped off the table's surface. Heat blasted our faces as the shouts of guides wondering what was going on came through amid the crackling roars.

I took a moment to start winding the crossbow again, loading a second orange bolt. My last one. I didn't want to use it, but if we needed a way out, or a deadly distraction, then the crossbow was our only, our best chance.

Behind us, the rear structure snapped as the roof, losing its front support, listed down towards the fountain. The clock, the heaviest part of the building, pulled the roof down with it. I glanced behind, over Selena's shoulder to see the burning boards at the back of the building simply split in two. Then the roof came crashing down on top of us.

"Go to the right, now," I said. "Bring the table."

As the building collapsed we shuffled, keeping the table over our heads to catch the embers and rocks and stone as they fell. Charged towards the right wall as it folded in at us. Holes opened, ashen and orange and burning. The raging heat licking our feet and our hair and running down our throat to scorch our lungs.

"We're not going to break out," Selena said.

"Stand up and run," Bryce said. "Lead with the table."

We hit the wall in ten steps, the side of the building bulging and bending and breaking. The table smashed into it first as Bryce, Selena and I were pelted with burning chunks of wood and rock. I felt the stings of embers burning through my coat, singeing my neck, and burrowing their way into my wrist and hands. But I held on. We held on. The clock tower's wall did not.

We burst through into the open alley between the clock tower and the next building, a shower of sparks heralding our exit. A shower infinitely dwarfed by the raging inferno behind us. We dropped the table and ran, sprinting down the alley to the right. Behind the clock tower and into Riven's endless maze. Kept the blaze between us and the guides for as long as we could.

Nobody said anything for a long time. We just ran. I took the lead and gradually shifted us towards the apartment. After another hour skulking through back alleys and broken buildings, we made it. Opened the door to find Nicholas standing and staring at us. At our wrecked clothes, our burned bodies, and battered souls.

"So, did you manage to find me some iron?" Nicholas said.

111

I wasn't used to seeing Bryce so defeated. He collapsed on one of the few chairs Nicholas had in his lab at the bottom of the apartment building. Bryce's eyes scrolled over the surroundings without seeming to notice any of them. Nicholas, usually ready to stream an opinion, fell silent when I told him what happened.

"We still need to get you back," I said to Bryce. "Even without the clock tower, you still need to go to the spot to cross."

"I know," Bryce said. "I know. But if I'm still asleep on the other side…"

"Alec will see to it," I said.

Bryce nodded, but it was the sort of nod given to stop a conversation rather than to agree. So I backed off and let Bryce confront his own demons.

"What are you going to do now?" Selena said.

"I have to cross," I said. "It's got to be almost morning. Anna and I, we have to get to New York. Have to stop Piotr."

"And us?" Selena said. "Do we sit here and wait for you to come back?"

I shook my head. "No, when Bryce is ready, you should try to get into the clock tower. Or what's left of it. If Alec gets him free, you may not have much time from him to cross out."

Selena and I went back up to her apartment, said our goodbyes, and then I laid down in the bed and crossed over to the other side.

Dawn broke over the town. Gold rising in a beautiful morning as woodland birds whistled. A few souls moving outside the window, beginning their daily tasks. Anna breathed slow beside me, lost in some dream. Not for much longer. I gave her what time I could as I readied. Went down to the front desk and acquired a schedule for the trains.

Twelve hours ride from here to New York. The sooner we started, the better.

"I thought you'd have had enough of trains," Anna said as we made our way to the station an hour later, *Pine's Rest* going without payment for our night courtesy of a back door. "Weren't you a hostage the last two times you rode one?"

"Almost. With my luck, airships aren't much better. At least it's easier to get off of a train," I said. "I don't have the money to buy a car, and we don't have the time."

"Twelve hours," Anna said. "I've never been on a train that long."

"If we're lucky," I said. "We won't meet anyone we know. The hours will pass by in peace. I'll even get a drink."

"Maybe," Anna said.

The train we were catching dwarfed the small station. A long passenger rail that stretched for car after car. I spent the last couple of dollars I had to get us tickets at the reduced rate for guides. Once we got to the city, we'd be relying on whatever we could scrounge. Whatever charity people would offer us, so long as they didn't know who we actually were.

The cars were ramshackle, and we only had a bench to ourselves. No money for a luxury compartment or any kind of sleeper cabin. Compared to the opulent airship, this was more my usual.

"Why do you think your mother gave up?" Anna asked after I told her what I'd read in my mother's diaries. "She just stayed there, in the hospital..."

"I don't think she had a choice," I said. "The way she wrote it, it seemed like they were coming after Katherine even before I was born. Piotr knew what I would be."

"But he couldn't use you until you grew old enough to make it over to Riven," Anna said.

"I think Piotr ran multiple schemes," I said. "I was one of his bets, and I think only at the end did he decide to use me. Or try to. He had plenty of time to let me grow."

"I want to know why," Anna said. "Why would he bother? Why risk so many guides, why risk everything to try to connect Riven to our world?"

The coffee car came by as the train rumbled through the sloping scenery of Western Pennsylvania, rolling green hills and fields cultivated for summer crops. I grabbed a couple of mugs and took a sip. Even that little bit of normalcy helped.

"For the same reason so many others have tried the same," I said. "I think he's frightened. He's older. He doesn't want to give himself up to what comes next. I can't be sure, though. It's just a guess."

"And the other leaders? The ones he had in the Mountain?" Anna said. "They must be working together."

"Think about it," I said. "In Riven, you don't age. You don't die. You can't really get hurt for long. At least not as a spirit. Bring that back here? You could live forever."

"You don't know what would happen if the spirits came over," Anna said.

"It's a risk he's willing to take," I said.

"What would you do, in his place?" Anna said. "Would you tear everything apart trying to find a way back?"

An easy question to say no to. A hard question if I actually thought about it. Who wouldn't want a chance to live forever, to see and do everything without a care for your physical health? On the other hand, the reason we were trying to stop Piotr was that opening the gateway could destroy everything we ever loved. Could make both Riven and our world fall apart.

"I think I would want what Piotr wants," I said. "But I hope I'd have the strength to resist. Would you?"

Now it was Anna's turn to look out the window and take a moment to think. Were we the same as Piotr, only without the power and position?

"I'm a selfish person," Anna said. "I do a lot of things for me, and to help accomplish my goals. I don't think I could do this. I don't think I could justify it to myself and say the chance of a strange, endless life would be worth this risk."

I nodded. "Only eleven more hours to go."

I wouldn't mind the wait.

112

Chicago is not a small city. It has its share of tall buildings and sparkling design. New York was something else altogether. A showcase for experimental architecture, in what the mad magicians of metal and glass could come up with. Structures of all shapes soared up and down the skyline, looping and curving at times through each other.

Elevated halls, supported by filled balloons, like stationary zeppelins, held sway between buildings and allowed people to cross without descending the many stories to the ground below. Lights and sounds splashed in the train windows and echoed through our compartment. An endless plethora of motorized vehicles, blowing horns, and hidden growls and rumbles that make up the background symphony of any bustling place.

Anna and I made our way out of Penn Station and slipped on our masks, the first time since leaving Chicago that I bothered to put it on. Pollution, it seemed, tied a common thread between our cities.

"Where do you think they're holding the conference?" I said to Anna as she stared at the chaos around us.

"I'd say we follow the motorcades," Anna said, pointing. I followed her eyes and saw the scattered cars emblazoned with various flags. The squat vehicles carted ambassadors and presidents through the traffic and throngs of people towards their destination. Even though we were walking, we easily kept pace.

In Chicago, downtown taxis kept the streets clear. If you walked over one of the lines, you were liable to get hit. In New York, there were simply too many people. No automated taxis, only the human variety. An endless array of cars and horses, walkers and riders.

As we neared what looked to be a large square, I heard the cries of a nearby newspaperman. Shouting out the evening edition, including tonight's various speeches and the schedule for tomorrow. I pulled us towards the crier and, after begging Anna to pay for a copy, grabbed the newsprint.

"He's not here tonight," I said looking at the lists of politicians from around the world. "Tomorrow, though, Piotr has the evening to himself."

"What are you thinking?" Anna said.

"Look around," I said. "There's so many people, so many police. There's no way we're going to be able to take him out on the street. But if we can tail him, maybe we can find out where he's staying."

"You're starting to talk like a sneak," Anna said.

"Maybe you're rubbing off on me," I replied.

"I can only hope so," Anna said. "If we're not going after Piotr tonight, we need somewhere to stay. And I'm broke."

"That makes two of us."

We stood in the street, Anna reading through the paper and me scanning the crowd. Trying to think of something to do. I couldn't lean on my guide contacts; the New York group would turn me in the moment I showed my face. We could just wander the streets until the next day, but I didn't relish the idea of taking on Piotr after going all night without rest.

"How about this?" Anna said. She lifted the paper and pointed to a printed ad calling out services for connecting people with their lost relatives. Either here or in Riven.

"Sneaks?" I said.

"You might be wanted by the guides," Anna said. "But I'm still a sneak, and on their good side. I think."

"Do you even know them?"

"Do you know every guide?" Anna replied. "Come on, let's go."

The ad noted an office in the lower east side of Manhattan. A solid twenty block walk from where we were now, but I relished the exercise. Taking in the sights and sounds of a different sort of metropolis. The buildings here were taller, more compressed in the smaller landscape. The sounds were different too: mixed accents and calls for foods of different types. There was a feel of motion here that I didn't have back home.

There were similarities: Mechs stood everywhere. The conference boosted security, made patrols even more prolific than in Chicago. Masks were the status symbol of the day here too, with the wealthier groups sporting artistic arrangements over their faces and the less well-off going with colored cloth filters.

The reaction to seeing a pair of guides was the same sort of nervous caution. Crowds parted around Anna and I as we walked along. Eyes crawled up and down my coat.

Eventually, with the sun vanishing beneath the horizon and the city basking us in bright lights, we made it to a squat building that seemed, quivering beneath the towering construction around it, not long for this world. The office and the apartments above belonged to the sneaks, or, as the sign outside declared, *New York's Finest Finders*. The door was unlocked, the inside lit by a plethora of lights.

"Look, they have electricity," I said to Anna.

"They have money," Anna said. "Laurence and I do what we can with what we have."

Inside, we were greeted by a row of chairs in a room ringed with doors. Private hideaways where clients could talk with a sneak without worrying about being overheard.

"Can I help you both?" said the woman as she came out of the back hallway. Unlike Anna, who made her way in a casual outfit, the sneak wore a professional dress. Ready for business, and for a certain type of clientele that I didn't think would bother leveraging a sneak.

"I have a favor to ask," Anna said. At the woman's nod we launched into our story. Filtered out details like bringing down the airship. Whittled it down to the two of us needing to spend the night in the city and not having the funds to do so.

When Anna finished the woman told us to wait a minute, and disappeared back through the door.

"Do you think she bought it?" I said.

"Not at all," Anna said. "But she'll come back with an offer."

"With an offer?"

"Sneaks don't give things away for free," Anna said. "My guess is if we can't pay, they'll find something else for us to do. Maybe you can use your mask and scare away bad clients."

"Very funny."

The woman returned and waved us back with her. We followed; through a bland hallway and back into the start of the apartments. A broad room with a small kitchen, table and chairs. A radio playing the current speaker from the conference. On the table sat three other sneaks, all in suits and collared shirts.

"You are a guide, aren't you?" the woman said after bidding us to sit down. I nodded in reply. "Then you know Riven is getting more dangerous lately. We've even lost one of us."

"I'm sorry," I said. "That's why we're here. We're trying to end this war."

"What I don't understand," the woman said. "Is why you're coming to us when you should have plenty of guides you can turn to for a night in the city."

"We're trying to keep it quiet," Anna said.

"Why don't you tell us why you're really here," one of the other sneaks, a thin older man said. "Or we'll send you out that door right now."

"We need to stop the leader of the guides from breaking Riven apart," I said.

113

"Of the ridiculous things I've heard today," the thin man said. "This one tops them all. Trying to kill the leader of the guides? Why?"

"Because he wants Riven to splinter and send the spirits back here," I said.

"Ludicrous," said another of the sneaks. "That would be suicide."

"Not if you're already dead," I said. "Then, you could wander the world as a spirit. Live forever. Or so the thinking goes."

"I've never heard of that happening before," the thin man said. "Where's the proof that it would even work?"

I shook my head. There wasn't any proof. Not that I knew of.

"Why take the chance?" Anna spoke up. "If Piotr succeeds, then our world will be overrun. If it doesn't work, if he can't make a gate, then Riven will still be too dangerous for anyone to cross to. You'll be out of a job."

"Now there's an angle I can understand," the woman we'd

met at the front said. "Regardless, all you're asking for is an overnight. That, we can provide. For a favor."

"A favor," I said.

"We have a client with a special request," the woman said. "She can cross over into Riven, and knows where she wants to go. However, Riven is a dangerous place to be right now. Too dangerous for us. An experienced pair of guides, though?"

"So we take this client of yours to somewhere in Riven, and you'll let us stay?" Anna said, then glanced at me.

"We can do that," I said. There wasn't any way an escort job would be difficult. Not with what we'd already been through.

"Then it's agreed," the woman said. "Silas, would you mind fetching Honora and telling her we can proceed this evening?"

Silas, the thin man, nodded, stood up and left the room. The woman turned back to us.

"If you wouldn't mind, I can show you to your rooms. I imagine you'll need to get your gear on the other side. So if you want to get started?"

"Launching right into it?" I said.

"I don't know where you came from, guide, but in this city we do not waste time," the woman replied.

"Fine with me," I said.

They set Anna and I up in a pair of individual rooms, twin beds set in blank-walled rectangles. At least the pillows were soft, the blankets good. The sneaks might not have cared about the ambient decoration, but they put quality where it mattered.

As I prepped to cross over, I realized that we hadn't ever asked for their names, and they had never asked for ours. I suppose if you're going to work with criminals, it might be better to remain anonymous.

I showed up in Riven next to Anna, an alleyway somewhere close to the ruin of the clock tower. I recognized the buildings, ones I'd wandered past countless times in my hunts through the gray world.

"To the apartment?" I said, and Anna agreed.

Both of us noted where we'd come in, as we'd have to head back to this spot to return to New York. On the ground around us, trash had been scattered. Broken beds and shredded sheets. A pair of dirty mattresses leaning against the wall. Guides took the time to set up true bases. Built and maintained spaces meant for frequent crossings. This, this was meant to look random and dirty enough to pass for an accident. I only picked up the garbage's true purpose because I'd crossed over to this spot.

Anna and I made our way through the alleys and avenues to the apartment. Other guides and the occasional spirit wandered by, causing us to duck out of sight. Still, compared with the chaos of Bryce's escape, I enjoyed the walk. The quiet, empty streets a welcome reprieve from the crowds of New York.

"Are you still doing all right?" Anna asked as we continued. "About your parents?"

"I'm hanging in there," I said. "It would be worse, except I spent most of my life alone. Now it's just back to the usual."

"I suppose," Anna said, though her tone implied otherwise.

"You?" I said. "I haven't noticed tears, and you've kept composed."

"Now if that isn't the nicest thing anyone's ever said to me..." Anna laughed. "I keep it to myself. Nurture their memory."

"Sorry," I said. "Sometimes I talk like a hammer."

"Sometimes?"

Anna kept her grief to herself. Bottled it up and hid it. I

wasn't all that different. Every day brought one moment after another that I wanted to share with Graham and Katherine. In Riven or otherwise. Saving Bryce, getting out of the burning clock tower, I could imagine talking every detail over with my parents and earning their praise, enduring their loving criticism.

At the same time, it had been easy to fall back into the habit of relying on me and me alone. Taking in the situation and depending on my own sense to get me out of it. I didn't *need* Graham and Katherine for me to survive, but I wanted them sharing my world.

When the two of us walked into the apartment, Bryce, Selena, and Nicholas were bent over the scientist's work-bench. Piecing together some new weapon or other invention.

"We're back!" I announced, and the group turned around. "And we need our stuff."

114

IF THERE WAS a moment when I felt that Bryce was no longer my mentor, it came when he let me go with Selena and Anna. Let me leave the apartment armed and ready for adventure, but without him. Bryce said he had to wait for Alec, as the guide was still working to see whether he could locate Bryce on the other side and free him. If Alec could cause a large enough distraction for Bryce to cross over.

On my own. The leader of our little band.

We headed back towards the trash-littered spot in the alley near the clock tower. Where the child would appear at some point soon. Selena, her cleaver idly hanging from her left hand, whistled an old song as we walked. Anna, for her part, seemed lost in deep thoughts.

I didn't say anything. Plenty of my own thinking to do. I could feel the conflict with Piotr barreling to a close. A fight that would likely leave only one of us left. The questions niggling at my head concerned what would happen after? Would the guides rebel or scatter, letting angry spirits run amok? Would they rally behind me or someone else? Stand up to the dead and force Riven back to sanity or collapse?

Of course, Piotr might cut me in half and solve all my problems, but that wasn't a fun path to go down.

"This is the spot, right?" Anna said, and I blinked, realized she was right. Same alleyway, same dirty mattresses.

"So we wait?" Selena said, then glanced at Anna. "Is this what you did before? Took people on trips through Riven?"

"Sometimes," Anna had a defensive edge to her voice. "Only if they could cross over, though. Most of the time it was find and report back."

"Running errands, you mean?"

I laughed. "Selena might've picked up some of my old prejudices."

"I noticed," Anna said. "They were only errands if the client wanted them to be. When you're helping someone heal an emotional wound, or get a last conversation with a loved one, that's not so trivial."

There was a rustling noise, a scattered clinking as bits and pieces of rock and junk fell off their pile next to us. Climbing out from beneath a sheet; a dark girl of no more than twelve looked out at us.

"They said to hide, so I hid," the girl said. "They said there'd be a man and a woman, were they talking about you?"

"Are you Honora?" I said and the girl nodded. "Then we're the ones you're looking for."

"Where are your parents?" Anna said, and Honora pointed, down the alley and away to the north.

"Why don't you hop in line behind Anna here, and you just tell me which way to go as we walk?" I said, leading us off. No reason to waste time. The sooner the girl could cross back, the less chance of something terrible happening to her.

North of the clock tower, the city broke into a crumbling range of parks and clusters of homes. A place that could have been, would have been a ritzy residential area if the ponds weren't dusty and dry, the homes razed, and the trees shattered bits of their former selves. Of the parts of Riven that had suffered over the centuries, the north part of the city had fallen the farthest.

"When did you first cross over?" Anna continued her conversation with Honora, peppering the girl with question after question. At first I didn't understand why, but then I noticed Honora was paying more attention to her answers than to the ruins around us. Ignoring the occasional spirit wandering by. The sparks bursting in the air above as guides called to each other.

"Three years ago," Honora said. "It was scary. I didn't understand."

"I bet," I muttered. Remembered my own first time vividly. I'd been seven, curled up on the couch, the only place to sleep in the apartment where my current foster parent lived. A grouchy old guide, Morton, who, his age and general annoyance with everything notwithstanding, kept a focused eye on me at all times.

Looking back, I realized that the old man kept me on that couch for a reason. It was tied to the top of an apartment in the Warrens, a room with one door that he'd locked from the outside. When I launched myself into Riven, without a clue of what I was doing, I'd been safe. The windows were barred; metal rods jammed into the walls. I could only stare out at the city below me, until he opened the door.

"Did you talk to your parents about it?" Anna asked.

"They told me it was just a bad dream," Honora said. "That I didn't have to worry."

Morton hadn't played games with me. That same night, when he'd opened the door, he'd given me a knife almost half as tall as I was. Told me that, no matter how old I was, every night had a chance of killing me. Morton, in his black, long coat and crag-covered face, had glared at me until I held the knife like I meant to wield it. The first of many lessons.

"Mine did too," Anna said. "Only you knew that wasn't true, right?"

Honora held out her left arm and nodded to a vicious scar twisting around her forearm. "I learned."

My first encounter with an angry spirit happened more than a year later. A year of crossing into that locked room and waiting for Morton to let me out. We'd avoided any real guide work in that time. Exploring, taking twisting routes that I'd thought were planned but, really, was Morton's work with a resonator to avoid any danger.

That night, not long after I'd turned eight years old, we'd stopped outside of a busted up store. Bare shelves broken and leaning on each other, ash flakes clustering in the corners. Morton had turned to me, taken one of his constant rattling sighs, as though dealing with me was a burden ill-promised and unearned.

"In there," Morton said. "Is a trial. Your first real test. Do you think you're ready?"

"Yes," I said with a child's invincibility backing my voice.

"You're not," Morton replied. "You're going to get chewed up. Torn to pieces. If you're lucky, I'll be fast enough to save you. If you're not..."

Morton had probably meant that line to leave me scared and cautious. Afraid of the consequences. Except after a year of enduring Morton's endless dire premonitions and grumping growls, I wanted to prove to him that I wasn't useless.

"So then what did you do?" Anna asked Honora.

"I learned to hide," Honora said. "Did you?"

"All the time," Anna replied. "I still do."

I had ventured into the store slowly, holding the knife out in front of me; a shield as much as a weapon. From the back of the place, hidden behind a counter, I heard a voice muttering to itself. Quiet whispers that blurted, every so often, a single syllable. I placed every step carefully, measuring the distance and letting the soles of my boots land evenly on the floor.

The counter itself was the best part of the store. Still more or less intact, still with a glass case. Nothing but empty shelves inside, but I could see through. Could catch a glimpse of the creature beyond.

My first angry spirit sat on the floor, a boy not much older than I was. His legs splayed out and, in his hands, he held onto what looked like some broken pieces of wood. He moved them together, pressing them at angles into each other. Trying to build something.

I could finally make out his words. A series of names, repeated to himself over and over. Back then I didn't understand. Now, I've heard spirits do the same thing. A way of remembering parts of their lives as Riven begins to take it away.

"When did your parents pass?" Selena asked Honora.

"Only a week ago," Honora said. "They made me promise to come see them."

"So that's why you're here?"

Honora nodded. "They were real sick. They couldn't get out of bed, and so they said they would say goodbye here. Where they could stand."

The boy's eyes had blazed with the pale fire. I remembered staring at that face for an entire minute, taking in the flickering anger. The contorting mouth. Then I glanced back towards the shop's entrance, saw Morton standing there, saw his grim nod.

I went around the counter, held the knife steady, and went up to the boy. He didn't even notice I was there until I was nearly on top of him, the knife an inch away from his chest. Then his face met mine, and he fell silent.

We stared at each other for a long beat. And then he

lunged for me, his hands grasping for my face. I yelled, fell back, and stuck the knife forward out of desperation. Felt it bite into something.

"Twist the hilt, Reed!" Morton had called from the other side of the counter.

I felt the boy's fingers brush my face as I turned my wrist. Opened my eyes in time to see the blue fire spread from the knife, cover the angry spirit. Saw the boy's snarling face fall into slack-jawed nothing.

"How do you know where to find them?" Anna said. "Riven's a big place?"

"I told them where I hid," Honora said. "My favorite spot when I crossed over."

"How much further is it?" Selena said.

"Right there," Honora pointed to a large grove of dead trees, and within them, a small shed. Its wooden sides were sagging and the roof had a small hole on one side, but otherwise the place seemed intact.

Morton had dragged me up, forced me out to the street to watch the boy walk away into the distance.

"He's going to the Cycle now," Morton said. "Where he's supposed to be. You did well, Reed. Seems you might be ready for the next step."

A week later, I'd left Morton's couch for good and boarded a bus to Chicago, where I met a man named Bryce.

115

I opened the crooked door to the shed. Inside, amid filtered rays of gray light and scattered bits of rubble, stood a pair of spirits looking at me with calm, understanding eyes. No sign of pale fire, no need to keep my hand on my lash.

"Are you Honora's parents?" I said.

"We are," said the woman. "Is she with you?"

That statement alone; a cognizant reply to a question, did as much as anything to calm my fears. Spirits that were on the verge of losing themselves didn't have that much composure. Didn't care what questions were being asked.

"She is," I said, then waved Honora in. "They're all yours."

Anna stayed in the shed with the girl while Selena and I took up a casual post outside.

"I'm happy for her," Selena said.

"Rare," I replied. "The two of them happened to cross close enough to each other to keep themselves sane over here. That's lucky."

"I doubt Honora would see it that way."

I nodded. Doubted that she would. Tough to wager a few extra days with a dying parent against the chance to say goodbye to both of them in Riven. I knew which option I'd take, though.

"Do you think your children ever tried to see you?" I asked Selena.

"I don't know if they can cross over," Selena said. "If they could, if they can, then I hope they moved on. I'm not the mother they knew anymore."

I let the thread drop and Selena didn't try to pick it up. Her children were a sensitive topic. Selena never mentioned them. I didn't know their names, what they looked like. For her, maybe, it was a piece of a life she didn't have anymore. We moved on to the Cycle, what Anna and I were planning for Piotr.

The shed door swung open behind me. Anna led Honora by us, the girl wiping away tears but otherwise standing tall.

"Her parents have something to ask you," Anna said to me. "We'll take Honora back and you can catch up with us."

I raised an eyebrow, but Anna dodged it and looked down at Honora, gave her a gentle push to start the walk back.

"Want me to stay?" Selena asked and I shook my head.

"I don't think this will take long," I replied.

Back inside the shed, I shut the door behind me. Honora's parents stared at me, their faces calm and set. Again her mother spoke first, after she had grabbed her husbands hands and held them tight.

"We would ask that you let us go," she said. "We have said our goodbyes, and have no wish to spend another moment in this wretched place."

The father nodded in agreement.

"You're certain?" I said. "Together, you two might be able to hold on for some time. Perhaps see Honora again?"

"We can hear it," the father said. "Feel it pressing against us. If we are to go, then I would have it be by our own choice. I do not want to turn into an animal."

Now the mother nodded.

I used the knife. Twisted the hilt, a light poke into their arms, and the fire washed them away.

As I left the shed, I twisted the door. Blocked it with some of the fallen wood from the dead trees. Hopefully it would delay their walk to the Cycle long enough for Honora to cross away. The last memory of her parents would be as they wanted it.

We went back into the city, and let Honora cross over on a dirty mattress in the alley. Anna followed, giving Selena her gear. I handed Selena mine too, so that she looked like a caricature, loaded down with a ridiculous number of weapons. Except, as a spirit, she couldn't really get tired.

"When will you come back?" Selena said.

"We're going to try and handle Piotr tomorrow night. Hopefully, after that, I'll find a way to cross in and give an update," I said. "If things go will, it will be over."

"Then the real battle begins," Selena said, her eyes flashing up to a set of exploding yellow sparks overhead.

"We'll save it," I said. "With all of the other guides? We can hold Riven together."

"Remember when I said I didn't like this place?" Selena said. "How I wanted a way out?"

"You nearly got me killed trying to find it."

She'd led me right to Graham and his vicious hammer. To be fair, Selena had also led Alec and Bryce to my rescue, but still...

"Sorry about that," Selena replied. "What I'm trying to say is that now, rather than feeling trapped by Riven, I feel like I'm a part of it. I'm participating in this world. I've found a new life, Carver, and I don't want to lose it."

116

WHEN I CROSSED BACK from Riven, it was mid-morning. Anna and the other sneaks were talking over breakfast, swapping strategies for dodging guides and breaches. All of them paused as I sat down, until Silas pushed over the plate of bread and cheese they were splitting. I stayed quiet as the conversation resumed. Let the words wash over me as I kept turning over ways to catch Piotr in my mind.

The day went by fast after that. Anna and I explored what we could of the city, keeping an eye out for signs of Piotr or other guides. Trying to keep our own heads down. The airship crash was all over the newspapers and blaring radios, but nobody had tried to pin it on us yet. Blamed as a mechanical failure.

You saw that all the time. Machines going awry were as common as each new day. A standard part of life. What wouldn't have been, what would have attracted more attention, was a claim that a pair of criminals had made their way into the engine room and brought down the ship. Why attract controversy when none was needed?

Eventually we made it to a wide square where, in the

middle, beneath a large marble dome and surrounded by a colonnade covered in the flags of all the states, a banner welcomed the participants in the world peace conference. The sun dipped low. Piotr's assigned speaking slot would be up soon.

"I guess it's time?" I said.

"My feet could use a rest anyway," Anna said.

We walked up to the entrance, a long series of thin steps that nonetheless brought us high enough to stare over the heads of the crowds shifting back and forth behind us. A large array of security stood in front, holding batons in wearing the deep blue uniforms of New York police.

"You think they're looking for us?" Anna said.

"I don't think so," I said. "Why would they think we'd come here?"

"Oh, I don't know," Anna said. "Maybe because we crashed an airship heading to New York?"

"Just act confident," I said. "Nobody's blamed us for the crash yet."

The confidence act got us of the front of the line, to the point where a police officer, holding a large set of papers with names on it, stared at us and shook his head.

"You're not on the list, you're not getting in," the police officer said.

"We're late additions," Anna tried.

"Sorry," the officer replied. "If you're with an embassy, or you have a sponsor, get them to come and add your name. Then I'll let you in. If you're just looking to listen, though, they'll play the broadcasts at any of the bars around here."

The officer gestured at a couple of establishments down the steps. Anna and I chose a place by the name of *The Guided Spirits*. It seemed fitting; a bar themed after Riven. It was empty inside, perhaps owing to the slightly early hour and the entertainment on offer. Speakers around the small bar, a place full of wood furniture and gray, speckled walls, blasted out one windy speech after another.

"How are we going to catch Piotr from here?" Anna said.

"All we need to know is when he leaves," I said, waving down the bartender. "Then we can follow them to his hotel, and try to get in there."

"With your bare hands?" Anna said, raising an eyebrow.

"With whatever I can find," I said. "We've come this far. We can't stop now."

The bartender gave us a nod, and a free drink. For being guides, he said. I asked how he name the place and the man said that he'd flamed out of guide training as a child, but still remembered how Riven looked. How it felt. He asked if it'd changed it all in the decades since he last crossed, before they blinded him to keep them safe.

I told him no.

The speakers burst with static, a change in the presenters. Whomever was leading the evening's schedule announced that the next speaker came not from any country, but was perhaps the most impacted of all of them.

"Piotr's talking," I said. "I can't believe it."

"What do you bet that he'll talk about opening the gate and sending all the spirits back from Riven?" Anna said.

"If that happens, I think the police might do our job for us."

Over the speakers, we heard the gruff tones of Piotr's voice. Thanking the various countries for attending, and that he hoped this summit could prove to be a beginning to ending the deadly war.

"All of you have seen your sons and daughters part ways with their lives in this bloody and miserable fighting," Piotr said. "Yet, for everyone that gives themselves in service to their country, my guides pay an added price. In a war that you cannot see, we are trying to keep all of you safe.

Throwing ourselves into harm's way day after day, night after night to send the very souls you lose to the Cycle.

"Remember, as the negotiations continue, that every piece of land, every town, every treaty becomes worthless if Riven falls. If the angry dead return to take what they've lost."

I took a slow sip of vodka. Burning anger bubbled up as Piotr continued to rail about the threats posed by Riven's collapse. The man who wanted to bring about that fall doing everything he could say to prevent it. Then again, there was a reason the guides followed him without question. Piotr was a leader. He knew when and what to say.

After another ten minutes outlining all of the dire consequences, Piotr concluded his speech with a plea for peace. Applause played him off the stage. The announcer declared the evening's events concluded.

And our night began.

117

I THOUGHT it would be harder to find Piotr in the masses leaving the conference center. Hordes of people in light and dark jackets, despite the warm weather. Masks on. But Piotr stood tall, and his gold and blue-tipped mask didn't fully cover the white hair streaming down from his head and over his shoulders. Anna and I stood outside the bar and watched as he made his way down towards a line of waiting motorcars. And then ignored them. Continued to walk along down the avenue, pursued by a gaggle of reporters throwing questions.

"Maybe he's got a close hotel," Anna said.

"Easier for us, then," I replied.

We started off, careful to keep some distance between us and our quarry. Not that it would've mattered. The sidewalk was so crushed with people, even at this time of the evening, the sun having set and lights popping on, that recognizing a random person seemed a ludicrous idea. If not for that flowing white mane, there would've been no tracking Piotr.

After several blocks Piotr turned and held up a hand. The reporters, along with their note-taking recorders, paused. I heard Piotr tell them no further comments, and good night. The man we were after vanished inside of his hotel.

We followed.

The *Avalon* looked as if Ezra's had transformed into a large hotel. Instead of a single crimson bar, dark wood made up most of the interior. A marble floor greeted our steps and a fleet of doormen attended to guests going in and out or seeking direction. Restaurants bordered us on either side of the lobby, places well beyond the small amount of cash the sneaks had given us for last night's work.

We drew eyes as we went in, our dirty cloaks and haggard appearance doing us no favors with a crowd looking for confirmation of their own high status. Not that I cared. I had no interest in the puffery of the city. The only thing I wanted was walking up the grand central staircase in front of us.

I'm not sure what made Piotr look our way. A sound I didn't hear. Or one of those itchy feelings of eyes on your back. Either way, the leader of the guides paused his climb and turned to us, rested his eyes on mine as we stood inside the door looking back at him.

"Is he going to run?" Anna said.

"I don't think so," I said. I didn't know why I thought that, just that the idea of Piotr, in his ornate official cloak, smothered with gold outlines of the guide's insignia, taking off and huffing up the stairs seemed ridiculous.

A moment later Piotr turned back and continued walking up. We followed. No reason to hide now. No hope of pretending. Piotr himself climbed slowly, giving us time to catch up and see every time he chose to take the stair to another level. Going higher and higher.

He stopped at the eighth floor, one beneath the roof. Turned and looked back at us at the landing below him.

"Carver Reed," Piotr said. "You've proved quite difficult to get rid of."

"Through no lack of trying on your part," I replied.

"I'm only doing what is best," Piotr said. "Riven is collapsing, and we need a way to remove the pressure."

"Letting spirits cross back over isn't going to help anything," I said.

"Ah yes, because you are an expert on such things," Piotr said. "Doubting me, someone who has all the wisdom of the guides that came before plotting his course."

"Can we shut him up already?" Anna said.

I took a running start, pushing myself ahead of Anna. For two reasons. One, I didn't want her as implicated in this. If possible, Anna could get away without drawing too much attention to herself. Without ruining her life the way I was destroying mine. And two, I really wanted Piotr to myself. For my parents.

Piotr turned and ran down the hall as I charged. I hit the top of the stairs and rebounded after him. Heard Anna pounding the carpet behind me.

"Why are you running?" I yelled after Piotr. "If you are so truly trying to save the world, then why hide your intentions?"

"Because they would never understand," Piotr replied. He abruptly turned to a room, jammed a key into a lock and twisted it. Open the door as I reached him. Pulled me inside as I grabbed his shoulder.

I heard the door slam behind me as we went into the room, a spacious suite with multiple beds and lanterns hanging from the ceiling. Outside the windows, Manhattan sprawled forth. I saw it for only a moment before I felt other hands pulling me off of Piotr.

I threw an elbow behind me, felt it catch a chin. The hands let go of my right arm and I swung a punch at the guy holding on to my left. He caught it, and I recognized that face. Bloodied and battered. Scarred and angry. Derringer.

Derringer shoved me back against a dresser, rattling the radio sitting on top. Brought his left hand in a hook towards my face, which I ducked and countered with a waist high tackle. I heard a click, the door locking as I shoved Derringer into a chair. He toppled over on the ground, groaning. And then I felt a point sticking into my back. The sharp pain of a knife kissing my skin.

"You'll want to stop now, Carver," Piotr said, sparing a glance for Derringer. "Or Polk ends your life right here."

I froze. Tried to look around the room and see if there was an easy out. Something I could use to turn the tables. Until then, I could ask questions. Keep them distracted.

"You and Derringer are impossible to kill," I said to the man behind me. "How did you even get here?"

"That reporter told us everything," Polk said. "A knife to the throat was enough to open him up. We caught the overnight train. It seems you and Anna were too slow."

That night we spent in the hotel. That had given them an edge. Nothing we could do about it now.

"Doesn't look like your travel did Derringer any favors," I said. "Are you as messed up as he is? A horror show for the eyes?"

I felt the knife shift, Polk's muscles tense. If I could turn fast enough, could take the blade away... I took a breath.

"Carver, if you move," Piotr said, nodding to Derringer. "He'll shoot you. No matter how fast you think you are, you can't beat both of them."

Derringer pulled a revolver from his jacket and leveled it at me. Caught between a knife and a bullet. Not exactly how I wanted this to go.

118

THEY SAT me down on the bed. Derringer going to the bathroom to clean up while Polk kept the revolver leveled at my face. Piotr stood in front of me, hands at his side and looking almost sad at the situation.

"The strange thing is, Carver," Piotr said. "When I made you the head guide of Chicago, I meant it. I thought you were up to the task. After Graham and Barth failed, I'd all but given up at using you as a way out. Riven is collapsing, but it would still need strong guides to keep the flood in control once the spirits had broken Riven apart. I thought you could be one of them."

"Thanks for the consideration."

"Now, though," Piotr said. "Even if you could help me, your death would be warranted. You caused terror, and hurt to people both in this world and others. You injured guides, civilians. Bound spirits rather than sending them to the Cycle. By any measure, Carver, you are a criminal. One that deserves nothing less than death."

"And yet, all of this is because of your actions," I said.

"Yes, yes," Piotr said. "Blame me. I'm the source of all your problems. It sounds satisfying, doesn't it? To throw all the wrongs in your life on the shoulders of someone else? Let me tell you, Carver, what feels better. Owning your failures, owning your successes. I will give you one more chance to redeem your life. Cross over, find me at the Mountain, and give me the chance to save Riven. There is still time for us to relieve the pressure. To use your miracle to help us control Riven's end."

"What if I say no?" I said. My mind swirled through options and opportunities, ways to get out of the bed and make a break for it. I could dive through the window, plummet to the street below and splatter all over the ground. I could make a desperate grab for Polk's gun, but even if I managed to wrest it from his hand, I'd take at least one bullet. Would still be outnumbered.

I didn't know where Anna had gone, but I was glad she hadn't followed. Glad Piotr didn't seem to care about her. If this was truly the end, then I hoped that she could find a happy way to spend her last days before spirits overran the Earth .

"A simple answer," Piotr said. "First, Polk here will shoot you. Then we will track down Bryce and Alec; make them pay for aiding you. We will send Anna, that sneak which you insisted on making into a guide, to receive a cleansing. At the end of it all, when the spirits break the Cycle and open a path out of Riven, all you will have caused is suffering."

"You've thought about this," I said.

"It gives me no small amount of satisfaction," Piotr said. "Now please, choose."

I looked at the barrel of Polk's gun, Piotr's face, and decided the only way I had a chance to help my friends was on the other side. A useless death here would mean nothing. So I closed my eyes, focused on Riven, and crossed over.

Except I felt myself getting pulled. Pulled far away. This bed had been used before, had already been tainted and tied to a place in Riven. A place well beyond any I had ever been. And when I opened my eyes in the gray otherness, I was lost.

491

ALL AROUND ME, reaching nearly up to my chin, were long white stalks of grain. They shifted back and forth in Riven's breeze. The swooshing sound coupled with nothing else, the near silence playing into my ears as I searched the surroundings. I'd crossed over outside the city, that much was obvious.

Laurence, the sneak that worked with Anna, had once shown me the maps in their office. Their basement lair beneath the building being constructed in Chicago, a city I might never see again. He said east of Riven's city lies an endless field of grain. Stalks like these. I was likely in that field, somewhere.

I couldn't see a skyline, no crumbling towers on the horizon. No landmark beyond the shifting stalks. Beneath me, the hard ground felt the same as in the forest. Dirt overlaid with dead grass. I had no weapons, nothing other than the shirt and trousers that crossed over every time. The coat I brought with me.

Still, I was in Riven. That gave me options. I fell within myself and reached out. Focused on the bond between myself and Selena. Sent my emotions soaring across our great divide and connected with her. Felt her warm rush of happiness that I held and treasured.

"Where are you?" Selena said through our bond. "Did you find Piotr?"

I told her the story. By turns experienced her shock, and her anger. I'm sure she felt mine as well.

"So now I'm here," I said. "Wherever here is."

"You're supposed to meet them at the Mountain?" Selena said.

"That's what Piotr told me," I replied. "I don't think he expected me to cross here."

"Then use it, Carver," Selena said. "Use the time to think of something. To find a way to win."

"I'll try, but I'm curious," I said. "Someone crossed in this bed, someone brought it here. Why?"

Selena didn't have an answer. I couldn't get a direction, so after a minute I decided to walk. To brush aside the grains with my hands and wander through the endless field. The stalks felt dry but not brittle. Hard and strong. For being dead, or whatever they were in this world, the grain wasn't ready to fold.

"How are the two of you hanging on?" I asked Selena as I walked.

"It's getting harder and harder to leave," Selena said. "More breaches are forming every day. The guides are everywhere. If I have to leave, I can wear my coat and take my cleaver, and they don't notice that I'm not one of them."

"Do you think Riven is falling apart?" I said.

"As we know it?" Selena said. "Yes."

"Then am I doing the wrong thing?" I said. "Should I give it up? Find Piotr and let him use me to open his gate?"

Selena stayed quiet after that one. Let me wander further underneath that unchanging cloud-covered sky. If I hadn't felt the stream of conflicting emotions coming through our bond then I might've thought she hadn't heard the question.

"He wants to bring himself back," Selena said. "He said as much to you. That's not what's meant for us, when we go to Riven. You took an oath to be a guide, one whose mission is to see spirits safely to their end. If you are who you say you are, then it is your job to make sure Piotr doesn't open the gate."

"Strikes me as almost petty," I said. "If he could save Riven at the cost of my life, why shouldn't I give it to him?"

"You don't know that," Selena said. "And he's already sacrificed how many guide lives? How much time and energy? If he had spent all of this time wrangling more spirits, putting together a strategy to stop the war in your world, then perhaps this wouldn't be a problem."

I nodded, even though she couldn't see it. Piotr's gate might save Riven in the short-term, but at what terrible cost to the rest of the world?

A line blurred in the distance, a part of the horizon that didn't match the rest. Darker than gray, and flowing upward. Smoke from a fire. A target.

"I found something," I said. "Thanks for the talk."

"That's all you can say to me?" Selena said.

"I'm sorry," I said. "Thanks, as ever, for being there. For making me understand that I'm not always as evil as I seem to be."

"You never are," Selena said. "Go, find your way back to me."

1 2 0

A SMALL HUT sat beneath the trail of smoke, made from stalks of the dead wheat. In front burned the fire, a large stacking of grain going up as the flames made their way through them. More slowly than I would've expected, but this was Riven. Natural laws didn't always apply.

The owner of the fire, or least I assumed that's what she was, stood off to the side and watched the stalks burn. She wore a fine coat, the same full-body length as the one I sported. Only it looked older, poorer craftsmanship of a simpler time. Rough cloth woven together with less of the precision than modern machines produced for us. Its hood hid her face, and the only way I knew it was a she at all was the hair coming out from the hood's bottom, long and silver, and her hands reaching out of the sleeves and clasping in front of her.

"It's been a long time since I've had a visitor here," the woman said without looking up from the fire.

"Where is here?" I said.

"Names should be exchanged before questions are asked," the woman said. "Mine is Nara."

"Carver Reed," I said. I stepped into the clearing around the fire and reached out with my hands, hovered them over the orange glow. I felt the heat, like the clock tower as it burned down.

"Carver Reed," Nara said. "Here is a long way off from anywhere."

"I crossed over in a hotel, in New York," I said. "It brought me over back there, in the middle of the field."

Nara nodded. "There are still some of those. Old places that will let you come to these dead parts of Riven. They are becoming ever scarcer."

"I need to get back to the city," I said. "Can you point me in the right way?"

Now Nara looked up at me, her face bearing traces of wrinkles, her eyes a cloudy blue. You could be whomever you wanted in Riven. You created the image of yourself. Nara eschewed youth for a wiser visage, yet one that bore its age lightly.

"I can," Nara said. "But I have so few visitors. Would you mind staying for a little while and telling me about the world that you came from?"

Nara wasn't a person, I realized. She was a spirit. I should've seen it earlier, recognized the nothing else would bother building a home out here in the wilderness. Only, a spirit that survived long enough to make a place like this one had to be bound by someone else, and the only person I knew binding random spirits was Piotr.

"Who controls you?" I said. Nara laughed.

"Controls me?" Nara said. "I'm far too old for that."

"You're not bound?"

"What purpose would I serve, way out here?" Nara replied. "Who would find me to bind me in the first place?"

"Your answers are creating more questions," I said.

"I'm afraid that's a habit of mine," Nara said. "So tell me, Carver. Have the Americans won yet?"

"Won?"

"Yes, I believe the last time I saw someone like you, the Americans were fighting for their independence. It was quite the story."

I paused. Nara wasn't talking about the current war, but something over a century past.

"They won," I said, not knowing what else to say.

"Then he would've been disappointed," Nara said, shaking her head. "He spent far too long talking about his great empire. As though he'd forgotten that all empires eventually fall."

"How long have you been here?" I said.

"A long time," Nara said. "When you want very much to stay, Riven doesn't try to move you."

"Spirits can't stay by themselves. Not forever," I said. I realized Nara standing there seemed to contradict that assertion. That the Cycle would always pull a spirit to it eventually. If that wasn't true, then the Cycle was not as strong as I'd been told, or Nara was lying and perhaps Piotr meant for me to come here.

"Have you ever asked yourself how Riven came to be?" Nara said. "Why all of this exists?"

"Only after I've had a few drinks," I replied.

"I've been dry for centuries," Nara said, slipping back to a former time. "The last of the wine vanished long ago."

"What?" I said, because what else was there to say?

"It doesn't matter. You said you wanted to find your way back to the city?" Nara said. I had the impression that she juggled dozens of simultaneous thoughts, leaping from one idea to the next without a clear connection. "Long ago, it actually was one. The city."

"Now it's ruins," I said. "And won't be that for much longer."

"Is it finally falling apart?"

"Too many spirits," I said. "Riven is being overrun."

"Which is why you want to go back?"

I told her everything. I wasn't sure why. Whether it was the soft tones of her voice, the feeling that Nara had infinite amounts of knowledge and equally infinite patience. She did not seem to judge me for my fate or for my part in making Riven what it was. She listened like someone who had no desire to ever talk.

"So I have my reasons," I finished.

"I should say that you do," Nara said. "Except, from what you've said, you lack the skill."

"I have to try."

"If you are victorious, what will you do next?"

"I suppose I'll try to help the guides as best I can. Assuming I'm not locked up forever."

"May I make a suggestion?" Nara said.

"I feel like you're going to regardless of what I say."

"When you're done, when your quest for vengeance ends, come back here," Nara said. "You say you want to save Riven. I can help you."

"I'm standing here right now?" I said. "I'll take any hints. Tips."

Nara smiled, a chill pair of lips. A look not flavored with kindness or joy. Rather, she made the gesture seem mechanical. An expected part of conversation and nothing more.

"I've been waiting for a long time," Nara said. "I can wait a little longer. I will help you find your way, and when you are done, you will help me find mine."

121

"So what do you know about Riven that's going to help me?" I said to Nara as we stood around the fire.

"Such a broad question," Nara replied. "A spirit can learn much in centuries of living here."

"Then, because I don't have centuries, how about we get right to it and you give me the thing that's going to help me the most?"

"Difficult to answer," Nara said. "But if you were to ask me what I could most easily give you, then it would be to tell you about the binding."

"I already know how to do that," I said. Binding a spirit was one of the first things you were taught once you had passed the basic training necessary to become a guide. Bending spirits to your will, if only for a brief time, was integral for searching out breaches, for gaining allies in dangerous situations, or even because you needed someone to talk to. All of that was fine, all of it accepted under guide rules, provided you let the spirit go after you were done. Selena and I chose to ignore that part.

"Then tell me," Nara said. "If you are so sure of yourself, how much of you have you given away?"

"Given away?"

"I mean what I say. Have you nurtured those you bound, or do you sustain them? Do you feed them your life to keep them strong or teach them to grow their own?"

Grow their own? Spirits were already dead. They couldn't have their own life. They didn't make any sense. But then, here I was talking to a spirit that claimed she lived for centuries in the middle of an endless field of grain. Sense didn't have a large part to play in this particular situation.

"I do what I was taught," I said. "Part of me goes to live with every spirit I bind."

"It doesn't come back?" Nara said.

"Not unless the binding is broken."

Nara nodded. "That is how it was taught. That is how it was learned. That is not how it has to be."

"You're saying there's another way to bind a spirit?" I said.

"I'm saying that you can get your strength back," Nara said. "While still keeping those you love from going to the Cycle."

"Those I love?"

"Even one as old and alone as I am can tell when a man is talking about one he will not part with," Nara said. "The defensive edge in your tone, the way your eyes find their way to the edge of the clearing. How you needlessly avoid talking about any specific person. It's all how you try to protect the one that you love. I can help you, help her protect you."

"Fine," I said. "Then tell me. Or show me. Or do whatever it is you have to do that's going to give me my strength back. We're wasting time."

I'd felt that boost once before. When the ghoul near the Mountain had broken my binding to Selena and Nicholas.

Having that strength back would be a boon against Piotr, an edge I would need to hold my own against him.

"Look for the missing part of you," Nara said. I nodded. "Find it, and find her."

I reached into myself and looked for that small itch, that missing part of me. When I found it, I touched Selena across our bond. Sent a wave of happiness through. She replied in kind. I felt a question come back from her, asking me where I was, what I was doing. I told her only to wait. To listen.

"Now you must with draw from her," Nara said. "Take it back. Take it all back."

"You mean break the binding?" I said.

Nara shook her head. "Withdraw it. You will see what happens."

Like flexing a muscle, like holding my breath. I took in the connection between Selena and I. Her worry seeped through, the concern she probably felt coming from me. But I didn't stop. Our tie to each other dwindled away except for one tiny sliver, a sliver that I couldn't seem to cut, couldn't seem to close off without severing everything.

"It's almost gone," I said.

"Hold it there," Nara said. "Wait for her. She will learn."

I tried to press reassurance to the tiny bond. Like trying speak through a tiny hole that I could not see. Like trying to find Selena's hand in the dark.

"If she is strong, she will begin grow her own. To open her own soul and let it grow," Nara said.

" I don't understand," I said. "If she's dead, how can she live without my help?"

"As roots may grow multiple seeds, a proper binding can allow many spirits to flourish without killing the host," Nara said. "What is left within her will grow to fill the space you have provided."

It happened quickly. I kept my focus on my bond to

Selena, small and slight though it was. Eventually, like a warm glow from a distant fire, our connection grew. Opened again to a broad and clear path between us. Only this time it was a knot tied with both of us. If before I had focused on myself to find Selena, to reach through our bond, now it was like another sense. Like listening, or hearing. She was a part of me and I a part of her.

My strength came back. Not all of it, but most. As though I'd recovered from an exhausting run.

"That's how he's doing it," I said aloud. "This how Piotr is binding all of those spirits."

Nara looked at me. "The leader of your guides?"

"He must have figured it out," I said.

"Or had my secrets told to him," Nara said.

Now it was my turn to glance her way. "Who would have known? You said I was the first one here in a hundred years."

"I'm not the only one capable of passing such knowledge," Nara said, and I felt dumb. Of course. If any one of those guides had known how to bind spirits like this, they could have passed it down from one leader to the next. A secret to keep all of their spirits awake. Waiting for a chance to break out of Riven's chains.

"Thank you," I said. Next I'd have to repeat the process with Nicholas. Grab every bit of myself back that I could.

"Save your thanks," Nara said. "You will give it when you come back."

"I will," I said. "You keep insisting on that, why?"

"Because none of the others have done so," Nara said, turning back to her fire. "They have taken my knowledge and left me here to rot."

122

TIME IN RIVEN was a fluid concept. There weren't days to track, movements of the sun to follow as it trekked across the sky. There was only a growing sense of exhaustion, a tingling awareness that my body back in the real world might need some attention. But there was no going back.

Nara and I even tried, after I insisted. Even if I crossed over into the muzzle of Polk's revolver, I might be able to get some water. A bite to eat. Keep my body from withering.

We followed my trail of flattened and broken stalks to where I crossed over. Under her watchful eyes, I sat down amongst the wheat and tried to cross back. At first, it felt normal. Riven fell away and my soul, or my consciousness, or whatever you want to call it drifted. The feeling of the grain stalks, a pile that we'd made to give me enough of a bed to cross back, fell away.

I floated on water in an endless sea of night. The void that all of us went through while crossing between Riven and our world. After a few seconds I should have woken up on the other side. Instead I kept floating. Something wasn't right.

If you've ever experienced those moments before you fall asleep, those instants where you can tell you're about to slip away into a dream, that's what happened to me. Where my formless, shapeless self started falling into that void.

"They're blocking my way back," Bryce said.

I couldn't wake up. Polk or Derringer, or Piotr, were keeping me asleep. I pulled away from that sweet urge, that surrender to the endless dark. Pushed my soul back to Riven. Focused on the bed of grain, that gray sky, until my eyes opened into Nara's curious face.

"Then you must hurry," Nara said when I explained why I'd come back.

"Any chance you could help with that?" I said. "I don't exactly know my way around here. It all looks the same."

"To an outsider, I suppose it does," Nara said. Then she pointed. "Straight that way. You will catch sight of the city walls before long."

"I will keep my promise," I said to her. "I'll come back for you."

"For me?" Nara said. "No, Carver Reed, I think you will come back for yourself."

Not knowing how to respond to that, I left with a nod. Trudged through the grain until the wall appeared in the distance. Its gray bulk shimmering in the view on the horizon and gradually becoming real.

I told Selena I was coming, told her to get Bryce and Alec ready. I had no idea how long Piotr would wait for me. How many days he was willing to lose. Or how much longer I had before Riven fell.

Once I was in the city, though, it was apparent that Riven teetered on the edge. Buildings like the Palace, once dusty but whole, were marred by broken walls and torn gates. Spirits and ghouls taking out their frustration, the telltale gouges of guides striking back with weapons of their own.

I'd asked Nara, asked her if with all the space in the grain fields whether Riven could survive. If the spirits could spread out into the infinite. To which Nara replied that it wasn't about the number of spirits, but their proximity to each other. The collective force that in small amounts can make a ghoul, but in larger ones could form breaches and eventually tear those same holes open.

"Selena said you'd be here," Anna said, stepping out from an alleyway. "I'm not quite believing it. I thought you would be dead for sure."

"I should be," I said. "But Piotr's not ready to give up yet. He doesn't want to risk a wide open gate."

"So instead he sent you east of the city?"

"I don't think he knew where I was going," I said. "Where are you?"

"I'm back with those sneaks in New York. Helping them with client work."

"At least you got away," I said.

"I'm trying to figure out how to rescue you," Anna said as we walked along towards the apartment. "Only it's not easy. Polk and Derringer are in the room all the time, and others usually aren't far away. Piotr himself is gone; I don't know where."

"You could try the police," I said. "Claim I'm being held hostage."

"You might have forgotten," Anna said. "But you're a wanted criminal."

"Hmm, good point," I said. "Still, it might be worth it."

"You want me to try?" Anna said. "They could prevent you from crossing over."

"Better than being used," I said. "If we can't win, then you have to. You have to get me out of their hands."

Anna nodded. "It's been three days, Carver. Where were you?"

"Lost," I said. "It was really, really boring."

Anna seem to buy the explanation. If she thought I lied, she didn't press me on it. Nobody else needed to know about Nara, for now.

By the time we made it to the apartment, everyone was already there. Ready and waiting. Bryce held his voulge, wore a new coat that Nicholas had made. Selena had her cleaver. Even Alec returned, shaking his head when I asked him whether he'd found a way to save Bryce.

"He's in lock down," Alec said. "Guides are posted at his house, keeping him in that bed. His family is in a hotel."

"I never thought they would do something like this," Bryce said.

"The punishment is supposed to be terrible," Alec said. "To keep other guides from getting ideas."

"Look at how well that's worked for them," Bryce replied.

"All right. After this, Anna, can you work with Alec to break Bryce out?" I said. "Leverage some of your contacts to get them out of the city?"

"It's like you think I'm some sort of spy master," Anna said.

"Aren't you?" I said.

"I might be able to figure something out," Anna said, shaking her head.

"You would have my gratitude," Bryce said.

"Consider it a thank you for getting me in this mess," Anna said, she twisted her face into a smile. "Without you hiring me, I'd probably have been caught by now. Or maimed by a spirit."

"So what's the plan?" Alec said. "We head right for the Mountain?"

I nodded. There wasn't much else to it. Carry the fight to Piotr and hope we do better this time than before. Hope that knowing what was coming would be enough. That we could do better than Graham and Katherine.

Nicholas elected to stay back this time. Claimed he'd be better served spending the journey working on other projects. Things he didn't want to get into until he was sure they would work out. I didn't argue. Without the scientist, it'd be one less body to protect.

This time, as we journeyed out, I stayed for the entire hike. The couple of days walking along Riven's avenues, through the wall to the forest and along the same trail traveled by the thousands of spirits going to the Cycle. Alec and Anna crossed in and out as they were able to. Alec took the train by himself, went back to Inman's camp and crime scene. The police had closed the investigation, leaving the cabins deserted. Beds empty and waiting.

As we went, sparks littered the sky. Guides communicating about this or that breach. The howls of spirits, of rage beyond comprehension echoed between the buildings. Riven tearing itself apart in war.

Still, for the first time in days, I had hope.

124

THE MOUNTAIN STOOD BEFORE US, its entrance glowing with the pale blue reflection of the Cycle from deep within. The last time I'd stood there, it'd been with my mother and father. Now, with my mentor and my friend. Selena, the spirit that I loved. With us, a woman I trained; Anna. The sneaks in New York had plenty of beds synced up with various parts of Riven. Including the forest.

Around us the endless march of the dead continued; spirits brushing past on their vacant walk to the Cycle. Behind us, the ghostly trees beckoned with their shivering leaves. I looked at all of my companions gave them a nod.

"Inside, let me handle Piotr," I said. "Keep the other spirits off of us. If you have to wrangle them, do it. If you don't have to, let them stay. Every bound soul saps a bit of strength from Piotr's swings."

I drew my lash with my right hand, and my left settled on the familiar long knife. Tools made to serve a purpose, to serve an order that no longer wanted me. An order whose leader would see me dead. It felt appropriate that these would be the means of Piotr's end.

We marched into the Mountain, staying in line with Anna at the back, Selena and Bryce and Alec behind me. We kept going past the offshoots, the tunnels that led to treasures left behind by guides long past. Soon we made it to that central landing, the spot where, before, Piotr's cloak and sword had been. Now, there was nothing.

"Carver," Piotr announced from down the stairs, towards the Cycle. "You've taken your time. I feared you would never show. That your body would simply waste away in that hotel room and you would die a coward."

I couldn't see him, could only hear his echoing voice.

"Piotr, this is between you and me," I called back. "Come out here and let's handle this the way it ought to be."

"A fair fight?" Piotr said. "That's delicious, coming from you. Who tried to ambush me with that girl in New York. No, I think it's best you earn your audience."

"Behind!" Anna yelled, and we turned. A group of former guides, sporting all manner of weapons and cloaks, broke through the line of dead spirits. They slid through the spirit crowd, dancing between the dead without pausing. Without getting tripped up by the many feet or pushed aside by apathetic shoulders.

I had to remind myself that these were not normal foes, but the best the guides had to offer. Leaders bound to serve the next one in this endless chain until, with the gateway or with the end of my lash, the chain could be broken.

"Go Carver," Selena said. "We can hold them."

Bryce push me towards the stairs as he drew his voulge. "Don't let this be for nothing."

My mentor, always inspiring. I took off down the steps as the clash of metal rang out behind me. My friends fighting for their lives.

About time I fought for mine.

At the bottom of the stairs the cave widened out into the

flat landing before the great blue ocean of the Cycle. Piotr stood near the edge, watching spirits step off into oblivion. Facing me, though, were two spirits that I thought I'd lost.

"Hello Carver," Graham said, his hammer sitting on his shoulder.

"About time you showed up," Katherine said to me, my mother idly tossing one of her batons up and down. "We were getting bored waiting for you."

"Isn't it a pleasant surprise, Carver?" Piotr said. "Your parents. Still alive, such as it is. Think about it; you could return them home. Just lie down and give yourself up."

There's a certain type of anger that takes you over. That leaves you breathless and focused. That obliterates all consideration of anything other than the source. That renders reality into a single white hot dot and you can't think about anything else. Can't do anything except lash out against it in a ceaseless frenzy. Piotr was that dot, and I would erase him.

I took a step towards Piotr and my parents closed the gap. Graham raised his wrist, that same contraption ready to fire one of its burning wires. I swung with the lash, cracked it against Graham's gadget. The lash's coil wrapped around the metal and I pulled back so hard that the gadget itself tore off of Graham's wrist and flew back towards me.

I snapped the lash, still coiled around the gadget. Aimed it at Katherine, coming in at me from my right side. She swept her baton up through the gadget, hooking it and pulling hard. Trying to tear the lash from my grasp. Only I wasn't the same guide that I had been. For one, with Nara's trick, I'd grown stronger. For two, I had no concerns. No hesitation.

No fear.

Piotr had brought me to the edge of reason. To the point where there was nothing left except this fight, this victory. So I twisted my shoulder and pulled. Swept my arm and dragged my mother and her baton with it. Knocked her into Graham as he stepped forward with the hammer. They fell over each other to the ground.

I didn't hesitate. Ran up, and used the knife. First my mother, and then my father. Two stabs, two blue fire burns, and my parents were gone. Again.

"Impressive," Piotr said. "Though I suppose I shouldn't be surprised. They didn't want to hurt you. They resisted so heavily."

"Resisted?" I looked into their blank eyes as my parents rose up.

"Have you ever seen Graham open with that wrist of his?" Piotr said, drawing his great sword and leveling out towards me. "Why would Katherine try to catch your lash instead of simply dodging, cutting underneath and delivering her strikes? Your parents let you win."

I reached my hand towards my mother. There was a chance, now that they had been separated from Piotr, that I could rebind them. Perhaps make this a three on one. Then I saw Piotr's sword shift in the corner my eye. Whistle towards me in a long cut the forced me back from my parents.

"Time for these two to have peace, don't you think?" Piotr said. My parents, oblivious to the world, turned and walked those fateful steps to the Cycle. Only moments until they fell.

"I think you need to stop talking," I said, raising the lash. Piotr shuffled back from my first strike, the lash falling short. Moved himself away from my parents and I, towards the left edge.

I followed, using the lash to keep Piotr and his waving great sword at a distance. Every time it cracked, I forced him back another inch. Closer and closer to that ever-present blue. I spared a glance as my parents walked out on that short precipice with the other spirits. About to leap into the Cycle.

I wouldn't be able to get to them. I wasn't sure I wanted to. They deserved their rest. They had suffered enough. If I wanted to pay back their memory, I would do it by sending Piotr along with them.

MY LASH'S shadow shot a curling line through the Cycle's glow as it reflected on the cavern walls. My knife partnered with it, a straight edge pointing up towards Piotr's throat. He stayed out of range, across the room. The crowd of wandering spirits divided us as they marched endlessly into the blue lake. Piotr's great sword towered above them.

"I can say that this is refreshing," Piotr said. "To finally meet someone worthy. A test after all these years."

"I'm not a test," I said. "This isn't a game."

"Then prove it to me," Piotr said. The large man shifted forward, elbowing his way into the line of spirits and through the other side. Right into my lash's cracking strike.

The lash hit him in the shoulder, the point digging into Piotr's skin. Boring a hole through his coat. But Piotr was too broad for the lash to wrap around. He shrugged off the attack, continuing his advance. Piotr lowered his shoulder and leaned forward, bringing the great sword in a cleaving swing that would've split me in two. If I'd stayed put.

I darted back, putting distance between us. The great sword missed my face by a foot, the black and silver blade flashing reflected light as it went past. Plenty of room for my lash to strike again. I snared Piotr's right arm as his swing carried it into the lash's path. The cord curled around Piotr's forearm and held fast. I tightened my grip, held the lash out wide to keep Piotr from moving the sword back into position.

For his part, the leader of the guides stared at my lash around his wrist, as though he couldn't believe he'd actually been tagged.

"The problem with upstarts like you," Piotr said. "Is that they don't understand their history."

"History?" I said as I dashed forward with the knife. One strong stab and maybe I could force Piotr over the edge. Into the Cycle, from where there was no return.

"Every leader that came before has trained me," Piotr said as I went for the stab. "Every tactic discovered through the years, through centuries, I have learned."

As my knife neared his chest, Piotr dropped the sword and swung his hand, the one bound with the lash, into my strike. My own knife cut into the cord and severed it as the great sword hit the ground. I kept my stab going, pushed forward as the blade pierced Piotr's coat, cut into his chest.

I felt his big hands on my arm, pushing the knife back and away. His knee shot up into my stomach, and Piotr threw me to the ground. The man's strength was incredible. I had no way to counter that. I felt light and loose in his grasp, like a thread in the wind.

Piotr grabbed his sword as I pulled up to my feet. I was down a lash, and my knife looked awfully small next to that great sword. I'd have to change tactics.

"But with all the benefits come the costs," Piotr said turning towards me. Raising his weapon. "I know everything, Carver. All of Riven's secrets."

"You think so?" I said.

"I know this place is doomed," Piotr said. "The only hope we have lies in finding a way out."

Piotr slashed the sword towards me, but it was lazy. Forced me back, but not fast enough to go for a kill. My hands felt the back wall of the room, the smooth rock carved out by whatever ancient engineer put this cave together.

"You're not dead," I said. "You don't need to stay here."

"We all come to Riven eventually," Piotr said following my retreat. "I'm choosing to plan in advance."

As Piotr stepped into another swing, I broke into a run. This time towards the line of spirits. They provided some cover, gave me a chance to think. I shoved my way through a pair of nurses, both bearing the scars of disease. Behind me, I heard Piotr's sword bite into the same spirits. Carving and twisting them away. Clearing a path by murdering the dead.

"Stop running, Carver," Piotr said. "I have other things I'd like to do."

"Sorry," I said, and as Piotr broke through the line of spirits, I drew and fired Inman's gun. Still had it, still had bullets even after all this time. Piotr didn't see it coming, only managed to widen his eyes in shock as the bullet bit into his chest.

I followed up the strike, throwing the knife ahead of me and, as Piotr moved to block it, grabbing his hands and fighting for his sword. Piotr might be stronger than me but I hoped that, with surprise on my side, I could wrest the weapon away.

I went for dirty tricks. Kneed Piotr in the stomach, jammed my heel into his foot, and dug my fingernails into his hands as we wrestled for the sword. It wasn't enough. For the first time, I heard Piotr growl, a gravelly aching rumble of pain, and he used his shoulders to clear me away.

"Unexpected," Piotr said. "I should have figured you would use that coward's weapon. It suits you."

Piotr leaned into another swing, and I did the only thing I could think of. I grabbed a spirit walking by on my left and threw him into the path of the blade. Piotr's attack bit into the spirit, but the ghost stopped the sword's momentum. Gave me an opening. I ran up and stuck my right foot behind Piotr's right ankle, pressed against the man's shoulders as he tried to free the sword from the spirit. Sent Piotr toppling to the ground.

Piotr's hands fell free of the sword as I tripped him, and I turned to grab his weapon. Pulled it the rest of the way out of the spirit, who stared at the wound without comprehension. Who turned and continued his walk. Who leapt into the Cycle without knowing that his miserable existence punctuated the end of a tyrant.

I stood over Piotr with his great sword held in my hands.

"Tell me one more time," I said. "About all that knowledge."

I saw the anger, the fury and fear drain out of Piotr's face in that moment. The man I'd once regarded as a wise sage, a leader in times of darkness, now simply looked like an old man.

"You've won," Piotr said. "I admit it; I'm done. Your victory is yours and, with it, a chance to see the ruin of this world."

"Looking forward to it," I said, raising the sword.

"There is something you should see," Piotr said. "Normally, when a guide leader falls, the transition is more orderly. The spirit has time to convey the information. To tell their replacement what they need to know."

"Already got that, thanks," I said, thinking of Nara, but I hesitated. Piotr might be telling the truth. Who knew what kind of secrets he had, or tools he knew about that might help after I sent him to the Cycle.

"Not everything," Piotr said. "Let me stand. Keep the sword. Press it against my back for all I care."

"Where?"

"It's not far," Piotr said. "As evil as you think I am, Carver,

I truly don't wish to see everything collapse to ashes. I did want to save Riven."

Part of me wanted to deliver the deathblow right then and there. Burn Piotr with wrangling fire and send him into the Cycle. But what if I would be throwing away the one thing that could help us restore Riven? To drive back the spirits and keep us safe? Didn't I have a responsibility?

"Go on then," I said. "If I see anything, if I see those hands move, I'll strike before you get anywhere."

"I would expect nothing less," Piotr replied, and then I let him stand. Let him lead me out of the chamber and back up the stairs towards the landing. Except, halfway up, he turned to the right and went through a small passage. One I'd skipped over, assuming it, like all the others, led to the lost bed of an old guide.

Instead the path wound steadily up, curling in on itself. Narrow steps carved into the rock led us through a darkened passage as the Cycle's blue glow dimmed. Soon a familiar gray light replaced it. Outside.

"Where are we going?" I asked.

"The guides used to live in the Mountain," Piotr said. "Hundreds of years before I was born the guides operated out of these caves. Only when the spirits began to cross over into the city did we move our operation. Over time, there was less and less need to come here. Less need to know where the spirits went after we took away their anger."

"That doesn't answer my question."

"So you understand," Piotr said. "We're going to where the guides kept watch. To where they could see spirits amassing, could see the ghouls do their work. Could plan their nightly raids."

A few moments later I saw that Piotr wasn't lying. The passageway opened onto a rocky slope, high above the door where we'd come in. The dark forest spread out beneath us and in the distance I could make out Riven's city; its wall a dark line on the horizon. Beneath us the crowded trail of spirits marched towards the Mountain from miles away.

"From here, a watcher could see a signal from anywhere. From the city walls, even, a guide could launch a spark when they were in trouble and expect aid to come," Piotr said.

"Why did we come here?" I said. "This won't help us."

Climbing the steps, making my way to the narrow passage, I hadn't been able to keep the great sword at the ready. I hadn't held it to Piotr's throat since we stepped up on the slopes. Had kept it gripped in my hands, but not in a position to strike. So I did nothing when Piotr pulled a sparker from his belt and held it up into the air.

"No," Piotr said. "But it will help me."

Piotr pressed the button on the bottom of the sparker and glimmering golden yellow motes launched high in the air, flaring bright against the ashen sky.

"What was that?" I said, bringing Piotr's sword to rest against his throat.

"The last signal I need to send," Piotr said.

"To who?"

Piotr only laughed.

I fell away. That's the only way I can think of to describe it. Me, the physical me, stood still on that slope with Piotr's great sword held against his throat. My spirit, my soul, shivered. Dropped as though I had fallen down an unending well.

Parts of me split away as I plummeted. First, with a tearing rend like scraping my knee on concrete, went the bonds I'd formed with Selena and Nicholas. Wrenched away and gone.

Next fled the tingling sensation, the warning my spirit had been giving me for days now that I needed to cross back. That didn't tear away. It vanished, as though the feeling had never been there at all.

I still fell, still rushed through oblivion as every part of me split and came back together, bent and turned and twisted. As though I was severely ill and, at the same time, crashing into the earth.

I blinked.

Piotr stared at me along the length of his blade. His eyes were questioning, curious.

"How does it feel?" Piotr asked.

I glanced down at myself. Everything appeared to be there. I could feel my fingers gripping the hilt of the sword, could feel Riven's chilled breeze on my body. Could feel my lungs attempting to breathe Riven's non-air. And yet...

"What did you do?" I said.

"Carver," Piotr replied. "You're dead."

I DIDN'T HAVE a rational way of dealing with the words. I hadn't prepared for this. No scenario I'd plotted that had this as a possibility. With my parents, Bryce and I had spent part of the journey over here talking about how they might show up.

I'd expected Piotr to try and persuade me to give up my life. One more opportunity to take the easy way out.

I'd planned to deal with a fight that I might lose, and had kept Inman's pistol as a surprise.

Bryce and I had practiced the grappling, him holding his voulge like a sword so that I'd know how to wrest it from Piotr's grasp.

If I was going to die, we all assumed it would be by Piotr's hand. Instead, it had been Derringer's gun, or a knife in a hotel room in New York. My body hadn't fought to survive. I'd been murdered.

"You gave up," I said. I searched, inside, for that connection. That tie to my physical self, but there was nothing. "You'll never open your gate."

"Does it matter?" Piotr said, nodding out over the expanse

of Riven in front of us. "Look at it. All of those points, those pools of light?"

I followed his eyes. Speckled like stars on the night sky were shimmering circles, the closer ones in the forest revealing themselves as Piotr called them. Pools.

"They're breaches," Piotr continued. "Every single one of them. More appear every hour. Riven is overrun. I'll either escape when one of those angry spirits tears a hole, or I'll be too dead to care."

"It'll be the latter," I said. I pulled the blade back and, with a single clean stroke, ended Piotr's reign as the leader of the guides.

His body crumpled to the ground, then rose. A pure spirit now. One that could live again. Except I was waiting. Twisted the hilt on the great sword and burned out the glimmer of a soul in Piotr's eyes.

He left me there on the slope, walked back into the tunnel on the path to the Cycle.

I don't know how long I stood there, watching the breaches glow on the sprawling landscape beneath me. There weren't guides operating in the forest. Spirits crossing from those breaches would continue to pour out, find each other, and feed off of their anger to become ghouls or packs of roving, maiming monsters.

Piotr was gone. The Master, as we'd called him during those months trying to find out who he was, had met his end. Riven, though, seemed as bad as it had been before.

"Carver?" Selena's voice came up out of the Mountain, carrying up the passageway.

"Up here," I replied and before long Selena joined me on the mountainside. "Is everyone all right?"

Selena took in the view, then settled on the ground next to me. She spared a long look for Piotr's great sword. "We're still here, if that counts. Alec took some scrapes, so he and Anna are crossing back over."

"Good," I said. "They'll need their energy. And Bryce?"

"He's waiting for us back near the Cycle. Watching to make sure all the spirits Piotr bound go in."

"Always about the mission with him."

"I saw Piotr go over the edge," Selena said. "That means it's over, right?"

"One part," I said. "Tell me, can you feel it?"

"Feel what?"

"The binding. You and I."

Selena paused. I watched her eyes as they closed briefly, as Selena searched for the tie that had kept us together for more than a year. Watched as she opened them, took her hand, and placed it over mine.

"I can teach you," Selena said. "How to resist the Cycle. It will get easier."

"And this?" I waved my hand at the view. "I don't know how to deal with that. There's no way we can face all of those breaches."

"Maybe not," Selena said. "But we've gone up against some terrible monsters before and come out alive. So to speak, anyway."

We stayed there on the slope for a while longer, counting the breaches and measuring our affection in the silence. For our entire relationship, Selena had been dependent on my binding to keep her away from the Cycle. Now, for the first time, I would need her help, her support, to resist it. To guide me.

THE WHISPERS STARTED on what Bryce said was the second day. We were in the forest, the three of us walking by spirits marching the other way, when I heard them. Soft and indistinct, like the remnants of a dream upon waking up. Less real words than urges. A pull to turn back, to return to the Cycle.

"Laugh," Selena said when she noticed I'd stopped, when she and Bryce made it a few paces ahead. "Think of something funny."

"That's hard to do on command," I said. But I did. Reached and replayed a memory of one of the many times Nicholas had detonated himself in his lab, all in the interest of research. A ruined oven and a scientist with his hair on fire, his coat charred and missing patches.

The whispers stopped with my smile. Faded away, though I could still feel it. Like the tiniest thirst, lingering at the edge of my senses.

"It worked," I said, and Selena nodded. Bryce, I noticed, kept his eyes on me a little longer. One of his hands had gone behind his back, ready to draw his voulge.

I was a spirit, unbound and capable of turning at any moment. I'd have done the same thing in Bryce's place.

Selena continued dropping tips as we made our way back to the city. Tricks like laughing, or focusing on a treasured memory. Or a loved one. Anything that brought you into your own humanity. That's what kept the Cycle at bay.

"It never truly goes away, does it?" I asked her as we went through the western gate to the city.

"You get used to it," Selena said. "After a while it's like anything else. Something you deal with."

As if coping with death wasn't enough.

Alec met us back at the apartment with a burst of good news. He'd been communicating with other guide leaders and, after pondering the situation, they'd decided to give Bryce his life back.

"And more than that," Alec said. "Since you're the ranking guide, Bryce, we're going to vote to make you the new leader."

"I don't want it," Bryce said. "I'm retired."

"Don't think you have a choice," Alec replied. "You saw all of those breaches. If we're going to have a chance, we need someone that can bring the guides together. It's not going to be me."

Bryce glowered in Alec's direction.

"Bryce," I said. "Take it. You'd be the best leader the guides have ever seen. You know Riven inside and out, already have connections on the other side, and with me over here, you've got your spirit emissary all figured out."

"Spirit emissary?" Bryce said.

"I figured you'd want to create a new position," I replied. "Someone that helps connect you with the spirits that aren't angry, that don't want to cross over quite yet."

"You're all assuming Riven's going to be around much

longer," Bryce said. "You're trying to make me the captain of a sinking ship."

"Because you're the only one that can save her," I said.

Bryce grumbled for a little while longer, but he didn't have any more fight left in him. By the time he left to cross back with Alec, the two were already talking allocations and adjustments, what regions needed more support, and how they could drive recruitment.

I watched them head towards the clock tower, a pair that I'd once made a trio, and felt lost.

"I see you picked up a new weapon?" Nicholas asked, kneeling behind me to inspect Piotr's great sword. I'd carried it back from the Mountain, as with the lash severed I needed some sort of defense.

"It's a trophy," I replied.

"Rather deadly for a trophy," Nicholas said. "The carvings on this are exquisite. I'd say it goes back at least a hundred years or more. Possibly ancient. Some of it, anyway."

"Some of it?"

"Yes. It looks like your sword is a composite. I can pick out at least three different types of iron and steel. Points at which they've been joined. If this were out on the other side, such a technique would make a weapon like this prone to shattering," Nicholas shifted his goggles up above his eyes. "In Riven? Perhaps it works differently."

I hefted the sword and looked at it, the black and silver streaks running down the blade. The runes I couldn't read appearing every couple of inches on the metal. The hilt, a curling gold and green design that bled into a bronzed guard. Piotr never explained where he'd found it. With him gone, the sword's origin would remain an unknown story.

Maybe I would use it to tell a new one.

129

"You say we have to go back?" Selena said. "Away from the breaches that we could be closing?"

"I made a promise," I said as we packed up our weapons. The crossbow hung over my back, the great sword hanging beneath it. My knife and lash, newly repaired by Nicholas, hung on my waist. Food and drink weren't necessary. They never would be.

"To who, again?"

"An old spirit. Goes by the name of Nara, though I'm not sure that's what she's really called," I said. "She says she can help."

"I thought you said spirits couldn't stay in Riven unless they were bound?"

"I did," I said. "Either I'm wrong, or someone's controlling her. I'm hoping for the former."

Nara hadn't said what she wanted me to do, why she wanted me to come back, but if she'd managed to survive unbound in Riven for hundreds of years, then I wanted to know her secret. I wanted to know how to stay.

Anna and Alec would be arriving soon, to help take us to

the city's eastern gates. I went out to the balcony, Selena's favorite viewing spot, and watched the sparks explode over Riven's broken buildings. Cries echoed down the alleys as ash swirled through the sky. A city of the dead full of life.

This was my home now, and I would fight for it.

CARVER'S ADVENTURES *continue in Spirit's End*

130

I HAD BEEN alive the last time I kissed her lips. Soft, cool to the touch. Mine were likely the same. Selena's eyes, though, still had life. Her soul was still there. Mine too.

We parted, grabbed our things from around the gray, ashy apartment. I slipped on my long black coat, a reminder of something I no longer was. A guide, meant to take the spirits of Earth's dead stuck in Riven and send them on. Send them to the Cycle to keep them from crowding out this world. This grand, desolate place.

My home.

I hooked my lash into my belt, a ten foot long cord with a piercing metal point at the end. On my left side, I stuck in a long knife, a foot and a half of pointed desperation. On my back went the great sword I'd taken from the man who killed me. The sword stood half my height and took both hands to swing. It's black and silver metal blade would have been heavy, but without a real body and its limitations, I had no problems hefting the weapon. I didn't get tired anymore.

My crossbow hung over the sword, three sets of bolts

looping around the shaft. Normal black-tipped quarrels meant to deliver pointed pain to anything they struck. Next were blue ones, ready to spit out wrangling fire that would deliver a spirit to its peaceful end. Last came orange. A shot that could be as dangerous to me as it was to the enemy. My favorite.

"You're sure this is what we should do?" Selena said as she set her cleaver, as long as a knife and as thick as my sword, with biting ridges on the front edge, in its holster attached to the front flap of her coat.

"I don't know," I said. "But if Nara doesn't have an idea, we're stuck. Breaches are erupting everywhere, and the guides don't have the numbers. We need a miracle, and unless you've thought one up in the last couple of hours, that spirit is our best shot."

I didn't bring up the other reason for speed. The voice whispering at the edge of my mind, calling me to drop everything I had and start on that long walk to oblivion. The Cycle murmured, always there. A honeyed hush inviting me to give up my troubles and embrace peace.

And they said the dead had no worries.

"Is it strong today?" Selena noticed my closed eyes. "Bad?"

She asked me every morning. Her passion kept the Cycle in check. If I focused on her, on what Selena was saying, what we had, then the Cycle's siren call would diminish. Selena gave me a reason to stay, one far more compelling than the Cycle's push to leave.

"No worse than any other." I ran my hand over my face, gave her a slapdash smile.

Selena gave me a hard stare for a moment. She knew when I wasn't telling her the whole truth. I didn't have time for that discussion now, though. Bigger things to worry about.

"You ready?" I moved to the door. "Alec and Anna should be coming soon."

"You're the one with a dozen weapons." Selena didn't need blades to be deadly, though the two she carried were enough. One harsh look from those icy eyes and any spirit ought to run away.

131

WE LEFT THE APARTMENT, the top floor of a three-story building that we kept frantically maintained as the rest of the city crumbled around us. Riven's gray light burned through the glassless windows, omnipresent and lifeless. A reminder of what I'd lost when Piotr had me murdered. The color of dawn's sunrise, the sounds of birds singing in the morning, even the roar and rumble of passing traffic. Riven stood a quiet ruin.

Most of the buildings in the city were decaying after centuries without care. Broken by fighting, by the tormented destruction of angry spirits, or left to rot away according to Riven's mysterious laws. Normally the gray sky was a blank slate, but now sparks peppered its dull infinite with colorful bursts. Guides alerting and communicating with each other across avenues and miles of city blocks. Letting others know of a breach, a swarm of angry spirits bent on revenge or chaos or both.

On the ground floor we walked into a bustling lab, a large square space full of burbling machines, twisting metal, and fiery forges. Devices constructed in Riven's harsh world by a madman I'd found years ago. Nicholas Salzer looked up as we came in and gave a quick wave before turning back to a large piece of fabric he'd spread out on a table. He held a stick with a burnt end in one hand. Paper was hard to find in Riven, so you used whatever dark ashes stuck to.

"What's burning up your mind now?" I asked and Nicholas paused, turned to me with a spacey look on his face, a man arising from the depths of concentration.

"I've been trying to find a good way to solve this problem," Nicholas said, holding up the ash stick as if it explained everything.

"This problem?" I tried to get a look at what he was writing, but the slew of mathematics etched on the fabric were foreign to me.

"The spirits," Nicholas said. "It seems the bottleneck is simply that the Cycle takes too long. That the spirits are allowed to stay past their expiration."

"You've found the obvious." Selena leaned against the wall, arms folded. "But what are you going to do about it?"

"That's precisely what I'm trying to determine." Nicholas talked at the table, his back to us. "When I have a suitable hypothesis, I'll be happy to let you know."

A probing question came to my mind, but before I could ask it, the scientist broke out rhetorical mutterings. Meant for his equations, no doubt. I glanced at Selena and shrugged. Nicholas was his own man, and he didn't suffer interruptions.

"Wait outside?" Selena said. I nodded.

The lab opened onto a broad road with various buildings on either side forming a low sort of canyon. The occasional spirit wandered up and down, looking lost or, in rare cases, nattering to themselves. Riven didn't have any bias. Spirits from anywhere could show up, well, anywhere. You might be walking down the street and see a soldier from the war on one side and a tribesman from a land you didn't know existed on the other. The afterlife was the ultimate melting pot.

Yet, among the ashen flakes and empty sidewalks, Alec and Anna were nowhere to be seen.

THE SKIES WERE clear of sparks. No panicked shouts came down the avenue. Unexplained absences in Riven usually led to dire conclusions, but I clung to a nicer reason.

"Did I lose track of time?" I said. Riven had no clocks, no day or starry nights with which to navigate the passage of hours. Only my intuition, that general sense of history inching forward, kept me from losing all idea of when I was.

"It feels right," Selena said. "Which isn't a guarantee."

Before, when I'd been alive, I had felt time. My body, still on Earth, on the other side, would tell me when to wake up. When I should cross back over. Anna had buried that body somewhere. Or burned it. I never asked her what happened to it, and she hadn't told me. I never planned to.

We both shouted at the same time we saw Anna, saw her stumble out from an alley half a block away, clutching at her side. Bleeding claw marks, the jagged lines left from finger-nails, rending through her coat. Her flail, chain and spiked ball extended, dragging on the ground. Limping.

"Alec needs help," Anna said as we ran to her. "There's a breach just back there. It opened on top of us."

We didn't hesitate. I yelled back into the lab, told Nicholas to come out and help Anna, and then Selena and I took off running. Our feet pounded on the stones. We ducked between the buildings. Hit a back alley and then saw the breach to our right. In a small clearing formed when the rear halves of some of the structures had collapsed into a large pile of rubble. Now a glowing pool covered those broken boards and stones, only instead of water, the surface reflected up part of Earth.

Spirits climbed through the breach, their hands rising up into Riven like swimmers emerging from the water. People dying from violence, from disease, or even simple old age. Normally scattered throughout Riven, the breaches drew spirits together. Pulled them into single areas where their confusion, their rage and despair over their lost lives fueled each other and drove them into the hysterical rage that made the dead so deadly. They crossed over in ruined clothes, in uniforms, young and old, however the spirits saw themselves as they traveled that final line between life and loss.

A guide stood in the middle of those clutching hands, snarling mouths, and wild eyes. Alec bounced from one spirit to the next, delivering a series of short jabs with the ridged gauntlets that cloaked his fists and forearms. Spikes on those gauntlets burned with blue fire that enveloped every spirit they touched and torched away the anger showing in those dead eyes. Pacified them and sent the spirits on their final walk to the Cycle.

It would've been easy to watch that dance, to stay back and admire Alec as he wrangled one spirit after another. Only we could see the toll. Cuts appeared here and there as one hand or another swung a lucky swipe. A sidestep that dodged one sloppy tackle led Alec into another spirit's bite. Being outnumbered in Riven was a death sentence, no matter how good the guide.

Selena and I waded in on either side. I struck with the lash first, sending its pointed tip out and wrapping around a spirit reaching for Alec's back. The lash looped around the spirit's arm and its point bit into his shoulder. The spirit, a posh gentleman in a suit that looked as though he came directly from a wedding, turned and snarled at me. His eyes burned with the pale fire, a lost mind.

I twisted the hilt of my lash and fire erupted along the cord, blue flames that matched the hue of the spirit's eyes. As the spirit lunged towards me, the fire caught up to his body and wrapped him in its purifying burn. I felt his hand touch my shoulder, but rather than rend, it fell away and I looked up into a vacant stare. The empty eyes of a pacified spirit.

"Your arrival is most fortunate." Alec dodged another spirit, delivering three swift strikes to its middle and sending it stumbling away, wreathed in a wrangling blue glow. "I have a tablet, and it is very nearly ready."

I glanced Selena's way and saw her with her cleaver in one hand and a knife in the other, dashing between spirits and severing their anger with stab after stab. A beautiful storm, a partner that I'd never realized I had next to me. I did not know where Selena found her ability, but watching her carve her way through those grasping arms and spitting mouths filled me with a kind of pride, a love that comes only from seeing the one you care about most exceeding your wildest hopes.

Yes, watching the love of my life carve up a bunch of dead spirits was the highlight of my day. I lived a strange life.

"Back away," Alec called. I looked as the guide pulled a tablet off of his belt, a stone block with a sapphire set in the middle. A sapphire that glowed a deep blue, ready to fulfill its mission. To close the breach and drive the remaining spirits away. Alec put it down on the ground and pressed in on the sapphire as two more spirits reached for his back.

Blue tendrils lanced out from the tablet, striking through the spirits and wreathing them in fire. Others shot towards the edge of the breach, seeming to dive into the ground and pull the portal closed. And then Selena tugged at my arm, pulling me away.

"We've got to run," Selena said. "If that thing gets us, we're gone."

My legs kicked into gear and we sprinted away down the alley. I'd forgotten. I was a spirit now. That tablet would destroy me as surely as it had our enemies. So many rules I had to relearn.

"Thanks," I said. "I'm not used to it."

"Pretty sure it was you who told me that Riven doesn't give second chances," Selena said. "That I had to keep watching my back."

"Not as long as you're around," I said. Selena rolled her eyes.

I looked back down the alley and saw nothing left of the portal. Only Alec, picking up the tablet. Content spirits staring at nothing. In another minute or two they would shuffle off and start a days-long journey to a mountain west of the city. Into cave and down to its depths, where they would find the Cycle, a great blue lake.

Each and every one of those spirits would drop in and erase themselves from existence.

133

So far as scratches go, Anna's weren't dangerous. Tears in the coat, a gash along her leg. Bruises on her wrists where spirit hands had gripped too tightly. Alec shared similar injuries. The common cost of doing business in Riven these days.

"Remember the times when we'd be able to walk in and out pain-free?" Alec stared at his wounds, shaking his head. We stood in the lab, getting ready for our jaunt to the other side of the city. "When all we had to fear was a little bit of bad luck?"

"I'm not sure what Riven you were in," I said. "It's always been dangerous."

"It used to be fun," Alec replied. "Now I cross over because it is my job, not because it is something I wish to do."

"You're talking to someone who's trapped here," I said. "Forever."

"Not if they break a hole," Anna said. "Then you could come back."

"To enjoy the world for the brief hours before the dead overran it completely," I said. "What a happy thought."

"Which is the reason for this adventure, no?" Alec said. "This woman, this Nara, she has a way?"

"That's what we're going to find out," I said, glancing at Selena. "Speaking of that, we should move. Anna, are you going to be okay?"

"I can handle it." Anna rose to her feet, her shoulders were set. Her head high. "Alec shouldn't be alone out there anyway."

The walking went slow. Anna still had to limp, and we were more cautious than usual. Kept our eyes scanning alleys, side streets, with one of us always watching our backs. I never relaxed while walking Riven's streets, but now I stood on edge. Every moment my eyes flicked in a different direction, trying to see into all the corners and shadows.

From the apartment we headed east, cutting through the central part of Riven. Streets broadened into wide boulevards and buildings grew to five and six-story heights. Hotels and offices that had never been used. As if a child had dreamed them up and discarded the idea halfway through. Dollhouses with no dolls.

We saw guides. Guides by the dozen. Dashing in teams towards popping sparks. Carrying wounded back towards where they could cross over, to where guides could heal and return again after some hours away. Cries for help mingled with shouts of victory down the corridors between the walls. Several times we broke off to help guides seal away spirits, close a breach or a wrangle cluster of mauling souls. Selena and I, with our coats and guide weaponry, stayed low. Didn't talk, didn't give our names. Did what we could while avoiding recognition.

Only once did another guide push the issue. He'd recognized Alec and, after we'd closed a breach together, the guide congratulated each of us in turn. Hesitated when he saw my battered features. His eyes, bagged and tired, squinted. Looked me up and down.

"I know this face," the guide said. "What is your name?"

"His name doesn't matter." Anna put her hand on my shoulder. "He's with me. And Alec."

The guide gave her a side glance. "Our laws are not kind to those who help fugitives."

"I never knew a guide to turn on someone giving them aid," I said.

The guide took a step back. "I cannot deny your efforts. And I have neither the energy or the desire to deliver justice to you today. On another morning, however, I will not hold back. You have lives to answer for, Carver Reed."

He turned and walked away, the other guides in his group following in silent judgment. His words hurt, but the pain filtered into the same numb part of me that had grown in the days since I'd been cast out as a guide. I made no pretenses that I was a saint. That I hadn't done terrible things in the name of grander objectives. But losing friends was never easy. Losing my place in life stung every day. Every hour.

As we neared the east edge of the city the buildings thinned out; broad courtyards became the norm. Patterned white stone broken up with the occasional statue or domed building. The largest of these, the Palace, marked the spot where Alec and I had fought our first ghoul months ago. A time when my life was different. When I had a life.

"So when do you think you'll be back?" Anna said.

"That's an impossible question," I replied. "Nara might give us an answer in fifteen minutes, or she could hold us there for fifteen months."

"Riven won't last that long." Alec glanced at his gauntlets, as though they were directly responsible for Riven's survival.

"We'll move as fast as we can," Selena said. "I won't let Carver waste time."

"You won't?" I said. "But it's my favorite thing to do."

Riven's east gate stood large and proud. An archway built of stone and bordered by twin turreted towers. The four of us stood beneath that arch, looking out to the hundred yards of clear space before the endless fields of waving white grain began. There was something inevitable in the stance, the feeling that we might never see each other again. This parting, this moment where the two pairs separated, with Alec and Anna returning to the war-torn streets while Selena and I ventured into the unknown.

"You are sure you don't want me to bind you?" Anna said. "I can keep you from the Cycle. We can talk over long distances."

"You need your strength," I said. "Can't afford to be anything less than your best. If you die because the binding saps your energy, then I'd be right where I am now. Binding me wouldn't help Selena either."

"We can keep each other sane," Selena said.

"The opposite of most loves of known," Alec said. We laughed, but it was the dry sore. Low and laden with future burdens. Still, I welcomed the chance to smile. While in my head, the Cycle continued its whispers.

It never stopped.

134

Selena and I put one foot in front of the other. Alec and Anna turned back and disappeared amongst the statues and the columns. Back to the world that I had known. In front of us stood stalk after stalk of great white grain. Some taller than I was, most at least three or four feet in height. All shifting back and forth in Riven's eternal breeze.

I took the lead, pushing and shoving the stalks apart. Like making our way through a thick forest, or swamp. There simply wasn't a motion I could take that didn't involve pushing aside the plants. If they could even be called that.

"How did you manage to walk this far before?" Selena batted a stalk away from her face. "Find your way to anywhere?"

"Nara showed me," I said. "Pointed me in the right direction, led me most of the way. Until I could see the walls."

"I remember the conversations," Selena said. "You talked about how endless this all was. I didn't really believe it but now these plants are the only thing I can see."

The last time I'd been through here Selena and I had been bound to each other. I'd been alive and we could send our thoughts, our emotions over any distance in Riven to each other. It'd been my only comfort as I'd wandered through the endless field alone. Even Nara, when she'd been there, acted less like a companion and more like a distant teacher.

"When we find her," I said. "Let me do the talking at first. I don't think she'll be expecting you."

"You think that'll be a problem?"

"I don't know what to think." I parted a pair of stalks with my hands, stepped between them and held them apart for Selena to follow. "She told me that she was old. Hundreds of years. That she'd seen Riven built from the ground up and turned into what it is now. You tell me whether you'd go crazy being in here that long, with no friends, no seasons, nothing other than this."

"Alone?" Selena said. "I don't think I would last a month. I don't think anyone would."

"You came close," I replied. Even after I'd found her, even after I had bound Selena, she'd spent most days in Riven waiting and watching. Drawing on the walls of the apartment; cityscapes that she could see from her window. I'd worried whether she was going to fall apart, whether I would come to visit her one day and find Selena destroyed by this world's unchanging pallor.

"I've always been a survivor," Selena said. "I leaned on you. I leaned on Nicholas. I leaned on the memory of my children and what it took to raise them."

Selena didn't mention the husbands she'd murdered. The willpower it must've taken to plot their ends and actually pull them off. To leave one life after another behind as a weeping widow until it finally caught up with her. That scar running along Selena's face an ever-present reminder of the sacrifices she'd made and the pain she'd suffered. And had inflicted.

Perhaps that was what drew me to her. What kept us

together in this crazy world. She and I had both lost so much, had endured broken lives and broken dreams. It was fitting that Riven would prove to be our home. The only place two souls like us could make an existence. Such as it was.

"How long will we be wandering?" Selena said later, as the city walls disappeared on the horizon and we continued our march.

"Depends on whether I can find her," I said. "If I get lost, then we might just be here, pushing through the stalks until Riven implodes."

"You're inspiring a lot of confidence."

"Hey, it was your idea to come with," I said. Selena had insisted on it, actually. Declared that if I went off on another quest without her, one of two things would happen: Either I would go insane and fall victim to the Cycle's constant whispers or she would. Made it a pretty easy choice.

We continued pushing further and further into the vast field for what felt like a day or more but without a body's fatigue or a sun's pattern to tell you the time, it was hard to know. Eventually, though, we both saw the wispy smoke rising into the sky. Nara's fire. Burning the grain one stalk at a time seemingly forever.

When I shoved through the last line of stalks and into the clearing, it looked the same as it had before. Nara's hut, a thatched structure, stood alone beyond a fire chewing its way through a large pile of grain. I wasn't sure if it was the same pile that'd been there when I'd first found the clearing, or if Nara actually cut more stalks. Either way it didn't seem like her constant burning was making headway. The grain crowded as close as it had been before.

"Where is she?" Selena said. "Didn't you say she would be waiting?"

I nodded towards the hut. "Guessing she's in there, or we've come all this way for nothing."

"For nothing?" Nara's voice came out of the hut's door, frosted and scratched. "For nothing? You have a very low opinion of your journeys, Carver. Even if you simply had to turn back now, would you not have gained even the slightest insight into who you are?"

Nara emerged from the hut, wearing the same dark robe I'd seen her in before. Her hood pulled up to cover her eyes, keeping her face in shadow. That strange combination of age that had Nara looking both wise but far from frail. Etched lines over strong arms, thick skin, and bright hair. Movement with purpose.

"Does she always talk like that?" Selena asked.

I could only nod.

Perhaps it was the way Nara looked in her robe, her slow purposeful walk as she crossed the clearing to stand in front of Selena and I, but I shivered. Wanted to but resisted backing away. As Nara came closer the light sneaking under her hood revealed more of her face, a look that had just enough wrinkles to convey wisdom if not desiccated age. If this had been Chicago I would've given her a senior's due, respected her as an elder. Here, in a place where spirits determined their own guise, choosing such a look had a purpose.

"You brought someone with you? Who is this?" Nara bent her head towards Selena, kept her eyes on me. "A spirit. An unusual choice for a guide."

"I'm not a guide anymore," I replied. "This is Selena. We're here for your help."

"My help?" Nara replied.

"You said you had a way to keep Riven from falling apart. It's only getting worse; the spirits continue to pour in and breaches are opening everywhere," I said. "If you have a solution, I'd like to know what it is."

Nara stepped over to me, reached out with her hand and touched my face. I flinched away. There was something strange about a person you didn't know touching you. Nara's cold hands, the wisps of her fingernails glancing on my cheek sowed unease. I noticed Selena's hand drift towards her cleaver. But then Nara stepped back, a frown crossing her lips.

"She and I are not the only spirits here," Nara said. "What happened to you, Carver Reed?"

"You see this sword?" I said, my hand rising to the hilt of the great blade on my back. "The man who owned it had me killed on the other side. He paid for it."

"Then you succeeded," Nara said. "I'm impressed. For you to be back, Riven must truly be in dire shape."

"Please," Selena said. "If you can help, we need a way to close the breaches quickly. A way to help the spirits get to the Cycle faster."

Nara gave Selena a frosted stare. "Riven is not a product of nature. It is not a random world of chaos, like where you came from. Where I came from. It is a construct. Built by those who refuse to take the last leap into the Cycle. I am one of those."

Nara held up one wrinkled hand.

"Before you start to ask your questions, before you panic, or assume I am something greater than what I am, take another look at the world in which you find yourselves. A place where natural law is scattered. Where the things you take for certainties come and go with the breeze. Where a house might be nothing more than bits of rubble and yet the next stands perfect. All of this, every inch you walk upon, comes from us."

I heard the words. They sounded like Piotr's. The mad ramblings of someone who thought they were above and beyond everyone else. Even if Nara was telling the truth, even if she was some sort of ancient spirit that had a hand in molding Riven to what it was, she was still here in the middle of the endless stalks of grain, alone in a hut. Hardly the existence I'd imagine for someone with the power to craft a world.

"If you are so strong, if you are truly what you're saying, then why let Riven slide into decay?" I said.

"Because I cannot," Nara replied. "Because, for everything we have learned over our centuries in Riven, we were once human. And humans are imperfect."

"That's not an answer to my question."

"I asked you to return," Nara said. "Because I want to save you. I want to save your guides and your order. To keep Riven safe. In our folly, in our fear, we bound ourselves. I can no more leave this clearing than you, a spirit, can choose to cross back home."

"Carver," Selena said. "She's manipulating you. I've seen it before. I've done it before."

"Your friend is astute," Nara said. "I do want something from you. I want you to go and find the other two. Bring them here. Together, the three of us can make Riven into what it needs to be. Can prevent this catastrophe and make it so that the guides never need die again."

"That's one hell of a promise," I said.

"It is one I can keep," Nara said. "Is it one you can afford to ignore?"

I glanced at Selena. Her mouth pursed, her eyes squinted at Nara. I'd been the subject of that scrutiny before. Had my soul weighed and measured. But it didn't matter. We had come out here for one purpose; to try and find help for the doomed city and our friends who were, right at this moment, battling for their own survival. Even if Nara wasn't giving us the whole truth, could we walk away?

"You said there are two others," I asked. "Where are they?"

Nara moved over to her burning fire and grabbed the unlit bottom of one of the stalks of grain. Held the torch up high. Her lips moved, a silent whisper that I couldn't make out. The flame at the top of the grain twisted, curling in on itself before launching out to the north and west. Back towards the city and then above it.

"Mali is the first," Nara said. "You will find her playing with her creations. If there was any one of us that truly wanted to be a god, Mali was it."

Once again Nara whispered to the stalk of grain. Once again the flame crawled in upon itself and shot out, south and west this time.

"Dolan is the second," Nara said. "He should be as idle as ever. Caught up in a past he cannot return to."

"And once we get the two of them, you'll be able to work together?" Selena said. "You'll be able to close the breaches?"

Nara gave a withered nod. I continued to get the sense that Nara hadn't spoken with anyone other than me for years. Possibly decades. The sheer act of holding a conversation was a struggle for her.

"We will do more than close the breaches," Nara said. "We will prevent them from ever happening again."

"That sounds too good to be true," I said.

"When you're dealing with gods, that is often the case," Nara said. "I suggest going to find Mali first. She will be the more difficult one, and you will need all your strength."

Nara turned her back to us and walked into her hut. I watched her disappear and held a thousand questions on my tongue. If there was one thing I'd learned from Bryce and the other guides, it was that information often came according to the wishes of others, not my own.

"She showed us the way," I said. "I guess we better start walking."

"Wait a minute," Selena replied. "We're just going to follow her orders?"

"You have any better ideas?"

"We could get more information." Selena looked towards the hut. "I get the feeling she's not telling us everything."

"She's not telling the whole truth," I said. "But I don't think pushing her is going to get us a better answer."

"Carver, she said the three of them created Riven. If that's true, then why does she need us to do this? You don't buy that nonsense about being bound, do you?"

I didn't know what to do. Or know what to say. All at once the feeling of being trapped, being locked into Riven forever seem to compress around my mind and fracture into pieces. I was never leaving this place. Never seeing another sky that wasn't gray, never actually breathing real air or drinking another cup of coffee. I'd gone from a world of order and laws, where reason ruled the land, to a world where the dead walked and mysterious figures claimed unimaginable power.

"Selena," I said, wrapping her in a hug so suddenly that her eyes widened with surprise. "I don't know what to believe. I don't know what other choices we have. If we turn our backs on this, then what else is there? What else do we do except fight and fight and fight until the Cycle claims our minds and turns us into nothing?"

"I..."

"We died, Selena. Our lives ended. And yet, somehow, we found each other here in this terrible place," I said, without really knowing the words I was speaking. They rolled out one after another as though coming from instinct instead of my mind. "Riven is great and hideous, but it is all we have. I am willing to do anything we can to save it. Help me."

I felt Selena's arms wrap around me, return the hug. It was both ridiculous and utterly necessary for the two of us to hold ourselves close. I could not hear her heartbeat, because she had none. I didn't feel the rise and fall of her lungs, because she wasn't breathing. I didn't feel the warmth of her body beneath the coat, because we were not warm. But I felt her love, and I embraced that.

A long moment later I released, stepped back and met Selena's eyes. "Are you ready to go find a god?"

"After all we've done already? I get the feeling I'll be underwhelmed," Selena replied.

136

WE MARCHED north for what must've been hours before noticing any change. Anything other than the endless grain. If Nara had been speaking the truth, then the vision her and the others had for Riven was a bland one. Who needed a field this large in a world where nobody had to eat?

Selena, looking around, was the first to notice we'd found our way back. My eyes had been buried too low into the stalks, pushing one after another out of the way.

"I think I can see the walls," Selena said. "The north side of the city."

"Then we're far enough west, according to Nara," I said. "Time to go north."

"Have you ever been up there? North of the city?"

"The farthest I've been was when we escorted that girl, Honora, from New York," I said. There'd never been much interest in going north of the city. There weren't enough spirits to make it worth your time. The Warrens and the Shambles were more fruitful hunting grounds. The crumbling factories in the Tar Pit more exciting than the dead grass and broken mansions on the north side.

I lived in Riven now, though. Might as well explore my new home.

We made our way to the wall, into that blessed hundred yard clearing between the end of the grain and the stone of the city. No gate in sight, only turreted stone splitting us from the chaos inside and the nothingness outside. I looked for sparks, but none lit Riven's gray sky. Either we were too far away from the fighting, or it had already ended.

"Never thought I'd see these walls and feel relief," I said, touching my hand to the smooth rock. "I'd be happy to never go back in that field again."

"Something tells me that's not likely," Selena said, glancing back at the stalks. "Unless Nara decides to relocate."

Nara's spark suggested we should continue along the wall until we hit the city's north gate. Compared to the trek through the field, the clearing beyond the wall made for easy walking. Every so often I'd remember how long Selena and I had been going, how I hadn't actually slept, well, at all since Piotr murdered me. I should have been exhausted. My body, after walking miles and miles, should have been aching. Instead, I felt the same. Not good, not bad. Just... there..

When we came to the north gate, we found it an equal partner to the one on the east side, a single curving arch with room for ten to fifteen to walk underneath abreast. Both Selena and I took a long glance into the city. Back that way went home. To the east, the field dwindled and died, as though cut off by an invisible barrier. There were waving stalks of grain, and then, not a foot away, hard dirt. That flattened land extended north as far as we could see. A razed, empty landscape.

"Can't say much about their imagination," I said, staring at the emptiness.

"Nara lives in a hut in the middle of that field," Selena replied. "I don't think they were the most creative group. If I could make a world, Carver, it would be the most amazing place."

"Oh? Tell me," I said replied as we set off on our walk north.

"First, there would be an ocean," Selena said. "Because I've never seen one. Towering waves along a beach that goes for miles and miles."

"Not a bad start," I said.

"The beach would transition into city. Not like Riven, or Chicago," Selena continued. "No, it would be both bigger and smaller. No pollution, friends and neighbors you actually knew. Buildings that flowed together so that you could walk from one end of the city to the other without seeing the same thing twice."

"I guess your sketches weren't all of your creative side," I said. The charcoal and ash drawings covered the walls of her, our, apartment. Riven cityscapes that Selena captured from the balcony.

"Maybe all this blandness brings it out in me," Selena said. "In the middle of the city, though, there would be this grand tree. A trunk miles wide. Whole species would live in its branches, and the most delicious fruit would hang down for anyone passing by."

"I like your Riven more than this one," I said.

Selena kept talking as we walked, adding more and more details to the world of her imagination. I contributed commentary, and we were so immersed in the idea that when we saw Riven split apart in front of us it was disappointing to leave the dream behind.

Canyons. That's the word that came to mind. Great rifts in the ground in front of us, the earth descending and spitting into trenches carved out of the surface. To the east and west we could see more, their ridged edges poking over the otherwise hard-packed earth.

The canyon in front of us stood wide, likely half a mile or more in distance. As though someone had stuck a shovel into the ground right at this point and declared this spot the start of it. I'd seen drawn pictures of, and read accounts about, the Grand Canyon back in America. Its painted sediments forming murals on the wonder's walls. Here, though, Riven once again proved its ability to reduce nature to its most desolate form.

Grays and blacks shaded up and down the canyon walls, though I couldn't account for the colors. Riven's light cast shadows, certainly, but the gradients along the ridged sides ahead of us followed no established pattern. More like someone casting about with a jar of ink, splattering its contents on a giant canvas with no thought to where it would lie.

"And we were just talking about how boring this place is," I said as we stood and stared.

"Riven always surprises," Selena replied.

Surprises. What might be lurking down in that canyon? I didn't see any spirits - this definitely wasn't the way to the Cycle. The canyon bent not far beyond where we stood, and anything could be beyond the corner. I remembered the ghoul in the forest, that age-old monster waiting to devour any poor soul that wandered by. Why wouldn't there be another one here as well?

"I'm guessing Mali is down in there somewhere," I said. "This is where Nara sent us. We'll just be careful."

"Because we haven't been careful before?" Selena replied. "Come on Carver. Whatever comes, we'll be ready for it."

Smart, creative, and cocky? So many reasons why I loved this woman.

137

WE WENT INTO THE CANYON, walls going up on either side. As we went deeper I noticed that what I'd thought was shade, or colored rock, was in fact a mossy plant. Something like dark leaves on trees in the forest. It grew in strings and stretches threading its way between rocky outcroppings and crumbling dirt. In fact it seemed as if this stuff might actually be holding the canyon up, preventing it from collapsing in on itself. After the trees and the grain, I wasn't exactly surprised over a new form of half-life in Riven.

Beneath our feet the ground became more uneven, the dirt filling with rocks and divots. More natural. The ever-present ash flakes faded away, as though being filtered out from the sky. A sky which had lost some of its gray cast. I even picked out a note of blue. The farther north we went, the more Riven changed to resemble the world I'd left behind.

"I don't understand this place," I said. "Riven isn't itself."

"Mali's a creator, isn't that what Nara said?" Selena replied. "What if she's making this?"

"Then why isn't Mali changing everything in Riven? Why only affect these canyons?"

"Carver, you're trying to ask why a spirit that's been stuck here for centuries isn't making sense."

"Point."

As we went further, the plants began to change. The black spidery moss began to shift to green. This too looked odd in its own way. The vines and leaves were perfect, spotless in their emerald color. Like the ghoul had been in the forest. Every so often flowers popped from one of the vines; florescent purples and blues. Beneath their feet the hard earth gave way to cushioned grass, all of uniform height. As though manicured by an especially attentive gardener.

Trees began to jut out around us, not the tall dead statues west of the city but brown, bark encoded with leaves. Between their tangled branches, more vines looped and swayed. Ferns, all sharing the same sort of banded leaf spring up between the trunks. The same designs, appearing again and again. It was on one hand beautiful and on another unsettling.

"Even when Riven does something incredible," I said. "It can't help but be a little bit creepy."

"I'm curious." Selena traced a finger along the bumped bark. "If Mali made all this, then Mali made the city and the forest and the Mountain, but those are not identical. The buildings in the city aren't one and the same repeated over and over again. This, though, it's the opposite of natural."

"I'm thinking we'll need to ask her a few questions," I said.

Of course, we'd have to find her first. The canyon widened around us until I couldn't see the walls anymore. Blocked by the jungle, the thick vines. We were moving forward, pushing through the brush and hoping to find some indication that we were heading the right way.

Yet, I would be lying if I said the yellow light filtering

down on us from a blue sky didn't bring me joy. And homesickness. For a few miracle moments I could pretend I was back on Earth.

"How does it feel for you?" I said. "You remember things like this? Sky this blue?"

"Were you ever told stories as a kid?" Selena said.

"It depended on who I was with. Sometimes, the guide would tell me tales. Or read from a book. More often, I was left to my own devices."

"Seeing the sky, the sunlight, it's like remembering a fairytale. That's how I recall the life I used to have," Selena said. "A story that I was told years before and now all I have are vague memories. Feelings and impressions."

"I suppose it all has to go eventually."

"You'll replace it." Selena threw me a smile. "You'll make new memories. Find new things to love here. Riven might not be everything you want, but it isn't empty. There are things here worth knowing. Worth loving."

"I can think of some."

I was in the middle of returning Selena's smile when I noticed a glint coming from the tree to our right. There's a certain shine to metal, a clear clue that it's not natural. A harsh glare. Living in Chicago I'd seen that reflection every day. Among the leaves and rock of the canyon, there was no hiding it.

With a single move, my right hand reached over my back and pulled off the crossbow. Caught the weapon in my left and aimed it at the light. Selena froze, followed my pointing.

"Tell me who you are and I won't shoot," I shouted into the jungle. I turned the crank, loading a normal bolt. It wouldn't wrangle a spirit, but it could hurt it plenty. Give us time to react if whatever held the metal proved to be less than friendly.

"Shoot him?" said a voice behind me, curious and light.

"Why would you do that? Neither of you look like you are members of the Right Hand."

I gave Selena a slight nod, didn't move my crossbow or my aim. Selena drew her cleaver and pointed it over my shoulder at whomever had spoken.

"Same goes for you," Selena said. "Who are you and what you want?"

"Me? I'm Cheo, and we're part of Mali's Left Hand," the man said. "Would you please come with us? It will be such an honor to bring two such as yourselves for the collection."

1 3 8

THE GLINT MOVED from the trees. Shuffled down through the branches and leaves. I kept my crossbow aimed at the shape as it shifted lower. Cheo, behind us, whispered words, names I didn't recognize, into the jungle. Around us more people came out from behind tree trunks and dropped from other branches. All of them dressed in orange garb, each and every one of their shirts bearing a left hand printed in smeared, dirty red.

"You can put your weapon away now; there are no Right-Handers here," Cheo said.

"You're going to have to forgive me," I replied. "I don't plan on taking my hand off this trigger until I know what you are."

"Carver, that's not exactly the best way to make friends," Selena said.

"It is okay. I understand. The Right-Handers are devious. Dangerous," Cheo said as I turned to face him, still keeping the crossbow ready. "Keep your weapons. We will take you back to our village. Teach you why we are not to be feared."

"We don't have the time," I said. "We need to get to Mali. You know where she is?"

"Mali?" Cheo said "The great one? Mali is all things. The giver and taker. The creator and the destroyer. We are not worthy of her. Neither are you."

"That's presumptive," I said.

Cheo shook his head. "No, it is only fact. None of us can be worthy while the Right-Handers survive. As they cannot so long as we exist."

I glanced at Selena. "Do you think they know they're spirits?"

Cheo slanted his head. "Spirits?"

"I don't think so," Selena said. "Nara said Mali could shape things. Maybe this is something that she's doing?"

"Cheo," I said. "Do you know about the Cycle? Do you ever feel a compulsion to leave here and walk away?"

Cheo shook his head. "You're both very strange for wanderers. Most do not ask so many questions."

"We're the curious type," I said. Sounded like Mali had her own little slice of Riven and was making something very strange out of it. If Mali could change all of this, though, then maybe she really did have the power to save Riven. To block the breaches or blunt the anger of the dead.

Power. That word, ever since Piotr and Graham, had taken on new meanings. Graham had shown me that spirits could have goals, and could work to achieve them. Piotr had bound both guides and spirits, formed a deadly force that chased his desires without heed for the consequences.

Riven wasn't as simple as it used to be. Wasn't only about wrangling angry spirits and going back to Chicago for a drink in the afternoon.

I missed that life.

The group of people that had surrounded us - I counted eight of them - stared with smiles on their faces. The blank happiness that comes from a life unburdened. Now that they were close I could see that each one carried a variety of weapons. None of the quality the guides had. Sharpened sticks, bows and arrows with metal tips, some crude knives and axes. Whatever war Cheo and his Left Hand planned to fight, it wasn't going to be a fancy one.

"So you're saying that the Right-Handers need to go if we're going to see Mali," I said, and Cheo nodded, this time with a vigor that had me worried he was going to pop his head off.

"Yes, yes that's it exactly," Cheo said. "Come with us. Help us. When we defeat the hideous Right-Handers, then you will get your audience with Mali. Then the world will be righted."

"What do you think?" I asked Selena. For their part, the group seemed endlessly patient. Willing to beam at us with hopeful grins as we took our time.

"It's either we try to fight our way through them," Selena said. "And keep wandering through these canyons, or help them and get a direct path to where we want to go."

"Agreed," I said, then, to Cheo. "You're up, captain. Lead on."

Cheo clapped his hands in what may have been the most pure display of sheer joy that I'd ever seen. Then he strode off into the forest, beckoning us after him. The rest of the Left-Handers filed in behind us as we marched, though I noticed more than half of them disappeared as we moved. Vanished back into the trees.

"Where are they going?" I asked Cheo after the third one dropped away.

"We are not done with the collection yet," Cheo replied. "They are going to find more lost ones for us."

"Lost ones?"

"Like you," Cheo said. "Wanderers that can help. Most,

though, are not so well-armed as yourselves. So great and powerful."

"Great? Powerful?" Selena said. "Don't feed his ego, Cheo. Carver doesn't need that."

"Apologies," Cheo replied. "We are a band of lost souls. What we have for weapons comes from what we can find. What we can build. I look at your might and see hope. Things that could win our fight forever."

"That's the idea," I said.

"Are the Right-Handers like you?" Selena said. "Spirits?"

"They may share our face, but not our hearts," Cheo replied. "All they are is evil. Terrible anger."

"How long have you been fighting?" I asked.

"Forever," Cheo replied. "There has always been a Right Hand and a Left Hand. Never has one completely wiped out the other."

I heard heat come into his voice. Cheo's shoulders stiffened, and he glanced at me with a twisted vehemence that I'd only seen in a spirit consumed by uncontrolled rage.

"That changes with the two of you," Cheo continued.

"Mali requires that you wipe them out completely?" Selena said. "She sounds vicious."

Cheo didn't reply. Didn't say anything as we continued moving through the jungle. Perhaps Selena had struck a nerve. Caused the spirit to revisit just what Mali was asking of him and the others. Then I caught myself.

Who cared if the Left- and Right-handers destroyed each other? They were already dead.

139

THE PLANTS THICKENED as Cheo led us through more groves of spindly trees and vines. He recovered, breaking out of his funk and promising that we would find ourselves amazed and awed by what the Left Hand had accomplished. By the paradise that they had put together here in the harsh land of the canyons. And of course, Cheo emphasized, they had done all of this despite the cold attempts by the Right Hand to hurt and kill every last one of them.

Cheo wasn't wrong. Whereas in the rest of Riven, the buildings and the cities had been objects of ruin and decay that lasted for centuries, moldering remains of dreams left to founder, the Left Hand had a home. A village of tree houses and thatched huts. A large square with a central dominating pillar inscribed with runes that I could not read or understand. Fires burned in large grilling pits, though I didn't see any food actively cooking. Spirits wandered, men and women and even children going about building more homes, weaving clothes from plants, or bending and shaping wood into weapons. Here, perhaps, was Riven's only society. A village of the dead that nonetheless felt alive.

"But all of you are spirits?" Selena said. "How are you doing this?"

Cheo looked at her quizzically. "Spirits again? What are you meaning with this word? We are all members of the Left Hand. We have all been collected and called to our duty. This is our home, our sacred place to protect."

Our sacred place. The words had a weird ring to them. Spoken with a reverence that I'd not heard in a long time. The same sort of reverence that, as a young child, I'd heard in churches. Or in town squares as criers delivered sermons of the day. Whomever these spirits were, I didn't think they believed themselves to be dead.

"Cheo, how many of you are there?" I said. "How big is the Left Hand?"

"Nearly a hundred," Cheo beamed. "One hundred souls ready to pick upe spears for Mali and vanquish the Right Hand."

"And the Right Hand? How big are they?"

"Sadly, they are larger still. I fear if we do not bolster our number soon, they will come to crush us."

Cheo said the words and frowned. Then turned to one of the larger huts, one that was more than three times the size of Nara's. He pointed to it. "Please, follow me over there. We can talk more about the plan."

"The plan?" Selena said.

"Of course! Our grand attack to bring down the Right Hand," Cheo said. "It must begin soon. Before they know we are coming."

As we walked through the village the spirits of the Left Hand looked over at us. Some even offered waves. All of them looked conscious and cognizant. None had the vacant stares of spirits caught by the Cycle. None had the pale fire eyes of one lost to Riven's insatiable hunger. No, whatever the spirits were, they'd found a way outside of what made

Riven a brutal universe. Selena and I caught each other's eyes and nodded. Mali had created her own little corner in this dead world.

Inside, the hut lacked even the basics. Only a small pit for a fire, this one unlit. Some sparse bundles of plants and grass forming little circles around the inside. As though someone had put the house together and forgotten how to fill it. Cheo sat down on the hard ground and motioned for us to do the same. I looked for beds, for any sign of the usual life comforts. The sort of things that any permanent village would have to have. But I saw none.

"Tell me," I asked Cheo before he could launch into his plan. "Has this village been here as long as the Left Hand?"

Cheo cocked his head at me. "Of course. How could there be a Left Hand without a home for them?"

"That doesn't make sense," Selena said.

"It doesn't have to," Cheo replied. "But it is, nonetheless."

Selena and I waited a moment. To see if Cheo would offer some additional explanation. But it seemed like with that recitation, the statement that sense and logic need not apply, that the matter was settled.

"When we go to attack the Right Hand,"Cheo said. "You should know that it will be hard fighting. It always is. They will not hold back, and neither will we."

"We're used to it," I said.

"I expected so."

Cheo laid out an intricate plan of assault on a village that seem to be much the same as the one we were now sitting in. A series of huts in a large clearing. At least, that's what it looked like going by the rocks Cheo laid out on the floor and the marks in the ground he drew with a stick to illustrate exactly how we would be approaching. If there was one thing I took away from the plan, it was that Cheo harbored an undying hatred of the Right Hand. He infused every sentence with insults and anger. Until I couldn't handle it anymore.

"What do they do? The Right Hand?" I said. "What makes them so terrible?"

"They tried to kill our goddess," Cheo said, his voice falling into an almost stunned reverie. "They tried to take her from us. There is no act more unforgivable than to try to destroy one's creator."

"How did they do that?" I said.

"They attacked her temple," Cheo said. "And we defended her. The Left Hand, we came to her aid and stopped them. Struck them down. But the Right Hand, they are like a disease. They will not leave us for long. They will try again. We must make sure they cannot."

Before another question could come to my lips, three more spirits entered the hut, some of the hunters from earlier. They bore the same bright smiles on their faces and waved their arms. They shouted that they had found more. More that were ready to join the Left Hand.

The collection had been successful.

140

WE WENT outside the hut to a changed scene. Where before the spirits had been meandering around the village in what seemed like a reasonable imitation of life, as if they had one, now all those same spirits gathered around the pole in the center. Men, women, and children stood staring at that pole, and the five figures assembled around it. A quintet of confused and lost spirits; two were dressed as soldiers, another a child no more than ten, with the sunken look of one who'd fallen to disease. The last two were older women in flowing dress from a region I didn't know.

Cheo guided the two of us to the front of the circle, calmly pushing aside spirits in our path. They made way for us with deference, bowing at our faces and our backs. I couldn't quite comprehend what was happening here. So unlike any other part of Riven. The spirits acted so differently. They didn't seem to be bound, and yet they moved with purpose. They didn't seem to have any recollection of who they used to be, but they were able to find a shared objective.

Riven made it difficult to communicate with many spirits.

Language and ideas didn't transcend death. While I might know English, a spirit may not. What I took as a gesture of hello, another spirit might interpret as an attack. All of which made Riven a dangerous place to make assumptions. Here, though, it was as though the spirits were wiped clean. Replaced with a common personality, a common goal, a common mind.

"Every second we're here, I get more worried," Selena said. "These spirits aren't normal."

If Cheo heard her, he didn't react. Instead, he led us to our part of the circle and then moved to the five in the middle. Cheo turned and held up his hands to the crowd. They began to murmur. Not individual speech, no, but the same three words over and over again in a low and constant hum.

We are Mali.

"Nara thinks this person is going to help her?" I whispered to Selena.

"I suppose Mali has an army of spirits? She could use them to help cleanse Riven," Selena said.

"Or rule it," I replied.

The murmur built up in volume and speed, until it became a shout. All the spirits yelling in perfect unison. The five in the middle cast their eyes around, curious but unconcerned. Unafraid. Difficult to be scared when you were already dead. When you didn't know what you were or what, if anything, was at risk.

"Bring the water," Cheo announced as the chant reached its height, loud to the point where I winced with every cadence.

A path parted through the crowd of spirits, a wide berth filled with a moving vat. A cauldron of black stone. Eight spirits carried it, the vessel suspended on wooden sticks held above the ground. I couldn't see over its lip, but it seemed, with the bend to the spirit's shoulders, that whatever was in that pot was not light.

"Set it down before our new friends," Cheo commanded and the carrying spirits put down the pot in front of, first, the young girl.

Now on the ground, I could see over the edge and into the vat. If you would have shown me the liquid back on Earth, on the other side, I would've told you that it was water. Perhaps dirtied, or tainted with some sort of dye. In Riven, the liquid's pale blue cast reminded me of the Cycle and the fire that both drove spirits mad and made them sane.

"Now she shall be the next to join us," Cheo announced. "How do we welcome a new soul to the Left Hand?"

"With the tightest grip," the crowd shouted back.

"And how do we thank them?" Cheo continued.

"With the sweetest wine," the crowd replied.

"I drank my fair share of wine," I whispered to Selena. "It never looked like that."

"Carver," Selena said. "If they offer that to us, I don't think we should drink it."

"I'm not thirsty anyway." I moved my hand to the lash's handle. We still had our weapons. Cheo hadn't bothered to take them away. Perhaps trusting that we were indeed his newest friends. His greatest allies in this strange war.

The young girl walked up to the pot, placed her hands on the edge, and lifted herself up. Stared into the shimmering waters. She hesitated. Cheo walked up behind her, put his hand against her head, and dumped the spirit into the water.

"Drink," Cheo said.

Another first in Riven. I'd never seen a spirit drink anything here, not that there was much in the way of liquid. I wasn't even sure they could until that moment. I certainly hadn't tried it since Piotr severed my cord with the living. The girl, though, took a large gulp. We could see her throat work as she swallowed. After a moment she stood back, turned to Cheo, and embraced him.

"Welcome sister," Cheo said. "Welcome to the Left Hand."

The rest of the five worked in turn. Each one going up to the pot, taking their drink, and coming back a loving member of the Left Hand. New additions to their village. After the final hug to welcome the newest brother, the second of the two soldiers, Cheo held up a hand. One hand, his left.

"With this collection, we are finally ready. Ready to make a last end upon our great foes. Go now and prepare. We will march on the third cry," Cheo announced. One of the spirits that had carried the pot put his hands around his mouth, curled them, and gave a sharp, high shout.

"The first cry," Cheo told us as the crowd dispersed. The same eight spirits that had carried the pot in, hefted it once more on the wooden carrier and lifted it away. "Are you ready?"

"What was that?" I said, ignoring Cheo's question. Selena and I were as ready as we were going to be. As ready as you could be in a place you suddenly no longer understood.

"The collection?" Cheo said. "They were pledging loyalty. Joining us in our crusade."

"Why didn't you try to do that for Selena and I?"

"Because you do not need it," Cheo said. "You are not lost. You are not searching for a cause."

"How do you know that we'll help you?" Selena said. "Maybe we're on the Right Hand's side?"

I shot her a warning glance, but Cheo laughed. Nodded past us. I turned and looked, followed Cheo's eyes and noticed that on many of the treehouses, standing on roofs and on thatched decks, were spirits with bows and arrows. Rudimentary stuff, but their points had an unmistakable blue tint.

"Dipped in Mali's boon," Cheo said. "Lethal to the Right Hand. Perhaps also to you."

"A threat. Because that's what this was missing," I said.

"Only a warning," Cheo replied. "One that will be unnecessary, I think. With your help, the Right Hand will fall. And then all of this can cease to be."

For the first time I saw Cheo's smile falter. I saw something in those eyes that spoke of a deeper longing, something beneath his drive to ruin the Right Hand.

"What are you looking for, Cheo?" I said.

"For an end," Cheo said. "To be free of this burden. To be free of this hate. To be free."

Another spirit sounded a cry. The second one. Cheo bid us a short farewell to go and get himself ready. To arm himself for what would be the last fight of his life, such as it was.

Selena and I went into the hut to grab a moment alone. Outside, spirits shouted each other, called for this or that or the other thing. Making ready for a war. Something not even death seemed to exorcise from existence.

"You know, you really do look ridiculous," Selena said. She stood across for me, the meager fire pit between us. Her hair splayed around her face and touched the collar of her coat. Normally she kept it up, out of the way of any potential danger. Yet when we started on the trek to find Nara, I noticed she'd let it flow free.

"I'd venture to say most of us do," I said. She stood there, messing with one of her gloves, trying to make it a perfect fit for her fingers. Her eyes and her smile followed me.

"Most of us don't have a sword, a crossbow, a lash, and a long knife sticking out of them," Selena said. "I have to say though, it's growing on me."

"Now that I'm dead and you start giving me compliments?" I said. In Riven, you didn't age. Selena would never change until she ventured to the Cycle. On the outside, at least. Beneath the skin, she was completely different from the woman I'd found wandering the streets.

"Don't want to miss my chance," Selena said. "And someone ought to. You've been looking awfully sad lately."

"Guess that'll happen when you die," I said. I didn't talk about how Selena had changed too. Riven usually had a dark effect on the soul, could desolate the most positive of people. Yet over these last few months, Selena had gone from dependent on Nicholas and I in order to crack a smile, to being the cause of our own.

"You'll get used to it," Selena said. "Death has its advantages."

"Does it? Like what?"

At first I think I fell for Selena because she was like me. Entirely without anyone else. I was an orphan, she was a spirit. Our secrets were shared with each other, because there was nobody to tell. Now, though, it wasn't about what kept us apart from the others but what brought us together. Literally, Selena kept me safe from the Cycle's song, and I did the same for her.

"It strips away your needs," Selena said, placing her hands above the small fire. "I don't need the warmth from these flames. Don't need to find food to eat, air to breathe. I'm never sick, nor tired. Centuries could pass without aging a day."

"But without any of those things, what do we have?"

Selena stepped over the fire pit, slipped her hand beneath my chin, leaned in for a kiss. Our cold lips touched, and though I may not have had a drop of blood in my body, I may not have had a heartbeat, I had a soul. And in that moment, my soul found a partner.

"You make a compelling argument," I whispered into her smile. A smile that faltered as she stepped away from me. Back over the fire pit.

"In a way, I think what we have is more pure now than it ever was before." Selena threw a look out the door, at the spirits getting ready outside. "Our survival is dependent on each other, and there are no other needs getting in the way."

"I won't think of it like that," I said. Now it was my turn to chase her around the fire pit. Gently fold her in my arms. "This isn't about survival. It's about you and I. Together."

"Careful, Carver, you're getting too sweet," Selena laughed. "Don't tell me my gruff guide is going soft?"

I didn't know whether the kiss made me soft or not. I didn't care.

"You realize we're about to fight a war for a bunch of spirits?" I said when we parted. "That we left the city looking for an end to the fighting, and only found more?"

"You and I have been fighting our entire lives." Selena started checking her weapons, arranging herself for a fight. "Why did you think it would stop once our lives were done?"

The great sword went over my back, the crossbow on top of it. No bolt loaded, as I wasn't sure what I'd need to shoot first. The lash; coiled and slotted into the belt holster on my right. My long knife, sharp and ready, on the left.

"For a while there," I said. "I held some strange hope that you and I would find a way. That we could curl up in this imperfect corner of the world and make a life. Or I'd find a way to bring you back."

Selena tied back her hair, and we stood across from each other. Two guides, heavily armed and ready to dive into another fight. Seeing Selena stand that strong pulsed a thrill through me. Seeing the one you love confident and capable, that rush didn't go away with death.

"You already did," Selena said. "You gave me a purpose. You taught me what I needed to know to survive. Now I'm returning the favor."

The third cry sounded. The call to yet another battle. I wouldn't be fighting it alone.

580

142

WE FLOWED through the jungle with the Left Hand. Cheo's band whispered between and above the trees, sliding through branches and around trunks with little more than the chatter of leaves to announce their passing. Cheo himself, along with us and some other spirits that I gathered hadn't quite mastered the art of forest travel, trod along on the ground. Trampled ferns and fallen leaves beneath our feet.

"Have you ever noticed, Cheo, that it all looks the same?" I asked our leader as we moved along.

"The same?" Cheo replied.

"The plants, the trees. They're all copies. The same types, and they grow the same way."

"When I first came here, every branch stood unique. Flowers of every color bloomed. Creatures even whistled in the night or scattered at our approach." Cheo's voice fell into reverie. "Over time, such things have gone."

"Over time?" Selena asked. "How long have you been here?"

Cheo looked at us, the corners of his mouth having

trouble deciding whether to turn up or down. "Mali is a wonderful goddess, and I stay at her pleasure."

A goddess? Her pleasure? Mali's private world kept getting more and more strange, and Nara wanted this person to help her?

"Do you serve someone?" Cheo asked me when I posed the questions. "Have you ever lived and died to help another?"

"Only with my own choice," I replied.

"Then perhaps you do not understand. Mali is not simply a master, or a person we obey. She is with all of us. Inside us. When we triumph, she celebrates with us. When we fail, she mourns our loss."

"Does she control you?" What Cheo was talking about sounded more and more like a group of bound spirits serving out Mali's whims.

"She expresses her wishes, and we do what we can to make them real." Cheo never stopped moving forward, always kept his eyes on the next piece of jungle to move out of the way. "You ask these questions as though you disapprove, yet you came here, yes?"

"We need Mali's help, but I'm not a fan of binding unless it's necessary."

"I have seen what happens to those who lose Mali's gift. This binding that you mention. They wander, lost, and disappear never to return." Cheo didn't sound all too disappointed by the prospect, though. In fact, I'd have argued the Left Hand leader looked losing Mali's gift as a blessing.

Cheo seemed to realize his own tone betrayed him, and he gave a heavy sigh. "If I am weary of the bow and the arrow, the spear and the sword, it is because Mali's service is not easy."

"You could lose, right?" I said. "Throw yourself into the Right Hand's attack?"

"Mali compels me to fight as best I can. Such an act would go against her wishes. Therefore, I await the day a Right-Hander bests me in combat. May it come soon."

I didn't know what to say to that. A spirit with a lingering death wish they could not fulfill. Riven never ceased its surprises.

The hike felt long, but without exhaustion or a day's passage to tell the time, it was impossible to know. Only when Cheo held up a hand did we discover that we were close.

"Beyond the next glade," Cheo said. "We will find their village. They will not be expecting us, so if we move quickly, then victory should be ours."

"How do you know they're not expecting us?" I said.

"Because they have completed their collection. We have not," Cheo said. "They no longer scour the jungle for new ones to add to their numbers, which means they are preparing to attack us. Which means we have one moment to capture the surprise."

Cheo unslung a crude bow from over his back, held an arrow in his left hand. His eyes adopted a focused glint that I'd seen in my fellow guides ahead of a battle; that iron focus, a steeled reserve against whatever ruthlessness was to follow.

"Guess it's time," I said to Selena, but she'd already drawn out her cleaver and knife. I followed Cheo's lead and brought out the crossbow. Slotted in the blue bolts and cranked one into ready position. Did I want to use any of the six bolts I had in a random fight with jungle spirits? Not particularly, but I didn't want to die either.

And if victory meant an audience with Mali, then there was no point in holding back.

Now we crept. Kept ourselves low as we shifted through the brush. Cheo and I on either side and Selena between us, just behind. The positions gave Cheo and I clear firing lines while leaving Selena free to step up and engage anyone rushing us. Standard tactics for engaging spirits. As for whether they'd work against the Right Hand, who knew?

The clearing looked identical to the Left Hand's village. The same number of huts in roughly the same places. A central pole standing tall, though the runes were different. As were the spirits crowding around it. The many spirits circling the pole. Far more than the Left Hand.

"Cheo, we're too outnumbered," I said. "They must have double ours, maybe more."

"Surprise, my friend," Cheo said. "Is the great equalizer."

Cheo stood, nocked an arrow. The Right-Handers continued to chant - I picked out Mali's name amid unfamiliar words - and glanced around the perimeter to see the other Left-Handers settling into positions. Picking their shots. I supposed I'd better find mine.

Looking down the crossbow, I squinted my right eye and took aim. Like the Left Hand, the Right Hand had spirits of all backgrounds, ages, races. Mali's devotees didn't discriminate.

I found a frightening man, one bearing a series of jagged scars around his face, body, and arms, and leveled my shot. He'd likely died in an accident, sudden and vicious. Crossed to Riven without realizing, without having a chance to change his soul to suit himself.

Now, I'd wipe what was left of him just as quickly. My finger tightened on the trigger, and I squinted. Dead on.

Cheo fired.

143

THE ARROW FLEW SILENT. My only clue came from the slight *twang* as the bowstring snapped. Cheo's aim was true, and the arrow re-appeared wedged in between the shoulder blades of a spirit on the outside of the circle. A man that yelled in wounded surprise, a yell that cut off abruptly as pale blue fire erupted from the arrow's point.

I hesitated. Blue fire? These spirits had arrows capable of wrangling? How?

Battle cries jerked me back to the present. Left-Handers calling from the trees as they peppered the Right-Handers with arrows. The Right-Handers scattering and calling for arms. Both sides wished Mali's vengeance upon the other. Both sides damned their foes in the name of the same goddess.

"Are you going to use that thing?" Selena said as Cheo loosed another arrow.

"Waiting for the right moment," I said, covering. Took aim with the crossbow. My scarred man had vanished into the swirling crowd, so I picked a target at random. A frenzied guy whose lanky arms waved, directing traffic. Pointing out Left-Handers in the trees and jungle. I pulled the trigger.

My blue bolt lanced out, pierced the spirit's chest, and wreathed him in the same blue fire as the Left-Hander's arrows. He stopped his arm waving and, a moment later, wandered off towards the jungle. A long, long walk to the Cycle from here, but the spirit would get there.

The first counters started from the Right-Handers. Arrows of their own shooting out from hut windows, or from spirits crouching behind stacks of wood, piles of brush. Our ambush had taken a good fifth of them, I estimated, based on the number of idling and wandering spirits staying in the middle of the clearing. That still left us outnumbered.

"We can't afford to let them get settled," I called to Cheo.

"Agreed!" Cheo replied, and then he cupped his hands and gave a ululating cry. "Charge with me, friends!"

"And now it gets interesting," Selena said as we took our first steps out from the brush.

"Stay close," I replied. "If those arrows hit us, we can't save each other. Can't use a binding to recover."

"You mean we might die again?" Selena laughed as we ran towards the village. "Carver, all that would give me is peace!"

I raised the crossbow as we charged, cranked the next blue bolt into position. Directly ahead of us stood a pair of huts, Right-Handers starting to pour out of the main doors. Hard to aim with every footfall pushing the crossbow up and down. Thankfully, a point-blank shot wasn't hard to find.

A hulking spirit shoved his way out of the hut on the right, and I blasted the man's monstrous chest with my shot, sending him falling back into the hut with blue fire burning along his body. A tattooed woman took his place, raising a pair of knives and starting towards me.

I threw the crossbow hard, striking her in the face. Keeping her in the hut's doorway, the only thing limiting the number of spirits coming at me. As she recoiled, I grabbed the great sword with both of my hands, planted my right foot into the dirt, and, leaning forward, drew the weapon in a long front slash. The sword sliced through the hut's walls, cut through the spirit's pitiful knives, and diced her in fire.

The doorway collapsed, the roof sagging as my cut undermined the hut's integrity. Instead of one, now three more spirits stood in front of me in the wide opening. Two with crude axes and a third holding a bow, arrow knocked and ready to fire. I braced for the shot.

A knife flew by my right shoulder, embedding itself in the bow-wielding spirit, causing the man to stumble back. Selena followed it, sidestepping an ax-man's swing to chase down her knife, grab the weapon with her left hand and twist the hilt. Blue fire raced down the blade, sending the bowman to blissful peace.

The first ax-man came at me, crying out in a language I didn't know and bringing his short-hafted weapon in an overhand strike towards my head. A suicide play - the spirit left himself wide open, ready to give up a hit in order to deliver a crushing blow. Instead, I pushed off with my right foot, went to the left of the wild swing and sliced with my sword as the spirit went past. My swipe caught the spirit in the back and sent the ax-man sprawling, burning blue lighting him up.

In front of me, Selena matched her ax-man blow for blow, clangs ringing out as the cleaver caught the ax-man's strikes again and again. The ax-man feinted a right-handed cut, which Selena moved to counter, and struck out with his left hand. Punching at Selena's face.

My love was too fast. She saw the punch coming, ducked it, and threw her right shoulder into the ax-man's chest. As he stumbled back, Selena reversed her right arm, sweeping the cleaver out in front and catching the ax-man with his arms wide. A burning blue cut opened in the spirit's stomach, and he looked at Selena, mouth agape, as all the rage and ruin drained from his eyes.

"Cheo!" Selena yelled as the ax-man fell away. I followed her eyes and saw our Left Hand leader pressed by a quartet of Right Hand spirits. At first I thought Cheo's end was going to be quick in coming, but our guide to this misbegotten land had no intention of going out quietly. He spun and kicked, blocked and countered, content to keep the swiping axes and knives at bay rather than expose himself for a killing strike.

"Guess we'd better help him," I said, running back out into the clearing. Beyond Cheo's dire dance, the rest of the Right Hand village had blown into one of Riven's surreal pitched battles. Vacant spirits, standing stunned or starting to walk off to the Cycle mingled with the furious fighting between both sides. The Left-Handers, either out of arrows or unable to find good targets in the melee, had left their ambush spots and dove into a Right Hand force gathering into its own.

Strategy's part in this play had ended. Chaos had taken hold.

Something smashed into me as I ran towards Cheo, picked me up and threw me ten feet across the ground. I hit the grass and rolled, keeping the great sword's blade flat against the ground. Looked up to see a foot sliding towards me. Felt it strike my head and snap it back.

Spirits in Riven couldn't suffer serious injury for long. Without organs, bones, or blood, there simply wasn't much to actually damage. Pain, though, that stayed. Not because of a natural process, or so Nicholas had told me, but because our minds still believed we had breakable bodies. Still believed we could be damaged and destroyed.

So when the kick connected, a banging blossom of thwacking agony wracked my mind and the jungle overhead spun like an over-wound clock. Instinct was the only thing that saved me. I rolled with the strike, lifted the great sword in the way of the attack, and caught my assailant's club on it.

My enemy's weapon was a nightmare instrument: a warped wooden shaft with shards of metal sticking out of its end at odd angles. Like the crooked claws of a hideous monster. Each and every one of those glinting pieces shimmered with pale fire waiting to be unleashed. I couldn't let it touch me.

I shoved up against the club, and against the corded arms that held it. Arms covered with scars. My first target, come back to find his would-be killer. The shove brought me a bit of breathing room as he stepped back to stay upright. I curled forward, planted the sword against the ground to get to my feet. Took my first good look at my foe.

The first thing I noticed was his club, coming right back towards me in a crashing blow I had no time to dodge.

144

So I DIDN'T TRY. I dropped the great sword and ducked into his swing, hoping to get close enough so that I dodged those metal pieces. I felt the club strike my shoulder and the left part of my neck. The thwack nearly drove me to my knees, but I didn't feel any stinging pain. No slicing cut. No blue fire. My shoulder, had I still been human, would have been dislocated. My shoulder, because I was dead, merely flashed between aching pain and numbness.

With my right hand I drew my knife and tried to stab the spirit in the stomach, but his left hand grabbed my wrist, holding my knife out wide. He reached back with the club for another strike and I slipped around him, pulling his left arm across his chest as I went underneath his right. Or at least, that's what I tried to do. As I moved behind him, the spirit dug in his left foot and pulled me back, whipping me down to the ground. Raised the club above his head and brought it smashing towards my face. I stabbed up with the knife, catching the club on the point of my blade. The knife drove into the wood, splitting club and shattering into pieces, the shards sprinkling down around me. The spirit stared at the stump in his hand, a few inches of splintered wood. Until I stood up.

"Quality matters, my friend," I said, brandishing my polished, forged knife.

The spirit growled at me, his face a menacing mishmash of crumpled bone and skin. His exit from life had been a truly miserable one. He threw the club stump at me and followed it up with a reckless charge, head down and arms outstretched. I ducked under his hands, caught his waist and, bracing my feet, lifted him up and over my shoulder and sent him flying behind me.

As he hit the ground I turned and drew my lash. The spirit planted his hands and shoved himself back up, just in time for my lash to wrap around his neck. The metal end pierced the scarred man's skin and I twisted the hilt, sending the blue fire along the length of the cord and wrapping the spirit in its pale glow, ending his pain.

I withdrew lash and turned around, hoping Cheo still lived. Saw that Selena had come to his rescue. The two of them were finishing off the Right Hand spirits. Cutting and slicing and tearing with wild abandon. Behind them the pitched melee died down. Cheo's surprise play had worked. Without a chance to get themselves formed up, the Right-Handers had been trapped inside huts, or scattered across the clearing where teams of Left-Handers divided and skewered their foes. Despite the numbers, the Right-Handers had no leadership, had no organization, and were picked apart.

Selena and I joined in the cleanup efforts, taking care of the scattered resistance and making sure no other threats remained. Eventually, when the jungle returned to its normal quiet, the two score Left-Handers that had survived the battle joined us in the middle of the clearing. Clusters of vacant-eyed spirits stared at us, while others wandered out under the Cycle's siren call.

"Then it is done," Cheo said to the group. "The Left Hand is victorious. Our enemies vanquished. Now, our peace can finally reign."

I glanced at Selena. "What peace do you think he's talking about?"

Selena shrugged. "You don't think they can live in their village?"

"Did you see it when we were there? Did you see this one? The only things they were doing were getting ready for war. Recruiting more spirits. They don't have a peace time function."

"Maybe now they get to find one," Selena said.

Cheo continued extolling their victory. He claimed the battle in the name of Mali. Claimed her grace caused the Left Hand's triumph. The rest of the Left-Handers echoed each of the statements with wild shouting. The sort of delirious victory I'd seen on occasion with guides when we closed a breach. When we took down a ghoul. Even so, the ecstasy on these spirit faces as Cheo pronounced them the favored ones had me shivering. I'd seen loyalty like that before. I'd seen the spirits in Barth's tower, the guides that followed Piotr. That sort of fervent obedience only ended in terror.

After Cheo's speech ended, the crowd dispersed. The Left-Handers wandered the clearing and found what weapons they wanted to take. Collected arrows and spears and axes. Then they disappeared back into the jungle to walk back to their home village. Cheo kept us behind, until only the three of us stood in the clearing. He held out his hand and shook each of ours.

"It's been a long time since I fought alongside a pair of your caliber," Cheo said. "Thank you."

"Glad we could help," I said. "This is what you wanted?"

"The Left Hand won. The Right Hand lost. I achieved Mali's goal," Cheo said, but the pronouncements sounded oddly hollow. "Now, I imagine you would like to see the goddess herself?"

"That is why we're here," I said.

"Then I will take you to her, as promised."

145

WE STRUCK out from the village a few minutes later, not heading back east towards the Left Hand's town but instead striking north. Deeper into the canyons whose walls seemed to grow ever higher and the jungle ever more dense. Even though the trees and ferns were the same, there were more of them. They pressed tighter around us until the thought of leaving the path and leaping to the branches as the Left-Handers had done, looked an impossibility. Instead we moved single file, the thick trunks closing in on either side. All signs of the blue sky above faded away as leafy canopies closed off light. Rays filtered down through tiny gaps, spotlights illuminating our steps. As though we were shifting between night and day.

"Quite the atmosphere," I said.

"Mali made beautiful things, once," Cheo replied.

"Once?" Selena brushed a low-hanging vine from her face.

"She hasn't left her temple for a long time," Cheo answered. "I suspect she has lost interest in us, in her people."

"How long have you been here?" I said.

"You know that is an impossible question." Cheo led us across a bridge, made from tree branches strung together with vines, over a shallow crevasse whose smooth bottom suggested it once ran with water. "But I feel as though it has been many, many years."

"I ask because you understand English. You understand our words. Yet, I don't think you came from America. Or England."

"I speak many tongues," Cheo said. "I have to collect many spirits, teach them and train them. As I find new ones, I endeavor to learn. When time is no object, mastering a new skill is not so daunting."

"And Mali? Will she understand us?"

"Mali will hear what she wants to hear. That is why you must choose your words with care."

Not really an answer, but as with most things Mali, it seemed like the only way we would know was when we met her face-to-face. Around us, the jungle shifted from its copycat form. Where similar trees had grouped together, now arced large trunks with spiraling bark. Mushrooms bloomed up to our waists. Flowers, static without any breeze, stood straight up and searched for any sunlight picking through.

"Mali's garden," Cheo observed. "What energy she expends is focused here, closest to her."

"Beautiful." Selena went over to one of the flowers, a purple and black menagerie with long, spindly petals. She ran her hand along the ends, then frowned. "It's hard. Not soft, like a flower should be."

I took a turn, ran a finger along the edge. The petal felt like stone. Rough and scratching. When I pressed on it, the flower didn't move. Cheo, standing behind us, said nothing and frowned.

"Can I say I'm uneasy?" Selena said as we continued our

walk.

"You can. I'd even agree with you," I replied. "Whatever Nara expected Mali to be, I don't think this was it."

"Keep that sword of yours handy."

"Always." I wasn't lying either. My hands had taken to resting themselves on the hilt of the lash, the long knife. Comfort in the thought that no matter what sprung out at me, I'd have a decent chance of sticking it first.

Such was our world.

Our single file walk ended with a rock wall. Only, unlike the black mossy vines that covered the rest of the canyons, this section, maybe two hundred feet wide, was carved out in gold. Or at least, rock that looked like it. Every square inch molded into one symbol or another. Characters I didn't recognize, swoops in lines and diagonals looping around each other. Some carried on for yards, climbing up to the very top where the leafy canopy brushed up against it. All of it sparkling as various spots of light slipped their way through and bounced off. An opening, twenty feet wide, yawned at us. Bordered on the edges by set stone. No light came from that cave, only a deep night. Alongside the entry stood a pair of pillars, on which the same four characters repeated from top to bottom.

"I'm guessing that's her name?" I said.

"My goddess is not a humble one." Cheo gestured at the face of the temple, the patterns laid into the rock. "Before, we brought spirits here for the collection. This served as their first introduction to the greatness they were going to see. Until Mali tired of the ceremony."

"There are so many symbols on these walls." Selena stared at the columns, and I watched her eyes move along the etchings. "They're hard to understand."

"You can read these symbols at all?" I said.

"It's in an old tongue," Cheo said. "I no longer hear any

spirits speakings its language. Earth must have forgotten it."

"I can't read it, Carver." Selena walked up to the left pillar, traced her hand along the carved runes. "But I've seen the symbols before. In museums."

"Do you know what it says?" I asked Cheo.

Our guide ran his eyes along temple's exterior. I chose to call it the temple because that's what it seemed to be. Mali's place of power. A goddess's place of strength.

"My translation is imperfect," Cheo said. "But I believe it says that this domain belongs to the maker. This world belongs to the one who built it. All those who do not recognize its brilliance, you are not wanted. Those who wish to pay their respects, enter and be recognized."

"I'm sensing arrogance is a thing with Mali," I said.

"That may be all she has left," Cheo replied. "If you have come to offer something Mali wants, you will fare better."

"I have no idea if Mali wants what we're offering."

"Who wouldn't want an invitation to walk through a bunch of dead grain to meet with a creepy old spirit?" Selena said.

"We're not giving her a choice," I replied. "She's coming with us."

Cheo looked at the both of us, confused. I shook my head, and nodded towards the doorway.

"Shall we?" I said.

"Before we go in," Cheo said. "I would caution you; be careful and courteous, or be prepared to face the fury of a goddess."

"Cheo, anyone ever tell you how good you are at giving ominous warnings?" I said. "Selena and I have seen the worst Riven has to offer. I think we can handle it."

"For your sake, I hope so," Cheo said.

We followed Cheo through the entry, into Mali's temple.

Into the dark.

146

As a child, I'd been scared of the dark for years. I think it had something to do with moving all the time. Never having a parent or someone that I could crawl into bed with, someone to chase away those phantom monsters. Instead I'd had one gruff guide after another, people whose nights were spent in another world. Who, when I cried out because of some nightmare, did not wake up. Did not come to comfort me or drive away my fears.

It took me more years than I care to admit to come to own my terrors. To fight the shadows. The night became a battleground, a place where I waged endless wars with the black corners of my room. When I started crossing into Riven, the spirits added shape to the monsters I'd been warring with for years.

So as we stepped into Mali's temple, as the details slipped away until only the silhouette of the door behind us was visible, I refused to be afraid. Refused to fear what I could not see. I placed my hand on Selena's shoulder, and felt Selena put her hand on mine. We walked side-by-side.

"Have to say," I said, my voice sounding strange in the

dark. Disembodied; coming from everywhere and nowhere. "I love the ambiance."

"There used to be lights," Cheo said. "Burning torches that never went out. Mali tired of the paintings."

"The paintings?" Selena said.

"Hold on," I said. I reached down to my belt, pulled out the long knife, and twisted its hilt. Blue fire wrapped the weapon, and lit up the hallway in its pale glow. Around us the walls burst forth with colorful images. Finely detailed strokes outlining landscapes and telling stories. Three figures repeated among all of them. Two women and a man. One woman with silver hair, one with black. The man had none.

One painting on the left wall showed the trio standing on a disk surrounded by lava. Or some other glowing, hideous liquid. The next one showed the three of them marveling at the land around them, the dark-haired woman's arms raised to the sky. On solid ground, a mountain soaring in the distance.

"Who made these?" I said. "Mali?"

"I don't know," Cheo said. "They have always been here. Since before even I. If Mali made these, then they were the only ones she ever painted."

The fire on my knife went out. It was not a torch - it would only burn for seconds at a time. I reset the hilt and was about to twist it again when Cheo, in the dark, put his hand on my wrist.

"Please," he said. "You come as a guest. It is best to obey the host's wishes. If Mali wants these paintings hidden, it is best that they remain so."

"And if I want to see them?" I said.

"Do it after I am gone," Cheo said, and I could hear his grin. "That way Mali will know who to blame."

I thought about it. True, I didn't want to annoy Mali either, but I wanted another look at those paintings. What they seemed to show. Three spirits, and one with Nara's silver hair. Mali, perhaps, the other woman, the one appearing to make the world. Who the man was, I had no idea. Nara had mentioned a name, Dolan?

"Are you thinking what I'm thinking?" I asked Selena.

"Carver, I learned a long time ago never to assume you and I are thinking the same thing," Selena replied.

"Fair point. When we get out of here, let's talk."

"We've got a long walk back to the city. Plenty of time."

Cheo ushered us along. Further down the dark path. I could feel the walls closing around me. The stone floor shuffled with the scuffing of our boots. No other sounds played out. No flowing water, no rustling of a breeze. No crackle of far-off flame. Riven was never a loud place, unless you were in a pitched fight with howling spirits or standing next to a building as it finally succumbed to the slow collapse of the place. But the passage achieved a new silence altogether. As though I'd truly died, as if all of my senses had disappeared.

I bumped into Cheo's back. Our guide had stopped.

"We are nearly there," Cheo said. "When I enter her chamber, I will cease to be myself."

"What do you mean?" I said.

"I am Mali's subject," Cheo replied. "Under her rule, and her will. Do not interrupt. After it is done, you will have your chance. I wish you every bit of luck."

"You won't stay?"

"I will do as Mali wills," Cheo said. "I do not think it likely that, after all of these years, she will have changed. It has been a pleasure to know the both of you. May the Goddess grant you good fortune."

"Not sure we want her blessing," Selena muttered. Cheo didn't reply. He started walking again and we followed.

I almost didn't notice the light. Didn't realize that the walls fell away as we walked into a larger chamber. A room with twin pools on either side. One glowing a faint blue and the other a lime green. A stone pathway ran between them. It led to a dais, on which, in a chair, sat the goddess we were seeking. INext to her, resolute and and staring at us with non-existent eyes on its metal face, stood a ghoul. Its golden skin shimmered in the pools' light. The ghoul wore a tunic coated in jewels, a rainbow of gemstones. Two arms, two legs, each a pillar of precious metal. As though Mali had molded the ghoul from both spirits and the earth.

Mali herself sported a silver dress, one that flowed around her and the throne on which she sat like liquid mercury. She wore no crown, sported no jewels. As if she didn't want to compete in opulence with her own ghoul.

Cheo kept walking as we stared. Left us standing there gawking at Mali's chamber. He took five steps forward and dropped to one knee, placed his hands on the ground and lowered his eyes to the floor.

"As it ever is, I have returned," Cheo announced. His voice dropped any friendly affectation. Every syllable pronounced as though giving an official notice. As though pronouncing, sentencing someone to their death.

"As it ever is," Mali replied from her throne. She spoke with a light voice, earnest. A person trying to seem more excited than they really were. Disguising the weight of her centuries.

"Shall I perform the rite?" Cheo said.

"Ten thousand times," Mali spoke softly. "Ten thousand times, Cheo, you have led the Left Hand to victory. And ten thousand times, you have conquered my realm for the Right Hand. It seems you are my greatest creation."

Ten thousand times? Both the Left Hand and the Right? I wanted to ask questions, but the idea of interrupting felt so far removed from any aspect of politeness, that I felt rooted to the spot. Unable to tear my eyes away from these two. From a goddess and her servant.

"I have fought many battles for you," Cheo said. "I will fight however many more you choose for me."

"I wonder, my Cheo, why you keep on winning?" Mali said. "Every time I pass the mantel to a new spirit, you wind up the victor. Are you truly the best that time has ever seen?"

"It is because you give me the strength I need."

"Yes," Mali replied, leaning forward in her chair and giving Cheo a glittering smile. "As long as I live, so will you. No matter how dangerous your duty becomes, so long as I am here, you will return victorious."

"As it ever is," Cheo said.

Mali nodded and Cheo stood, went over to the lime green pool and dipped in his hand. Took a sip of the water. Shivered.

"I stand for the Right Hand," Cheo announced to the chamber. "With your blessing, I shall destroy the Left Hand. I will end their vicious attempts to hurt you. To damage your kingdom."

"Go then, and seek their most deserved doom," Mali replied.

Cheo turned to her, bowed, and then marched past us. I thought about stopping him, but it didn't look like our friend lived anymore in those eyes. The Cheo that had brought us here was gone.

147

HAVE you ever had an elder stare at you? A look from someone who seems know who you are and who you would become?

When Mali turned her gaze to us from Cheo's departing back, I felt those eyes. Her Riven-gray colored pupils on me. They ran to and from every inch of my soul. And when Mali slid over to Selena I'd be lying if I didn't say I relaxed.

But exchanging stares wasn't going to get us anywhere.

"Mali," I said. "Nara sent us. We need you to come work with her to save Riven."

Mali sat back on her throne. Her fingers bounced constantly up and down, as though playing a piano that no one could see. I watched her eyes flick towards me. Instead of matching mine, Mali's look landed somewhere over my shoulder. In a space and time far away from the temple in which we stood.

"Nara sent you," Mali said. "Are you certain?"

"The woman in the field of grain," Selena replied. "Riven is falling apart, and she said you could help save it."

Mali laughed. A sort of strange, despairing chuckle that

comes when someone hears about yet another folly committed by a notorious friend. Another error in an endless series of mistakes. Where redemption is so far gone that the only reaction is a sad chuckle.

Then Mali, goddess of her own making, stuck out her arms, palms up, and began to hum. The water in each of the pools started to rise up, droplets breaking free of of the rest, hanging in the air like diamonds. Then the drops shifted to the center, over the walkway and between Mali and us.

They formed a square, a moving sheet of water hanging in the air. The droplets began to shift, re-arrange themselves. Some combining to darken their color and others splitting, becoming lighter. Until before my eyes sat an image like that of the painting in the hallway. A deep green disk on which stood a trio of blue figures. Two women and a man. Around them a sea of light blue, nearly transparent water.

The water moved, blue droplets gathering and weaving through the green. Smaller figures. Blue lines stepping off and scattering away.

"I think that's the Cycle," Selena said, and I agreed.

The parade of spirits continued as the three figures watched. Then one of the women appeared to reach out with her hand, to touch one of the blue lines. The droplets stopped their walk across the green disk. Waited until the blue figure pointed above. Then droplets marched their form up and off of the disk. Once more, they scattered into the transparent sea.

Now the second woman moved, tracing her hand along the outside of the green disk. More drops from the green pool raced up to join the water curtain, adding their color to the expanding disk. Widening it until nearly all the transparent water had been pushed off the edge. As the disk grew, the first woman continued reaching out and touching the smaller blue spirits, keeping them in a large huddle. Building an army.

The transparent water, the Cycle, had almost been removed from the curtain entirely when the male figure reached out. Pointed to the first woman's growing group of spirits. At the wandering blue lines that no longer had a place to go. The second woman shifted, her arms corralling the Cycle into a small circle and sending it to the left side of the watery curtain. Surrounding it in a triangle of deep green. The Mountain, and the Cycle within it.

I noticed now, wandering through the curtain of water, more deep blue figures appeared. Not so large as the main three, but more defined than the spirits. The man reached out to those figures, and each one he touched seemed to alight their hands and arms in light blue drops. The pale wrangling fire. The first woman, the one with the expanding army of thin blue figures, grew agitated. Some of the thin blue figures surrounded one of the man's burning allies. And quenched it. This prompted the man to send his other servants after the woman's army. They clashed around the disk, with many of the woman's thin blue figures racing off towards the mountain as they fought.

Meanwhile, the green disk changed. Instead of a flat and uniform surface, everywhere the second woman brushed her hand, new features arose. The green lightened and darkened, clustered and shifted to form a familiar outline. A map I knew all too well.

"This is Riven's history," I said. "How it came to be."

"But who are they?" Selena said, pointing past me at the three figures. "I get that the one making all the green things, that must be Mali."

"The other two? I don't know."

"You think the other woman is Nara?"

"The one binding all the spirits?" I said. "Possibly."

That would explain how Nara knew so much about bindings. If she had been the first one to learn, with centuries to perfect and perform the process. Only in this rendition, it almost looked like Nara was the evil one. Her army of spirits fighting constantly against the man's smaller, pale-fire-wielding force.

In the water play, it looked as though the man and first woman had fought themselves to a stalemate, an equal line of figures continually replacing and destroying each other. The second woman, Mali, moved apart from them and watched. The view changed. Zoomed in on the city, the droplets shifting and expanding to show alleys and blocks. Thin blue figures moving and appearing to work with each other. Spirits running a town. Moving carts of goods, illustrated in green droplets. Operating stores. Gathering together.

Then, from the left and north sides, came the deep blue figures and their pale-fire arms. Streaming down through the streets and burning away the spirits. Sometimes they appeared to smash through buildings, scattering green droplets. The swirling battles went on for a while, until the view shifted out again. The smaller figures vanished entirely, reforming into the man and first woman, standing on a green plain. They grappled, their fingers locking with each other. Behind them, the green shifted and broke, droplets scattering and forming themselves back together.

Mali entered from the right, her dark blue form appearing to plead with the pair. Being ignored. And, finally, raising her arms to the sky. Deep green lines came down the water curtain, splitting the man and woman. Splitting Mali apart from them. Mali's figure hung her head, and then the water curtain dissipated. Scattered back to the pools.

"Now you understand," Mali said. "I cannot free them. I cannot free Nara, because she will try again."

"Try again to what?" I said. "Bind spirits? It didn't look so bad, there, in the town."

"She kept them," Mali said. "All the spirits. They did her bidding. Worshiped her. You believe Riven is in danger now, then freeing her would only bring the hordes under her control. What you saw there was a city bent to the desires of its leader."

"Then why did you make it in the first place?" Selena said.

"Because Nara asked me to," Mali said. "We were the first ones. The first who kept ourselves from taking that last step into the Cycle. No doubt you have found its call easier to resist when you work together? So it was with us. When Nara wanted a city, I built it. When Nara wanted the Cycle gone, I tried to destroy it."

"You put it in the Mountain," I said.

"I would have sealed it off completely, were it not for Dolan," Mali said. "If he hadn't held me back. Argued that there might yet be some use for it."

"So if you think Nara is going to ruin Riven," I said. "Can you help us? Can you drive the spirits into the Cycle?"

Mali shook her head. A frown came over her face. "Meddling has only brought me pain, little spirits. I should have vanished into the Cycle when I first came here. Instead, here I am. Trapped in a prison of my own making."

"I don't understand," I said.

"I learned to create this world," Mali said. "I do not know how to destroy it. There is no way to free the Cycle. And I will not let Nara go. Whatever befalls Riven, she will not have a hand in it."

I glanced at Selena. If Mali wasn't going to help us, then there wasn't much use in staying here. We were wasting time.

"Let's go back," I said. "Nara might have another idea."

"Didn't you hear her?" Selena said. "She's saying Nara's evil."

"Mali also said she didn't want to help Riven," I said. "That makes them the same to me. At least Nara gives us a chance. Maybe she's changed after all these years."

At my nod, Selena and I turned back to the passage. The dark path to the surface.

"You are not the first," Mali announced to our backs. "Nara has sent others. All begging for her release. All of them turned as you did. Determined to help Nara find a way free."

"What happened to them?" Selena asked.

"I did not let them go," Mali said, her voice dropping to a whisper. Once again, Mali's hand shot forward. The stones bordering the passageway out shivered, then crumbled in on themselves. Blocking our escape.

"We don't want to fight," I said, turning back around.

"You are free to die," Mali replied, then nodded at the golden ghoul beside her. Its head turned, and though its eyes were golden ovals, I met its gaze.

And when the ghoul marched towards us, Selena and I met its advance.

148

SELENA RAN TOWARDS THE GHOUL, cleaver raised in her right hand, her long knife held at her waist, point forward and ready to stick Mali's creation. The ghoul more than tripled our height; Selena didn't come up to its waist. As the two approached, the ghoul swung out with its right hand and connected with Selena's side, knocking her across the ground and into one of the pools. The ghoul didn't bother to look at what happened to her. Came right on towards me.

Most of the other ghouls I'd seen had been horrendous creatures. Misshapen masses of arms and legs and limbs that bore no other description. The spirits that they'd consumed shifted beneath their skin, faces popping to the surface and giving you a reminder of who had been consumed to create the abomination. Mali's ghoul looked different. Golden, pristine, a model of a person, if one without any clear gender features. Smooth skin and sporting a long gold tunic that stretched from collar to knees. I'd seen similar things before, in museums of ancient artifacts. Exhibitions on tours through Chicago. But it was one thing to stare at an artifact beneath a glass case and quite another to have an object of antiquity reaching for my throat.

I cracked the lash, wrapping around the ghoul's outstretched hand. Waited for the telltale sign that the metal tip had pierced the ghoul's skin. Then I'd start the fire and send it to its next life. Only the lash's point bounced off the ghoul's skin and hung, limp, as the ghoul continued its advance.

"It's skin isn't... skin," I shouted to Selena as she pulled herself out of the pool. The bluish liquid clung to her, bits of it dripping off onto the ground. Thicker than water.

"Maybe if you actually hit it harder." Selena shot back.

I didn't have time to hit anything. The ghoul swung at me with its right hand again, just as it had attacked Selena. I dropped to the floor, flattening myself and feeling the ghoul's fist fly overhead. Through the ghoul's legs, I saw Selena coming up behind, cleaver ready. If I could get its attention for another moment, Selena could hammer home.

I glanced up and saw the ghoul's left fist rising high. Ready to deliver a strike to my back that would bash me into nothingness. Then Selena's cleaver bit into the ghoul's calf. She swung her large knife with two hands, hacking at the monster's skin. This time, unlike my lash, I saw flecks fly off. Selena's blade breaking through. I expected a roar, but the ghoul stayed silent. A look at its face confirmed that it didn't have a mouth, only a metal line. Still, her attack made the ghoul pause, turn and regard the flea biting at its leg. Which let me get back to my feet.

Selena's cleaver had another trick. She twisted the hilt, the blade sticking into the ghoul, and wreathed the cleaver in blue fire. I waited for the cleansing flames to wash over the creature, to burn it to a cinder and leave nothing standing. Except the flames failed. They didn't burn. They didn't catch on and torch up and down the creature. They stayed on the cleaver, as though the ghoul were made of water. As though a steady breeze blew the flames back. Selena stared at her weapon as though it had betrayed her.

"Watch out!" I said. The ghoul, rather than smash me with its fist, swung its left arm back, catching Selena with its barrel-sized hand. Again she flew through the air, this time landing at the foot of Mali's throne. Crumpled to the ground.

"Hey," I said to the ghoul. "My turn."

I did not want the creature mashing Selena to spirit-mush. The ghoul didn't seem to care which of us it crushed, so long as it was crushing. Its right fist came at me in a lumbering hook. I sidestepped the attack, back out of the ghoul's reach. I let go of my lash and drew my great sword. Lifted the weapon out as the ghoul pulled its arm for another swing and brought Piotr's large blade down on the ghoul's hand. It cut through, lopping off three of the creature's fingers. They hit the ground; heavy, solid gold blocks.

"Have to be more careful," I said. "You only have ten of those. Well, seven now."

The ghoul didn't seem to care about my jabs, physical or verbal. Its left hand made a grab for my head. I pivoted, swung the great sword at it, and at the last minute the ghoul jerked its hand back. My strike missed by inches. That was okay. All about buying time.

"Mali, call it off," I shouted. "We don't want to fight you. I don't want to break your toy."

Mali, for her part, ignored me. Ignored the fight. Her eyes were closed, her hands still playing that rhythm in the air. Either living in a memory or doing something I didn't understand.

If she wasn't going to stop the ghoul, then I'd have to destroy it.

The ghoul swept its broken right hand towards my legs, bringing it in low. I crouched, and then jumped over the swing, bringing the great sword down on the ghoul's wrist. My blade bit in, and, as I fell back to the ground, I twisted the hilt to send blue fire down into the creature. Again it failed. I stared at the cleaving cut, incredulous. The fire should burn away the rage, clear the binding that held a ghoul together in Riven. If it didn't work, then we had no hope.

The ghoul's left hand caught me unaware, bashed me into the side of the room. I bounced off and landed on my knees. My head rang with the impact, and I realized the great sword still hung from the creature's right wrist, stuck in the ghoul. The monster turned towards me, and I drew the long knife from my belt. A pathetic choice to go against the giant creature.

So I ran.

I went around the ghoul and towards the blue pool on the far side. The ghoul turned, but its bulk made it a slow mover. A good thing, as I had to figure out a strategy. My knife wouldn't help much. I had my crossbow. The normal bolts would be useless. A blue bolt, that would only send the same fire that had so far failed to hurt the creature. The orange. That was an option, if I wanted to bring down this entire temple on top of us. The space was too small; Nicholas's invention would burn its way through the rock and us in its quest to devour anything within reach. So I backpedaled. Tried to get my distance. For its part, the ghoul didn't seem to be in any hurry. Why bother running when the rat has nowhere to go?

My retreat around the pool brought Mali, and her throne, into view. A thought - if I couldn't defeat the ghoul, then maybe I could take out its creator.

I took four steps towards her before Mali realized what I was doing. With her eyes still closed, Mali held out her hand. The floor around her began to shake, stone blocks rattling loose from their frames. Revealing dirt and grime underneath. They shot together, forming a wall in front of me, between Mali and the point of my knife.

"Please," Mali said. "Stop this. Give in and let the end come. Embrace your fate as Cheo embraced his."

Cheo. That was an idea. If I could get the ghoul to the right place...

BUT I'D RUN out of time. The ghoul had closed, its hands wrapping around each other in a heavy overhead smash. I tried to dodge, squeeze around to the left along the chamber's back wall. The ghoul, keeping its hands raised, kicked out with its right foot instead of smashing down. The swipe wasn't dead-on, wasn't very strong, so I only flew up and bounced off of the wall, landing near the corner with my head and back aching. The knife out of my hands, which were trying to push me up. I knew the ghoul's follow-up would be coming, and as I scooted forward, the ghoul's left fist flattened the spot where I'd fallen.

I didn't make it past the right hand. Despite only having a thumb and pinkie finger, the ghoul wrapped its palm around me as I ran. Lifted me off the ground. Only, without the fingers, I could still move my right arm. The ghoul's thumb pressed against my head, like squeezing a fruit. I tried to think of what I could grab, but all my weapons were gone. My crossbow pinned to my back. In a second, I'd snap apart.

"Let him go," Selena growled, her voice trembling with

pain, strong. The ghoul turned towards her, letting me see her running jump onto the creature's tunic. Selena climbed, using her knife and cleaver to slice new handholds. With its left hand, the ghoul tried to pluck Selena off itself, but its movements were too slow. Too clumsy. Selena was a wiry spirit, slippery and quick when she wanted to be. She dodged the scrabbling hand and pulled herself up onto the ghoul's shoulders. Took her cleaver in both arms as she wrapped her legs around its neck, and slammed her blade into the ghoul's head, biting off flakes of metal. And then the ghoul jumped. Press its legs down and elevated, ducked its head. Slammed Selena into the ceiling and crushed her into the stone blocks.

The impact knocked the ghoul's hand open, let me loose from the fingers. I splashed down into the blue pool, its icy water soaking my clothes. The chill seemed to scare away the pain, bring reality back into focus.

"Selena!" I called, sputtering away the water. She didn't answer, her broken body motionless on the walkway. The ghoul, after staring at Selena's form for a second, turned to me. I stood in the pool. Right where I wanted to be.

The ghoul's hands came for me again, smashing down. I dodged back, towards the far end of the pool and the entrance that Mali had sealed. The ghoul's hands splashed into the liquid in front of me, finally shaking the great sword out of its wrist. The blue, gooey water ran into the cuts and holes, the scratches we'd made on its hands. Filling them.

The ghoul shuddered. Paused.

When Cheo drank the green stuff on the other side, it seemed to erase his mind. A trap, or some sort of binding. Maybe, maybe the blue would do the same to the ghoul.

The monster seemed to fall asleep for a moment. It stood back, straightened. I stayed in the pool and watched. Did nothing to interrupt its reverie. If this didn't work, if the ghoul decided again to pound us into dirt, then I didn't think there was anything we could do to stop it.

Instead, the ghoul jerked. Turned towards the chamber's exit and, with a strong swing of its left hand, punched through Mali's broken wall. The golden ghoul walked away, vanishing into the darkness.

"Unexpected," Mali said. "I've never seen that happen before. Not in all my years."

"So glad we could make it interesting," I said, running over to Selena's form. If she'd been a human, I had no doubt the ghoul would have killed her. Every bone in her body would have been shattered into dust. As a spirit, however, Selena had no bones. Had nothing other than her soul. So when I held her, I saw her eyes flicker. Her mouth move. Selena would come back.

"Indeed," Mali said, her eyes moving to the pool. "Nara's gift, it seems, has proved to be a trap all this time. Always ruining the beautiful things Dolan and I built for this world."

"I'm starting to think you're the evil one, not her," I said. "You keep spirits for centuries, replaying the same conflict over and over. You said that you murdered everyone Nara sent before."

Mali considered. "Let me ask you, spirit, what you think I should have done? Should I have welcomed Nara's pawns with open arms? Accepted her overtures, released her?"

"The way I see it, you all had the power to keep Riven safe. So why didn't you?"

Mali sat forward, looked hard into my eyes. "I wonder if she has her claws in you even now. This far distant, you should be free, and yet..."

"Help us."

"There is no helping you. I will not give this cursed world into Nara's grasp." Mali pressed her hands on the arms of her throne, digging her nails into its grooves. "Come now, servant. Let's see if Nara has chosen well this time."

As I held Selena in my arms, my weapons scattered around the room, Mali, the spirit that built the Riven I knew, that crafted its buildings, its forests, its ashen sky, rose from her throne with my end in her eyes.

150

Mali slid out of her throne, stretched, holding her arms together above her head. I set Selena back down on the ground, picked up her knife in my right hand, unsure of what to do. What strategies worked against a spirit thousands of years old? What haven't they seen? I decided to flip the knife to my left, lunge forward and stab.

Mali made me pause.

Two stone blocks in front of her feet rattled, broke out of the floor. One flew into each of her hands and melted into a ring, the stone seeming to liquefy and reform in her grip. The rings were as big around as a melon, only with serrated edges. Mali held them lightly, though I couldn't see how she didn't cut herself on the gleaming rings. Perhaps she did. Perhaps she didn't care.

"It's been such a long time," Mali said. "I might be rusty."

"That would be such a shame," I replied. "Really wanted another hard fight after that last one."

"Oh, I wouldn't worry about that."

Mali raised her right arm behind her, getting ready to throw the ring. Which meant I had to strike first. I stepped over Selena, and took a long lunge forward. Bursting out with the knife towards Mali. A third stone flew up out of the ground in front of her, striking the middle of the knife and sending it flying. The blade splashed into the green pool, leaving me barehanded and staring into Mali's devilish grin.

"Come now," Mali said. "Such an obvious attack? You'll have to do better."

"Most people can't pull blocks from the ground," I countered. "Not fair."

"You were expecting fair?" Mali said. "How have you made it this far?"

Mali whipped her right arm, then her left, the sharp disks flying towards me. I had no time to dodge - only a few feet separated us. The first one burrowed its way into my left shoulder, and the second into my right leg. They whirled like saw blades; grinding, spinning, and tearing. My left arm went numb, and I fell to one knee as my leg stopped being able to hold my weight. As fights go, I'd had better starts.

"That's all you've got?" I said, trying to buy time. Spirits healed fast in Riven, and if I could keep her talking, I might get some function back. "All those centuries and you make a couple of rings? Why not another ghoul?"

"Dolan gave me the ghoul," Mali said, sending a quick frown up the passage. "I covered it with gold after a while. There's only so long you can stand to see swirling spirits and grotesque flesh."

"That didn't answer my question."

"I don't answer to you," Mali replied. She sucked another pair of blocks up from the floor, once again pulling them into the circular rings. I still wore the crossbow on my back, but without two arms, drawing the weapon and loading it wasn't possible. Not to mention it would be obvious, and I didn't think Mali would stand there and let me crank a bolt into position.

"The same rings again. Very creative," I said. "It's like you're stuck on them."

Mali worked a smile at me. "When you've already made everything, you find yourself returning to your favorites."

Behind me, Selena groaned. She'd been barely moving since the ghoul crushed her into the ceiling. If she could wake up, then we'd have a better shot. Goddess or no, Selena and I were a tough team to handle.

Mali wasn't going to let that happen. She walked around me, and I watched her. I couldn't do anything, could barely focus over the burning pain from the stone disks, which were still embedded in my skin from Mali's attack. The goddess stood over Selena and looked down at her, shook her head. "I forget how hard it is to actually destroy a spirit. Without Dolan's weapons, you'll keep coming back."

She wasn't wrong. I took Mali's moment of distraction and used my right arm to pull the stone ring from my left shoulder, ripped out the one from my right leg. Tossed them to the ground. Immediately, I felt my spirit tying itself together. Like drinking water after a long thirst - a cool, nourishing glow. It would take hours to get full movement back, but every little bit helped.

"You know what?" Mali said. "Nara and Dolan called me the creator. You call me a goddess. It's an incomplete name. I cannot make whatever I want. Inanimate things, yes. Facsimiles. Those trees in Riven's great forest. The grain covering Nara's fields. All of it is so close to life, none of it is living. The flowers in the canyons, the endless copies of ferns and vines. None of it is alive. All of it stays as I wish it, and will as long as I want it to. But if I want souls to play with, I have to find them. Same as you."

"I don't play with souls. I send them to the Cycle."

"Yes, and how noble of you," Mali said. Selena twitched and Mali gave her a vicious kick, stilling her. Then Mali walked over to the green pool and dipped her rings inside of it. "You feed souls, creatures of mind and memory, love and loss, into the one thing that can destroy them completely. Have you ever wondered why?"

"If I didn't, Riven would be overrun," I said. "This world, and Earth, would only be home to the dead."

"Would that really be so bad?" Mali said. She pulled the rings out, dripping with green. I knew what she was going to do. I'd seen it with Cheo. With the ghoul. Cut us, get that liquid inside of our souls, and bind us to her. Or to her left hand. Or right hand. I couldn't remember which color meant which. I didn't want either.

"You tell me," I said. "You've been living with the dead all this time. You don't seem too happy about it."

I twisted around, faced Selena. The motion tapped the crossbow against my back. An idea, maybe, but I needed a distraction.

"All due to a lack of variety," Mali said. "A little more space. Freedom from this place. Then, I think, I would be as happy as a spirit could possibly be."

"You'll be as alone then as you are now," I said.

"Maybe, but it's worth a try, don't you think?" Mali replied. She walked up to me, raised the ring in her left hand. "Now I will give you one last choice. Yourself, or her? Which of you will be the first to enter my service?"

"She will," I said.

And Mali laughed.

151

"So gallant," Mali said. "Even the men in my own time were better than that."

Mali turned her back to me, and gave me my chance. With my right hand, I reached behind my back. Grabbed the blue bolts loaded into the side of the crossbow and slipped one out. Twisted it in my fingers as I brought my arm back forward. Threw it. Like a dart, hard and fast. The bolt stuck between Mali's shoulders, bursting into blue flame. I could see Mali shudder, and I'm sure her eyes would've been wide had I seen her face. But Riven's creator did not scream. Didn't shout, or howl, or curse my name. As the fire covered her, she dropped the rings to the ground and knelt.

"There's the freedom you were looking for," I said, pulling a second blue bolt out. Just in case.

A moment later, Mali's spirit rose, vacant and ignorant to the world she'd made. The goddess's ghost walked out of the room, vanishing into the dark passage.

After Mali left I stayed in the chamber, sitting on the stone floor for what felt like hours. Letting my soul knit itself back together and playing over in my mind what had happened. Nara had sent us a request to find Mali, to convince her to come back. Instead we found her, enraged her, and destroyed her. A spirit that Nara said was key to saving Riven, and we'd sent her to the Cycle.

Add to that everything Mali had told us. Her show with the water. Her statements about Nara, that the old spirit was playing us. That Nara wanted to undermine Riven and all that it stood for. That all Nara believed in was binding spirits by the dozen; creating a world of her own making.

"Carver?" Selena's voice sounded weak. Tired. "Are we still here?"

"Against all odds, we are," I said. "How are you feeling?"

"Oh fine." Selena groaned. "You know, broken everywhere. Every possible part of my soul is aching. The pain is canceling itself out, I think. As though my mind can't reconcile all of it."

"It'll get better," I said. "We're safe now. Mali's gone."

I replayed the fight for her. When I came to the part where I suggested Mali take Selena first, Selena laughed. Still lying there on the stones, her head flat against the rock, but I saw the smile, and it made me feel happy. Needed those moments. A little bit of love and levity in the twin pool's dim light.

"Of course you'd send me first," Selena said. "Always about you."

"I had to," I protested. "If she hadn't turned her back, then I wouldn't have--"

"Sure, sure," Selena said. "Of course that's the reason. Couldn't you have done that any other time, like when she was dipping her rings in the pool? Had to wait until she was going to take me out?"

"The pool would've been a far shot," I said. "I had to be sure."

I could tell Selena wasn't being serious. Could see the play in her eyes. We spent a while there, sitting, then standing, and then limping out of the chamber, picking up our weapons on the way. With every step our spirits put themselves back together. By the time we made it out of the temple, we could make a fairly good pace, leaning on each other for support.

"I feel like an old man," I said. "Like my body doesn't work anymore."

"You don't have a body, remember?" Selena replied.

"If this is what they feel like, maybe I'm glad I never saw mine broken."

Outside, we turned to look back at the temple entrance. All those runes, those stories about the goddess that lived inside. No longer. The temple would stand empty, potentially forever. Riven didn't have natural forces, and unless something came by and actively destroyed this place, Mali's home would stand for more centuries than she did.

"So what are we going to tell Nara?" Selena said as we turned back to the jungle.

"That we tried," I said. "Maybe she'll have other ideas."

"Do you think we should trust her?" Selena said. "Because if we don't, and we're wrong, Riven's going to fall apart. But if we do, and we're wrong, then Nara's version might be worse."

"We play it both ways," I said. "If what she says seems to be right, that we do it. If it's wrong, now we know that we can wrangle her just like any other spirit. Mali showed us that much."

Selena nodded. We passed by the same rock-hard flower from before. Again, Selena reached out to touch it. No change. No sign that the flower knew its creator had disappeared. Like the buildings in Riven's city, the only thing that would tear the plant apart would be our weapons, our struggle.

"Strange that this flower will likely last longer than all of us," Selena mused, looking at the plant.

"So will the stones, and the rivers and the clouds," I said. "The difference is that they aren't doing anything with their time. They aren't risking themselves to save this place."

"Doesn't sound so bad."

"You'd get bored."

Selena laughed, then grimaced and steadied herself on my shoulder. Still putting ourselves back together.

We continued walking, past the ferns and trees that took on a stranger cast now that we knew none of them truly lived. That they were all figments of a bored spirit trying to find something to do with her imagination. Onward into the canyon, until the whispering wind gave way to harsher noises. Shouts and cries. The sound of metal on metal.

"Is Cheo already fighting another war?" I said.

"I don't think we can wage another one," Selena said.

"We may not have a choice."

Because the sounds were coming straight for us now. A rolling mix of snapping branches, crashing brush, and clashing iron. And we didn't have the strength to run.

152

IN FRONT of us a tree simply disappeared, vaporized and blew apart as the golden form of Mali's ghoul smashed through it. Cheo and a group of other spirits came hot behind the monster, all throwing knives, spears, or firing arrows at the ghoul's back.

"Do not let up," Cheo shouted over the noise. "The Left Hand's monster must not be allowed to live! It is a perversion, a slight against our goddess!"

The ghoul ran straight for us, but as it noticed our limping forms, it slowed to a stop. Stared down at us with its solid, unseeing eyes. Behind it, arrows and thrown spears clinked off the ghoul's back, bouncing away. Cheo and the others, four spirits, caught up and stared at us as well, halting their attack as they realized the ghoul had done the same.

"Didn't realize we were that stunning," I said. "Do we really look that bad?"

"Who are you?" Cheo said, pointing one of his crude knives towards us. "Are you part of the Left Hand?"

"He doesn't remember," Selena said to me. Cheo's other spirits fanned out around us, setting a trap. In our condition, even with our weapons back in hand, neither Selena nor I would be able to fight them off. If Cheo truly had no idea who we were, if he believed we were the enemy, there was no way we could win.

"Remember you?" Cheo said. "I don't understand."

"You know who Mali is?" I said.

"Of course," Cheo replied. "She is my goddess."

"Don't take this the wrong way," I said. "But she's dead."

Rather than flying into a rage, or sitting down in despair, Cheo reacted with a nod. A slow, sad motion. The other spirits mimicked the move. "Her voice changed. A whisper, now, telling us to go far away from here. I assumed it was a Left Hand trick."

"The Cycle," I said. "You'll get used to it."

"I do not understand?" Cheo asked, and Selena and I told the spirits about the Cycle, how Mali fell. By the time we were done, the spirits had put up their weapons. I couldn't tell if the ghoul listened as well, but it stood tall and shining over us the entire time.

"It seems we have nowhere left to go," Cheo said. "Except to this Cycle."

"You've been a spirit for a long time," Selena said. "You don't have to be one anymore."

"And this one?" Cheo pointed at the ghoul. "Does it belong in your Cycle as well?"

The ghoul, standing above us in silence, reached out and pointed at me with one hand. The one that only had two fingers left.

"Think it's mad you cut off its fingers?" Selena asked me.

"I hope not," I replied. The ghoul pulled its hand back. Stared at me with its blank gold face. On an impulse, I pointed to a tree next to me and spoke to the ghoul. "Grab that."

The ghoul stomped around me, reached down with its

intact hand, and pulled the tree from the ground. Held it aloft like a club.

"It's obeying you?" Selena said.

"Looks like I got myself a ghoul." I waved for the monster to toss the tree away and the golden ghoul launched it through the brush. "You better be real nice to me now."

"Aren't I always?"

The ghoul, along with the other spirits, belonged in the Cycle. But as I started to tell them to march that way, I paused. The spirits had wrangling weapons, and the ghoul could certainly pound some breaches into pulp.

Bryce and the guides could use a force like this.

"Selena," I said. "I think we've got a new plan."

"I get nervous when you say that."

"This one's good, promise," I said. "How many spirits do you have, Cheo?"

"Between both hands? The number would be around one hundred. There have not been many new collections lately. Spirits are becoming rare."

"The breaches are drawing them south," I said. "Cheo, I need you to gather up both hands. Even the spirits you hate. We're going to the city."

"The Left Hand will not march for me," Cheo replied.

"No." I glanced at the ghoul. "But they will for this."

153

Convincing Cheo to round up the other spirits in the jungle and hike back to the city with us didn't take much doing. I guess living without a purpose means there's nothing to hold on to. They weren't giving up anything to come with us, and so they took to the new adventure without complaint. The ghoul followed us everywhere. Tromping along behind me. I wasn't sure what drove its actions either, except, perhaps, a loyalty to whomever had destroyed its master.

Mali had said the ghoul was a gift from Dolan, the third one of their trio. I'd never heard of anyone making a ghoul before, perhaps this one was different. In any case, I wasn't going to say no to a giant monster for a bodyguard.

After a long trek, we made it back in sight of the city's walls. Then to the north gate. Selena and I walked on our own now, almost back to full strength. Truly, being dead did wonders for one's health.

The north side of Riven held a scattered series of large houses. Parks and dried lakes. Empty, ruined from fighting. We didn't even encounter a guide until we entered the city center. Then a pack poured into the street in front of us.

Their weapons at the ready. Several guides hung out of windows from buildings bordering the street, aiming at us with guns and bows of their own making. Our band, nearly a hundred strong, boasting our own military menagerie, and a giant golden ghoul, probably had them nervous.

Understandable.

"Never expected to see you again," said the guide leading the pack. He pulled up his mask and I knew him. My most likely murderer. Polk stood a thin and wiry man. A weaselly face. I hadn't known the guides still counted him a member. Didn't know what he was doing here.

My hand drifted to my lash. Selena grabbed it. Stopped me.

"Now is not the time," Selena said. "There's too much at stake."

"You know why we did it," Polk said to me. "Piotr's orders. He told us he had a solution that would save everybody. We didn't want to die anymore than he did."

"That's not an excuse," I said.

"Why I'm here," Polk replied. "Trying to pay it back. Closing breaches. Buying you time."

"You want to buy us time?" I said. "Then let us through. This group is reinforcements. To help you. They know what they're doing, and they can wrangle spirits."

"And that thing?" Polk said, nodding at the ghoul.

"He's mine," I said. "I'll send him after anyone that annoys me. Like you."

Polk laughed, but it was a weak chuckle. Laced with nervousness. Good.

The guides didn't fight us. They let us into their territory. From there it wasn't a far walk to the square with the fountain, near the clock tower's charred ruins, where Bryce had set up headquarters. We were lucky. We'd come in at a time when both Bryce and Alec had crossed over. They were there, looking over a large board on which a crude map of Riven had been drawn. Markers placed, moved on and off to indicate breaches. Still other pieces, bits of debris cut into squares and circles, indicated groups of guides and where they had been sent.

It didn't take Bryce long after I told him our tale to send the ghoul, Cheo and his army to a new target. The west gate into the city.

"It's the best choke point we've got," Bryce said to Cheo. "You'll have constant action. There's too many breaches in the forest and we can't get out there. But if you hold them with the walls, funnel them to the gate, that will give us time to clear the city. Right now we're just hanging on."

Cheo accepted the new duty with the same solemn expression he'd given Mali. Pledged his devotion to the new cause, and then marched his force off.

Bryce came to Selena and I. Waved Alec over.

"It's not looking good," I said to my former mentor. "We killed the person Nara said was going to help us."

"There's no backup plan?" Bryce said.

"We don't know," Selena said. "We haven't been back to her."

"That's where we're going now," I said.

"Can you spare an hour or two?" Bryce said. "Anna is missing. She and that sneak of hers, Laurence, were helping us out. I don't have any guides left that I can send after them. Especially not any that want to risk themselves for a sneak."

"I'd go alone, but the breaches make it too dangerous to travel solo," Alec chimed in.

"Where'd she go?" I said.

"She said she was going back to where they cross over. They wanted a tall building to help scope the city. If we can secure a vantage point, we'll be able to send guides to breaches quickly. Keep us living a little longer," Bryce said. "You know where a building like that might be?"

"The Warrens. We can check it out. How's everything else?"

Bryce sighed. "If there was any hope that we could survive this by strength of arms, I'd have you stay. I'd have you fight with us and close as many breaches as you could. We've lost the forest. We're facing more ghouls every day. On the other side, with Piotr gone, the peace talks are wavering. Nobody wants to give up their stake. While they argue, their armies keep fighting."

Bryce spared a glance to the spark-filled sky.

"Carver, if you don't succeed, we won't hold out much longer. Neither will Riven."

154

RUNNING THROUGH RIVEN FELT FAMILIAR, and in a good way. The same back alleys, crumbling buildings, and ash strewn streets felt like home. No more canyons, no more identical jungle flora. Just hard stone and wood. Selena, Alec, and I made our way south from the clock tower and towards the Warrens.

"How's the other side?" I asked Alec as we walked along.

"Chaotic as ever," Alec said. "Chicago, it is a mess. All in a flurry trying to make things for this endless war. On top of that, everyone is sick. This disease continues its rampage. Everyone uses their masks now. Even inside."

"Sounds like fun," I said.

"I used to live like that." Selena's eyes stared into a distant past. "Wiley, my husband, he worked as a meat cutter. We never had clean air in that part of the city. Everyone wore their masks. Sometimes the purifiers would break and you'd wear them indoors too. Because anything could make you sick, we wore gloves all the time."

"Yuck," I said.

"Indeed, of the worlds we have, yours appears the most miserable," Alec said.

"You'd think that," Selena said. "Except we were so careful that few of us actually became ill. We were happy, healthy in our own way."

"I would take a chance with disease in order to breathe out of my own mouth every once in a while," Alec said. "When it's hot out? Nobody wants a mask wrapped around their face."

"The price you pay, I suppose," Selena said.

"Is Ezra's still around?" I said.

"Carver, you've been gone a week. The world hasn't changed," Alec said.

Fair enough. I hadn't been dead for that long. Only it was hard to tell. Already it seemed like my memories of the time before, of Earth and walking the real streets, were fading. Like childhood or a boring day the next morning. Bits and pieces falling away and being replaced by the perennial gray. I didn't know how to hold onto them. How to hold onto who I was.

We reached the Ghoul's Gateway, the arch that led into the Warrens. Spirits were more common here, the tall, packed buildings providing plenty of space for them to cross in after their demise. Usually you'd find a few angry spirits running around, ready for wrangling. Now, there were guides patrolling in groups and nearly every spirit had already been pacified. Their eyes blank. None of the frightened curiosity you'd see in a spirit before the fire claimed them. No, all of these had been wrangled. If Riven had a scorched earth policy, the guides were employing it.

"Do you think it will ever go back?" I asked Alec. "Where you won't have to walk every block with your hand on your weapon?"

"Can't answer that question," Alec said. "We can choose. If

we succeed, then Riven may know some peace. If we fail, then we may know ours."

After four more blocks we came across a large building, nearly a block long in and of itself. Seven stories high and serving as Anna's crossing point. Her room, the place she and Laurence crossed over from their hideaway in Chicago, sat in its basement. We stood in front, looking into its entrance, and saw nothing.

"Should we go inside?" I said.

"Where could they be?" Alec peered up the building's wide facade.

"Two choices," I said. "Up or down. They cross into the basement, so I say we check there first."

The three of us moved into the lobby, a spacious place that deserved to be decorated with potted plants and marble columns. A bronze desk with a receptionist, a doorman to tip his hat and greet you. Instead stains splattered the inside, faded reds and browns, the occasional black mark of fire. Holes punched in the floor and tears in the walls gave distant fights their due. Large rooms off the lobby on either side played homage to the life the apartment building was meant to have. Restaurants, perhaps. Or meeting spaces. Social clubs, as if Riven had ever had any. Towards the back of the lobby a wide stair opened up, going both down and towards the top.

We fell into the typical silence that guides adopt when investigating a new area. A space where danger might be around any corner. The slightest sound, the quietest laughter could serve to drive a spirit angry. Not a chance we were willing to take. I led, the great sword in my hands. The stairway gave me enough room to swing, though I was less sure about the hallways beneath and above. Then again, these walls wouldn't mind a few extra cuts.

The basement resembled a catacomb. I'd crossed over

here with Anna more than a few times, but never alone. Always with her to lead me out. So I had to pull the floor plan from memory. Whether it was because we were standing right there, or because the thought concerned Riven, the layout came back clear.

Who needed memories of childhood when you could recall basement arrangements at will?

"It's a grid," I whispered to Selena and Alec. "We're at the back middle. To the right, there are three main rooms. All square, I think maybe meant to hold supplies. On the left, it's one large space. Ductwork. A lot of ruined stuff. Probably where power would've gone, if this had been Chicago. I say we start there."

I didn't say that the large room would make it easier to see each other. To cover corners and make sure we weren't getting ambushed. Alec, Selena and I needed a warm-up. Needed to get back into the groove of clearing out rooms where angry spirits could hide behind anything. Could reach out from any shadow to grab your throat and tear it apart.

The door to the large room, a double affair, had been ripped away. On the other side, it was easy to see what had done it. A trio of slathering spirits stood at the far end of the long room, scrabbling at its back door. Pounding and tearing. What they were trying to get at, why they didn't just come back out our door, I didn't know. No reason, except that spirits tended to think in straight lines.

We crept into the room, stepping over pipes, rubble, and broken bits of wood. The spirits didn't notice. So focused on that far end. On whatever was on the other side of that door. We made it within five feet of them before one turned, a middle-aged man whose eyes burned bright with that blue angry fire. He opened his mouth to scream and his fellows turned, and then I ended all of them with a single cut. A wide slice with the great sword, its blade wreathed in blue fire.

Each of the three cuts from my single slash ignited, burning the spirits and collapsing them to the ground. In a minute they would rise up again, no longer dangerous.

"Quite the weapon that," Alec said. "For a second there I thought you would miss. Give that one an opening."

"Glad you have faith in me," I said.

"You're recently dead," Alec replied. "Figured you need some time to adapt. Might be a little slow."

"Haven't lost a step, believe me," I said.

Selena stepped past us and lifted the door's handle, an action the spirits hadn't thought to take. The back of the basement sat on the other side, a dark empty hallway. We went out into it, and turned to the right. Towards the rooms on the other side of the basement. I recognized this place; Anna and I crossed over into the last room on this side. The door into it was shut, and when I tried the handle it didn't move. Locked. So I did what no spirit would ever bother with.

I knocked.

155

"Who's out there?" I heard the voice on the other side. Recognized it.

"Laurence, it's Carver. And some friends. We're trying to find you, and Anna," I answered.

The door clicked a moment later, and swung open to reveal Laurence, Anna's fellow sneak and Chicago resident. He looked, to put it charitably, not good. His eyes were wide, and I noticed his mouth had picked up an unnerving twitch like he couldn't decide whether to frown or open up into a chilling scream. Laurence, who hadn't made any secret of his disdain for the guides, hugged me tight. So tight that I had to shift my arms up, keep the great sword out of the way as the man burrowed his head into my shoulder.

"I never thought we'd see another soul," Laurence muttered as he stepped back from me. "I never thought I'd be able to get out of this basement. That Riven would be closed to me forever."

"Seems kind of dire, doesn't it?" I said. "It's not like there aren't a bunch of guides running around."

"How many would come in here?" Laurence asked. "You

can't see the breach, not from the street. We realized that after the first day. It's in the middle of the building, along with all the spirits. They weren't making much noise when we came back here. Went up to the rooftop, and they caught our scent."

"Anna's on the roof?" Selena said. "Why?"

"We thought we could find a spot," Laurence said. "This building is one of the tallest in all of the city. From the roof you can see across every neighborhood. You can spot breaches miles away. If we held it, and established a line of communication to Bryce and the rest of the guides, we could direct them to any breaches quickly."

"So why are you down here, when she's up there?" I said.

"We took the risk," Laurence said. "Anna diverted their attention, and I made a run for it. We agreed that because she had a weapon, because she knows how to fight, that Anna should stay up top while I went down. I barely managed to trick the three spirits in the next room."

"We found them," I said. "They're taken care of."

"Pardon, I believe we should make a move up to the roof," Alec said. "Any delay seems improper."

"Yes, yes," Laurence said. "I had planned to travel to Ezra's. To tell you what happened. But now here you are."

"Always arriving just in time, that's us," I said. Then we turned and ran up from the basement. Our feet pounded on the stairs, Laurence taking the back. Up to the lobby, and then to the second floor. Up to the third. And then we stopped.

You could hear it, the growls and knocks of crazed hands beating on the walls. The hissing and half-whispered rage. The breach was here.

"Is there another stair?" I said to Lawrence. I'd been up this apartment building once before, when Anna and I tried to talk to the spirits we bound over at the Mountain. We'd taken the central stair all the way up. She never mentioned if there was a back way, but it seemed strange these steps were so empty.

"Thin and treacherous," Laurence said. "A fire escape. I never understood why one would need one of those in Riven?"

"There's a long story about where this all came from," I said. "I'll tell you later. If the spirits aren't running up this one, then they've got to be going the other way."

"That's a good thing, right?" Selena said. "Fewer obstacles before we get to Anna?"

"Theoretically," I replied.

"Hold on," Alec said. " I have a tablet. We can close the breach."

"Alec and Selena," I said. I pulled out my long knife, handed it to Laurence. "You too. Find the breach, close it. I'll go after Anna."

"You are sure?" Alec said. "We could split evenly?"

"The breach is more important," I said, and then I held up the sword. "And have you seen this thing? I'll be fine."

Selena rolled her eyes. I gave her a wide grin. Spirits liked to play hero too.

The trio broke off, headed down the hallway one step at a time. I hefted the great sword in front of me, both hands wrapped around the hilt, and dashed up the stairs. Once again, I was aware of how a spirit's endless stamina made running up floors holding a heavy weapon as easy as a light jog back in Chicago. I just hoped Anna would still be there for me to save.

156

I HIT the fourth floor and things became messy. A pair of spirits stood on the landing, snarling at each other. Fighting over who would get to go first. Two soldiers. Still sporting their ragged uniforms. I'd noticed as the war had gone on that the quality of gear worn by the spirits became thinner, shabbier. Used to be that they would cross over in clean colors, medals and ranks sewn into the sides. Now they wore barely more than rags. Whatever the countries could churn out fast enough to cloth their troops.

And yet, those simple uniforms sealed to the soldier's identity so tight that when they died, those rags came over with them.

"I wish more people would fight over me like you're fighting over those stairs," I said, coming up to the landing.

The nearer soldier glared my way, those eyes burning blue fire. Turned and leapt towards me, hands outstretched. The stair's height gave him plenty of reach, but proved little defense against my great sword. I swept it from right to left catching the spirit mid-jump and throwing him down the stairs as blue fire curled up and over him. Wherever the soldier landed, he would be walking to one place. The Cycle.

The second spirit tackled me back down the stairs, catching me before I could get the sword in position. We bounced off the wall, rolled over each other down the steps. Halfway back to the third floor. I kept rolling until I sat on top, level on a step. The spirit bit at me and I jammed the hilt of the great sword into his face. Knocked him back.

I would've loved to have had my long knife. To grab it with my left hand, take a quick jab to finish the fight. The great sword didn't do much in close quarters. So I did what I could. Raised the hilt again and jabbed the thing in the face a second time. Bought myself a moment of stunned confusion. Used it to bring up my knee and plant my foot on the spirit's stomach. Stood myself up and climbed back a couple of steps. The spirit rolled up after me, grabbing at my ankles. Fine. I rotated the sword in my hands and jabbed it straight downward. Right into the middle of the spirit. Sent him away with a burst of blue.

I went up the stairs, past the fourth floor to the fifth. I could hear the noises at the far end of the floor. Towards where Laurence said there might be a back stair. I had a choice. I could go that way, engage spirits here and fight my way up. Or take these stairs, the easiest route to get to the roof.

I favored the path of least resistance.

Up to the sixth floor and then the seventh. Or rather, to the door opening onto the rooftop. I listened before twisting the handle, but heard nothing on the other side. No clashing metal, no growls, no fighting. If Anna still lived, she'd cleared herself plenty of room.

I used my shoulder, pushed the door open with the sword held ready to stab forward into anything on the other side. Only I didn't see anyone. Not a soul on the entire rooftop.

Empty stones and the wide expanse of the city beyond the edge.

"Anna?" I shouted. "Where are you?"

"Carver!" I heard Anna's voice, off the side of the building. Down below the roof. I ran over, stomping across the flat stones. Stared over the edge and saw that Laurence had been right. A second stair clung to the building, black iron climbing up the side in a crisscrossing pattern. On top of that escape, holding a long line of gnashing and thrashing spirits at bay, stood Anna. She wielded the flail Nicholas had made for her in both hands, crushing it down on a spirit as it attempted to climb its way to her. Anna swung slowly, and I noticed she bled from plenty of cuts. Particularly a long gash above her left eye.

"Mind switching spots?" Anna said without looking up at me. Her voice was layered with exhaustion. "I've been here for a long time now."

"Give me some room," I said. Anna backed up, allowing a pair of spirits to gain a few more steps without her flail sweeping out in front of her. That was a mistake. I dropped off the rooftop, slamming the great sword in front of me as I fell. I caught the platform at the top of the stairs, and brought the sword down on both of the spirits. As I cleaved into the pair, I realized why Anna had chosen to fight here, rather than on the broader base of the rooftop.

The spirits that I'd wrangled stood there for a moment on the stairs, blocking the path forward for the angry ones behind. Confused and lost. Buying us time.

"Not a bad plan," I said. "Though, why didn't you use your sparker? That's what they're for."

"We did," Anna said, slumping back against the railing. "I used every spark I had. Only the sky is too crowded. So many lights now that it's impossible to know which ones truly need help. Or maybe nobody even noticed."

Coming back into Riven from Mali's canyons, I'd noticed the same thing. The sky a changing rainbow of colors as endless sparks splashed against the fog. Our main method of communicating became less effective the more we used it. If there were sparks everywhere, we couldn't tell which required the first, or any, response.

"So you were trapped up here?" I said.

"No, I stayed because I felt like it," Anna retorted. "Doesn't it seem like fun?"

"Sorry, bad question," I replied. The two spirits shuffled back through the line of angry ones and I took Anna's spot. Waved my blade at the grasping hands of the next wave, kept them at bay. And if they came too close, carved them in two.

"Did you find Laurence?" Anna said.

"He was enjoying the basement," I said. Jabbed at a spirit and sent him reeling back down the stairs, burning away. "You have to teach that guy how to fight."

"I will, with all that extra time we have," Anna said, then she perked up. "But if we can take this building, then I think it will help. Bryce doesn't know where to send his forces. We're responding, not being proactive. The more breaches we catch early, the less ghouls we have to deal with."

"We'll take it," I said. "Selena and Alec, they're busy dealing with the breach. Once it's cleared, we should be able to mop up the rest of these guys no problem."

"Thank you, Carver," Anna said.

"My fault you're in this mess," I said. "Think I owe you at least one escape."

We stood there, holding ground at the top of the roof for a while longer. Until shrieks started down below. Alec and Selena had closed the breach and were working their way up to us. When the spirits turned their back to me, I made quick work of them. We met up in the middle, on the fifth floor. Alec and Selena with grim looks on their faces.

"Where's Laurence?" I asked.

"He crossed over, after we saw the two of you up top. Apparently the two of you have spent a little while on this side?" Alec said.

"My body's probably dead," Anna said. "I'm only half joking."

"Then go," Alec said. "I'll tell Bryce about the building. Do not worry."

"We have to get moving too," I said. "Nara is waiting."

"She is not the only one," Alec said. "Everyone's waiting, Carver, go. Find a way to save us. Selena, do not let him mess it up."

"You're asking the impossible," Selena said as we pushed our way through stunned spirits.

"Carver," Alec said, and I saw him holding my long knife by the blade. "Forgetting something?"

He tossed the weapon to me and I caught it, felt the edge cut into my palm. Felt the slash start to knit itself back together immediately as I slipped the knife into its holster. My spirit covering for my mistakes.

We left the Warrens and headed east. The first time we left the city, Alec and Anna had given us a personal escort. Now we had none. Now the guides running around barely noticed us. We didn't have blue fire in our eyes, we didn't have a breach behind our backs, there was no time to investigate a pair of spirits. No reason if we weren't trying to kill them.

Riven was dying from a thousand gashes. The guides had to focus on the largest ones.

157

THE GRAIN FIELDS weren't as endearing as Riven's dark streets. Something about those endless stalks, knowing that they been made by a sick goddess with no love left for the person Mali had trapped made the waving plants even worse than before. I saw Selena shudder, felt like doing the same as we pushed our way through. Each and every one of these mirrored stalks the product of one person's delusion.

We made it to Nara's clearing quickly. Neither one of us cared to spend an extra minute in these fields. Her fire still burned, the grain stack the same height as when we left. The charred ruin sending thin smoke up to the sky and leaving the air with the smell of dry kindling. Nara herself wasn't out as we came in. Only appeared after we'd been standing there for a full minute or more. As though waiting for the proper moment to make her grand entrance.

Not that her frail form, robed and tired, could pull that off.

"I count only two of you," Nara said.

"Mali didn't like your offer." I sighed. "Didn't like us much either."

I launched into the story. The fight with the ghoul, Mali's water show, and kept an eye on Nara's face throughout. Her expression never changed. Not even when I shared Mali's comments, those harsh statements about whether Nara should be trusted. About whether her motives were true. That Nara would only bring Riven into further chaos. In fact, the only reaction I saw came when I told her how I'd stabbed Mali with the crossbow bolt. The blue fire burning away Mali's power, her consciousness. At those words, Nara closed her eyes for a second and I swore, I swore I saw a tear make its way down the creases in her cheeks.

When Nara's eyes opened again they were as fierce as ever.

"I should have expected that Mali would have lost her sight," Nara said. "Mali was ever the most attuned with the present. With what she felt in the moment. It made her such a great and terrible creator. Her whims built the city, built the forest, built this massive field. She gave no thought to where it was going, gave no thought to what she was doing."

"I wanted to ask you," Selena said. "If you knew why Riven's city is so close to modern? If Mali had been here for centuries, then why would she build a place that must be completely different from her time?"

Nara smiled, glanced over at the fire. "It wasn't always like that. The city has lived and died a thousand times. I haven't seen it in so long that I barely remember how it looks. As new spirits came to us, Mali would have them tell her of the world, and she would remake Riven to suit their tales. You say that she kept new spirits of her own. I assume, whenever she felt like it, Mali rebuilt the city."

"Wouldn't we notice?" I said. "If, say, a hundred years ago, the city changed itself?"

"Perhaps you did," Nara said. "Are there records? Written journals?"

"Some," I said. "But most are concerned with guides. Names and titles. Positions and laws. Riven itself always seemed to be the same. An endless task."

"Then perhaps that is your answer," Nara replied. "If the focus is ever on the spirits, then a world that changes slightly once in a lifetime may not be so remarkable."

Nara had a point. If I'd wandered into the Warrens tomorrow and found it made over with newer buildings, I might be confused for a moment, but at the first sight of a tortured spirit, I'd be back to the usual. Riven tended to kill the curious.

"Mali mentioned prisons," I said, switching back. "With the water, she seemed to show the three of you being divided. Is that why you didn't come with us?"

"When we parted," Nara said. "We had our differences. We realized that we posed a great danger to Riven with our struggles. So we sealed each other away. I had hoped Mali could part the barriers."

"I don't see any barriers," I said.

"The field," Nara said. "That is my prison. Dolan has his desert, and Mali her canyons."

"I don't understand," Selena said. "How? How can you seal someone to a single place?"

"Surely by now you accept that Riven has secrets to which you are not privy?" Nara said. "Perhaps, in time, you will understand."

I'd listened to guides give me vague statements all my life. Growing up with one sentence after another telling me to accept what I'd been told and not ask questions. To deal with the fact that some things weren't meant for me to know until some undefined 'time'. I'd bested the leader of the guides in combat, rescued and damned my own parents, and been murdered. What else could I possibly do to be ready to understand something?

"Nara." I unsheathed the great sword. Pointed it towards the woman. I felt Selena's eyes burning into me, but ignored her. "Explain. Or I'll assume what Mali said is true. I will end you here and take my chances with the spirits."

"A bold statement," Nara replied evenly. "And no doubt, Carver Reed, you are willing to take your chances. But what about her? What about your friends back in the city? Are you willing to risk all of them on your rash judgment?"

I narrowed my eyes and she held up a gnarled hand. "Still, perhaps you are right. You want to know why we are sealed? Go, find Dolan. He will tell you. If Mali can't help, then he is our last option," Nara said. "While the three of us would have been better, Dolan and I can still do what needs to be done."

"And why can't you tell us? Why can't you give us the answers?"

"Would you believe me if I did?" Nara replied, and I had to admit she had a point there. Already I'd started taking her every sentence with a heaping helping of doubt.

"You said he lived in a desert?" Selena said, shoving us past the tension. I lifted the sword away, put it back in its sheath.

"South of the city," Nara said. "In a sea of sand much like this field. If you keep walking, you will find him. Bring him here, and together we can help you."

Nara turned to go back into her hut, and Selena looked back the way we came.

"Wait," I said to the spirit's back. "I have one more question."

Nara looked back at me, her face a set line. No surprise, no irritation, no anything. "Ask."

"Mali. What she showed to us, it looked like you bound spirits. Many, many of them. How did you do it, if you weren't alive?"

Nara smiled, but I didn't like the hunger that came over

her crinkled eyes. A person reminded of her brilliance and eager to show it. "A living soul binds another through by giving part of their life. Like setting fire to kindling. A dead spirit binds the other way. By stealing what remains of the one they seek to control."

Her words clicked. Barth's tower, on the far edge of the city. The mad former guide had more than a dozen spirits doing his bidding, but most had lost their personality. Had been stock still and silent, save for the one Barth had directed to greet us.

"How many?" I asked. "How many spirits could you bind like this?"

"Why do you need to know?" Nara replied. "Are you getting ideas?"

"I'm trying to find yours," I replied.

"I have told you, time and again, that my true wish is to save my home," Nara spoke, annoyance drifting along the edges of her voice.

"You haven't said how."

"You are in no position to ask," Nara said. "Now, go. Your friends are dying while you dawdle."

I had no argument against that point. As Nara went back into her hut, Selena and I once again set forth through the field of grain. Marching back to the city, and then south, to another part of Riven I'd never seen.

Hopefully the desert, and Dolan, would prove less hostile than the jungle and its queen.

158

To get to the desert, we once again had to choose: go back through the city or around it. We made it back to the east gate without facing that decision, and, looking in at the broken Palace and the parade of sparks beyond, I glanced at Selena and shrugged.

"We go in there, we're liable to get bogged down," I said. "You heard Alec, there's no time to waste."

"You hear me arguing?"

"I, uh, no I don't," I said. "Guess I wanted to state my opinion."

Selena nodded, matched my eyes through the archway. "Come on, Carver. Let's go around the outside. Bryce and the others can keep it together long enough."

So we followed the wall south. Spent most of the journey bantering back and forth as to whether Nara would turn out to be the worst decision we'd ever made. After seeing Mali's show, I felt less and less like the old spirit in the hut would turn out to be a good call. That in trying to save ourselves, we'd wind up bringing Riven into an even darker ruin.

"Hard to get worse than world-ending," Selena replied when I'd spoken the thought.

"Do you trust her?" I replied.

To our right, the city wall continued. We walked on hard dirt, staying clear of the grain off to our left. Above, the same gray sky loomed over a breeze that blew ashen flakes around the air. I never really understood where those flakes came from, but they made Riven feel as though it was constantly snowing. Light flurries. Without any of the seasonal charm of the natural, chilly kind.

"I see someone who wants something, and thinks we're the best way to get it," Selena said. "My first husband, the alcoholic?"

"The one who fell from the apartment window?"

"Matthias, yes. We had a similar understanding," Selena said. "I didn't want to stay in the country. He wanted a wife and lived in the city, where I thought all that really mattered took place."

"That's naive," I said.

"What do you expect from a fifteen year-old girl?" Selena replied. "For a brief time, too, it was everything I imagined. Matthias used me, his new, pretty wife to get into the sorts of clubs and parties he'd not been invited to earlier. It was a deal, and we both made our profits."

"You're such a romantic."

"Please," Selena said. "You're no better. It's why we're perfect for each other. We're so bad at sharing sentiments that it took both of us dying to really fall in love."

I laughed. Couldn't argue with that. Before, when I'd bound Selena, there'd always been our unequal standing hanging over us. I could jaunt back to the other side while Selena had to stay in Riven. If I'd died, the binding would be broken, potentially sending her to the Cycle. Now, we needed each other. Needed each other's stories, their hand to keep the Cycle's whispers at bay.

Riven didn't have dinner dates. Didn't have theaters or a circus. But it did have time. We didn't sleep anymore, didn't get tired. Our moments came when we worked to wrangle a spirit, when we navigated the crowded jungle in Mali's canyons, when we filled the endless gray with stories we'd tell to each other. What we had wasn't a fairy tale, but I loved it all the same.

"So how does Matthias make you trust Nara?" I said.

"Because she will not change until she has what she wants," Selena said. "And when people get what they want, they let their guards down. If Nara starts to do something we don't like, we take care of her."

"Don't know that there are many apartment windows to push her out of in that field," I said.

"We don't need one. Not here," Selena said. I could tell without looking that her hand rested on the cleaver's handle. In that, Selena was right. If Nara decided to play a different game, tried to change the rules, we could end her just like we did Mali.

159

When we reached the south gate, on the other side of the Shambles and the busiest spot in Riven, I stopped and stared at the train of spirits. Thousands of them milled through the gate, heading out of the city and towards the Cycle. On a downbeat path that journeyed into the dark forest and up to the Mountain beyond. Technically, the west gate would have been closer, but the path went this way and the spirits followed it.

Maybe that's how Mali had designed it.

To the south, Riven's scraggly dead grass continued off towards the horizon. I wondered if it would be like the canyons, where we would be walking towards nothing at one moment and, in the next, see a new world open up in front of us.

"Why is it so crowded?" Selena said, marveling at the gate. "It wasn't this bad when we rescued Bryce."

"The breaches," I replied. "Normally spirits are spread out all over Riven, but now they're concentrating. When a battle on Earth forms a breach, it pulls in other spirits crossing over. Then you've got a big group. The guides wipe them out, and they walk here together. Join the rest."

"It's eerie," Selena said. All of those faces; men, women, children from across the world shuffling their feet one after the other. Looking straight ahead. Quiet and numb.

"It's peaceful," I said and Selena cocked her head at me.

"Suppose you could see it that way," she replied.

"I choose to," I said. "Easier to deal with if you look at it that way. A peaceful march to an endless sleep."

We ventured south, padding along the ground until I noticed that it began to give away. My footfalls landed on less firm soil. The dirt shifted, and my footprints left deeper indents. What grass there was died away.

"It's white," Selena said, looking ahead. In front of us, Riven's dirt fell into a silky sand, laid out in small drifts as though someone had spread a fine blanket of snow in front of us. Ash flakes fell on and vanished into the landscape, buried by Riven's slight breeze.

"At least it's not gray," I replied.

Trudging through the sand would have been a slog had we been alive. Able to get exhausted. I figured that's why nobody had explored these regions before. The canyons and the desert were so far beyond the walls of Riven's city that any living guide would have had to turn back. Perhaps with a succession of different spots to cross over you could gradually make your way farther and farther, but that begged a different question.

Why?

For nearly two thousand years, guides had operated in Riven without chasing the origins of its structures. Had stuck to their prime goal. Wrangle the spirits, keep the dead moving to the Cycle. Our numbers never gave us the luxury of sending guides out on expeditions.

Our. Still talking like I'm one of them. Not only was I a

spirit, no longer alive, but I'd killed Piotr, the last leader of the guides. He might have been chasing disaster, but I don't think I still qualified for membership in that esteemed group. I glanced at Selena walking beside me, her eyes bright in the light reflecting from the sand. I had what I needed.

The column appeared in a slow unveiling. A shaded obelisk on the edge of our vision that resolved itself and its fellows behind it as we came closer. As tall as the ones bordering Mali's temple, and similarly carved in runes. Behind the column, splitting it on either side, were more. A long row leading back to what appeared to be a wide cluster of buildings.

Laurence had a map, back in Chicago, that hinted at a town like this. A ruined place. If there was anyone that would take the leaps to get so far afield, he'd be the one. Now I wished I'd studied that map more closely. Much as I enjoyed walking into the trap in Mali's temple, I'd prefer to avoid the same situation here.

"Do you see it?" Selena said to me. "On the statue?"

I took a harder look as we walked up. And recognized it. The disk, the three figures plastered on the hard stone. The same image as Mali's show with the water. Nothing else adorned the statue, just a pile of sandy brick stacked on top of each other.

The next column continued the tale. The figures moving now, some of the thin blue outlines that I'd taken for spirits appearing on the disk. The same illustrations, the same story. It played out across the statues, each one showing the next scene as we went deeper and farther down the row.

"I guess that means Mali told the truth," Selena said. "Unless she made these too, and it's all a lie."

"Seems like a lot of trouble, but I can't put it past her." I ran a finger along one of the paintings. To see if it would flake off, but the columns were sturdy. Hard brick. "From what Mali said, it sounded like she made all of these places."

We made it to the warring scenes. Where the dark figures with the blue fire attacked the spirits. Drove them into the Cycle. Without Mali pushing the story along, we took some time to examine the figures. The paintings that brought them to life.

"Do you think these are the guides?" I said the Selena. "Wrangling the spirits and sending them back to the Cycle?"

"Can't think of anything else they'd be," Selena said. "Which would make that third figure the reason we exist."

"We?"

"Feel like I've earned it, Carver." Selena folded her arms. "Keeping you alive has to be worth something."

"The pleasure of my company isn't payment enough?"

"If only." Selena gave me a slight grin. "I know I shouldn't care. That it's pointless, given that we're spirits, but I never *belonged* to anything. Not once."

"Until now," I said, earning the full smile this time. "Of course, that means you can't walk away. Can't retreat to the far corner of Riven when things get dangerous."

"Because that's so like me."

"Just saying that the guides don't take freeloaders."

"They took you, so I think I'm good," Selena replied.

"Good point."

The next column held a picture of the three figures, standing apart and split by thick green bars. Mali had hinted that this had been when the three of them had locked each other away. But she never explained the prisons. Nara said she couldn't leave the field, but why? How?

"Do you think she couldn't leave the canyons?" I said.

"I think Mali was as trapped as Nara," Selena said. "And Dolan, he's trapped here."

"I hope he knows how to free himself," I said. "If we're going all this way as a waste of time..."

I went to the next column, the last. Like the first, it stood in the center of the path. The other columns fanned out on either side, regaling us through painted pictures the story of the three spirits and how they had made Riven into what it was today. This one, on three of its four sides, showed one spirit. Mali, Dolan, and Nara. Each one painted with green circle around the figure. The circle seemed to extend the line from one to the next. Mali, her hand outstretched, appeared to push the circle around Dolan. Who did the same to Nara, who brought the arc to completion around Mali.

Nara's reach cut across the blank side of the column, the entirety of that side a single green line lancing through the stones. As though something could've been there that was left off at the last. I felt a hand land on my shoulder, heavy. At first I thought it was Selena, and then I looked.

The wide, lost eyes of a spirit new to Riven stared back at me.

160

YOUNG, a boy not much older than twelve or thirteen. No marks of disease, no mortal wounds. The boy had the presence of mind to turn his spirit into who he wanted to be, rather than what he was.

"Carver, I have him," Selena said from behind the kid, her voice tight. Her cleaver no doubt ready to strike.

"Wait," I said. "Spirits shouldn't be showing up here. He should be pulled to a breach, or one of the other places in the city."

"The city?" the boy said. "Do you know where I am?"

I started to answer, but the boys eyes drifted away and, in the middle of my sentence, he began walking back behind the column. Further into the desert. Not unusual. Spirits had a lot on their minds, and their minds weren't exactly whole to begin with.

"Should we wrangle him?" Selena asked, coming up beside me.

"No," I said. "I didn't see any fire. Let's follow."

We paced the spirit deeper into the desert. Past the

columns and into what seemed like a small village. Single-story houses, their pale adobe-style bricks rising up from the white sand in square shapes. They felt old, but also pristine. A set constructed by a historian, or someone making a model in a museum. The spirit moved past the houses, didn't bother checking or looking in any of them.

"Who are you?" I asked the spirit, called ahead to it. Sometimes, pushing a spirit to remember who it was could give it a measure of sanity. Bring it back from the brink. The boy glanced back at me.

"My parents called me Turner," the boy said. "You don't suppose they're here, do you?"

Again, when I started to answer, the boy turned away and walked. Further into the town.

"He's not going towards the Cycle," Selena said.

"Which means he's taking us to where he came from," I replied. "We'll wrangle him there."

After a few more twists and turns through the desert streets, we came to a large courtyard. Stones paved across the center, and the wide square stood surrounded on all sides by more of the brick buildings. Several of these pushing two stories and one, across from us, standing a full four. The large building looked designed with a fine hand, its doorway bordered by twin columns culminating in an arch. Mali's temple, in desert form.

"There's a breach," Selena said, pointing. In the center of the courtyard the wide shimmering pool of a breach stared back at us. More spirits hovered around the edges. Looking around, curious. It must've formed only moments ago. The spirits not yet angry, not yet vicious and intent on tearing us apart.

"Turner," I said. "Is this where you wanted to take us?"

"I thought you could help my friends," Turner said. "We're all lost, you see."

My hand drifted to my great sword. There was only one direction for these spirits.

I UNSHEATHED the great sword from behind my back, leveled it out towards the boy. Selena drew her cleaver and long knife beside me. The two of us hadn't taken a breach solo, but this one wasn't burning. Not yet anyway.

"Carver," Selena said. "We don't have a tablet."

"Then we clean it up as best we can," I said. Without a sapphire tablet I wasn't sure how we'd close the breach, but leaving spirits around would, eventually, create an angry swarm. The breach would grow. Swallow the desert town and start pouring spirits north. Delaying that as much as possible still mattered.

Turner didn't move as I went up to him, as I twisted the hilt, as the blue fire burned up and over him. The other spirits turned to watch, gawking as I made my way around, sharing slashes with Selena. Wiping what was left of the spirits out of Riven so that their mindless souls could start on their last walk to the Cycle. Within a minute we'd cleared most of the courtyard. Or at least, that's what I thought.

I almost jumped at the first howl, so at odds with the silence of the place. The rustle of the wind on the sand, the occasional whisper of the breeze looping through a nearby house. Otherwise, the only noises came from the swishing of our blades. Until the newcomers made their presence known. They crawled from the breach without us noticing, one hand at a time. Hauling themselves out, looking like soldiers. Or natives from a land I didn't know. Breaches didn't discriminate.

A pair of spirits stood up from the pool, looking around. Their eyes flickered with the pale blue fire that meant all shred of sanity had left their souls.

"And just when I was getting bored," I said to them, waving the sword their way. The spirits hissed and charged towards me, their arms outstretched and clawing for my face.

I stepped forward with my left leg, leading into a wide swing that bisected both of the spirits and sent them burning away to the ground. Behind them, though, four more sets of arms appeared through the breach, pulling the spirits through.

"Finish up the rest," I said to Selena. "I'll handle the newcomers."

I ran over to the spirit arms as they appeared, and swiped down. First one, then another, and another with consecutive slashes. Burning them away as they crossed through into Riven.

Something snatched up my ankle, and I fell flat on my back. The breach spread up beneath me, a window into a ruined mountain town. That accounted for the variance. A war-torn village in a country I didn't know, soldiers and townspeople crossing through as shelling continued.

Not that I had time to appreciate it. The same spirit that had knocked my ankle aside clamored out of the breach on top of me. Clawing my coat as he climbed up towards my face. With my left hand, I grabbed my long knife off my belt, and jabbed it into the spirit's chest, twisted the hilt and burned him away. Only those seconds had already cost me too much time.

I pulled up to my feet, and two more spirits hit me from behind. I managed to move with the push, using the my jacket's loose skin to tear away from them. Left them holding shreds of leather. The two spirits continued coming for me, joined by another three to my right. Behind me, I could hear Selena hacking away at the others outside the courtyard.

"Guess I deserve this for being cocky," I said. Not that the spirits listened, or cared. Their burning blue eyes were interested in only one thing. Me.

I sidestepped left, and the two groups of spirits ran into each other as they turned to follow. Slipped the long knife back in my belt and gripped the great sword, went for a wide slash. One that should've chopped clean through all of the spirits. That would have, except the first spirit dove at me in a frantic tackle. Caught my arm before my swing could build momentum. Knocked away the great sword with his scrabbling hands. The rest followed in.

I raised my arms, tried to knock away the fists and claws, the teeth. "Selena!" I shouted. If nobody came in a second, I'd be torn to pieces. No idea if my spirit could recover from something like that, and I didn't want to find out.

Selena didn't answer, but I heard plenty of growling rage from her side of the courtyard. We were outnumbered, and we were losing. As a spirit bit at my face, I jutted my head forward, bashing into it and knocking the spirit back even if it made the world blur. I reached for the long knife, and when I jabbed it forward, I felt it bite, saw the flames take hold. Then the next spirit swatted the knife away. The lash wasn't any good here, too close.

A pair of hands grabbed my shoulders from behind and threw me to the ground. Another spirit, leering down at me with a smile full of rotten teeth. Wild eyes and frayed eyebrows. A wrinkled, splotchy face that suggested more than one encounter with the disease. The spirit leaned in towards me, his mouth opening to reveal craggy teeth sinking towards my face.

Pale fire erupted from his chest, as though the spirit had been stabbed through. Then something lifted the spirit up into the air and launched him away. Threw it to the other side of the breach. The other spirits reaching for me paused. A fatal mistake. A man, wearing a tan cloth shirt and pants, stepped over me and swung his arms, stabbing in through the air. Instead of weapons, every time his leather-wrapped hands came close to a spirit, wrangling fire would shoot out from his knuckles, spreading forward and catching the souls in its cleansing burn.

As the man swept the spirits away from me, I heard his laughter; bright, free-flowing joy.

The man, for I didn't know what else to call him, cleared out the breach with smooth strokes. Punches and kicks, mainly, but in the manner of one exercising. Testing his muscles, his reach. Several times the man glanced back at me, apparently making sure another spirit hadn't caught me unawares. He didn't wear a helmet, and his dark head was hairless, his eyes bright and burning around the edges with the same fire as the angry spirits. His teeth were as white as the desert sand, bared in a fierce smile. Before I could say anything, he bent down and picked my great sword off of the ground. Strode to the center of the breach, jammed the blade into it, the point cutting down into the stone. Twisted the hilt.

Blue flame poured out of the sword, spreading and covering the breach like an oil lake lit in flame. Everywhere the fire touched, the image of Earth, the ruined town disappeared. Crinkled away and revealed the white stones beneath. I searched for Selena and saw her at the edge, banishing a remaining pair of spirits with synchronized swipes and slashes from her cleaver and knife. In a minute it was over.

"Been a long time since I've seen this sword," the man said as I stood up, his voice tinged with ash and fire. "Like meeting an old friend. One you never thought you'd see again."

"Dolan?" I said, because who else could it be?

"Seems you know I am," the man replied. "Now I'd ask the same of you? Who comes to play out here, in these desolate ruins?"

"People who come to find you," I said.

Now Dolan's grin faltered. Sank into a line. He glanced at the sword, still held in his hands. "Not much use coming for me," Dolan said. "I had my time, and this isn't it."

"Not sure that's your decision to make," Selena said. "Riven needs you, Dolan. Whether you like it or not."

The spirit laughed, a loud grumbling thing that bounced off the walls of the houses around us. "A bold announcement. And you may not be wrong, as I haven't seen a breach in this ruin for a thousand years or more. Unfortunate then, that I cannot leave it."

"Are you sure? Nara sent us," I said. "She wouldn't have, if you couldn't come with."

When I said the name, Dolan's eyes flared, and his teeth bared into a snarl. Before I could move, before I even knew what was happening, Dolan darted forward with my sword and stabbed me with it. Blue fire ran up and around me, and burned my world away.

When I died, I mean when Piotr had me killed back on Earth, it'd felt like falling down an infinite well. Bits of me disappearing as my soul untethered itself from my body. This, this was more vicious. Whereas before my physical body fell away, now my mind dissolved. My memories, my sense of who I was, where I was, what I was vanished. I would say that everything went black, but that's not true. It didn't go anywhere, didn't become anything.

Just ended.

I came back on the edge of the courtyard. Dolan stood in front of me, his hand on my forehead. His eyes still burned, not in the pupil's center as with the angry spirits, but more as though the edges glimmered with that pale flickering flame.

"I'm sorry," Dolan said. He stared at my eyes, apparently searching to see if I was really there.

"Yeah, you can back off now," I said, pushing him away. "What did you do to me?"

"I brought you back," Dolan said. "Something I haven't done in centuries."

I'd done it before. With a binding, you could restore a spirit to some semblance of their former self. Rescue their mind. I'd brought Selena back after the ghoul on the way to the Mountain demolished her. I hadn't known what it felt like to be torn away and put back together. I didn't want it to happen again.

"Well that's lovely," I said. "Mind explaining why you decided to torch me in the first place?"

"You said Nara sent you," Dolan said. "That alone is reason enough."

"They don't like each other," Selena added.

"Got that, thanks," I replied. "Mali told us the Nara wasn't exactly your best friend. You have to look past it. If you don't, then everything falls apart."

Dolan glanced at the courtyard, where the breach had been. "I believe you. Except, there is a difference. You do not release a river to extinguish a candle."

"Excuse me?" I said.

"Whatever she said to you," Dolan said. "Nara will doom Riven more surely than anything you could ever imagine. You are a spirit, and you would be in her chains. She would rule over all of you without a second thought, and you will have no say in the matter."

"Do you have a better idea?" I said. "Because if our options are to die horribly as Riven tears itself apart, or be ruled by a power-hungry spirit, then we might as well torch ourselves here and now."

Dolan stared back at me, then let his eyes cast around the ruins. "You mentioned Mali. I assume Nara sent you to her first?"

"She's gone," Selena said. Before I could speak up, Selena launched into the story.

Dolan took the speech in stride and, by the end of it, nodded as Selena wrapped up with our return to Nara. "Then you have happened on a stroke of luck," Dolan said. "You won't need Nara anymore, because I can do it better."

"Do what better?" I said.

"You are staring at the founder of the guides," Dolan said. "If anyone can lead you to victory against a horde of angry spirits, can cleanse Riven of the foul stench of the dead, it is I. And with Mali gone, at last I am free."

Oh, good.

163

DOLAN DECIDED our instruction in Riven's history at Mali's hand hadn't been good enough. As we began the long walk back towards Riven's city out of the desert ruins, the ancient spirit began to tell us his version of the tale.

"If you want to know how Riven came to be, it starts with the three of us," Dolan said as we went through the sand. His eyes wandered the distance, floating back through memories. "We came into Riven within moments of each other. Each of us, all of us, victims of an attack on our village by a neighboring one. All of us were young, barely fifteen years old. That didn't matter. The attackers came in fast, slaughtered everyone and presumably took everything that was ours. The next thing I knew, we were standing here, on a flat piece of rock fifty or sixty yards across."

"How do you know what a yard is?" I asked him, and Dolan blinked at me, annoyed that I'd broken his recitation.

"If you want to jump ahead," Dolan said. "I'm happy to do so."

I shook my head, as it was obvious that Dolan was not,

would not, in fact be happy to do so. After a moment, the spirit turned back to his story.

"If you've seen what Riven looks like now, it shares nothing with the Riven that I knew when I came here. There were no trees. No mountains. No walls. No city. The dead were our only companions. They came to the one spot they could. An endless river of spirits and souls dropping onto our little patch and stepping off into the great blue ocean of the Cycle. I watched them. I don't know for how long.

"If you think time holds little relevance in Riven today, it held less then. Nothing measured how long we stood there. No buildings to tell a history of wars, no scraps of paper to write down the passing of days. Eventually, the three of us noticed each other. Found in our inaction, in our hesitation to walk off the edge, a common bond. Nara and Mali's eyes, like mine, tracked the endless walk of our countrymen without joining their journey. Mali spoke first.

'Are you alive?' Mali asked us.

"We did not know, then, what had happened. Whether we had died or whether some mystical event had forced us into this strange new place. Our gods had no stories of a world like this one. Our elders had no tales to prepare us for such a void as Riven. So in our confusion and our loneliness we bonded over the endless years.

"Our friendship kept the Cycle at bay. Its whispers quiet, hovering at the edges of our consciousness. As children will do, we started to play. To test the boundaries of the world we were in. The dead spirits us didn't mind as we pushed them around."

"You three were the only ones that stayed?" Selena said. "No other spirits came over questioning where they were?"

Dolan paused, his foot settling into the sand at the top of a rolling dune. The look he gave Selena held the same sadness I'd seen on a thousand spirit faces. Regret that cannot be righted.

"That patch became our castle. Our sanctuary. Anyone that didn't start the walk to the Cycle became a problem. Someone that might attack us. Attempt to rule us." Dolan twisted into a defiant mask. "We are not saints. We were a trio who found ourselves in a strange and unfamiliar place. Without guidance, without knowledge. But Riven was ours, and we kept it."

"That's evil," Selena said.

"Selena," I cautioned.

"She's right," Dolan said. "My, our, only defense is that we knew nothing better. Only that the spirits that fell into the infinite blue never returned. That our patch was small. And that, in our experience, newcomers only meant loss."

I could see more questions dance around Selena's lips, but she kept them closed. Dolan waited a moment, then began his march. Continued his story.

"Over time we began to see the cracks in Riven's facade. The pieces of this world that didn't quite connect. It started when one spirit fought back. When I managed to overpower it, and break its neck. Only to have the same spirit heal itself and stand back up an hour later. That was our clue, that the normal rules did not apply.

"Nara was the first. She realized she could find a way to attach to the spirits. To hold their hand and gain their trust and eventually, control them. Those were momentous hours. Mali and I watching Nara go up to each spirit in turn, take its hand, and speak softly to it. You must understand, such an act as the binding came to us as out of one of our legends. Magic, you might have called it, though in time we understood binding to be more akin to love than to sorcery.

"As Nara proved to us that our conception of reality didn't hold sway in Riven, Mali played with a different sense.

Projected her dreams and desires out into the gray. I never understood quite how, and Mali never explained it to us. A jealous keeper of secrets, that one."

"Seems to fit with her character," I said. "She didn't want to talk much with us."

"Always more interested in her own mind," Dolan said. "It's why I wound up trusting her more than Nara. Mali wanted her own world, but she didn't feel the need to destroy this one to get it."

164

<hr>

"So she didn't tell you how to create things yourselves?" I said. "And you didn't ask?"

"We asked," Dolan said. "Both Nara and I. Except, as you've seen, talent still chooses its targets in Riven. Mali harbored hers, and neither Nara nor I could ever master more than the simplest creations. For me, that meant these."

Dolan nodded at the columns we were walking past, the ones coated with paintings.

"Spots of color," Dolan sighed. "That's all I could ever make. Nara even less. Her attention tuned inward, to the workings of the soul. With Mali's growing ability, we became kings and queens, living in grand castles in the middle of the city. Nara bound spirits and questioned them, brought us information from the world outside. I acted as the enforcer, working with Nara's spirits to push any reluctant souls into the Cycle.

"I began, before long, to have Mali make weapons to arm Nara's souls. To arm myself. A few of the spirits had become aggressive, resisting our escorts to the end. With the long shaft of a spear I found my own talent. A curious dip in the

Cycle, the spear's point vanishing beneath the surface, sent the pale fire up its length and into my body.

"I should have been destroyed then," Dolan paused, brushed at the edges of his eyes, where the faint blue hue still shone. "Except Nara's spirits, my bound allies, pulled me back from the brink. Brought my passive body back to Nara, where she ignited me. Brought me back."

"Then you owe her your life," I said.

"To a degree," Dolan admitted. "A debt I have long since paid back, I assure you. After Nara returned me to myself, I could feel the fire raging in my soul. If the Cycle whispers to you, it screams at me. And like a shriek, I found I could let it out. Pour its energy into things, like that spear. Like your sword.

"It didn't take long for the city to crowd with lost spirits. Nara became more obsessed with binding them, demanding that I take care only of the ones that appeared sentient, to know where they were. Nara turned to Mali to create streets and stores, buildings large and small. Replicas of places the spirits would tell us about. Riven's city grew larger, and I found more spirits wandering its alleys. Lost and growing angry."

"So you took action," I said.

"No," Dolan replied. "Though I wonder what would have happened had I started sooner. Before Nara became enraptured with the lives she was spinning in our dead city. As your world grew, more souls crossed into Riven. Nara couldn't bind them fast enough. The spirits would turn on her, on ones she had already charmed. The bright streets became dangerous, and Nara looked to me.

"Mali and I created the weapons together. She molded the edges, I imbued them with the fire. At first we gave them to Nara's spirits, and they patrolled the streets with deadly efficiency. Tireless warriors. With only one master."

"You didn't like that," Selena said.

"We were a trio." Dolan nodded. "Now, we were Nara's prisoners. Mali realized it first. When Nara requested a change to part of the city and Mali denied it. Said she preferred that neighborhood as it was. Only when Mali refused, a pair of Nara's spirits holding my weapons appeared at her door. This time, it wasn't a question.

"From then on, Mali and I began to recruit and harbor those sane spirits we found. Built them up and trained them in secret, in a mountain on the edge of the forest. Well away from Nara's fantasy world."

"We've been there," I said. "To the Mountain."

Dolan looked north and west, towards where the Mountain would be. "Mali made it to cover the Cycle, to hide what we were doing. She claimed to Nara that it would allow us to control the spirits coming in, and it did. We took and trained those we could. In time, we had an army of our own.

"I don't know how long the war lasted. Only that Nara ran out of weapons before we ran out of souls. At the end of it, standing in Nara's grand room, we made our worst mistake."

"You trapped yourselves," Selena said. "That's why you split up."

"We tried to bind her," Dolan said. "Rather than simply send her to the Cycle, which is what we should have done."

"It didn't work?" I said.

"Nara tried to do the same thing," Dolan said. "Bind us as we bound her. The conflicts wrecked our minds. Nearly drove us all to insanity. Mali herself leveled half the city, built it up and brought it down. As though a thousand voices yelled in our minds at once. Nara, you don't understand, she can command your every idea. Your every feeling, if she chooses. So Mali and I clung to the only thing we could control, which was our connection to her.

"We sent Nara east, into the fields. Made her walk every step, and then forced her to remain in that clearing. At the same time, we could hear her whispering to us. To Mali and I. Soon after, I found Mali at my throat, coming for me with Nara's curses spilling from her lips. After that, we left the city. I came here, where the desert sand and distance kept Nara's voice quiet. I think Mali and myself would have thrown ourselves into the Cycle years ago, except doing so would have freed our enemy."

"If what you're saying is true, then bringing you back is a risk," I said. "Can't Nara overpower you?"

"Maybe," Dolan said. "Though all things change with time. Perhaps I can resist her urging now, or control her with my own binding. Better still if we do not test the theory. Better still if we can quiet Riven without involving Nara."

After what Dolan had said, I was all in favor of that.

165

Bringing Dolan, an ancient spirit, into the middle of the guide headquarters went over about as well as I expected. Guides are taught to treat anything new with more than a bit of suspicion. Especially spirits, and one that looks like Dolan, wearing clothes no guide would sport, was just an excuse to take extra precautions. Guides watched us from buildings as we walked, sneaks trailed us from the moment we entered the city.

Bryce had an operation running, and it ran well.

Even so, I saw the cracks. Other guides crossed our paths, dashing by in front of us and ducking down alleys. Calling for help to close a breach, or wrangle a group of spirits. Still, the chaos seemed better controlled than when Selena and I had first left the city for Nara days and days ago. I even let myself feel a rush of hope. That maybe, somehow, we'd manage to control the city. Break out and stem the tide of angry spirits.

Bad idea.

By the time we made it to the clock tower courtyard and Bryce's haphazard command center, the leader of the guides expected us. Alec walked the three of us into a cluster of senior guides, standing around a large table cobbled together from doors torn off of their hinges. On it, marked by chunks of broken stone, sat landmarks I knew.

The Mountain. The city walls. The gates on the south and west sides.

"For a makeshift war, I'm not impressed," Dolan announced after introductions were made. "You are letting the spirits come right up to your doorstep. You should be driving them back. Take the breaches one by one until there are none left."

"I don't know what the numbers were like in your day, sir," Bryce said. "We have neither the manpower or weapons to make such a move."

"With me, you do," Dolan said. "I will lead your finest to the west gate, into the forest, and clear it. From there we will forge a straight path to the Cycle and keep it patrolled. Make it easy for spirits to find their way to their everlasting home."

"You talk as if the breaches are not constantly moving," Bryce said. "They pop in and out. We close one and another appears in a completely different part of the city. There are no paths to patrol, there are no single regions to hold. They are everywhere, and we're not."

Dolan stared back at Bryce, thinking hard. Or at least that's what I thought he was doing. Perhaps, after so many centuries, the idea of holding a strategic conversation was new to him. So I figured I'd better step in.

"Bryce, I think Dolan has a point. If nothing else, cleaning out the older breaches in the woods can buy us time get rid of some of the ghouls and maybe bring us to another solution."

"Leaving the protection of the walls will allow such a force to be surrounded," Bryce said. "Here, if a breach appears, we have reinforcements. Help is all around you. Out there, in those trees, you will be swarmed by spirits looking for souls to devour. Ghouls by the dozen. The west gate is constantly pressed as it is."

Bryce spared me a nod. "That spirit, Cheo, and his tireless force is the only reason we are not there now fighting for the city's life."

"Your guides are too terrified to risk their lives for Riven?" Dolan said. "Too scared to wade into danger?"

"They have no fear of danger," Bryce said. "No love for suicide, either. We have families, Dolan. People on the other side that depend on our return. Throwing that away in an uncertain attempt is not an order I can make."

"Then you are a coward," Dolan replied. The rest the room looked at the spirit, and the stares weren't friendly. Including my own. "I created the guides as a force for Riven. To face its dangers without fear. A sword against the plague of the dead. Now you say that you are nervous about the cost you might pay? You should be honored to pay it!"

All of us sat silent for a minute. I wasn't sure what to say. How to calm the tension. Then Bryce did what he'd done for me countless times. Found a way.

"I cannot understand where you came from," Bryce said to Dolan. "I do not know your life. What circumstances brought you here to us. Carver says you are a force for our side and I choose to accept his judgment. But here, in this place, you are not the leader. Whatever you might be, you are not a guide, and here guides make the choices, and we do so without threats." Bryce turned to me. "Carver, you left to find a woman. Where is she?"

Selena and I explained what happened. How we found Dolan, and how Nara still lived in her hut in the field. Dolan said nothing. No outburst of anger, no harsh asides casting aspersions on Nara's motivations and her character. No, he stood there and stared at Bryce. His eyes calm.

If I knew anything, I'd guess Dolan was finally evaluating Bryce. Taking a measure of my mentor's person against Dolan's centuries of experience and finding where Bryce landed among all the spirits Dolan had ever known.

"So you're proposing that Dolan is as good or better than your original option?" Bryce asked me when we concluded, and I nodded. "That we should listen to him?"

"I don't know if his plan will work," I said. "But I do know that doing nothing will get us killed. Going back to Nara may well be worse, if what Dolan says is true. With those facts in hand, in my view, we should at least try."

Bryce turned back to Dolan. Gave the spirit a nod. "We will allow you to take a force of spirits. My guides may follow. Provide support at a distance. If things go well, and I hope they do, then we will commit more of us to the attempt."

"If that is what you can give, then that is what I would ask," Dolan replied, nodding his head. "Now, if we can get started. It has been many, many years since I have had the pleasure of a good fight."

"So who goes?" I asked the group around the table. "Who wants to brave the ghosts of the forests, the ghouls and the breaches? Because Dolan and I can't do it alone."

Dolan caught the inclusion. Adding myself to his cause. The old spirit gave me an appreciative nod. Selena, behind me, chimed in her name.

"I'll go," came Anna's voice, from the back of the room. I hadn't even seen her there. "Laurence can take my shifts watching from the Warrens."

"I can't let Carver get himself killed, so I will go," Alec said. A number of other guides echoed his cheery observation and before long we had a group of thirty ready and willing to risk their lives in our impossible mission.

166

WE STARTED out west from the clock tower courtyard. Went through crowded avenues and by the apartment that I'd long since left to Nicholas. Which reminded me that I hadn't seen the scientist for a while.

Selena and I split apart from the pack and dropped in. I briefly wondered if Nicholas had blown himself to pieces, given that, from the outside, his lab appeared quiet.

What we found inside, what we saw, wasn't what I'd expected. The machines that once covered his lab; crude furnaces and forges, gadgets crumbled together from whatever junk Nicholas could lay his hands on, were gone. The only thing that still remained in the room sat in the center. A spherical device that Nicholas hunched over, back to us, looking like a man madly devouring a meal.

"You've changed things around?" I said to Nicholas and he jumped at my voice.

"Carver," Nicholas said, turning his goggled eyes towards me. I noticed more than a few singes along the man's face, and his ever-dirty coat had reached a stage of filthiness that rendered its definition as clothing suspect. "I was not expecting you. With more notice, I could have prepared a better presentation."

"Presentation of what?" I said.

"Ah, this." Nicholas stepped aside and waved at the object. Without the scientist in the way, I had a better view. The ashen-metal ball resembled what I'd seen of artillery shells used in the war. Nicholas had been reaching through a flipped-up access door. I tried to peer inside, but, without sticking my head in, I couldn't make out anything. "You remember my orange rays? From the crossbow?"

I nodded. The rays jumped from one object to the next, devouring and destroying anything close by. And by destroying, I meant ruining utterly. Disintegrating into nothing. Obliterating souls seemed dangerous, so I tried not to use the weapon all that often.

"This device will send out so many more," Nicholas said. "At twice the range. It will keep burning until there is nothing else to grab."

"Where do you think we would use it?" Selena said. "Spirits don't sit still and wait for you to detonate a bomb."

Nicholas looked beyond us, out the window on the first floor and into the street. "The city is crowded enough. The rays should be able to leap across the streets. If we used the device in your clock tower square, the entire city should go up."

"That doesn't sound like victory," I said.

"I am not aiming for victory. I am aiming for survival," Nicholas said. "The device will annihilate most of the spirits. If the guides cross out ahead of the explosion, they will remain. Riven will be reset, and we get another chance."

I let the words sink in. A reset button. If we triggered the device as the war wound down, as disease stopped the insane flow of spirits, then a reset might be all Riven needed. A chance to escape. We just had to keep Riven going long enough to set it up.

"I like it," I said.

"You like it?" Selena said. "You like that he's made something that can destroy all we have?"

"Please, Selena. We don't really have anything. Mali thought this up ages ago. It's not ours. It's not real. The only thing that is, is you and I. What we have. That doesn't need the city."

"Nicholas," Selena said. "Who's going to trigger the bomb?"

"I will," Nicholas said. "I'm the only one can. Who knows how. And I won't teach you."

"What? Why?" I said.

"Because, Carver," Nicholas said. "You have Selena. Graham and Katherine are no longer here. That leaves me alone. With as much time as I've spent with these cold machines, I'm getting tired. Getting lonely. This device is my way out. A swan song, I believe they call it."

"We'll buy you enough time to use it," I said.

Nicholas nodded. It felt strange; talking about the end of someone. Normally, a spirit's end came through the Cycle. A slow walk to peaceful nothing. A journey triggered, perhaps, by my wrangling lash. Yet here was a soul planning self-sacrifice. To remove himself and take our troubles with him.

"You're a good man," I said to Nicholas. "A great scientist."

"Do not tell me what I already know," Nicholas said, the man's smile flavoring his words. "Now go buy me some time. The device is not ready yet."

167

THE WEST GATE leading out of the city stood tall and grand, the opposite of the factory remnants of the Tar Pit that came before it. I could make out Cheo's golden ghoul from blocks away, standing in the middle of the gate as though single-handedly barring the passage into the city. Only when we closed did I realize that's exactly what the ghoul was doing. It braced its legs against the ground, a pair of large stones from one of the factories dragged behind it, to help the ghoul keep its balance. Its hands were outstretched, palms spread out against the gate. A gate shut for the first time in my memory.

On the other side we could hear the clamoring of angry spirits. The hammering as their fists struck the solid wood barrier. I couldn't tell how many spirits were out there, not from the ground. So Dolan, Selena and I made our way up to the top of the left turret.

Cheo stood up there, staring down at the horde attempting to gain entry. A true mass. More spirits than I'd ever seen in one place. They stretched out in a wide semi-circle all the way from the clearing at the gate to the edge of the forest. A hundred yards or more. All of them were shrieking, wailing, waving their hands in anger at some distress that I could never know. The spirits were all types: men, women, children, grandmothers and grandfathers. Races from across the globe. Cultures equally varied. A man in a soldier's uniform might stand alongside a woman in a tribal headdress, both of their eyes burning with the pale angry fire.

"This is not a battle we can win," Cheo said. "The Right Hand does not have the forces for this. The ghoul will not hold forever."

"Seems to be doing a good job so far," I said.

Cheo shook his head. "They are starting to climb on one another. Eventually, they will climb these very walls. Once that happens, the real battle will begin. It will end shortly thereafter."

"Everyone's all doom and gloom today," I said. "First Nicholas, now you. Dolan, cheer me up?"

The old spirit looked out over the mob. The wave of burning blue eyes. "I've seen a force like this before," Dolan said. "Nara did similar things. Brought an endless stream of enemies to our doorstep. Thrust them against us like a battering ram. Do you know how we beat them?"

"Do we look that old?" Selena said.

"We used what they did not have," Dolan said. Tapped his head. "The spirits do not think. They are not bound, they cannot adjust their tactics. We lay a trap, we open the door, and we bring this fight to an end. So think, my friends. What snare can we set?"

"I have an idea," I said, thanking Nicholas for reminding me of the very weapons I already had.

First, we took my crossbow and unloaded the orange bolts. All three of them. Then, we laid them out on the ground, one spaced out from the other across the gate. Safely behind the door as the ghoul held it. Once the bolts had been spaced out we drew back, assembled our guides and the Right Hand's spirits around the opening. Far enough back to be out of the range of those blistering orange rays.

"Fair warning; the rays might destroy the gate," I said.

"We won't need it anymore," Dolan said. "After this, we strike out. Carry the fight to the breaches in the woods. Slow them down and end them. If your man on the other side can fulfill his part of our bargain, then that should be enough to tip the scales."

Bryce had crossed back when we left. Crossed back in yet another attempt to warn the world against its cataclysmic course. For his part, Bryce said that the war was dying down anyway. A lack of soldiers. A lack of national will. But the faster the conflicts could be resolved, the sooner we could gain control on our side. The sooner Nicholas would be able to flip a switch.

"Let's go," Dolan ordered and the ghoul complied. The beast rocked back on his heels, his hands leaving the door. Immediately the pounding grew, and without the ghoul's hands supporting the gate, the sheer pounding force from dozens of tireless spirits began to break it apart.

A crease appeared in the gate's middle, then a crack. The hinges groaning alongside the archway. You would've thought that such a massive thing would give way slowly, but no. When the gate lost its hold it was open in an instant. The large doors twisting and breaking along their sides. An endless flood of horrors pouring through towards us.

"Weapons ready," Dolan said. He shifted the great sword, my great sword, into a forward stance with his hands. Point facing towards the spirits. I drew my lash and long knife. Selena held her cleaver at the ready. Then a spirit stepped on the first bolt.

The orange ray exploded, blossoming and dancing and cutting and burning its way into the charging ranks.

Nicholas' weapon worked best if the targets were close, and these spirits were as close as you could get. Smothered into one another as the stampede surged forward. The burning orange rays shot through all of them. Jumped and split from soldier to sailor. From bartender to baron. The spirits vanished as the blossoming glow consumed them.

By the time all three bolts had been triggered, by the time the growling roars had ceased, the only thing in front of us was a charred ruin that had once been a gate. The stone walls had burned away, the archway collapsed, but there were no spirits.

I didn't know how many thousands upon thousands had been obliterated by those bolts, but I did know the idea had come from Dolan. The ancient spirit had proved why he deserved to lead. Why I was happy to follow.

"Do not rest," Dolan announced. "For this is only the start. Ready yourselves, for now we charge."

168

DOLAN COULD RUN. The ancient spirit wasn't willing to wait an extra moment, and after we saw him sprint ahead five long strides, dancing around the rubble and the scorched remnants left behind by Nicholas's burning rays, we joined him in the rush.

The guides fanned out behind Selena and I, along with Cheo's squad of spirits. A motley crew. Our number, compared against the angry souls we'd just decimated, was nothing more than a pittance.

Dolan wanted to get to the breaches before more spirits came through. I knew we wouldn't make it. We weren't that lucky.

We were halfway across the clearing when the next wave began emerging from the woods. The forest's gray trees and their dark leaves hid the spirits until they broke out. Appearing as if from nowhere and running headlong across the open plain towards us. Their blue eyes burned with hatred. Hatred that they didn't know or understand, yet acted upon regardless.

Dolan lifted the great sword high. "Never stop running!" Dolan shouted to us as he led. "Take them as they come and move on to the next. Find the breaches, seal the gates, and reclaim your world."

And then the spirits were upon us.

I tried to stick close to Dolan, to Selena. But in the melee, that was an impossibility.

The first spirit coming towards me looked like a soldier that had caught the wrong end of a mortar. His torn arms outstretched, reaching towards my throat as he ran, and without stopping I cracked the lash in front of me. The point burrowed into the soldier's chest and I lit him up in blue. Yanked the lash away as he collapsed in front of me.

I whipped the lash at another spirit on my right, heading straight for a guide. Caught him in the shoulder and twisted him, burning, to the ground.

Turning back towards the woods, I saw another rushing at me. This one a woman wearing a hospital gown. Another disease victim. She died a second death on the fiery edge of my knife. I shoved her off and kept forging ahead. We were nearly to the tree line.

Dolan had already hacked his way into the woods, but his shouts, loud whoops of thrilling excitement and encouragement, gave plenty of clues as to what way he slashed. Beside me, Selena finished a thorough dicing of a suit-sporting man and took a second to look across our line.

"We're not going to move fast," Selena said. I agreed. Too many spirits poured from the forest. Our band was being surrounded, despite the fact that we were working our way through with brutal efficiency. Plumes of blue fire erupted constantly around us as spirits were wrangled and sent to the Cycle. Yet, between the snarls of rage and howls of anger, I caught cries of pain. Strikes inflicted on the wrong side.

"We can't stop here," I said. "Dolan's right, our only chance at slowing the spirits down is right now." I didn't wait for Selena's nod, but dashed into the dark trees.

691

169

THE FIRST BREACH sat a few yards beyond the forest's edge. A lime green pool expanding to fill a clearing beneath the dark canopy. Dolan, as I approached, ducked beneath a pair scrabbling arms and dished out a fatal cut. Then, without pausing in his move, he twisted the hilt around in his hand and stabbed the sword straight down into the earth. Just as I'd seen in the desert; bright flame poured into the ground and burned away the breach. Different than the sapphire tablets we used. Not necessarily better.

Spirits on the edge of the breach crawled away, escaping the flames. Our tablets, they would grab everything within the area. Every spirit would be pulled back and cleansed of their fury. But then, a tablet would have grabbed me too.

"On to the next one," Dolan said to me and Selena as we caught up.

"We're getting ahead," I said. "If we leave them behind, they might be trapped."

"If we don't move," Dolan said. "We will be."

The ancient spirit turned and advanced, slicing through another pair of burning blue souls.

"He's losing it," Selena said. "Dolan's going to get us killed if he keeps going like this."

"We're already dead," I said. But she was right. The guides straggling behind us were scratched, wounded, or were fighting through exhaustion. Spirits continued to pour from between the trees, and my lash cracked again and again and again. My knife stabbed more times than I could count. I didn't have muscles that tired, but my friends did.

I had to get them out of here.

"Anna!" I shouted. And I heard the answer, somewhere in the woods. "Sound the retreat. Get the guides back to the gate. Hold that line. We'll take it from here."

The guides around us heard my words and backed away, formed a tight cluster then went towards the west gate. I went the other direction. Cheo and his Right Hand joined us, and I noticed some taking to the trees as they had in Mali's jungle. Their wrangling arrows split the air, piercing and cleansing spirits we didn't see.

Battered, we happened onto the second breach. Followed Dolan's trail of wrangled spirits and slashes biting deep into the trunks. Except this time, Dolan wasn't having it so easy.

In front of him loomed a ghoul, a two legged thing seemed that had no arms, like a living archway. It lunged forward and shifted its legs to any angle it wanted. As though made out of rubber, or sand. As we entered the clearing, Dolan rolled forward, ducking under a wide sweep of the creature's front leg. Rather than continuing its motion, however, the ghoul sank back to the ground, and scooped its legs the other way, wrapping itself into a circle and pinning Dolan into the middle.

The ancient spirit tried to move the great sword, but the ghoul crushed him too tightly. No room, no range of motion.

I started to make a move, then Selena shouted and I turned. Too slow. A spirit, some sort of ragged deliveryman, tackled me and shoved me to the ground. His claws, sharp fingernails, raked my cheek. I felt the heat, and if I'd had blood, I'm sure it would've been running. I rolled to the left, using my shoulder to shove the spirit off of me. Stabbed with the knife in my left hand. Sent the spirit away. And then two more replaced it.

"Help Dolan!" I called, not sure Selena could hear me. The spirits bit and tore at my cloak, at my arms and legs. But they couldn't kill me. At least not for a while. If that ghoul took Dolan, then this whole thing was lost.

One of the spirits wrapped its arms around my neck and tried to crush my throat. I jammed my head into its face, which I didn't bother recognizing. There were too many, simply too many souls to note specifics this point. All of them burned the same, all of their teeth clicked and gnashed towards me. Their hands were all cold and hard. They weren't the people they had been.

My head knocked the spirit's own back, which gave me enough room to move my left hand and jab upwards towards the spirit's hip. Or at least, I tried. A third spirit joined the pile, pinning my arm and my knife to my left side. I felt my legs go numb. The second spirit ripping my knees apart.

I wasn't sure how much damage I could take until I ceased to be. I didn't know at what point I could be overwhelmed. Whether I could be ripped so far that my soul would not be able to put itself back together. I didn't want to find out.

With my right hand, I dropped the lash and gripped the spirit that sat on me. Wrenched my arm to the right and threw the ghost off. Grabbed the knife from my left hand by the blade and pulled it out of my own grip. The spirit I'd thrown off tried to dive back on, but it wasn't fast enough. Still holding the base of the blade, I jammed it into the spirit as it tried to regain its position. Slipped my hand down to the hilt and twisted. Ignored my own searing pain to save what was left of my life.

I withdrew the knife and lunged into the spirit tearing into my left arm. Took care of it. Though I could no longer feel my left side, except for the pain. All of the pain. I'd been burned, I'd been beaten, I'd been slashed and bashed in this world. But this ripped a new layer of agony through my mind. I think the only way I maintained any concentration at all was by focusing on the shouts of Selena and Dolan as they tangled with the ghoul.

They were my friends, and they needed me.

I leaned forward, sat up and stabbed. Brought an end to the spirit that had made a meal of my legs.

I tried to stand up, only I couldn't feel my feet. Couldn't feel anything, in fact, outside of my right arm and my neck. The ground rumbled beneath me. Overhead, swinging in a lazy arc, came the large left foot the ghoul. More like an elephant, or a large Greek column than any human appendage. The ghoul's leg hovered over my head, and I could see the dripping scars, the slashes made from Selena's cleaver and Dolan's sword. I could see that leg come down towards me. And I could do nothing to stop it.

A flash of gold, and then the leg flew away. The ghoul, from what mouth I did not know, roared its outrage as Mali's creation battered it away. Pounded the ghoul with large gold fists. I looked over and saw the two-legged monster collapse under the fbarrage. Saw Selena and Dolan, limping, stick it with their blades and send their blue fire racing along the ghoul's body. A moment later, Dolan did the same to the breach.

For the moment, we were clear. For a moment, we were alive.

170

"You're hurt." Selena walked up to me as I sat on the ground, looking and feeling pathetic.

"You've seen the obvious," I replied.

"We have to keep moving," Dolan announced from where the breach used to be. "If we stay here, they'll catch us. On to the next one."

"Carver is wounded," Selena said. "You can't walk, can you?"

"I'm going to have to sit this one out," I said. "Think Goldie over here can carry me back to the gate?"

Selena glanced at Mali's ghoul, its formless face looking back at us. "I don't think you're that heavy, Carver."

"Then go with Dolan," I said. "Close the breaches. And make it back."

Selena bent down, gave my forehead a quick kiss, and then she and Dolan were off. Sprinting further into the dark forest. Cheo and the others followed, the ghoul staying behind and lifting me up.

I'd never been carried like this before, in the arms of a giant creature like this one. Lofted above the ground. The peace didn't last long. Not thirty seconds into our walk, the first spirits arrived. Drawn by the sound of our crunching and grinding through the brush. The ghoul snapping branches as we pounded through them.

The spirits dove at the ghoul's legs, biting and clawing at its metal skin. So far as I could tell, they weren't doing any damage. At least, not physically. But they were wearing it down. The ghoul slowed, every step held back by the grasping arms. Spirits clinging to the legs; pulling and dragging. Trying to force the ghoul down. With both its arms holding me, the ghoul didn't have much in the way of defense.

But I did.

I reached inside my coat, to the holster Nicholas had made for me after I'd found Inman's pistol. I kept the weapon loaded, had more bullets inside my coat's pockets. The guides had plenty of ammo, although the bullets were made from Riven scrap. Nothing compared to the quality you'd find on Earth.

I drew the gun, it's gold barrel seeming very out of place in the gray dark forest. Aimed it, and fired as the ghoul stepped forward.

The bullet picked off a spirit on the ghoul's left ankle. I cocked back the hammer, aimed, and fired again. Another spirit knocked off to the ground. The shots didn't burn with blue fire, just hard metal. But every spirit I knocked away allowed the ghoul to speed up. Pulled us closer to that gate.

I fired another four times until, with a click, the pistol told me it was empty. I'd have to reload with one working hand. Not exactly something I knew how to do.

Maybe I wouldn't have to.

The ghoul crashed into the large clearing in front of the wall. Shouts and cries of guides and battle blew into my ears. I could see it; the mass chaos around the ruin where the west gate once stood. The guides that had come with us, along with reinforcements, manned the line of rubble. Held back a wave of spirits trying to claw their way through. Dolan's idea; those burning orange rays, had given us an opening, had damned our defenses.

"Anna," I yelled as we came closer. I could see her, wielding her spiked flail and waving it back and forth, bashing and burning spirits as they charged towards the guides. "Let the ghoul through. It can hold the line for us!"

The guides, whether they heard me or saw the golden beast, cleared a path for us to pound through. I had the ghoul set me down on top of some broken shards of the gate. Not exactly comfortable, but the sooner I was out of his hands, the sooner the ghoul could go back to doing what it did best: mashing spirits to a pulp.

Like Inman's pistol, the ghoul couldn't wrangle the spirits. Couldn't burn them in blue flame and send them running. But it could stamp them out. Knock them down and render them incapacitated so a guide following along could finish the spirit off.

And the ghoul was tireless.

I watched, crippled and useless, from my vantage as Mali's monster tore through the spirits. Had there been the thousands from before, I had no doubt the ghoul would have been overwhelmed. Covered and simply borne into the dirt by the weight of the spirits. Now, with only dozens, the ghoul was free to wreak its destruction.

"What happened to you?" Anna said, walking over. I could see the sweat shine on her face, the fatigue evident in how she held her weapon low. Breathing hard even though Riven had no air.

"Outnumbered," I said. "Turns out letting spirits tackle you is a bad idea."

"Thought you'd have learned that by now," Anna said. "Selena? Dolan?"

I told her where they were. Told her that the success of this whole mission stayed entirely with them.

"If they can't close more breaches, then we sacrificed the gate for nothing," I finished.

"Not for nothing," Anna said. "We closed some, and we gave us hope. A chance that the guides might do something rather than die in alleys and dark rooms."

"That hope won't last long," I said.

"That's up to you. How long before you're able to move again?"

I could feel it; my bones, such as they were, knitting together. Feeling returning to my arms and legs. Slow, but it would get there. Before too long I would be back, as dangerous as ever. Such was the magic of being a spirit. Such was the benefit of being dead.

"When Selena gets back," I said. "I'll be ready."

What I didn't know is what I would be ready for. Either another raid deep into the woods, or a retreat to Nicholas and his desperate bomb.

171

AT FIRST GLANCE, they didn't look good. The two of them, Dolan leaning on Selena as they emerged from the woods. The great sword dangling across Dolan's back, held on by its sheath. They stumbled across the clearing, spirits bursting out after them. I heard Anna call for the guides to assist. Saw my friends and fellows break away from the line and guide Dolan and Selena home. And I saw in my love's eyes that we had lost.

"You're still here?" I said to Selena as she came up to me. As she sat Dolan down alongside my shredded body. As she collapsed to the ground.

"I shouldn't be," Selena said. "They should have torn us apart a thousand times. I should have died a thousand deaths, Carver."

"But you didn't," I replied. I glanced at Dolan. The spirit's eyes were shut. He bore a number of nasty gashes and wounds. Perhaps, like me, he was waiting for them to heal. "Is Dolan alive?"

"He'll be okay," Selena said. "No worse than you, I think."

"Cheo? His spirits?"

Selena took a breath. How funny that instinct should live out past our lives. Past the point where our brains cease to be. Yet here we were, still taking a moment and inhaling nonexistent air before delivering bad news.

"Five," Selena said. "We'd been moving fast. Breaking in, Dolan sealing each breach with the sword, and then running. By the fifth one, though, we'd lost some. Too many."

"Lost?"

"The ghouls," Selena said. "They can't kill a spirit, send it to the Cycle, but they can consume them."

I saw the fear in her eyes. Then remembered that it had happened to her. Devoured in the forest by an old ghoul, Selena had ceased to be. At least until Anna and I had rescued her. Ghouls were simply products of spirits, a mass of cold anger and hate. Confusion and loss. Brought together to spread ruin.

"They caught up to you," I said. It wasn't a question. I knew from her look that Cheo and his spirits were still out there. Were now a part of some creature that would likely be making itself manifest before too long.

"There were two more waiting," Selena said. "Two more ghouls around the breach, attacking each other. Absorbing one spirit after another as they crawled through the breach. They were feeding, Carver."

"I suppose there's enough for them to eat," I said.

"They stopped when we came in. I don't know how to describe them to you, but they were shapeless things. Gluttons that had lost any limbs that they may once have had. They came for us," Selena's voice trembled here. Wandered up and down in pitch. Traumatized.

Sometimes I forgot, with all the we had seen, that it was always possible things to get worse. You could happen upon some new terror that rendered you at a loss.

"There wasn't anything I could do," Selena said. "Dolan

tried. Made a charge into the center of the breach and stabbed the sword down. That's when the first ghoul hit him away. Knocked him into the edge of the clearing. Both ghouls went after him. So I closed the breach. Went to the blade and twisted the hilt and sent the fire down."

"At least you closed it," I said, the words sounded lame coming from my mouth. Not nearly enough to fill the void for emotion.

"I didn't realize it," Selena continued. "Behind me, Cheo and the others, they attacked the ghouls. They were trying to save Dolan. In a way, they did. Distracted the ghouls long enough for me to pull the sword out, grab Dolan and run. I left them there, Carver."

"You did what you had to do," I said. "Cheo wanted peace. Now he has it."

Selena laughed, a hopeless chuckle. "Peace? Inside of a ghoul? I don't know, Carver. That's not any peace I would want."

"I can't argue with that," I said. "Except to say that maybe it will be worth it."

Selena looked back out across the spirits. The guides. Fighting each other in an endless dance. More guides were arriving from the clock tower, from the city, while others backed away from the front lines. Wounded or exhausted. A rotation that would be carried out indefinitely.

"We should use it," Selena said. "Nicholas. His device. Let's use it and end this madness."

"You know as well as I do that's not a permanent solution," I said. "You know as well as I do that if we leveled the city, the breaches would come back the same as before. We need something better. We need Bryce to succeed on the other side."

"Even if he does," Dolan said, his voice creaking up from beside me. "Even if your man stops this war. Even if this disease ends. There will be more. There will always be more people, more souls flooding Riven. It will be impossible to hold."

"This, from the most optimistic spirit I'd seen in a long time?" I replied.

"This, from a spirit that has seen the end. We have no other choice, Carver," Dolan said. "We must go to Nara."

"Didn't you say, not all that long ago, the Nara was the worst choice we could make?" I said.

"She's the only one that can create an army big enough to keep Riven safe," Dolan said. "The only one who can save us from total annihilation."

"Then we failed?" I said.

"We have," Dolan replied. "There is no other way. We cannot close all the breaches, and if we cannot cut off the spirits, then we cannot survive."

172

As time went by, with us laying in the rubble knitting our souls ack together, the guides formed a more organized perimeter. Runners established routes, carrying ammunition, weapons to those who had broken theirs, and calling for reinforcements as needed. Injuries were carted away on makeshift stretchers. Crossing points close to the west gate were identified and communicated so guides on the other side could have an easier time of coming to the wall. To the ruins.

But the swarm never ended. The spirits kept coming. Yes, they were mindless. Yes, they stood in each other's way. Those that had been wrangled often waited around for some time, giving guides a moment of relief before they were shuffled out of the way by the next wave of attackers. It wasn't easy. The repetitive boredom of the attack played into our human instincts. To where a guide might expect a moment after wrangling one spirit only to find the next one right behind, reaching for their throat.

Eventually, I was able to stand. Leaning on Selena. Dolan,

less hurt than me, went along in front of us. We set off, leaving Alec and Anna in charge of holding the wall. I'd never left a fight like that before. Walked away from the guides who needed me.

I recalled my parents, in the bowels of the mountain, fighting Piotr and yelling at me to leave them. Those had been impossible odds like this one, so perhaps the fights weren't so different after all. Or perhaps I was a coward.

"You'll do them no favors by staying," Dolan said after I'd glanced back one too many times. "However many spirits you destroy, there will be double that coming after them. The best way for you to help your comrades now is this."

"And what is this?" I said, pouring my frustration in the my voice. "What are you expecting Nara can do? What you couldn't?"

"I told you," Dolan said. "She will take the spirits, she will bind them together, and she will make an army that can cover Riven. Restore it to peace."

"Then why didn't we go to her from the start?" Selena said.

"Because it took both Mali and I to contain her ambition before," Dolan said. "I'm not as confident in myself alone."

"We'll be there," I said. "And besides, if Riven falls, Nara falls too."

Dolan only nodded, then lapsed into silence. I remembered the paintings, Mali's show. If Nara truly represented a terror greater than what was already happening, well, we'd have to risk it. Certain failure on the path we'd tried. With Nara, we had a slight chance of success.

By the time we reached the clock tower courtyard both Dolan and I were walking normally. Our souls repaired. Bryce hadn't yet returned from the other side, which I took as a positive sign. If he was making headway over there, then that might make up for the lack of it here. We didn't stay long. I gave a quick update to the guides holding the command center, and then we were off. Marching east towards the grain field once again.

The trek to Nara's felt shorter this time. Perhaps because Dolan, as soon as he was able, pushed us to run. Claimed that because we could not get tired, we may as well travel as fast as we could. Lives were in the balance. I didn't argue.

Running without end felt strange. As though at any moment my muscles would wake up and realize that they shouldn't be doing this. That sprinting down one block after another, through neighborhoods and towards the east wall, past the palace and out towards the green without a single pause for breath was wrong somehow. But I didn't. My legs never protested. I didn't drown in sweat, or fall apart as my body gave out. Eventually the strangeness of it all faded. I was living in a new normal. I had no body, not a real physical one anyway, and it was time I learned to use it.

Nara stood outside her hut when we approach this time. Stared past us right at Dolan. Locked eyes with the spirit, but otherwise let no expression cross her face.

"It's been a long time," Dolan said first.

"I'd forgotten what it felt like," Nara said. "To have you close enough to feel the binding. I don't like it."

"If I could stay away, I would," Dolan replied. The spirit then told Nara what had happened. Our failed defensive. The overwhelming numbers of any spirits flowing from the breaches. Not once did surprise cross Nara's face. Not once did she show fear. Instead, that same straight gaze stared at Dolan the entirety of his tale.

"So can you help us?" I asked when Dolan had finished.

"Help you?" Nara said. "It sounds like you need a little bit more than help. You need a savior."

"Don't let it go to your head," Selena said.

"Why shouldn't I?" Nara replied. She moved over to the ever burning stack of grain and poked it with a loose stalk. "Here I am, tending this fire for all eternity, until the three of you decide to pay me a visit after trying every possible way to avoid doing so. You tell me that all is lost. That your friends and families are suffering. That I am your only salvation. If I am not your savior, than who could ever be such?"

"When I first came here," I said, brushing over the argument. "You told me that I could help you. I've done that. Brought you who you asked. We need your end of the bargain."

"I cannot argue with that," Nara said. "I believe I know how to repay you. I can do as you asked. I can reach out, once I'm close, pull the spirits in and drag them into my net. Save your friends. Your world."

Hesitation hung in the air as her voice trailed off.

"But?" I said.

Nara turned away from her burning grain pile and came towards me. Closed until she was barely a foot away. I stood my ground.

"The problem with being a savior," Nara said. "Is that everyone expects you to save them. Even from themselves."

"Explain," I replied

"Carver, back away from her," Dolan said, a different edge to his voice. I heard the great sword being lifted from its sheath.

And then I felt something alien. Nara reached out and touched my chest. Her hand pressing onto me, and then into me. I've binded spirits before, but this was different. Rather than joining, Nara's technique felt more like theft. Nara took my will, my voice and my choice way. My senses were replaced with shadows of themselves, held by strings leading back to her.

In a moment I went from knowing who and what and

where I was to waiting for Nara to tell me, for her mind to inform me. I stood still, rigid. Stared into Nara's eyes and knew what had happened, knew there was nothing I could do about it.

173

"CARVER, WHAT'S GOING ON?" Selena said. I wanted to turn my head to her. To warn her. But I was a prisoner in my own body. I couldn't move. Until Nara gave me an order. The compulsion, Nara's binding pushing my mind to take Selena and throw her to the ground. Less an outside command and more an irresistible urge.

Knocking Selena to the ground was the *right thing to do*.

I turned, looked at Selena and gave her smile. "It's fine," I said. "Nara is going to help us."

"What?" Selena said. As she squinted her eyes at me, I stepped forward, wrapped my arms around her shoulders, and pulled her over my leg and onto the ground. Nara bent over Selena while I watched, but before Nara's hand could touch her, Dolan shoved his great sword in between. Pushed Nara back.

"Dolan," I said, drawing the lash in my right and the long knife in my left. "Nara is trying to help. This is how she does it. Stand aside."

Dolan glanced at me, then turned to Nara. "I had hoped the years had softened you. It appears I was wrong."

Nara slanted her head at him. "Softened me? I waited, trapped here in this field, for centuries. The only thing I had to nurse was my vengeance. Now I shall have it."

"Even if it costs you everything?"

Nara laughed. "It won't. After you, I will take Riven back and turn it into the paradise it was always meant to be."

"You don't deserve to be a god," Dolan replied, then lunged forward with the sword. Straight for Nara. Selena backpedaled away, while I stepped between Nara and Dolan's strike. Deflected the spirit's sword with my knife just enough for Nara to shift away.

Dolan settled his eyes on mine. I gave him a nod. I respected his skills. I did not respect his stance.

"Please," I said. "You know this is our only choice. Do not sacrifice yourself for nothing."

"She speaks through your mouth now," Dolan said. "I am sorry, Carver. You deserved a better end."

Dolan lifted the great sword, pulled it up and left, then stepped forward into hard swing at my head. Not something I could counter. So I rolled, fell to the right and let the blade whisk over me. Came up to a crouch and flicked the lash at Dolan's ankle. Caught it as the spirit slowed his swing, and I pulled. Should have swept Dolan off his feet.

Instead, the spirit dug his heel into the dirt, halting my yank, and then swiped down with the great sword. I dropped the lash, so it fell loose and Dolan's swing missed the cord. Didn't want my weapon severed this far away from Nicholas, the only one I knew who could fix the thing.

I stood up, backpedaled as Dolan strode towards me, the lash dragging behind him. My empty right hand reached into my coat, pulled out Inman's pistol. Properly loaded and ready. Aimed it at Dolan's face, and he paused.

"You're not fast enough to catch this," I said.

"Resist, Carver," Dolan replied. "This is not your doing."

The problem with Dolan's words is that they didn't go into my ears. Or rather, the mind that heard those words was not my own. So I pulled the trigger.

Dolan staggered, the bullet punching a hole in his chest. No blood, of course, but every blow still hurt. More importantly, it kept Dolan's attention on me. At least, until he heard the scraping sound of Selena's cleaver leaving its sheath.

Dolan looked behind him, saw Selena moving into position. I saw in my love's eyes the same spirit that had taken mine. Nara, watching from the edge of the clearing, held a small smile. Two new prizes to start her collection.

"Give it up," I said to Dolan. "This is a fight you cannot win."

"Don't you understand?" Dolan said, holding the great sword in one hand, the other over the bullet's wound. "She cannot leave if I do not let her. Or unless I am dead. Which do you think she has chosen?"

I struggled in that moment. Pushed against Nara's voice, whispering in my head. Telling me to fire again. To knock Dolan down and allow Selena to end his misery.

Do it. Nara spoke in my mind. *Let him free.*

My finger tightened on the trigger. Dolan's sad eyes watched, rimmed with the pale fire that had been burning him for a thousand years or more. And I stopped.

No. I replied.

Nara's fury flowed through the bond, and I felt myself losing control. If Nara wanted to move me herself, I couldn't stop her.

Dolan must have seen the flickering fight in my eyes, because he shifted his feet. Darted in an attack. But not at me. Not at Selena. At Nara. The great sword sweeping along the ground, burning with blue fire, to destroy our hope and our damnation.

My next bullet struck Dolan in his right shoulder, but the spirit barely flinched, racing across that clearing. A brief panic flashed over Nara's face, and then a long knife appeared, jutting out of Dolan's back, burning with blue flame. As Dolan crossed the last couple of yards towards Nara, he stumbled, the sword fell out of his grip, and as the fire began to crawl over him, the old spirit collapsed in the dirt at Nara's feet.

Selena drew back her arm, empty without her knife, and watched. As did I.

Nara bent down, picked up Dolan's head with her hand and angled his face towards her. I couldn't see his eyes, couldn't read the pain on his face, could only feel the immense satisfaction flowing through my connection with Nara. Could only hear her words as they slipped out of her sanguine smile.

"Goodbye, old friend."

174

I SLID the great sword into its sheath, slung over my back. Looked towards the break in the grain where, a moment ago, Dolan had disappeared on his vacant journey to the Cycle. A hand landed on my shoulder, light and firm.

"It feels good, doesn't it?" Nara said. "To have your weapon back?"

I nodded. My mind, otherwise, ran blank.

"It is a proper sword for a champion," Nara continued. "Did Dolan tell you that part when he lied to you?"

"He did not," I replied. Nara's words prompted a question, a thought: *lied to us?* But the idea of asking it fled, vanishing from my consciousness without consideration.

"Riven used to be a bustling world," Nara said. "Where every spirit had a home. A new beginning. A chance to pursue passions without the weight of reality upon their shoulders. With no need for food, for shelter, no fear of death or time, anything was possible. Until Dolan and Mali saw fit to destroy it. They were scared, I suppose. Thought my methods cruel. Dangerous. As do all who see things they do not understand."

Nara turned me around to face Selena, who had put her weapons away and watched us with a solemn face. Waiting for the command of her leader.

"Until he decided on another path, Dolan was my sword. Was my champion. He protected my city, Carver. Now I ask the same of you," Nara said, then broke into a low laugh. "Well, *ask* may be the wrong word. Once you've seen the faults in loyalty, it's easy to see the advantages in obedience. In ownership."

Nara pointed towards the grain, and we moved. I heard her walk behind us as my arms pushed the stalks aside. Clearing a path for Nara's new freedom.

As we moved, I tested the limits of Nara's control. She'd set me to a task - clearing the path - and within the bounds of that task, it seemed I could adjust my approach. Move a stalk with my left hand, then the next with my right. Or use both arms. I tried just bowling them over with my shoulders and that worked too. Try and stop moving, though, and nothing. My body simply didn't respond.

Earlier, with Dolan, I'd felt Nara direct my thoughts. Alter my mind. My words. But when the spirit wasn't focusing on me, my soul came back. Like waking up after a deep sleep, I had to connect with my senses, my limbs. Understand what I could and couldn't do.

I glanced over at Selena, who marched resolute beside me. No idea if she was finding out the same things.

"Selena?" I said, more to see if I could speak than anything. I felt Nara's glance snap to me as I said the words. Felt her mind press in on mine, searching for my objective. Relaxing when she found only curiosity.

"Carver?" Selena replied, meeting my look. "What are we going to do?"

"Whatever she wants us to," I replied.

"Correct," Nara said from behind us. "Take the opportunity to get used to your new existence. Understand that you are on a leash. One that can be long or short, according to your actions. I have no desire to hurt my champions, and would rather focus on things other than your next move, so please, treasure our relationship."

"Treasure," Selena said. "You just killed our friend."

"No," Nara said. "You did."

"That's a lie," I replied. And then dropped to one knee. My eyes shut. Mouth clenched. Not my doing. My mind ran away from my body, curled up against a crushing headache. Dolan was going to the Cycle because of what Nara made us do. Right?

Or had we done it on our own?

Hadn't Dolan turned on us? Drawn his sword while we spoke with Nara? Discussed the plan to save Riven?

He'd tried to kill Nara. Unprovoked. She had no weapon.

"We had to stop him," I said to Selena. "There was no other choice. He would have ruined our last chance to save Riven."

I saw Selena's slow nod in reply. "I had to," Selena said. "It was the only way."

"Regrettable," Nara said. "But we do not have time for grief. Come now, keep moving."

I stood back to my feet, reached out, and brushed the next stalk out of the way. Put one foot in front of the other. Dolan had turned traitor at the end. Tragic, but inevitable. His plan had failed, after all.

Now we had a new leader.

175

THERE WERE two guides waiting for us at the east gate. Watching to see if we had succeeded. One of them I recognized; the wiry guide that had worked with Piotr. Who may very well have killed me on the other side, trapped in the hotel room in New York City. The other I didn't know, but it didn't matter.

"This is Nara," I said as we walked up. "She's going to save us."

Polk looked past me, nodded at Nara. "Where's the other one? Dolan? Where you all traveling together?"

"Dolan has to see some other problems," Nara said. "I'm pleased to meet you."

Nara stepped forward and reached out her hand. Polk took it. I saw the change come over his eyes, the moment when he lost control. The moment when Nara took him for one of her own. The other guide, however, didn't seem to pay much attention. He was looking at Selena, and I realized my love had drawn her cleaver.

"You won't be needing that here," the guide said." "There's no breach nearby. Kept it clean for you."

"Just in case," Nara said, placing her hand on the guide shoulder. In a moment he, too, belonged to her.

From down the street, we heard a noise. A shuffling as another guide stepped out of a squat guard post, just inside the gate. I knew him. Derringer. Only instead of friendly eyes, his face was covered with suspicion.

"Derringer," I called. "Come here, say hello."

"Don't think I will," Derringer said. "See, I saw a lot of Piotr's work. Saw how those bound spirits reacted when he talked. Saw how those eyes matched his stare the way yours all match hers. I know what I'm seeing."

And then Derringer ran. Nara didn't speak, didn't say the words, but I felt the order. The call to catch Derringer and bring him to heel. To make him respect our leader. So the four of us took off at a dead sprint. Chased Derringer over the wide stone courtyards between the Palace and the statues that made up Riven's east side.

Derringer wasn't a small man. Wasn't slow, either. Chugged ahead, pumping his arms and his feet the way a true runner does. But he was human. His muscles burned. Selena and I picked up ground, running closer, harder. Derringer tried to duck behind columns, weave between streets and take back alleys at random, but it wasn't enough. He couldn't avoid our endless energy.

The streets had closed in by the time we finally caught up with him. Buildings lined either side of the broad avenue. The ashen flakes so common to Riven blew into my eyes. Then Derringer stopped, huffing, hands on his knees.

Selena and I came up behind him. I had my lash and knife ready, Selena with her cleaver. Inside my mind I felt Nara pushing me to end him. To burn him and turn him into a spirit that she could then rebind when she caught up with us. Beneath that call I felt my own boiling heat. Derringer had been with Polk, with my body in that hotel room. One of them had pulled the trigger, cut my cord to the other side.

I wanted him dead as much as Nara did.

"You know what happens if you kill us?" Derringer said. "The line's barely holding at the west. It's going to fall any day, any hour now. When it does this whole city will be razed to the ground by rampaging angry spirits. You think your new one can save it?"

"I don't think," I said. "I know she can."

"Well this is a hell of a way to start," Derringer said.

I raised the knife and Derringer glared back at me. Time to a erase that face. I moved forward, drew my arm back. And felt searing pain tear into my shoulder. I fell back onto the street, heard the gunshot's echo as it ricocheted down the avenue. Not what I'd expected to happen.

"It's not going to work," said the familiar voice. "You are covered, Carver. Surrender, and perhaps we can free you from your curse."

"Alec," Selena called, and yes, she was right. I knew that voice. "You are in the wrong! Nara wants to help Riven!"

I counted faces in the windows, a number of them aiming long guns down at me. The resources they must've pulled from the wall at the west gate to wait for our return. A return they expected to be triumphant, to bring miracles. To save their dying friends on the other side of the city.

Now the west served only to safeguard the doomed.

"Selena, it is a tragedy to see you so," Alec said, walking up the street towards us with a pair of guides on either side. "Our offer is for both of you. Put down your weapons. Talk peace with us."

I stood up, the pain from the bullet starting to recede already.

"We cannot," I said. "And you cannot win."

One of the guides in the building next to us shouted and

vanished from the window. Attacked from behind. Nara's voice filled our minds, telling us to run. To pull back down the street and find her some blocks away. Another guide yelped across the way. As Derringer turned, as Alec turned to the noise, Selena and I bolted. I heard bullets strike the ground around me, but then we dashed into an alley and were gone. Blitzing through buildings and around corners and curves. The route Nara wanted us to run appearing like a map before our eyes. A compulsion telling me to take a left, then a right, then to go straight through a ruined store.

We found her at the top of the decrepit apartment, the haphazard stairs giving us a stumbling hike to the top floor. At the edge of the center of town. Nara stared out a window over Riven. Neither of the other guides were there.

"Two sacrificed for your folly," Nara said. "Next time, catch your prey more quickly."

Selena and I apologized. In unison.

"It seems your guides have improved over the years," Nara said. "The kind of organization needed to have layered formations never existed in my time. Dolan must've been proud of his legacy."

"The guides are strong," I said.

"But not strong enough," Nara snapped back. "Still, the guides need not be our first foe. There are easier paths for us to walk. Fear not, Carver. We will save your world and we don't need the guides to do it."

176

We moved south. South and west, skirting the edges of the main guide territory around the clock tower. We stuck to alleys, to side streets. Cut through buildings. Crept along little canyons between ruined structures. Whenever we happened upon a spirit, Nara would have us restrain the lost soul while she bound it to her. Then she would send the spirit out ahead of us and in various directions, scouting to see where danger might be. We avoided breaches, which would attract guides. We dodged clusters of spirits that could be seen by others. Or that could, potentially, attack us before we were ready. But as we went further and further, and Nara bound more and more, I began to notice around the edges of my vision, in the windows of buildings we passed and down streets that we did not walk, spirits flashing by. They were always there, always watching. Forming a ring around us.

Nara did not speak, and Selena and I had no words to say. I felt a growing sense of despair. Despair that nonetheless mingled with the slightest hope. Nara herself may not be the savior we were hoping for. Neither, however, did she want to see Riven destroyed. She might save Riven, even if what remained wouldn't be the world we knew.

We reached the Shambles and the southern gate, the beginnings of an army walking around us. Several dozen spirits trod in our wake, or led our advance. Nara bound everyone we came across. With a quick shake of her hand, a palm on an unsuspecting back, she added another one to our force. I began to see how she had accumulated so many spirits so quickly. How Dolan and Mali had grown to fear their friend. If in a matter of hours she could collect hundreds of souls, in a matter of days she could have thousands. Eventually, millions. Then there would be no force capable of stopping her.

Yet, I felt there was some chance of survival. The guides, after all, could cross out. Could leave Riven behind. If Nara ruled an army of the dead, at least they would not touch the other side. They would not come back to Earth.

We were not long into the forest, walking along the trail the spirits took to the Cycle, when a familiar rumbling shift the ground. The trees to our right emerged several ghouls. Ones I'd seen earlier, chasing Dolan and Selena on their quest to close the breaches.

"What should we do?" I asked Nara. She only grinned at me.

"Watch," Nara said.

The ghouls stomped towards us, all three of them large, vaguely humanoid monsters with random collections of arms and legs. They pounded the ground and scooped up spirits as they went, devouring them into their bodies and growing larger with every one. Until Nara sent her wave.

Her new army moved in a giant cluster, charging and wailing and carving into the ghouls. They scaled those ghastly arms and legs. Clawed into their bodies and tore the ghouls to shreds. The giant creatures threw spirits off of them by the dozen, but two dozen more ran in to replace the ones lost.

In minutes, the ghouls had been shredded, scattered and broken into pieces. Nara gave us the command. Selena and I, with my lash and long knife, her cleaver, we went up to the broken ghouls and burned them in fire. Split them into their masses of spirits. Then Nara bound those too.

"Do you doubt me anymore?" Nara said to me when they were done. "Do you not think I can save your world?"

I could only shake my head. Nara was truly great, truly terrible. She was our Savior.

177

THE MOUNTAIN. The last time I'd seen the place, I'd been walking to my eventual death. It hadn't changed much. Still the one entrance hollowed into its rocky walls, full of spirits walking into the Cycle. Spirits that were being bound one after another by Nara in a feverish blitz. From one to the next she took and chained their souls to her. Growing and expanding her force. Sending the new spirits to form ranks in front of the Mountain itself.

Just before the cavern entrance we turned to look at the force spread out in front of us.

"Do you see?" Nara said. "This is what you came to me for, Carver. This is what you needed. With these souls, we can clean our adversaries from Riven and take the world for our own."

"One question." I looked at the army, at all of the spirits standing with nothing on them. No weapons, no hooks, no swords, no sparkers. A mob, yes, but one lacking in the ways to wrangle spirits. "How will we shut the breaches?"

Nara glanced at me. "You have the sword with you."

"I cannot be everywhere at once," I said. "Here, come with me."

I felt Nara let me make the statement. Let me guide her to the top of the Mountain, through Piotr's passage to the slope high above the forest. Selena followed.

From up there, we could see all across the wood into the border of the city. The breaches popped, yellow and blue and green lights glowing throughout the forest and beyond. So many it looked like the stars in the sky on that night I'd gone with Inman to his camp along the river.

"Even with a dozen of me," I said. "We would never be able to close them all. We would never be able to keep Riven alive."

"Then we shall make a hundred of your swords," Nara said. "A thousand. Enough for every spirit to wield."

"How?" Selena asked. "Can you do it without Dolan?"

Shock, followed by frustration poured through the bond as Nara remembered Dolan was gone. The only spirit that had ever mastered the art of creating the burning weapons had vanished. And while the guides taken the original tools, had restructured them into an new swords and axes and bows over the centuries, without Dolan, there wasn't a way to make more.

"Dolan was a spirit," Nara said. "Anything he did can be done by another. All we have to do is find the right one."

Neither Selena nor I were given permission to reply. Instead, we followed Nara down, back into the Mountain, to the edge of the Cycle. She positioned us near the ledge, and we watched her step up to a passing spirit, an older woman, and touch her on the shoulder. Bind her to Nara's will. Then, Nara pointed towards the Cycle.

Dolan had said that he'd captured the flame by accident. By touching the Cycle and corralling its burning energy. Nara sent the spirit to do the same.

The woman reached down over the edge and touched the blue. Fire raced up her arm, over her body until we could see none of it. Nothing except the blinding light. The spirit toppled over the edge and vanished.

"Only the first try," Nara muttered.

But the next one had the same result. And the third. The fifth. Into the hundreds. I couldn't track how much time Nara spent tossing spirits to their doom, only that it must have been many hours before Nara backed away, her face a mask of barely controlled rage.

"It will not work," I said. Nara wasn't paying attention to my will, her focus on other things. For once, I had the freedom to move my own lips. "We might stand here for an eternity waiting for the another spirit like Dolan. If that doesn't happen soon, then Riven might well be gone by the time you find one."

"Be gone?" Nara said, looking at me with a question in her eyes. "Before, when you first came to me in the field. You mentioned that you wanted to save Riven. To save it from what?"

"It is being overrun," I said. I felt Nara pushing, questing after a deeper answer. "Guide history says that if there are enough spirits in Riven, a hole back to Earth might open. A way back to the other side. Where they could hurt our families. Our friends. Destroy everything we know."

Nara nodded. "That is what I needed to remember. Come, let us return to the slope."

Back at the overlook, we again stared out at the breaches.

"You asked me to save your world, Carver," Nara said. "But it seems that Riven cannot be so saved. There is no other choice than to let this calamity befall us. To ride the wave into the unknown. If these spirits will create a gateway, then we will walk through it."

Even with the connection, even with Nara suppressing

my feeling, I turned over in anger. Betrayal. For a moment, that urge overwhelmed our bond.

"You lied," I spat. "You were the one that let Dolan go. That stopped our only chance. It's not that Riven can't be saved, it's that you destroyed any hope to save it."

"We are all human, are we not?" Nara said. "Flawed, pushed by our ambitions to something beyond our ability to obtain? Only rather than focus on our failures, I choose to take advantage of the future, and our future lies with those."

Nara's arms swept out across the view, taking in the breaches peppering the countryside. As she did so, one, a glow coming from inside the far-off city wall, winked out of existence. Nara stopped her gesture, blinked at the space.

"The guides," I said, answering her unspoken question. "They are still sealing what breaches they can inside the city."

"Delaying our victory," Nara said. "It seems, Carver, I may have a use for you yet. My champion still has a cause against which to wield his sword."

"How might I serve?" I said, hating the words as they came out of my mouth, loving them and the way they pleased Nara through the bond. I was her puppet, and adored it when she pulled the strings.

"You will take some my legion," Nara said. "You will march along the spirit's path and enter the city from the south. Drive the guides before you. Slaughter those that stay. Chase away those that run. Cleanse Riven of them and their souls. Open the door to our new home."

1 7 8

Nara lined the souls up for me in row upon row before the Mountain's entrance. Bathed in the Cycle's glow, I stood before hundreds of spirits bound to follow Nara's, and through her, my command.

The spirits came from anywhere and everywhere. Young and old, rich and poor, dressed in rags and the finest suits. Through and around them wandered souls Nara hadn't yet bound, like a river breaking around a dam of the dead.

Every few seconds another spirit went around me and took its place in the ranks. Another binding, another soul that would stop at nothing to tear every guide apart. I only needed to tell them when.

"March!" I shouted into the swirling ash. Into those dark trees. Nara heard my words and sent the command to those in thrall to her. Including me.

Without conscious effort, my legs moved forward. Long strides that took me through and past my army until I walked at its head. I held the great sword in my hands, ready to fend off any attackers.

And there were plenty of those. Angry spirits from

nearby breaches bit at the sides of my force. Crashed out from the trees in snarling waves only for my spirits to beat them back. Descended on my forces in gnashing piles until, with our superior numbers, we tore the attackers apart.

Of course, without the wrangling fires, the spirits would heal with time. Would return to their rampages. Would continue pushing Riven until it collapsed.

"Why the Shambles?" I said to Nara through our bond. "Most of the guides should be concentrated at the West gate?"

I could feel her back there, near the Cycle, gathering more spirits and adding them to her force. Yet, the strength of that bond dimmed as the distance between us grew. It would take two days march to get to the Shambles, and in that time her ties would slip. By the time we reached the city, I might be able to resist her entirely.

"Because I want to crush their resolve," Nara replied through the bond, her voice crashing into my mind. "Because when you threaten to cut them off from their home, they will not fight. They will flee. Scatter and break."

"You're underestimating them. The guides are better than that."

"Are they?" I could hear Nara's laughter. "You forget, Carver. I once had to choose between dying for my beliefs or living, trapped for centuries. They will choose as I did. They will run for their chance to survive."

Around me streamed the blank-eyed dead. Wrangled or, less likely with every hour, a spirit naturally seduced by the Cycle. I caught their eyes as they missed mine. How many of them would Nara turn to her side?

"We should make for the clock tower." My mind turned towards the attack, trying to find the angles for Nara's victory. "That is the center of the guides' forces."

"Then take it," Nara said. "Wield my force like a hammer and smash the guides to dust."

Had we been in person, I might have bowed. Or said how much I loved the opportunity to carry out her order. However, as I crunched along the path, Nara felt my pleasure through our bond. Knew that I would not hesitate to tear apart the city at her word.

The hundreds of souls behind me would do the same.

179

THE SOUTH GATE STOOD A MENAGERIE. A focal point for all the city's spirits coming together before pounding down the path to the Cycle. I'd not stood on the outside of it, looking in, before.

At least, not as an invader.

On either side of the gate stood turreted towers. Staring out over the right one leaned a guide, locking eyes with my army. As my forces formed up, the guide held up a sparker and launched a bright bolt into the air.

I pointed my sword at the guide as the spark burst high in the clouds, scattering a series of azure points high and low. They dimmed and fizzled as my souls ran around me, towards the gate.

Which slammed shut, its large oaken doors sliding closed before the first of my forces could make it through. Apparently, I was wrong. The guides were not entirely invested in the West gate.

Perhaps Bryce had learned from the others what Selena and I had become. Perhaps he had prepared for the worst.

It wouldn't be enough.

I jammed the sword in the ground before me. Took the crossbow off of my back and slotted in an orange bolt. Poor fortune that Nicholas had replenished my supply after Dolan's ill-fated charge to the woods.

I raised the crossbow, aimed, and pulled the trigger. The orange bolt streaked towards the gate, hit the thick doors, and burst into a blinding nova. The searing rays crept along the outlines of the doors, like spilled paint spreading across a canvas.

After a minute, the rays drained away, leaving nothing more than some blackened bits hanging from the sides. A trio of guides stood behind the ruins, stunned.

"You should run!" I called as I went towards the gate. The crossbow over my back, the great sword yanked up from the ground as I walked and sheathed behind my back. "There is no need for you to die here."

The guide in the middle, a woman with axes, whom I recognized dimly as one of Bryce's wardens after his arrest, stiffened but stayed. The two guides next to her, each one with the sword and knife combo of greener recruits, matched her resolve.

"You are no longer welcome in the city, Carver Reed!" replied the woman, her voice thick with the knowledge of impossible odds.

"If anyone has the power to decide who comes and goes from here, I do not think it's you." I raised my left hand and the first spirits of Nara's force shuffled up beside me. Matched my stride step for step. "I say again. Depart, cross back over, and await your fate with your families."

These three guides would die if they stayed. Would be washed away by the force at my back. Their sacrifice would not buy time. Would not prove a point or change the outcome of this certain war.

So when the woman crossed her axes in front of her

chest, ready to meet the charge, I held my spirits back. Nara, through our bond, urged an all-out attack. Told me to drive forth into the city and break them. But where before her voice had smashed through my mind, now it was closer to a conversation. Words that could be ignored.

I went ahead of my army. Met the woman and the other guides just on the inside of the arch. The Shambles, the scattered apartments, slums, and warped streets sat in front of me. Somewhere in there were my mother's journals, still sitting, as they would forever, in an empty house.

"There is no need for you to die here," I repeated to the three of them as I closed. "I cannot hold back Nara's spirits, or my own sword, much longer."

"And I will say what I said before. It is our privilege to die for our city and our order." The woman looked for a second like she was going to attack then and there, but a last glance at the younger guides next to her stilled her hands.

"Then do so when it will matter," I said. "Go, run and warn your fellows of what is coming."

Nara couldn't control what I said, not at this distance. Even so, my skin began to crawl. My head began to hurt. I wasn't quite defying her command, not yet, but the pressure to strike these three down, to send in the spirits, grew.

"Why are you giving us advice?" the woman asked. "Why should we trust you when you're bound to the enemy?"

"Because who else is there?" I said. "Also, this."

I drew the sword from over my back and the guides stepped back. The spirits behind me edged forward. This was the moment.

"Five seconds," I began. "Four."

The woman looked again at the guides. At the spirits behind me.

"Three."

At impossible odds. I saw her eyes shift.

"Two."

They ran. Turned their backs and sprinted down the road. Past hapless spirits marching towards us.

"One."

I pointed the great sword forward and Nara's spirits surged past me into the city. I walked with them, one foot falling after another.

On my left, Nara's spirits wound their way up an apartment building. Breaking through windows and doors, searching every room for hiding guides. To my right, the spirits found where the three guides had kept spare weapons. Took them and armed themselves.

Everywhere I looked, Nara's army spread. A wave crashing through the city, and bringing terror with it.

180

THE THREE GUIDES must have made it back. Must have warned the others. I encountered no resistance moving through the Shambles. None at all in the Warrens. Even Anna's apartment building had been abandoned.

A dangerous gamble - without access to its basement, Anna wouldn't be able to cross back. At least, not if she'd continued using the building as her entrance into Riven.

I doubted she was the only guide taking such a risk.

The guides had set themselves up in the clock tower square. My home in Riven for years, the clock tower itself loomed as a burned out ruin on the north end of the square. A fountain, now surrounded by shanty shelters, served as the nexus for guide operations.

I formed the spirits back into a line as we moved into view of the square. A block away. In front of us, looking out from building windows and standing in a line across the avenue, stood the guides that I had called friends. Brothers and sisters that I planned to drive away or grind into dust.

Front and center stood my mentor, his twin-edged voulge standing taller than he did. Bryce glared at me with a mixture of anger and disappointment, a look that had as much directed at himself as it did me.

Beside him stood Anna and Alec. I suppose in some sort of attempt to twist my emotions with my friends. An attempt that worked, that made me lurch, that nonetheless did nothing to stop me from ordering the charge.

Nara's army would lose many spirits, but we could afford to. The guides, on the other hand, would be decimated by every casualty.

From the buildings around us, rising two and three and four stories, guides shot their sparkers. Anna, Bryce and the others as well. The bright light and heat saturated the air, caused me to pull up, shield my eyes with my hands. Warmth brushed my face, and when I pulled my hands away, the buildings around us burned.

The guides that had been on them were nowhere to be seen. The fires spewed smoke into the street, the sky, the alleys. Weakened walls collapsed, spreading debris and sending charred rubble into the way of my spirits. While not deadly, the hot ruins hampered our progress. Set spirits aflame or shattered their legs. Trapped them under falling balconies.

Our advance floundered.

Nara could feel the anger and agony through her bindings, and she pushed those feelings to me, and I used them. Charged forward through the blaze to the other side. Where instead of dozens of guides, I saw a scattered few. Bryce had disappeared. Retreated.

"Carver, it's good to see your tactics haven't improved." Alec struck fast, his gauntlets flying towards me from my side.

I rolled with the blows, turning as his fists hit my shoulder to bring the great sword between us.

"With Nara's spirits, I don't need them." I countered.

Stabbed the sword forward. Alec grabbed the blade with his hands, tried to turn it away. Only I pushed forward, forced him back.

He'd been stronger than me as a man. With human limitations. As a spirit; no longer.

Alec pushed the sword to the side as he felt a building's burning pyre draw close. Accepted a cut on his right shoulder as he twisted from under the blade. Danced into me, and then rolled out again as I reversed the stroke and forced him back.

"You can fight the binding, Carver!" Alec fell back as some of Nara's spirits pushed through the smoke behind me. I nodded, and they rushed my friend.

"You can run, Alec," I replied. The guide took a step into the first spirit, delivering a gauntlet-armored right uppercut to the soul's chin. Striking and setting it aflame.

The second jumped into the air, arms outstretched, towards Alec's left shoulder. Rather than turn, Alec stuck out his left hand and let the spirit impale itself on the gauntlet's spikes.

The third, however, caught my friend out of position. Striking him low, with Alec's right hand still pushing off the first spirit. Knocked Alec's legs out from under him and sent the guide to the stones.

In a flash I stood over him, Nara's remaining spirit holding down Alec's arms. I pinned Alec to the ground with the point of my blade.

"You're better than you were," Alec said to me.

"I always let you win," I replied. Raised the sword. Nara's voice screamed in my head to end him. To stab Alec and burn away the guide's tie to Earth. To life.

Difficult to ignore a direct command through a bond, even from one so distant. But I could hesitate. Could try.

Only for a second.

"That, I will never believe." Alec pulled Nara's spirit, clinging to his arms, over his head and in between my sword and his chest. I stabbed down, felt the sword bite, and twisted the hilt. Burned the spirit away.

Alec pushed himself out from under my legs. Scrambled to his feet as I worked my sword out from the spirit. Dropped into a ready stance, which loosened as he looked over my shoulder.

I could hear them. Nara's spirits making their way across as they found ways through the flames. As burning rubble died down. The guides had delayed our advance, yes, but their gambit was at an end.

"Much as I would love to continue," Alec said. "I believe these odds are against me."

"You're giving up the clock tower? How will you cross back?"

"If we don't end this now, there won't be anywhere to cross back to!" Alec gave me a slight nod, then turned and ran. The square behind him was deserted. Guide gear, tables, and maps remained behind.

Nara's spirits flooded into it, tearing everything apart with abandon. I went up to the main table, where not long ago I'd sat with Dolan, Selena, and the others to plot our last best hope for salvation.

On the table sat the same map they'd had on there before, only instead of breaches, there now was drawn a single thick line. From the center of the city towards the Mountain.

A small ball sat at the end of it, right over the Cycle.

181

I FELT Nara's pulse as I looked up from the map. Her words crossing the distance between us.

"You have driven them from their home?" Nara asked.

"Riven is their home, and they are still in it," I replied.

"Then you are failing."

"I do not wish to succeed." I watched as spirits armed themselves with remaining gear. Long knives and swords. Spears and axes. Guide weapons in the hands of those they were designed to destroy.

"But I do, and you belong to me." Rather than hot anger, a cool acceptance flowed through the bond. Assurance that I was indeed hers. That I would do whatsoever she asked.

Nara was right.

"I believe they mean to come to you," I said, explaining the map. "Though what they plan to do when they get there is harder to know."

"Try to destroy me, of course. Though what their hopes are after that, I do not know."

"The Mountain is too far for most of them," I said,

glancing at the clock tower's ruins. "They won't be able to cross back before their bodies die on the other side."

"A pity. You will follow from behind. Chase them. I am building up a secondary force that shall meet the guides head on in the forest. They will have nowhere to run."

With that command, Nara's voice faded away. Her mind turned to other matters. Mine turned to the army, now staring at me and waiting for further orders.

So we marched west. Towards the Mountain, Bryce and the guides.

As we went through the city center, I realized we were passing close to the apartment I'd shared with Selena and the others. To Nicholas' lab.

I directed the spirits to continue their destructive walk after the guides and dipped down the right side street. Nara was paying less attention than usual. Focusing on growing her second army, no doubt.

The apartment sat as I'd last seen it. Three stories of shabby, yet sturdy construction. The balconies that Selena loved to look out from stuck their black iron out from the top, a fire escape ladder marring the side view.

I went inside Nicholas's lab, which occupied the entire ground floor, and stopped. Empty, except for a couple of old tables. One of which held, on it, a piece of paper, next to a box no larger than my hand.

Conspicuously absent was the bomb. The reset button. I'd half expected it to be waiting for us in the clock tower square. Thought they'd push it and send us back.

Carver,

Anna tells me you're on your way to ruin us at the behest of some ancient spirit. I can think of no more appropriate way for our time here to end than at your hand, though I confess my own thinking has you too headstrong to simply follow orders.

However, I've come to understand Riven as a place of para-

doxes. A world where science ties loose with the spiritual, and where our strongest friends may need the most help. And so I offer you a gift, with all my thanks.

Your humble scientist,

Nicholas

I looked at the box, small and squat and black. A gift. What Nicholas could have for me at this stage, I didn't know. I reached for the box, no latch bound its contents, and pushed up on the top.

I heard the bang. My eyes caught the flash before they closed by reflex. I felt the fire burn. In both the harsh heat of orange flames and the purifying blue.

"Come back, Carver."

What? I floated. Or rather, existed in a place that did not. A vast emptiness. One I recognized, from when Dolan had wrangled me. A place of shadows and flitting images.

This was, I understood, the place where spirits stayed as their mindless forms walked to the Cycle.

"They told me I should leave you. But you saved me, so I feel I have to return the favor."

I looked around, but couldn't find the source of the voice. Couldn't remember to whom it belonged. The shadows shifted. A face? Hair?

Something tugged me, yanked me off of my feet, such as they were, to my back and I fell. Through the shadows and the lights. Until the world gradually brightened around me and I realized I was looking into Anna's eyes.

"There you go," Anna said. There was a noise, somewhere outside, and a worried frown crossed along her expression. "I'm sorry, but I can't wait for you. When you get better, come find us. We're going to the Mountain."

Anna stood up. I tried to speak, but my mouth wouldn't work. I couldn't feel my legs, my arms. Pain began to leak through.

Anna pulled out her flail, let the chain dangle near my head. "Good bye, Carver. I hope I see you again."

And then she was gone. Leaving me lying there, on the floor of the lab, with hordes of Nara's spirits running through the area.

Nicholas's bomb had broken my spirit. It would take hours to heal. Hours I didn't have.

182

FEELING RETURNED TO MY ARMS, tingling sensations that gradually grew into the cool touch of the stone floor or the ragged scratch of my ruined coat as it brushed my leg. The ceiling blurred in and out of focus as my eyes pieced themselves together.

Nicholas hadn't gone easy on me.

If Anna hadn't been there to bring me back, I'd still be in that dark nova. Lost. Unknowing.

The first time, when Dolan burned me away, I hadn't known what was happening. He'd yanked me back so fast that I didn't have a chance to process the event. We'd moved on out of the desert and I hadn't given it a second thought.

Now I understood what had happened. Who to thank for bringing me back to Riven's ashen world.

I reached out through Anna's bond. She was growing distant. On her way to the Mountain. I felt a rush of warm encouragement from her. She still believed in me, somehow.

My right hand came back to me. I traced the floor. Felt my way around, as my neck refused to turn.

Nicholas' bomb had devastated my coat, leaving a

shredded mess behind. At least the thick jacket had done some work protecting the shirt and pants beneath. They felt crisped to the touch, but intact.

I couldn't say the same about the lash. The heat, it seemed, had burned through the cable. The hilt sat in the holster, but as a weapon, its days were done.

The scrabbling came soft at first. A grumbling rasp. The lab's door swinging open and banging against the wall. I couldn't turn to see, but I could feel its eyes on me. The rasping stopped.

A spirit, and based on how fast it shaped up, one of Nara's.

"He is here, yes," the spirit spoke to no one. At least, nobody here. "Alive, yes. Eyes are open. His hand moved."

My left hand only hurt. I couldn't move it. Legs could twinge, but couldn't bend. The only thing I had was my right.

"I am sure, yes." The spirit came closer to me. Its head popped into view. Long, stringy hair. A face that should have been young, but had been worn hard. She blinked down at me. "Alive, yes."

"She can't feel me, can she?" I said. Playing for the delay.

"He is speaking," the spirit muttered. "Asking questions."

"Ask her," I said. The spirit snarled at me, then pulled back. Stared straight out at the wall of the lab.

"He wonders if you can feel him?"

I shifted my right hand. Pulled it across my body. To my left holster. Towards the long knife I hoped would be there. When the spirit jerked her eyes back down to me I paused.

"No, she says. You are no longer hers."

"I can feel her," I protested. My voice scratched. Again the spirit looked away. Listening.

My hand made it farther. Grasped the end of the long knife's hilt.

"She says you lie." The spirit leaned in close to me. Her

manic eyes locked on mine, her lips pulling apart. "She says you are not to be trusted."

"What's your name?" I said the words. A tactic I'd used before on spirits, especially ones on the edge of sanity. Even if they had no intention of answering, for a moment the spirit would think of their name. Many could no longer remember it, and that realization would throw them into a panic.

As it did with this one. Her face went slack, then widened with worry. Until Nara clamped down on those feelings. Pushed the spirit back to its goal.

"She says you are to be ended." The spirit opened her mouth wide, the inside of it far too close and visible for comfort. Teeth, bent and broken, came in close for my eyes.

The knife bit in hard, though I didn't have the angle to twist the hilt. My wrist wasn't turning. The spirit fell back, my long knife sticking out of her abdomen. Hissing in anger, pain. Whistling screeches that echoed around the lab's hard walls.

I lunged with my right arm, pulled my body over. Presented my back to the spirit, then my left side. But I saw what I wanted.

Trapped beneath me, under the ruins of the crossbow, sat the great sword. I rolled slightly, giving my right arm enough room to grab its hilt. Bent my elbow to swing the point of the sword up, maybe a foot.

I had never realized how heavy the blade was till now. I suddenly wasn't sure I could actually use it. Could keep it high enough.

The spirit wrapped her hands around the knife and pulled it free. Looked like she was about to throw the blade away, then paused. Nara again.

This much direct control from so far away. If nothing

else, keeping Nara so busy would buy my friends some time. Leave a few more spirits unbound.

The spirit burst at me, stumbling forward with the knife swinging in her right hand. Holding it forward in a stab.

I pushed with my right hand, levered the great sword's hilt into the floor as I slid onto my back. The point went up as the spirit closed. My blade hit the knife, knocking it from the spirit's hand. But then my move was done.

The great sword stood upright, but it was all I could do to keep it that way.

Outside, from the street, I heard the pounding of footsteps. Reinforcements, and I doubted they were mine.

The spirit sidestepped nearer my head, her eyes locked onto my sword. I couldn't move it to follow. I tried to think of what tricks I had left. Came up blank.

As the spirit realized I couldn't counter, a gnarly smile spread over her face. She came in to kill me.

As she dove towards my face, I shifted my shoulder, pushed my right arm forward. Let the hilt tilt back towards my head. The heavy blade fell, right towards me. I locked eyes with the sword for a second, before the spirit's wild face blocked my view.

I felt her teeth bite my skin, and then heard the thick slice as the great sword fell onto, into the spirit's head. This time, I had the leverage to turn my right hand, twist the great sword's hilt, and send the pale fire burning.

The flames covered my vision as they consumed the spirit, lying on top of me. I closed my eyes for a second. Started to relax. Until I heard the feet again. Close.

I'd lived through one spirit, only to die to the coming dozen.

183

<hr>

I PUSHED the vacant spirit off of me with my right hand. Felt a bit of life in my left leg, so I pressed that foot against the ground and scooted back. Bought me some space and an angle with which to look at the door to the street.

There I saw madness.

Spirits were tangling with spirits. Diving at each other, rolling around in the street. Some had the telltale blue eyes of an angry soul, enraged and mindless. The others were likely Nara's forces, pulled into a fight they weren't looking for.

That many angry spirits meant a breach would be nearby. A breach that, right now, was saving my life.

A clang drew my eyes back towards the spirit I'd wrangled. The great sword had fallen to the floor when the spirit stood up, her head at an awkward angle from the sword's cut. Her eyes were blank, staring straight ahead without emotion.

She took one step, then a second and a third. Towards the door and out into the chaos. Without interruption, she would go all the way to the Cycle.

Where, if Nara stood ready, she could be bound back into service.

Nothing I could do about that, though. So I pushed my way over to the great sword. This time, I moved over to the wall, dragging the sword behind me as I crawled.

I jammed the sword into the angle between the floor and the wall and pushed into with my right hand. Pressed down and slipped my left leg under me. With my right leg still straight, the position was profoundly uncomfortable.

But if I couldn't stand, I'd be defenseless against the next spirits that came in, whether they were Nara's or wild ones from the breach.

With my right hand, I let go of the sword. Shifted my weight to my left side. Leaned forward, grabbed my right ankle, and bent my right leg beneath me.

Pain sparked and splashed. My vision swam. I tried to focus. Suppress it.

The pain isn't real, Carver. You don't have nerves.

If only it was that easy.

Outside, shrieks grew louder. More of them. Spirits howling frustration without reservation. Which meant Nara's side was losing. Or abandoning the field.

Soon I'd have company, once one of those angry souls wandered in here.

Again I picked up the sword, now in a kneeling stance. Pressed it against the wall with my right hand. My left foot, its shredded boot sticking to the skin, moved until it rested flat on the stone. Then I pushed, hard.

I may have screamed.

But, leaning on the sword, I stood. My right leg, still a broken mess, touched the floor. Did not want to put weight on that yet.

I looked across the lab. To the tables two yards away. The sword would be my walking stick. My left leg my only balance. If I could get to the tables, then I'd have some support. Could free my right hand to swing the sword, at least somewhat.

A body smashed against the outside of the lab, scrabbling hands and tearing teeth telling just what was happening to it.

I lunged with the sword, turning and driving the point into the stone. Hoping Mali had made Dolan's sword stronger than the city. That her gift to her fellow spirit could bite into rock.

The sword struck the floor and sparks flew, but I felt the point lodge into the ground. It held my weight as I moved my left foot forward a long step. Did it a second time.

Now I could reach the tables. Once more lurch with the sword, and I'd be perfect.

But I'd run out of time.

Behind me, I heard the mad mutterings, growls from a pair of spirits. I risked a glance. Soldiers, their military minds long gone. Looking at me as though I were lunch.

They darted towards me, eyes wide and burning. I waited a long second, then shifted my weight to the left foot. Pressed down with my left leg, and then swept the great sword with my right hand.

As my body twisted, I shoved off with my left leg. The spirits' hands brushed my ragged coat as I turned, the sword scraping along the ground. I saw their faces, their burning eyes, as I fell. They kept coming.

My back hit the edge of the table, and Nicholas' workbench held firm. I used the leverage, dragged the sword up in a crossing cut that the spirits, without any sense in their souls, ran into.

I twisted the hilt as the sword slashed, drawing burning blue lines across the spirits' outstretched arms. And then they landed on me, bearing me off the table and to the floor. Collapsed.

I saw the underside of the table, and had an idea. The burning spirits rolled off of me, and in seconds they would be gone. Leaving me again open to attack. Unless the spirits couldn't tell I was there.

With my right hand, I hefted and hacked at the table's front right leg, nearest to the door. After a pair of whacks, the leg snapped in half and the table tilted forward, then fell. As it listed, I pushed myself behind the falling barrier.

The table sat between me and the door, blocking all view of the outside. The screams had died down. The breach would still be drawing spirits, but with nothing to keep them here, they would be ranging farther in search of souls to maul.

Me, I curled up behind that fallen table. Pulled my legs together, held the sword close, and willed my soul to heal.

184

Hidden behind the table, waiting for my body to heal, I reached out across my bond to Anna. Felt her nervous excitement, and spoke to her.

"Where are all of you?" I said the words in my mind and, like directing a shout towards a distant friend, sent the question to Anna.

"We're in the forest," Anna replied. "Closing breaches and marching towards the Mountain. Bryce is leading. Determined."

"Not surprised. Sorry I can't be there."

"Yet, you mean."

"I'm hiding behind a table, Anna. Nicholas' bomb really tore me apart."

A wave of concern passed through the bond, along with a little bit of laughter.

"We couldn't take chances," Anna sent. "If the fire didn't break the bond with Nara, we didn't want you up and running again."

"Right. Instead I get to stay here and fight off spirits with one working arm."

"I thought you were hiding?"

"Now." I paused. Listened. Spirits were still running through the streets outside, but nothing pulled them into the lab. "How are you going to last until the Mountain?"

"We will because we have to. There's no other choice."

"Nicholas thinks his bomb will work?"

"Same answer, Carver. It has to."

"Know what'll happen if it works, right? I'll be gone."

Silence from Anna. A tinge of sadness.

"We know," Anna's words came slow. "If Nicholas can do what he's promising, he'll be swept away too. And Selena. And, really, all of us still here."

"That's a high price to pay."

"Set against the cost of not doing anything?"

"I see your point."

"I believe you said to me, shortly after we met, that guides have to be prepared to die at any time, right? That we couldn't expect long lives?"

I nodded to nobody in the lab. It'd been a bravo sentiment to share. Words that made me feel strong and important, especially when shared with a kid on the train into Chicago, or in a quote to Opperman for one of his stories.

"Comes with the job," I said to Anna. "Only, just because it's likely, doesn't mean you have to be all right with it."

"Tell me. Would you really want to stay here, in Riven? Forever?"

"It's not all bad." I surprised myself with the words. How true they were. "With Selena, and all of you, there's plenty of adventure. Places to explore. Things to do. The scenery could use some work, and the food is terrible..."

Anna didn't say anything. Not that there was much you could say to someone who'd already died, who was about to die again, if his friends got their way.

"Except," I continued. "You know what, I am angry. I'm

frustrated. I never had a chance to raise a family. To lead a normal life. To fight in a war for my country or find a normal job. By chance, I could become a guide, and before I knew any better I was one. All of the things I could have done, I can't do."

"As it is for all of us," Anna's reply came soft. "We're pawns in a game bigger than we are. Carver, even with all the horrors, all the danger, and all the fighting, at least we have the chance to affect the world. You and I, Bryce and the other guides, we're shaping everyone's future."

"I know. Which is why I wouldn't change this for anything," I quirked a smile that I hoped made it into my words. "I need catharsis every now and again."

"Know what you could be doing instead?"

"What?"

"Getting yourself up and coming after us."

"That might be a good idea." I tested my legs. My hands and feet. More feeling. I could probably stand, maybe limp. Brave a step or two.

I curled forward, sitting up. Put my right hand on the top of the table, pulled myself standing. My right leg wasn't thrilled about it, but between the twinges, it held. I leaned down, picked up the great sword. Lifted it with both hands. Shifted the weapon to my right and took a step, left hand ready to catch myself on the table.

I didn't fall.

Took another step. Reached the end of the table. I could do this.

"Anna, it's going to be a while, but I'm on my way."

THE TAR PIT'S factories and warehouses were empty. Its streets bereft of the wandering spirits that I would normally see. The breaches pulled the souls elsewhere, and the guides had kept the city as clear of those as possible.

My limp straightened as I walked. I flexed the fingers on my left hand. Even managed to turn my head from side to side without pain. The miracles of being dead.

Within a few hours I could see the West gate, or rather, its ruins. The long line of rubble where the archway had once stood. The half-crumbled guard tower on the south side.

And the guides fighting a desperate battle outside of it.

I couldn't quite run, but as my shambling jog brought me closer, I saw the pair of guides outside the tower's lone door. They were fighting a group of spirits, armed as well. Nara's army, then, chasing down some stragglers.

The clash of metal on metal confirmed that the spirits weren't the usual hands and teeth crowd. I slowed as I approached, taking cover in the torn ruins of a guard house. Through its ripped walls, I took in a better view.

I didn't like what I saw.

Holding their ground in front of the door, fighting in solid tandem, were my least favorite guides; Polk and Derringer. They barred the door with their bodies, driving Nara's spirits back. The odds weren't great; eight against the two of them, and Nara's spirits seemed to be fine with biding their time. They darted in an out, looking for a quick stick, rather than the reckless charge I'd come to expect from spirits.

Polk and Derringer were human. They would bleed, they would tire. They would lose.

While I wasn't quite my sneaky self, I hadn't been noticed. I could wade into the back of the spirits, could take them down. On the other hand, Polk and Derringer had killed me. Took a knife to my throat or put a gun to my head and pulled the trigger. What better justice was there than seeing their cruelty matched?

I watched Derringer duck a swing from a spirit's sword, then saw Polk stab over his partner's head, driving the point of his rapier into the spirit's chest, alighting it in blue flame.

A strong move. One that left Polk open.

The hatchet came down into Polk's back, the spirit wielding it in both hands. The guide collapsed against Derringer, who by reflex or skill threw Polk perfectly back through the doorway while retreating himself to fill the entrance.

One on seven.

Even I'm not that mean.

I stumbled out of the guard house into the dirty street and started shouting. Waved my arms. Trying to draw attention. The spirits, and even Derringer, turned at the noise. Stared at me.

Then Derringer took advantage. Used his swords and stabbed the spirit closest to him. Burnt it up.

Two on six now.

The spirits split in half, three turning to tackle Derringer and another trio facing me. I had hatchet man, another spirit with a pair of long knives, and one holding a spear in both hands. All three spirits looked like shabby ghosts of a hospital ward, clad in stained gowns with pocked faces.

"Nice variety, guys," I said, drawing the great sword.

The one with the spear had the reach, and he led the attack, darting forward with a straight stab while the other two broke out to either side of me. A good ol' pincer move.

So I stepped forward. Slid just to the side of the spear's thrust, and as the spirit started to pull back his weapon, I sliced the great sword across. The spirit wasn't far enough away to avoid the blazing point.

I kept my momentum, pulling the sword and rotating my feet to the left, forcing hatchet man back. Which left long knives free to jump on my back, stabbing into me with those damned daggers. But I kept turning, and he failed to account for his own momentum, and even as those knives stabbed into me, he flew off and hit the ground.

I lifted my swing, pushing past the searing pain, cut my rotation in half, and brought the great sword over my head and down on the knife-wielding spirit. He wouldn't be getting up again.

Which left hatchet-man all alone.

"Carver!" Derringer's pained yelp jerked my eyes back towards the tower. One spirit left for him, but Derringer, leaning against the entrance, had a knife sticking out of his side. One of his swords sat on the ground. The last spirit, holding a big ax, wheeled it back for a deathblow.

So I did the only thing I could. I twisted, put my weight into it, and launched the great sword through the air. It flew, spinning, and thwacked into the ax-man's legs. Sliced in and tripped the spirit.

I didn't see what Derringer did then, because the hatchet

man came for me. He swung towards me chest, and I dove forward. Caught his forearm before the weapon could come down, and drove both of us into the dirt.

Unfortunately, this meant seeing the spirit's face up close; its sore, oozing nightmare a true feast of terror. I responded to it in the only sane way I could imagine - taking my own head and bashing into his nose.

With my left hand, I tried to get a grip on the hatchet. Failed as the spirit moved his arm out of my reach. Ready to slam it down on my back. So I slipped my right arm underneath the spirit's back and pulled as he swung the hatchet. Pulled the spirit over on top of me, causing his strike to miss wide right.

The hatchet hit the stone hard and bounced off, out of his grip. Leaving us both weaponless. Two spirits clawing and tearing at each other. At least, that's what I thought would happen, until the spirit, snarling in my face, froze and collapsed as blue fire burned around it.

Derringer's sweaty, bloody face appeared over the burning spirit's shoulders, searching to see if I was still alive.

"Barely," I answered the unspoken question and threw the spirit off of me. My back burned, but compared to Nicholas' bomb, this had been cake. Nothing to it.

"Thanks." Derringer helped me up. "Came out of nowhere."

"Still not convinced I should have helped you." I leaned on him as we walked back to the tower.

"Polk and I were the guards." Derringer showed me into the tower, and I saw, lying there in various states of injury, were a dozen guides or more. Most leaned against the walls. A few sat on the ground. A couple were on their backs.

I felt faintly ill. I'd almost abandoned all of them to their deaths, just for my own grudge.

"Hurt too bad to go on," Polk coughed as he stood to

shake my hand. "Bryce sent us back with them. Circled around that band of spirits you were leading. Guess you aren't doing that anymore?"

"Changed my mind," I said. "The rest of the way shouldn't be too bad. A breach, but it's not crowded."

Derringer nodded. "Suppose you won't want to escort us?"

I shook my head. "Have to catch up to the rest of them. If they don't succeed, it won't matter if you get back alive."

None of them protested. They all knew.

1 8 6

DERRINGER WALKED UP to me as I stared at the ruins of the West gate, already coating over with ash flakes. The breaches in the woods, and the spirits pouring forth, were likely chasing after the guides. Nara's army. A rare moment of quiet for this part of Riven.

"Polk and I can go with you. We can help," Derringer said.

"You won't be able to keep up," I replied, not bothering to look at him. "I won't get tired. Any spirit that catches me, I'll heal up in minutes. You're already hurt. Polk can barely walk."

Derringer didn't say anything for a second. Then I felt his hand land on my shoulder. "We're with you, Carver. I know you have no cause to like us, and that's fine, but we're behind you. All of us want you to go back to that Mountain, take care of Nara, and save Riven."

"You say you're behind me?" I looked at Derringer, then spread out my arms. I think he thought I was going to wrap him in a hug, but no, I had a better idea.

"Anything we can do."

"Give me your coat."

"What?" Then Derringer looked at mine, which wasn't a coat so much as a pile of cloth scraps. "Oh."

In Derringer's coat, a little loose in the shoulders but otherwise solid, I left the guard tower and headed west. Beyond the gate and into the clearing before the forest. As I neared the trees, I paused and turned back. Looked at the ruined wall, the fractured gate, and the city that lay beyond. I would never go back there. I knew this as much as I knew anything.

Either we would succeed, and the Cycle would wash over and burn me from existence. Or we would fail, and Nara would bind me to once again become her thrall. And we would wait the end of everything there in the Mountain.

I hadn't felt sadness thinking about how I wouldn't see my apartment in Chicago again. A smile at the thought of Ezra's, never tasting another glass of their frothy beer or warm coffee on a cold winter morning. Riven had none of those charms, but I realized, standing there, that it was more of a home to me than any place had ever been. I knew its streets, its breaking buildings, it's endless breeze and ash flakes. Riven was never safe, but it was home.

Now to protect it, I had to destroy it.

With the great sword held out in front of me, my back still sore from the hatchet, I moved into the forest. The gray trunks rose high into the air, the dark canopy filtering out the fogged sky. Sounds of spirits fighting each other gnashed their way through. Echoing off of the trees, the ground, to make it seem as though all the world around me engaged in a deadly struggle.

I knew which way was west, and that is where I walked.

I reached out to Anna, to see that she was still there. Confidence fled back to me. A slight bit of sadness. Perhaps they were losing guides. Perhaps they were understanding that this might cost them their lives as well. Resignation to a necessity.

Several hours into the walk, or at least that's what I guessed, the constant crashes and growls and chatter burst forth closer to me than before. I could see movement beyond the next tree and I steadied myself. Waited for something to come crashing through. The sounds turned away at the last moment, a sharp change. They were loud, a struggle between more than just spirits.

I shouldn't investigate. No reason to be curious now. Should just keep going. Except I didn't know if it was like Polk and Derringer. A friend in need of help.

So instead of running from the noise, I went towards it. Went into a clearing, one that hadn't been there before, but now, through the felling of trees by blow and body, a broken circle appeared. In it, their large and thick arms swinging at each other, stood Mali's golden ghoul facing off against another, stranger one.

This ghoul, made from the molded bodies of consumed spirits, had six arms, and used them as legs and anything else that needed. It grappled with the golden ghoul, and they alternated throwing each other around the clearing. I couldn't tell who was winning, both battering the other in equal measure.

The monster stood on two of its arms, and grabbed the golden ghoul's paired hands with two more, and then with its uppermost pair snatched the golden ghoul's head and began to twist. To tear the golden ghoul the pieces.

Mali's creation had been my friend.

I ran forward and slashed with the great sword. Caught the back of the monster and bit deep into the dark, swirling flesh. The blue fire from my blade danced along the edges of the cut, but failed to take hold.

The ghoul, however, noticed. Broke off from its grapple and cut loose with a high-pitched howl that came from, I realized, a mouth in the middle of what I'd taken to be its chest. The ghoul turned and kicked with its lower left leg. Hit me square in the ribs, though I managed another cut from the sword in the process. I flew back, landed on broken branches.

What was another bruise anyway?

The attack gave the golden ghoul a chance to regain its footing. It bashed down on the six-armed creature, driving it into the ground with the force of its golden fist. However, from its new position hugging the earth, the ghoul grabbed and threw Mali's creature's feet out from under it. The golden ghoul tumbled to the ground.

The monster used its advantage; scrabbled on top of the golden ghoul and began to hammer on it with four of its six arms. Beating and breaking down my monstrous friend.

"Mali should have made you better," I muttered as I stood up. Adjusted the sword and charged with it, leading its point like a spear.

As I came close, the monster slowed its beating with its middle left arm, and swung it out to meet me. I stepped left, around the swing, and then brought the sword around and down on the arm. With the added force, the sword sliced through and severed the ghoul's limb.

It shrieked, and stumbled back off the golden ghoul. This time, the blue fire from my sword burned away the severed hand and licked at the stump. As the ghoul fell back, I followed in. Slashing every time the ghoul tried to drive me away with its arms. It had no defense against the sword.

Or so I thought.

The ghoul paused and I drove in for a stab right into its mouth. And then all three of its remaining arms, the ones it wasn't using for legs, came in at me from different angles. I adjusted my swing to aim for the right one, slashed across the ghoul's reaching hand, but it kept coming.

The ghoul pressed the sword into my body and accepted the blue burning flame. I felt the pressure on all sides. Crushing, grinding. In a moment I would break apart entirely. Flattened to nothing more than dust.

Until Mali's ghoul, the thing that had nearly killed me back in her temple, dove headlong into the beast's midsection. Knocked me out of its arms and drove its golden fists over and over into the other ghoul. I hit the ground and stayed still for a moment, trying to find which parts of me worked.

Thanks to Mali's ghoul, I could feel my arms and legs. Wasn't destroyed like after Nicholas' bomb. I creaked to my feet, hefted the sword up off the ground, walked around the golden ghoul as it continued to bash the thrashing beast, and then jammed my blade into the top of the six-armed monster. Let the blue fire run down the sword and into the creature, burning away the ties that bound together.

Mali's ghoul stood as the fire finished consuming its foe. Stared at me with a nod. And then turned back to the burning remnants.

I saw why. As the ghoul burned, spirits emerged. The source of its power and its rage. Tose spirits were those of the Right and Left Hand. Cheo's warriors, torn and confused. Bound together in lost anger.

"Cheo," I said when I saw the leader emerge from the fire. He was not, however, the man I'd known. Like the others, the ghoul had torn apart any connection he still had to sanity. If I'd still been human, still had life, I could have bound them. If I knew how to use Nara's technique, I could've done that as well. But I saw the calm on that face, the steady, clear eyes, and I rested my hand on his shoulder.

"I'm glad to give you the peace you sought," I said as Cheo looked at me. "You're fighting days are done."

A moment later, Cheo walked away. On his last steps the Cycle.

187

I SLID the great sword back into its sheath and turned west-ward. Ready to follow in the footsteps of Cheo's spirits and catch up with the guides heading towards the Mountain. I took one step forward and then heard a rumbling sound behind me.

Oh. Over my shoulder, I noticed the golden ghoul looming over me.

Took another step forward. Heard the ground shake under my feet as the ghoul shifted, following.

Guess he wanted to come with.

From there we kept walking. The ghoul followed me almost to the line, brushing aside trees as if they were twigs and staying within inches of my back foot. If the idea of a ten foot tall living statue, with bits and pieces broken off, walking behind me didn't seem odd, well, I'd been in Riven a long time now.

Things didn't surprise me much anymore.

As we moved, spirits occasionally appeared, from breaches or lost contingents of Nara's army. The ghoul and I handled them with equal amounts of disdain and skill. I would either slash or stab. The ghoul would stomp, or hit the spirit with its fist so hard that the soul would go flying through the trees and not show its face again. So we progressed. With every step I felt stronger. My soul knitting itself together.

I don't know how long it took, but we caught up with Nara's army. Or what was left of it. When I'd set out from the Mountain, as commander of Nara's force, there had been over a thousand spirits walking with me. But over time, as breaches and guides and angry spirits had torn away at the sides, what remained were only a few dozen marching in any semblance of order. As the ghoul and I approached, they paused in their march. Turned to look at us.

"Carver!" I heard the voice; Bryce's call. "How about you take them from the back, and we'll take them from the front?"

I held the sword high, signaled a yes. We charged. Nara's spirits turned, half of them to greet me and the ghoul, and the other half to stand against the sudden appearance of a dozen guides. Guides I recognized. Anna and Bryce, Alec and more. They dove at the spirits with a viciousness that I treated to desperation. We all knew this was it, and we weren't going to let the snarling traces of Nara's army stand in our way.

The fight was swift, uneventful. An unbroken line of cuts and swirls, tweaked with blue fire and Nara's spirits were laid to waste.

When it was done, I helped some of the guides tend to their wounds. Bryce found me setting a man's shoulder, dislocated when a spirit he'd wrangled fell onto it, back into place.

"Nicholas is just beyond the next set of trees. The remainder of our forces around him." Bryce looked me up and down. "Glad you're back, Carver."

"If you wanted me back, you could have found a nicer way to ask," I said. "Leaving a bomb, really?"

"We didn't know if you'd even find it," Bryce said. "More a last-ditch shot than anything. Anna had more faith than I did."

"Thanks."

"But now that you're here, we need to decide what to do."

"I saw the map," I said. "You want to detonate it inside the Mountain."

"Nicholas believes his device will burn far enough to bring the Mountain down. To set the Cycle free." Bryce led me into the trees, away from the cleanup. Towards Nicholas. "If that happens, the Cycle will wash through the forest, over the city–"

"It'll wipe out everything," I said. "I know."

"Including you. And Selena."

"We're already dead Bryce." I gave him a halfhearted grin. "I've died once, I can do it again."

My mentor gave me a quick nod. "Thank you for understanding. The other part of it, of course, is the rest of us."

"We'll give you time to escape." I wasn't going to detonate the bomb while Bryce and Alec and all the others were still in here. They had families. This whole thing was pointless if it meant killing the ones I loved.

"We can't trust this to you," Bryce said. "If you fail, if Nicholas can't detonate the bomb, then we lose everything. Who knows what Nara has waiting for us up there - if it's only you, there might be no chance of success. If that means we lose ourselves, then so be it."

As we went into the main force of the guides, I could feel stares on me. Some hands went to their weapons, before relaxing at Bryce's look. My fellows, having last seen me carving through their own ranks, no doubt had some grievances. Debts they felt they needed to settle.

"Nara's hold is broken," I announced to the guides. "I'm here as I am. I will take Nicholas and the bomb into the Mountain, we will detonate it, and end the risk Riven poses to you and your families."

I saw a few nods, but it seemed like the guides weren't in the mood for speeches. That's when I realized that they had been traveling for days already. Crossed over for far longer than a normal hunt. Their bodies, on the other side, were at risk.

"Bryce," I turned to him. "You have to get them back. You have to get back."

"How would we do that?" Bryce replied. "They're exhausted. Only some of us, the strongest and most experienced, have been able to keep their endurance. To send them back now, through that forest, would be sending them to die."

"Not if they had an escort."

"There's no time."

"We split them up," I said. "Mali's golden ghoul goes with all of you, back to the city. Nicholas and I go to the Mountain."

"You, Nicholas, and some of us," Bryce countered. "As I said, Carver, we mean to see this through."

Bryce gathered up the rest of the guides, those who could walk, and those who could carry the ones who couldn't. I sent the ghoul off with them. Pointed and told the creature to protect the guides with its life. I didn't know if it really understood me, but when the guides shuffled off back towards the city, to the places where they could cross over and return to their homes, the ghoul followed.

They would make it. They would be saved.

Alec and Anna stood near Nicholas, looking over the bomb, which was attached to a cart nearly as tall as I was.

Crude wheels on the bottom, and ropes around the device that tied it to the signs. Keeping it level, keeping it safe.

"Sorry I nearly killed you," I said to Alec as I walked up.

"Me? Why, I decided not to kill you." Alec glanced at Anna. "For her sake. I, I had declared that you had outlived your usefulness. But she argued that you should have one more chance."

"Well then, thanks Anna," I said. "Alec, I won't be saving you when you get into trouble."

"My friend, if I get into trouble, it will be trouble's problem, not mine."

Anna laughed. "Carver, without you around, he's only become more insufferable."

"I didn't think that was possible." I looked at Nicholas, bending over the bomb, adjusting something on the left side. "Will it work?"

The scientist paused, then stood up and looked at me, his face straight. "Always you question me, and always you are wrong. Why would this time be any different?"

"This time is different because you trying to blow up a mountain. Not make a lash, or a crossbow."

"They are all miracles, and I am a miracle worker."

"If you're wondering, Carver," Anna interjected. "I stay sane around these two by taking long walks. Long walks where I find and wrangle every spirit I see."

"Healthier than drinking, which was my solution," I replied.

"You imply that I am in nuisance in some way," Nicholas drew in a fake breath. Smiled. "You are likely correct. Glad to have you back, Carver."

"Couldn't miss the finish."

"We will need that sword of yours," Alec said. "It would be nice if we had Selena as well."

"She'll be there," I said. "Just not on our side."

"Yet," Anna placed her hand on my shoulder, the drew me in for a hug. "We'll get her back. Before the end."

"I hope so," I said. And I did. Really. I hadn't said goodbye to Selena yet. I didn't want to go away the vast nothing, into the next grand adventure, without one last time to talk to her. We had our life stolen from us, and it was time to take it back.

Bryce sounded the call a moment later. Time to head off, to the Mountain. To drive one more mad spirit into the ground.

188

THE MOUNTAIN ROSE out above the forest; no longer a natural wonder but a trap constructed with hopeful intents. To trap the and turn Riven into a second home for humanity. A dream turned nightmare.

The Mountain was, at the heart of it, the only reason Riven existed in the first place. Without it, the Cycle would be free. Spirits would wander into its blue oblivion soon after arriving.

No breaches. No ghouls. No guides.

But there the Mountain stood in front of us, and before the wide cave entrance through which hundreds and thousands of spirits passed through on their walk to the Cycle, stood Nara's new force. Smaller and concentrated, and led by the love of my life. Of my death.

Selena led at least a hundred spirits. They arranged behind her, standing in rank-and-file, in sections. Perfect lines, perfect soldiers.

A couple dozen of us walked out of the forest. Bryce, Anna, Alec, myself and a bunch of other guides that had made the journey. All of them exhausted. All of them slow.

All of them knowing they weren't likely to make it home. Today, they were here for their friends. For their families. For their homes.

I wouldn't let them down. I wouldn't fail them.

Not again.

Nicholas stayed at the back, hidden in the lost spirits that continued to move around us in their blank walk to the Mountain. Had to keep him protected. If Nara destroyed Nicholas' device, then this was all lost.

Me, on the other hand. I was expendable. The only spirit on our side. Which meant I walked out in front. I kept the great sword on my back as I went toward Selena, who stood several yards in front of Nara's troops. Their many eyes followed me and I flashed briefly back to that moment in the Tar Pit when my father, Graham, threw a torch. So many single-minded faces, locked on mine.

"Nara suspected that you'd been turned." Selena didn't smile as I walked up. Didn't draw her weapons. Instead, she looked at me as someone might stare at a particularly ugly house. An object both ordinary, and unimportant. To be dealt with if necessary, or ignored.

"I have problems picking sides," I said, spreading my hands as I came close to her. "But I think you'd like the benefits over here. The people are nicer, for one."

"They won't win," Selena replied. "Look at them. Half are about ready to fall over right now. And the others... can they even lift their swords?"

"My love, I dare you to find out."

Love. That word seemed to penetrate Nara's binding. Made Selena flinch, look away for a moment. Her hands, I noticed, balled into fists. For a second Selena had her own body back.

When her face came back to mine, Nara's mask had slipped on again.

"Nara is willing to offer all of you one last chance," Selena said the words not to me, but above and around, to Bryce and the other guides. "If you leave, she will let you go back to the city unmolested. You can head back to your families, safe."

"Till when?" Bryce called back. "Until your army grows again, and chases us down? Or until you let Riven fall to pieces under the weight of the dead?"

Selena turned back to me. "I see Bryce hasn't changed. He's never been a man of reason."

"Is that you, or Nara talking?"

"I suppose you'll never know," Selena said, and then she frowned. I noticed a single tear slip out of one eye. "But Carver, you should know, what happens next is all her."

Selena's hand moved faster than I thought possible. Sliding in her coat and drawing the cleaver into a slash at my stomach. I didn't jump back so much as fall, my feet dancing quick under me to keep my balance. The cut snagged the edges of my borrowed coat and tore through it. But not me. No blue fire burned my skin.

I reached behind my back and drew the sword out in a wide swing that forced Selena to stop her advance. I had reach. I had power. Selena had speed. Tough to say who would win this one.

"Resist her," I said, keeping the sword in a guard stance. Ready to swivel to any side Selena chose.

"I can't." Selena rose her cleaver into the air, twisted the hilt, bursting the blade into blue flame. Behind her, the spirits roared as one, and began their stampede towards my friends. This would be it, and I didn't know how the guides could survive. They were too tired, too drained.

Selena brought her cleaver down, dropped into a crouch. Ready to spring at me.

Only I wasn't standing still.

I jumped to the left, bowled into a bunch of charging spirits ignoring me to rush the guides. Swung the great sword in through their ranks. Felt the weapon bite and cut and burn. Tried to take as many as I could with every lunge and spin. Dolan's sword sang, and it played a fiery tune.

And then Selena was on me. Her cleaver blocking my strike, stopping the sword. Her knife stabbing towards me. I reversed first my grip on the sword and spun backwards. Away from her knife.

With my wrist reversed, I didn't have the leverage to keep the blade upright, and my sword went down into the ground. Dropped away from Selena's cleaver.

I flipped my wrist again, underneath the sword, and swept it up. Selena dodged to the right, into the path of one of her own spirits. The charging soul shoved into Selena and knocked her to the ground.

I had a clear shot. Lifted the sword, about to swing it down, when I felt Anna's panic through our bond. A paralyzing fear, numbing cold through my body. I turned, looked down the hill.

I'd done what I could, but the guides were still being overwhelmed. Anna herself, flail swinging, was holding four spirits at bay alone. She was already bleeding, already hurt.

"You stay here," I said to Selena, who was trying to free herself from the spirit.

I sprinted down the hill, using the weight of the sword to give me extra momentum. Swung at spirits on my way down, hacking their legs out from under them, or pushing them into each other. Anything to disrupt their numbers. To keep them from simply overwhelming over my friends like a wave crashing over a small rock.

I hit the spirits from behind, slicing through three of them in one broad swipe. Anna's flail caught the fourth. She gave me a quick, tired grin. "Like I said, it's good to have you back."

"Doing what I can," I replied, twisting and laying into another two with a couple of chops. Unlike Nara's first army, the one I'd taken into the city, these spirits lacked weapons, lacked discipline. Nara was panicking. I could see, in the stream of occasional spirits coming out of the Mountain and diving towards us in suicidal charges, that Nara seemed more bent on numbers than strategy. Her forces lived and died by hordes, not skill.

"Watch it, Carver!" Alec called as I took care of another spirit. The guide, his gauntlets lit with flame, darted in between Anna and I, catching another spirit that I thought had gone down, but had only tripped, its hands grasping for my ankles.

"Get back to Nicholas." I needed them by the scientist. I needed them away from me. "I can take their claws. You can't."

But I couldn't take the cleaver. I couldn't take Selena's knife. She came after me, relentless. I barely had my sword up in time to block a straight ahead stab, the ridged edge of the cleaver making that as lethal as the sideways chop. She tried to stick the knife in my right leg, but I shifted to a side stance, her knife only grazing me. Not enough to set me aflame.

I drove her back with a quick series of in cuts; short jabs that leveraged the sword's reach to force her into a defensive stance.

"Nara says that she'll forgive you," Selena said as she whirled around me, moving her feet from side to side in a circle, continually testing my movement with the great sword. Looking for me to get out of position. To not follow her around and leave myself open for a quick strike.

"So kind of her." I shuffled my feet well. If there's one

thing that had I learned with Bryce and our hunts, it's that being nimble was the key to survival. Movement kept you alive, which wa more important than getting a lucky blow. We rotated until Selena stood downhill from me. A bad move.

"She thinks it's generous," Selena said "I think it's your only chance."

"I think you need to pay more attention." I lunged forward. Used my higher ground to deliver an overhead blow at an angle she couldn't counter without sticking both her blades above her head. But I didn't count on her roll. Rather than block, she dove down the hill. Towards were Anna stood, fending off another spirit. Selena came out of her tumble, rose, and jabbed Anna with the knife.

I saw Anna's eyes widen. Saw her mouth drop, saw her turn at the pain and knock Selena's knife away with her flail. Anna stumbled back against a tree trunk. The sneak that I had found, that I met on the train all those days and months and years ago, held her hand on the blossoming red coming from her side.

Through our bond flowed pain, and a sudden weakness.

I ran. Followed my swing. Selena turned towards me with the cleaver, but I stepped by her. Delivered a cross chop that caught a spirit reaching to finish Anna off. Selena had a clear shot at my back.

I expected the bite of her cleaver, even as I planted my feet to turn around.

Anna pressed herself off of the tree, her left hand leaving a bloody print behind. Swung the flail forward, over my head as Selena thrust forward. Anna's spiked, burning ball hit Selena's shoulder, knocking her strike away and bursting her into fire. The blue flame covered my love, and washed her away.

I wanted to hold her. To stay with Selena and never, ever

leave. But as Selena burned, I had to turn. Had to keep swinging the sword and fight with my fellow guides.

Some fell, other stood strong. Bryce lanced with his voulge over and over again. Alec used his gauntlets to devastating effect. Other guides use their knives, their swords, their axes. By the end of it, eight of us were left standing amid a hoard of vacant spirits.

Nara, it seemed, had taken her own lesson. Resolved to keep any new souls for later. She gave us a moment to breathe.

Anna looked gray. Pale and lost. Her eyes caught mine as I stepped over to her, back leaning against the tree, her flail on the ground, her hands clasped over the wound in her side where Selena's knife had cut deep.

"You have to release me," I said, looking at the wound. "Cut the bind. Take your strength back."

"But we need you to finish this."

"I need you to live," I said. "We're so close to the Cycle now, so close to Nara. I'll be able to fend it off for a little while."

Anna stared at me. Then shook her head. "I won't. I won't take that chance."

"Then promise me," I said. "Promise me that if you have to, you'll cut me loose."

"Only if I must."

Bryce and Alec were there a moment later. Alec moved Anna's arms away, started binding the wound. Tearing treads off of his own coat and wrapping the stab. "It's a long way back, Anna, so we better get moving."

"You can't abandon them here," Anna replied, shaking her head.

"The way's clear," I said. "Nara doesn't have the forces left. I can take it."

"No," Bryce said. "You'll need help."

My mentor turned and went over to Selena, just standing up, lost to this world. He put his hand on her shoulder, and started talking to her. Establishing the familiarity, the relationship to form a bond. And in a minute, Selena, my Selena, looked at me.

"Carver?" Selena said. "Are we free?"

"Not yet."

Minutes later, the entire group sorted itself into two sections. Bryce and the other guides in one. Selena, Nicholas and I and the other, along with the cart holding the bomb.

"Take Anna back," I said, my eyes drifted over to her again. Sweating and pale, Anna's own eyes were closed. "Go as fast as you can. We'll take care of this."

"I'll let her know when we're clear through our bond." Bryce nodded at Selena. "So you can detonate."

As good a plan as any. As spirits roamed by us, my friends began the long trudge back to the city. Back to where they could cross over. On the way, they'd doubtless have to fight other spirits, pouring through breaches and in scattered angry waves prowling Riven in ever greater numbers. They would make it. They would survive.

It wouldn't matter if we failed.

189

Surrounded by the walking spirits, the three of us, with Nicholas pulling the device on its cart behind him, entered the Mountain. Spirits filled the tunnel, all moving down towards the Cycle. On either side, branches broke off, empty and unexplored. I remembered them from when we were here last.

"It's sort of fitting," I said. "The end of the guides will be the place where they first began."

"Where they began?" Nicholas asked.

"Mali created the Mountain to house the Cycle. It was here, Dolan said, that he first found how to make the weapons that burned. Here where the guides stayed when they first were building up to fight Nara."

I wasn't sure what else to say. There's something about actually confronting history that leaves you at a loss. Myth and legend becoming real and tracing a direct line to you. All of those events, those mistakes and those successes leading to the three of us trying, in one last attempt, to erase all of it.

We made it to the cavern where Piotr had crossed over.

Where those months ago I had lost my parents. We had scored our first real victory, and had our first real loss.

It would've been nice to have Graham and Katherine beside me. Graham's cocky optimism, his big hammer would have suffused us with confidence. Katherine's kindness, her knack for knowing the best way forward... but they weren't here. We were on our own.

To the left, stairs continued down, descending deeper into the cave. At the bottom of those steps would be the gray blue ocean of the Cycle. At the bottom of the steps, I had no doubt, would be Nara.

"I'll lead," I said, with the great sword out in front. "Selena, you take the back. Stay between anything and Nicholas. And you, genius, you get that bomb to the cliff and get it going."

"Don't we need to wait for Bryce and the others?" Selena said.

"We wait if we have time," I said. "I want them to live, but we can't risk it. If we have no choice, Nicholas, you blow this thing."

The scientist nodded. I didn't notice any moral qualms flashing through his eyes. Any concern that he wouldn't be able to follow through. Nicholas knew the objective. He would do what he had to do.

We took the last set of steps, past the cave leading up to Piotr's overlook, slowly. At the bottom the steps opened into a wide chamber dominated by the Cycle. Its blue light flashed through everything, covering our faces, our coats our minds in teal. Ahead of us a parade of spirits shuffled off the precipice into the endless sea. One after another, like animals. Or machines.

"I've never seen it," Nicholas said. "It's beautiful."

"Just don't get too close." I shifted the great sword, looked around. Where was Nara?

Nicholas move the cart into the chamber. Pushed it near the cliff's edge. Spirits ran by him, by all of us.

"You came back to me," Nara's voice echoed down the steps. She was above us. Back the way we come.

"Where are you?" I shouted. Ushered Selena by me, and pointed her over to Nicholas. We had to keep him safe.

"Why does it matter?" Nara said. "It won't change what is going to happen."

"What do you think that is?" I said. Part of me wanted to keep her talking, though I didn't think we could keep up the back and forth for an entire day. Or longer, depending on Bryce and the others. Nara would come out sooner or later. We would be ready.

"You're going to lose," Nara said. "You won't even see it coming."

I positioned myself in front of the steps. Glanced back at Nicholas and Selena. They seemed okay.

I felt hands grab my mouth, my throat, pull me back and pin my arms to my sides. Shouts came from my friends, and spirits that I'd swore were walking to the Cycle a second ago pulled them away from the device. Away from the Cycle. Against the cave walls.

Spirits held each of us, resolutely obeying their leader's command. Nara, who walked down the steps and into the chamber. Walk towards the bomb and stared at it.

Two other spirits, both soldiers, followed her. Personal bodyguards.

"What are you trying to do with this?" Nara said, and she looked back at us. "What is it? Some sort of weapon?"

I realized, hopefully as Nicholas did, that Nara may have never seen a bomb before. May not have any idea what such a thing could do. After all, explosives had no place in Riven. Perhaps the idea of detonating the Mountain would never even occur to her. Wouldn't even be a possibility.

"It's mine," Nicholas said. "I'm trying to find out more about the Cycle."

"It doesn't matter," Nara said. "The Cycle won't matter soon. We'll all be going back home."

Nara walked across the chamber, through the spirits, and up to Nicholas. Reached her hand for his face.

I saw Nicholas move his shoulders. Saw them shift, and then I recognized the coat he was wearing. The lines crossing it. I'd had a coat like that once, until spirits had torn it away. As Nara reached for it, the coat burst into blue wrangling flames. They covered the spirit holding onto him. Nara jerked her hand back in surprise.

I felt the twinge. The spirit holding me tight wavered as Nara lost her own binding. Her own focus on the spirits falling away in her fear. I took advantage. Pressed my feet to the ground and shoved the spirit back into the wall behind me. Broke it against the stone.

The spirit's hands fell away and I stepped free, the great sword in my right hand. Ready to end Nara's madness.

I reversed the sword and stabbed behind me. Felt it bite into the stunned spirit. Burned it. Nara ran away from Nicholas, back up the cave's stairs. Coward.

"Carver!" Selena yelled, and I saw her spirit dragging Selena up the stairs. Up and away from the Cycle.

I moved to follow when Nara's two bodyguards cut me off. They were tall, hulking creatures. But they held no weapons.

So when they dove at me, I used the sword. A right swing, then a whirl to the left. Two cuts, two burning spirits. The way was clear.

Nara needed better guards.

Nicholas darted over to the device, the glanced at me. I could go after Selena. Or I could stay, keep Nicholas safe.

"Go," Nicholas said. "That's not my last surprise." He

opened his jacket to reveal a number of blue bolts on the inside, leftovers for my crossbow. "I'll be fine."

"You'd better be," I said. "Yell if something changes."

I ran up the stairs, chasing after Selena. Chasing after Nara. Trying to survive.

190

I WENT up the stairs and paused as I passed the pathway to the overlook. There were two places they could go. I didn't know which. I could still hear Selena shouts, but they echoed through the cave, bouncing off the walls and making it hard to tell where they were coming from.

Everywhere, really.

I was about to cry out, to ask which way, when pain flowed through me. It wasn't mine, though, it was Anna's. Coming through our bond. It went away almost as soon as it came through, but our tie continued to weaken. I could feel it, feel her life slipping away. If she died, our bond would be gone.

I shook my head. I couldn't do anything for her now. Had to find Selena, had to keep Nicholas safe.

"The overlook!" I heard Selena's cry, and went that way. She'd realized, perhaps, that giving directions was a better use than anguished yelling.

There weren't spirits wandering Piotr's path, so my progress was fast. I leapt up the steps. Pushed off the walls and kept the great sword ahead of me, held steady. Burst onto the overlook.

The forest expanded below, falling away from the Mountain. I could see, almost like city lights, the glow of dozens of breaches. Riven was being overwhelmed, and it was happening faster. Some breaches looked like they were connecting, large pools of yellow swallowing up trees whole. Somewhere down there, Bryce and the others were running for their lives.

At the edge of the overlook, Selena fought for hers. The spirit had her, a scrawny but strong soldier that had lifted Selena's feet off the ground. Was moving her towards the edge, getting ready to drop her off.

I couldn't make it there in time. Selena was going to fall.

I lifted the great sword over my head, in both hands, and threw it forward. Let go as my hands started down.

The sword flew through the air, whirling end over end. It struck the spirit. Embedded itself into its back. Burst into flame. Then the spirit fell over the cliff.

And Selena went with it.

I ran towards them. Where they had been. Dove and slid across the rock, reached with my hand to see if there was anything to grab. Felt nothing.

"You'll have to reach farther," Selena's voice sent a jolt through me. I peered over the edge; she hung a few feet down, her cleaver and long knife biting into the rock, giving her enough of a handhold. I scrabbled further, leaned down, and gripped onto the rock with my left hand. Reached out with my right. Selena glanced at it, glanced at the cleaver and the long knife.

"Leave it," I said. "It's not worth dying for."

"You keep forgetting Carver, we're already dead." Selena let go with her left hand, and the cleaver fell out of the mountain and tumbled into oblivion. She leaned on the knife, and reached up and grabbed my hand.

As I pulled Selena up, the knife fell free. Selena kept her right hand wrapped around its hilt. Not willing to give up that last weapon. I rolled over, used the leverage of my back to pull Selena up and onto the overlook. She rolled across me, and we both laid still for a moment.

"How many times do I have to save your life?" I said to her.

"I could ask you the same question."

And then I remembered Nicholas. Alone down there by the Cycle. With Nara roaming the caves.

191

Selena and I sprinted down the stairs. Back through the hidden passage and down towards the cavern and the Cycle. Every second we weren't by his side, Nara could find a way to tear the scientist apart. Destroy the device.

Selena and I burst into the chamber, shoving spirits aside, and saw the device still intact on the cliff. Nicholas stood in front of two smoldering spirits, watching to make sure they didn't rise up again. Behind him, stepping out of a cluster of spirits marching to the Cycle, Nara walked towards his back.

Nicholas looked up, saw us held up a hand. Didn't see Nara approaching.

I shouted his name. "Behind you!"

The scientist, thin lanky eyes shining with adrenaline, turned in time for Nara to grab him by the face. Her bony fingers wrapped around his cheeks and I saw the life drain out of them. The independence, freedom, gone.

She bound him.

I ran towards them. I could hear Selena doing the same. Despite the fact that we only had Selena's knife, I was determined to try something, anything.

Nicholas turned back to me, between Nara and I. Held up his hand, gave me a single wave. "Goodbye, Carver."

The scientist turned and jumped off into the Cycle.

We all watched Nicholas vanish into the blue. Then the old spirit, the one who was supposed to help us save Riven and who had scattered those dreams to ashes, spoke. "He was the greatest risk remaining," Nara said. "An unknown. I do not know what that thing is, but there must be a reason you brought him here. There must be a reason you were trying to save him."

"It doesn't matter now." I didn't know what to think. To feel. With Nicholas gone, I didn't know who could trigger the device, if anybody. I didn't know what the plan was. I just never thought we'd fail. I never saw it coming. We had the advantage, we had the equipment. But here I was, unarmed, at the end of the world.

"What's next?" Nara said, and she looked at Selena. "Do you stab me? Burn me and throw me into the Cycle? Even though it will do you no good?"

"Maybe not, but it'll feel great," Selena said. She took a step towards Nara, and then the old spirit lunged towards me. I had no hands, no weapons to strike her, so I did what I could and met her grasping hand with a tackle. Pushed her back, along the Cycle's edge. We danced, me trying to keep her hands from grasping mine, from touching my face, my throat, my wrists, anywhere that could allow her to connect to what was left of my soul.

"You are such a disappointment," Nara snarled as we wrestled. She was stronger than I expected. But again, appearances could be deceiving in Riven. Muscle and bone didn't matter once you were dead. The only thing that did was your determination. Your skill.

Nara had learned a lot in her centuries.

She twisted her leg and caught my calf, threw me to the

floor. Reached down towards my face. I kicked up with my foot and struck her in the stomach. Drove her back.

"Can't you see that Earth doesn't deserve to die so you can live?" I shouted at her.

"I happen to think it does." Nara rushed at me again. I could see Selena behind her, angling for the right spot to stick Nara with the knife. That was my hope, that was my plan.

But Nara knew that as well as I did. She kept twisting us, rotating our grapples to get Selena out of position.

I had to try something different.

So when Nara charged again, I let her wrap her fingers around my throat. Felt her start to tear my soul. Felt Nara's whispers pour into my mind. And then I felt them vanish. Pushed away by Selena's burning blue knife.

Nara took a step back for me, surprise showing on her face. She couldn't possibly imagine such a thing. As though the concept of defeat had never never crossed her mind.

"Stabbed in the back," Selena said. "Should be familiar to you." Nara took one step, her mouth worked, and then she collapsed into the flames. They dwindled around her body on the ground. I didn't let her stand up. I pushed her over the edge.

As Nara disappeared into the deep blue of the Cycle, I realized that all three of the spirits that had build Riven were gone. Fitting, then, that their creation go with them.

I gave Selena a smile, and started to move to the device, when my world exploded.

Pain lanced through me again, coming out of nowhere and everywhere. Through the bond I shared with Anna. It was wild, uncontrollable, and I knew there was only one way to stop it.

"Let me go," I said the words aloud, but sent them through our bond. Sent them to Anna across the distance between us. If she was going to get back alive, she needed all her strength. She needed the part of her that she had given to me. I needed her to take it back.

Confusion, relief, flowed through our bond. Anna was hesitating. So I urged her again. Begged her. Tried to be confident, to let her know that this was my decision. That I would be okay. Despite the fact that I knew none of those things.

Selena knelt next to me, her face a mask of worry, when she asked what was going on I could barely form the words tell her.

Then I felt it. The strange rush of my body putting itself back together. Of Anna leaving me, and cutting me off. I knew that she would be feeling a similar feeling. Strength returning to her limbs. Like waking up after a long nap, or a good meal. I hoped it would be enough.

When the severing was done, I stood, pain-free.

"It's done," I said to Selena. Only, it wasn't. I heard the voices leaking into my head. The whispers. The endless parade of statements one after the other. Urging me, urging me to walk ahead. Take a few steps and disappear. All of my worries, all of my troubles would cease.

I knew where they came from, I knew that calling.

The Cycle wanted me.

192

Selena had her arms around me before I could move. Her mouth close to my ear, and I heard her voice.

" Carver, Carver come back. Push it away. Listen to me."

The words came and went, blending with the growing chorus of whispers. Demands. Urges that I dive into the deep blue. Like the craving for tobacco, alcohol. Deep needs that had to be satisfied.

"I can't fight it," I said, and pushed Selena way. Stood up. Moved my left foot, then my right foot. Closer to the edge.

Selena tackled me from behind. Knocked me down. Jammed her elbow into my back and pressed me to the ground.

"You're not going to leave me here," Selena said, I could hear her voice break. "After all this, you're not going to leave me alone. Not here. Not now."

The raw emotion in those words broke through. Blunted the force of the Cycle's call just enough for me to pause. To feel my hands, my legs, my mouth. To take control. But I didn't tell Selena to get up. Not yet. Not until I was sure.

"Keep talking," I said. "I need you."

Selena did. She spoke in stories, and memories, and poems. She told me about how she felt the first time we met. When I'd saved her from the spirit and the streets. She told me about the apartment, the long days drawing and trying to find a passion in Riven, loving it when I came to the door to offer excitement.

She told me about the first time she held the cleaver. More than a weapon, it was a symbol of independence. Something that said this was her world too, and she had a place in it. Was no longer at the mercy of others. She could drive her own destiny.

She talked about how she felt closer to me than any other. How when the two of us journeyed through the strange world, those were the best times of her life. In Riven or without. That the two of us as a team, facing horrors, or just walking together through the endless desert or stalks of green, those moments are what she treasured.

Selena buried the Cycle under her words. Her love quieted the whispers, softened the cries. I fell into a kind of trance, meditative and listening to everything she said. When she finished, before she could launch into something else, I held up an arm. My face still lay against the rock, but I spoke anyway.

"Thank you," I said. There may have been more to say. But right then, that's all that seem to matter.

Selena let me up a moment later, but I noticed she stayed ready. Willing to throw herself under my legs again, and again and again if necessary.

Around us spirits continued their doomed walk as though none of this was happening. An audience unaware of the play in front of them.

The device sat there. Waiting for us.

I went up to it. A solid dirty metal sphere, with a small hatch that opened when I pushed in. Inside sat a smaller sphere, connected to the outer one with many spokes. A simple switch, one that you could press, sat inside.

Carved into the metal above it, was a message.

To whomever happens to be the one activating this device, I would pass along the following:

Pressing the switch will activate the procedure. Precisely 10 seconds after, the inner core will ignite. The rays will admit shortly thereafter, triggering the chaining reaction as expected.

Glanced at Selena. "He said this was complex, it looks like it's just a switch."

"Maybe he knew," Selena said. "Maybe he understood at the end that it wasn't going to be so simple. That he might not make it."

I looked back in towards the switch, and noticed another series of etches. Below the button. These in a messier scrawl.

If you are reading this, then forgive me. The Cycle calls to me, and if I am to see it, I needed a reason. This was my chance.

Your friend,

Nicholas

"I always knew Nicholas was sly one," I said after letting Selena look at the message.

"He got his wish," Selena answered.

"So when do we press it?" I said.

"When Bryce gives us the signal."

I don't know how long we sat, telling stories, holding each other, and basking in the Cycle's blue glow. Watching the spirits go by in their endless march. It was a long, perfect goodbye. The two of us together in our wait for the end.

When Selena sat up, I knew the call had come in. Bryce had made it home.

"He says to thank us," Selena spoke, repeating prices words to her. "That they made it back, with surprise help from a golden ghoul who, wandering back from the city, found them."

"Mali's finest creation."

"Anna made it," Selena said. "Alec says Laurence is going to take her to the hospital. Bryce says to detonate it."

"Are you ready?"

Selena nodded. I moved towards the bomb, stopped. Turned back to her. "Together."

We both reached in, her fingers rested lightly on the switch. Selena whispered *now* and we pressed down. The only sound was a slight fizzing, as though something had started to burn.

I shut the hatch. We stepped away. Selena met my eyes, I met her lips, and the world swirled away.

193

Anna walked down the avenue, on a wide sidewalk beneath towering buildings. More and more every day, scaling upwards ever higher. Now that the war was over, plenty of energy and materials were being thrown into the city's growth. Zeppelins filled the sky, fewer mechs walked the streets. Still, Anna felt relief when she came in sight of Ezra's. A home of sorts. Through the purifier, and into the rich bar. That mantle above the back counter showing a fantastical orchestra, jazzy tunes pouring out from speakers beneath. Alec was already there, sipping coffee. On the table, a mug of tea just for her.

"It's been a while," Alec said as Anna sat down.

It had. Months. Not much reason to get back together this far from home anymore. They didn't have regular meetings. The guides, as a whole, had more or less stopped existing. Bryce said he checked every so often. Crossed over and stood on the small piece of Riven that remained. Anna hadn't tried it. Most of the crossing points, the beds they were used to, would take you right to your own demise. They'd lost a few guides that way, immediately after. Now there were only special places, tied and designated to the small scrap of Riven remaining.

"He's coming today, right?" Alec said. Anna nodded.

They spent the next hour rehashing their lives. Catching each other up the way, Anna supposed, normal people did. There weren't toxic ghouls, angry spirits interrupting. No discussion of hidden enemies, vile maneuvers. No, for once all they had to complain about was the rent. New restaurants. The conversation went flat.

Then a third person joined the table. Anna stopped. Looked at the man.

"So I hear you've got a story to tell," Opperman, the reporter, said.

Anna could only nod.

WILD NINES

For Davin and his crew, running security on Europa should've been easy, and was, until a deadly mistake makes the Wild Nines the number one enemy in the solar system.

WANT MORE STORIES?

Sign up for my mailing list to receive free books like STARSHOT, along with new releases and sales. No spam, ever.

ACKNOWLEDGMENTS

There's this idea that writing is a solitary act, but that couldn't be further from the truth. Every writer depends on friends, family, and, yes, the readers to keep spinning their stories.

Specifically, I'd like to thank my wife, Nicole, who's endless love and encouragement make every day brighter. My brothers, Jonathan, Justin, and Matthew, and parents, Bob and Mary, who help keep a smile on my face.

And, of course, all of you readers that make this life possible.

Thank you.

ABOUT THE AUTHOR

A.R. Knight writes sci-fi and fantasy in the frozen north of Wisconsin. With a pair of cats keeping him company, he enjoys delving into adventures that are as much about the villain as the hero.

After getting a degree in journalism and touring the country installing healthcare software, A.R. Knight thought it would be good to get back to what he loved. So now he's got a small office and early mornings to spin whatever tales come into his imagination.

When he's not writing, A.R. Knight tends to travel anywhere he can, whether that's islands off the coast of Ecuador, the rainforest, snowboarding in the Rocky Mountains, or sipping scotch in Edinburgh. That's the nice thing about the writing life, you can take it anywhere.

To contact or see what he's up to, visit www.adam-rknight.com

arknight@blackkeybooks.com

Riven:
Jonathan

The Cycle:
Justin

Spirit's End:
Matthew

The Riven Trilogy:

Ebook ISBN: 978-1-946554-53-6

Print ISBN: 978-1-946554-57-4

www.ingramcontent.com/pod-product-compliance
Lightning Source LLC
Chambersburg PA
CBHW031602180726
48284CB00005B/1361

"Following this fantasy experience is addictive and thoroughly satisfying."

- The San Francisco Review of Books

Blood and Mercy

"The series excels in using allegory to mirror contemporary issues and explore them in a unique, thoughtful manner. Frustration, hope and the transformative power of righteous fury ooze from the...The underlying optimism of the series, balanced with unflinching realism regarding the difficulty of change at personal and systemic levels, is a testament to the possibilities of the fantasy genre—and a worthy read for our times."

- Aurealis Magazine

Books by V. S. Holmes

BLOOD OF TITANS

REFORGED
Smoke and Rain
Lightning and Flames

RESTORED
Madness and Gods
Blood and Mercy

REBEL
*Treason's Tears**

STARSEDGE: NEL BENTLY

Travelers
Drifters
Strangers
Heretics
Fugitives
*Emissaries**

SHORT FICTION
"Nowhere Fast" (*We Came to Dance*)
"Starfall" (*Vitality Magazine*)
"The Tempest" (*Out of the Darkness*)
"Disciples" (*Beamed Up*)
"Familiar Waters" (*Love and Bubbles*)
"Mere Primordium" (poem, *Mystic Blue Review*)

**forthcoming*